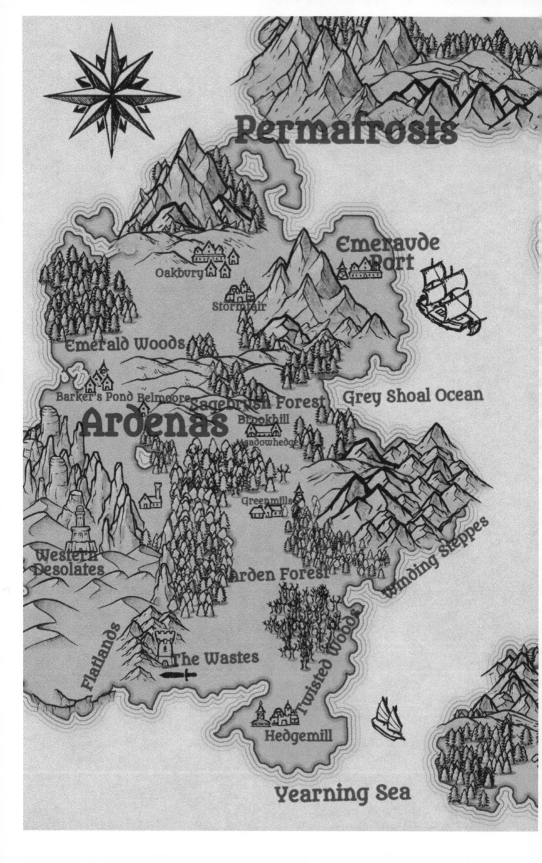

SONGS OF THE WICKED

C.A. FARRAN

SONGS of the WICKED

BOOK ONE OF
A DREAMER'S
MISFORTUNE

C. A. FARRAN

CONTENT WARNING

This story contains content that might be troubling to some readers, including, but not limited to, depictions of and references to death, harm against animals and children, references to sexual assault, graphic depictions of violence, and sexually explicit content.

For Lance, whose faith in me is limitless, and for my wildling, who makes me believe in magic.

CHAPTER 1

*S*pring brought purple lupines back to the riverbank. A whisper of their sweet scent reached out as they swayed gently in the warm breeze. Dappled sun undulated along Aislinn's goose-pebbled arms.

She lay in the tall grass, clutching the earth like a lifeline. The dirt beneath her nails was an anchor when her body threatened to float away. The river drowned out the rasp and crackle of her lungs struggling with each inhale as light danced across the ripples, casting sharp beams of sunlight to kiss her face and broken body.

Aislinn's golden hair, once braided into a crown adorned with wildflowers, was torn from the scalp in some places. Blood trickled down her forehead, and her cheeks were tight from dried tears.

Her lavender gown—the one she'd promised her sister she'd keep clean for the ceremony—was torn and bloodied, and each breeze that ghosted against her skin breathed through the tears in the silk. The ground beneath her was wet with blood, and the throbbing in her ribs from his knife as well as the pain between her legs had grown numb.

This would have been her nineteenth season.

Where were the gods? The ones the elders swore would protect her? They hadn't come when he took her body. They hadn't come when she begged for mercy.

Aislinn let her head fall to the side, squinting through blurring vision until her eyes found the faint outline of a human shape.

A hooded figure stepped out of the shadows, bearing unearthly darkness. The being's shroud of black devoured the light around it, and a blanket of quiet wrapped around the forest.

This was no god she'd ever prayed to.

Death had come to claim her. Aislinn knew it in the farthest corners of her heart. Softly closing her eyes, she conjured a warm memory—running through this very forest with her sister Yera. Barefoot over soft moss and cool grass. She could almost hear Yera's laughter as she resigned herself to her fate and took one last strangled breath. Tired of counting her heartbeats and clinging to the riverbank with desperate fingers, Aislinn relaxed her grip, letting go.

IT WAS A CURIOUS THING, to look down on one's own body. Aislinn watched, puzzled, as the hooded figure placed a gentle hand over the corpse that wore her face.

Aislinn lifted a shaky hand to her hair, finding the plaited crown intact and free of blood. A curious thing, indeed. "Is that me? Is that... my body?"

The stranger stood, turning. "Do you know what I am?" The voice was somehow both soft and hard. A gentle rush and a harsh scrape.

The trees groaned and their leaves shook in a sharp breeze—a breeze that failed to meet Aislinn's skin. Part of her wanted to believe this was her mind's final moments, conjuring images as her body shut down, but Aislinn knew better.

"You're death," she whispered.

The figure lowered her hood to reveal long red hair in a simple plait running down her back. Her smooth skin held an unearthly glow, unmarred by time and nature, though there was nothing youthful in her forlorn expression. With her brows drawn over her amber eyes, she gave a short shake of her head. "Not exactly." She pointed toward the body on the ground. "That is the face of death. I'm merely your guide."

Aislinn always believed there was more to life than the here and now. She wasn't the most pious, especially by Ardenian standards. Her mother always said Aislinn's father had returned to the earth, but she knew there was something after death. She could feel it in every hum of the wind. She didn't believe in much, but she believed that her father wasn't far. Wasn't that enough?

"It's time to go now, Aislinn." The girl twirled a lupine between her fingers, vibrant purple spinning to a blur. When Aislinn's gaze fell to her hand, she dropped the poor flower to the ground.

Why pick a flower only to leave it forgotten?

"How do you know my name?"

"I know much about you."

Aislinn's hands fisted by her side. "That's not an answer!"

"It isn't, is it?"

Why was this strange girl speaking in riddles? Was it not enough to face her mortality? "Can you at least tell me your name?"

The ghost of a smile hinted against her mouth. "Lark."

"Lark," Aislinn said, testing the name on her tongue. She never thought death would come in the form of a fire-haired girl, hardly older than she, bearing a human name. Then again, she hadn't thought she'd encounter death so soon.

"It's time."

Aislinn glanced at her broken body that still lay on the riverbank. "I'm not going anywhere." She stepped back from Lark. "I want to go home."

If she'd known she'd never see her mother again, perhaps she would have sat still while she braided her hair. Or she wouldn't have shrugged out of her embrace. She should have told her sister, Yera, how much she'd always admired her, that she envied her smile. Not for its beauty but for the ease with which it came. There were many things Aislinn should have done, but instead, she'd run off after the ceremony, desperate for a moment alone before the wedding feast began.

Lark remained silent, watching.

"Do you see what he... did to me?"

"I'm sorry, but I can't undo it. All I can offer you is peace." Lark held out a hand. "Please, let me help you."

Aislinn recoiled and stepped around Lark. Why couldn't she feel the wind? Why couldn't she smell the lupines, the river and its scent of rotting moss, earthy and comforting? She rubbed her arm, but felt no goose pebbles on her skin. It was as if her hands had fallen asleep—tingles of sensation—nothing tangible but over her entire body. She stumbled and landed on her knees next to her corpse. When she first looked upon it, she felt nothing. Now, her chest constricted with panic. It was her face, but it was all wrong. Like her features weren't where they were meant to be. She'd only ever seen her face in a mirror, to see it like this—frozen in pain...

"Tell me this is a dream."

Lark knelt across from her, adopting slow, careful movements. For a moment they remained in silence, the only sound the gentle rushing of the river.

Aislinn squeezed her eyes shut, seeking the scent of this place she once considered home. Slowly, the soft florid scent of lupines filled her senses, the warm earthy smell of moss and dirt surrounded her. She opened her eyes and the aroma faded, but she held onto a hint of it.

"You have questions, I understand that. But none of these questions will bring you the peace you seek, the peace you deserve, after everything you've suffered." Lark's amber eyes softened. "I can show you the way, but you have to come with me now." Again she held out her hand.

Aislinn glanced down at Lark's hand, making no move to reach for her.

"I know it's daunting. But you need to trust me. *Please.*"

Lark's ethereal face had softened into an almost human expression. A soft realization dawned on Aislinn; anything was better than facing down her used and discarded body. The evidence of his crimes, still worn on her skin.

Was it her choice? Could she choose to remain? There was nothing here for her. Not if she was dead. The only pieces left would be carried by those who remembered her.

But memory was a powerful thing.

Aislinn remembered her father's laugh, the way his smile crinkled his moss-green eyes—the eyes she inherited from him. She wanted to see his smile again.

Aislinn lifted her hand and placed it in Lark's. A small seed of hope took root in her chest.

Aislinn lagged half a pace behind her guide as they wove through the forest. She paused to look up at the trees, craning her neck to see how tall they were. They towered high in the sky, as high as any bird would dare to fly. The sun hinted at its presence between lush green leaves. The light that once seemed so cruel and unforgiving, highlighting the marks on her body, now felt safe and inviting as it illuminated the expanse of skin unmarred by his touch.

Aislinn's gaze fell to Lark, the mysterious being with kind eyes and fire for hair. Aislinn's mind buzzed with a thousand unasked questions. She tightened her mouth in an attempt to smother them back down her throat. "What's it like?"

Aislinn never did have much self-control.

Lark turned. "That's an awfully vague question."

"Being what you are. Is it lonely?"

"Not for most of us."

"Us? How many of your kind are there?" Aislinn never considered there'd be numerous harbingers of death. She also didn't consider her words to hold any insult, but the way Lark's mouth tightened, she must have said something wrong.

"As many as there needs to be."

Aislinn pondered the unspoken meaning behind Lark's words. "Are you at peace, being what you are?"

Lark's face hardened. Her eyes drifted over Aislinn's shoulder. She froze, a preternatural stillness coming over her. The only sound was the thrashing of leaves, trees swaying wildly in a breeze Aislinn no longer felt.

A low groan seeped through the treeline.

A sound of desperation.

Of searching.

"*Run*," Lark hissed.

Before Aislinn could react, Lark gripped her elbow and yanked her, propelling her through the forest. Each time her foot caught a gnarled root, that inhumanly strong grip tightened and pulled her harder. Faster.

Only when they broke through a clearing, Aislinn stumbling over a rotting log, did Lark relent their pace. She turned, watching the tree line.

Aislinn panted. Her lungs were near to bursting, and her heart threatened to leap from her chest. She placed a hand against her breastbone. Did she still have a heartbeat? If not, why could she feel it thundering in her chest?

Lark didn't appear winded.

"What... was... that?" Aislinn choked out between breaths she was sure she didn't need.

Lark continued listening for a heartbeat or two before turning her head to look at her. "Something I have neither the time nor the patience to deal with today."

"I thought I was already dead. How is there any danger?"

Lark hissed a curse. She turned to regard Aislinn with a darkened expression. "As long as you exist here, there is always danger."

Here as in the mortal world? Was it so dangerous for her soul to remain? It wasn't her place to ask questions and she should let this strange girl keep her secrets. "But what was it?"

Aislinn wasn't well versed in adhering to what she should do.

Lark pointed in the direction they'd run from. "That is what happens if I fail my duty."

Aislinn paused, letting Lark's words sink in. "If I don't move on, whatever that thing was will come to get me?"

Lark exhaled a sharp breath. "You could become its mirror."

As if that didn't send a thousand questions climbing up Aislinn's throat.

"We need to leave," Lark said with a note of finality Aislinn couldn't bring herself to argue with.

When they reached the edge of the forest, they stopped short. Rolling hills stretched ahead, and clouds cast shadows that ambled across the brilliant greenery. Aislinn stood with her hands on her hips and squinted into the distance.

"That's Finn's land. He owns this stretch for miles. Will he be able to see us?" Hope bubbled in Aislinn's chest. If Finn could see her, maybe she could convince Lark to let her see her mother and Yera one last time. To say goodbye before accepting whatever came next. Her heart that shouldn't beat, squeezed.

There would be no goodbyes for her. Not in this life.

Lark's mouth tightened before she turned back to the sprawling landscape before her. Without a word, she slid one hand into the air. The light around it seemed to ripple and refract. Like she was slipping between a gossamer curtain.

Aislinn gasped at the sight. "Is that... the door to the other side?" Would her father be waiting for her? Would she ascend to Avalon? She didn't hold any stock in the notion that every mortal sinner was bound for an eternity in the Netherworld. That seemed too cruel.

"Think of it more as a path leading to an entryway. You still have to choose to cross the threshold."

"What an odd place for it to reside." Aislinn frowned. Did all souls have to come to this spot?

"The veil is everywhere. It's the access point that varies. Each soul has a unique passage." Lark looked her over, assessing. "I didn't even know for certain it would be here for you. I had to let it call to me."

Aislinn pursed her lips. "That seems unnecessarily complicated."

"Yes." Lark gave her a knowing look before waving a hand in invitation.

Aislinn took a staggering step forward, reaching her arms toward the rippling surface. Lark guided her through, following behind.

Before them lay another forest, and once they cleared the juncture of the glimmering veil it closed behind them. Disappearing as if it had never been.

A vibrant world of color surrounded Aislinn. Instead of warm browns and lush greens with hints of sunlight and blue skies, this forest held rich purple and red leaves. Soft lavender light illuminated the forest floor.

An overwhelming sense of belonging crashed through her as if she should build a house right in this spot and never leave.

A turquoise blue pond stretched before her with a simple wooden bridge stretching across. She leaned over to see where it led, but a dense cloud of fog obscured anything beyond it.

"These last few steps, you must take on your own." Lark's voice cut through Aislinn's consciousness and she turned to face her.

"Where does it lead?"

"To where you were always meant to go." Lark wasn't looking at her but beyond her.

"What does that mean?" Panic rose in Aislinn's throat. This wasn't what she agreed to. Lark said she'd guide her, not abandon her. Aislinn wasn't ready to part from the oddly comforting girl yet. The full weight of the truth, her mortality, pressed down on her.

Lark's brows furrowed as if she was in pain. "It means, I don't know where it goes. My job is to bring you here, I can't force you to go any further, I can't tell you what you'll face." She closed her eyes and took a breath before leveling a stare that reminded Aislinn she wasn't human. "But if you stay, there will be nothing for you but your bitter lament."

Aislinn broke free of Lark's stare to gaze across the bridge. What if the village elders were right? What if her sins had bound her to a cruel fate in the Netherworld? She tried to be kind, but she wasn't selfless, not in the way the elders demanded. Relinquishing autonomy to exist for others. She was selfish, preferring her own company and solitude to congregational worship of gods that had long abandoned them. Was thinking ill of the gods a sin?

Fear and panic clawed at her, but the words her mother had woven into the fiber of her being from years of repetition filled her mind. *Fear is not weakness, it's your compass. When fear beckons, dare to find your strength.* Aislinn took a deep breath, squared her shoulders, and turned one last time to face Lark. Her guide.

"Can I ask you one question with the promise of a real answer?"

"Ask it."

"The man who... hurt me, am I the only one he'll do this to? Is there any way to stop my fate from being shared with another?" Aislinn held this fragile hope that she could leave this world and find something beautiful.

"I promise, he will never hurt another soul again."

"Thank you." It was a small comfort.

With a determined stride, Aislinn marched up to the bridge pausing for only a moment before beginning her ascension across. She stopped halfway to look back. "Lark! If I can send you a message, a sign of some sort, I'll tell you what's on the other side!"

Much to Aislinn's surprise, Lark's expression melted into a dazzling smile, her face appearing youthful for the first time. Perhaps in these moments, when mortals moved on to find their peace, Lark found her own.

Aislinn gave a little wave before facing down the unknown. To whatever semblance of peace awaited her. With unwavering footfalls, she walked forward, disappearing into the fog.

LARK LET HER SMILE RELAX, as the temporary warmth of this young soul faded and the tether to her soul ceased. She awaited the cool numbing that always spread through her veins after relinquishing a tether. But a glimmer of something remained. It smoldered in her chest. Her hands flexed, itching for something she hadn't felt in a long time.

Bloodlust.

She promised Aislinn that the man would never hurt another girl again. Lark always kept her promises.

CHAPTER 2

*A*midst a sea of revelers and drunkards, Lark stood unseen and silent as death. The sun had slipped beneath the horizon, and the first stars began their watch.

Lark preferred the uncovered sky. Had she been reaping across the seas in Koval, the same wedding ritual might have been performed behind closed doors. In Ardenas, communion with nature was the truest flattery of the gods. Weddings especially took place under open skies so the Paragons of virtue and the Warriors of Avalon might look down and grant them favor. As if the gods cared. Her master—Thanar, god of death—valued balance and uncompromised loyalty. Loyalty to duty. To death.

Nereida, the witch-queen of the Netherworld was another goddess the faithful mortals feared. She valued punishment and destruction. Reapers were forbidden from crossing paths with her.

And the Paragons of virtue, the Warriors of Avalon—they were the worst. Mortals built altars and statues to their likeness. Worshipped and revered their power and strength. Only to be met with ambivalence.

Lark surveyed the grand celebration. Long tables overflowed with food and candles. Wooden casks had been tapped, and one man was so bold as to lay beneath the torrent of wine spilling out and slurp at it. A young woman and her fellow could be seen atop a bench off to the side, audibly coupling with no sense of discretion.

Lark thumbed the small scroll in her pocket—Aislinn's name was sure to have disappeared by now. The moment she had first made physical contact with her small golden scroll, newly scribed with her mark's name, she'd felt Aislinn's destiny taking shape. Like threads weaving together to form a tapestry, each decision woven into the culminating moment of her demise. Once in possession of a scroll, a Reaper was duty bound to guide those listed to the beyond—to forge a tether between their souls until the task was complete. Lark learned not to arrive early; the temptation to alter fate was far too inviting. But she always tried to arrive soon enough to be with them when they died. She couldn't bear the thought of letting them slip away alone. Knowing what would befall Aislinn, what she'd suffer before death claimed her—Lark couldn't prevent it. But she could offer her this.

Lark knew she shouldn't be here. Without Aislinn, her tether to this world was no more, and her power was waning. Without a connection to a mortal soul, it took considerably more effort to remain among the living.

But Lark made Aislinn a promise. Whatever the cost.

This, though. This was disobedience. Meddling in the lives of mortals, interfering in any way, threatened the balance. She would be punished. But right now, this moment was pure freedom.

Lark tucked her loose tendril of hair behind her ear and closed her eyes with a deep breath, letting her guard slip. Her barriers fell away, and she projected her consciousness out, sifting for her target. Many of the souls she touched held a haze of drink and merriment. Though they weren't to be discounted, she pushed past.

Lark caught a distinct note of worry... *can't believe she's not here... should have been here hours ago... this isn't like her... is she avoiding me...*

Lark opened her eyes, searching for the source.

The bride. Aislinn's sister, Yera. She wore a brilliant white gown with gold embroidery on the bodice that matched her hair. The resemblance between the sisters was uncanny, but her verdant, green eyes were muted with concern and lacked the inquisitive brightness of Aislinn's. Yera gripped the deep umber hand of her handsome groom, as he rubbed his thumb across her bone white knuckles. He ran his free hand through his thick wavy hair, and his warm hazel eyes shifted between scanning the crowd and turning to gaze down at his new wife in yearning.

"Yera! Has Aislinn arrived yet?" The question rang from a voice hardened by age. Lark's focus landed on an older woman who held the same intense beauty as both Aislinn and Yera. Her features were set in fierce determination, but Lark tasted her fear. Gut-wrenching and all-consuming.

Mortal emotions were known for their potency. But these emotions were both strange and unwelcome. The human's fear seeped into Lark's pores, and her guard plummeted.

Lark clenched her teeth as the onslaught of thoughts, emotions, and urges rushed through her all at once in a dizzying kaleidoscope. The deepest despair to the brightest joy jolted through her awareness. Her defenses were being stretched in all directions, on the brink of tearing.

In the distance, a cool haze permeated the furthest barriers of Lark's perception. A creeping sense of darkness licked at the edges of her mind. A soul, putrid and foul, overpowered the others to fade into the background.

Lark's gaze found him. He faced away from her, and he tipped his dark head of hair back in laughter. He donned a fine, dark tunic, a gold braid detailing his broad shoulders.

"Corwyn!" a voice called out.

He turned, and Lark finally looked upon the face of the beast. His pale green eyes were empty. Stubble dusted his square jaw and he wore the satisfied smirk of a man used to getting what he wanted.

The party continued in a whirl of colors as Lark tracked her target. His rancid soul festered in her senses, but she didn't dare let it slip away. She delved deeper, beyond his present state of mind to unveil layers upon layers of his rotten core.

Images of the wedding replayed at the forefront of Corwyn's

thoughts. Feelings of warmth and pride as he watched his best friend marry Yera. When the picture shifted to Aislinn, predatory ownership collided with the memory. Lark held onto that thread and tugged, pulling deeper into his impulses. Yanking hard, she lurched forward into the dark recesses of older memories.

A memory of when he was ten. He cut open his sister's cat to see its unborn babies. He blamed it on the stable boy and delighted in the lashings he received for it.

The image shifted. Corwyn delivered the final kick to a man's face, already beaten to a bloody pulp beyond recognition. It squelched on impact.

Lark was about to pull back when she caught a whisper of memory he was trying not to think about. Tugging at the thread, she held firm until it unraveled. She felt his hate, his rage at Aislinn. Corwyn's hand pressed a knife against Aislinn's side as she thrashed against him. He wasn't used to them fighting back. She managed to claw at his chest, drawing blood.

Lark snapped out of Corwyn's mind, stumbling back as pure revulsion danced in black sparks across her vision. She clenched and unclenched her fists. She could shatter his mind and leave him a drooling, obliterated mess. It would be so easy and *so damn satisfying.*

The call of her power, its seductive and wicked song, was almost too loud to ignore. The steady beat of a cadence she was all too familiar with. The allure of giving in to these urges—urges that whispered great and terrible things—sang through her veins. But on the murky edges, a cold whisper took root.

Lark couldn't do that, to disturb the balance was too great a risk. She pushed the clawing desire aside. She'd have to find a more creative way to deal with him. One that didn't create another tear in the veil to her world. A method of restraint, control.

She peered across the crowd, following Corwyn's every movement. She waited until his head was turned to will her form into view. Just for him, no need to startle the revelers. She pushed at his mind, silently calling him to see her. His head turned instinctively, and his gaze latched onto her, unable or unwilling to look away. Like she was the target.

Lark curved her mouth into a suggestive smile. His grin was enough of an answer. With the slightest tilt of her head in silent invitation, she turned away to saunter toward a nearby lodge. She didn't have to check to see if he followed. The steady thrum of his heart was well within her awareness, but still, she cast her chin over her shoulder now and then. Corwyn answered each glance with an eager stride, his legs propelling him forward, his mind of a singular purpose.

Lark reached the far side of the empty cottage, and leaned against it. She was distantly aware of the stone cladding that pressed against her shoulder blades.

When Corwyn emerged beside her, panting and desperate, he all too quickly invaded her space, caging her between his hands.

So predictable. Of course, he was the type to think one look from a woman named her as his.

"You're a quick one," he whispered inches from her face. He brought his lips to her ear. "Shall I call you my little rabbit?"

Lark clenched her fist, fighting the instinct to kill him. Aislinn's family deserved to know what happened to her. "Corwyn, your reputation precedes you."

He pulled back, a cocky smile still poised on his lips. "You've heard of me? I'm flattered." He bent his head toward her neck.

Lark's hand snaked out, halting him at arm's length. The look of surprise that crossed his face was downright petulant.

"I know everything about you." She pulled down the collar of his tunic until she could see the tip of the scratch marks Aislinn had given him. "I'm going to give you one chance. Confess your crimes to the bride and her mother—" she tugged him closer "—or you'll incur my wrath."

Corwyn's expression yielded from disbelief to rage. He yanked her hand free and pulled away, straightening his tunic. "You're mad in the head, sweetheart. I can call for a healer, but next time don't bring your particular brand of crazy anywhere near me, lest you incur *my* wrath."

It was meant to sound threatening, but to Lark, it sounded like a plea for her talents. "Oh, Corwyn. I was so hoping you'd say that." She flipped their positions so he was pinned to the wall and gripped his throat. His eyes widened as he clawed at her arm. It was futile, she'd never feel the sensation of his nails against her skin. "Now," she continued. "As you've chosen this route, there are a few ground rules we need to set. Firstly—" she squeezed his throat "—no speaking. I gave you a chance to use your words, and you declined." She released him.

Corwyn gasped and coughed as he massaged his throat. "Crazy bitch."

"There's no need for name-calling." Lark planted her hands on her hips. "And already you've broken the first rule. Skies above, what am I ever going to do with you?" She lashed a hand onto his throat again, holding but not squeezing.

He glared at her, eyes venomous.

"Have you ever wondered what it might feel like to have your tongue ripped out?" Lark forced her awareness into his mind, tying in a new thread, writing in a false memory of having his tongue torn from the root.

Pain clouded Corwyn's gaze. His low warbled moans of anguish were music to her ears. "You don't have anything clever to say anyway. Now you can be a better listener. We need to remove the temptation of the sin itself. Isn't that right?" She glanced meaningfully down at his trousers. The panicked noises he made hardly seemed human. "Not a fan of that idea? Then don't tempt me."

Corwyn nodded, silent tears streamed down his face. She let her hand drop from his throat again, and his eyes darted to track the movement.

"Secondly, no sudden movements. In fact, don't move at all. I might think you're up to no good." She opened her black cloak and walked her fingers along the handles of her blades one by one. Before she could lift one from its sheath, she felt a slight tickle along her side.

He'd sunk a small stiletto through her black leather cuirass and in where her liver would be if she were human. Its ornate handle was adorned with filigree and a family crest depicting a bear and a serpent. Lark ripped it free. She didn't have to look at the weapon to know there'd be no trace of her left on it; her presence here was little more than an illusion.

Holding the dagger up for a closer inspection, Lark peered over at him. He trembled as wetness bloomed across the crotch of his trousers and down his thighs. "You seem incapable of following any of my rules." She heaved a gusty sigh. "I suppose the time for talk is over."

Lark kicked in Corwyn's kneecap hard enough for the audible crunch of bone. He dropped to the ground like a stone and tried to drag himself away.

Such a wondrous thing, the desperation of survival.

Lark grabbed his ankle and flipped him to his back. She climbed over him and sat on his gut, bringing the blade to his chest. He wiggled beneath her, but mortal strength was no match for hers. She sliced through the fabric of his tunic and with quick, practiced strokes, she carved. Steel against flesh. Deep enough to draw blood but not so deep to puncture anything. She couldn't risk him dying by her hand.

Corwyn's blood was distantly warm against her fingers, and with a final flourish, she inspected her handiwork.

I killed Aislinn

"I wonder if these will scar."

Corwyn stared up at her, panting. Tears stained his cheeks. Lark wiped the blade against his tunic and stood. The words angrily bled, dripping down his chest as he staggered to his feet. His eyes were dazed and unfocused.

Lark gave him a quick pat on the head before turning him toward the party and steering him toward the crowd.

"I'd much rather you own up to your deed. Consider it your

penance." She shoved him to the middle of the dance floor. He stumbled and landed hard, startling those nearby into silence.

With a wave of her hand, Lark restored his tongue by erasing the false memory of losing it. Beneath the garlands of roses and awash in warm candle light, Corwyn curled on the ground and sobbed, bleeding from the confession on his skin. Aislinn's mother stood dangerously still, and Yera clung to her groom as they approached, her fingers digging into his arm. His mouth hung open in shock as he folded Yera into his side.

Corwyn's face pinched in anguish as he caught sight of his friend.

"Freddy... there was a madman... he must have hurt Aislinn and left this message for you to find."

Lark rolled her eyes at his pathetic attempt to play the victim.

"Where's Aislinn?" Yera ignored Corwyn's plea to her husband. At least she wasn't so easily swayed.

But Lark was done being patient. She pressed her awareness into Corwyn's mind, seeping into every twisted corner. He howled in agony as Lark weaved the sensation of having every bone in his legs smashed. He fell forward, bracing his hands on the ground before vomiting. "No more!" He gagged, tears rolling down his cheeks. "Please, have mercy."

Where was his mercy on that riverbank? When Aislinn fought to survive, and he took and took until all that was left was the tattered remnant of her soul awaiting Lark's guidance.

Lark plunged to her violent depths, but she found no mercy for him. This time she broke his fingers. Each one that held Aislinn in place, that angled the knife between her ribs.

Corwyn groaned, pain snatched the strength from his voice. "I confess," he rasped, quiet enough only Lark's inhuman ears could detect.

"Louder boy!" Lark called, unable to halt her grin.

"I confess!" he shouted, lifting his head. "It was me."

With a wave of her hand, Lark wiped the pain free of his mind.

"Confess what? What have you done?" Yera took a determined step forward. "Where's my sister?"

Aislinn's mother grabbed a knife from a nearby table and stomped up to him, pulling his head back by his hair. Blade poised against his throat. "Answer my daughter."

Corwyn went limp as he sobbed. "I left her in Ferus Woods, by the river."

A myriad of emotions crossed Yera's face, shock, grief, rage, ending in a composed veneer of calm. "Frederick." Yera's voice was steady. "Please send a search party to the riverbank."

Frederick nodded and placed a gentle kiss on his bride's forehead. As he turned to walk away, Corwyn pushed himself up.

"Freddy, please."

Frederick stopped, and without looking over his shoulder called back. "Aislinn is my sister now. When we return, I am invoking the rite of blood justice."

Lark was familiar with the custom, having reaped many souls who had befallen it. The family of the victim harmed can lawfully invoke the rite to inflict equal damage to the offending party. She had a feeling they would get creative with their methods of balancing the scale.

Another wave of exhaustion reminded her she had expended too much energy and had no desire to reap Corwyn's soul when they found Aislinn's body.

Lark never prayed to the gods, knowing what manner of beasts tended to answer. She prayed to the skies that Aislinn's family found peace. That Aislinn had found her peace as well.

Lark walked away from the mortals into the plane of existence where she belonged.

The Otherworld.

CHAPTER 3

*E*ntering the Otherworld was like stepping onto dry land after treading water. Though Lark would never feel the true weight of her living body again, the Otherworld mimicked the sensations of the mortal world—equal parts illusion and memory.

Each time Lark returned to the Otherworld, she appeared in front of the castle of stone nestled into the foggy mountains. The grounds seemed to stretch endlessly, but it was an illusion. She could walk away from Thanar's castle and find herself upon it again in less than a day. She used to try to run to see how far she could get. She could circle the world before dinner. Reapers didn't need room to explore.

Although Lark lived in luxury, given any trinket, and fulfillment of any desire, returning was like entering her cage.

Lark buried the familiar feeling of dread and pushed the oak double doors open.

An empty entryway greeted her. Grateful for the chance to recover without prying eyes she dashed up the grand staircase to her room, avoiding her weary reflection in the polished gold. A garish feature of the castle, but Thanar loved his displays of extravagant wealth.

It wasn't wealth. It wasn't real.

Reapers weren't alive. This world was a shadow of the real one. An attempt to imitate what Lark desperately longed for. Life.

Lark never admitted it to anyone, not even her closest friend, Ferryn. But she'd give anything to remember what it was like to be mortal. She had been human once, many lifetimes ago, but she'd given up trying to remember what it felt like. Lark couldn't even be sure of how many lifetimes had passed. Unchanging.

She must be exhausted if her internal whining had started so early in her return.

"Lark! Where do you think you're going?"

Skies, not now. Not when the door to her chambers was so close.

Lark leaned her head over the banister to see Ferryn, eager as ever, grinning up at her. His beautiful face was all angles and edges. Perfectly chiseled and always at odds with his childish expressions.

"Go away." Lark turned to trudge the rest of the way.

"You've been summoned for debriefing."

Lark glanced over the side again.

Ferryn's face was positively gleeful.

"What if you didn't see me? What if you came looking for me but I was already closed up in my chambers for the night?"

He shook his head, shoulder-length golden hair falling in his face. "I'd have to drag you out. Most undignified, if you ask me. Normally I wouldn't dare, but judging by how long it took you to climb the stairs, I'll take my chances."

"You waited until I reached the top to call me?" Lark glared down at him, and his face broke into a boyish smirk in response. She rolled her eyes. "I hate you."

"No you don't!" he called back in a sing-song voice he reserved for when he was being an obnoxious twat. With a sigh, Lark lumbered down the stairs.

"Chop, chop little onion! I just returned from the Western Desolates, and I can still feel the sand on my skin. I desperately need a bath." At Lark's expression, he ran a hand through his thick hair. "You know what I mean."

Reapers didn't feel. Not in the physical sense. The memory of

21

sensation and an aptitude for pretending sustained most of them to relish their fine luxuries.

Not Lark though.

But she found comfort in Ferryn's friendship. His presence was a balm, his blue-green eyes twinkling with familiar mischief. Falling into step with him felt like finally coming home. Their paths hadn't lined up lately, as they'd taken staggered missions. She didn't realize how much she'd missed him until his familiar form was pacing along-side hers. He was her counterweight. The only one who kept her from sinking so deep she couldn't find a way out.

She'd been made before Ferryn. It wasn't a time she recalled fondly. But then he came into the Otherworld, this bright and burning beacon of joy and laughter. He was annoyingly beautiful and seemed well-aware of that fact. His death should have been one marred by despair—a life cut short. But he barreled into the Otherworld as if he was always meant for this existence, indulging in everything Thanar crafted to keep his Reapers entertained.

Lark had hated him for it.

But Ferryn was the type of soul that drew everyone in like moths to a flame. He'd been determined they would be friends, and not even Lark could resist his carefree spirit.

Despite the calming effect he always had on her, each step closer to the Great Hall seemed heavier than the last. Lark hoped her extended absence hadn't been noticed.

She'd broken Thanar's number one rule: don't interfere in the lives of mortals. Lark wouldn't be surprised if he already knew of her antics in the mortal world. Nothing seemed to escape his notice. Nor the notice of his spymaster, Nyx. She cast her network far and wide enough not a single Reaper was beyond her awareness. Her little shadows seemed to hound every corner. If Thanar already knew what she'd done, he'd punish her.

Something bumped into Lark's hip, ripping her from her thoughts. She glanced up at Ferryn who raked fingers through his hair as he tied it back, staring straight ahead. Ferryn was so childish sometimes. Lark had half a mind to—

Ferryn's arm came around her neck, yanking her into a headlock, and Lark stumbled along at his side. Her laugh echoed though the hallway as she elbowed Ferryn in the ribs. He grunted and released his hold, looking down at her with his considerable height.

"We'll call it a draw," he said with a nod as if he was being generous.

Lark scoffed. "Sod off to the Infernals."

The sentries posted outside the Great Hall didn't offer them so much as a glance as they approached. Dread knotted in Lark's gut. But she couldn't bring herself to regret pursuing Corwyn. The bastard deserved it.

Ferryn tugged on Lark's elbow before she could open the doors. "Good luck."

THE ECHOES of Lark's steps resounded in the otherwise silent hall. At the head of the room, giant windows spanned from the floors to the ceiling's high arches. The illuminated space glittered in opulence of ivory and gold as dust motes glimmered and sparkled in the streams of warm light.

Golden arches lined each side of the grand room with vestibules, offering a semblance of privacy. Lark passed the antechamber where she and a fellow Reaper once met when the hall was vacant and she yearned for something she couldn't name. Heavy kisses, clumsy hands, and torn seams of her favorite tunic. And all she felt was empty. That was the first time Lark's suspicions were confirmed, that this world was a shallow reflection of the realm she longed to be part of.

She didn't even glance at that room, her eyes remained locked on the throne in front of her.

Thanar, god of death and master to all Reapers, lounged on the ornate throne of gold and marble. Formal black robes hung from his frame and pooled at his feet. His sleek black hair framed his pale face. He was all jagged planes and features sharper than a blade. His defined cheekbones and angular nose made severe what would otherwise have been a handsome face, and his dark eyes followed her steps with a look of stern calculation.

Standing to his left was Commander Ceto. Rumor had it she was Thanar's first Reaper, and Lark didn't doubt it. The power she could taste in the air whenever Ceto was near was a testament to that. Ceto was as beautiful as she was lethal. Her deep russet skin and sharp cheekbones only accentuated the unearthly symmetry of her face, and she wore her hair shaved close to the scalp. Ceto preferred to stare down her enemies with the full strength of her gaze instead of obscuring it behind a curtain of hair. There hadn't been a battle in centuries beyond counting, not since the Warriors of Avalon descended from the heavens to challenge the Otherworld. But that was long ago, before the balance was mastered and the alliance was struck. Reapers were to guide mortal souls to their crossing, and the Paragons of virtue would determine where those souls went. The Commander's role had shifted to maintaining Thanar's numbers, but she still always appeared ready for battle. Ceto donned her armor of glittering obsidian, forged by darkness. Her full lips pulled back in a sneer, large brown eyes narrowing in disgust as Lark approached.

To Thanar's right, stood his spymaster Nyx. She was a predator of a different kind. Where no one could miss Ceto's presence, Nyx lived in the shadows. She could be anywhere at any time. A hidden danger, presence unknown until it struck. Nyx's hazel eyes peered beneath her sharp edge of black hair, burning with unspoken promises of pain. Her simple, black leathers were burdened with more blades than Lark could imagine needing.

The three of them were a fearsome sight.

Lark focused on Thanar. With a slight incline of her head, she clasped her hands behind her back to await his response. She wouldn't kneel.

Ceto emitted a low growl.

Thanar didn't acknowledge the slight or Ceto's ire. His eyes bore into Lark with a quiet intensity. "Report."

"Sir, I guided the soul of a young woman to her place in the afterlife."

"No encounters with Undesirables."

"There was one lurking in the forest, but I managed to complete the soul's journey without interference." Lark swore she caught the instant on Thanar's face when she'd said too much, but he was far too controlled to reveal any tells. She dared a glance at Nyx. The spymaster smiled. It was a slow creeping threat.

"A shame you couldn't manage to take one out. Their numbers must be brought under control." Thanar's gaze shifted, almost looking past her like he found the wall infinitely more interesting than their conversation. "Continue."

Lark did her best to feign confusion. "That's all. I led her soul to the afterlife."

"And after?" His day stare flicked back to hers and he angled his head, staring down at her with the ghost of a smile on his face. He was baiting her.

Lark wouldn't bite. She maintained a rigid posture even with the weight of his attention slowly bearing down on her. Her gaze drifted to Ceto. There was no warmth in her dark eyes.

"I was summoned here." Lark tried to keep her voice flat and disinterested. Let him tip his hand first.

Thanar shifted in his seat. Bringing one hand to rub his chin he studied her. Lark refused to break his stare, even as her resolve began to fray at the edges.

All Reapers were under Thanar's authority. He was the master and gatekeeper of death and all who dwelled in his domain were subservient. It was instinctive to be submissive to him. But Lark always rebelled against that impulse.

The only places his influence didn't extend were the human world and Avalon. The uppermost dwelling for only the rarest of souls. Unfortunately for Lark, she belonged to neither.

"Larkin," he said darkly, the authority in his voice pushed down on her.

Had she sworn fealty to Thanar, he need only have plucked the thoughts and memories from her mind, like pulling petals from a flower. It would have been the deepest bond of allegiance to swear the oath. Her thoughts would flow through him. Every urge, every desire, at his mercy to command. She'd never know what thoughts belonged to her, and which were planted by him.

Many Reapers swore the oath. It was a show of good faith. The ultimate loyalty to their master. But Lark could never bring herself to submit.

She stood taller and lifted her chin ever so slightly, challenging. Thanar's eyes narrowed as they dug into her deeper. The pressure of his will pressed even harder. Lark gritted her teeth against the strain.

"Speak." His voice boomed, rattling through her mind.

"I took a short detour, sir." His power was still an invisible weight. Lark had to strain not to drop to one knee under it.

"Is that what you call it? You disobey direct orders, have the gall to lie to my face about it, and then you dare to suggest it was a minor infraction?"

Lark squeezed her eyes shut against the pressure. "I didn't think it worth your time... sir." She managed to spit the words out between her teeth. Her knees were beginning to buckle.

The weight of his influence lifted. Fighting hard not to sag in relief, Lark lifted her head when his deep laugh rang out.

He wore an indulgent smile, deepening the shadows on his face. "Leave us."

Ceto and Nyx stepped down from the dais, offered him a bow, and stalked off. Lark debated stepping into the Commander's way if only to cause a distraction. She'd rather face Ceto's wrath than face Thanar alone. One day he'd tire of her presence, of her insubordination. Perhaps he'd simply dismiss her from his inner circle and let her live out her miserable existence in peace.

A fool's hope.

Still smiling, Thanar pushed off the arms of the throne to stand. Crooking one finger at her, he turned away to walk behind the dais toward one of his private rooms.

Lark blew a stray strand of hair out of her face and followed.

Hopefully, Nyx had returned undetected to keep her ever-watchful eye on her. Not that she'd be of any help.

"Close the door."

She shut the door behind her and crossed the crimson carpet, taking a seat in one of his ridiculous chairs that belonged in a Kovalian monarch's castle. The mahogany back was carved into the likeness of a giant tree. Lark leaned back against twisted branches.

Thanar's study was understated compared to the rest of their dwelling. The solid, oak desk he sat behind was empty save for a neat stack of vellums and a pristine quill and ink bottle. One small window allowed light into the room—the rest of the walls were floor-to-ceiling shelves of perfectly aligned books. Lark had the sudden urge to rip them all down.

Thanar's hands formed a steeple in front of him as he stared at her. Lark resisted the impulse to cross her arms and instead settled for placing her elbows on the armrests of her chair.

"There is a far more interesting account of your whereabouts from my scouts." The corner of Thanar's mouth twitched as if he was fighting a smile. "But you completed the task and remained discreet. So, no harm done."

If he wasn't going to punish her, why did he demand a private audience? "Sir, I don't understand."

"Larkin, what would you have me do?" He stood in one fluid motion and perched on the edge of his desk before her, close enough to almost touch. Lark resisted the urge to scoot her chair back.

"Hmmm?" Thanar leaned over her, his black hair falling in his eyes. "Do you doubt I would punish you?"

Lark stared up at him, and something akin to fear crawled along her skin, an unease she wasn't accustomed to. "No, sir. I don't doubt that."

"Do you doubt I would end your existence if I felt your loyalty was compromised?" He ghosted his feather-light touch against her jaw. Lark's stomach churned.

Her fingers dug into the armrests. The wood splintered beneath her nails. "No, sir. I don't."

Thanar's mouth spread in a slow smile. He eased back so he wasn't looming over her. "You're wiser than you pretend to be. Don't play the fool, it's an absurd look for you."

Lark didn't care how she appeared to him, so long as he left her be.

Thanar turned the full force of his gaze back to her, pinning her in place. "There is no room for doubt in my court. Your loyalty must run deep." He looked down the strong line of his nose at her. "I haven't forced the oath on you. Not *yet*."

He'd never threatened her with that before. The oath would be the total and complete loss of her autonomy. So far, he'd been satisfied with her assurances of loyalty and successes.

But the day was coming he'd demand more.

"Nevertheless, I expect your only ties to be bound to me. Is that clear?"

She nodded her traitorous head.

"You may have a day's rest. Wash yourself." Thanar lifted a dark brow. "I can smell the memory of his blood on you. Then you will accompany Ferryn on his next assignment. Leysa should have sent one of her acolytes to inform him."

Leysa. Another member of Thanar's inner circle. If Ceto was his force, Nyx his eyes and ears; Leysa was his soul. The beating heart of the entire realm, and his seer. All deaths traveled through her mind before they came to pass. She had her legion of seers who dispersed the assignments among Reapers. It was a wonder she hadn't made an appearance to scold Lark for creating more work for her. Though any visit from Leysa was a welcome one. Ceto and Nyx resented Lark for her role within Thanar's circle, but Leysa had always been kind and welcoming.

Lark still didn't know where she fit in. Her role resided in guiding souls and slaying Undesirables. But she needn't remain in his inner circle for that. His court was complete without her. There were rumors he was grooming her for the role of second in command, to one day inherit his throne and role as god of death. But that was gossip, he'd made no such promises. Lark would never want such a thing. Her unwillingness to swear the oath should have earned her a lower ranking, and yet he refused to release her from his side. On the outside, it appeared as favor but Lark saw it for what it was.

A cage.

Her only true reprieve was her travels to the mortal world.

Ceto had long since retired from reaping human souls, that was beneath her. Nyx too utilized her talents elsewhere, usually in reporting on Reaper activity.

It made sense a Reaper on active duty would remain in his court, but somewhere deep in her soul, Lark knew there was more to it. He indulged her more than the others, gave her allowances others wouldn't dare to hope for. For a price yet unnamed.

She hoped it was to earn her loyalty rather than command it.

"I expect a full report upon your return. No details omitted." Thanar wasn't looking at her now. His attention had fallen to the stack of parchments on his desk. He eyed them with a look of disdain, though made no move to reach for them. Lark knew this was her dismissal and stood, still reeling from the dichotomy of his reactions.

"Oh, and Larkin?"

She paused to turn and face him. His dark eyes held every promise of pain.

"Disobey me again and you'll wish for death."

SITTING ON HER BED, Lark finally unclenched her fists to reveal half-moon imprints on her palms where her nails dug in. They hadn't drawn blood, and they never would. She wasn't even sure what ran through her veins in this form. Neither living nor dead. Any sense of touch had dimmed to a faint wisp of memory when she'd become a Reaper. Physical sensation in this world was akin to trying to remember a dream.

Lark's thoughts flitted back to Aislinn, traipsing through the forest, head upturned to greet the sun. Lark closed her eyes and tried to imagine the sensation of the sun warming her face. The closest she came to feeling human was the echo of fear Thanar instilled in her.

She'd seen him pass a sentence before—another soul who dared defy him. She couldn't remember his name, but his screams were forever burned into her memory. As was his face, twisted in agony, as his mind unspooled until his soul was ripped to shreds. Only then did Thanar release him to true death.

Lark stood and walked around her bed, hanging off the poster rail as she swung herself toward the window. There was once a time she marveled at how grand her private chambers were. Thanar was eager to craft them to her liking, spinning the image from thin air. She chose every crimson drape, the walnut floorboards. In the corner, her clawfoot bathtub sat ready and waiting. Steam rose from the illusion of a hot bath, always waiting. Even her vanity was grand, gold filigree framing her mirror. There was once a time when the surface of her dressing table overflowed with useless and glittering trinkets, each more beautiful than the last. But they were all empty. Lifeless. The day she tossed each piece of jewelry out the window was the day they stopped appearing in her room.

Lark sank to her knees on the bench beneath the window and pressed one hand against the panes. The glass was cool, or a pale imitation of what she remembered cool to feel like. It was dark, only a spattering of stars in the sky. They offered no comfort, she had seen real stars in the mortal sky.

There was a soft knock at the door. Lark lowered her hand from the window.

"Yes?"

The door opened, only a fraction of the way, before her visitor slipped in and shut it behind her. Blonde hair cascaded down her back in soft waves. She spun in a graceful movement, her pale blue gown swaying.

"Leysa."

"Larkin." Leysa's voice was soft, and her movements were lithe and airy. Lark wouldn't have been surprised to learn she was a dancer in her human life. Whenever that had been. She was one of Thanar's most ancient possessions.

That's what they all were. Possessions.

"I trust your journey to the mortal realm was pleasant." Leysa's sapphire eyes were wide and childlike. She looked so small and delicate. Even her words were gentle, like they might break if she released them too harshly.

"What do you think?"

Leysa played with the silver ring on her finger. "Yes, well. I wanted to say I'm glad you accepted the tether."

Leysa was the keeper to all mortal tethers. She knew the moment every mortal would meet their end and the circumstances, and she trained the seers who helped divide the assignments among their kind. Sometimes she took extra care in assigning those to more seasoned Reapers. Trying to ensure no soul was left behind. But some souls were too lost to recover.

"Was there ever any doubt?"

"No, but all the same. I'm glad you were there for her." On silent feet, Leysa walked over to where Lark sat and perched on the bench next to her. Her normally glazed eyes held a smoldering fire. "I assigned someone to take care of Corwyn. I'm glad for that too."

She was glad? That was strange. Leysa valued all human life but Lark placed no value on mortals like Corwyn. The image of his skin weeping blood, of him crawling away flashed in her mind. "I could have killed him, I wanted to, and I would have altered the balance in doing so."

"But you didn't." Leysa's voice was resolute. If only Lark could be so sure.

"Didn't you always know it would come to that?"

Leysa shook her head. "The future isn't as stable as you might think. Paths can always change."

"My path seems steadfast."

"I wouldn't be so sure. You acted according to your conscience." She placed a small hand over Lark's. "You have more power over fate than you know."

Lark pulled away from her touch. Leysa was kind, but it felt like a test. Like any minute Thanar would materialize in her chambers and demand she swear the oath. "I was reprimanded for my offense."

"That doesn't mean you weren't right in doing so."

Lark stared into those ancient eyes, flames of blue. This conversation was edging on treason. "I lost sight of our purpose. It won't happen again."

Leysa let the burning intensity of her gaze subside and turned away. She stood and strode across the room, her gown fluttering. When she opened the door she paused to look over her shoulder.

"Pity."

This time when the door closed, the sound reverberated off the recesses of Lark's mind.

With a sigh, Lark stood and paced to her bed. As she peeled the silk covers down, that same hint of unease crept along her chest. Her soul was burdened with fatigue, and the tug of sleep was a heavy and tempting offer. But the threat of what her dreams would hold gave her pause.

Reapers didn't dream. They rested their souls with a level of peace only the dead are familiar with.

Lark dreamed though.

A closely guarded secret she kept, too afraid to discover what it might mean.

CHAPTER 4

"*I* see you're still alive, so he couldn't have been too vexed."

Lark looked up from her breakfast to meet Ferryn's gaze.

They sat across from each other at a long table in the dining hall. Large windows spanned floor to ceiling, allowing the lie of a morning sun to illuminate the grand room. Most of the tables were empty and clean as if no meal had even taken place, taper candles unlit and wicks pristine as if they'd never burned.

Lark still couldn't understand why they still dined as if they were living. Ferryn's plate was overfilled with sausage, sugared pig fat, honey glazed rolls, and herbed boiled potatoes. She glanced down at her bowl of wheat and sweetened milk frumenty, and her mug of black tea. She could have feasted on the finest foods if she chose to, but what was the point when she could taste nothing?

"Although, that's no surprise. You're the favorite," Ferryn said, rolling his eyes as he lifted his chalice of wine to his lips.

"Stop," Lark said. "You know I hate that."

"Doesn't make it any less so."

To be under the harsh scrutiny of Thanar's gaze was nothing to long for.

Lark spooned a glob of frumenty before dropping it back in her bowl. "How am I favored if I refuse to swear the oath?"

Ferryn's answering smirk begged to be slapped from his face. "That only proves my point."

Biting back her response, Lark returned to her tasteless breakfast. She ran her finger along the rim of her cup, numb to the billowing steam. Ferryn seemed determined to argue today. Some days the banter was a welcome diversion, but not on this subject.

Before Ferryn could continue his taunting, the heavy thud of the Commander's boots echoed through the silent hall, coming to a stop before them. Lark glanced up.

"Tell me, Larkin, does your hypocrisy know no bounds?" Ceto's lovely face was twisted in disgust.

Lark sighed and pushed her bowl to the side. "I don't know or care what you're talking about."

Ceto's lips curved in a cold smile. "Don't you? Tell me something, how does it feel to be a protected pet? What does he require of you to grant you such immunity?"

"Back off, Ceto," Ferryn said.

Ceto's eyes narrowed. "This doesn't concern you."

Ferryn opened his mouth to retort but Lark shook her head. It wasn't worth it for him to attract Ceto's ire as well. He tightened his lips and glowered.

"You think you're above the law." Ceto gripped the pommel of her sword, fixing Lark with her dark glare. "You do as you wish with no thought to the consequences."

Consequences. Ceto had no idea how often she thought of the consequences yet to be revealed. Lark clenched her fists and remained silent, refusing to turn away from her harsh scrutiny.

"There is no honor in you, Larkin. One day you won't be able to hide behind Thanar," Ceto said. She wrinkled her elegant nose in disgust before she turned and stormed away.

"*Bitch*," Ferryn whispered, watching her leave with an unreadable expression.

"No, she's right. I've seen him punish for far less." Lark dragged her bowl back in front of her. "I only fear he's tallying up my debt before he reveals the price."

He shook his head, snatching up his wine once more. "That's not true. She's just pissed he's chosen you as his heir apparent."

"Don't say that."

"It's true, everyone knows it."

Thanar couldn't choose her over Ceto. The Commander was everything she was not. Strong, ruthless, authoritative, and loyal. He'd be mad to choose Lark when he had the perfect candidate primed and ready.

Lark pushed down the ghost of unease curling in her chest. She'd never accept the position.

Ferryn swept a hand through his unbound hair. He arched his back in a stretch and waved at a pair of Reapers who hadn't left the hall yet. He wore his self-assured smile, the one that rarely failed him in the past. Ferryn enjoyed all their privilege had to offer.

Lark rolled her eyes.

Ferryn's ease with which he savored their existence left a bitter taste in her mouth. Why couldn't she enjoy anything?

"Have you even glanced at your scroll yet?" Lark couldn't keep the venom from seeping into her voice.

"Hm? No, I have time." Ferryn hadn't even broken his staring contest with his conquests across the hall and was now beckoning for them to join him with a crook of his finger.

"Thanar commanded me to accompany you."

Ferryn snapped his attention back to Lark, wide-eyed. "He did not!" His shrill tone made those same ladies who'd been susceptible to his charms a heartbeat earlier laugh as they strode out the door. He ignored them. "Say you're lying. Say you're a cruel and wicked liar!"

Lark took a bite of her neglected breakfast, grimacing at the vague sensation of texture on her tongue. She washed it down with a sip of her tea, before sliding both her bowl and cup away. "I'm not lying."

"I don't need you as my shadow. Why am I being punished for your mistakes?" He pointed at her. "Now you can't deny his favor."

The moment the words left his lips, instant regret was evident in his features.

Lark didn't care.

She slowly stood and leaned over the table. "You know damn well why I have to shadow you, Ferryn. How many souls have you lost in the last month? The last year?"

Guilt flashed across his face.

"Undesirables are on the rise. Every soul counts," she said, looming over him. "The balance must be maintained or else the veil will be compromised. Do you really think the Paragons will take kindly to our failure?" The war with Avalon was from before Lark's time, but she'd be a fool not to dread a resurgence. "If you don't want to be overseen, take your duty more seriously." Lark shoved away from the table.

Ferryn needed to remember their purpose, and it wasn't rutting, and feasting, and savoring. Their role was vital, or those souls would be lost to the abyss. If the Otherworld went to war with Avalon, there'd be no one to guide the mortals. Death had a way of festering amongst humanity.

Ferryn was right about one thing though.

Any other Reaper would have received punishment. A repeat offense would result in a year in the hole. Thanar would empty the recipient of every emotion, every memory, and fill them with nothing but pain and misery. What was a year when a Reaper's lifespan was infinite?

The fact that Lark remained unscathed by her bout of insubordination did little to ease her worry. The threat of an unknown punishment, to be called in and delivered at any time, ensured she remained on edge. Balancing on a needle-fine point. It was a fool's hope to write it off as nothing more than a necessary means to keep her on active duty—that she was worth sparing to lessen the numbers of Undesirables that stalked the mortal lands.

Souls that escaped the Netherworld, clawing their way back to the land of the living, were a dire threat to the balance. Any Reaper who crossed paths with an Undesirable was commanded to kill on sight.

Lark was usually good at following that particular order.

But after watching Aislinn's fate unfold, helpless to prevent it or aid in any way, Lark hadn't had it in her to fight the Undesirable tracking them. It scented Aislinn out, hoping to find a soul deviating from its purpose, its destiny. To turn a human from their path was to make a monster. Lark couldn't risk it getting its claws, either physically or proverbially, into Aislinn. Not after everything she'd suffered.

Between Lark's failure to slay the Undesirable and her disruption in mortal affairs, it was difficult to ignore Thanar's favor.

Restlessness itched through Lark. She exited the dining hall through the back gardens. A familiar noise reached her ears. She strode purposefully toward the sounds of cheering and metal clanging. As she neared the sparring ring, she threw off her cloak and grabbed twin daggers from her hips. Spinning them on her fingers, the closest thing she could experience to excitement blossomed in her chest.

WHEN THE SOUNDS of the sparring ring no longer echoed in Lark's ears, and the phantom pang of muscle soreness whispered along her body, the numbness returned. It was always a steep drop after seeking an echo of sensation.

Anger, fear, anguish, any of those feelings were better than this.

She was a void.

Half alive, and never knowing peace, despite leading countless souls to theirs.

When Lark reached the privacy of her chambers, she closed her door, and a deafening silence filled her ears.

She was alone. She was alone.

Sinking to the floor, she buried her face in her hands.

Reapers had no tears to shed. Nothing to dim the ache she nearly felt.

FERRYN WAITED for Lark at the bottom of the gold staircase. He leaned against the banister with a sour expression as he fiddled with his gloves. Like her, he was dressed head to toe in black, and he'd tied his golden hair at the nape of his neck.

"Ferryn, about yesterday..."

His turquoise eyes locked on hers as he lifted a brow. "You wish to fall to your knees and beg my forgiveness? Very well, then."

Insufferable ass. "Nothing I said was untrue."

Ferryn fought a smile. "Nor what I said."

Lark blew a loose tendril of hair from her face. Was it too much to expect the barest hint of humility from him? "All right, fine. I'm sorry." She crossed her arms and cocked her head to the side.

Ferryn maintained his composure for a heartbeat before a laugh burst from his chest. "My word, Lark, you are dreadful at apologies. All is forgiven, my little bird," he said, patting her on the head. "I'm sorry too."

With Ferryn, it was always easy. Lark could almost forget how much she loathed this existence. He was the closest thing to family and if she could love anyone, it would be him.

But Reapers didn't love.

Ferryn gave her a warm smile, one she couldn't imagine her face recreating. She promised herself to never try to wipe that smile off his face again. At least for a day or two.

He turned for the giant double doors without waiting to see if she kept up.

"Wait, who's the mortal? What are the circumstances?"

Ferryn paused. "I don't know, I only skimmed the assignment."

Lark had wanted to go at least a day without getting annoyed by how little he cared for his duty. She slapped his chest with the back of her hand in admonishment. "Do you know when the mortal will die?" His answering silence offered little in the way of comfort. "Do you even know where we're going to materialize?"

Ferryn pressed a finger to her lips, she swatted his hand away. "Shhhhhh. Hush little bird, I'll take care of us."

"You should know where we're headed. How in the blazes do you expect to lead the soul to their crossroads if you don't have any idea where the next entrance is?"

"Ugh. If I'd known you were going to be this dour I'd have started the day with something stronger than tea."

Lark resisted the urge to hit him again, as tempting as it was. Ferryn yanked the doors open, bathing them both in blinding light.

CHAPTER 5

They stepped out into a bustling village. Lark glanced around, unsure of which mortal settlement they were in. It was Ardenas for sure, the rustic architecture was a dead giveaway. But the continent was vast. They could be anywhere.

"Is this the right place?"

"Madame, you wound me." Ferryn placed a hand on his chest as if scandalized. He turned, and Lark followed the line of his gaze to land on a stone clad well, painted to resemble a field of wildflowers. Ferryn hummed thoughtfully. "All right, fair question. But yes, this is it, I'm positive." He scratched the top of his head, studying his surroundings with a furrowed brow. "I'd say it's a fifty/fifty shot we're within a mile of the dying mortal."

Lark repressed the urge to sigh. "Is this your first reaping?" If she could have accepted the tether on his behalf, she would have. But unless Ferryn formally offered it to her, the mark was his to locate and guide. "Project your awareness, and feel the pull."

"Okay, okay. Calm yourself." Ferryn closed his eyes. His chiseled face smoothed into serene concentration as he fell silent. The gentle hum of the wind carried the scrape of a shopkeeper's broom and fragments of conversations.

Lark glanced around. They were in a small village abutting a large sunflower field. The bright yellow flowers towered on green stalks, reaching for the sun. The road ran alongside the field, and at its bend sat a notice board. Lark stepped up to it, ignoring the notices posted in search of workers and missing people.

Green Mills.

She turned and assessed the village sprawled before her. Shops lined the path while mortals hurried through their chores and errands. A woman with dark hair and shadowed eyes lowered her bucket into the painted well. A man dusted in flour emerged from his shop, setting out his loaves, freshly baked that morning. Lark couldn't remember the aroma of fresh bread, but she imagined it smelled warm.

What would she be like as a mortal? Would she collect those bright flowers in a basket? Maybe she'd don a homespun dress as she twirled through the streets, hugging her basket of flowers. She'd give them away, for how could one put a price on the simplicity of beauty found in nature? They weren't a fabricated illusion of a flower, she could pluck one from the earth.

Lark snorted at the absurdity of her thoughts.

"You'll be pleased to know we are very close. It's just up there." Ferryn took off in a determined stride toward an inn with a thatched roof and a rotting wood exterior.

Lark trailed behind him. "Right there?"

"Don't sound so surprised." He ghosted right past the barkeep and up the flight of stairs to the bedrooms.

Lark could hardly keep up with him and wished for once he might take his time with this assignment. If only so she could spend the time observing the curious mortals gambling by the fireplace. Usually such sport was reserved for a later hour. She recognized the expressions of grim regret from losing a day's worth of wages, to the smug grin of the man raking in his winnings.

Lark reached the top of the stairs in time to see Ferryn disappear through a closed door at the end of the hall. Lark passed through the solid wood door—and collided with a firm body. "Ugh, Ferryn, really?" She peeked around his broad shoulders to see what had rooted him to the spot.

The scent in the air was one she hadn't forgotten, despite having no recollection of her human life. One she could remember enough to conjure as if she still possessed a sense of smell.

Sickness.

And death.

A young man lay on the narrow bed in a heap of sweat-soaked sheets, silvery-blond hair sticking to his pale, glistening forehead. He writhed, eyes clenched shut, as his head lolled from side to side. Blankets twisted in his fists, and a guttural groan loosed from his chest.

It wasn't the sight of the man who lay dying that transfixed Lark to stare and commit every feature to memory. It was his companion that kept vigil at his bedside. His brown hair was cropped short, and the unfathomable depth of his green eyes was alight with fire as he watched the man on the bed. His jaw, sharper than any mortal man's had any right to be, and dusted in dark shadows of a night without sleep nor the edge of a razor. A deep line scarred his left cheek and a faint scar bisected his upper lip. The scar deepened as he frowned. Sat atop a wooden stool, he rested his lips against his laced fingers. Lark couldn't make sense of why her chest seized at the sight of him.

"Gavriel, they've found me!" a voice weakened by illness rang out. His murky eyes blazed in understanding and lucidity as he stared directly at her. "I knew you'd come." He tried to sit up but he broke into body-wracking coughs, spraying droplets of blood across the coverlet.

"You mustn't strain yourself, brother. The healer has not yet come." A deep, soothing voice pulled Lark's attention from the dying man's stare. *Gavriel.* He wiped at the dying man's lips with a blood-stained cloth. "There's no one there."

"They're right there!" the dying man insisted. "Are you blind? There's a red-haired woman, and..." He squinted his bloodshot eyes. "A beautiful blond man."

Lark ignored the smug look that crossed over Ferryn's face.

"No, Emric." Gavriel pulled a wet towel from the wash basin on the night table and placed it over Emric's forehead. "That's the Waking Nightmare taking effect."

"Serves me right for not paying attention when we studied poisons." Emric barked a laugh punctuated by a wet cough and ripped the cloth from his head.

"That's not funny," Gavriel growled, tossing the cloth back into the bowl and sloshing water over the side.

"No, it's not funny at all."

Gavriel clenched and unclenched his hands, and Lark was overcome by the urge to grab one of those hands. To let him know he wasn't alone—she was here, and she could see his pain. But she suppressed the foolish impulse and instead looked down at her boots, unable to stomach watching the intimacy between these two mortals.

Ferryn turned to approach the bed. Emric's watery eyes locked on him, and Gavriel followed his friend's gaze to see what he was looking at.

"Are you death?" Emric's voice was a scrape, somehow both dry and bloody.

Ferryn's face was uncharacteristically full of sorrow. In a soft voice, he answered. "In a way. But I prefer to think of myself as a tether."

Emric's grey eyes widened as fear danced across his features. He licked his dry, cracked lips. "To life?"

"To your destiny."

Gavriel's expression was worn with despair as Emric conversed with the shadows. Or so it would appear to him.

"What's your name?" Emric asked.

Different mortal, same questions. Always longing to understand, as if that would help.

"I'm Ferryn." He gestured behind him. "That's Lark. We're going to make sure you find peace, my friend."

"Ferryn," Emric said with a nod. "And Lark. I'd say it's a pleasure to meet you both, but that's not true."

At the sound of her name, Gavriel's head snapped up, pinning her in place with the intensity of his stare. Lark froze, even though there was no earthly reason he'd be able to see her. Finally, he released her from the hold of his gaze, turning back to Emric, and smoothing his stringy hair off his damp forehead.

Another bone-rattling cough wracked Emric's body. "It's time, isn't it?"

Ferryn nodded. "I'm afraid so."

Gavriel shook his head. "You need to hold on."

"I can't. My grip's gone weak," Emric said with a smirk.

"That's not funny either."

"No, it's the truth." His smirk softened into a genuine smile. A reassuring one.

Gavriel seemed equal parts rage and anguish. His green eyes were shards of rough emerald, dark and wild. Pain etched lines into his face, carving a haunted path in their wake. If only a man's willpower were enough to delay the inevitable—that his mortal soul could cling to another so tightly, even death had to abate.

But fate answered to no man. And Emric's death had been cast into stone.

Lark didn't wholly understand how fate was written; it was above her rank. Avalon was where fate weavers originated. It wasn't her place to question, just to guide. If there was a way she could give Emric back, let him stay, if only so the agony on Gavriel's face didn't look so permanent, she would halt the skies in a heartbeat.

The thought left a searing trail of disgust through her. Why should she care if some mortal man grieved the death of a loved one? Death was inevitable. She had nothing to apologize for.

"The healer will be along soon enough. You'll be fine," Gavriel said. Was he reassuring Emric or himself?

"You did well in poisons, Gavriel. Is there an antidote for Waking Nightmare?"

A litany of expressions crossed Gavriel's face, rage, fear, and then sorrow. A quiet acceptance of something out of his control.

Emric's breathing slowed as he took Gavriel's hand, pulling him close to whisper in his ear. Gavriel's rigid posture slumped, shoulders lowering as he nodded. Something about his quiet acceptance struck Lark harder than his anger or pain.

Emric took one last rattling breath, filling his mortal lungs before his body went still. There was no illusion of slumber in the silent stillness of his form. Even in dreams, the weight of living is carried, but he'd gone slack, like he might, at any moment, float away without a soul weighing him down. Gavriel placed his hand back on the bed with heartbreaking gentleness.

Lark felt a presence beside her.

Emric's soul stood, restored to what he should have been. His white-blond hair, spiky and wild, and his tan face, a stark contrast to the deathly pallor his corpse wore. His dark eyes were no longer glassy, but alert. Lark had thought them grey, but they were the ocean under a night sky.

Gavriel ran a hand down his face as he stared at Emric's empty body. He stood, pacing the length of the room. Each step boomed against the wooden floor.

"What happens now?" Emric asked, staring at his body.

"You come with us." Ferryn placed a gentle hand on Emric's back and led him from the room.

Lark hadn't moved from her spot, mesmerized as Gavriel continued his agitated gait. He picked up the clay pitcher and hurled it against the wall. The sound of it shattering rang hollow in the silent room. Gavriel turned, chest heaving and jaw clenched. Again, his stare found her face.

It was impossible. There was no way he could actually see her.

His eyes tightened, smoldering with the anger only mortality is awarded. The anger of living, and being left behind.

Lark turned and fled.

EMRIC DID nothing but complain as they trudged through the field. Tall pale grass swayed in a breeze Lark couldn't feel, and the evening sky darkened as dense clouds rolled in. There was a time when the thought of rain would have excited her, but now she'd experienced too many rainstorms without feeling the drops on her skin to care.

"So you're taking me on a jaunt before I crossover?"

Lark clenched her teeth and ignored Emric's haughty tone.

"The journey is part of the process," Ferryn said.

Emric laughed. "That's a load of shit."

Lark turned to regard the man with sharp edges of hair and a sarcastic smirk permanently etched on his face. It was a far cry from the sweating, bleeding man that held Gavriel's hand as he took his last breath. "Are you so eager to greet your end?"

Ferryn sucked in a breath. "Lark..."

"Did you miss my end back in that sodding inn? Because, from where I was laying, that looked pretty final," Emric said.

"Have you no desire to live?" Lark snapped. Gavriel was alone in his pain while Emric prattled on like he hadn't a care in the world.

"Princess, I've lived. Believe me, I've lived ten times over." Emric stretched his arms over his head and threw an indulgent grin her way. "Were I in my own body, I could show you how to live a little too. Unless...?"

Lark's face twisted in disgust.

"I'll take that as a no." Emric glanced at Ferryn and arched a brow. "What about you?"

Ferryn offered a wicked smile and shook his head. "If it were possible."

"Ah, what a pity."

Lark yanked a fistful of wheat-colored grass from the earth, and rolled it between her hands as her thoughts returned to Gavriel—the one who mourned this mortal's passing. Witnessing him lose Emric, the pain etched on his features, it was as close to pain as Lark could ever recall feeling. She clenched her fists and pushed the thought away.

"Is she always this expressive?" Emric asked. "It's like watching an entire lifespan of emotion. So fascinating!"

"I no longer wonder why someone would poison you," Lark said without missing a beat.

Emric paused before a fence, resting his arm atop the woven wood, and stared at her. His face was unreadable until he broke into an affectionate smile. "You and me both, Princess."

The corners of Lark's mouth tugged. For an arrogant twat, he was somewhat endearing. Not that she'd ever admit that out loud. "Do you know? Who poisoned you, I mean?"

"I have my suspicions. They don't matter much now, do they?"

"I suppose not."

They had to be nearing their destination, and Lark's curiosity was beginning to win out over her logic. She was running out of time and knew she had to ask. "That man back there."

Ferryn stopped dead in his tracks and turned his head to the side.

A forlorn expression crossed Emric's features, the only evidence of regret. "Gavriel. He'll be all right. Likely he'll burn the world to ash to ensure my death is vindicated."

Lark froze in horror. Skies, that man better not make more work for her.

Emric's answering grin offered no comfort. "I'm only joking. Sort of."

"Is he your brother?"

"In a manner of speaking, but not in the way you're thinking."

That was obnoxiously vague. "In what way then?"

Ferryn regarded Lark with a dangerous expression of warning. One she chose to ignore. The stretch of sky painted the horizon charcoal as the first few drops of rain fell and landed without touching Lark's skin.

Emric's eyes narrowed. "What, are you writing a book?"

So, Emric was chatty until it came to talking about Gavriel. Interesting. "He seemed quite upset over your passing."

Ferryn glowered at her. He was likely sore that she was supposed to be shadowing him, and here she was slowing this soul's journey instead. Lark didn't care. Ferryn had his *diversions* and could hardly judge her for being curious. "Who is he?"

Emric studied her as if weighing the cost of sharing anything about Gavriel. "Why do you ask after him?"

"Mortals fascinate me." It was true enough.

Emric didn't appear convinced. "He's a close friend." He leaned in close. "And an even better assassin," he whispered.

"Really?" It was a wonder why she hadn't crossed paths with him sooner, if death was his profession.

"Believe me, Princess, that man is keeping you lot in business."

She considered his words as she stared out over rolling hills of farmland. So Gavriel was an assassin, in a way so was she. If souls were the difference between life and death, she'd collected more than he could have killed in a dozen life spans.

Hers was a necessary role, protecting the balance and guiding souls to whatever afterlife the fates deemed fitting. If she left them, if she failed to aid their journey, they'd decay and wither. Until they turned into something else.

"Gavriel is the only reason I lived this long," Emric said solemnly. "He always made it his mission to look out for me. He was someone I didn't deserve."

Before Lark could respond, a hint of magic pricked her awareness. Whispering against her as soft as a caress. The entrance was near. It was only a matter of slipping through the veil. But an idea gave her pause. She had willed her form into view for Corwyn, a decision she steadfastly refused to regret. Perhaps she could go to Gavriel, assure him his friend wasn't alone as he faced the afterlife.

As if sensing her thoughts, Ferryn gestured for Emric to enter the crossroad before he grabbed Lark's wrist and shoved her through.

"I WALK across the quaint little bridge, and poof—I'm in Avalon dining on virgins and enjoying the finest foods? Wait, I think that was backward."

"I doubt that's where you're going," Lark muttered. Emric didn't hold the same reverence Aislinn had when he reached the crossroad. Lark always enjoyed watching the rapturous attention mortals gave to the violet forest and turquoise waters. Emric's lack of interest was a disappointment.

Ferryn offered Emric a soft smile. "You will find peace, my friend. That is all I can promise."

Emric looked at the bridge with a skeptical brow. After a moment's hesitation, his broad shoulders shrugged. Glancing back, he gave a soft wave. "Farewell, Princess."

Lark couldn't halt her answering smile as she waved back. He strode across and disappeared into the mist. The tension between Lark and Ferryn thickened. Having Emric with them had been a buffer. She couldn't believe she was starting to miss him. Rather than begin what was sure to be a long and uncomfortable conversation, she busied herself with inspecting her nails.

"What in the Infernal Regions was that?" Ferryn's face tightened in anger. The effect was jarring.

"What answer would offer you comfort?"

Lifting his head to the sky, Ferryn ran a hand into his hair and let out a frustrated growl. Lark considered making a snide remark but thought better of it. She was tired. Like the weary traveler with no destination. Or whatever nonsensical allegory mortals peddled these days.

"You know I love you, Lark."

"Ferryn—"

"I respect you. I'm honored to follow you," he continued. "But damn it, why do you make it so difficult?"

Lark opened her mouth to respond but nothing came out.

"Why are you so intent on being miserable? After the stunt you pulled on your last mark, you know what he'll do to you if thinks you're disloyal."

He meant Thanar. Lark glanced down at the lavender light that spilled over her boots. It was a far safer sight for the moment, rather than the full force of Ferryn's judgment. An uncomfortable silence stretched between them. Finally, she met his eyes and wet her lips, searching for the words. "I can't explain it."

His face remained unmoved. "Try."

Why was she risking Thanar's rage? It seemed like all she could do lately was see how far she could push, testing the boundaries to see how far they bent. It frightened her to think how thrilling it was, these quiet moments of rebellion. An ember of hope had sparked in her heart when Leysa told her fate didn't have to be a certainty. The words she hadn't dared speak out loud danced on her tongue, demanding freedom. "Do you ever think our existence is unnatural?"

"Lark..."

"I know it sounds mad, but I can't help but feel this is all wrong. I've felt it for some time now." A dam ruptured, releasing the rush of words that needed to be said. Lark threw her arms out, letting them fall against her thighs with a smack. "We sleep but don't dream. We feast but can't savor." She ran a hand into her hair, gripping it at the roots. "It's not living. What we're doing. And every day I feel less and less real, like I'm becoming another one of *his* illusions. But seeing that mortal... Gavriel...

"I hate what we are. I'd forgotten what it feels like to want something. And for a moment—" What did she want? Lark wasn't even sure anymore. The mortal? Did she want him, or envy him? The agony on his face, the fire in his eyes. It burned in her—a memory of something she couldn't quite recall. She'd never felt distant echoes of her former human life before.

Finally, she glanced up.

Ferryn had his face buried in his hands. "Skies above..."

"I wish Thanar had never made me. I'll never be what he wants me to be. I can't. I'd rather die than be his puppet."

"Stop. Don't say another word."

It made sense Ferryn might be disturbed by this conversation, but he shouldn't be surprised. Hadn't she alluded to this countless times before? Lark never said the words, but he should have known it dwelled in the shadows of her silent heart. "Ferryn..."

He shook his head, wearing an unreadable expression. In two strides he was upon her. He grabbed her shoulders, his face contorted in pain as he searched her eyes. With startling swiftness, he pulled her into a crushing embrace.

"You're my best friend, and I'd do anything for you," he whispered. "But you can't speak to me like this again."

His warnings, laden with desperation, halted any response before it could take form on Lark's tongue. The heavy implication of what he might be saying weighed in her chest like a stone. She didn't dare glance at the shadows lurking on the fringe of where they stood, fearful she'd see that Nyx was indeed watching. Ready to report to Thanar.

Nodding her head, Lark let her gaze lose focus until the forest became shapeless swirls of colors.

CHAPTER 6

*G*avriel lingered in the dark and silent room. Small embers glowed with a whisper of warmth among the ashes. He'd let the fire die hours ago, and the healer still hadn't come.

The finality of Emric's death seemed a cruel joke, as though any minute he'd spring up and laugh at Gavriel for believing even for half a breath he could be slain. His friend, the man he'd fought side by side with, could not possibly be taken from this shit-stained earth.

Gavriel scanned the darkness, knowing he'd find nothing, but he couldn't shake his unease. Emric had succumbed to the hallucinations, as all Waking Nightmare victims do. Gavriel had witnessed dozens of lives cut short by poison. Never by his hand, of course; it was an artless kill. In his line of work, deaths by poison were personal, intimate. Punishing its victim before death came, and Waking Nightmare was especially cruel. It lacked the sharp-edged mercy of his blade.

Never before had Gavriel witnessed a victim converse so coherently to their hallucinations. Even after Emric was gone, ghosts of his delirium took shape out of the corner of Gavriel's eye. He could almost see the flame of red hair Emric described.

Lark.

He pinched the bridge of his nose and squeezed his eyes shut. He knew no one by that name—there was no reason for its inexplicable hold over him.

Maybe he was going mad.

There was no sense in dwelling on the ramblings of a dying man. Of taking any stock in the fever dreams of Waking Nightmare.

Gavriel glanced at the greying corpse that hardly looked like his friend anymore. Emric deserved a better death than this. He deserved to go down fighting—at the end of a blade. Not bound to bed, writhing in agony, anonymously poisoned.

But there was no glory in death, only inevitability. Death came for them all.

He should report to the Guild immediately; that would be protocol. The Guild of Crows offered little room for personal vendettas. It was effective—cleaner that way, and Gavriel still needed to debrief on his completed mark. Green Mills Tavern had been merely a rendezvous point for him and Emric to travel back to the Guild together, to shake off whatever remnants of death they still carried. A promise was made, what felt like a lifetime ago. It wasn't Gavriel's jurisdiction to investigate any further without explicit permission. It was the nature of the beast. Live by the sword, die by the sword, or some such nonsense.

But the thought of letting Emric's killer escape retribution didn't sit well with him.

Waking Nightmare took hours for symptoms to manifest. Finding the culprit would be damn near impossible. Gavriel clenched his jaw and offered one last glance at Emric.

"Farewell, brother."

He stalked to the open window with the same silence all his movements possessed, stepping over the shattered remains of the white porcelain vase. He yanked his hood up before slipping through the window and leaping to the adjacent rooftop. He'd find the bastard who did this to Emric, and when he did, Waking Nightmare would seem a merciful death in comparison.

GAVRIEL WAITED on the edge of The Wastes for nightfall. When the dark was deep enough, he was confident of the shift switch in patrol at the Guild. Sebastian guarded the eastern wall, and he was known for his frequent trips to the latrine. Gavriel needed only to wait, and patience was his strong suit. He scaled the stone cladding of the tall fortress, his feet and fingertips finding well-known grooves and holds. As a boy, he used to sneak in and out of the Guild to visit his mother in that vile place on the other side of The Wastes. He hadn't thought he'd resort to boyhood violations of the rules, but he couldn't afford anyone stopping him.

The corridor was dark, and the braziers were left unlit. No surprise there. A fortress filled with shadow dwellers needs no excess light.

The lock to Emric's private chamber offered little resistance. Gavriel couldn't decide if gaining entrance with such ease was suspect, or further evidence of how little Emric had learned in his years at the Guild. Gavriel shut the door and made his way across the dark room—avoiding the floorboards that groaned underfoot. He'd memorized them from countless nights of checking on Emric after he'd moved out of the apprentice bunks. Whether to sneak him willow bark for pain after a brutal training session or offer a quick word of encouragement.

Emric's desk was riddled with parchments and melted wax. Gavriel didn't dare light one of the candles that littered every surface of his quarters. His desk, tiny end table, wooden crates and dressing table were all adorned with varying states of burnt candles. Whenever Emric was at the Guild, his room looked like he was performing a damn summoning ritual. Gavriel suspected Emric harbored a secret fear of the dark.

In the low light of the moon, Gavriel set about reading document after document. Open tabs at The Tawdry Steward and The Coveted Jewel, a bill of sale for a racehorse that never made it to the Guild, and dozens of death threats. Everything and nothing blended to weave a tapestry of chaos. Lists of names, some crossed out others still boldly written, waiting to be eliminated—all marks assigned to Emric. Of course, he kept lists laying out in the open behind barely locked doors for anyone to see. Gavriel shook his head, biting back a curse. It was bad form to think ill of the dead, but he started to wonder if Emric cared little for his well-being.

What other missteps had he taken before his death?

Guilt churned in his gut. It was his fault Emric was so careless. Emric never had to learn the hard way, always having Gavriel ready and available to cover his ass. From the moment he spied that bruised and battered kid, cowering beneath his coverings, he'd taken him under his wing and ensured none of the other recruits targeted him outside of the sparring ring. Perhaps he should have let him fight his own battles.

Perhaps he'd turned him into a liability.

The words, *"Dearest Emric,"* peered up at him from beneath a tower of parchments. Gavriel snatched the paper, forgetting himself for a moment, and stepped closer to the window to use moonlight to illuminate the page.

Dearest Emric,

I fear for my safety. You promised you'd return in two weeks. If you delay, I fear I'll be dead. I feel eyes on my back everywhere I go.

He knows of us.

I don't want to die. Not here. Not alone.

I pray you come.

-V

Gavriel glanced up at the ceiling, searching his memory for any mention of a woman from Emric's stories. There were far too many to sift through.

He slipped the letter back in its spot underneath several documents. Emric was a fool to have left a personal letter on his desk. But the question remained, was the letter the snare or the target? Gavriel couldn't decide what role this "V" played.

Gavriel sat in the chair, staring with unseeing eyes at the chaotic desk. He'd met Emric at their designated rendezvous point, but the effects of the poison had already reached a critical state. Emric had been administered at least half a day before Gavriel had gotten there.

Gavriel rubbed his temples, willing the exhaustion to remain at bay. He'd need to investigate the towns surrounding Green Mills. Based on proximity, that left Barker's Pond, and Ever Glade.

Ever Glade was the more likely of the two. Travelers and traders, fresh from the docks of Emeraude Port, frequented the town and its impressive marketplace, making the ingredients to Waking Nightmare easier to attain. It was no Stormfair, or Brookhill, but it was one of the larger towns in Ardenas. Barker's Pond was more of a fishing trade. But Ever Glade was nestled in Sagebrush Forest—a far wasted effort if it proved fruitless.

Gavriel swept a hand over his face. Every moment he waited, Emric's killer got further away. But with each passing hour he failed to report, he jeopardized his holding among his ranks.

He glanced at the corner of the letter that peeked out from the pile. That pain in the ass wouldn't have made this easy on him. Ever Glade. It had to be. Skies, what did Emric get himself into?

With a sigh, Gavriel turned back to the window, catching his reflection in the glass. His mouth formed a tight line beneath his dark hood. Protecting his position meant reporting to Master Hamlin immediately. If he didn't, he'd likely receive some form of punishment for the offense. Or a demotion, forcing him to work his way from the ground up once more. He'd spilled enough blood to earn his place, did he want to risk his position? Was he really that foolish?

Gavriel pushed open the window, mind made up. He was a fool.

CHAPTER 7

"*R*eport."

Lark dragged her gaze to Thanar's. The hollows of his cheeks were deep and shadowed, his eyes, black as unfathomable darkness. He hadn't donned his usual garb, but his untied black tunic and breeches were a stark contrast against his pale skin. Surrounded by gold and harsh light cutting through the white marble throne room, he was a harbinger of dark promises. Ceto stood beside him—Nyx was nowhere to be seen. Ferryn's eyes remained forward. Words spoken under the cover of the forest still rattled around Lark's head. She shifted uncomfortably, trying not to read too much into Nyx's absence. Had the shadows been stirring in the woods, whispering of her treachery?

"Sir, Ferryn guided the soul to the afterlife." She wet her dry lips. "He was efficient and effective." She glanced over at Ferryn. He still wouldn't look at her.

"Undesirables?"

"No, sir."

Thanar's smile turned feral as he leaned forward in his seat. "Anything else you wish to share?"

Dread coiled like a venomous snake in her gut. "No, sir."

"Larkin."

She almost flinched at the severity of his tone. Instead, she leveled him with what she hoped was a bored expression. "Apologies, would you have me describe every blade of grass we tread on?"

A hiss escaped from Ceto's lips.

Thanar's expression turned murderous, but almost as quickly it smoothed into a veneer of calm. He gripped the armrests of the throne, the wood groaning beneath his clenched hands. "Your glib tongue does you a disservice."

Lark held her neutral expression, hoping it was convincing. If he expected her to cower, he could go to the Nethers.

"Ferryn, you are dismissed." Thanar's icy tone whispered promises of punishment.

Ferryn hesitated, finally glancing at Lark. Fear shone in his eyes.

"I said, dismissed." Thanar's voice dropped to a dangerous rumble.

Ferryn offered a tight bow to the dais and turned with measured movements. He trudged out of the throne room, pausing once, before closing the doors behind him.

A heavy silence settled. Lark tightened her fists. Thanar was drawing it out, letting the seconds drip.

"Ceto, have you any counsel on what I should do?"

Ceto's lip curled in a snarl, her dark eyes immolating with rage. "Strip her of her rank, and send her to the hole."

The hole? That would be a cruel fate, trapped where darkness never ceased.

"A tempting punishment, but not what I had in mind." With a wave of his hand, Thanar dismissed Ceto.

She bowed low and turned to prowl around Lark, close enough to be a warning. Her heavy boots punctuated each step, echoing off the walls of the bright throne room. Ceto held Lark's gaze for a heartbeat, then stalked off.

Lark remained rooted to the spot. Was it to be another veiled threat about swearing the oath? A small voice whispered in her head. *It will be far worse.*

Thanar watched her through his black hair, looming above on his garish throne, his posture rigid. Rather than cast her eyes downward in submission, Lark held his stare, absorbing the full force of his fury. He could demolish her with a single thought, shatter her very existence. But an unwillingness to submit tensed every muscle in her body and strengthened her spine to stand taller.

His posture relaxed, and his grip on the armrests loosened. He stood and descended the steps. He towered over her, and as he drew closer, Lark had to tilt her head to maintain eye contact. She wouldn't break first. Lark set her jaw and glared at him.

She would not yield. Not to him. Not to anyone.

His gaze softened to tender fondness as he stared down at her. As he exhaled, his breath blew errant pieces of hair from her face.

"I have given you everything you could ever long for. Provided every luxury in death you never had in life." His whisper ghosted against her face. "But still you treat my gift with disdain. There are rules in place—"

"To control us." Lark couldn't keep the words from spilling from her lips.

Thanar closed his eyes, his brows knitted together. And for a fleeting moment, this terrifying being almost appeared vulnerable. "No." He opened his eyes, searching hers for understanding. "All I've ever wanted was to protect you."

His words dug into her, clawing their way through her chest, and squeezing. The back of her throat tightened, her stomach churned an angry torrent of emotions. She shouldn't have felt them. Reapers didn't feel.

Lark stepped back, putting some space between them. "I don't understand." She hated the waver in her voice. Panic fluttered in the corners of her traitorous mind like a caged bird desperately trying to take flight.

"I know, Larkin." He held out his hand. "You don't have to understand. You have to trust me." Never breaking eye contact, he took a step toward her.

Lark couldn't get enough air, and the room spun. Cold shot through her veins, giving her a moment's clarity.

He was forcing his way in.

Thanar's hand closed around her arm.

Lark's skin set ablaze. Her mind and body were caged by his power. Heat licked up her arms, clutching and smothering her lungs, her breath both fleeing and rushing back in ragged stutters.

All her defenses were ripped away. Walls crumbled to ash. His influence seeped into her soul, sieving through every thought and feeling. Ripping them to shreds and reforming them into something twisted and wrong—her soul shattered and pieced back together over and over.

A guttural scream loosed from her chest as she sank to the floor, clawing at smooth marble to desperately grasp at something. Unearthly pain lanced through her nerves, leaving her raw and open as he shattered her again. Lark didn't exist outside the pain, diminished to this never-ceasing torture of being torn to shreds over and over. Her mind was a broken mirror. Shards of glass blown apart, hastily fused, and smashed again into jagged pieces. Pieces that would never fit together again.

Her back arched and fell, her muscles unable to fight or even tolerate the onslaught. Were she mortal, the blessed reprieve of shock would lend itself. But he could keep her aware for weeks while he tortured her. Months. Years. No respite from falling unconscious until he allowed it.

Gritting her teeth, Lark dug deeper into her soul's well. Searching for something, anything to keep the tattered edges of her mind from fraying entirely. It was only a matter of time before she succumbed to his will completely.

An unbidden image rippled to the surface of her consciousness. Short brown hair cropped close to the scalp. Scars across his left cheek and splitting down the side of his lip. Dark green eyes. Sharp jaw set in determination as anger contorted his face. *Gavriel.*

Lark held tightly to that image as parts she didn't know existed in her were ripped open. If she survived this, she'd find him. She didn't know how or to what end, but through her suffering, she summoned a pulse of hope.

LARK AWOKE on the floor of the throne room to swirls of gold glittering against white marble beneath her cheek. It was obscene how such an awful place could command so much light. Her soul was still sore from the memories of the pain. She pushed herself to sit upright, and a firm hand gripped her elbow.

Thanar hovered above, pulling her to her feet.

On trembling legs, Lark looked into the face of her tormentor. His wrinkled brow and softened eyes were a mask of concern. He lifted a hand to push her hair from her eyes, and she flinched.

"It's all right, you're all right." His voice was gentle as he stroked her hair. "I admire your spirit, Larkin. You're strong." His praise twisted her gut. "But without control, darkness will consume you."

It took every shred of Lark's control not to snatch his hand away. Every instinct screamed to run, to put as much distance between them as possible. Gritting her teeth, she gave a slight nod.

Thanar's mouth pulled into an indulgent smile. Like a parent tolerating their child's half-hearted apology. He let his hand fall and turned to leave, his footsteps echoed in the empty throne room. Without looking back he called out to her. "Together, Larkin, we will do great things."

Lark waited for silence, listening for the final note of his departure before sprinting to the doors and making a mad dash to her chambers. She didn't slow until she burst through her door, slamming it closed behind her.

She staggered to the vanity, bracing her hands on its smooth surface as she stared into her gilded mirror. Half-formed memories of pain hovered along the edges.

Lark studied her reflection, auburn hair hung in her face. Her amber eyes were tight and dry, free from the burden of mortal tears but her features twisted in lingering fear. He penetrated her defenses so easily. He'd invaded her soul, the very essence of her being, and stripped away any free will she'd clung to. The panicked sense of violation still gripped her chest, forcing her breaths out in stuttered staccato.

A slippery feeling of shame slithered in her gut. What was that mortal phrase? Wishes made in haste always bring suffering. She'd wanted to feel, this was her penance.

No. Lark didn't believe that. Thanar was a bastard, and she hadn't done anything wrong by wanting something.

I will never submit.

The thought roiled in her until rage replaced guilt and fear. Rage she shouldn't feel, and yet she commanded. Her hands clenched, fists trembling. Such sweet, exquisite fury. Baring her teeth at her reflection, she gave herself over to the anger, reveling in its hypnotic embrace.

A HESITANT KNOCK on the door broke the silence. For hours she'd sat, until the last notes of fury curled up inside her, twisting and weaving into every fabric of her being. She was a fugue of emotions that finally resonated.

Lark didn't look up from where she sat by the window, legs tucked underneath her, hands resting in her lap. "Come in."

Her door swung open, and the heavy drag of footsteps crossed her threshold. The door heaved shut.

Lark glanced over to find Ferryn covering his face, leaning against her closed door. Her room seemed smaller with him in it. She turned back to the window to gaze upon the fabricated scenery. Not a single blade stood out from another. A sterile recreation, void of life. It was a thoughtless rendition of what the midday sun might look like soaking into lush green grass. Even the misty mountains looked flat in the distance.

"Lark..."

"I know," she murmured. She should have known from the instant his gaze failed to meet hers in the throne room. He'd found a way to report to Thanar before they'd returned. Or he was in league with Nyx's shadows. It hardly mattered at this point.

All that remained was this heavy burden between them. The unvoiced betrayal, a line in the sand.

He'd chosen Thanar over her.

Ferryn made his way across her room until he stood beside her. "I am so sorry."

She felt nothing at this. No swell of anger that threatened to spill over. Perhaps the emotions Thanar had punished her with had finally run their course.

"Lark, please say something."

She forced her eyes to meet his face, studying him, unsure of what she was searching for. Dark shadows nestled beneath his blue-green eyes. His face was downcast. Curious. Lark didn't know Reapers could feel guilt.

"I didn't know he'd..."

Lark tilted her head, waiting for him to continue. "You didn't know he'd what? Punish me?"

Ferryn cringed and squeezed his eyes shut.

"Rip me apart and stitch me back together over and over?"

"Avalon's mercy."

Lark turned her attention back to the courtyard. It lay under a harsh stream of golden sunlight. Bright, but empty. That familiar sense of longing seeped through her chest.

What sky was Gavriel under?

The image of the scar across his cheek sprung to mind. The one bisecting his lip even as he tightened his mouth. What had he survived in his years?

Ferryn exhaled, clearing the thought from her head. "I swore fealty to Thanar. Before our trip, I took the oath."

Lark whipped her head to level him with a glare. "How could you do that? You wanted his favor badly enough to give him full and unrelenting access to your mind?"

Ferryn ran his hands to grip his golden unbound hair. "Are you even willing to hear reason?" He stared her down, both challenging and begging her to listen. To understand.

"Do you mean excuses? Because I've heard them all, I just never thought I'd hear them from you."

His features contorted in anguish. "Lark, please. You know me better than anyone. I take my duty seriously. And I'm trying to overcome my mistakes. My *shortcomings*." He spat the word out, echoing their earlier conversation. "I don't want to be a liability."

Lark recoiled. She was at fault for his actions? For words spoken in haste?

No, he made his choice and sealed his fate.

Ferryn rounded her four-poster bed to stand before her. "I know I can make things better. Not just for us but for mortals too. I wanted a chance to prove it. Whatever the sacrifice, it's worth it."

Lark rose to her feet and took a moment to examine him. The chiseled edges of his face seemed hardened, each shadow deeper. There was a tension in his mouth Lark hadn't seen before.

Before she could close herself back off, she pulled him into a tight embrace. He sighed as he hugged her back and rested his cheek on top of her hair.

"I'm sorry," he whispered against the top of her head.

She shook her head and hugged him even tighter. Forgiveness mattered little, for Lark now knew she was well and truly alone.

CHAPTER 8

*G*avriel resisted the urge to tug at his collar. He'd stopped along the way to trade for less conspicuous attire. The scratchy wool of his grey cloak was driving him mad. But he was used to blending in.

Though he was counting down the minutes until he could change back into his sleek wardrobe with minimal chafe.

Ever Glade's tavern was no more distinguished than any other inn he'd stayed at, though the decor seemed to favor dead animals. It was no surprise. Sagebrush Forest surrounded the town and roads with plenty of grounds for hunting. Gavriel refused to glower at the head of a buck looming over the mantle. He had no disgust for the slaying of animals for warmth and food, but for sport? It would be in poor taste for him to mount the heads of his kills. How was this any different?

The Haberdash Inn and Tavern bustled with activity. In a small village such as this, there wasn't much entertainment to be found after dark. The locals crowded the space. Boisterous voices sang loudly and off-key from a group of men who'd all entered together. Their rowdy energy only grew with each round of drinks. It was a song Gavriel had heard many times in many taverns across Ardenas. The drunk men muddled the words, but they always managed to pull together to shout the words, "with breasts the size of melons!"

The barkeep, a balding, portly man, overcharged for rancid swill. His wife, the dark-haired proprietress masquerading as a barmaid, was all smiles and warmth. A few curls had escaped from the section of hair she'd coiled at the back of her head, and her cheeks were flushed as she strode across the room, pitcher in hand. The patrons fit the same archetypes he'd met hundreds of times. It made keeping up the ruse of being a traveling writer all the easier.

Gavriel kept his eyes wide and inquisitive and his posture open and inviting. Conveying enough curiosity about the world that no one found it suspicious he was asking so many questions. He already had a quaint anecdote prepared should anyone ask about the scars.

No one did.

He took another sip of what was meant to be ale but tasted like warm piss. He tried to avoid grimacing at the flavor. Dragging the back of his hand across his mouth, he was certain he left a trail of ink along his chin. He was supposed to be a writer. He was nothing if not thorough. He made sure the pointer and index fingers of his right hand were stained as well. As if he spent hours clutching his quill and penning stories. It was the little details that mattered most.

"Dorin!" A hand clapped him on the back.

Gavriel did his best to appear startled at the contact as if this drunkard hadn't announced his presence from two arm's lengths away. "Peter!" Gavriel forced his lips into a warm smile. This particular gentleman was known for drinking away every coin he earned. Two nights in a row he'd held Gavriel's ear, weaving story after story about his life, certain he would inspire the traveling writer.

"Did I ever tell you 'bout the time I saved my brother from the mine collapse?" The reeking stench of his breath blasted Gavriel in the face.

"Twice actually."

"He woulda died if I hadn't dragged his sorry ass outta the rubble!" Peter clenched his empty tankard, peering into it.

"Right, and come to find out he was sleeping with your wife." Gavriel kept his tone bright, despite his annoyance.

"Shoulda left that son of a bitch in there to suffocate!"

"Peter!" A female voice cut across the crowded room. "You best not be bothering my customers!" The proprietress strode toward them, tray tucked under one arm, and loose curls bouncing with every step. Her wide nose and high cheekbones were dusted with freckles, and even with a severe expression she looked ready to break into a smile. Turning to Gavriel, she pasted an apologetic look on her face even as her almond shaded eyes sparkled with mirth. "Is he bothering you?"

"No one's botherin' anyone!" Peter waved his tankard around, spilling droplets all over the table. "Now make yourself useful and bring us another round."

She placed a hand on her slim hip. "And how will you be paying for that?"

Peter scrunched his face up and examined the ceiling as if searching for his answer.

"Shoo now, off you go."

Peter shuffled away, grumbling under his breath. Gavriel pretended to watch him leave, all the while tracking the proprietress' movements in his periphery. She hovered over his table, seemingly occupied with scraping something off her shoe.

Gavriel allowed an easy smile to cross his face. "I appreciate the save. I thought I was going to hear the story of him finding them in bed for the third time."

"He does seem to enjoy telling that one."

"But his descriptions are so vivid I feel like I can see the mole on his brother's ass."

She threw her head back and laughed, exposing the long column of her delicate throat. Her eyes were bright with lingering laughter as she tucked a curl behind her ear. "You're not the first to need rescuing from Peter's penchant for oversharing."

"Oh?" Gavriel kept his voice light with mild curiosity. "Do many travelers come through these parts?"

"Not worth saving." Her mouth slid into a suggestive smile, dimpling her cheeks.

Gavriel coughed into his hand uncomfortably. Her smile widened.

"That can't be true, I'm sure there are opportunities for far more diverting company," Gavriel said.

Her eyes narrowed. He must have struck a nerve. "Dorin is it?" Her gaze had turned somewhat cold, calculating.

"Yes, that's right. I never caught your name." He offered the same crooked smirk he'd seen Emric charm dozens of women with. One that had never failed Gavriel in the past.

"I never gave it." She gave him a coy smile and sauntered away.

BY THE TIME Gavriel stood and stretched his arms over his head, the barmaid was wiping the tables of the empty tavern. Empty apart from Peter who had passed out in the corner, a dark bottle tucked under one arm.

Gavriel crept to the drunkard's sleeping form and placed his cloak over him. He wouldn't need these clothes for much longer anyway. As he turned away, he caught the eye of the barmaid, who had stopped cleaning to watch him. Just as he'd hoped. Small acts of kindness were currency for trust.

"We don't get many kind folks around here."

He stared at the floor and rubbed the back of his neck, feigning embarrassment. "I'm sure that can't be true."

"No, it is. You wouldn't believe the type of men who come through here. Always wanting more than they give. Taking more than they deserve." She strode past him, slamming the tray down on the bar hard enough to stir Peter.

"I'm sorry to hear that." Gavriel swept his gaze over the darkened corners of the tavern. "Your husband must worry for you."

Although her back was to him, he could sense the moment her ears perked up. "Indeed, he is very protective of what's his." She let her words hang between them as she turned.

"Your name." Gavriel wasn't asking this time.

"Vana."

V. She penned the letter to Emric. She was the reason he'd dragged himself to this sodding town. The reason Emric was buried in a shallow grave marked with a stone Gavriel had bent one of his knives carving into.

Vana shrugged and leveled him with an empty stare. "I'm guessing your name isn't Dorin."

Gavriel remained still, watching her.

"Have you come to kill me?"

He cocked his head in confusion. What role did she play in all of this? The bait, or the snare?

"My husband, he must have hired you." Vana tugged at her sleeves. "Well, let's get on with it."

"I'm not here to kill you." Not yet, anyhow.

She furrowed her brows and wrinkled her nose. "You're not? Then what do you want?"

Gavriel took a step forward. She shrank away but her back hit the bar, locking her in place. "I'm here for Emric's killer."

Vana's eyes turned glassy until they spilled tears over her cheeks. One hand flew to her throat, violent sobs shaking her shoulders. She fisted her skirts in her hand and crumpled in on herself. Gavriel's face burned as he watched her unravel. He glanced about the room for the thousandth time to ensure nothing waited in the shadows. Only Peter, snoring.

Gavriel took an unsure step toward her until he stood an arm's length away. He offered a quick pat to her shoulder. She turned her body into his and buried her face in his chest, throwing her arms around his neck. Gavriel stiffened, his hands itching to deflect any hidden blades that might make their way into his side. Her tears trickled down his collar. Far too quickly, his neckline was soaked. He pushed her away to search her face for any signs of duplicity. All he saw was pain.

She met his gaze, her eyes and nose reddened from crying, and her cheeks wore a slick trail down to her neck. "I hoped my husband was lying, but I should have known he was capable of such evil."

"You need to tell me everything."

WITH THE DOOR LATCHED, the curtains drawn, and a blanket running along the bottom of the door, Vana sat on Gavriel's bed, hugging herself.

Gavriel sat on the chair in the corner, resting his lips against the top of his clasped hands.

"I loved Emric from the very first moment he walked into my inn. It didn't take long for me to catch his eye. He was handsome, rude, and so arrogant. But he was also warm, and kind. I knew it was wrong, and I tried so hard to keep my distance." Vana took a deep sip of water from the cup Gavriel passed her. "But how do you fight against the tide? Or stop the sun from rising?" She ran her finger along the rim of the mug. "I was always going to be his."

Gavriel resisted the urge to roll his eyes. It was just so Emric. "Go on."

"He was relentless in his affections. And to be honest, he was a breath of fresh air compared to my husband. He seemed to enjoy everything about me. Oh, the hours we spent exploring one another's bodies—"

Gavriel cleared his throat. This part of the tale was unnecessary. "Skip."

"I begged him to take me with him when he left. But he said it was too dangerous. Finally, he told me why I couldn't follow him. I'd never be safe at the Guild."

"He told you?" Gavriel shouldn't have been surprised. Emric was notorious for failing to blend in. Were it not for how lethal he was with a blade, he'd be the worst assassin in all of Ardenas. The Guild of Crows tolerated little—indiscretion one of the worst offenses a member could commit. It was a precarious balance. The Guild offered a certain level of impunity but it came at a cost.

"He did. Which is why I knew what you were almost immediately."

"That's impressive."

Vana shrugged, dismissing the compliment. "I let him go, but only with the promise he'd give me an address to write to."

"Don't tell me—"

"Of course not! He gave the name of a place in Green Mills, The Lantern Inn. A courier would be along every so often to retrieve anything for him. I took it as a farewell gesture and made peace with the fact that I'd likely never see him again." She stood and paced back and forth next to his bed. "It wasn't long before I realized he'd left me with a parting gift." She halted to place a hand on her stomach.

A flash of cold struck Gavriel in the chest. "You are with child." Emric rarely spoke of his own father. They were all bastards, in a way. But Gavriel searched his memory for any inclination that Emric would be stupid enough to want a family. Theirs was a life unsuitable for foolish ideals. The closest they came to family was their fellow Crows, and even then one never knew when a mark might pit brother against brother.

"I *was*. Emric's perfect child." Vana hummed. "If only my husband had not learned of it. I wrote to Emric. He never responded, but I kept writing, hoping he'd come back to me and take me away from my husband."

Gavriel ran a hand over his mouth, processing her words. "I don't mean to sound callous, but how much do you know about the Guild?"

"I know you're not free men. Otherwise, Emric would have taken me with him."

He sidestepped the remark. "Then you know bringing his child there would be the last thing Emric would want."

She laughed darkly. "What other choice did I have?"

Gavriel's jaw clenched. When backed in a corner, there are many choices one never thought to consider. "You never thought to tell your husband it was his?"

The warmth of Vana's brown eyes evaporated. "My husband is sterile."

"Ah, shit."

She began pacing. "Needless to say, when he discovered my condition he put an end to it."

Gavriel stared at the floor as her words sunk in.

"He suspected something for a while, and he must have read one of my letters. He slipped something into my tea, an herb that reversed my"—she took a steadying breath, her fist clenched at her side —"ailment."

The unbidden image of what Emric's child might have looked like flashed through Gavriel's mind. Wild blond hair sticking out at odd angles, but with Vana's dark, keen eyes. Perhaps Emric would have left the Guild. No way would he have let her bring his child there. "And Emric?"

"He must have used my letters as a means to put an end to Emric too." She ceased pacing, bracing one hand against the wall and hanging her head. "My Emric," she murmured.

"I'll look into your husband tomorrow. For now, keep away from him and try to stay safe."

Vana nodded, wiping her cheeks. "We can't meet like this again, it isn't safe for you. There's a place where Emric and I used to..." She bit her lip, a fresh round of tears dancing in her eyes. "Meet me in the barn on the edge of town, after you... deal with my husband." Her voice fell soft.

"I will." Gavriel stood, gently leading Vana to the door.

She spun to face him. "Promise me."

Gavriel searched her eyes, finding desperation mingling with hope. "I promise." Softly, he led her out, and closed the door on her tears.

A common barkeep got the jump on Emric? Waking Nightmare wasn't exactly sold at any herb shop. The most skilled alchemists and apothecaries brewed it. Unofficially, of course. Even Gavriel wouldn't bother attempting to mix a poison as temperamental as Waking Nightmare without help.

Gavriel rubbed his forehead, willing reason to prevail. They had trained at the Guild, tasting and smelling all sorts of poisons, Waking Nightmare included. Could Emric have been so careless?

Something wasn't adding up.

GAVRIEL COULDN'T SLEEP. His head pounded, his small room was stifling. He lay back, arms tucked behind his head. Cracks in the clay plaster spider-webbed in black streaks from the tops of the walls across the ceiling. As if the room was about to split in two.

Again, the image of Emric's child, a mess of sharp blond hair and dark eyes, appeared in Gavriel's mind. What kind of life would the son of a Crow and a married woman have had? Would Emric have abandoned them for their own safety?

No. Emric would have run.

Despite the enthusiasm Emric always showed for their work, it was all in service of escape. To earn enough coin to buy his life back. Emric always seemed to revel in the bloodshed, but when all was quiet and no one was around to boast to, unease would set in. The overwhelming silence of their burden smothered them. The things they did. The horrors they carried. He'd never lend words to it, but Gavriel knew that deep down Emric was too soft for their life.

Gavriel stood and pulled his clothes from the sack hidden beneath the straw mattress. He hadn't bothered unpacking or placing anything in the bureau against the wall. He'd known he wouldn't be here long. Dressing head to toe in his usual black, the familiar weight of his blades settled the steady throb of his pulse. He was done waiting. There seemed to be no reason to keep up the charade. If this barkeep did kill Emric and his unborn child, he deserved a swift execution.

Gavriel slid the window open, the cool night breeze slipped into the room. He hoisted one leg over, straddling the sill and for the briefest of moments, considered what life might be like if he'd never become an assassin. Would he have led a quiet existence, with a pretty wife, content to spend their humble days working and raising children? A peaceful mundane existence. The thrumming in his blood answered his unspoken questions. He never had been suited to normal life.

When the wind began to push back his hood, he pulled the rest of his body through and into the night. Dawn would be soon approaching. Gavriel had just enough time to wait in the barkeep's cellar. The man would have to grab a new cask; the last one had been emptied the night before. Courtesy of Peter.

Gavriel leapt from the lower part of the roof and landed beside the tavern. The cross-hatched windows were still dark. But he had no idea how early a riser Vana's husband was. Gavriel ducked into the hidden alcove where the cellar doors were padlocked shut. He removed the last of his lock picks, and with dexterous fingers felt around each of the tumblers until it clicked in place and the lock swung open.

He pulled the doors open just enough to slip through. He reached one hand back through the space between the rotted wood planks to position the padlock so it appeared shut. He'd need an exit that wouldn't draw the attention of the local law enforcement. Gavriel had no desire to spill innocent blood today.

Gavriel settled into the humble, dank cellar, finding a stool to perch on. The dark was a welcome comfort. Supply shelves filled the space, overladen with barrels and bottles of nothing he had any interest in. Drinking on the job was something Emric would have done to pass the time, but Gavriel preferred to keep his wits about him.

He crossed his arms and leaned back, extending his legs forward and getting comfortable. Now, he'd wait.

The cellar was sweltering. Beads of sweat rolled down Gavriel's neck and under his tunic, the material clinging to his back. If the barkeep didn't show himself soon, he might have to resort to climbing through the man's window to finish him off. If only so he could find a secluded stream to dunk in afterward.

The creak of the wooden door swinging open pulled Gavriel from his thoughts. He wet his dry lips, anticipating what came next. He knew there'd be pleading, denial, and possibly an attempt to bargain for his life. Never once had a target swayed him from his purpose, and this would be no different.

Footsteps thudded down the stairs in a faltered rhythm. A bald head came into view, glistening with sweat. He grunted as he carried an unmarked crate to the opposite corner. A flickering lantern balanced atop the crate, illuminating the space in a modest glow. His heavy footfalls jostled the row of canning jars—the pickles jumped in response. Gavriel stood, surprised when a sudden wave of dizziness threatened to blacken his vision.

Damn this heat to the abyss.

Gavriel resisted the urge to pull one of his stiletto blades and offer a warning strike. Instead, he watched, obscured by the shadows. The oaf of a man dropped the crate and lifted the lantern to continue sorting through his wares completely oblivious to Gavriel's presence.

The barkeep had let the door shut behind him. It was almost too easy. Most people would at least have the good sense to glance around their surroundings. Even those not trained in the art of detection might have that small semblance of instinct—to sense when someone watched from the darkness. That primal part, the part that exists purely on survival, might give pause.

This particular man had no such sense.

From beneath the cover of his black hood, Gavriel decided to be sporting and gave a loud, hard clearing of his throat.

The man froze. When he caught sight of Gavriel, he jumped and the lantern hit the dirt floor with a sharp crash. He placed a hand over his chest. "Good heavens! You trying to kill me, boy?" Though he had a startled fear in his eyes, he sounded disapproving, as though it was a minor inconvenience for someone to be waiting in his dark cellar.

Gavriel pursed his lips. "That remains to be seen."

"There's no coin to be had down here." The man eyed him as if still assessing if the threat was real. As if Gavriel was just in the wrong cellar. An honest mistake.

"I don't want your coin." Gavriel gestured to the seat near the wine rack. "Now sit down before I slit your throat out of sheer impatience."

The man threw himself into the chair hard enough he almost toppled it. "What do you want from me?"

Gavriel stood and stalked over. The man wasn't as old as he originally thought. "Answers."

Beads of sweat trembled on his forehead, and his widened eyes darted around in a panic. "What sort of answers?"

Gavriel crouched in front of him, pulling his hood back to fall away from his face.

Immediate recognition dawned on his features as he sat further back. "You're that writer."

"Not exactly. But in the spirit of civility, I will offer you my name and you will tell me yours. I am Gavriel."

"Eli." His gruff voice wavered.

"A man came through here some time ago, Eli, and then again, recently. He was blond and very hard to miss."

Understanding dawned on Eli's face. He looked up at Gavriel, fear replaced by a calm acceptance. "I remember the man," he said quietly. "Emric."

Gavriel glared at him. Eli's answering expression held no guilt, no fear, and no satisfaction. Only a quiet sadness that angered Gavriel more than any other reaction. The pounding in his head intensified. He surged forward and grabbed Eli by his threadbare tunic, yanking him to stand. "Is this your admission to murder?"

Eli shook his head, bewildered. "He's dead?"

Gavriel maintained his murderous glare, but his hold on Eli loosened. "Are you suggesting you didn't know?"

Eli's shocked expression was answer enough. Gavriel dropped his arms letting the man take a few staggering steps back.

Shaking his head, Eli adjusted his rumpled shirt. "I thought you were a distraction while he left with my wife."

Gavriel rubbed his temples, pressing against the pulse that threatened to split his skull. "Tell me what you know."

"I know he and Vana were quite taken with one another." Eli settled back into the chair and eyed Gavriel with a softened expression. "I've always known my wife didn't love me. The way she lit up for him, she never looked at me that way."

Gavriel frowned, watching him carefully.

"I pretended not to notice, but it was hard not to. She was heartbroken the day he left." Eli wiped his hands on his simple cotton trousers. He left streaks of dirt against the light fabric. "He came back a few days ago, just to stop in. I thought for sure she'd be gone with him."

Gavriel's back hit the wall, and he allowed himself to sink into a crouch.

"When he disappeared again, it didn't seem to hit her as hard as the last time. I figured she'd either gotten over him, or they'd made arrangements for her to join him." Eli met Gavriel's eyes with a fierce intensity. "I've always known that woman's worth. And I've thanked the Paragons and the skies above for joining us. But I've also known my luck wouldn't last. A woman like that is meant for more than this. More than me."

Gavriel sighed and squeezed his eyes shut. He could hardly listen, the pounding in his head was unbearable. He was starting to feel nauseous from the pain. When he opened his eyes, the shadows in the corner seemed to move. He whirled his head around, regretting the sudden wave of dizziness it caused. He must have been dehydrated, though he'd sustained without food and drink longer than this before. The next time he waited in the dark for his next victim, he'd bring sustenance.

Eli stood over him, concern etched on his face. He pressed the back of his hand to Gavriel's forehead.

"Son, you're burning up. You need to go lie down."

Gavriel stared up at him. "You didn't kill him."

Eli shook his head. "No, I didn't. But I'm real sorry for his passing. That's sure to be hard on my Vana." He offered a hand and with surprising strength pulled Gavriel to standing. "Does she know yet?"

Sod it all to the abyss. If there was one thing Gavriel despised above all else, it was a coward who couldn't own their sins.

"Do yourself a favor. Steer clear of her. At least until I have a chance to deal with this," Gavriel said.

Eli's brows furrowed. "What's that supposed to mean?"

Gavriel shook his head and made his way to the cellar doors. His footsteps were heavier than normal. This blasted heat would be the death of him.

"Hey! Where are you going?" Eli called after him.

Gavriel threw a look over his shoulder. "I need to talk with your wife."

CHAPTER 9

A day passed. Lark received no summons from Thanar. No marks, no assignments, and no visits from Leysa.

Sitting by the window, Lark wrapped her arms around her knees. She leaned her head against the glass and watched the illusory sun travel across the sky and disappear behind the hills. Exhaustion pulled at the edges of her weary mind, but she feared sleep would only make her vulnerable to Thanar's will. He hadn't forged the oath, not entirely. But still, his influence prodded as if waiting for her guard to fall.

When the last bit of color faded from the clouds, and the shadows rose to creep along the knolls, she finally looked away from the window.

Her room was the same. A large ornate bed, the crimson covers unperturbed. In the corner sat her clawfoot bathtub. She'd given up on pretending she could feel the water against her skin. Her large vanity with the gold filigree mirror stood the same. And yet, she hardly recognized it. Nothing and everything had changed.

"I have given you everything you could ever long for. Provided every luxury in death you never had in life."

Thanar's words seeped like poison in her mind. Lark clamped her hands over her ears as if she could drown out the sound of his voice.

But memory was a wound that can't be silenced.

It would be easier to give in to Thanar's influence. To let him carve his way in. But still, she fought. She'd reject the bond even if it killed her. She'd thrash and fight until the darkness consumed her if she had to.

The pull of influence subsided. Lark tipped her head back against the cool glass, allowing herself a moment's respite. Her soul was exhausted and raw. Thanar must have sent her to the deepest circle of the Netherworld and this was her twisted purgatory.

Lark curled into herself, awaiting the next wave against her will.

She met silence.

A day and a night of fighting the intrusion, and finally, silence.

A new day's sun peeked over the hills, basking the landscape in a soft glow and yet Lark felt no intrusive stirring within her. In the soft light of a young morning, her soul finally settled into a quiet calm, inner voices silenced.

Lark smiled, and a low sound escaped her lips. She thought it was a laugh. A second one followed soon after.

She'd done it. She'd resisted the strength of his will. How long would it take to rebuild her walls, to erect her fortress around her mind and soul once more?

Perhaps it was a premature victory, and yet she claimed it.

AFTER DONNING a pair of dark breeches and a loose black tunic, Lark almost looked like herself again. If one could ignore the manic gleam in her eyes. She left her hair loose and made her way to the dining hall.

When she crossed the threshold into the hall, she searched the tables looking for Ferryn. They hadn't spoken since he'd come to her room. Although they'd left things on a note of reconciliation, she couldn't quell the worry that flickered at the memory.

Ferryn had sworn the oath to Thanar. Anyone who demanded unrelenting access to someone's thoughts and will wasn't to be trusted. Working directly with him was tumultuous at best, and even she had a hard time drawing the line. The impulse to submit was hard to ignore. But under the weight of the oath? Would Ferryn even be able to tell the difference between his thoughts and those planted?

"Lark."

Ferryn's long golden hair, usually unbound, was tied back from his face. His blue-green eyes scanned her, assessing.

Again, the notion that she couldn't trust Ferryn to be himself anymore tugged at her.

"You know, I forgot I have something to discuss with Leysa." Lark pulled his hand from her shoulder, attempting a hasty retreat. But he slung his arm around her, steering her between long tables overflowing with loaves of bread and unnaturally bright fruits.

"Nonsense, you must be starving." He threw her a sideways glance. "Well, you know what I mean."

"I'm not a child, don't treat me as such."

"Of course, not. But I am glad to see you've left your chambers. I was beginning to worry you were growing mushrooms in there."

He seemed like Ferryn. It was a precarious comfort to fall back into this with him. For a moment, Lark could almost pretend nothing had changed. But the ghost of what lingered hung heavily above their banter.

Lark slid onto the bench facing the windows, keeping her back to prying eyes. She met Ferryn's questioning stare. Blue-green reflected the pain he hadn't lent words to, but his mouth lifted in an affectionate smile. "I'll go fetch us food."

"It's not real food." She snatched a bright red apple from the silver bowl. "There's no reason we eat other than to sate a yearning for life—"

"—that we no longer experience. I know, you've spouted this exact speech to me hundreds of times." Tipping his head back with an exaggerated sigh, Ferryn stood.

Very theatrical, even for him.

"Be here when I come back, or I shall be so cross I might never speak to you again." He strode away.

"Promises, promises."

Ferryn always dismissed her claims, but if their existence was so revered, such a gift, why did they play at being mortal? All the luxuries provided were empty echoes of what it meant to live. To be alive.

Lark couldn't remember her mortal life or death. But the first moment she opened her eyes and sucked in a mouthful of air through lungs that weren't functional, she felt the wrongness of it all. Even as Thanar proclaimed this existence to be a privilege, a gift not to be squandered.

Gift. The word was vile in its application. To consider this life that was forced upon her as not only desirable but in need of gratitude...

"I leave you unattended and you start to brood."

Ferryn stood over her, balancing plates of bacon, sausages, bread, eggs, and skies knew what else. He placed them on the table, and with a pointed sigh, dropped to his seat.

"I wasn't brooding." Sulking, she supposed. She was sulking.

Ferryn stabbed a sausage with his fork and pointed it at her in accusation. "If brooding was a contest, you'd be the reigning champion." Stuffing his mouth, Ferryn somehow managed a satisfied smile.

Lark grabbed a loaf of bread and bit into it with more force than necessary. Keeping her focus on her plate, she chewed in silence. It was tasteless, nothing to savor. She had the vague sensation of a brittle crust surrounding a softer, airy interior. She couldn't remember what bread tasted like; perhaps if she could, she would have been able to fool herself into enjoying it. Ferryn certainly enjoyed his food if the noises he emitted were any indicator.

He cleared his throat. "While I was assembling this feast, we were invited to play Paragons and Sinners. Baize managed to draw up a new deck, and I'm itching to restore my honor after the last game. A bit of quality wholesome diversion might do you some good. Shall we head over there after breakfast?"

Lark shook her head, swallowing hard. No, she didn't want to play the mortal game where cards determined the outcome. "I need to check in with Leysa and see if I've been given any new assignments."

Ferryn fell silent, looking anywhere but at her.

"What is it?"

Preoccupied with his silverware, he tapped the handle of his butter knife. "I, erm, don't think that will be necessary."

Lark dropped the bread and dusted the crumbs from her fingers. "Why?"

"There's a teeny tiny chance you've been... suspended." Finally, he met her stare, bracing himself for her reaction.

Lark glanced down at her clenched fists and with great effort, unclenched them. It must be a mistake. "Where did you hear that?" She kept her voice flat and disinterested.

"Ceto." The name squeaked out of him. "Under Thanar's orders."

So, she was to stay here, on suspension, until Thanar deigned to release her. Probably, until she submitted and swore the oath.

Without an assignment, Lark couldn't leave the Otherworld. She was a prisoner.

Lark stood. She may have offered a word of farewell to Ferryn but she couldn't be sure.

She had to get out of here. She had to find a way.

In the meantime, the sounds of the sparring ring called her name.

EXHAUSTED AND STILL NOT SATED, Lark returned to her quarters.

Her pride had been her downfall. She'd thought herself infallible. Thanar had always overlooked her mild indiscretions with mortals because she got results and helped keep the number of Undesirables at bay. But once he'd known the full extent of her fascination, Thanar found her weakness.

Ferryn.

What possessed him to swear the oath? She recalled what Ferryn said, about wanting a chance to make a difference, but there were other ways.

Lark wrapped her arms around her waist. It was a tragedy. The beauty of his soul had always been its wild freedom, his reckless abandon with which he approached living. Or whatever it is they did. Now it could be snuffed with a thought.

She sat on the bench by her window, devising a plan to knit the pieces of her life back together. She needed to get back on Thanar's good side. But she didn't have a clue how to achieve that end. Perhaps a show of good faith, volunteering her presence at his side, as loathsome as that would be.

The sound of her door bursting open was the only warning she received.

Ferryn stood, hand still on the door that left an impressive dent in her wall.

Lark leapt to her feet. "What—"

"There's no time." Ferryn crossed the room in three strides and grabbed her hand in both of his. "I can't change the past. But I can offer this." His gaze never faltered from hers as he pressed a small, torn parchment into her hand and closed it into a fist. "I offer you a chance. I only ask that you accept my atonement and trust what I said. All I want is to make things better."

Lark closed her fist around the parchment. "I don't understand."

"I won it today, I'm giving it to you. I'm formally offering it to you, Larkin."

She stiffened.

He could only mean one thing.

"What did you do?" Lark extended her arm to keep her fist as far from her as possible. "Ferryn, what is this?" To formally offer another Reaper a mark was to place that soul in their care—to begin the process of forging the tether to track the soul in question. If she was suspended, this was a direct violation of Thanar's orders.

Ferryn's expression softened. "Open your hand."

Lark shook her head fast enough her vision spun. "Tell me the meaning of this."

"It's a mark."

"I gathered that much. Won't this land you in trouble with him?"

"More than you can even begin to imagine."

Lark grabbed Ferryn's hand and tried to press the parchment back into his palm. "Then take it! I don't want it!"

He closed her hand again and pushed it away. "Please, Lark. Take this knowing I accept whatever happens next."

Lark tried to begin several responses. Only to close her mouth each time, words failing her. This was important enough for him to risk Thanar's rage. With great care, she opened her hand to peer at the crumpled mess in her palm, smoothing it to lay flat.

The entire world narrowed to one name.

Gavriel Pearson

CHAPTER 10

*G*avriel braced a hand against the wall of the barn. He lifted his head to regard the curved timber of the barn ceiling. It was a simple enough hold, with only a horseless plow rusting in the corner and two rickety wooden chairs to occupy the abandoned space. The shadow of a bird flying overhead shot across the sunlit floor. Gavriel closed his eyes against the sting of sweat that dripped down his forehead and into his lashes. Every muscle ached. He still couldn't believe his stupidity.

Of two things he was certain: he'd been poisoned, and he had no idea what the toxin was.

On the trek from the cellar to the barn, the place where Emric used to meet Vana, Gavriel had cataloged the poisons in his arsenal. At the Guild, he'd studied every known lethal substance, methods of administering, scents and flavors to be on guard against. He'd been so careful. And yet something had slipped past his notice.

Vana.

He'd been so blind. Of course, it was her. Now all he could do was wait. Wait and hope whatever was killing him would have the decency to let him eliminate her before his final breath.

Soft footsteps crept behind the door. It swung open, hinges groaning with age.

Vana. The architect of Emric's destruction. Her face was void of any reaction. She strode into the room with all the grace of a lady far above her station and closed the door behind her. She raised her chin and tucked her hands behind her back.

Gavriel pushed off the wall and staggered to stand before her.

"You don't look well," she said.

"I've been worse." Speaking was like swallowing glass.

Vana laughed. "I doubt that."

Gavriel offered a shrug that took more effort than it should. He'd have to act fast or he'd pass out before he had the chance to kill her.

She gave him a pitying look. "You figured it all out?"

Saying nothing, he tracked her every movement with eyes trained to detect her intentions—eyes that had failed him once already in her regard. He wouldn't make that mistake again.

"At this juncture, being forthcoming would be wise, seeing as how you're on borrowed time." Vana waited, with a pleasant smile on her face that didn't reach her dark eyes. He gave a terse nod, and her smile widened. "Splendid. I'm going to assume you are Gavriel?"

He didn't respond. She didn't deserve whatever satisfaction she sought.

Vana tucked a brown curl behind her ear. "Now, Gavriel, we agreed to be transparent here. Don't make a woman plead for common courtesy from her would-be killer."

His jaw clenched. Narrowing his eyes at her, he nodded again. Her answering sigh was all unspoken disappointment.

"There never was a child," Gavriel said.

Vana tilted her head at him as if seeing him for the first time. "Hm... not bad. No, I was never with child." She glided over to the chair in the corner and hoisted it up to carry it back to her spot. She slammed it with a thud. "Since the gentleman won't offer a seat." She sat, crossing one elegant leg over the other.

"Does this amuse you?"

Vana seemed to consider his question. "I suppose it does. But truth be told, I find everything amusing these days."

Gavriel wiped the sweat from his eyes. This fever seemed likely to boil him from the inside.

She watched him with a calculating expression. "I have to say I am fascinated to witness your symptoms. You're not my first case study but certainly my strongest. The others died so quickly." She leaned her delicate chin on her clasped hands. "How long did it take Emric to die? It kills me I never got a chance to observe him."

Gavriel could snap her thin little neck. "You killed Emric for sport?"

"No, I did love him. Well, as much as a carpenter loves his hammer."

Were any answers she could offer worth listening to her spew poison?

"I'm not naïve. I know what happens to women who travel alone," Vana said. "But traveling with a trained assassin? That would be my one chance to leave this cesspool and do something for myself." She gestured to the chair in the opposite corner. "Please, let us have one last civilized conversation." A wry smile played at the edges of her mouth. "It's a long story, and I'd hate for your strength to wane before your thirst for revenge is sated."

Gavriel glanced at the chair, weighing his options. The tremble in his legs won out over his pride. He scraped the wooden legs of the chair to the center of the dirt and straw-covered floor and dropped into the seat. Bringing his ankle to cross over his lap, he yanked his dagger from its sheath to balance on his leg. He'd never falsely promise mercy.

"I was never destined to be an innkeeper's wife or to even stay in Ardenas where the pigs outnumber the people and everything smells of horse. My father promised he'd send me to Koval to study."

It was a story Gavriel heard many times. Koval was the center of culture and educational advancement. The University and the Great Library were housed in the Royal City. But people fell through the cracks, and dreams of grandeur all too quickly evaporated into servitude. Ardenas might be the backwater country Vana claimed, with its reliance on beliefs and practices handed down generations, but at least slavery was criminal. In Koval, they dressed up the word, calling it *indentured servitude* or sent criminals to work in the mines until death claimed them.

The islands of Vallemer and Anquan were—

"Are you even listening?"

Gavriel blinked through the haze of sweat. "Apologies, it would be easier to focus if you hadn't poisoned me."

Vana huffed a laugh. "Right, as I was saying. I was fascinated by everything the world held for me. I wanted to learn it all. I knew I'd never be satisfied; I'd always crave more knowledge. My father always said ignorance is darkness. A candle snuffed out in a windowless room. But knowledge was *freedom*. A lighted path. Any destination within reach."

Gavriel watched an unspoken emotion cross her face. She blinked, slipping her mask of indifference back into place.

"When my father died, my sister's husband became head of the household. That bastard gambled away our inheritance. Including my tuition to University." She snapped her fingers. "In an instant, gone were my dreams, my purpose. He sold me and my pathetic dowry to Eli. I had to take action; this was my life he was selling for a few coins. So I slipped nightshade into my brother-in-law's meal. I knew he'd never notice the slight change in flavor. The man doused everything I cooked with a disgusting amount of salt. Including the roasted herbed chicken I made that night." She huffed a tight breath. "I didn't account for my sister eating off both plates while he washed for dinner, her cursed voracious appetite. She was, after all, with child."

Gavriel stared at her unflinchingly unapologetic face. "You killed your sister and her unborn child?"

Vana's nostrils flared and her mouth twitched. "By accident. No one suspected anything. She collapsed before we even sat to eat, too quickly for her symptoms to progress at an observable rate. Even the midwife thought it was the baby who killed her." A muscle feathered in her narrow jaw. "I've learned a thing or two about proper dosage."

"How very fortunate for you," Gavriel spat.

"It changed nothing. I was still sold to Eli. The legal papers were already drawn up, and just like that, my life ended. My candle was snuffed out. Nothing but darkness." Vana leaned back in her chair. Turning to look out the window. "Then I met Emric. Gods above, was he stupid. But handsome and wild. Everything Eli was not. I knew if I could travel with him, I could start over. He once referred to the library at your Guild as 'enormous and full of dull tomes.' He thought it had great acoustics for rutting in, but I knew the value. If I could have made it there, I would have devoured every piece of knowledge within those pages."

Gavriel clenched and unclenched his fists. Listening to her speak of Emric filled his mouth with bile.

"But Emric would never hear of it. Couldn't be bothered, not even when I told him of our child."

Gavriel glared at her. "You mean the child that never existed."

She waved her hand. "I was so sick of others deciding my fate. I slipped the Waking Nightmare into his ale, knowing he'd discover it. He'd told me of his poison studies at the Guild. It was reckless and impulsive. But I had to do something, you understand I had to! He could use me and cast me aside, and I was expected to roll over and take it?"

Gavriel grit his teeth hard enough his jaw ached. "You murdered him."

"Yes well, unfortunately for him, he was more skilled between the sheets than in his actual occupation."

Gavriel closed his eyes and exhaled. He always tried to avoid killing in anger. Ever since his first kill, he endeavored to maintain a clean track record. But he wasn't infallible.

Vana leaned forward. "Aren't you the least bit curious about what's killing you?" Excitement and pride shone in her eyes.

"Do you have the antidote?"

Vana laughed and shook her head. "I'm not going to tell you that until you ask what I gave you!"

He took a deep breath. "What did you poison me with?"

"Waking Nightmare, of course."

His stomach sank. He chronicled every drink he'd wafted before letting it touch his lips, each testing bite of food he'd taken before resuming his meal. He'd been so cautious. On his guard. There was no way she'd slipped it past him. "That's not possible."

She crossed her arms. "It isn't? My mistake, your symptoms must be a coincidence."

Gavriel had the vague sensation of his head shaking while he stared past her, searching for the moment he'd slipped up.

"Ask me how I did it. Go on, ask!"

The shadows moving in his periphery suddenly seemed ominous. "How?"

A self-satisfied smile played on her mouth. "I found a way to isolate the compounds and administer them separately. The Abrium flower, ground up to a fine powder, is odorless and harmless. Unless combined with Salinata essence, which if brewed to maximum potency, creates Waking Nightmare. The flavor, though, is very salty and easily identified in foods, so it's best to rely on skin contact for exposure."

Skin contact.

She'd flung her arms around his neck and soaked his collar as she sobbed.

Her tears.

The bitch poisoned him with false tears. He wasn't sure if he was angry or impressed.

"I turned your body into an alembic." She still wore that smug smile.

"That's very impressive," Gavriel said.

"I know."

He summoned every ounce of strength he possessed and stood. "It's a shame those talents of yours are a waste."

A flicker of fear flashed in her dark eyes. "What if I told you I have the antidote?"

"You don't."

Her chin gave a slight tremble. It was the only tell Gavriel needed to confirm what he already knew. He was going to die. "Perhaps I do, perhaps I don't. Killing me only ensures your death."

"A fact I'm well aware of."

"Then you are a fool."

Gavriel marked her quickened breaths, the fear he could practically smell. He edged a step closer to her. "Wrong tactic."

Vana balled her hands up into fists. "What strategy do you suggest I employ to sway your decision?"

She was grasping at straws here. He'd seen this before. "Convince me you're not a danger."

A blank look of shock came over her. As if that was the last answer she'd expected to hear. "I'm not."

"I don't believe you." He took another step closer.

Vana shrank back in her chair, hands bracing the sides of the seat. "With death breathing down your neck, you'd still deny me mercy?"

"Did you really come to expect mercy from me?"

Her eyes widened. "You're a dead man anyway. You don't fear for your soul?"

"Vana, I have no illusions where my soul is headed." Gavriel could see the racing pulse in her neck. It was rare to find anyone who welcomed their death. Fighting the moment of imminent mortality. He hated to draw it out.

She jumped up, hands fisted by her sides. "Even knowing my story—"

"Changes nothing." There was no anger anymore, no remorse either. It was all a means to an end. Perhaps he could have spared her life were it a mere quest for revenge. But he'd never know. "You're too dangerous."

His mind barely registered her reaching into the pocket of her skirt before his blade snaked out and sliced across her throat. She tried to stifle the blood spilling down her neckline, and she pitched forward. Red pooled on the floor.

A shadow moved out of the corner of his eye. Gavriel snapped his head up to see a figure clad in black, hood raised, watching him from the corner. He shut his eyes, rubbing them to wipe the illusion from his sight.

The Waking Nightmare. It must be.

When he opened them, the figure remained. Small hands dropped the hood, revealing an ethereal face. He squinted in the poor light of the barn to assess her features. Golden-brown skin and black hair framed icy blue eyes. She was lovely, but there was a dangerous edge to her beauty. "Are you Death?"

She laughed behind her hand. "I suppose so," she said in a soft, lilting voice. "But fear not, little mortal. I'm not here for you. You belong to someone else." Her smile was full of promise and mischief. If he'd had the time or energy, he would have questioned her further. But then again, why interrogate a figment of a poison-induced hallucination?

Gavriel staggered back and stumbled out the door.

If Waking Nightmare granted him another illusion, he hoped his soul collector was as pretty as Vana's.

CHAPTER 11

*L*ark stared down at the parchment in her hand. "Ferryn…"

Ferryn placed a hand on Lark's shoulder. "I can't know what you plan to do about this."

"What do you mean? I have to guide him." Lark shook his arm off. "I'm duty-bound. I can't leave his soul to fester on the earth." She gripped a fistful of hair in one hand, Gavriel's name in the other. "You call this an offering? Is this a test from Thanar?"

"No, I promise! I just thought if you wanted a chance to see him one last time or even…" Ferryn turned away, his gaze falling to the floorboards.

"What?" Lark pulled him to face her. "Tell me."

Reluctantly, he met her eyes. "There are whispers of a power that could offer an alternative to death."

Did he mean the witch of the Netherworld? She was the only one, besides Thanar, to hold such a power. But to contact the Netherworld without permission was to invite Thanar's wrath, and Lark had no desire to make herself a target.

Lark paced the length of her bed. "Nereida? You want me to consort with the witch of the Netherworld?"

"Queen," he quietly corrected.

"Curse you, Ferryn. Why would you put this on me?"

"I've told you, Larkin." He ignored her cutting glare. "This is a chance. Change the path, forge a way. Isn't that what you wanted?"

Lark stared down at Gavriel's name. Perhaps she could do it: alter fate. But what if Nereida sold her out to Thanar? Thanar would know one way or another, he always knew. And if his punishment for perceived disloyalty was any gauge...

Was this mortal worth it?

Damn. Damn it all.

"How do I find her?"

"You don't," Ferryn said. Lark opened her mouth to protest but he continued. "That would be wildly dangerous and an affront to Thanar."

"I don't know what kind of games you're playing—"

Ferryn held up a hand. "If I were to *hypothetically* converse on entering the Netherworld free from prying eyes, I'd mention the use of paint for these markings as the entry point." He withdrew a slip of parchment from his pocket and handed it to her.

She stared at it. "How do you know of this?" All communication between the Otherworld and the Netherworld ran through Thanar or his inner circle. A way to slip past unnoticed? This information was enough to earn a fierce punishment.

Ferryn scowled. "I know things too, Larkin. I can read."

His response offered little in the way of comfort. "Ferryn—"

"Hush now, listen closely. Use said paint to trace markings here." He took the tip of his finger and drew it down the center of her face. "And here." His finger ghosted across her cheeks.

Why was he taking this risk? Lark searched his face for answers. He held her stare with a forceful hope in his eyes.

"But chatting among friends about forbidden subjects, I would be remiss if I didn't also mention the words needing to be spoken." Ferryn snatched the paper from her hands and flipped it over, returning it to her grasp. "Here."

He was risking much. All Thanar needed to do was ask the right question, and he'd know to sift through Ferryn's mind and find this very moment.

Lark laced her hand in his. For all his flaws, all his shortcomings, he was still her friend.

"But it's a good thing you won't be doing those things we only discussed hypothetically."

Her mouth twitched. "Yes, it's a good thing."

He kissed the top of her head before pulling his hand from hers. Turning on his heel he strode to the door.

"Thank you."

Ferryn paused. "I don't know what you're thanking me for," he said with a blank stare. "I came to find you, but you were resting." Without another glance, he was gone.

LARK SCRIBED the intricate symbols on her floorboards. Sweeping lines and cutting forms Lark had only glimpsed in Leysa's private library, where ancient texts of Avalon were hidden. She couldn't understand it, so Lark hadn't paid much attention. Now, she wished she'd asked Leysa to explain their meaning. Shapes snaked around where Lark kneeled, red paint seeping into the dark grains of wood. Could Thanar have put Ferryn up to this to see what she'd do?

Lark couldn't dwell on that thought.

She'd already had the red pigment on hand. A gift from Thanar because he liked the way her eyes looked smudged with red kohl back when he used to throw parties. It was easy to run down to the kitchens to collect a few eggs so she could make the paint. For once, she was grateful for how much her fellow Reapers played at being mortal.

Lark dabbed her finger in the bowl and brought her circle to a close. The wick of her candle was almost burnt to nothing. Hours had passed, and yet she hadn't accepted the mark. The tether to Gavriel's soul. Fearing what she'd see of him, she'd put off forging the mental connection.

Finally, she completed the last symbol. Now all she had left was the incantation. But first, she needed to see what he faced. She reached the parchment she'd left out of the circle, and sat legs askew to avoid smudging the paint.

Gavriel Pearson.

Letting her eyes slip closed, Lark sent her awareness out, feeling for the tether. A gentle tug in response was all the invitation she needed.

She was in a forest. The dense tree line surrounded her. Movement out of the corner of her eye snapped her attention to him. Gavriel. A deathly pallor lightened his skin and dark purple bruising curled beneath his eyes. His hair was matted with sweat as he staggered forward, deeper into the woods, a look of determination etched on his face.

He wheezed, a thick sound, but didn't slow his pace.

There were no visible wounds on his body.

Lark pushed her awareness even deeper. Into the very recesses of his mind.

Jagged fragments of images pelted her. A woman with dark hair and green eyes smiling down at her, thumbs wiping away her tears. A whip held in an unfamiliar hand. A flash of red hair, a vase shattering against the wall, a blade in her hand swiping across a delicate throat.

Lark fell back against the floor.

Her chest rising and falling, she stared up at her stamped bronze ceiling. She was no closer to any understanding, which had never happened before. When she tapped into a mark to determine what she'd face, she would ease into their mind and weave herself through the end of their story. It was her right and privilege as their guide.

Gavriel was different.

She should travel to the mortal realm and fulfill her duty. She was honor-bound to help his soul cross over, to aid him in his path to his destiny. The last thing she needed to do was cross Thanar again, and this... there was no greater offense than to interfere with the balance of life and death.

Was it worth it?

Was he worth it?

Lark could still complete the mark. She'd forged the tether, she could walk away from the symbols on the floor and lead Gavriel's soul to the afterlife. She hadn't done anything that couldn't be undone.

Thanar's punishment flashed in her mind.

Lark might not be able to fight his compulsion next time. She still hadn't regained all her strength. If he chose to dominate her will now, she would be powerless to stop him. But if the fear of his punishment could sway her from her purpose, he'd already won. This choice was hers.

Thanar would not be her master. Neither would her fear.

Lark clenched her fist. She was running out of time. She grabbed the bowl, dipped her index finger until it was coated in a sheen of red, and drew a line down her face from hairline to chin.

Taking a deep breath, she dowsed two fingers this time and ran them across her cheekbones.

"Aperi portam."

The circle of symbols on the floor began to ripple. Lark held both palms flat and pushed into the floor. She sank deeper and deeper through the wooden boards as if they were the veil that separated the worlds. An illusion of a barrier.

Lark slipped through, tumbling through a yawning chasm of nothing, and her stomach dropped. She didn't land, she just... stopped. Time halted, suspended in midair. She still sat on the floor, palms against now bare wood. The symbols had vanished. She glanced up to find her chamber door. She hadn't left? It hadn't worked?

She was in her room, nothing had changed.

Lark wiped the paint from her face, only to find clean skin. As she stood, the entire illusion of her bedroom disintegrated into dust—a dark billowing cloud that evaporated until she stood in a stone corridor lit by glowing braziers.

A single red door stood at the end.

There was no turning back. The only way to go was forward, to the red door.

Lark took a shaky step forward. Her stomach was a stone. The only other time she felt this much was under Thanar's power. This must be the Netherworld, it was the only place a soul absent a body could experience visceral reactions. How else would they punish the souls of the damned?

Fear is not my master. I will never submit.

Lark ran her fingers along the walls. They rippled under her touch as if she disturbed the image reflected in a pond.

Lark reached the door and hesitated. This was the realm for souls in the afterlife—provided they failed to earn a spot in Avalon. The Netherworld had many circles. Lacuna was the pocket between the Netherworld and the Mortal world, a unique place of suffering. Arcadia was known to be a blessing in the Netherworld, a second chance at a happy afterlife. One of the great Warriors of Avalon had crafted it as a gift for mortals who fell short of passage to the heavens. But one would be a fool not to fear a descent into the Netherworld. For deeper still, the pits resided. The pits were a prison where only the darkest, most twisted souls dwelled. The birthplace of Undesirables, souls who clawed their way back to the living, only to be contorted beyond what little shred of humanity they had left. Rumors had circulated that the most fearsome of Undesirables were souls of the Netherworld released by the very witch Lark sought.

Lark reached for the ornate brass doorknob and twisted, letting the door slowly swing open.

Whatever Lark dreamt she might encounter traversing the depths of the Netherworld, this was not it.

She'd heard tales of the witch of the Netherworld, the mother of darkness, and evil incarnate. The only being to match Thanar in both power and cruelty. But nothing could have prepared her for what lay ahead.

Lounging in an oversized black leather chair—legs dangling over one side with heeled boots crossed at the ankles—was a woman. Her thick curls of snowy hair hung over her shoulders, and a large leather-bound book hid her face. She donned a black, silky gown that pooled on the floor, and her pale legs flashed through a thigh-high slit. She still hadn't deigned to look up from her book.

Lark cleared her throat.

One finger shot up in the air, signaling to wait a moment. The fire, crackling in the hearth, cut through the silence. Unsure of what to do, Lark took the opportunity to survey the space. Books filled the large room. Floor to ceiling bookcases with numerous volumes wedged in. Spilled across the desk, stacked on the floor, more books than Lark could count. The only other private room she'd ever encountered with these many books was Thanar's. But where his study was cold and organized, this was warm and messy. Homey. Perhaps that was to give a false sense of security.

With a sigh Nereida lowered the book, swiping her delicate spectacles from the tip of her nose. "I love a slow burn, don't you?" She had a decadent timbre to her voice, deep and rich. "Is there anything more satisfying than all the unspoken promises of that first kiss?"

Nereida turned the full force of her gaze onto Lark, violet eyes alight with intelligence and age. Regardless of her centuries, her face was smooth and youthful. Her delicate, upturned nose was situated above thick, full lips painted a deep burgundy, and despite her white tresses, dark eyebrows and lashes framed her narrow eyes.

It was then, Lark realized she hadn't answered the question. "Um, I'm sorry I don't understand."

The witch held the book up and quirked her dark lips. "A tale of romance rife with twists and turns. If it comes too easy, it doesn't feel earned, does it?"

Lark frowned. "I thought love was meant to be freely given, if it's earned that isn't much of a gift."

The witch flashed a smile that sent shivers down Lark's spine. "Oh, you are a sweet thing." She stood and stretched with feline grace. "You didn't come here to discuss my love of filthy romantic literature now, did you, sweet Larkin?"

Lark shouldn't have been surprised. If Nereida was as powerful as was claimed, she would have sensed her coming. "No, witch. I didn't."

She raised a dark, elegant brow. "Nereida, child, and mind your manners. You're in my house now."

The fear Lark had commanded at bay fluttered in her stomach.

"Aren't your kind afraid of me?"

"I'm not afraid." Lark's words were automatic, a knee-jerk reaction.

Nereida rested a hand on her generous hip. "You should be," she whispered. "Tell me why you've come down here, little Reaper."

Lark did her best to hide her discomfort. "I need your help."

Nereida smiled sweetly and nodded, twirling the end of a white curl.

Lark swallowed the unexpected lump in her throat. "There's a mortal, whose soul I've been tasked with claiming."

"That doesn't sound like anything you can't handle yourself, dear." Fire and amusement danced in Nereida's eyes.

"I don't want to guide him." Lark took a deep breath. "I want to save him." The last vestiges of uncertainty faded, and Lark was more certain of her path than ever before.

Nereida hummed, casting her violet gaze to the side as if in thought. "Is he handsome?"

"What? Why would that... I don't know." Handsome? Why should that make a difference?

"Liar. He must be very handsome indeed to have you twisted in such knots."

Lark's lips tightened. It was absurd to expect help from a witch.

Nereida smoothed the black silk of her gown. The deep angular plunge of her neckline accentuated her generous cleavage. "Is that why you sought me out? You've risked much asking for my help, little Reaper. He'd best be handsome enough to be worth the trouble."

"You seem fascinated with physical beauty. Do all your allegiances run only skin deep?"

"Ooh. She bites." Nereida laughed, tossing her head back. Her white teeth gleamed in the firelight. "You speak of allegiances you know nothing of, child. Bitter ramblings from your master I suspect. But again, you didn't answer my question. Perhaps because you don't even know why you seek to save him?"

Lark grit her teeth. "Will you help me or not? I haven't much time." She still hadn't gleaned any understanding of Gavriel's death. He could be dead already, his soul stuck until she arrived.

Nereida clicked her tongue. "My help hinges on your reasons, sweet Larkin. Come, now. Venture a guess."

Lark enunciated every word. "If I can keep death from him, I have to. Whatever the cost." Why did it matter? Was it the mortal or control? A need to save Gavriel, or a chance to prove she would never be Thanar's slave? "Perhaps I've slipped into madness."

"Love is madness. Anyone who tells you otherwise is either a fool or a liar." Nereida studied her for a moment. Assessing.

Lark stiffened, knowing whatever came next, she'd accept it. Perhaps that made her a fool. But her foolish heart knew the truth. There was no turning back now. Whatever price demanded, she'd pay. This was her choice.

Thanar would punish her either way. She might as well give him a good reason.

"Very well." Nereida strode over to stand behind her large wooden desk, her black skirts billowing in her wake to reveal thick, pale thighs. She yanked open a drawer and began rummaging around.

"I'm sorry, what?" Lark asked. Nereida wasn't going to make her beg or crawl on glass?

Nereida ignored her and continued searching the drawer. A triumphant expression came over her face. "Ah, here we are." She pulled out a dainty glass vial filled with iridescent blue liquid and shut the drawer with the side of her rounded hip.

Nereida placed the vial in Lark's palm, folding her hand shut, and pulling her close. Lark had nowhere to look but into those narrow, violet eyes. They crackled with energy like the sky before a storm.

"This will save your man. It will stitch his earthly body as well as his eternal soul back together, good as new," the witch said. Lark attempted to peer down at their joined hands, but Nereida yanked hard enough to force her attention back to her face. "This is transference magic, so you must restore the balance."

"What does that entail exactly?"

"You will have to swear to take on his injuries, open your soul to accept his pain. Your promise must be true, or it won't work. Come now don't look so grim, you aren't alive so no harm should come to you."

No harm *should* come. Trifling with technicalities was always dangerous.

It didn't matter. It changed nothing.

Nereida nodded, as if aware of Lark's thoughts. Her expression turned serious. "But be sure this is the path you wish to take. There will be no turning back, Larkin."

Lark nodded. There was a glimmer of something, excitement? It curled in her chest as she made her decision. A foolish decision, to be sure. But oh, how it was hers to make. Was this freedom? Eyes wide open, choosing pain?

But Lark wasn't a complete imbecile. "Name your price."

Nereida shook her head, deep burgundy lips tugging at the corners. "The first one's free, sweet thing. Now go. And remember, if your promise is false, it won't work. The bright side is mortals have short shelf lives, so even if he dies, you can rest assured knowing his end was coming soon, anyway." She released Lark's hand and took a step back.

Lark tightened her grip on the small vial, as her own heart clenched. "Why are you helping me?"

Nereida held up a finger. "Ah, ah. Like I said, I enjoy a slow burn. When you finish the story, you'll understand more than you possibly could right now."

CHAPTER 12

Gavriel was familiar enough with death to know his end was near.

Like a dying animal, he'd crawled away for some peace. In the end, that was the only luxury he could afford.

Hidden among the dense greenery of the narrow trees, he'd made it far enough into the Sagebrush Forest that it would be private. Nestled in the leaves, Gavriel awaited his demise with the patience he'd honed from years spent waiting in the dark for his targets.

But he was no danger to anyone today. If there was an afterlife, Emric would be waiting. Ready to beat him bloody for being so foolish. For walking straight into a trap. Perhaps grief had made him sloppy.

Now, Gavriel was just tired. Through his bones, deep in the pit of his soul, he was tired. Tired of death. Tired of life.

A bloody cough rattled through him. He rolled to his side, granting his lungs reprieve. The forest floor cushioned his head as beads of sweat trailed down his face, stinging his eyes. His vision turned hazy as he stared at the swirls of green and pale sunlight. This seemed like a decent way to die. He could think of far worse ways to go. Not even Gavriel had the stomach for the time he found one of his men tortured, ribs severed from his spine and lungs pulled through to create wings like a crow. A vicious mockery of the Guild symbol. Gavriel had vomited right on the stone floor at the sight.

There was a quiet dignity to this death. Poisoned by a brilliant woman. But what a waste, her talents could have been applied to greater fates than this. Perhaps even the Guild could have used a mind like hers, had they found her before all this.

Gavriel barked a laugh, blood trickling out the side of his mouth. He'd never have let her anywhere near the Guild. It was a shite home, made worse by the social-climbing of pissants like Connor Briggins, and the hand that fed you was as likely to leave a blade in your back should you misstep. But it was home.

Home. After his mother sold him to the Guild, Gavriel never dared hope to call it that. But that's what it became.

Memories of bright mornings, of his mother's laughter as she cooked him breakfast, the smell of freshly baked bread—they were hard to hold onto. They slipped through his fingers like water. The memories from after, the landlord casting them into the street, his mother's determined stride after she left him on the steps of the stone castle, Hamlin's heavy hand on his shoulder, and all his time training at the Guild—those were easier to recall. Almost as easy as memories of visiting her in that infernal place where she'd disappear up the stairs with strange men. Each time he saw her, her eyes held less light.

If there was an afterlife, would he see her again?

A hint of movement swept through his periphery. Gavriel turned, regretting the way his head spun. He'd forgotten one crucial side effect of Waking Nightmare—the hallucinations—the torture of a slow, creeping madness. He groaned and rolled to his back, staring up at the wavering trees. The leaves swayed in the wind. He let his eyes lose what little focus remained, obscuring the sight overhead to a muddled series of shapes and shadows.

Perhaps if he gave in, death would come swiftly and without malice.

Not that he deserved such kindness.

The snap of a twig ripped him from his thoughts. He whipped his head to face the sound, the action sent stars dancing in the corners of his vision.

A mass of black and red came barreling out of the thicket, straight toward him. Before he had time to react, a body landed, hard and heavy beside him. He angled his head to see what was disturbing his death.

A young woman clad head to toe in black kneeled beside him. She reached into her pocket with desperate hands, clawing for something. Her red hair was windswept and wild as she yanked a small vial of glowing blue liquid out of her pocket. She sighed in relief and looked at him with panicked eyes.

The whole world narrowed to her face.

A warm glow emanated from her skin as if she'd swallowed the sun. Pale pink lips parted as she stared down at him. Her amber eyes peered to the very depths of his soul.

Waking Nightmare wasn't as bad a death as Gavriel thought.

She tipped his chin up, and he pulled away; he wasn't done looking at her. Her lovely face tightened. Such mesmerizing eyes, like the sunset he'd once seen over a lake. The orange sky had lit the water on fire—ripples bathed in liquid honey.

He must be going mad if he was willing to resort to poetry in his head.

She made an impatient noise and placed a hand behind the back of his neck. "You must drink this." Her voice was the most beautiful sound Gavriel had ever heard. This hallucination must have been a parting gift. A farewell from life with an offering of one last beautiful thing to take with him on his journey.

He smiled, and her face twisted. Perhaps he had blood in his teeth. Still, he reveled in the stunning beauty that hovered above him. The small crease between her eyebrows. The impossible smoothness of her skin, as if she'd just entered the world, perfectly molded, free from the burden of suffering.

He could think of no sweeter death.

"Please, Gavriel." Something about the plea in her voice gutted him. That or his name upon her lips. Either way, hallucination or not, he'd do anything she demanded of him. He'd walk through the fiery pits of the Netherworld. Scale the peaks of the Forbidden Highlands. Reason be damned.

His fever must have scrambled all of his good sense.

Gavriel let her lift his head. She slammed the vial against his lips, rattling a few teeth in the process. He frowned at his beautiful illusion, before opening his mouth and letting the liquid slip past his lips, onto his tongue, and down his throat. It was obnoxiously sweet with an edge.

When she'd emptied its contents, her face relaxed.

He smacked his lips, wrinkling his nose. The cloying flavor tingled in his throat. "That was disgusting."

A look of disbelief came over her before a sharp laugh startled from her chest.

He'd been wrong. *That* was the most beautiful sound he'd ever heard.

LARK BREATHED A SIGH OF RELIEF.

She'd done it. She'd defied Thanar and rescued a mortal from his fate. Shirked her duties and acted on her conscience. This was different from punishing Corwyn, which could be reasoned away with logic and a sense of justice.

This was purely selfish.

Lark ran a shaking hand over Gavriel's cheek, tracing the scar she'd been dreaming of. Softer than a whisper, she dragged her fingertips to the faint line that slashed through his lip. She couldn't believe this was real, that she was here, his head in her hands. He smiled as if she hadn't just forced some foreign liquid down his throat. He was perfect.

Gavriel gazed up at her, his eyes struggling to stay focused.

That wasn't right, he should have healed by now. His skin still held a waxy shade of fever, somehow both flushed and pale.

It hadn't worked. She risked everything, and it hadn't worked.

Blasted damnation!

Gavriel weakly reached for her, and Lark froze. He tucked her hair behind her ear. His dark green eyes, with golden flecks she hadn't noticed before, were unreadable. The emotion in them began to wane.

This couldn't be it. The witch swore it would work. All Lark had to do was administer the healing draught and swear to pay the price.

Of course. This was transference magic. Nereida told her as much.

"The price is mine to pay."

Gavriel's brows furrowed at her words. Feeling more foolish by the moment, Lark tried again. "I swear to inherit the debt this mortal bears to his name."

Nothing. The sickly pallor of death clung to his face, even as the fever raged.

"I don't mean to sound ungrateful for your presence. But what exactly are you doing?" Gavriel's rich voice held a polite cadence with a hint of amusement. His mouth curved, stretching the scar across his lip. Lark placed a hand onto his sweat-slicked forehead. She searched his eyes, seeking answers they couldn't offer.

She'd failed.

Come so far only for him to die in her arms.

"I'm trying to save you." The words were spoken through her teeth.

Gavriel still wore that maddeningly serene expression, as if slowly fading into the abyss was a wonderful way to spend the afternoon. "Tell me your name," he said softly.

"Lark," she grunted, mind still racing. If declaring the promise to absorb his injury wasn't enough, there had to be another way to swear her sincerity.

The witch was no help. Nereida hardly seemed inclined to aid her, awaiting Lark's departure so she might return to her romantic tale.

Oh.

A kiss.

Nereida had mentioned a kiss was an unspoken promise.

Yes, those ancient beings certainly did enjoy toying with people.

Lark glance down at Gavriel—

His face contorted in disgust, staring at her like she was a monster.

"You were real. You took him," he said between gritted teeth.

Lark took a deep breath punctuated with a sigh. There was no time to debate this. She'd deal with the consequences when she knew he would survive. Not exactly what she'd had in mind, but she was short on options.

With rough force, Lark slammed her lips against Gavriel's in a bruising kiss. There was no finesse, no intensity, save for the physical force of her mouth against his, and his hands trying to push her away.

Lark pulled back to see hatred burning in his eyes—eyes that were already clearing up. The veil of death lifted, and as he crawled back, color stained his cheeks. Anger. Life.

"You stole Emric from this life," he spat.

Lark rolled her eyes, ignoring the wave of dizziness that came over her. Stupid, ungrateful mortal. "Technically, it was another who guided him. I simply shadowed."

She should remember, to a mortal, death was the end. Even she had fought to prevent Gavriel from meeting his end. But he glared at her, as if she'd been the one to choose Emric's fate.

"You're a monster. Some sort of demon."

"You're alive because of me." Something constricted in her chest before it settled to a cool anger. How dare he? If he knew what she sacrificed, the danger she put herself in, all to save him, would he still look at her like she crawled out of the Netherworld?

"I didn't ask for it. I didn't want your help."

Lark stood on shaky legs. She knew this was transference magic, but she hadn't expected to inherit his poison induced weakness so quickly. "I believe what you mean to say is thank you."

Gavriel shook his head and clenched his fists. He rose to his feet, such smooth movement. He'd been sweat-soaked, shaking on the ground when she'd found him. "Can you bring him back?"

Exhaustion weighed heavily on her. She was without a tether in the mortal world, bearing the weight of Gavriel's death, and he demanded more.

"I can't."

"I'll take his place." Gavriel towered over her, fixing her with his intense stare. "Let him live in my stead."

"It doesn't work that way," Lark said.

"You could at least try!"

"He's gone!" Lark regretted the energy it took to yell. This was all wrong. He shouldn't be looking at her that way. "He's gone."

Gavriel's shoulders lowered. His rigid posture collapsed at her words, and the fire fled his eyes. "I am to accept that fate chose to spare me?" he asked, quiet enough she knew it wasn't a question meant for her.

Lark didn't care.

She chucked the glass vial at a nearby tree, reveling in the way it shattered, and the way Gavriel whipped his head to glare at her. "Fate had nothing to do with it, mortal. I saved you. Of my own free will."

Another wave of dizziness swept through her, threatening to buckle her knees. She'd lingered before when she hunted down Corwyn after Aislinn crossed over. But without Gavriel's death, her connection had no basis. Already the poison that once coursed through his veins, dimming his light, infected her. Where does death go without a body to claim?

"Why?" The word left Gavriel's lips with all the force of a murmur.

Lark opened her mouth. Biting words threatened to spill, but they vanished from her tongue just as quickly. "I had to know I could."

She turned back the way she came from, needing and loathing departure from his sight. After a few paces, she dared a backward glance over her shoulder.

He remained rooted to the spot where she'd left him. Eyes downcast. Fists clenched.

More broken than when he'd been a mere whisper from death.

LARK SLAMMED to her knees on the floor of the garish foyer, ears ringing.

She'd barely had the strength to open the heavy doors to her home.

Her cage. Transitioning to the Otherworld was always an adjustment, but never like this. The weight of Gavriel's death pressed upon Lark. The phantom flush of heat boiled beneath her skin; her skull throbbed. A wave of dizziness rolled through her again. Is this what poison felt like?

Gavriel's face, serene and euphoric, before it twisted to malice flashed in her mind.

That had not gone the way she thought it would.

What had she expected? That he'd be grateful for her assistance?

She was a fool. A lonely, misguided fool.

What was Gavriel to her? Some mortal who'd never even known of her existence until the moment she crashed into his last few dying breaths.

But still, Gavriel seared her thoughts with an edge of longing. Every image of his face, burning with intensity with passion and rage, had been replaced. His utter disgust and horror as he glared at her, was etched in her mind.

He was right.

She was a monster.

It was time to stop playing human.

Heavy footfalls broke Lark from her wallowing. The Commander marched toward her, guards in tow. Lark glared up at Ceto before the back of an armored hand came barreling across her cheek.

Reapers didn't bleed, but laying on the floor, Lark had the vague sensation of blood trickling down her face as darkness overcame her.

CHAPTER 13

*I*t took three days for Gavriel to make his way back to the
Guild.

For three days, rage and regret propelled him. His muscles and
ligaments ached with every footstep that drew him closer to the
fortress he'd called home for the last twenty years.

Finding Emric's killer did nothing to assuage the gut-churning pit
that Gavriel had come to know as his constant companion. Ending
Vana's life had granted him no peace but instead carved out a new
wound.

Facing death, Gavriel found a moment of peace. As if dying might
restore some semblance of balance to a world without Emric. Skies
knew Gavriel's hands weren't clean. If anyone deserved to be lost to
the abyss, or whatever awaited him when he drew his last breath, it
was him. Vanishing from existence, or sent to the deepest pits of the
Netherworld, it made no difference. At least his death would serve as
atonement for the loss of Emric.

Then *she* had to wreck it all. What seemed like a parting gift from a
shit-stained world was really one last bite in the ass. The fire-haired
demon—sent to torment him.

She'd saved his life, only to reveal it was she who'd ferried Emric's soul to the afterlife.

Expelling her from his mind, Gavriel forced his gaze and thoughts to the horizon.

The Guild stood proudly at the edge of The Wastes, the only land-mark inhabiting the barren soil. A fortress of stone and blood atop scorched earth. Cursed land. It was once the site of one of the last great battles, before Ardenas and Koval found peace. During the battle of Emerald Knoll, when Lord Blackstone's children were brought onto the field and slaughtered, their mother slit her wrists, bleeding her curses onto the once lush ground and sentencing the enemy armies to certain death. They felled the Kovalian forces the next day, despite their strength and numbers. From that day on, nothing grew, and all men who walked upon the soil were cursed to outlive their children.

Gavriel was sure the Guild had peddled those rumors and salted the earth regularly.

Not that they needed any help steering unwanted visitors away. There were no armed forces in Ardenas, aside from privately owned city guards easily bought for a few silvers. The worst the Guild had ever faced was a group of rowdy villagers, assembled and bloodthirsty in a misplaced rage. But that was before Gavriel's time. The Guild of Crows had a reputation that preceded them, and in no man's land where coin is the common tongue, their blades were the sharpest.

He scanned the outer walls of the castle, as if he'd locate a sudden change in its façade. The same stone tower loomed over the dead earth, both a beacon and a warning.

Entering the foyer in the light of day was strange. He usually entered at night, through a window to avoid detection. He'd overseen the training of all their watchers and each one of them had their blind spot. Blind spots he'd committed to memory in case of emergency.

He strode right down the hallway to the stairs, ascending until he reached the northern turret to Master Hamlin's private office.

Upon reaching the heavy, oak door, Gavriel stilled. With no small amount of trepidation, he rapped on the door with his knuckles in two hard successions.

"Come in," the voice of Gavriel's childhood answered. The same voice that had bellowed at him again and again when his form was all wrong. That snapped at him when he bent to his weaknesses. That comforted him after the death of his mother. His mentor, his master, his jailor.

Gavriel opened the door and glided in. Offering a quick nod, he clasped his hands behind his back, feet hip-width apart.

Hamlin remained fixated on the parchment in his hands, his greying hair tied back. He mumbled to himself as he read over the report. Although Hamlin was thirty years his senior, there was no doubt he could kill Gavriel without breaking a sweat. Hamlin had the heart and soul of an assassin, and the years hadn't dulled his speed or senses.

Gavriel peered across the desk adorned with gilded iron inlays, columns, and quatrefoils. In his youth, Gavriel spent hours staring at the intricate designs. Hamlin had a way of insisting on patience, even now as he ignored him. But Gavriel was used to impromptu lessons of discipline.

Above them, the iron hoop crowned with candles groaned as it gently swung in the breeze from the open window. Thankfully, it was early enough no one had lit it. Hamlin kept to the old ways, utilizing animal fat instead of beeswax for his candles. They stank something fierce when they burned.

Hamlin finally lowered the page to peer at Gavriel. The lines on his face had grown deeper. He gestured to the chair.

Gavriel sat. Waiting.

"Did you find his killer?"

That had always been Hamlin's style. No bullshit, no sparring with words. He saved his fancy footwork for the fighting ring.

"I did indeed," Gavriel said.

"And I take it they are no longer a problem?" Shadows curled under Hamlin's blue eyes, casting weary energy to his face.

"That is correct."

"Hmm." Hamlin gazed out the window.

Two crossed swords glared at Gavriel from the stone wall behind

Hamlin. They were sealed within the bronze symbol of the Guild, a crow taking flight. Once, Gavriel stood on a chair to reach those swords, his insatiable curiosity compelling him to investigate their authenticity.

They were real and sharp. The deep gash in his palm was a testament to that. Gavriel ran his thumb over the scar at the memory.

"I hate what's come of this place," Hamlin murmured. "Times used to be far simpler. The whole world's gone to hell. Us with it." He turned back.

Gavriel caught himself under the full weight of Hamlin's stare. He resisted the urge to shift in his seat.

"You disobeyed orders. Wrote a mark for yourself in a quest for vengeance, completely disregarding the chain of command." Hamlin's voice held no sign of anger, only calm disappointment.

Shame threatened to burn Gavriel's cheeks like he was a seven-year-old boy once more. But time had granted him a knack for hiding such things.

"You are hereby stripped of your position and banished."

A cold shock spread through Gavriel's legs, hardening them to stone.

It was a familiar sensation—a numbing sort of terror. Like the memory long buried of his first mark. He'd completed the task without conducting the barest of research. He wasn't trained to question; he was trained to follow, and without thought, he obeyed. How quickly his arm had shot out to deliver a killing blow. Gavriel had been sure his own face matched the shocked expression of the stranger whose life he cut short. If only he'd known who'd been sentenced to the end of his blade.

Gavriel schooled his expression into one of cool indifference. "That seems a bit harsh even for you."

"Damn it, boy, do you realize what you've done?" Hamlin's face reddened. "You compromised the integrity of what we do here. The minute you took matters into your own hands"—he snatched his glass off the corner of his desk—"you tied mine."

Hamlin downed his whiskey before pouring two more. He slid one across the desk.

Gavriel studied the glass, amber liquid sloshing against the side. Gavriel had been confident in his ability. But the ease with which he snuck in and out of the Guild, the evidence he needed atop Emric's desk, and how quickly Hamlin pieced together what had happened, there could be no mistaking.

"The letter was a trap," Gavriel said. Not set by Vana, but by someone much closer. Gavriel slid his gaze up to find his guess confirmed on Hamlin's face.

Gavriel lifted his whiskey and threw it down the back of his throat, only catching wisps of vapors on his tongue. "Shit."

How could he be so foolish? Had he been so unobservant not to see what was spelled out in front of him? Had grief lodged his head so far up his ass?

Apparently so.

"Connor?" Gavriel knew it was him, the conniving little shit. He'd been a thorn in his side since his earliest days at the Guild, a boyhood rivalry he'd hoped they'd grown out of.

"Most likely. I received word of Emric's demise ahead of your return—the first time." The muscle in Hamlin's jaw rippled. "I would have thought you'd bring the news to me yourself."

The familiar weight of shame sank in Gavriel's gut. So, they'd guessed his response, and kept eyes on him from the moment he snuck in to when he crawled back out the window. He wanted to regret his actions, but he knew Hamlin wouldn't have permitted him to chase Emric's killer right away, appearances and such. The instant the Crows seemed little better than common mercenaries and thugs, the armor would weaken. The Guild was built on strength, skill, and image. "Can I take the night and be off in the morning?"

Hamlin shrugged. "Sure, but if I were you I'd be gone as soon as I could."

"Why's that?"

"There's a bounty on your head to be issued at first light." Hamlin raised his glass to his lips, a haunted look in his eye. "I was hoping to give you a head start."

CHAPTER 14

*L*ark woke in a dark, damp cell. She sat up, relieved when her vision didn't spin. The poison must have run its course. Her hand flew to her cheek, where Ceto's blow had drawn blood Lark shouldn't possess. Her fingers came away clean.

Had she imagined it?

She reached for the bars and yanked until she was upright, leaning her head against iron.

No windows. Lark never thought she'd miss the fabricated sky of the Otherworld. The only source of light flickered from braziers halfway down the hall. Sooner or later, they had to retrieve her, for her sentencing at least.

Unless they left her to rot.

Reapers couldn't die. Not from earthly threats like starvation. Her only death now would be if she were wiped from existence. Only Thanar or one of the great Warriors of Avalon could kill a Reaper.

Which was beginning to sound more and more like a bargain.

"Skies, what have I stepped in?" Lark said to herself.

"The same taint I have, no doubt," a familiar voice echoed in the dark chamber.

"Ferryn?"

Footfalls resounded off the stone walls until Ferryn stood in front of her cell. A grim smile lifted on his face, never reaching his eyes. "Hello, little bird."

Lark threw her arms around his neck, despite the barrier.

Ferryn stepped back but placed his hands over hers. "Why did you come back?"

"I had no choice. Once the tether severed, I had to return."

He closed his eyes, face drawn tight as he exhaled slowly. "Nereida didn't offer you mortality."

Besides the transference draught, the witch hadn't offered much more than ridicule. Lark shook her head.

Mortality. It would be a means to escape Thanar, temporarily, albeit. Death would still come for her and when it did Thanar could do with her what he pleased. But the price for mortality must be far steeper than anything Lark had to offer. Especially on this side of the iron bars.

Ferryn dragged a hand down his face. "Well, so much for that."

The sound of armored footsteps rang from down the hallway.

"Ferryn, you have to go!"

He gave her hand one quick squeeze before taking a casual stance, leaning against her cell door.

Ceto and two of her men rounded the corner. It was impossible to tell who they were, blackened iron helmets obscured their faces. Something flashed across Ceto's face, a glimpse of shock that melted into her usual brand of disgust.

"I thought I told you to stay away from the prisoner," Ceto said to Ferryn, her voice low and dangerous. "You can't be here."

Ferryn's shoulders tightened in an uncharacteristic line of tension, like he was holding his breath. "You say many things Ceto." He exhaled, a fragile sound. "It's hard to keep track of which words mean anything at all."

Ceto's expression darkened, a storm brewing on her face.

"Go, Ferryn." Lark gave a gentle shove through the bars. Ferryn's defense, although appreciated, wasn't worth the Commander's anger.

Ferryn leveled Lark with an apologetic look, before stalking off.

Lark almost missed the glance he cast over his shoulder at Ceto. His expression was undecipherable in the shadows, and then he was gone.

Ceto jerked her head. The guards marched up to Lark's cell, unlocked the door, and swung it open. Before she could react, they clamped manacles on her wrists and dragged her out, one at each elbow. Lark pressed her heels to the floor and yanked her arms free. "I can walk."

With a scoff, Ceto turned on her heel and strode down the hall. The guards made no move to grab Lark again, only tucking in behind to hound her steps.

They passed rows of empty cells, making the trek to the upper levels a yawning chasm of silence. Prisoners didn't last long down in the dungeons. Thanar had a special place for those he punished over time.

Ceto paused at the bottom of the stairs. She gave a faint nod; the two faceless Reapers bowed and marched down the opposite hallway.

When the sounds of their footsteps faded, Ceto turned the full strength of her dark stare on Lark. "This won't be pleasant."

"I was under no illusions it would be." Lark shook the manacles.

"Before we go any further, I need you to answer a question."

A hard laugh escaped Lark's lips. "Why should I tell you anything?" Ceto had done nothing to garner a shred of trust from her.

"Once we enter that room, I can't say for certain what will happen." The intensity in Ceto's dark stare gave Lark pause. Those eyes that had always cast hateful glares her way, cutting across halls and grand rooms. Now they held all the fire but none of the disgust.

"I never knew you cared."

"Why did you do it?" Her nostrils flared, as her penetrating stare swept across Lark's face. "Why did you spare him? Are you playing at something here? Or was it foolish sentiment?" There was an edge to her voice. Desperation? It couldn't be.

Lark glanced down at her bound wrists, weighing her words with care. "I suppose I was sick of someone else deciding the fates of the world. Of feeling bound and tethered." She wouldn't be another cog on the wheel. Never again.

Ceto's eyes widened.

"I'm sick of being an instrument of power," Lark continued, "without any control of my actions." She clenched her fists tight enough she could almost feel the bite of her nails in her palms. "I wanted to forge my own path."

Lark unclenched her fists. Debating the foolishness of telling the Commander the truth. "And I guess, I thought he was worth the risk."

Ceto clenched her jaw. Her mouth set in a firm line, and her armored hand gripped the pommel of her sword. "Tell me, Larkin, are you prepared to do whatever it takes to achieve your goals?"

"What are you asking me?" There was no possible way Ceto was anything less than unswervingly loyal to Thanar. To consider otherwise was madness.

"You know what I'm asking." The warm light of the braziers caressed Ceto's dark features, bathing every line with fire and shadows. She regarded Lark as if truly seeing her for the first time. "You want to change fate? Tell me, what would you sacrifice? What would you give?"

Lark refused to shrink away from her scrutiny. To escape destiny? That unrelenting specter that haunted them all? "Whatever I had to."

Ceto nodded once, appearing satisfied. "When we get up there, you will tell him you were lovesick. Temporary madness that forced your hand." She grabbed her by the shoulders. "You will not tell him what you've just said." She relented her grip and made to take a step up the stairs.

"Why should I lie? Thanar deserves to know exactly how I feel about being his servant." Lark realized too late how freely the words were spilling from her lips in the presence of the Commander.

But Ceto merely scoffed. "You would do well to learn to swallow that bitter taste, it's the only way you'll survive long enough to see the end."

"Perhaps, but at least I'll die knowing I'm not a coward."

The anger returned to Ceto's expression, that familiar disgust. "Do you have a death wish? Is that all this is? If so, tell me now to spare me the effort."

What effort? Unless Ceto was planning to petition Thanar on Lark's behalf, there was no conceivable effort on her part.

Lark lifted her chin. "There are worse things than death."

Ceto advanced on her in an instant. "Yes, there are. There are bigger things at stake than you, Larkin. Decisions from centuries ago will finally bear fruit and I will not have you destroy everything." She pulled back, baring her teeth. "Be certain your quest for absolute freedom isn't at the cost of everyone else around you. If you aren't willing to make the necessary sacrifices, would you let someone else?"

Lark couldn't make sense of anything Ceto was saying—still shocked by the notion Ceto might not be Thanar's pet. What sort of sacrifices was she expected to make?

Without an answer to her question, Ceto gripped Lark's elbow and hauled her up the stairs.

LARK SHOULD HAVE BEEN COWERING. She wasn't oblivious to the fact that this was the worst-case scenario. Oddly enough, a steady calm had made a home in her heart and damned if she was going to rationalize that away.

Thanar sat on his throne of gold and marble, his ominous presence bathed in harsh light.

Lark met the stares of the gathered onlookers as Ceto dragged her through the massive ivory and gold throne room. Her chains clanged with every step, and her boots squeaked against the polished marble floor, an undignified sound in the silent hall. If Thanar commanded silence, not even the sound of breathing would be tolerated. Lark felt the weight of Thanar's steely gaze, and twisted her heel, reveling in the obnoxious squeal it made. Her gaze snagged on Ferryn where he stood at the back of the fray. He wrung his hands and worry creased his brow before it smoothed in his veneer of cocky indulgence.

It was unfamiliar to see Thanar's throne room full. It seemed like eons since he last held a ball or gathering of any kind. He used to throw extravagant parties, requesting her presence by his side. He'd even gone so far as to send ornate gowns to her chambers. But she'd refused enough times he stopped asking, and somewhere down the road, he stopped hosting.

Thanar must want to make an example of her. Oh, his poor pride.

Ceto jerked Lark forward, dumping her on the floor at Thanar's feet. Lark slowly lifted her head to take in the full weight of his stare. Dark eyes glared down at her like a sky without stars.

"Larkin is hereby charged with corruption of a human soul and willfully sabotaging her duty as a Reaper." Ceto's voice rang out.

Lark rolled her shoulders, rising onto one knee.

"How do you plead?"

Lark opened her mouth, a snarky reply dancing on her tongue, but the thought of Ceto's warning halted the words. She schooled her expression into that of contrition. "Guilty."

"Rise." Thanar gazed at her with a mixture of rage and grief. He leaned to one side, resting on his armrest in a forced appearance of casual disinterest. His eyes still burned with that intensity he seemed to save for her, a muscle feathering his sharp cheek. "How did you receive the mark?"

Lark blinked. She hadn't been expecting that question. She couldn't risk throwing Ferryn into the line of fire, but if she claimed the mark was hers then Leysa would face judgment. Lark didn't even know the name of the Reaper assigned the mark.

"I—" What could she say? "I stole it."

Thanar tipped his head to the side, an elegant finger pressing against his lips. "That would be difficult to do since you know you can't forge a tether by theft."

Shit.

"Ferryn." Thanar's voice echoed in the silent hall. "Come forward."

Ferryn sauntered up to them, long hair unbound and fluttering with every step. He offered a bow that seemed more sarcastic than reverent. "Yes, Master?"

"Care to shed some light on the situation?" Thanar held a hand toward her. "Lark doesn't seem to recall how the truth works."

Ferryn ran a quick hand through his hair. As if this was an inconvenience, rather than a sentencing. "It was my mark, and I gave it to her."

Stupid, impulsive, senseless, idiot! Lark shifted, the rattling of her chains grated against her ears.

"Why?" Thanar's voice was low and deceptively calm. Lark had been on the receiving end of that tone far too many times to find comfort in it.

Ferryn shrugged. "I wanted to see what she'd do."

Lark didn't dare breathe.

Thanar's dark brows were drawn in concentration. "You know how easy it would be for me to pluck the answer from your mind, Ferryn."

"Yes, I do."

"But I much prefer honesty, loyalty, and integrity over force." Thanar's gaze flicked to Lark.

"I know these things, which is why I swore the oath," Ferryn said in a voice commanding and firm. Lark almost believed him.

Thanar frowned but nodded. "Very well, I accept this answer." He dismissed Ferryn with a wave of his hand, turning his full attention back to Lark. She tried to keep the shock from her face at how easily he swallowed Ferryn's lie. Thanar continued, "How you came to receive the mark, isn't where my interest lies."

Of course not, his interest resided in making Lark squirm.

"Care to offer any words in your defense?" His tone was both sharp and pleading. Anger and hope.

Lark didn't dare a look over her shoulder at Ceto. "I was blinded... by love."

"Love..."

This was the first time his voice ever sounded small to Lark.

"Yes. An affliction I'd never felt before."

Thanar's brows raised in an almost human expression of surprise. "You betray our laws" —his hand gripped the arm of his throne— "our very existence, for the fascination of a human?" He stood, taking a step closer to her.

Lark resisted the urge to spit in his face as he brought it so close to hers.

He took her chin in his hands, forcing her neck to tilt up toward him. "And were you *satisfied* with your affection for this mortal?" His grip on her chin tightened.

"Nothing came of it." Lark wasn't sure if that answered his question.

"Why not?"

"It was a one-sided affection."

Thanar's eyes appeared to soften at that. If she played her cards right, perhaps she could get him to pity her lovesick act enough to grant her immunity from this offense.

Unlikely. Impossible even. But still, she dared to hope.

Thanar released Lark's chin hard enough to jerk her head back. He returned to his throne and sat, bracing his elbow on his thigh. He rested his chin on his hand as if considering his next move.

What a farce. He knew what her punishment would be. Knew it before this silly trial even began.

Heavy silence filled the hall. The air, laden with gruesome possibilities.

"I have the solution to both of our problems, Larkin. Would you like to hear it?" Thanar asked, wearing a smile that twisted her gut.

Lark braced herself for whatever punishment he deemed fit and managed a demure nod.

"This mortal has made a mockery of us both. You, jilted by his fickle nature, and I—" His smile turned predatory. "I will not suffer even an unworthy rival of your loyalties. You will travel to the mortal world and end his life. Upon your return you will swear the oath, to ensure this never happens again."

Tightness clawed at Lark's chest, like the first moment she drew false breath as a Reaper.

"No."

"No?" He cocked his head to the side, assessing her without any sincerity in the expression. Calling her bluff. "Allow me to rephrase, you will follow these orders, or I'll wipe your soul clean."

When he'd punished her last, he filled her with guilt and shame, a mockery of the emotions she dared to wish for. If he wiped her soul clean, she wouldn't be herself. She wouldn't even remember her own name. She would be whatever he made of her, filled to the brim with whatever he decided her to be. She might be bound to fate, but at least her mind was her own. To take that away... "You... can't."

He shook his head. "You're too valuable to waste. But if I can't trust you, you're a liability." He angled an eyebrow. "You are familiar with what the intrusion of my influence feels like. That will be nothing compared to this."

A violent rush in her ears deafened the murmuring of the crowd. It was a good thing she didn't need to breathe.

"I'd rather die."

"That's not your call, is it?"

Ceto's firm grip found her arm.

"Take a day to think it over, Larkin." Thanar waved a hand, dismissing her from his sight.

Reapers didn't feel. But something dark thrummed in Lark's veins as she was led away.

CHAPTER 15

Ceto slammed Lark's cell door shut. "You can't really be this selfish."

Lark glared at her. "It's selfish to refuse murder now?"

"You had the stomach for it before."

Lark would never regret what happened to Corwyn. He deserved worse. "That was different."

"Why?" Ceto cocked her head. A sure sign she was baiting her. A contrived question to elicit the correct response.

"He was a monster, this mortal—"

"You have no idea who this mortal is. Your childish fascination is based on a fantasy."

Lark tightened her mouth in a firm line.

Ceto wasn't wrong.

Lark was well aware of her shortcomings. She'd been willing to risk everything for a mortal she knew nothing about. But it was more than that.

"You see what you wish. I thought, perhaps, you were more than this. Could be more than what you seem." Ceto's voice had gone uncharacteristically soft. "But you're blinded by your desires. Your short-sighted, selfish desires." She turned away.

"And what do you think I desire?" Lark called out, unable to stay silent.

Ceto continued her steady pace down the hall of the dungeon.

"Ceto!"

"Bury your head in the sand, Lark. That's where you're most comfortable."

Hours passed.

Hours spent waiting for Thanar to force her hand.

Letting Thanar empty her and fill her with his own will was not an option. Lark had hoped true death would be his threat. He'd wielded that punishment before. It wasn't as if he couldn't make more Reapers.

But he'd never let her escape.

Ferryn belonged to him now. Leysa hadn't sought Lark out since they spoke of Corwyn, hadn't even attended her sentencing. There was only one person she could call on.

The witch.

Nereida didn't seem opposed to undermining Thanar.

Behind a locked door, Lark would never get her hands on the ingredients needed to access the Netherworld, but Nereida seemed to know Lark was coming last time. Perhaps the witch had eyes and ears everywhere as Thanar did.

Lark clenched her fists. Taking slow steadying breaths, she relaxed her stance. Her eyes slid shut. She was a tether—searching for a connection. Her soul existed to forge bonds. She could forge one of her own.

Lark opened up her awareness and reached out, lowering any walls she'd constructed to keep Thanar out.

Silence.

Lark exhaled a slow breath and let herself feel the truth of her conscious thoughts. Let them fill her.

Nothing happened.

Lark grunted her frustration and focused all her energy on pushing her awareness out. As she had at the mortal wedding feast. Only this time, it was her soul on the line.

What if Thanar was expecting her to try something like this? What if he had no intention of waiting to force the oath on her, and she'd just made herself vulnerable? What if—

Lark swallowed her fear and drowned out the thoughts spiraling in her mind. Only one thing mattered.

She had to get out of the Otherworld.

"Nereida, please answer me."

The ground shifted beneath Lark's feet. She peered down to find the symbols burned into the stone she stood upon. She fell to her knees and pressed her hands to the scorched markings, as she had when she'd drawn them herself.

Then she slipped through.

"My, my you have excellent manners when you need something, sweet thing." Nereida leaned against her desk, amusement dancing in her violet eyes as Lark struggled to stand.

Something wet trickled over Lark's lips, and she wiped her nose with a shaking hand. Dark red blood slithered down her first knuckle. That was impossible. Reapers didn't bleed. "What's wrong with me?"

Nereida tucked a lock of snowy hair that had escaped her thick plait behind a delicate ear. "Did I forget to mention? You took a small morsel of humanity from your pet mortal when you saved him."

Lark gaped at her hand. At the thick, crimson trail. "What does that mean?"

"I'm not sure, you're the first to try it." Nereida yanked a handkerchief from the pocket of her black leather breeches and held it out expectantly.

Lark reached out a cautious hand to accept her offering and wiped the blood away.

Nereida paced over to her desk, hands clasped behind her back. "Now, to what do I owe the pleasure of your visit today?"

Lark tucked the blood-soaked cloth into her pocket. "Thanar is going to force the oath on me."

Nereida turned. Her white snake of hair slithered over her shoulder as she appraised Lark. "What do you need from me?" Her stare bore the heat of a ritual pyre the mortals were so fond of building.

"You could let me join your ranks. I've been told I'm quite adept at handling Undesirables."

"You know his reach extends this far, Larkin."

Lark knew that. That wasn't what she wanted, anyway.

"He can come collect that which is his whenever he pleases," Nereida said, leaning a hip against the edge of her desk. She crossed her arms, her black leather jerkin creaked with the movement.

Lark's jaw clenched. "I'm not *his*."

Nereida's mouth twitched, fighting a smile as she hummed.

Lark wasn't his. Even if he was the creator of all Reapers, the god of the Otherworld, death incarnate—

—she would never be his. Not unless he wiped her soul clean and filled her with whatever he saw fit. But would she even be herself anymore? Would a small part of her always rage, locked away in the darkest corner of her heart while she was dragged along?

Lark didn't think Thanar had ever done this before, kept a Reaper but remade them to suit his whims. He'd always discarded and reforged. Why would he keep her when she was everything he hated?

The words leapt from Lark's lips before she could think better of them. "Could you make me mortal?"

"Not for free, sweet thing. Can you pay the price?"

Without waiting for Lark to respond, Nereida began yanking out her desk drawers and dumping them unceremoniously onto the floor. Scattered parchment and quills plunked across the intricately woven rug. An ink bottle shattered, and black oozed along the red and gold threads.

"That depends on what it costs." Lark didn't care for riddles. What would Nereida ask of her?

Could she afford to say no?

Nereida ignored Lark and the ruined carpet, rummaging until at last, she stiffened. A triumphant smile stretched across her features.

"Ah, here it is." Nereida raised a golden bone—sharpened to a very fine point.

A sharp bone wasn't an answer. Not to Lark, anyway. "What are you offering?"

"A way out." Nereida offered a feral grin, shadows dancing across her face. They sank beneath her violet eyes and full cheeks. "Where not even *he* can get you."

The flicker of hope was far too enticing for Lark to dismiss. Nereida could only mean two places, the mortal world or Avalon. There was no chance she meant Avalon.

"You could walk amongst the mortals." Nereida took a step closer, the sharpened bone gleaming in the firelight. "I can remake you as a mortal."

To be free of Thanar at least for one lifetime was worth a thousand deaths.

No price too steep, no demand too great. One word and the witch could have anything.

A sobering thought.

It was in moments of desperation; grave mistakes were all too easy to make. Lark couldn't let her guard down, not now. She'd need her wits about her to forge such a deal.

"You are fascinatingly expressive my dear," Nereida said. "As much as I enjoy watching that little mind puzzle, time is of the essence." She raised the bone and all its grim implications. "Do we have a deal?"

"Terms. Name your terms before I agree to anything." Lark managed to spit the words out. The price must be high for such a tempting offer.

Nereida's eyes flashed and an easy smile spread across her face. "Of course, sweet thing."

Nereida strode to the oversized armchair by the fire that crackled in the hearth. She plopped herself down, crossed her legs, and peered over at Lark. "Have a seat." With a wave of her hand, a small wooden chair dragged its way across the floor.

Lark sat, unsure if excitement or nerves gave a rapid flutter in her belly. Lark couldn't hold onto an emotion long enough to discern it.

Nereida interlaced her fingers across her knee. "I offer you mortality. That is one mortal lifespan, no more, no less. This does not grant you immunity from any natural and or normal causes of death that mortals face. Examples include; old age, murder, illness, childbirth, exposure, starvation, if you trip and fall into a large hole and break your neck—"

"I got it."

"Furthermore, you can choose any age to begin your mortal lifespan at. From that point on, you will age as mortals do, rapidly and gracelessly."

"I suppose I'd want to be whatever age my form is." Lark never thought of age as anything tangible before. She wasn't even sure how long she'd been a Reaper—living each day the same as the last, feeling nothing but fleeting hints of emotion. It left her with no real concept of time. Reapers were locked in whatever age they were at death. Lark couldn't say with any certainty how old she was when she died.

"A wise choice," Nereida said with a short nod. "It might be a touch awkward to have your soul trapped in a baby."

"Will I look like this?"

"I can make you look however you want, darling."

Lark peered down at her hands, wondering how strange it would feel if she didn't recognize them. "I want to look like myself."

"As you wish. There might be slight differences, chalk it up to species discrepancy."

Although tempted to inquire more on that subject, Lark let it drop. "When I die, where will I go?"

"I can promise you'll come straight to me, no chance for Thanar to get his grip on you again."

"No Reaper to guide me?" Lark couldn't see how that was possible. Mortal souls needed a guide or else they'd remain and fester. Could she become an Undesirable?

"I assure you, your soul will know where to go," Nereida said. Her voice held an edge.

Lark breathed a sigh of relief. Short-lived when she realized one simple unanswered question. "You haven't said what you want in return."

Nereida arched an elegant brow. "No, I haven't. How familiar are you with our world, dear?"

"As much as anyone's allowed to be, I suppose. We exist on a different plane than the human realm, separated by a veil of sorts. When a soul passes through, they create a temporary door through the veil to enter the afterlife. From there, souls go on to either Avalon." Lark pointed up. "Or the Netherworld." She gestured around them.

"Very good. The little Reaper has attended to her studies. But I'm more curious if you understood how our world exists. What it thrives on."

Lark hesitated. Avalon, The Netherworld, The Otherworld, The Mortal world, Lacuna—they had always been and always would be. Provided the balance was maintained. Lark always assumed the bastards up in Avalon ran things for themselves. Thanar handled everything in the Otherworld and delegated to Nereida for the Netherworld. The Mortal world simply held fast amidst everything else. A fragile state of being that they all were duty-bound to protect.

The how of it all fell on the shoulders of the gods. Let the mortals ponder the meaning of it all. Lark had better things to do.

Nereida continued. "Each soul you aid leaves an imprint, a memory of power. This essence grants us our abilities and strengthens the veil between worlds. It's no coincidence the rips in the veil and failing to aid souls in crossing over occur in tandem."

Lark failed to guide Gavriel. "Did I create another tear?"

Nereida chuckled. "Oh, yes. A rather impressive one, at that. Even the least motivated of souls could accidentally fall through." She placed a comforting hand on Lark's knee. "But don't fret, I can fix that too."

Lark pushed her hand away. "You're offering quite a lot without stating my debt."

Nereida sighed. "Your distrust and impatience cloud your logic, dear. Now pay attention." She leaned in close. "Your master is losing his grip on the realms. Each tear allows for souls to claw their way back to the mortal world. What do you think happens to a soul that twists its way back to the land of the living?"

Lark's knees bounced with impatience. "Undesirables."

Nereida nodded gravely. "A pretty word whispered among Reapers. I prefer to call them what they are. Monsters. Demons."

"Why don't you stop them?"

Annoyance flashed across Nereida's features. "I can't, child. Thanar has tied my hands. Only he has the power to restore the veil. But he's so paralyzed by fear of disturbing the balance he won't dare risk it." Her violet eyes burned. The sort of fire Lark yearned for. "Give me your power, and I can change everything. All you've accumulated, from every soul you've aided, strengthens the veil. Let it pass to me when I release you from your cage, and I promise to use it to aid our world."

Lark ran a hand through her hair. If what Nereida said was true, it was Lark's duty to ensure her transition left the least amount of damage as possible. She had already acted out of selfishness and caused further problems for her kind. The least she could do was this small mercy for her people.

People she would never see again.

Lark couldn't believe it had taken this long for her mind to catch up to this fact. In escaping Thanar she was also cutting others out of her life. Gentle Leysa would never again check on her after an assignment, with her soft words and kind eyes. Ferryn would never force her out of her dour moods with his easy nature. Never yank her into an embrace when she was on the verge of losing herself.

Lark never had the chance to say goodbye.

A faint echo of regret tightened in her chest. The type of ache that needed the mortal release of tears.

But Reapers had no tears.

"I agree to those terms."

Any reaction Nereida may have felt, she hid well. Without another word, she held out her hand, conjuring a scroll. With a flick of her wrist, it unfolded, rolling down halfway to the floor.

"There's something you should be prepared for." Nereida still held the sharpened bone. Firelight crept along golden ivory, casting a sinister glow. "There will be side effects, as you become accustomed to your new body. For three days, you will make no sound, your tongue will be silenced. Each step you take will feel like walking on knives. Every footfall will be agony. But when the sun sets on the third day, your voice will return to you, the pain in your steps will lessen, and all you'll have to contend with is seeing to all of your mortal needs." Her full lips parted to reveal white teeth. "Humans don't keep well."

"I don't fear pain," Lark said.

"You don't know pain, child. Not anymore."

There would be no turning back. Once Lark signed her life away, it couldn't be undone. She'd be human, mortal, vulnerable. She'd be alone, weak, exposed.

She would be free.

Lark's fingers closed around the glimmering shard; it was light in its weight. Before she could change her mind, she scrawled her name across the bottom line.

She was free.

CHAPTER 16

*S*harp pain sliced up Lark's arms and legs. Her raw lungs ached with each breath. All edges and corners pressed into her vulnerable flesh. Everything was too tight. Like she'd been stretched taut over uneven ground. Forcing her now mortal eyes open, she squinted against the bright shards of light filtering through twisted branches that creaked overhead in a punishing wind. The sharp scent of overturned earth and rotting wood filled Lark's senses. Eagerly, she tried to sit up.

She couldn't move.

Gnarled roots wrapped across her bare stomach and down her legs in a suffocating embrace. Lark clawed, fingers raking against thick, unforgiving roots.

She lifted her head to stare up at the great tree that acted as her cage. Ancient and unyielding, it towered above her—mocking her for her frailty. A whimper died in Lark's soundless throat. She would have no voice for three days. An odd side effect, but inconvenient enough to make her newfound vulnerability that much worse. She opened her mouth to test her voice once more—

Silence.

With shaking hands, Lark pushed her hair out of her face to survey her surroundings.

She was in the middle of an unfamiliar forest.

All the trees within sight were neither living nor dead. Barren and desolate despite the usual warmth of spring. If this was Ardenas, this was the season when mortal children wore their hair adorned with flowers as the sun warmed the land. If Lark was in the Permafrosts, well, she'd have died of exposure already. Vallemer wasn't much better, a harsh landscape of extreme cold and rocky terrain. Koval would be far warmer this time of year, at least in the regions Lark had reaped. No, this must be Ardenas. Not the Desolates, but most of the rest of the country was spotted with forests and small towns.

Lark had no concept of distance, having spent her existence walking through invisible veils to arrive at her destinations. Would her mortal body last until she found a town or village?

She caught sight of a nearby tree. Its roots appeared sturdy enough for leverage. Twisting, Lark stretched as far as she could while trapped beneath the yew. The muscles in her shoulder burned. She scraped the dirt and as she yanked her body forward, the confining roots pulled against her flesh. No sound emitted from her throat as they ripped her now delicate skin.

A sharp breath and Lark's hand finally closed over the thick root. She pulled, and warmth spread across her skin as the first sensation of her blood smearing lit her already sensitive nerves ablaze.

She wrenched free from the giant yew's grasp and rolled to her back, staring up at the cover of branches. Naked and bloodied, she shook with silent laughter.

The witch wasn't lying.

With each step that pushed her deeper into the forest, Lark's strength dimmed. More times than she could admit, she rested to avoid passing out from the pain. Her feet pulsed with the steady thrum of her heartbeat, and her bloodied steps were slick against the cold ground.

No voice, and every step made her want to scream.

Lark set her heavy body down, once again, and rough bark scraped against her back. Each sensation was both exciting and terrifying. She *felt* cold. Running a tentative hand along the gooseflesh of her arms, she marveled at each one. The dried blood on her stomach and legs pulled her skin tight across her muscles.

She had to find shelter before nightfall. Death by exposure wouldn't be a welcome start to her new mortal life.

With a sigh as heavy as her limbs, Lark stood, wobbling against the onslaught of her aches. Invisible blades cut through every nerve along the bottoms of her feet, severing the appreciation of her responsive body.

A wave of dizziness threatened to crash Lark to the ground. Propping herself up against a tree, she lifted her head to the sky. The forest spun.

The light had sunk to horizon level. She'd been traveling west for what felt like hours. Surrounded by endless trees. A dead forest with no end.

Lark exhaled a stuttered breath. Something burned in her belly like she'd swallowed a heated blade. Was this what fear felt like in a mortal body?

Lark surged forward and stumbled over a thick root. Her knee slammed into the dirt. She bit her fist against the pain, wishing she could cry out. Bracing a filthy hand against a fallen log, she pushed to stand, only for her weak legs to buckle beneath her. She crawled on her hands and knees, ignoring the sharp edges of the pitiless forest floor.

Half dragging her body out into a clearing, Lark curled on her side, hugging her knees to her chest. Roots and sticks dug into her skin and shivers wracked her body. The cold she'd been fascinated by hours ago was now harsh and biting.

She was going to die.

Perhaps fate was stronger than all of them. Stronger than even Thanar himself.

An oddly comforting thought, that something, this great and terrible thing, could be more than Thanar. More than his darkness and the incessant shadows that haunted Lark's steps.

She was tired.

Sinking deeper. Drowning in a never-ending sea of inevitability.

I will never submit.

Forcing her head up, Lark dragged her body, lasting another moment before she collapsed. The dark trees looming above twisted in her despair. An unbidden image of Gavriel, glaring in disgust, fluttered through her mind before the overwhelming heaviness of sleep smothered her under its suffocating embrace.

THE HAZINESS of a dreamless sleep cleared. Beads of sweat rolled down Lark's back. The sound of a crackling fire pricked her ears, and the light between her fluttering eyelids tinged an angry red. Tightness in her sore muscles brought her attention to the pile of blankets wrapped around her. Lark peeled a heavy layer back enough to peer over the mountain of coverings.

Darkness had crept over the forest, but a roaring campfire illuminated the space and filled the sharp shadows of naked branches.

Across the fire, a woman sharpened a stick with effortless finesse, her silver ring glinted with every pass of her hand. She didn't seem to notice Lark watching, so Lark took the chance to study her.

Her long black hair was swept in a thick braid over one shoulder. The firelight danced across her smooth, dark skin, highlighting the deep warmth of her bronze tone and illuminating her high cheekbones. Her neat eyebrows were relaxed. If she was concerned about Lark, she certainly didn't show it.

"Finally awake?"

Her husky voice, like a whisper of smoke, swept across the makeshift camp in a forest that was still far too quiet. Her face was serene and expecting, while her hazel stare assessed with unflinching honesty.

Lark sat up, ignoring her aches. One fist gripped the blankets to preserve what little sense of modesty she might have left. She wasn't used to mortals seeing her without willing herself into view.

Lark opened her mouth to ask a question that died in her throat. She still had no voice.

The woman continued staring, blade and stick frozen in her hands. "Can you speak?"

Lark's hand lifted to her throat. She shook her head.

The woman nodded, placed her tools aside, and held her hands over the fire. "I'm Daciana. No harm shall come to you, provided you don't attempt anything rash." She offered a small smile that dimpled her smooth cheek.

Lark owed the woman her life, with nothing to give in return. She glanced down at her coverings, soft and smooth beneath her fingers, an intricate weave of gold against black velveteen. Far too fine a thread for a simple traveler.

Daciana tracked her glance. "When I found you, you were stark naked as the day you were born. You remember this?"

Lark would have laughed at the choice of words. Technically this was the day she was born. Or yesterday was. Skies, three days were beginning to feel too long. She nodded.

"I didn't think it right to dress you, so I wrapped you the best I could and made camp beside you." Daciana had turned her attention to her tent. "There are clothes in my tent. They're yours if you wish."

Why was this mortal helping her?

Daciana seemed to understand Lark without the help of words. "It's the least I could do."

Lark stood on shaky feet, nearly buckling under the sudden slice of pain.

Once she reached the canvas flaps, she yanked them open and climbed in to escape the human's kindness and the discomfort of an ever-mounting debt. But that didn't stop Lark from yanking the breastband in place and the smallclothes up her legs. Lark pulled the white, threadbare tunic over her head and the dark leather leggings up over her hips. Finding a spare pair of boots, she yanked them onto her feet. Sharp pain bloomed, and her eyes stung as the hardened leather bit into her sensitive heels. She ripped them off and cast them aside.

Lark emerged and saddled over to the mound of blankets on the other side of the fire. The space atop the barren earth that had been her first bed since becoming mortal. The image of her ornate four-poster bed back in the Otherworld swept through her mind.

"You seem to try to speak as if you've forgotten you can't." Daciana rubbed her chin, watching Lark with her ever-inquisitive stare. "Must be recently afflicted."

Lark nodded. For someone to have any grasp of what happened to her, even in their limited sense, was a relief. The wind whistled against Lark's ear and pricked the hairs on her neck. She rubbed her arm, marveling at the fabric beneath her hand. It wasn't quite rough, but it was textured. And she could *feel* it.

"I can't in good conscience leave you to fend for yourself like this." Daciana seemed to speak more to herself than to Lark. "Nor can I force you to go anywhere you don't wish to go."

Lark bundled her arms around her knees, eagerly awaiting whatever sentence this mortal would pass. The absurdity of that was not lost on her.

"You can come with me if you wish. We need to make it back to the others." Daciana's hand ghosted along her hip to the gleaming hilt of a dagger. "This place isn't meant for the living. I can't even hunt here."

Lark frowned. Though Daciana's words confirmed something she felt deep in her bones, sitting in this desiccating forest, what she suggested couldn't be right. The mortal world was tied to mortal rules. A forest with no animals? Sounded like some superstition peddled by people who dwelled in the woods and sought solitude.

"Listen," Daciana said, as if sensing Lark's thoughts. "Have you heard any birds? Any rooting in the underbrush?"

Lark stilled. No, the forest was dead silent. Perhaps that was why she couldn't recall reaping here. One can't have death without life. But then why was this human here?

"This place is many things, but safe isn't one of them. Come with me, fill your belly. Then go wherever you wish." Daciana picked up her knife and continued her task of sharpening her stick. "Or don't. The choice is yours, as I've said."

Lark bit her dry, cracked lip, tasting salt and blood. She was still weak and vulnerable. But Daciana could lead her anywhere, like a lamb to the slaughter. There was no telling who or what would greet her at their intended destination. Daciana seemed like a good, honest human.

But even wolves could hide in sheepskins.

Die now, or possibly die later. This human didn't have to help her. What purpose would it serve to save her only to lead her to her death?

Lark locked eyes with Daciana across the fire. She poured every shred of trust she had left into them and offered a curt nod.

Daciana's answering smile crinkled her eyes. She handed Lark the sharpened stick. "I can't let you travel the forest unarmed."

Lark glanced down at the sad little stick, trying to feel grateful.

Daciana laughed, high and bright. "It isn't much, but you'll forgive me if I don't hand you a blade just yet. You look likely to fall over and skewer yourself."

Lark felt her lips curve into an unwilling smile. She held her hand out, gesturing for the knife.

Daciana hesitated. She looked over Lark and her outstretched fingers, before placing the knife in her palm.

Lark carved away at the handle of her spear with quick practiced movements. She was reborn as a mortal without strength, clothes, or her voice, but at least she carried her dexterity with a blade to this life. When she finished, she flipped the knife, holding it out handle first to Daciana to show off her handiwork.

Lark.

Daciana ran her eyes across the inscription. "Your name is Lark?"

Lark nodded, smug that her weak fingers hadn't lost their tactile coordination.

"Well met, Lark." Daciana held out her hand. Lark slipped her own into it, marveling at the strength beneath its smooth surface. She gave it one quick shake before retreating.

Daciana smiled. "Wait 'til you meet the boys."

IF DACIANA MINDED TAKING frequent breaks and bearing Lark's weight from time to time, she didn't show it.

Though it seemed impossible, after traveling for a day, the trees began to thin, revealing more of a grey sky. The heavy gloom failed to diminish the sparks of excitement bubbling in Lark's chest. She was free. She was human. And she felt *everything*. The way the leathers formed to her legs, crinkling with every step. The scratch of the wool cloak against her neck. The cool, damp air that misted her hair to cling to her forehead.

Though, she could do without the sensation of knives piercing the bottoms of her feet.

At last, they stepped out from under the cover of unforgiving branches. A sprawling field stretched before them. It separated the two forests with an expanse of open land. Without the cover of gnarled branches and a sky overcrowded by trees, Lark took a deep breath and lowered onto the grass. Daciana took a seat beside her. Across the valley, a lush, green canopy of leaves swayed in the wind, beckoning. Arden Forest. Lark had reaped in Arden Forest before. Hunters, lost travelers, young couples running away together. Death made no exceptions, and humans were notoriously delicate to afflictions such as starvation and exposure.

Lark tugged her cloak tighter, attempting to stifle her shiver.

"It's not far now," Daciana said before she stood. Lark glanced up at her, not quite ready to walk on knives again.

Daciana held out her hand. "When was the last time you had any water?"

At the mention of water, Lark's throat screamed its dry protest. It would take some getting used to, these needs of life. Lark let Daciana yank her up, wincing.

Daciana slung Lark's arm around her neck, gripping her hand and wrapping her arm around Lark's waist. No room for arguments.

They trudged, one step in front of the next, closer to the far more welcoming woods ahead. Lark gripped her carved stick. A tightly wound coil had made its home in Lark's gut. Apprehension or hunger. Likely both.

Lark stumbled, leaning into Daciana. Strength was never a tangible thing as a Reaper. Mental fortitude and awareness shaped her notion of strength. Daciana was lean with streamlined, firm musculature. She half carried Lark along, showing no symptoms of exhaustion. It struck Lark how comfortable it was to be this close to her. A comfort she'd only known with Ferryn.

A knot formed in her throat at the thought of him. She swallowed it down as the pressed forward.

Arden Forest surrounded them in rich tones of deep browns and verdant greens. Taking a deep breath, Lark let the earthy aroma fill her lungs. A damp, intoxicating scent of life. She took her next step with purpose, ignoring the familiar bite of pain.

In the distance, Lark could make out a campsite. Four linen tents were situated around a circle of stones, grey ashes in the center. Beside it sat a stack of pots and pans, bowls and utensils. How very civilized.

The sound of footfalls crunching over twigs and leaves faltered Lark's steps, causing Daciana to pause. A boy stepped into view. His white tunic, rolled to his elbows, revealed pale arms as he cradled an arm's load of kindling. His thick, dark hair was windswept and messy as if he ran his fingers through it. As he caught sight of them, he froze. Grey-blue eyes, wide in shock.

"Um... who's this?" His lilting voice was both baffled and amused.

"She needs water," Daciana said.

"Of course." He dropped his armful of branches and twigs at his feet and strode toward a tent.

Daciana led Lark over to the fireside, placing her on the ground. "I'll only be a moment."

Lark scrambled to her feet. To do what? Hobble away?

"No, no, don't strain yourself." The boy had returned, full lips pulled in a gentle smile, waterskin in hand. He wasn't as young as Lark thought from a distance. A man, rather than a boy, with delicate features. He had a lean but solid build, and his pale face was soft, despite his sharp cheekbones and piercing eyes. "Here, drink." He held the leather waterskin out to her, waiting for her to accept.

Lark grasped the container, bringing it to her chest. Lifting it to her lips, she ignored the tremors wracking her hands as she closed her mouth over the opening. Tipping it back, ice-cold water rushed out, filling her mouth and flooding her throat. She sputtered, water dripping down her chin. Coughs shook her body, pulling from a deep place in her chest and ripping through her stomach.

Lark wiped her chin with the back of her hand.

She lifted again, this time tempering the amount of water as it flowed. Instant relief fled through her mouth and down her throat, soothing the ragged edges that thirst and choking had carved. She gulped it down until a gentle hand at her back urged her to stop. Lark lowered the waterskin to find Daciana taking it from her grasp.

"You'll purge if you drink too fast." Daciana's brows were drawn in gentle concern.

Lark turned back to the man gaping at her.

"Right," he said. "So, Daciana, could we talk privately for a moment? It's not about you," he offered far too quickly to Lark.

They stepped far enough away that Lark's mortal ears couldn't pick up their words. Heads bent, they whispered to one another, occasionally glancing her way. Lark turned her attention to the campsite.

Unsure if they slept two to a tent or not, she counted a possibility of six more people that might make an appearance at any moment.

Two sets of footsteps made their way back.

The man sat beside her. "It seems introductions are in order. I'm Langford. A pleasure to make your acquaintance." He extended his hand.

"This is Lark," Daciana answered for her.

Lark shook his hand. His eyes searched her face for answers like she was a puzzle he was determined to solve.

Langford's gaze dropped. "Oh dear, look at your feet!"

Lark followed his incredulous stare to glance at her filthy, bloodied feet. She wiggled her toes, ignoring the unfamiliar flood of warmth on her cheeks.

"Where are your shoes? Why didn't you give her something?" He turned to Daciana.

Lark touched his arm to gain his attention, shaking her head.

"No?" His dark brows lifted. "Well, this should be interesting when Alistair comes back."

Lark's stomach issued another mind-rending cramp. She doubled over gripping her midsection. Definitely hunger.

"Do you have anything she can eat?"

Langford shook his head. "You were supposed to be back two days ago. Alistair and Hugo set off a few hours back to gather supplies."

Daciana muttered something about helpless children.

Lark wished she could apologize. She wished she could explain her weakness was only temporary. Had she been in her previous form, she'd be a formidable force. Now, she was a burden.

Lark ran a hand into her tangled hair. Pulling her fingers free, she managed to yank a few strands from her head. She gripped them, turning them over to examine for the first time. Her hair was darker than she remembered, but still, a reddish hue caught the light.

It was still her. She was still herself.

DACIANA BUILT the fire beside Lark. Dusk was approaching, and so far, no signs of the one called Alistair. Though it pained Lark to admit, she was relieved. Langford seemed no further endeared to her, she could only imagine how the other fellows would react.

Distrust, fear, annoyance.

She wouldn't blame them. She must seem strange to their sensibilities. She'd reaped enough mortals to know a silent, shoeless woman from the forest would be an odd find.

Lark caught Langford staring at the ground in front of her. She followed his gaze only to land on her blackened feet, blood and dirt crusted. Refusing to feel self-conscious, she stared back at him. His eyes immediately pulled to her face, a blush creeping up his neck as he turned away.

"You should wash up," Daciana said.

Lark shrugged. The action pulled at her grime-coated skin.

"You don't want to cause infection. Such a simple thing but it can make all the difference."

Lark had no doubt. It seemed anything could harm her these days.

"I'll take you to the stream."

Lark wanted to protest. She wanted to insist she could care for herself and didn't need coddling from a stranger. A stranger who'd already tipped the balance beyond what Lark could fulfill.

But her voice was still missing. And she needed help.

Face hot, she nodded.

Daciana offered her a small private smile. How did Daciana come to find her anyway? What was she doing there, in the forest not meant for the living? Lark shouldn't question her fortunate circumstance. What if someone else had happened upon her? She'd been completely at Daciana's mercy, a lesser person might have left her for dead, or worse.

After they returned, Lark's skin cooled and clean from the icy stream, Daciana built up the fire. Lark shivered, delighted at the feeling of skin that wasn't taut with blood and grime. In the Otherworld, she'd always had a steaming basin of water waiting in her private chambers. But she couldn't feel the heat when she sank into the tub. As a mortal, even as a silent shriek sprang from her lips at the freezing water, she marveled at how much her new body *felt*.

Daciana stood, watching Lark warily. "All right, I'm off to gather something for you to eat. It seems Langford has picked the berry bushes clean in my absence."

"You know they aid my digestion," Langford said, hands on his hips.

Daciana sighed. "Yes, I know. If Alistair comes back before I'm gone, make sure—" Daciana froze, angling her head and staring into the distance. Two beats later, Lark heard the unmistakable sound of footsteps approaching. Whoever it was had no intention of trying to be quiet.

"You're back!" a deep voice crooned. "I thought for sure you'd found a new pack to run with." The man in question came into view, dark hair hanging in his brilliant green eyes. His jaw was dusted in dark scruff that failed to hide the cleft in his chin. He donned shiny black leather pants, a gleaming cutlass at his side, and his unbuckled crimson gambeson revealed a black tunic and the top of his golden-brown chest. A burlap sack hung over his shoulder as he strutted toward them.

"And leave you to fend for yourself?" Daciana stretched her legs out. "Never."

"That's a relief," he said, his verdant gaze landing on Langford. "What about you, did you miss me?"

Langford rolled his eyes, cheeks reddening. "How can one miss a pebble in their shoe?"

He answered with a crooked grin until he spotted Lark. His smile faltered, and his gaze darkened. "And what do we have here?"

Lark could feel every ounce of his assessment like needle pricks against her skin. She raised her chin.

"Lark, this is Alistair, you'll learn to ignore him. Alistair, this is Lark. Our guest." Daciana's tone left little room for contradiction. "And she's in dire need of sustenance."

With a sigh, Alistair lowered the bag to the ground. He reached his arm in and pulled out a loaf of bread. He went to break it in half, only for Daciana to snatch it from him and hand it to Lark.

"I was planning on waiting for Hugo to eat." Alistair watched Lark with thinly veiled annoyance.

"Where is he?" Langford looked over Alistair's shoulder.

"We split up. I was to find a merchant." Alistair bent over and pulled out a large, brown bottle. "Which I did, and he was to go hunting." He cast a pointed look at Lark. "So, we could feast tonight."

Daciana warmed her hands over the fire. "We'll make do. It's no fault of mine you failed to acquire supplies until we'd run out."

He crossed his arms and tilted his head. "We were expecting you back two days ago."

"I got held up."

"Clearly."

Lark thumbed the bread. The way they bickered made it difficult to determine the hierarchy of the group.

Daciana noticed her hesitation. "Please, eat. We have more than we need."

Alistair scoffed and took a swig from his bottle.

Lark broke the loaf in two and handed the bigger half toward Daciana.

She waved her off. "I insist. I'm going to find Hugo."

"No need," a deep brogue drawled. From behind Alistair, a thickly muscled man approached. He towered over them, a head taller than even Alistair, who was of formidable height. His dark hair was shaved on the sides and peppered in grey. A thick mustache and beard obscured half his face, and he carried a deer carcass over his shoulder. Intricate tattoos covered his large hands and wrapped around his wrists, shapes and symbols encircling his neck and throat, ending just below his jaw.

Did they run his entire body?

Lark was familiar with the human practice of hammering ink beneath skin to form permanent lines. She used to ask mortals the significance of their markings. Sometimes they answered. His symbols looked familiar, but she couldn't quite place them.

"I'd appreciate your quick hands on this," Hugo's deep voice rumbled as he regarded Daciana with an expectant stare.

Daciana grinned and immediately jumped up to help him.

"Don't you want to introduce yourself?" Alistair's voice was all honey and sarcasm.

"No," Hugo grunted.

Lark preferred it that way. Wasting no more time, she sank her teeth through the crust of bread and ripped through the crumb. It was hard and sharp, cutting the corners of her mouth. Chewy enough her jaw was already sore. But if she'd had her voice she would have groaned at the taste. It was the most magnificent thing to ever pass her lips.

In the Otherworld, she'd dined on all sorts of delicacies. Dishes only mortals of extravagant wealth could ever dream of. Once Ferryn forced her to eat a chocolate cake that spouted a river of decadent chocolate and raspberry filling, and she'd tasted nothing. But here in the forest, across the fire from strange humans, eating a stale piece of bread, she savored every bite, every taste.

For the first time Lark could ever recall, tears rolled down her cheeks at the sensation of filling her hungry belly. The rightness of sating a mortal need. So simple. And yet so significant.

This was what she was fighting for. Sacrificed everything for.

To feel.

To live.

Lark glanced up; her chewing slowed at the twinge of pain across her jaw. They all stared at her. Daciana's face tightened. Uncomfortable by the emotion reflected there, Lark's gaze darted to Alistair, and his dark brow furrowed. Hugo's stare was trained on the ground, anywhere but on her. Langford had pressed a finger to his lips—as if holding back a litany of questions.

Lark wiped at her cheeks with filthy hands, collecting the tears to inspect them. She smiled around a mouthful of bread at the wetness glimmering in her hand under the moonlight.

Alistair rose taking slow, measured steps. He clutched the brown bottle, keeping both hands in plain view.

Lark tracked his movements but didn't shrink away as he sat at her side. Despite his closeness, he was careful not to touch her. His eyes were impossibly bright and green, like the sun pushing its way through the leaves. This close, she could see the stubble along his deep golden jaw and imagine how rough it must feel. Curiosity begged her to run her hand across his skin, just to find out. Her eyes traveled lower. His throat bobbed.

"Do you have anywhere to go?"

Anywhere to go? Lark knew no one on this plane, save for Gavriel. And she was the last person he wanted to see. She shook her head.

"Is there anyone you need to find?"

Again, Gavriel's face filled Lark's mind. His fire, his anger. Once directed at death, now reserved for her in the only moment they shared. Chewing slowly, she gave an almost imperceptible shake of her head.

"I see," Alistair said, voice distant as he studied the ground. "I don't know what you've been through. But if you wish, there's a place for you with us." Lark glanced back to the remaining three. "I promise no harm will come to you." He extended his hand to her. A garish ruby glinted on his first finger, the reflection of the flames dancing along its smooth surface.

Lark wiped a hand on her leggings and grabbed his hand, giving it a firm shake.

Alistair grinned, casting a boyish expression on his face. He gave her hand a small squeeze before dropping it to uncork his bottle of ale. "Well, company, I'd say we have something to celebrate." He drank deeply before lifting the bottle overhead. "To Lark. She may not have a way with words, but damn if she doesn't have good taste in friends!" He held the bottle out to her.

Lark grabbed it and took a long pull. Thick, bitter liquid filled her mouth, and a cough pulled from her throat as she choked.

Alistair laughed and clapped her on the back.

Across the fire, Hugo frowned at the ground, while Langford offered a tight smile that didn't quite reach his eyes.

Daciana beamed at her, and Lark found herself smiling back.

And for one moment, thoughts of what she once was, of where she'd come from, of what she'd fled, all disappeared. As Lark filled her hungry belly, a warm ember of hope burned within.

She was human. She was alive.

CHAPTER 17

The first rays of dawn slipped through the worn stitches of the tent. Lark wished the sun would hurry its pass across the sky and fulfill her third day.

After Alistair's proclamation, and only another sip or two of ale, she'd drifted off by the fire. She only knew she'd been moved when she awoke alone, in a dark tent, thrashing against her nightmares. If she'd had a voice, she was sure she'd have been screaming.

In her dreams, Ferryn was on his knees in that skies forsaken throne room. Thanar's command resonated like an unintelligible hum, and Ceto's broadsword lifted, the blade catching the light of the false sun. A whistle rang through the air—the thud of Ferryn's head, cleaved from his body and rolling across the floor. Lark couldn't scream, she couldn't move. Gavriel appeared, and turned his hateful glare, chips of emerald ice, upon her. "Was he not worth saving?"

Shaking the last vestiges of the nightmare from her mind, Lark stretched her aching limbs. No one told her being human would make her feel so creaky.

Glancing down at her now clean feet, she inspected the gashes and scrapes she'd earned from walking barefoot. The wounds were shallow, but the skin around them was red and hot to the touch. She crawled from the privacy of her bedroll, poking her head out between the flaps.

The spring morning carried the scent of damp earth and moss, almost drowned out by the musky scent of the campfire.

Langford sat fireside atop a wet log. His dark hair, mussed from sleep, stuck out at odd angles. He opened his mouth in a gaping yawn.

Where was Daciana?

Alistair strolled into view and handed a plate of what looked like eggs to Langford. "Lark, if you intend to break fast with us you'd better hurry. We won't save anything for you."

Lark sighed and stepped forward. She winced, wishing again for her third day to be up. Limping over to the fire, she leaned heavily on the makeshift spear Daciana had carved for her, and sat beside Langford. He passed her a plate. The wood was smooth beneath her touch, and warm from the fried quail eggs.

Her first bite exploded the yolk on her tongue along with its rich almost buttery flavor. Eagerly, Lark dug in, trying not to pay too much attention to the all consuming joy she experienced in response to hot food. If she could avoid tears, that would be preferable. The first time was unavoidable, but another episode like last night might be awkward.

"How did you sleep?" Alistair's voice was cheerful.

It should have been an innocuous question, but horrifying memories of her dreams assaulted her, and she clutched the plate tight enough her hands shook.

Lark once treasured her ability to dream. Reapers didn't dream, and yet her mind would come alive whenever she laid down her head.

"It's probably for the best you can't speak." Alistair popped an entire egg into his mouth, and orange yolk peeked out the corner of his lips. He wiped his chin with the back of his hand. "I took the third watch last night and almost ran into your tent to make sure no one was attacking you. You must have some vivid dreams to justify all that thrashing. Unless you were merely enjoying some *alone* time. In which case, I like your style." He gave a rakish grin that crinkled the corners of his verdant eyes.

Lark bit the inside of her cheek, willing the conversation to steer anywhere else. It was fortunate she hadn't needed to share a tent with anyone. Daciana was quick to set up her lodgings with little more than rope, and some spare canvas.

"I have nightmares too."

The first words Langford uttered to her since the night before. Lark met his stare, dark circles etched beneath grey-blue eyes.

Alistair was quick to sever the silence. "So, are you ready for your first day?" He stretched, exposing the top of his golden-brown chest. Did he ever bother lacing his tunics? "You'll have to earn your keep."

Lark wasn't sure what annoyed her more. His arrogant smirk or the fact he was right. She pursed her lips and nodded.

"Wonderful, you can help Langford."

Langford looked about as pleased with the notion as she. "I don't think that's such a good idea."

Alistair ran a hand over his unshaven jaw, appearing deep in thought. "Lark, dear, in your current state, can you hunt?"

Lark gritted her teeth and shook her head.

"Hm, can you track? What about heading to the nearest village to collect us a contract?"

Lark glared at him. Insufferable ass.

Alistair scratched his head. "I don't know, Langford. What do you think?"

Langford ran a hand into his hair. "I can find something for her to do."

Steaming, and not the least bit impressed by the humiliation that burned the back of her neck, Lark wolfed down the rest of her meal fast enough not to taste it.

"I SAID, valerian! Not water hemlock. Are you trying to kill us all?"

Lark clenched her teeth, resisting the urge to slap Langford. She glared at him as he pinched the bridge of his nose.

Dropping the cluster of white flowers in his outstretched palm, her cheeks burned. She shouldn't be off collecting herbs. She'd been remade, her fate undone. Her path was uncertain, but she would not spend her days picking flowers.

"I'm sorry, I'm sorry. I spent years studying herbs at University." Langford sat on a nearby rock, leaning forward to rest his elbows on his knees. The gentle rush of the narrow stream carved through their silence.

So, he'd gone to the University in Koval? What was he doing in Ardenas?

Lark pushed the question from her mind and planted herself on the bank near his feet, running her fingers across the grass. Each blade was warm under the midday sun. The forest had thinned, allowing the azure sky and wisps of white clouds to capture the day. They hadn't gone very far, with Langford having to help her nearly every step of the way. He was quick to have her lean on him, but less patient with trying to communicate.

Langford pulled two apples from his bag, holding one out to her. She grabbed it and took a large bite. Crisp, tart juice exploded on her tongue. The satisfying crunch of the fruit's flesh had her attacking it with vigor.

Nothing in the Otherworld compared to the flavors she experienced here in this weak, sore, human body. She sank her teeth into the apple again. She swore she could taste the sun against its skin—she could taste the earth the tree grew from that bore this fruit.

She could taste life.

When all that remained was the core, she lifted her eyes to Langford. He schooled his expression into feigned disinterest, but the way he gripped his apple tight in his hand betrayed the tension he tried to hide.

Lark wiped the back of her hand across her mouth. She needed to stop acting as though she'd never tasted simple foods before.

A bird sang out its call. Lark held a hand to her brow, shielding her eyes as she searched the sky.

"What did you do before you came here?"

Lark huffed a strand of hair from her face. Even if she could speak, would he believe her? Mortals were quick to bend a knee to Avalon. But to ask him to accept on faith she was a tool wielded by death, the servant of the god of death—she'd sound crazy at best. And if he did believe her...

Gavriel's face swam into view, his once lazy smile melted into pure disgust and hatred.

No one harbored affection for the hand of death.

"Can I guess?" Langford had the ghost of a smile on his face.

Lark nodded.

"Let's see." Langford leaned back, turning his gaze to the leaves above them. "You're a princess who escaped the vengeful clutches of her evil stepmother?"

Lark wrinkled her nose and shook her head.

His responding laugh rumbled from his chest. His laughter transformed his features, banishing the shadows that curled beneath his eyes and made him appear fragile. His full lips parted to reveal straight, white teeth and dimples that creased his cheeks.

With a satisfied smile, Lark settled on her back and let the sun kiss her face. Bathed in the warm glow dancing between the trees, she let her eyes slip closed. The wind was a gentle whisper against her skin, ruffling wisps of hair in its wake. Alighting her nerves with each passing caress.

"You behave as though—" Langford paused. "You've lived your life locked in a dungeon and are only now seeing the sun for the first time. *Feeling* the sun for the first time."

Lark's eyes opened, and she lifted to lean on her elbows. This was her first time feeling any true sensations. The way the wind rose goose-pebbles on her skin or tickled her neck when it whipped her hair. The saturating warmth of basking in open sunlight. The relief of resting a weary body. She couldn't wait to know what rain would feel like against her mortal skin. After a heartbeat or so, she nodded.

Langford's grey-blue eyes widened.

Not waiting for his response, she dropped back to her spot in the grass, content to enjoy this moment and banish thoughts of her old life.

She couldn't bear to think of those she'd left behind, what punishment they might be facing. She hadn't thought it through when she took the witch's deal. Barreling forward, trading her life, her friends, and leaving her destiny behind.

She wasn't ready to question her decision. Not yet.

"HOW DID OUR NEWEST MEMBER DO?"

The sun was still high in the sky when Lark and Langford made it back to camp.

Langford placed the bag of herbs he'd gathered by his tent and turned to Alistair. "She certainly won't poison us on purpose."

After their break lying in the grass, Langford was quick to show her exactly which herbs were necessary for which aches and pains. What to take if one had trouble sleeping. Herbs that promoted mental clarity. Once he got to explaining, Lark was enthralled. The way his eyes would light up when he told her something she didn't know, which was admittedly quite a bit.

Alistair sighed. "I was afraid you might say that. Oh well! I have a new chore for you. Take care of the wash." He gestured to an enormous canvas bag stuffed beyond its capacity with clothes. "Travel east until you hit the large stream. Shouldn't be too far." Alistair threw a pointed glare Langford's way. "We used to camp closer to freshwater, but *some* people complained about bodily freedom."

"You were constantly naked. It isn't my fault you dangled your phallus in Hugo's face," Langford said.

Alistair rolled his eyes, turning his attention back to Lark. "In any case, you'll head east and wash the laundry."

He had to be joking. Walking was agony. How was she supposed to carry that sack and remain upright?

Lark threw a pleading glance at Langford.

He brushed his hand on his trousers, stepping forward. "I can accompany her."

Alistair spun on his heel. "No. This is for her alone." He turned to Lark. "You can do this."

Lark limped to the oversized bag of dirty clothes. Gripping it by the handle, she dragged it behind her as she made her slow trek to the same stream Daciana had taken her to the night before. She remembered the path well enough.

Lark pressed further, trying to ignore each tortuous step.

After what seemed like hours, the rush of the stream pricked her ears. She pressed through the thicket. The familiar bank and the scent of damp earth greeted her. The sun bathed the steady, coursing water in a warm glow. Moss clung to the stones peeking out from the water's edge.

Lark couldn't marvel at the natural beauty of the quiet moment, she still needed to wash the clothes.

She lowered to her knees on the bank and ripped the sack open, yanking everything out. Without inspecting too closely, she leaned over the stream and began dunking each garment into the icy cold water, swishing them around beneath the clear surface, scrubbing and agitating until bubbles began to rise. Langford had given her soap cake for any stains, a concoction of his own that smelled faintly of lavender. Lark scraped it over the wet clothes before swirling them beneath the surface of the cool stream.

After some time, the motions became almost soothing. It was mindless work, but it kept her hands occupied which was a nice change after feeling so useless. If Alistair thought this was going to be a regular thing, she'd have to deposit a few snakes in his trousers for him to find.

The sun was still relatively high on the horizon. Several more hours before Lark could speak or walk without wincing.

As she hung the last tunic over a nearby branch, the birds she'd been half-listening to fell silent. An unnatural quiet draped over the forest.

The hairs on the back of her neck rose, and her ears pricked.

Lark peered over her shoulder. She reached for the spear she'd used as her walking stick thus far.

As a Reaper, the only thing Lark had to fear was Thanar. Everything else trembled in her wake. She was formidable. Unstoppable.

But as a human, Lark suddenly understood what it was to be afraid of the shadows. To feel the icy chill of fear breathe down her neck as she faced the inevitable truth of mortality.

The breeze ceased—its loss made every nerve in her body heighten in anticipation.

A low growl emanated from the far bushes.

Lark spun around, cursing her stance, and aimed her weapon.

The leaves trembled, and terror rooted Lark to the spot.

Shit.

The shrubs parted—a pair of antlers pushing through. The rest of its dark body dragged its way out from the cover of the forest, slowly approaching where Lark stood paralyzed.

The beast sniffed the air, grunting, and rose onto its hind legs to its full height. Flesh hung off its body in open flaps, exposing its rib cage. Its bones expanded with each breath. Massive paws were adorned with long, thick claws meant for tearing human flesh. A deep guttural growl reverberated from its chest as it stepped elongated limbs further into the clearing.

Lark's heart hammered in her chest. Her blood rushed in her ears. Palms slick with sweat, she gripped her weapon even tighter.

The creature bared its teeth, loosing another growl, and putrid saliva dripped from its jowls. Its eyes glared an unnatural red, sizing her up as prey.

Lark's stomach dropped, and her insides churned, threatening to dump its contents.

An Undesirable.

A Wentiko. Souls of mortals plagued by insatiable greed. The punishment for such a soul twisting its way out of the Netherworld was to become a monstrous beast, always hungering, never sated. A hunger for flesh that drove them to madness.

If Lark were in her old form, she could shatter the beast without breaking a sweat, provided her tether remained strong. But as a mere mortal...

The Wentiko threw its head back, howling in rage. It lowered back to the ground, head bowed and antlers low.

A heartbeat passed. The pressure, near painful in Lark's throat. The wooden spear shook in her hands.

The beast rushed.

Energy exploded through Lark's veins as she sprang, instinct moving her too quick for her mind to keep up. She feinted left, narrowly missing its antlers aiming for her belly. It reared up, and its claws raked against her side. Heat bloomed from the wound. A wet, sticky heat.

Lark spun back, pivoting on her heel, and aimed the spear at its jugular. Antlers slammed against her chest at an angle, knocking the air from her lungs and sending her flying to the ground.

Lark tried to push herself up, arms shaking. All she'd sacrificed, and for what? A blink of a lifespan. A drop of life that evaporated before she could taste it.

No.

She would die. But not yet. With every fiber of her soul, *not yet*.

The unmistakable sound of claws ripping the earth barreled toward her. Lark rolled to her back just in time to thrust her spear into the belly of the Wentiko. The shriek it emitted was almost human.

Her mouth open in a silent scream, Lark twisted the spear left and right, as the beast thrashed on top of her. The Wentiko slashed at her again, its claws catching Lark's shoulder. Tears rolled down her cheeks as she tugged her spear up through its chest. Cracking and squelching filled her ears, and hot breath fanned her face as it snarled its rage, teeth mere inches from her face. Warm blood spilled over her chest and Lark squeezed her eyes shut, not wanting the last thing she saw to be the hate in an Undesirable's eyes. She conjured the image of Gavriel. When he looked up at her with wonder and tucked her hair behind her ear. That was the image she'd take to the Netherworld.

The Wentiko shuddered above her. Lark opened her eyes, blinking back tears. Its stare finally glazed over. It collapsed, trapping her beneath its massive body and ripping the breath from her lungs.

159

Lark dragged her bloodied body out from under the creature's heavy corpse. Every scrape, every slice, and every bruise pulsed their reminders. Lark gingerly touched her side and winced at the bolt of pain that lanced through her. Her shoulder stung with a strange heat, and her entire body seemed to rumble its protest. It would seem her mortal form would be put to the test right from the get-go.

Lark forced herself to stand when a wave of dizziness nearly knocked her off her feet. She attempted to wrench her weapon free but gave up when it wouldn't budge from the Wentiko's sternum.

One shaky foot in front of the other, Lark threw herself toward the stream, trying to get the ice-cold relief of water against her wounds. The shock of the freezing temperature numbed her aches.

Soaking wet, and her vision dimming with black spots, she made her way back to camp.

One thought rang in her head with each throbbing step.

Survive.

"You sent her alone?"

"I didn't realize I'd been demoted to the babysitter. Would have been nice to receive that in writing."

The unmistakable sound of Daciana grunting in frustration reached Lark's ears.

"Years I've known your faults. I always told myself 'there's a limit to Alistair's selfishness'. But here we are and, damn it, you find a way to surpass my wildest expectations of your incompetence!"

"Dac, wait."

Lark staggered out of the trees and into the clearing. With a wince, she attempted another step forward, only to fall to the ground.

Daciana was at her side in an instant and pulled Lark's arm around her neck, supporting her weight. She brought her to Langford, depositing her beside him.

"Build a fire." Daciana offered no room for argument, and Hugo jumped to the task.

Langford's soft hands were already busy inspecting her wounds, peeling back her tattered clothing. His eyebrows pinched together as he reached into his bag and produced a salve Lark recognized from their afternoon together. He spread the murky substance along her gashes.

Alistair watched in silence, tugging at his hair anxiously. His mouth twisted as if trying hard not to speak.

"The wounds are superficial." Langford finally spoke. "And don't appear to be the work of a blade. Though this does beg the question of what exactly happened." He turned his piercing gaze on her face, searching for answers Lark couldn't give. Not yet anyway.

"See? I told you she's fine," Alistair said.

Daciana's expression turned murderous as she rounded on Alistair. "You sent her unprotected to complete some asinine task. She comes back wounded, and you have the gall to profess no mistake was made?"

Alistair backed away, hands up in surrender. "Now, now. I made no such claims. If you would only listen to my reasoning—"

"Your reasoning is why she was almost killed!" Daciana spat on the ground.

"We don't know that. If she could act it out, like a game of charades, we could decipher where the fault lies."

"You arrogant ass!"

Alistair's face darkened. "Bad form. No name-calling."

With a noise of disgust, Daciana turned and crouched beside Lark while Langford bandaged her side. "Are you all right?"

Lark nodded. She was... better than all right. She killed an Undesirable with her own mortal hands. The pain was worth the warm sense of pride filling her chest.

Offering her a tight smile, Daciana squeezed her non-injured shoulder and handed Langford another roll of wrappings.

"Wonderful! This only proves my point, yes? She's more than capable of accompanying you."

Daciana slowly stood—the movement of a predator that had even Lark on edge—and glared at Alistair. "We're not discussing this."

"You know I can't go with you; Hugo is too conspicuous—he'll be noticed the minute he crosses the threshold. And Langford—" He threw a disparaging look Langford's way. "No offense, but you have the face of a twelve-year-old milkmaid."

"None taken. You'll be wishing for my skin when you're dried up and wrinkled."

"That leaves you going alone. Or you bringing Lark." Alistair ventured a step closer. "And you are *not* going alone."

The fire crackled against the charged silence.

"She isn't ready." Daciana crossed her arms, hazel eyes flashing. "Some of us value human life."

Human life. Lark couldn't help but wonder if Daciana would be so keen to protect her if she knew the truth.

Langford wrapped the last of her bandages and patted her arm.

"You may not agree with my methods, but my reasoning was sound. You can't keep her guarded night and day. If she's going to run with us, she needs to take care of herself. I don't want to create a liability. For us or her." Alistair paced to Lark, dropping into a crouch beside her. "You know what I'm saying, don't you?"

Lark took in the full force of Alistair's stare. His dark brows pinched over vivid green eyes. Of course she understood. There was no use coddling someone if you wanted them to thrive. She nodded, grabbing a hold of his hand.

He clapped the top of her hand before standing. "She can do this."

Dusk had settled over the camp. The shadows grew taller, slicing through rich orange and pink that spilled across the rocks and canvas tents of their campsite. A buzz of energy began to build in Lark's chest as the last few rays of sunlight completed their descent.

The sun had set on the third day.

Lark's mouth curved in a satisfied smile.

Finally.

CHAPTER 18

"Then we don't take the job."

"Money or not, he needs to be taken out." Daciana crossed her arms.

The sun had sunk below the horizon as twilight crept over the camp, and the fire glowed against the dark forest. Lark bit her lip to hide her smile, waiting for her opportunity to speak.

Alistair nodded. "I agree, so we send you and Lark."

Daciana shook her head. "You abandon reason for the sake of stubbornness."

"No, I weigh my risks economically." Alistair's face tightened. "And he's not worth the risk. We go in numbers or not at all."

Daciana groaned with enough exasperation to silence him, finally.

Lark's knees bounced and she wet her lips. She should prepare an explanation with cunning and foresight. A touch of patience could go a long way.

"Don't I get a say?"

Lark was never great with patience.

Four sets of eyes trained on her.

Lark's voice was hoarse and unused, but it was hers.

The fire crackled against the harsh silence of the group.

"You can speak?" Langford arched a brow, wiping Lark's blood off his hands.

She cleared her throat. "I can now, yes." Oh, it felt so good to use her voice. Even if she sounded like she'd swallowed dirt and pebbles. Lark cleared her throat again. "It's a long story."

"Well, that's wonderful news." Alistair seemed to recover first. "My idea worked so spectacularly, it even cured your hysterical muteness."

Hugo scoffed, coughing to cover his reaction.

"You said it was a long story. I'm a patient listener," Daciana said, eying Lark with stern calculation.

Lark wasn't ready to tell them everything. To risk being cast aside. "When you found me, you said it was clear I was recently afflicted." Lark stood, wanting to cry for joy at how good it felt to be on her own two feet—absent of the sensation of walking on knives. "It was a temporary curse, nothing more." Lark swallowed, realizing she needed to offer more if she wanted them to believe her. "The rest... I would share another time."

Daciana's hazel eyes flashed with something Lark couldn't quite name, before her face softened. "That's asking a lot, but I suppose I asked for your trust first."

"I didn't have much of a choice."

Daciana smirked, thumbing the daggers she wore at her sides. "No, I suppose not. But I have a pretty good sense of these things. And I'm inclined to accept this as answer enough. For now."

The rest of the group breathed a collective sigh of relief. Daciana held more sway than it appeared, and deep reliance on her instincts. One they all seemed to share, despite Alistair behaving as if he called the shots. Lark tucked that detail away for safekeeping.

There was still more to reveal.

"There's something you should know," Lark said, keeping her hands at her sides. Just in case the others were feeling twitchy. They took her in. Clothed and fed her. The least Lark could do was warn them of what they might face. Hopefully, they'd never face an Undesirable. But hope was a fragile thing. "The creature who attacked me isn't of this world. Not anymore."

"What do you mean?" Langford asked with a nervous laugh.

"What was it?" Alistair ignored him. His expression, unusually grim.

Lark held his stare. Did he really accept her words as truth? "An Undesirable."

"A what?" Hugo asked. These were his first words spoken to her.

"A beast. A soul that's clawed its way back to the world of the living, only to find it's been twisted from its original state. Made into a monster by the journey." The memory of its gnarled body, worn by death and decay, ghosted a shiver down her neck.

"Lark," Langford said with a tone so gentle it grated. "You've been through so much—"

"I didn't imagine it," Lark said through her teeth. She needed to remember this was hard for mortals to accept unless they'd witnessed it firsthand.

Some mortals believed. The ones she had reaped after falling victim to Undesirables certainly believed. Some were taught the old Ardenian ways, whispering stories around dying hearths and bundling protective herbs. But believing in monsters had fallen out of fashion back when Ardenas broke away from Koval. There were still mortals who hired Hunters: fighters born and bred to hunt monsters and beasts. But even they seemed a relic of the past. Many viewed Hunters as little more than charlatans, preying on the desperate and meek, assuming the monsters they slew were imagined. How easy it was for mortals to convince themselves in the warm light of day that the shadows had grown tall and played tricks on their minds.

"Those are just fairy stories," Langford said, eyes tight. "We discussed this very thing in my philosophy class. They're ancient myths, repeated to keep the superstitious branch of the faithful in line." He shook his head, running an elegant finger over his mouth. Even as he said the words, he appeared ever the scholar, dutifully debating and pondering.

"If it was some manner of beast, maybe it was a bear or a boar?" Alistair said. "You're sure it was an animal?"

"It was an Undesirable," Lark said, hugging her knees. Why did it matter so much if they believed her? "Langford confirmed it wasn't the work of a blade."

"I did," Langford said hesitantly. "Your wounds are consistent with blunt force trauma, and lacerations thicker than the width of most blades." He frowned, shooting a significant look at Alistair. "But I'm still trying to piece together what happened."

"I'm telling you what happened," Lark said between gritted teeth.

"People are more than capable of cruelty, Lark." Alistair's voice held an edge and a shadow passed over his face. "No one would fault you if something happened."

"Look here, is that the work of a human?" Lark gestured to her shoulder, her side, where the wrappings Langford applied hid the tracks of angry claws. Was Alistair willfully ignorant?

"Yes, Lark." A muscle feathered in Alistair's jaw. "That could be the work of a human. I've seen far worse than that."

Aislinn's gasping form, bloodied and broken, sprang to Lark's mind. "I'm not lying."

"You could be lying about everything," Alistair responded smoothly. "Daciana trusts you aren't a threat, but that doesn't mean you're telling us the truth."

He wasn't entirely wrong. She was going to have to take them to the bank to show them the Wentiko, when all she wanted was a warm meal and to retire to her tent. Why couldn't she have landed with a group of superstitious mortals?

Daciana cut in before Lark could speak. "I believe her."

Alistair rolled his eyes, lips parting to offer some retort.

"So do I." Hugo's gravelly voice silenced the others. His words hung heavy in the night air amidst the crackling flames. "I've seen all kinds of monsters, mostly human." Hugo met Lark's stare. "Some, not."

What horrors had Hugo seen?

"Well, that's just wonderful," Alistair said, leaning back to put his boot-clad feet by the fire. The picture of calm disinterest. He laced his hands behind his head. "So, what? We're saying monsters prowl the shadows now? Why haven't I ever seen one?"

"I can show you. Its body is still by the stream." Lark hated how excited she was to prove him wrong.

Alistair arched a brow, a dark smile lighting up his face. "All right, Lark. You show me this creature, and I'll let you go into town with Daciana for the job." He smacked the back of Daciana's arm. "See? I told you she'd be handy. And if she's telling the truth, which you and Hugo seem to think so, then that proves she's more than capable of handling herself." He crossed his arms, his self-assured grin nothing short of triumphant.

"How do you always manage to twist things to serve your purpose?" Daciana asked.

Hugo began sharpening his knife, done with the conversation now that he'd spoken more than two words. Langford stared up at the night sky, mumbling to himself about historical inaccuracies, trying to sort out which theory led him astray. All the while, Daciana and Alistair bickered about whether or not Lark would accompany her on this mission they had yet to tell her anything about. Lark traced the stitches on her trousers, tiring of the way they spoke as if she wasn't sitting right there.

"She'll need training," Daciana said.

"Each day that passes, we risk someone else finishing the job or worse, him getting tipped off." Alistair ran a hand into his dark hair.

"He's not going anywhere." Daciana's eyes glinted dangerously. "So long as he winds up in the ground, I'm content."

Fed up with listening to them, Lark interjected. "There's no use in fighting over my fate, it's mine to decide."

Finally, they broke their staring match to look at Lark.

Daciana's eyes softened. "I didn't explain what we do, did I?"

Lark shrugged. "No, but I can read between the lines. You're assassins."

Langford snorted again, shaking his head. "Assassins."

"Not exactly. We collect contracts." Daciana threw him a withering glare. "We do delve into that territory. But only if the cause is just."

"And the coin is heavy," Alistair added.

"And if our consciences remain lighter than the gold offered," Langford said.

"But it isn't our typical job," Daciana continued as if they hadn't spoken. "I don't enjoy taking another life. Not without cause."

"This is cause," Alistair said, voice closer to a growl.

Lark nodded. It would seem death would remain her fated companion. "What's the contract?"

Daciana's jaw tightened. "A few girls at the tavern let slip that Talbot Morris frequents for wine and women. He's a known operative within the slave trade between Ardenas and Koval."

Lark was familiar with the slavery in Koval. They called it indentured servitude because it sounded prettier, but calling filth by another word didn't make it reek any less. Ardenas had long abolished any forms of slavery, even going so far as to rebuild the nation without the rule of a monarch. Koval maintained its royal line. The current ruler... Lark couldn't remember his name. Or her name. Skies, why didn't she pay more attention to the marks other Reapers received?

"Talbot has found a way to line his pockets?" Lark asked.

"His men round up whomever he deems suitable and ships them off like cargo, sold to the highest bidder." Daciana seethed. "Men, women, children, any he sees on the streets that won't be missed. You speak of monsters, Lark, he's the worst kind."

Children? Lark's hands clenched at her sides, the steady thrum in her ears a reminder: she was alive, and she could take matters into her own hands.

"How do we kill him? Tell me we're going to kill him."

Alistair's grin turned feral. "I knew I liked you."

"THE THING TO remember about handling a deadly weapon is not to get hurt," Alistair said.

Lark rolled her eyes and crossed her arms. The midmorning sun was cool against her skin but the promise of a warm day hung in the air. Parts of her still ached, but it was a rewarding sort of pain.

They'd blessedly given her a meal and a full night's rest before hiking to the stream. After she'd taken them to the site of the attack, Langford had set to work studying the beast and murmuring to himself. He'd made her say the name Wentiko, several times. Repeating it to himself and rolling the word around as he poked and prodded at the carcass. Thorough in his examination. Hugo stayed with Langford so he could work in peace; the large man hardly said a word, so he'd be least likely to distract him. Alistair, far too smug for a man who was just proven wrong, was eager to begin Lark's training. Daciana was right, Alistair had a knack for twisting everything to suit his purpose.

"Any weapon you wield can be disarmed and used against you," Alistair said, pointing the curved edge of his cutlass at Lark's chest. His stance, wide and assured.

Without wasting a moment Lark's foot darted out, landing a sharp kick to his inner thigh. He stumbled back, but before he could raise his sword, her elbow landed in his chest, knocking his arm away, and he dropped his cutlass to the ground. Her other hand jabbed his throat, sending him back coughing and sputtering.

With a small smile, Lark placed her hands on her hips, ignoring the way her shoulder and side stung. "Go on Alistair, tell me more about how things work." Pressure points were always easy to manipulate, it was a relief that even in her weakened state she could aim for vulnerabilities.

He rubbed his throat, a grin already spreading across his face. He straightened. "I wasn't sure how much of the basics you were aware of." He picked up his sword, and flipped it to hold out, handle first. "You'll forgive the mistake, I'm sure. Only last evening you couldn't speak or walk without falling like a drunken scoundrel. I think you enjoy proving me wrong in dramatic fashion."

"It's not my fault you never asked the right questions." Lark grasped the hilt of his weapon. The steel trembled in the light.

"Your muscles have atrophied," Alistair said, frowning. She was grateful he didn't take this chance for ridicule.

"My muscles are new and untested," Lark muttered through gritted teeth.

Alistair's head snapped up to look at her, eyes narrowing. "What does that mean?"

"Nothing."

He tilted his head, his face lighting up with curiosity. "You speak in such riddles. Utterly fascinating."

If Lark told him the truth, it would make even less sense. Instead, she waited for him to continue.

He waved his hand in dismissal. "No matter, that's a task for another time. This particular undertaking," he said, raising an eyebrow, "requires a more delicate hand." He moved to stand behind her, shaking her arm to dislodge the weapon from her grip. "You won't be needing that. He'll likely select Daciana for the night, tasking you with keeping his guards entertained. But if not"—he placed one hand on her hip and pulled her close, his other hand gripping her throat—"focus on maintaining your composure."

Lark fought the instinct to wriggle free of his grasp, keeping her hands loose at her sides.

"Now assuming he's selected you to wile him with your charms, this is likely a position you'll find yourself in." She shivered as Alistair's words fanned against her ear. "Daciana will search for a way to come take care of him, but if our reinforcement is somehow delayed, pardon me." He yanked her tighter against the firm planes of his body. Lark's cheeks burned. "What do you do?"

Lark slid her hands over his as if to lace their fingers. She ripped his hands away and spun out of his hold.

Facing her, Alistair smiled. "Good, but now you've given yourself away; either he'll attack, or he'll holler to his men, and you will have compromised your only advantage of a surprise. And then you'll face a frontal attack."

Lark huffed an impatient breath. He was right, damn him. She put her back to him and yanked his hands into place. "Fine, go again."

Alistair chuckled. "Easy love, if you want me this badly you need only say so."

"Shut up."

His hold was firm, but not tight against her skin. She doubted a real attacker would be so gentle. "Do it right."

He angled his head to peer at her with calculating curiosity on his face. Dark hair fell into his eyes. They narrowed in suspicion like this was a test.

"Come on, stop playing," Lark said.

"Very well."

Alistair's grip tightened, making it harder to breathe. Lark's injuries throbbed in earnest, but she sharpened her focus on the warm body pressed against hers. Lark's hair caught in the dark scruff along his jaw, and her heart hammered in her chest, echoing in her throat. Her palms pricked with sweat. This was only practice, this wasn't real. Why did her body seem to think she was in danger? Were mortals so designed for fear this way?

Lark exhaled the quietest of breaths and brought her hands back over his. This time, she wove them together. Turning, she plastered a mask of serenity on her face, before lacing her hands behind his neck.

"Good. I'm under the false impression you enjoy my touch and are mad with desire to be taken." The corner of Alistair's mouth lifted. "Now, incapacitate me."

Lark slammed her knee to his groin. As he dropped, she brought her elbow down on the back of his neck, before she slammed the heel of her palm into his face with a slight crunch.

He gripped his nose as he stood, a small grunt escaping his throat with the action. "Shit, Lark. That was perfect!" He lowered his hand, revealing the blood streaming from his nose, over his mouth and chin.

"Oh skies, I'm sorry."

"Don't be." Alistair waved her off. "I think we're all pleased with this outcome, yes? As I said, Daciana will likely be his choice, you understand, so you probably won't even need to put this lesson into practice." His angular nose still wept blood. "Now I'd better make sure no permanent damage was inflicted. I'd hate to disappoint my usual in

Belmoore. Langford!" he called. "I need you to fix my nose and make me pretty again!"

"Wait, you aren't coming to Brookhill with us?"

Alistair paused, half turning to respond. "No, sorry. I can't be seen anywhere near this. I need a good alibi when word gets out." He ran his sleeve over his face, smearing his blood. "Hugo, Langford, and I all have plans to make such a ruckus at the Horse and Feathers tavern, we may very well get blacklisted." He gave a devilish, bloodied smile before disappearing into his tent.

THE AFTERNOON SPENT PRACTICING close-quarter combat only served to increase Lark's concerns. She was weaker than she thought she'd be as a mortal. The weight of carrying around a physical form fatigued her more than it should.

After Alistair concluded their practice, Daciana took up the mantle and instructed Lark. Different holds and how to evade them without arousing suspicion. More than anything, Lark just needed to let the full weight of what was to come sink in.

Langford was helpful in their quest to prepare her for subterfuge. He'd spoken of maintaining a vague disinterested expression on her face all the while listening to every conversation around her.

Hugo didn't say much, which was hardly surprising. Though she caught his stare more than once from across the fire. Nothing was leering to it—it was more of a quiet consternation. Unsettling, nevertheless.

Something about relying on these humans made Lark feel small. Insignificant.

"I'm turning in for the night." Lark hadn't realized she'd stood. She ignored their stares, opting to head straight for her tent.

Crickets churred in the darkened forest. Even in the dark, life teemed around her, and a swell of some unnamed emotion stirred in Lark's chest. The skeletal moon filtered pale light through dense leaves, piercing the forest floor. A soft spring breeze whispered over her skin and made the white flame of light flicker beneath shadows.

"Lark, wait." A deep, gravelly voice came from behind. She turned to see Hugo had caught up with her, his eyes darting back and forth. His tattoos were dim obscurities along his thick neck and forearms. "I didn't know how early you two will be off in the morning."

"Early enough to give us time to hit the market and find a bed for the night."

"Yes, that's what I thought." His dark eyes were tight. A muscle clenched in his jaw, making his mustache twitch.

Lark stared up at the huge man. "Why Hugo, I don't believe I've ever heard you speak this much."

He grunted. It may have been a laugh. "Yeah, well." He fumbled with his pockets. "Here." He pulled out a small, curved blade, sheathed in simple leather. Intricate markings adorned the oaken handle. Lark couldn't quite make them out in the dark, damn her mortal eyesight.

She took the knife, tracing delicate hands over it. She pulled it from its sheath, marveling at the steel blade and glinting blood groove. "Thank you."

With a large hand, he rubbed his beard. "Just don't hurt yourself."

Before he could object, Lark stood on her tiptoes and placed a quick kiss on his cheek. His answering scowl did nothing to diminish her happiness. Grumbling to himself, he stomped off.

Upon arriving at Brookhill, Lark was stunned with the sense of familiarity. It seemed like not that long ago, she was standing in the center of Ever Glade with Ferryn imagining life as a human. Right before she stumbled upon her first glimpse of Gavriel, the mortal with fire in his eyes.

So much had changed.

Daciana and Lark found their lodging. The Ashwick Inn was a small establishment on the outskirts of town. It was a decent enough place to lay low before they infiltrated the tavern in the town square.

The innkeeper and his lovely wife, her belly swollen with child, greeted them with warm smiles and promises of hospitality.

The simple room came equipped with a few homey comforts Lark marveled at. The pliancy of a mattress filled with straw rather than a simple roll on the forest floor. The modest oak end table where her candle burned. Thanar never could create an atmosphere of ease.

A soft knock sounded in the early evening. Daciana opened the door to find a young boy with a soot-covered face. He carried a burlap sack over his shoulder. Bowing his head, he handed the sack to Daciana.

She opened it to take a quick look and tossed it inside the room. Pulling ten silvers from her coin purse she deposited them in his hand.

"Thank you, miss," he said and strolled away.

Confused by the exchange, Lark waited for Daciana to explain. There must be a good reason a strange boy was delivering a mysterious satchel. Especially when no one should know where they stayed.

Daciana tossed her the sack. Larked tugged it open to find simple homespun dresses. Of course, they'd need to blend in with the other workers.

With a heavy sigh, Lark placed it on the floor. Despite the weariness in her bones, and the aching weight of her human body, Lark's mind buzzed with anticipation. If they were going to pull this off, she'd need to play a convincing human barmaid.

Daciana began disarming her countless weapons hidden all over her person. Lark counted each gleaming blade in the dwindling candlelight until finally, the heaviness of sleep beckoned.

IT WAS ALL TOO easy to convince the barkeep they were freshly hired. One look at Daciana and he would have believed anything she told him.

The Tawdry Steward was a popular place. Boisterous voices filled the room, muffled by the steady pounding in Lark's head. The air was heady with warm bodies and spirits. Every seat was filled, save for a small, dark corner. Lark imagined hiding in that corner or slipping out the door into the cool night. As a Reaper, walking amongst a crowd was like running a hand through smoke. As a mortal, every nerve seemed over-fired.

Lark cast her gaze upward, collecting her thoughts. Dark beams ran along the ceiling like a cage.

A man with a bushy, red beard spit his ale out as he laughed, spraying the side of Lark's dress. Lark clenched her teeth, adjusting her skirts as she kept her revulsion from spilling across her face and resisted the urge to tug at her leather bodice. Her gown cascaded in layers of white cloth that swept along the grimy floor, no doubt collecting filth along the hem. Her neck and shoulders were exposed, baring her skin. But nothing sat where it was supposed to.

Lark glanced over at Daciana who filled out her dress in all the right ways. Her thick, black hair was coiled in braids on each side in the Northern fashion. Her dark skin glowed, bronze undertones shining in the candlelight as she beamed at each customer, refilling their tankard and occasionally stopping to perch on a man's lap. She'd saunter across the room, catching the eye of everyone she passed. Swaying her hips in that manner that looked neither unnatural nor rehearsed.

Lark concentrated on not tripping over her unfamiliar shoes. In her previous form, she could exploit every weakness humanity had to offer. But now uncertainty seemed to falter every step. Do mortals swing their arms when they walk?

Lark huffed a strand of hair from her face. Daciana had expertly plaited it on either side, keeping most of her hair down and flowing down her back. Wisps were already coming loose as she flitted about the room, carrying a full jug of ale.

With a cheeky wink and a toss of her shoulder, Daciana managed to charm the gentleman gazing at her with rapt attention and signal Talbot's location. Talbot sat in the center of the room, holding court with all the surrounding men. He was unremarkable, nondescript.

Nothing to hint at the monster beneath. His was the face one could see a thousand times and still have trouble recalling.

The leg of a stool caught Lark's foot, and she nearly stumbled to the floor. She needed to focus on how to keep Talbot's men occupied once he was upstairs with Daciana. An easy distraction would be a great, disastrous fall.

"All empty over here, wench."

Lark forced her mouth into a tight smile and made her way to the charmer who called for her. Filling his tankard, she did her best to look politely disinterested, as Langford had instructed. The comforting weight of Hugo's dagger in her boot was a reminder she wasn't helpless.

"Here too, lass."

Across the table, a man with a confident smirk held his mug out expectantly.

"Of course." Rather than climb over anyone's lap in the cramped path, Lark leaned over the dark walnut table to refill his cup. The gouged wood was rough beneath her palm. A possessive hand gripped her backside, making her squeeze the handle so tightly her fist shook. The image of smashing the pitcher over his head was a temptation and a distraction from her anger. Without a backward glance, she pulled back from the table, ignoring the roar of laughter that followed.

Taking a deep breath, Lark glanced up to see Daciana watching her. She inclined her head. As if asking if she was all right.

Lark smiled and gave a short nod. Resuming her rounds, she almost missed the hooded figure shrouded in shadows by the corner. He sat alone, holding a tankard and never lifting it to his lips. If someone else was here to work their job, she had to let Daciana know. She slowed to allow her periphery a full appraisal.

He dressed in dark, fitted leathers. This was no simple village garb. Even his vambraces that wrapped around his wrists and forearms were pure black boiled leather. A dark hunting hood shrouded his head, his face half-hidden by shadows. Even without the confirmation of his gaze, Lark's skin prickled. He was tracking her movements.

She turned, about to offer to refill his mug when her eyes landed on his mouth.

Cutting through his upper lip was a very familiar scar.

Lark rooted to the spot, and ice froze her veins. It couldn't be. The odds were insurmountable. The very chance that he'd be in this tavern, on this night, was impossible. And yet, Lark found herself transfixed. Every nerve in her body hummed.

Lark willed life back into her feet, forcing them to turn, and tripped over a nearby bench. She hurtled to the ground, jug shattering and spraying ale all over herself and nearby patrons. Cursing her throbbing ankle, she sat up.

A strong hand grasped her wrist, pulling her to her feet.

"You're bad at this," a baritone voice rang out.

Lark found herself staring right into the beady-eyes of Talbot Morris.

Shit.

CHAPTER 19

Of two things Gavriel was certain: the barmaid he couldn't tear his eyes from was the demon who incessantly haunted his thoughts, and he was not about to let her go.

He'd known before he'd even seen her—felt the change in the room. She was disguised as a mere girl, and even her hair seemed different, darker, less a living flame and more the burnished embers. But still, he knew.

It was her, and she hadn't noticed him.

It made sense. He was some nameless bastard whose very world she turned upside down for sport. In this dimly lit tavern that reeked of piss and sweat, he was insignificant while he silently stewed in his rage.

But she knew his name. Said it in her melodic voice—a voice that undoubtedly lured many a man to their deaths.

The previous glow of her skin had softened. Her simple dress and bodice accentuated the column of her neck and her delicate collarbones. She appeared almost normal, with her long hair trailing in a mess down her back, a fresh splatter of freckles across her nose. A blush, high on her cheeks from nerves or excitement.

He clenched his hand tighter around his tankard. *Don't fall for the demon's illusion.*

A ruddy faced man grabbed her ass, and his companions roared with laughter. Gavriel's jaw clenched of its own volition at the sight. Demon or not, an unwanted touch made his hands itch for his blades.

Gavriel tracked her every movement, observed every mannerism. She'd taken great pains to create a convincing façade. It was eerie. Not even he had the skill to slip into character so fully.

She huffed, blowing the hair from her face. Tripped over obstacles like a weak colt.

The sight of it gave Gavriel pause. Perhaps this was a mere girl.

At once she stilled, seeing him, finally. The panicked shock froze on her face as she gawked at him. The full weight of her scrutinizing gaze bore down on him. Those sodding amber eyes that he wanted nothing more than to forget. Every nerve hummed under that gaze, and a small part of him reveled in it. How just the sight of him could ensnare her into paralysis.

She turned and fell smack onto the floor, shattering the pitcher.

Gavriel stood before his mind caught up.

He couldn't confront her here. His discretion was vital to his survival, or at least the survival of those hunting him. Yet another reason to hate her. She'd managed to upend everything in his life. He'd been lucky enough not to face any Guild members since he fled his home like a coward.

Before Gavriel could decide what to do, a man approached her. The tavern was too damn loud, he couldn't discern the exchange.

Gavriel remained in the shadows until they walked hand-in-hand to the stairs.

The upper levels held private rooms for one purpose.

She threw a frightened glance over her shoulder at the other barmaid.

So, she wasn't alone.

Gavriel knew he'd have to follow, either to help her or to save the poor sod who dared to proposition a demon.

CHAPTER 20

*L*ark's heart hammered in her chest. She'd have to distract Talbot long enough to get the upper hand.

Two sets of heavy footsteps sounded up the stairs behind them. Talbot's men. By the skies, they better remain out of the room to stand guard. Lark swallowed against her tight throat. What had she to fear? She'd walked the planes of existence longer than this mortal had been alive.

But that was different. None of it was real.

Hours spent in the sparring ring yielded nothing for her mortal muscles. Lark's body seemed to remember the movement like a distant dream but lacked the strength for any real damage.

Mentally, she ran through the litany of holds she'd practiced with Alistair and how to extricate herself from them.

For the thousandth time since her mortal life began, she reminded herself this was what she'd always wanted. She clawed her way back to the land of the living, forsaking her master, her friends, her old life. This was what she wanted.

She curled around her fear, savoring it.

This was *life*.

Lark drummed her fingers along the splintering threshold as

Talbot unlocked the door. He arched his brow, grinning crookedly back at her. As if her impatience was her desire to bed him.

One of Talbot's men, with glassy, bloodshot eyes and a lazy smile, gave her a wink. The other glared down at his Paragons and Sinners playing cards—mortal depictions of Paragons of virtue and Warriors of Avalon graced the card faces. The paragon Basilius stared up from the guard's hand, his blond hair nestled behind a crown of fire and his bulky form shrouded in gold armor. Lark had seen a true likeness to Basilius once, drawn by Leysa. He was bald and scrawny with a mischievous glint in his eye. What else did mortals get wrong?

The guard muttered to himself and shuffled the deck as he took up his post beside the door.

They didn't follow them inside, a stroke of good fortune. But Lark still needed to ensure they heard nothing to rouse alarm. Her stomach fluttered its nerves. Human emotions were so visceral.

As soon as they entered the candlelit room, Talbot's greedy hands grabbed her dress. Lark danced out of his reach, offering a sly smile. "We have all night, do we not?" She gave herself over to the part, words slipping from her tongue low and throaty.

She tucked her shaking hands behind her back and eyed the stone window. It would be a long fall. If she could only get him to that side of the room...

"Ay, but I'm not a very patient man. And I've been watching you long enough." The candlelight danced along his face, forging harsh shadows.

"What did you imagine, as you watched me?" Lark drifted past the poster rail, putting as much distance between herself and the bed as possible. What a relief that mortal men were all the same, easily pliable with a few well-placed words. It was when words failed that worried her.

"Less talking," he said.

Why hadn't Daciana shown? And why do mortal hands sweat so much? "Ah, ah. We do this my way, good sir."

Talbot's expression darkened, brows pulling together. "In my experience, you don't get a say." He lunged for her, pinning her to the wall, his hands caging her.

Lark swallowed her terror and plastered an amused smirk on her face. "Oh darling, you've never experienced anything like me." Lark dug her fingers into the spot behind Talbot's ear, eliciting a surprised gasp as she spun their positions. She pressed an elbow into his throat and trailed her hand down his forearm. Praying to the skies this would work, and that he wouldn't turn violent. "Now behave, lest I make you beg for my favor."

His eyes glassed over, making her feel filthy. "As you command."

Lark slunk away, keeping her gaze glued to his and quelling nausea that threatened to rise. She didn't have all these pesky human reactions when she'd done the same song and dance for Corwyn. She almost wished for her emotions to vanish, as if they never were.

Almost.

"Undress."

Talbot immediately unbuckled his leather cuirass. It hit the wood floor with a thunk. He threw his tunic over his head and started fumbling with his trousers, his hands flying wildly. He yanked the belt from his waist, tossing it and his sword aside.

Lark hid her grin behind her hand. With any luck, she'd get him naked and tied to the bedpost before Daciana even made her grand entrance. That would make for a good story to tell the boys.

He yanked his pants down to his ankles with a ferocity that forced Lark to cover her laugh with a cough. Talbot straightened, hands firmly planted on his hips. Awaiting her next instruction.

It was almost too easy. Such a human thing, to trust that which seems weak. She'd endeavor to remember that particular mortal failure to use to her advantage.

"Now, be a good lad and—"

The door slammed open with enough force to leave a hole in the wall. Standing in the doorway was the hooded figure from downstairs, a short sword at the ready. It glistened in the candlelight.

Blood.

Both she and Talbot froze.

The man stepped through the door, dropping his hood.

"Gavriel." His name left her lips in a strangled breath.

Gavriel's eyes, a dark unfathomable forest, flashed. "Demon." The curve of his mouth stretched the scar across his lip. Lark itched to wipe that hateful smirk off his face.

Gavriel kept his sword at the ready as he advanced with a predatory movement. "I do hope I'm not interrupting."

Talbot had the good sense to look embarrassed, but when he bent to lift his trousers Gavriel advanced, angling his sword to his throat. "I think you look comfortable as you are, wouldn't you agree?"

Talbot glared back at him. "My men will rip you limb from limb."

"The men who were stationed outside your door?" Gavriel appeared to consider. Talbot's gaze dropped to the blood-coated blade, and Gavriel edged a step closer. His formidable height made the room seem small. "You should be thanking me for not leaving you alone with"—he pointed at Lark with the tip of his sword—"this."

Talbot's eyes darted between the two of them.

"Here I thought you were finally going to offer me the gratitude you owe. How disappointing." Lark hoped the waver in her voice went unnoticed.

"Yes, quite." Gavriel cast a glance at the man still standing naked in the room with them. "Does he owe you gratitude as well?"

Lark let her hand drop and marched right up to him until the cold kiss of steel pressed against her chest. Gavriel's gaze dipped.

"What is it exactly you're accusing me of? You cast aspersions, and yet you know nothing." Lark's heart thundered against her chest, hard enough she wondered if he could feel it reverberating off his sword. She didn't know why, but deep within the recesses of her fragile human heart, she knew he wouldn't hurt her.

She hoped it wasn't a human failure to be so certain.

Gavriel's eyes burned into hers, all-consuming. "I know enough to keep my distance, Demon."

That little nickname was going to get old fast.

"Lower your sword."

Daciana's voice cut through the room.

Lark hadn't even heard her enter, too consumed by the cold yet heated stare Gavriel transfixed her with. Daciana brandished the dual-edged blade of her haladie and a short sword she pressed against the back of Gavriel's neck. "I won't ask you twice."

Gavriel relaxed his arm with a sigh. "You don't know what you're doing."

"I'm protecting a friend." Daciana's voice held such conviction.

"Friend? She's a monster. Death follows her, resides in her shadow." Gavriel hadn't torn his gaze from Lark's.

Daciana pressed in closer. "Says the man creeping in the shadows all night. Yes, I saw you. Which one of you is the monster again?"

Gavriel turned to face her. His sword hung loosely in his hand, but one flick of the wrist is all it would take. Daciana seemed to realize this; her gaze never wavered. Neither did her weapon's silent threat.

From out the corner of Lark's eye, Talbot began inching toward the sword he'd discarded along with his belt. It was all the distraction Daciana needed. She linked an edge of her haladie on Gavriel's sword, twisting it away.

Talbot hobbled toward his sword. Swift for a man with his pants around his ankles.

"Wait!" Lark lunged, slamming into Talbot's back. His head caught the stone windowsill with a sickening squelch, as the sharp slice of a blade cut down her back. She landed half on Talbot, half sprawled on the floor. The blood pooling beneath his still form soaked the hem of her dress. Hands shaking, Lark rose to her feet. Sharp pain lanced through her back, and she cried out. Reaching over her shoulder, she flinched as her fingers pressed against the tear in her dress, in her skin.

The back of her gown was warm and wet.

A look of shock and regret bloomed on Gavriel's face. He took a step toward Lark, but halted to block Daciana's swing. The harsh notes of clashing steel filled the room. Lark took shallow breaths as the sharp tang of blood permeated the air. Talbot's lifeless body was a silent but heavy presence. And still they fought.

"Stop!" Lark yanked Hugo's dagger from her boot lacings and threw herself between them.

Gavriel wrapped an arm around Lark's waist and hoisted her to the side. Dizzying warmth spread through her at the contact. Her pulse quickened as his scent hit her—like warm hearth, leather, and northern wind. He blinked at her like he couldn't remember how she found her way into his arms.

Lark slammed the hilt of her dagger into his shoulder. Daciana swept his weapon away with a sharp clang, and it clattered to the ground. Gavriel shoved Lark and bent to the floor, but Daciana had already placed a firm boot on top of his blade.

"Enough," Lark said, ignoring the way her skin sang from his touch. "We don't have time for this, we need to leave." She bent down to retrieve Talbot's medal of honorary service to the city. Alistair had requested evidence and Lark wasn't about to bring a body part. The bronze sunburst pin pricked her finger, and a teardrop of blood swelled against her skin.

"What about him?" Daciana snatched up his sword. "He can't be left alive."

From the moment Lark saw Gavriel, fighting the inevitable tide of death, something called to her. Something she couldn't quite name. In all her years as a Reaper, never before had she felt so human. No, his death could never be by her hand.

"Quit pretending this is some sort of moral dilemma," he said.

Lark kicked him in the shin, eliciting a sharp hiss. "Shut up so I can think, Gavriel."

He bore his teeth at the sound of his name. "Get on with it. At least I'll finally be free of you."

Lark held his stare, trying to rein in the erratic pounding against her ribcage. She wondered if he knew she hadn't been free of him since the first moment she saw him either.

Daciana held his short sword in her hand, testing the balance of the steel. "This is a good weapon."

"I won't have your blood on my hands. But Daciana's right, we can't leave you," Lark said. "You're coming with us."

Gavriel's jaw clenched. "I'm not going anywhere with you, Demon."

Daciana abandoned her appraisal of Gavriel's sword. "Lark, you're injured. By his hand. I value the sanctity of life as much as the next person, but he isn't worth taking a knife in the back."

Lark hoped it had been an accident, that she wouldn't have to worry about getting her throat cut in her sleep. "All the same, he's coming with us." Lark placed a gentle hand on Daciana's shoulder. "You put trust in me before. I'm only asking you to do it again." She hoped she was convincing. They needed to gain distance and fast. Being so close to death meant a Reaper would be on their way to collect. Or was already in the room with them.

Daciana stared at her a moment then groaned and sheathed her dagger. She tossed the sword she'd acquired on the bed, claiming Gavriel's as her own. "Fine, but if he attacks you again, I'm killing him."

"Perfectly reasonable," Lark said.

Gavriel stilled, a calm storm brewing on his face. "The day will come when I will revel in your death."

Lark offered him the sweetest of smiles that felt tight against her face. The slice down her back throbbed. "Don't make promises you can't keep."

Daciana yanked the braided pull cord from the draperies and sliced a piece off. "C'mon lurker, hands out."

Gavriel frowned and crossed his arms. "Absolutely not."

GAVRIEL'S BOUND hands twisted in impatience.

Lark tugged her grey cloak tighter, relieved Daciana had the foresight to stash their belongings up a tree so they wouldn't travel in their disguises. They'd kept off the roads in case Brookhill's guards were on the lookout.

In the first hours of the morning, fog clung to the moors, a specter of light filtering through the grey mist. Each breath Lark took was wet with dew. By afternoon a warm sky settled over the landscape of soft green hills and valleys. What would have been a journey of a few hours stretched to last most of the day.

Gavriel remained sullen. Daciana paused their trek a few times to check that his bindings held. Each time shooting Lark a dark look.

The outskirts of Belmoore finally cut across the horizon. Farmland stretched beyond them, beckoning under the fading sun. Rich hues of crimson and orange blended in swirls of violent color across the sky—never had Thanar been able to create such a sky in the Otherworld.

They arrived at Horse and Feathers as night settled its dark embrace over the town.

Daciana paused at the door. "What's the plan, Lark?"

It was a fair question—one Lark had wondered herself the entire journey. "We avoid killing him." She glanced at Gavriel, who still hadn't spoken since they left Talbot's body in that room. "But we can't exactly let him go."

"So, he's to be our captive indefinitely?" Daciana arched a brow.

"No, don't be ridiculous," Lark said with a wave of her hand. "Just until he can be nice."

Daciana's lips parted, her face drawn in disbelief. She recovered quickly, running a hand through her thick, black hair. "This won't end well. You have my support, infernals if I know why. But I can't promise the others will agree to this madness."

"They'll follow your lead." Lark was almost sure of it.

Daciana narrowed her hazel eyes, her gaze shifting between Lark and Gavriel. "Why are you protecting him?"

That day in Thanar's dungeon, Lark thought it was because Gavriel represented something important. Other times, she wasn't so sure.

Why was she protecting him?

Lark met Daciana's stare unflinchingly. "Go get Alistair."

With a sigh Daciana slipped into the tavern, closing the door behind her and leaving them to wait. All at once, the air grew too thick. Something significant hovered between them in the cool night air.

"Why are you doing this?" Gavriel's low voice interrupted Lark's thoughts, sending them scattering about.

"You wouldn't believe how many times I've been asked that since you crashed into my life."

He gaped at her, scanning her face before reinstating his composure. "I think it was you who came barreling into my life, Demon." The way he said it this time lacked any bite.

The door swung open. Alistair charged through with Daciana hot on his trail. "Is this him?"

Gavriel had the good sense to remain composed and still as Alistair sized him up.

"Alistair, calm yourself," Daciana said.

Alistair turned to Lark. His eyes were somehow both piercing and burning. "Daciana said you were wounded. Show me your back."

"It's not— "

"Show. Me. Your. Back."

With a sigh Lark turned and shifted her cloak so he could inspect the shallow graze across her skin. It didn't hurt. Much.

Alistair hissed out a curse, turning the full force of his anger on Gavriel. Darkness she'd never seen on Alistair's face stretched its shadowy wings across his features.

"You did this to her?"

Gavriel said nothing, glowering.

Alistair's fingers twitched by his side. The rage in his eyes softened to just this side of madness. "Lark, why is he here," he said through clenched teeth. "Instead of in the ground?"

Lark wasn't certain what would happen if they crossed blades. Gavriel's body was carved for violence, all hard edges, but Alistair's face, hardened and cruel, sent a warning through her mortal heart.

"His skills are worth his weight in gold." Lark hoped the mention of one of Alistair's favorite things would dampen his anger.

Alistair yanked on the lapels of his jacket, smoothing his clothes before running a hand through his dark hair. His cool smile returned, though his eyes still held the wicked glint that promised blood. "I say we gut him. It's not worth the risk, no matter what *skills* he possesses."

"That's not going to happen," Lark said. She'd fought too hard to save him. Lost too much in the process. What a waste it would be to end his life now.

"I can fight my own battles." Gavriel reached for a sword that no longer hung by his side. His bound hands flexed in frustration.

"So brave," Alistair said. "Brave enough to slice a woman up when her back is turned."

Gavriel bared his teeth.

"We are not debating this." Daciana clapped a hand on Alistair's shoulder. "We're not going to kill him. Yet."

"I don't need your protection either," Gavriel said.

Daciana laughed. "Oh, yes you do, but I'm not looking out for you." She pushed Alistair toward the tavern. "Let it go."

Alistair glared at Gavriel. "Lay a hand on any of my crew, you'll wish I killed you." He stormed back inside, leaving Daciana, Lark, and Gavriel to the night.

Something jagged ached in Lark's chest—a weight with sharp edges. Guilt? These humans had taken her in, cared for her, and trusted her. And she demanded more.

"How long am I to be your prisoner?" Gavriel's voice was hard.

"Don't be so dramatic, I'd hardly call you a prisoner." If Lark had known he had such a flair for theatrics, she might have introduced him to Ferryn.

"No? You've bound me, confiscated my weapons—you decide where I go and when, even though I want to be rid of you."

"You seemed determined to kill me back there. That makes your wanderings my business."

"Now I'd settle for being as far from you as possible."

Daciana shifted uncomfortably before leaning against the stone cladding of the tavern. She quickly cast her gaze elsewhere.

"I saved your life. Why has that earned me your contempt?" In the darkest moments under Thanar's punishment, Lark saw Gavriel's face. When she held his name in her hand—his fate, sealed by death—

she'd banished the inevitability of destiny. Seeing him in that tavern, something resonated in her chest. Some deep-seated need to know he was real.

She was no longer a harbinger of death. She was flesh and blood. If he could just see past his hatred—

"Saved my life?"

Lark hadn't realized how close Gavriel had gotten until she felt his warm breath on her face. His eyes blazed with that fire. His sharp jaw, dusted with dark shadows, was clenched in anger. "You ruined my life. Everything from that moment has been one shit storm after another. If you were going to haunt my steps, you should have let me die."

That single act. That one choice. The moment she defied fate and destiny, forging her path. Everything she'd burned, the destruction she'd wrought. The new life she'd bled for. All of it, he saw as a curse. Here she'd been so empowered by her commanding of the tide, her control over the threads of fate.

And she was but a fool. A misguided fool who burned and salted the earth, expecting something beautiful to grow.

Lark realized her cheek was wet. Reaching a shaking hand up, she wiped away the traitorous tear. Cursing the tremble of her chin, she met his stare.

Something flickered in his eyes.

"You're a bastard." She hated the way her voice shook. "Daciana, could you watch the prisoner? I'd like that drink now." Without waiting for a response, Lark opened the door, and warm air blasted her in the face. On steady feet, she marched straight through the tavern. Soft light from the large stone hearth and the candlelit chandelier washed over her. She refused to meet the eye of anyone inside. Whatever corner Alistair, Hugo, and Langford were in, she had no interest in finding. The steady thrumming of her blood filled her ears and muffled the sounds of merriment. She reached the backdoor, ushered herself through, and closed it behind her.

Lark leaned against the cladding, running her fingers along the grooves between each cold, rough stone. A raw breeze ruffled her hair as she stared up at the starless sky.

The warm light from the tavern shone through the small window at the top of the door, her only source of light in the darkness.

Sitting beside that small shard of light, Lark silently wept.

CHAPTER 21

"This seems like a bad idea." Daciana's frown deepened.

"You always say that, and my ideas are always brilliant." Alistair grinned. "Maybe not always, but they tend to work out."

In the wee hours of the morning, when the rising sun set the indigo sky on fire, they left the Horse and Feathers tavern. Alistair, Hugo, and Langford had been all too happy to go. Judging by the men shouting after them as they swept out the door, the feeling was mutual. Something about Langford cheating at cards—an accusation he denied.

The quiet dawn was spent in the nearby woods of Ash Forest, where they set up camp. Daciana had refused rest, unwilling to let her guard down around Gavriel. Lark fought sleep, but in the end, exhaustion and over-worn eyes won out. She awoke to find most of the camp already packed up, Gavriel still bound but this time with a proper rope that encircled his entire body to a tree.

Without looking, Lark knew each time his eyes landed on her.

"Fine," Daciana said reluctantly. "You and Hugo made the deal. The two of you should collect."

"I'll be the third rider." Lark had never ridden a horse. It wouldn't be as fast as traveling through the veil, but it would be faster than walking everywhere. Why didn't these mortals keep horses? It seemed an unnecessary inconvenience to travel on foot.

"Good call." Daciana glared in Gavriel's direction.

"Splendid, and we'll meet you in Sagebrush. I don't want you waiting around here. Too many roads," Alistair said, all humor wiped from his voice. He had a way of switching his careless cad persona on and off, like the turn of a lantern key.

Lark's head throbbed from a night spent spilling tears into the dirt. She chalked it up to adjusting to humanity. It was like listening to the world behind a door, then slamming it open—everything that had been merely imagined flooding in. Everything still felt too bright. Too loud. That was why she spent the evening sobbing on the dusty ground. It certainly wasn't that she cared what Gavriel thought of her.

Daciana crept up to her, placing a hand on her shoulder. "Be safe. Alistair's contacts are hardly trustworthy." She gave Lark's shoulder a quick squeeze and turned to ready her pack for travel.

Langford produced a jar from his pack, offering it to Lark. "This salve is due for a second application at sundown. Ask Alistair to help you reach your back."

"Thank you." Lark took the canister and busied herself with stashing it in her satchel, carefully avoiding Gavriel's cutting stare. It was unsettling, the way he silently presided over the camp. Bound and utterly still. For some reason, it would be easier if he at least appeared to be struggling to escape. She shouldered her bag and trudged over to Alistair and Hugo. "Ready?"

Hugo grunted. Without asking, he grabbed her bag and hauled it over his shoulder. She opened her mouth to protest but Alistair cut a hand between them.

"Don't bother. Let our oxen man prove his chivalry."

Hugo grumbled something about breaking bony fingers.

"Fare thee well, comrades!" Alistair gave an exaggerated wave. "The next time we meet, may our pockets be lined with enough gold to drown ourselves in drink and very fine company." He seemed to reconsider. "Well, adequate company. We need this gold to last."

Lark kept her back to the assassin. She should cut Gavriel loose.

Let him get himself killed if he was so determined. She could have freed him last night if she'd wanted to.

What kind of person did that make her?

In the far recesses of her heart, a familiar ache had made its home.

"TELL IT AGAIN!" Alistair laughed. "Omit no detail, love."

Lark grinned back. "I commanded him to undress, and he yanked his trousers down around his ankles, where they stayed."

They strode along the narrow path, through the bright forest. Alistair called it a foot road, too tight for a carriage or many riders to fit.

"You have no affinity for detail. What color were his smallclothes? Any embarrassing tattoos? On a scale of shallot to eggplant, how big was his cock? Give me specifics, woman!"

Lark laughed, her face sore from smiling. "Nothing of note, though I confess I was a bit preoccupied trying not to laugh."

"Ah, to have been there to see it."

The unbidden image of Talbot's cracked skull, lying in a pool of blood, wiped the humor from Lark's face. She hadn't let herself think of the aftermath, tension of the moment prevailing over thought. But now it came crashing into her with a vengeance.

Death was as inevitable as the rising sun, nothing to be feared. But she'd had a hand in his death. Accidental in completion, but not in nature. She'd set it in motion as surely as if she'd written the scroll herself. One moment he drew breath, and the next he crumpled to the floor. His blood painting the stone.

"Hey," Alistair said gently, stopping Lark with a hand and stepping in her path. He dropped his gaze to catch her eye. "It's okay. He deserved to die."

"Who decides that?" Hadn't she wanted a hand in deciding who lives and who dies?

Corwyn got what he deserved; she certainly didn't mourn him. Talbot was equally horrible. Was it a mortal weakness for death to be so heavy a burden? Lark wished she could remember her previous life

—before she became a Reaper. Perhaps the answers to her ceaseless questions were in the past.

Alistair gripped her shoulders, anchoring her to this moment. "We do. For those who couldn't take matters into their own hands. For anyone too weak, or too afraid to break the cycle of torment." His vibrant green eyes burned with a fire he so rarely showed. "I sleep soundly at night, completely at peace with what we've done, do you know why?"

"Because you weren't there?"

Alistair huffed a breath. "Because it's right. I never said it was easy, but it's right. There's comfort in that, isn't there?"

So simple. His world was a clear divide between right and wrong, so sure of his path. Lark's seemed determined to remain in darkness.

Alistair's gaze never left hers as he patiently waited for her confirmation.

Talbot had to die. She might regret the hole it carved in her. But not his death. Lark gave a short nod.

Alistair released her arms and walked ahead of them.

She'd almost forgotten Hugo was there. She turned to him. "Why doesn't that make me feel better?"

Hugo furrowed his brow, his mustache twitching. "I don't know what it's worth, but it never gets easier. For any of us. We keep going, keep doing what needs to be done. But the burden stays with us."

For some reason, that helped a little.

"You're late."

A woman leaned against a massive ash tree. Its trunk was more than three men thick, dwarfing her. Despite her slight frame, she held an air of authority. Her long, dark braid hung over her shoulder, and her black leathers were similar to Gavriel's in both style and quality. Her cold, blue eyes flickered over Lark, before returning their hold on Alistair.

Alistair casually sauntered to where she waited. She didn't seem amused by his charms, if her frown was any indicator.

"Allow me to offer my sincerest apologies." Alistair sketched a bow a respectful distance away. "But we were held up by unforeseen complications."

Lark's cheeks burned. Gavriel certainly was an unforeseen complication of her own making.

"Complications?" The woman repeated. "They were dealt with, I hope."

"Of course." Alistair grinned.

Hugo stood behind Lark, his presence was a towering mass of comfort.

Sun-dappled light filtered through the emerald leaves of Ash Forest's giant trees. The woman edged toward them. Rays of the midday sun kissed her bronze skin and glinted off the hilts at her sides. She crossed her arms, revealing two more small blades along her forearms. "Don't tell me you came empty-handed."

Alistair pulled the medal of valor from his pocket and tossed it to her.

Her arm snaked out to catch it. Turning it over in her hand, she inspected it. "How did he die?" The question hung in the air, there was nothing innocuous about it. Like it was a test they weren't meant to be aware of.

"Blow to the skull," Lark said before Alistair could speak for her.

The woman's icy gaze slid to Lark, pinning her in place. She took a full moment to assess her, head to toe, sizing her up. "And I'm to believe you delivered the killing strike?" Humor and acid in equal measures sharpened her voice.

"I didn't need to. He did it himself."

Her expression gave away nothing. "Explain."

"There was a scuffle, and Sir Talbot—" Lark swallowed the bile that threatened to rise at recalling the image of his last breath. "He cracked his skull in the commotion."

She waited. Expecting to be called a liar, to spill blood, and call upon death once more.

The woman simply laughed. Loud and bright.

Alistair chuckled nervously. Lark turned to see Hugo watching the tree line. She followed his gaze to find an archer poised in a tree, crossbow trained on them.

Shit.

When her laughter finally subsided, the woman wiped at her eyes. "That is a befitting end to the bastard's life." She pulled out a purse. Alistair reached out as if to catch it.

"Not so fast," she said, pulling it back. "I require one more thing."

Alistair groaned. "The deal is done."

"Consider it a change order." Her mouth twitched. "I want a name." She jutted her chin toward Lark. "The name of the girl who gave me a moment of amusement amidst these dark times." The hand at her side twitched.

"My name for yours." A bead of sweat slithered down Lark's brow as she waited for the woman to signal her archer.

Her lips curved in a brilliant smile, transforming her face—all but her eyes. They remained cool and calculating. "Hazel."

"Lark." Her gaze flitted between Hazel's face and her hands.

"Lark, like a bird?" Hazel angled her head in fascination. "Well, Lark, I expect we'll meet again. Soon, I hope."

Without another word, she tossed the coin purse. Lark caught it in her shaking hand, and Hazel swaggered off into the woods. Her raven black braid, trailing down her back. None of them breathed until the sound of her steps faded and all they could hear was the forest.

Alistair was first to speak.

"Did anyone else shit their pants?"

Lark exhaled a tight breath. Heart hammering in her throat, she handed the bag to Alistair. "You saw the archer in the trees, yes?"

Alistair nodded before running a hand into his dark hair. "Yeah, I saw him." He opened the bag and began sifting through it.

Hugo stared at her, his face drawn in concentration. This was the first time they stood this close in the light of day. His broad nose was crooked, likely from a break that never healed right.

Lark rubbed her arm, her skin goose-pebbling despite the warmth of the spring day. Now all they needed to do was acquire horses and go meet the others. Then she could see about letting Gavriel go free. His fate should be his own to command.

Hugo's gravelly voice interrupted her lamenting. "We need an archer."

CHAPTER 22

Gavriel found pleasure in little things—he always tried to appreciate the glimmers of light among the shit of this world.

In this instance, he was appreciating the fact that every movement he made seemed to scare the piss out of the healer they called Langford.

Rope still encircled both Gavriel's wrists, a futile effort, really. He could escape without even trying. Perhaps the boy sensed that. But as much as Gavriel hated to admit it, this couldn't have come at a more opportune time. His only chance at eluding the Guild and all those who hunted him was Koval. He could disappear there. The Crows didn't maintain major strongholds in Koval. But here in Ardenas, they'd be watching the ports. Watching the roads, the forests, the taverns, the inns. Anywhere he might show up. Ever since he'd fled Master Hamlin's study, gaining mere hours in advantage, he had a target on his back. He hoped the bonds of loyalty ran deeper than empty pockets, but he wasn't naïve enough to count on it. Many of the Crows knew him personally, others by reputation and description, but allegiances forged in blood didn't guarantee permanence.

What better way to blend in than with this ridiculous group of people? One of whom, Gavriel suspected as a Vallemerian warrior, if his tattoos held any significance. Though he caught the outline of a lion's head, blending in with the rest of the symbols on his forearm. A Vallemerian warrior, and a member of The Den of Lions? The demon sure knew how to pick her allies.

The demon's face flashed in his mind, the look of hurt she wore when they spoke last. Gavriel ignored the tightness in his chest and reached for the apple the warrior, Daciana, had left in the dirt by his boot.

The pale boy jumped for the hundredth time.

Gavriel smirked as he held the badly bruised apple between his hands. Maintaining eye contact with the jumpy fellow, he took a large bite, savoring the ruined fruit with more verve than necessary. Langford quickly averted his eyes and busied himself with organizing his herbs.

"You know," Gavriel said around a mouthful of apple. "She was very thorough in her search." He wiped his mouth with the back of his hand and gestured over his shoulder at Daciana. "You have nothing to fear from me."

Langford's hands stilled their task. "It would be a mistake to consider you unthreatening. One doesn't need a weapon to be dangerous."

Gavriel watched him for a moment and nodded.

After parting with the others, it took mere hours to locate a suitable camping site and set up. The afternoon sun was warm enough Gavriel was sure he'd have interesting burn patterns on his hands and wrists from the binds. He considered shifting to a spot in the shade, but thought better of it.

Daciana tended to her blades. The sharp ringing of whetstone on steel was oddly relaxing. The demon was far from him, lending him the ability to take a full breath for the first time since seeing her face in the crowded tavern.

Her presence was unsettling. She was a painful reminder of everything he'd lost: his livelihood, his home, any sense of honor he'd scraped from the bottom of the barrel, and Emric.

For some reason Gavriel still couldn't comprehend, the demon found it important to keep him alive. Likely to torment him. Whenever she was near, his blood scorched through his veins, his heart thundered against his ribcage, and his mind edged closer to madness. She was a poison, as dangerous as Waking Nightmare but without the release of death.

She could seep into his mind, fill it with thoughts he'd never claim as his own, and just as swiftly rip his soul away. Those delicate hands were more lethal than her companions knew. That's the only explanation for why they guarded her so fiercely.

"I wonder about your disdain for Lark."

Gavriel turned to find Daciana studying him.

She continued running her whetstone along the blade, eyes scanning him while her hands worked efficiently. "What has she done?"

"It's complicated."

"That I believe, still I'm asking."

Gavriel sighed. "She made a decision that wasn't hers to make." It was true enough. "And I suffered the consequences."

"You hold her to such standards." Daciana shook her head. "Is she not permitted to make mistakes? To err as all humans do?"

Gavriel scoffed and flexed his fingers that were beginning to fall asleep. "She's no human." She was something far more. And far worse.

"If she's not human"—Daciana canted her head imperceptibly in the way an animal senses the air—"then what is she?"

He stared at his bound hands; dirt lined his palms and darkened his nails. These were the same hands that once tucked a tendril of fire behind a delicate ear.

"A monster."

This time, it was Daciana's turn to scoff. "We're all monsters here." Her full lips curled in a humorless smirk. "You included."

She couldn't possibly know how right she was—or that she was probing at old wounds that never fully healed. It mattered little. The fester and rot of a life bred for violence left little room for sentiment.

"I never said I wasn't."

Daciana studied him with piercing scrutiny. Gavriel refused to break her stare, as unsettling as it was.

"I need to wash," Gavriel said. "And relieve myself. Things are going to get unpleasant real fast if I'm not given basic human decency soon."

Her mouth twitched as if fighting a smile. "Are you threatening me with soiling your pants?"

Gavriel said nothing, waiting to discover just how ruthless this woman who seemed determined to protect a demon could be.

Finally, she sighed. "I'm not untying you. Nor do I have any desire to guard you while you tend to your needs." Daciana crossed her arms, narrowing her eyes in calculating thought. "Perhaps we'll consider this a test, shall we? Go wash, go shit, whatever else you need to do. If you don't come back within the hour, I'll know you ran."

Gavriel huffed a small laugh of disbelief. "Just like that?"

"It matters not if you run. I can promise I'll find you, and you won't like it when I do."

Something about her calm, matter-of-fact delivery made Gavriel certain she would make good on her word.

He stood, hands still bound in front of him.

"There's a river east." Daciana resumed sharpening her set of blades, his long sword, and numerous daggers among her supply. The glint of her haladie, beckoning him. It had been ages since he'd wielded one, preferring simple knives and daggers over the show-manship of a double-edged blade.

"I don't suppose I could have one of my weapons back?"

She stared at him, expressionless.

"I didn't think so," he muttered before wandering off.

IT DIDN'T TAKE LONG for Gavriel to reach the water. Even less for him to slip his hands through the intricate knots Daciana had tied and pocket the rope. He'd quickly sneak his hands back into position before he reentered their camp. It was the least he could do, offering them a false sense of security. He'd never do anything to harm them, not without fair warning. It was only sporting.

With a heavy sigh, he stripped down, unwilling to spend the day in wet clothes. He was no more naked than he already felt, stripped of his weapons.

Wading into the river, his muscles clenched at the cold. Though spring had been in bloom for a few weeks now, the water retained its icy grip. Gritting his teeth, he sank his head beneath the surface. The utter quiet, save for the throbbing in his head, was a welcome relief. Opening his eyes under the murky water, he was only able to make out the muddled shapes along the river's bottom. He let the air escape his mouth in a torrent of bubbles, before kicking off the sand to break through the surface.

Tilting his head back he floated along the surface, bobbing weightlessly. The sun slipped behind a thick cloud. Again, the thoughts returned to him.

He could leave. He could cut his losses, leave his weapons behind. Clad only in the clothes on his back, he was free to go. Daciana's warning was a distant thought. Sure, she'd hunt him. She could get in line.

But he wouldn't go until he was certain they couldn't be of use. If he could nudge them toward Koval, he'd stay until they became a nuisance to his plan. Then he'd disappear.

The thought carved a pit in his stomach. He wouldn't be able to escape the demon, not while she lived. Shadows would dance in the corners of his mind, her illusion their image.

His hand cut through the water, creating ripples in its wake.

He still remembered the feel of her lips. Bringing his fingers to his own, the memory flooded his mind. The memory of fire, of a scorching kiss.

He hated her. He hated that she'd found a way to worm into his mind and plague him with thoughts he had no wish to entertain. He hated that the sight of her tears had hollowed out his chest.

With both hands he splashed his face, willing his thoughts to cease their torment. The image of his hand around her delicate throat, holding but not crushing. Of her lowering to her knees, her amber eyes burning up at him. Of threading his fingers through her hair and—

"Well, well. What have we here?"

He snapped his head in the direction of the tree he'd hung his clothes on. A woman leaned against it, black hair down to her waist, not a stitch of clothing on her pale, shapely body. Her eyes were a startling blue like the hottest part of a flame. A sharp smile cut across her beautiful face.

"I was certain I was tracking a different sort of beast," she purred.

"Who are you?" he demanded, wiping droplets from his brow. A naked woman alone in the woods seemed an awful lot like a trap. He scanned his surroundings, searching for enemies hiding in the tree line, waiting to ambush. Finding none failed to assuage his dread.

"Where is she?" She ignored his question, wicked amusement written on her striking face. "Where is your little Reaper now? Rumor has it she's decided to play human."

She couldn't possibly mean the demon. What could she want from her?

"Come, come. Don't be shy. Where is Larkin?"

Gavriel's jaw clenched hard enough to ache. "I have no idea who you're talking about."

She threw her head back and laughed. Her long, black hair skimmed the tops of her thighs. "You lie. I can smell her on you." She took a step closer to the water's edge.

"Are you like her? Forged from the same darkness?" He wasn't even sure what he was asking as his toe swept the bottom of the river, searching for a rock. She called the demon a Reaper. Is that what she was?

She ran a hand down her ample curves. Despite her obvious allure, Gavriel wasn't enticed, he was too familiar with danger not to recognize it. "She is nothing compared to me now. A drop of water to an ocean. My darkness, you've never seen the likes of."

He cursed Daciana for not allowing him the mercy of a blade to protect himself. "And what exactly are you?"

"Come here little mortal, and I'll show you."

Gavriel's foot slid across a smooth stone roughly the size of his fist. Hooking onto the side of it with his toes, he pulled it just enough to free it from the sand and sediment.

Her grin turned predatory. "Your desires smell so... *potent*. Let's see how they taste in your blood."

Her hands shifted, fingers growing into elongated claws. Canines, sharpening into fangs. Black pooled across her eyes until they were nothing more than a dark void. Her mouth pulled into a snarl, as she lowered into a crouch.

Gavriel grasped the rock and yanked it free. She dove in, her naked body sliced through the water like an eel and disappeared beneath the surface.

Gavriel gripped the rock in his fist and searched the murky depth for movement. To have any chance at fighting this thing, he needed to get onto dry land.

Sharp claws raked down his back, and hot pain seared across his skin.

He spun and slammed the rock down with a thud against her skull. Momentarily stunned, she reared back. Gavriel didn't wait. He threw himself forward, landing against the surface of the river with a hard smack, and swam toward the shore. The muscles in his arms and legs shook, and he choked on a mouthful of water.

He dragged himself over stones and branches, staggering out and onto the bank. Needing a weapon, he grabbed a thick branch and turned—

Just in time to see her grotesque face break the surface. The veins beneath her skin bulged and slithered. Wide, black eyes and an exaggerated mouth split open to reveal sharp teeth gleaming in the sunlight. She stood, and water sluiced down her body, over curves hewn for only one purpose. She leapt toward him, screeching her bloodlust.

Gavriel held the branch out like a bo staff. But the wood was soft and would offer little in the way of protection. If this beast was going to take him out, by the skies, he'd drag it to the darkest circle of the abyss with him.

"That's not going to work," a new voice rang from nearby. An acerbic, feminine voice.

Gavriel turned, to see a figure obscured by a red, hooded cloak. She sat atop a small boulder, legs crossed.

Snarls filled his ears. The naked beast crept toward him. Black blood trailed along her hairline where he'd struck her. She snapped her teeth.

"I wouldn't do that if I were you," the hooded stranger murmured.

The creature straightened to glare at their bystander. "I'll get to you in a moment."

The figure dropped her red hood to reveal a girl with straight black hair tied back at the nape of her neck. Her pale face was splattered with freckles, and her deep-set brown eyes glinted in amusement.

"It hardly seems fair. He's naked. Although you're naked too, so I suppose there's equality in that. But he's unarmed and you"—she gestured in appreciation—"are well-equipped."

Claws slipped back into hands. Gavriel's blood still stained her now human-looking fingers. She retained her black eyes and fangs as she regarded the girl. "Who are you to be so determined to die today?"

The girl laughed, bright and unrestrained. "Tell me, are all Vrykolaka this incompetent? Do they all prey on the most vulnerable?" She cut a glance to Gavriel. "No offense."

The creature laughed, stepping over moss covered rocks to approach the girl. "I'm drawn to unspoken desires. I do not question where they come from."

"Of course. A man alone and naked must be full of unspoken desires."

Gavriel might have felt humiliated were it not for the years spent mastering useless emotions. Instead, he recognized the opportunity of distraction.

"And what of you?" the creature taunted. "I can smell your unspoken desires. They reek of fear and weakness."

The girl sighed. "Yes, I know, but we're not talking about me."

Gavriel crept behind the beast. The ground was soft beneath his bare feet. The spongy earth absorbed the droplets of water that dripped from his skin. The girl didn't glance at him once, keeping her stare trained on the naked woman.

The creature tossed her head back and laughed. "Oh, child. The blood is sweeter when desires are locked inside. I find myself at a loss deciding which of you I'll devour first." Her fingers grew back into claws, and a low growl rumbled in her chest.

The girl sighed. "Try to stay focused on the point."

"And what is the point?" The beast hissed, taking a step closer.

The girl's eyes darted to Gavriel, and she smiled. "Gluttony is your downfall."

With the thick branch, Gavriel swept the creature's feet out from under it. Without wasting a moment, the girl leapt onto the beast, sinking a jagged-edged blade through flesh and bone. It's face twisted in anguish, and one final roar tore from its throat. The girl raised her blade, slamming home with a force that shook the squelching body.

When the creature stilled, its eyes empty, the girl lifted her head. Her pale face was splattered in freckles and gore. "Ugh, put some clothes on," she said, shielding her eyes.

Gavriel grabbed his clothing off the branch, hastily pulling his breeches back into place and yanking his tunic over his head. "Who are you?"

"Today, I'm the one who saved your skin. But you can call me Kenna." She wiped her dagger on the grass before sheathing it and held out a bloody hand.

He shook it, blood smearing against his palm. "Gavriel."

"Well, Gavriel, I'd say don't venture far in the woods on your own unarmed, but truth be told she would have killed you anyway. You need this to kill a Vrykolaka." She held up her dagger now encased in a braided leather sheath. "She probably assumed I didn't have one. It's near impossible to find a blacksmith in Ardenas skilled enough to forge silver. Now, if it had been a Wentiko, or a Leshy, or even a Bubak, you might have stood a chance."

None of these words meant anything to Gavriel. He studied her blade, the only part of her rambling that made sense. It was no secret Kovalian blacksmiths were far superior. The mines held the strongest ore alongside ample opportunities for apprenticeship. Ardenian smithies, though formidable in their own right, tended to rely on the old ways passed down through generations. He'd have to see about having a few blades made once he crossed the ocean. He had plenty of daggers and a reliable short sword—or, Daciana had plenty of his daggers and his short sword—but there was always room for more. "Silver, huh? That's what it takes to kill a naked demon woman?"

Kenna grinned. "Vrykolaka, you uncultured swine. This one's not just silver, it was blessed by a priestess."

"A priestess blessed your *daggers*?" The priestesses were a superstitious bunch, honoring gods Gavriel couldn't remember the names of.

"You wouldn't believe what someone will do if you promise to hunt a Valafer."

Now she was just making up words.

Kenna slung her weapon back in place at her side. "Supposedly, the Valafer was tempting the faithful to commit all sorts of sins." She rolled her eyes. "I haven't found her blessing to make much of a difference, though it makes for a wicked story."

Gavriel was familiar with myths and legends of beasts and monsters, but none by these names. Demons, ghouls, Vampyres, Werewolves—all stories whispered in the dark when the other children at the Guild couldn't sleep. Older trainees were bastards that way, scaring the piss out of new recruits. Emric was just a kid when Connor told him a Vampyre was going to come to suck him dry if he kept his window open. Emric had night terrors for years. But those were just stories.

This beast lying slain on the grass was real.

"How long have you known of their existence, these monsters?"

"All my life. But they seem more active lately. I've stumbled upon five just this past week, without setting snares or anything." Kenna raised her red hood back up over her head.

The beast said she was hunting the demon. Were more out there looking? What would happen when they found her?

"I need to get back to camp." He turned to leave and the sound of footsteps followed. He turned back to glare at her.

"What? You need an escort. I'd hate to waste my time saving you only for you to get eaten." Kenna motioned for him to continue. "Lead on."

He should warn her they wouldn't get a warm greeting, that he was a prisoner willingly returning to his cage, but he was too tired to care. With heavy footsteps, he paced back through the forest, avoiding overgrown roots that stretched across the path.

Hoping and not hoping the demon was back.

Kenna caught up quickly. "How many are you traveling with? Why hasn't anyone come looking for you? Unless no one misses your absence."

He stared straight ahead. One person might miss his absence. It's not like he could explain his predicament. "There are two, maybe five, back at camp. If the others have returned."

She clapped him on the back, ignoring the way he winced. The claw marks, though shallow, burned in his skin. "That must be it! They're waiting for reinforcements to collect your body."

He ignored Kenna. It didn't make sense; why was a monster hunting the demon? Can one hunt death? Unless becoming whatever she was now, made her easy prey. It didn't matter. She wasn't his problem.

But even as he thought it, shame flickered in his gut. An image came to him; her face—her skin practically glowing, golden eyes burning like embers, her pink lips parting—as he slowly succumbed to poison. Her anguish. Desperate and—

The rustling of leaves and underbrush tore him from his thoughts. Some manner of creature was racing through the forest. He stepped in front of Kenna. "Get behind me."

She scoffed and pushed around him, brandishing a short sword he hadn't known she was carrying. "That seems like a terrible idea. Why don't you get behind me?"

Was everything a joke to this girl?

"Give me a weapon." If another of those things attacked, Gavriel couldn't rely on the element of surprise again.

"Nah, although you have my permission to rifle my corpse should I fall."

Before he could react, a figure came crashing through the thicket; dark auburn hair, unbound and flowing freely. As soon as she caught sight of them, she stopped, swaying on her feet before dropping to land on her knees in the dirt. "Gavriel," she gasped.

The demon.

He shoved past Kenna, almost reaching out, but he hesitated, uncertainty weighing his arm by his side.

Kenna edged closer. From the corner of his eye, Gavriel watched her lift a hand to her chest. "What are you?"

The demon opened her mouth but said nothing.

Gavriel tensed, preparing to lie. He wasn't even sure why, but he knew he would.

"Lark!" Daciana hacked through the brush, clearing a path with the slice of an axe Gavriel hadn't seen her wield yet. How many weapons did this woman own? "I told you to wait," she said, lowering into a crouch. She angled the demon's chin to inspect the tiny cut across her cheek from the thorns she tore through.

"I'm fine," she insisted, allowing the warrior to pull her up.

Daciana's face froze in shock when she caught sight of Kenna before her expression melted into cool indifference.

Kenna kicked her boot into the dirt. Her dark bangs slipped into her eyes.

"What are you doing here?" Daciana demanded.

Odd. He locked eyes with the demon. She frowned.

"Dac," Kenna said softly, eyes trailing over her face, searching. She took a step forward, only for Daciana to retreat a step.

"You can't be here," Daciana said. "You need to leave."

Kenna's hands twisted in her red cloak, thumbing the fabric.

"We need to hear her out." Gavriel didn't know why Daciana would welcome the demon but not Kenna. It didn't matter, she had knowledge they needed for survival. "She saved me from a... uh... "

"Vrykolaka."

"Yes, a Vrykolaka."

The demon startled and inched closer, scanning him head to toe. He ignored the way his stomach dropped under her scrutiny.

"She says there are more out there. Creatures we know nothing about. I know it sounds crazy, but I can show you proof. Whatever attacked me wasn't human."

"No need to be so dramatic." Kenna's shaky chuckle betrayed her nonchalance. "Besides, Dac knows all this."

"Wait, you know about these monsters?" Was this common knowledge Gavriel was just learning? The existence of unearthly beasts should warrant more of a reaction than this.

"Yes," Daciana said. "We don't need her help. She's free to go."

If Gavriel could stomach being near the demon, Daciana could get over whatever her issues were.

He was about to argue but Kenna placed a hand on his arm. "She's right, I shouldn't be here." She yanked her hood back up over her face and trudged back the way they came.

Daciana nodded, staring at the ground.

"Wait!" the demon blurted, and she ran after Kenna. Kenna slowed her pace and turned, expression unreadable. The demon leaned in, grasping her hand tight and whispering in her ear.

What in the abyss was she up to?

Kenna nodded. She pulled her hand away in a fist and marched off.

The demon exhaled a breath, watching Kenna leave before turning back to Gavriel. Her honey eyes widened in alarm. "You're injured."

Gavriel's attention immediately swung to the blood dripping down his back. He'd almost forgotten the beast's claws and the deep tracks they'd left. Feeling lightheaded, he shrugged, an action he regretted when his wounds stung. "I've had worse."

She rolled her eyes, such a human action, before turning and stomping back in the direction she'd come from. He watched her go and noticed her hair was matted with leaves and twigs. A sudden headache throbbed in his temples.

Daciana finally lifted her eyes from the ground. "Langford should look at your wounds before you pass out."

CHAPTER 23

"Oh, good. He lives." Alistair's scowl greeted them as they returned to camp.

Lark breathed a shaky sigh, the echo of a terror she couldn't quite name sat heavy in her chest—a sharp pang that made it difficult to catch her breath. Whether it was fear for Gavriel's safety or fear he'd gone, never to return, Lark didn't know, but the moment she'd realized he was missing, she'd darted off in search of him. Mortals were funny that way, the rush of undiluted panic knew no limitations.

On the far end of the clearing, Hugo tended the horses they'd returned with, paying Gavriel no mind. They couldn't afford the expensive breeds the horse-master boasted of. Instead, they settled for three Ardenian chargers. The sturdy horses could easily carry two riders and would serve them well on their journey north to look for more work.

Lark already bonded with one of the horses—a chestnut mare with the flaxen mane. Alistair warned her not to get attached, and Lark responded by naming her Apple. Alistair laughed at the name, asking why she'd even bother naming it only to select something ridiculous.

If the man could refer to his manhood in the third person, she could damn well name her horse.

In the center of the camp, Langford built a small fire within a stone circle. The tip of his tongue peeked out the corner of his mouth as he struck a large rock against a glimmering piece of quartz.

Alistair crossed his arms, frowning. "I see you had an adventure."

Gavriel ignored him and headed for Langford.

"He found himself a new friend too. I can tell you what little has been shared with me if you like," Lark said.

"And why is he free?"

"Give it a rest, Alistair. The knots weren't going to stop him," Daciana said as she strode right to her tent and shut herself inside.

Alistair stared after her. "What happened?"

"Daciana seemed to know whomever he met along the way," Lark said with a sharp exhale.

She'd have to ask Daciana about her connection with Kenna at some point.

Alistair frowned. "I should check on her." He started his determined stride before pausing to add, "Don't let anyone leave, die, or worst of all, take any of my property before I'm back."

"Does that mean I've been promoted to third in command?"

Alistair saluted, turned on his heel, and marched toward Daciana's tent.

As Lark watched his retreating form, something hot and slippery slithered in her gut. Were these nerves? The moment Kenna touched the pendant hanging from her neck and regarded Lark with naked curiosity, she knew: Kenna was a hunter. Either that or someone who bore the talisman of one. Unlikely, since they tended to guard them closely. A hunter had to know what was happening with Undesirables. It was their duty to slay any they came across. Perhaps it was a leap in assumption, but Kenna's knowledge of the Undesirable that attacked Gavriel and her ability to remain unscathed was proof enough.

When Lark realized what Kenna was, she'd whispered in her ear to meet back after nightfall. Her knowledge would be invaluable. Now all Lark had to do was wait.

LARK'S KNEE bounced as she stared intently into the fire. Langford's pale hands moved with a languid pace as he stitched the gashes on Gavriel's back.

"If you can't desist your ceaseless fidgeting, I'm going to ask you to leave." Langford didn't even look up from his task as he admonished her. His steady hand weaved through Gavriel's skin. The delicate needle glinted in the firelight.

Lark stilled, and Gavriel eyed her warily.

"Do you think the beast that attacked him was the same that you fought?" Langford's voice held its usual note of curiosity. Always puzzling. "One of those *Undesirables?*"

"I think so," Lark said. "It would stand to reason."

"Was it a Wentiko?"

"It was a naked woman, actually," Gavriel said.

Langford raised a brow. "Alistair would approve of that particular beast." He snipped the extra thread, finishing his work. "Why do you think it attacked? Is there something about being near a body of water that attracts them?"

Lark's mouth went dry. What unspoken desires of Gavriel's had lured the Vrykolaka to him? Probably the desire to kill her in her sleep. "How should I know? I wasn't there."

"Of course. I'm merely postulating. I suggest no absolutes, merely pointing out the similarities in the attack." Langford offered a sheepish smile. "It doesn't hurt to talk through any theories."

"The creature was drawn to a specific emotion," Gavriel muttered. He stared at the ground while Langford finished bandaging. Gavriel had stripped off his tunic for the procedure, a fact Lark was determined to pay no mind. Nor to his solid build—or the map of scars he bore on his skin. She certainly hadn't used her periphery to appraise him.

"Ah, I supposed that's it then." Langford placed the last bandage, pulling away to give him room to sit up. "What emotion was it?"

Gavriel yanked his tunic back on, ignoring the question. "Thanks." He clapped Langford on the shoulder before disappearing into Alistair's tent. Why they'd decided he was worthy of this much trust was beyond Lark.

"Since when does Gavriel share a tent with Alistair?"

Langford cleared his throat. "He doesn't, Alistair will share mine."

"Are we sure that's wise? No one's worried about Gavriel anymore?" Lark should have been pleased by this. It was she, after all, who wanted him along. But annoyance flared in her gut.

"I wouldn't say no one." Langford cut a meaningful glance in Hugo's direction. The large man kept a wary eye on Gavriel's tent, even as he ran a whetstone down his blade. A permanent frown pulled at his face—the determined look of a man with nothing but time and distrust.

Lovely. That would make sneaking off difficult.

Lark settled in for a long wait. The flames flickered and danced among the shadows.

THE HOUR GREW LATE, and Lark's eyes were heavy with exhaustion. But at the sudden realization that Alistair snored soundly in his tent, a surge of energy spiked through her veins. Hugo hadn't returned from wherever he'd gone off to, likely to relieve himself, and she hoped he'd remain there long enough for her to slip away.

She rose silently to her feet, taking slow, deliberate steps. She tiptoed along a fallen tree, creeping further and further from camp until the fire was a mere glow in the distance.

Tightening her cloak around her, she strode in earnest toward the river. Hopefully, Kenna was waiting and her efforts wouldn't be a waste.

The forest was different at night; more akin to her first days as a mortal. Under the pale light of a lonely moon, shadows grew taller and trees reached out their desperate branches, eager to snag her cloak. Without the warmth of the sun, the wind had a bite—a cold threat that whipped through her hair and clung to her skin. Lark shivered, clutching her cloak tighter. Her first memory in this body seemed a lifetime ago but it was mere weeks.

Two weeks. Was it only that long?

The gentle rushing of water whispered through the night air before she broke through the clearing. Tumbling out of the thicket, Lark froze at what lay before her.

Silvery light glinted atop the ripples, sparkling against the black water. Beyond the cover of trees, the moon cast such a glow as to make even the sun jealous. The velvet sky was spattered with uncountable stars; in the Otherworld, their gaze was cold and lonely. But here, her chest swelled as she stared up at a sky glimmering with promises.

"Took you long enough."

Lark jumped, squinting at the shadows beside the large oak that stretched over the water.

Shrouded in red, Kenna emerged wearing a wry grin as she twisted a small, white flower between her thumb and finger. With a sweep of her hand, her red hood fell back, and her dark bangs fluttered in the wind.

"I waited until I no longer had an audience."

Kenna nodded. She dropped the pitiful remains of the flower to the ground. "Why all the shifty cloak and dagger nonsense? Don't get me wrong, it's great fun. But what could you possibly have to say to me you couldn't say in front of them?"

There were many things Lark wouldn't say in front of Daciana and the others. They looked at her like she was someone worthy of them. She wasn't ready for the loss of their warmth.

"You're a hunter."

A broad smile crossed Kenna's face. "Figured that out on your own, did you? What about you?"

Lark ignored the question and the unease in her gut. "You hunt Undesirables."

Kenna snorted. "I prefer to call them monsters."

"Fine, you hunt monsters." Lark shifted, and the familiar weight of

Hugo's dagger pressed against her boot. She doubted she'd ever grow used to relying on mortal weapons for protection. "You sense them, and you end them."

Kenna waved her hand impatiently for her to continue.

"What do you know of Reapers?"

Kenna stilled, dark eyes glittering with avid curiosity. "Is that what you are?"

"Not anymore."

Kenna stared at her for a long time, her brow furrowed in concentration. "How?"

Lark wet her lips, unsure of how much she needed to divulge. "I was remade. I crawled into this world just two weeks ago."

"How were you remade?"

Lark hesitated. How much was this hunter aware of?

"Fine." Kenna held up her hands. "I only ask because I've been ass-deep in monsters for the past two weeks with no explanation as to why. Until now."

Lark released a staccato hiss through her teeth. "What do you mean?"

"I think you've got something to do with it," Kenna said. "A Reaper is remade into a human, and suddenly I've got more work than I know what to do with?" She shook her head, laughing. "It sounds like you ripped through the veil and invited all those delightful Untouchables to hitch a ride."

"Undesirables," Lark corrected, heart hammering in her chest as she stumbled back to lean against a sturdy tree. Nereida said she'd caused a tear when she saved Gavriel and would cause another when she reentered the Mortal world. But she'd promised to mend them. Had so many slipped by before she'd had a chance to sew the veil shut?

"Shit." Lark ran her hand through her hair, gripping it at the roots. What was she supposed to do now?

Kenna gave her a tight smile. "Well, thanks for the work. The paid work, that is. The monsters I stumble upon? I'm not as grateful for."

Fate was determined to punish Lark.

Ceto once called her selfish. How disappointing that she was right. Her single-minded goal blinded her to what might happen if she got her wish. What other consequences were yet to be revealed? If only Lark could speak to Ferryn, to know he was all right and discover the extent of her reach.

Lark pushed off the tree to step toward Kenna. "You seem to know a great deal about a lot of things, hunter."

An impish smile graced Kenna's face even as she tracked Lark's movements. "It's my job to know these things, Reaper."

"Maybe so, but you're schooled in aspects of my world I wouldn't expect," Lark said with uncertainty. "How?"

"Let's just say, I happen to know an expert."

"An expert on the veil? The Netherworld? Who?" What earthly person would know these details, and how could Lark find them?

Kenna hesitated, scrunching her nose. "Eh, she doesn't like it when I send people her way."

"This is important, Kenna. I need to find out what's going on." Lark hated to resort to begging, but she'd do it if she had to. "Please."

"She's going to be so mad at me," Kenna whined as she tugged on the silver clasp of her cloak. "Fine! Go see the hedge witch up north in Emerald Woods."

Lark grinned, even as she tried to make sense of the misshapen pieces of information Kenna was giving her. "That's a start, how can she help?"

"The little hermit knows *everything*. A bit curious that someone so determined to avoid the populace knows all sorts of secrets. More importantly, she can make contact beyond mortal limitations." Kenna raised her eyebrows. "If you catch my meaning."

A shaky and wild hope gripped Lark's chest. If such a thing were possible, she could reach Ferryn. "How do I find her?"

"In the heart of the Emerald Woods, is an isolated cottage. You'll head as far west as you can until you hit the lake. You'll see her place." Kenna reached beneath her cloak and tunic to pull out a black leather cord. "Show her this, and she'll help you."

A pendant forged of stone and wood dangled from her fist, casting an eerie green and blue glow. A sloping mountain range bathed in a night sky lit by ancient magic.

Lark reached out hesitantly, unsure if she should take a hunter's protection. A hunter's talisman amplified its owner's awareness, alerting them to Undesirables and Otherworldly beings. "Your talisman?"

"Its an insurance policy." Kenna dropped it in Lark's palm and stuck her hands in her pockets. "She's not likely to trust you. Show her this, and she'll know I sent you. Skies, help me." The last part, she mumbled to herself.

Lark ran her thumb over its smooth surface. The pendant hummed under her touch. Calling to a part of her, long forgotten. Like a song she didn't know the words to—begging to be remembered. She shivered. Both drawn and repelled by it.

"Oh, and Lark? Don't get killed. I'm gonna want that back."

Lark tore her eyes away from the pendant.

Kenna answered with a crooked grin. "I almost forgot." She turned and leapt up into the tree, scaling so high Lark had to strain her neck to see her. Kenna yanked a bag out of hiding and scrambled her way down. Lowering to one knee, she ripped the bag open, yanked out a few pages of parchment, and handed them to Lark.

"What are these?" Lark thumbed through the pages. Charcoal sketches of Undesirables along with their properties and weaknesses. The soft parchment shone in the pale light of the moon. The drawings weren't perfect. There were spots where the artist had pressed too hard, the sketches smudged from a hand sweeping against the page. "An index of sorts?"

"I like to think of it as imparting wisdom." Kenna could barely maintain her serious expression before it melted into a grin. Like her face was always meant to wear that smile. "I'll want those back too. But take your time."

Lark bit the inside of her cheek. As a Reaper, Undesirables were a pesky nuisance. They required power to be dealt with, sure, but nothing she couldn't handle. Now, they had strengths and weaknesses. Details she needed to commit to memory to ensure her survival the next time they crossed paths.

She was beginning to realize how much she'd taken her strength and abilities for granted.

"Thank you," Lark said.

"You're welcome."

The air hung heavy between them. Her secret was out, along with her next task. She couldn't push away the discomfort of owing another stranger a favor.

"Why are you doing this?" The words left Lark's lips before her mind had a chance to catch up. "Not that I'm ungrateful."

"Daciana cares about you. I might not agree with every decision she makes, but I've learned to trust most of her instincts." Kenna turned to leave.

"How will I find you again?"

Kenna's red cloak curled around her in a sweeping motion as she turned and offered that crooked grin. "I'll find you. I've got a feeling danger is drawn to you like a Vrykolaka to celibate men. I'll just follow the bodies."

SNEAKING out of camp was the easy part. Lark failed to realize sneaking back in would be the real task.

She crept under the cover of shadows, hoping and not hoping she could easily make it to her tent without incident. If she couldn't, she'd have a difficult conversation ahead of her. If she could, then their defenses were seriously lacking.

"Where'd you go?" A gruff voice she knew growled from the darkness.

Slowly, Lark turned to see Hugo sitting in the dark—a deep inhale of his pipe, and the orange glow of burning embers illuminated the disapproval on his face. She'd tucked the pages deep in the pocket of her cloak.

"I needed some time," Lark said. "Alone."

His blank stare told her nothing.

Remembering advice Alistair had given her previously on how to rattle Hugo's calm, she cleared her throat. "Lady reasons."

The effort it took to maintain his unmoving expression looked near painful. "I have no follow-up questions," his low voice scraped out.

Hugo put his pipe back between his teeth and resumed stringing what looked like a freshly whittled bow. Rather than ask him about his task, Lark took his dismissal as the gift it was and scurried off toward their sleeping arrangements. She should go straight to her bedroll, put the night behind her, and tomorrow, with a rested mind, figure out what to do next. But there was something she needed to deal with first. Assuming Gavriel hadn't disappeared when no one was looking.

Before Lark could change her mind, she steered toward Gavriel's tent, ducking low to the ground. With no finesse and only a modicum of discretion, she peeled the flap back and crawled in.

One fact she'd failed to remember: Gavriel was a trained assassin.

Before the flap of his tent had even fluttered closed, a warm, calloused hand gripped her wrist tight enough to bruise. The world spun as she flipped, landing flat on her back. The air rushed from her lungs, and her shoulder blades dug into the ground. The pages she'd hidden beneath her cloak rustled as they pressed into her skin. Gavriel's solid weight bore down on her chest, pinning her beneath him. A flare of heat surged through her as she gaped into the darkness.

"I knew this moment would come," Gavriel whispered. His warm breath in her ear sent a shiver down her neck. He was so close, every nerve in her body awakened in a heady rush. The squeal of a lantern key illuminated the space with a dim glow. The small flame teased along the hardened edges of Gavriel's face, bathing his sharp jaw and scarred mouth in warm light. The firm plane of his body pressed down on her, stirring something she wasn't prepared to feel.

"You play at being human so well, but I never forgot what you are."

At once, the fire in her body was doused. Sharp annoyance took its place. His never-ceasing hatred was becoming tiresome, and she would no longer handle him with care. "And what am I? Stop playing the victim and tell me the truth. What is it you think I am?"

"The kind of coward who sneaks into a man's tent to finish the job they started." Even in the dark, his green eyes glimmered with fire.

She had fire too.

"You're the coward. You blame me for Emric's passing because it's easy. You're too afraid to face the fact that I'm not to blame. And you know why that terrifies you?"

He surged closer, wrapping one hand around her throat just shy of cutting her air supply. "Silence your poison tongue, Demon."

But she would not be silenced. Not by anyone ever again. Certainly not by him.

"Because your hate is far safer. Without it, what are you left with? A graceless sky that cares little for what's ripped from your hands. Fate or chance. It makes no difference. You are not in control. You're just a scared little boy." She seethed, one hand gripping his arm and the other clenched to the side where he still held her wrist.

Gavriel eased his hold on her throat and wrist, rolling off of her. Lark tried to even her breath without revealing the tremors in her muscles. She sat up and scooted away so they weren't touching. It was safer this way. She focused on the canvas tent wall, studying the stitching pattern. Reaching a finger up, she ran it down the rough-textured cloth.

"I'm not a demon. Are you that stupid you don't know what a real demon is?"

He huffed a laugh, letting his head fall to his hands. "It's an entity not of this world that exists to cause human suffering and torment."

Lark rolled her eyes. "And that sounds like me? What a charmed life you must have led if keeping you from death equates to torture."

Gavriel fell silent for a heartbeat. He sighed softly, and a shiver ghosted along her spine.

"That thing I faced, she called you a Reaper. Is that what you are?"

"Was," Lark said automatically. Now she was nothing more than a weak mortal, vulnerable and foolish. And free—free and out of Thanar's clutches. "I hated being a Reaper."

He remained silent, so she took it as permission to continue.

"My entire existence felt almost imagined. Like a dream that isn't vivid enough to remember. I forgot what being human was like. The taste of bread. The touch of a lover. The rain. I couldn't even remember what it felt like to experience pain, or warmth, or cold, or anything at all. I was just—" She ran a hand through her hair, finding a few dried leaves she'd need to comb out later. "I was numb."

Gavriel studied her, saying nothing. Even in the dim tent, his frown transformed his features.

"No one else could understand why I was so unhappy. Becoming a Reaper is one of the greatest gifts of the afterlife. An honor bestowed only upon those souls deemed worthy—chosen for a specific purpose. But it was no gift to me. It was a prison sentence. My every move, every action was preordained. I was a bound by *fate.*" Lark's mouth twisted around the word—the very taste of it was enough to turn her stomach. "I watched you humans, your passion, your violence, your despair. And I burned with envy. I wanted what you had so badly..."

Lark's vision swam with unshed tears. Blinking them away, she continued.

"My master was ruthless to those who flouted the law, who intervened and changed destiny. We were punished without mercy for such offenses." She dropped her hand into her lap, balling it into a tightly enclosed fist. "I was punished greatly for the mere thought of interfering in your life. I hadn't even done it yet, but my sin was in the desire to do it. Loyalty without question, in mind, body, and soul." She pushed away the memory of her hands and knees on the marble floor, of Thanar forcing through her mental walls. "When Ferryn told me of your destiny I knew I had to save you."

"Why?" Gavriel finally spoke. "I asked you before, and I'm asking you again, why save me?"

Lark exhaled a soft breath. "I told you, I had to know I could. I couldn't let you die, and I *needed* to prove I had power over fate. Because if I could change your fate, maybe I could change mine."

A heavy silence fell over them. She'd given words to the whispers skirting along the edges of her mind. The sounds of the forest filled the weighted moment, and the churring of crickets called through the dark.

Lark searched Gavriel's face, but his far off expression told her nothing. "I'm sorry I couldn't save Emric. He seemed like a good friend."

"He was reckless." Gavriel smiled, but it didn't reach his eyes. "He was good in a way I will never be."

"That's not true." Lark inched closer. He watched her but made no effort to distance himself. "The way Emric spoke of your friend-ship, I'd think that goodness you speak of he recognized in you, Gavriel."

His eyes flashed, confused and surprised. "You spoke to him?"

She nodded, letting a small smile curl against her lips. "I did, and he's partly the reason I saved you." Perhaps if Emric hadn't been willing to indulge her curiosity, her conversation with Ferryn would never have happened. Thanar never would have punished her. And Ferryn wouldn't have felt obligated to give her the mark. So many moments. One misstep could have yielded a completely different outcome.

Gavriel's mouth pulled into an unwilling grin. "So, I can blame Emric for that as well? The man certainly knew how to plant me square in the middle of trouble."

"That, I believe."

He dropped his gaze, his smile slowly retreating. "I'm sorry too. I've been... unfair."

"You've been an ass."

He huffed a laugh, shaking his head.

Since this moment seemed the least hostile they'd shared, Lark yanked the pages from beneath her cloak. They crinkled in her hands as she tried to smooth them. "Now we can discuss the real reason I snuck into your tent in the middle of the night."

Gavriel frowned. "I assumed you either wanted to kill me or bed me. I certainly didn't expect this."

"I met with Kenna," she said, ignoring his comment even as heat stained her cheeks. "She gave me these for us to copy." She held out the parchments depicting all the dangers she was leading to them.

He flipped through the pages, one finger pressed to his lips as he devoured the information. "Hm, we'll need to find a priestess." He muttered to himself. "Blood of a virgin—good luck finding one south of the Permafrosts." Finally, he looked up. "These are very valuable. We can defend ourselves against some of these creatures."

"There's more." Lark pulled the pendant out from beneath her tunic. His eyes darted to it.

"A friendship necklace?"

"If I'd known you were as insufferable as Alistair, I would have let you hate me forever."

"I'm sorry, I'm sorry." He let the smile fall from his face and returned to his usual dour expression. "You're being so mysterious, I thought I'd play the fool, but I'm out of practice." He held his hand out. "May I?"

Lark pulled it over her head and dropped it in his palm. She ignored the warmth of his hand and turned her attention to the blue glowing stone. "It's a hunter's talisman imbued with magic. Kenna said to bring it to the witch in the Emerald Woods."

"And why would you do that?"

"I need to make contact with Ferryn, or anyone trustworthy from the Otherworld."

Gavriel waited for her to continue.

Lark sighed. "I need to be certain Ferryn is alright. He risked much for me, and I'm afraid I've landed him in trouble."

"Ferryn is your lover?" Gavriel's expression was blank.

Lark shook her head. "No, he's my friend."

"Doesn't that seem a bit ridiculous to travel that far north just to speak with someone you didn't care enough about to bring along when you became human?"

"It's not like that. I need to make sure the tear I caused has been sealed up, otherwise more Undesirables will be upon us."

"So, you essentially created a problem, and now need to inconvenience others to fix it?" Gavriel's eyes sparkled with mirth as the corner of his mouth curved.

Was it possible for the blood in a mortal body to boil? It sure felt that way to Lark. "I could just go live my life. This is what I fought for, this existence. I could let someone else deal with the trickle of ilk from the Netherworld and carry-on arranging flowers in my hair and riding off into the sunset—"

"You should leave the poor flowers out of this."

"—But I can't until I'm free of this burden. Until I know I didn't set everyone around me on a path of destruction." As her anger dimmed, something cold and desolate took root in her chest. How far-reaching were the consequences of her actions? All she wanted was to escape, to be free to feel. Now that she had what she wished for, how selfish was she to feel cheated? Why couldn't she live her life in peace, without this incessant guilt?

Human emotion was a strange and fickle beast.

Gavriel swallowed. "I was attempting a joke again. I must be woefully out of practice since it seems I keep pissing you off. Of course we'll find a way to get you to the, well I'm unfamiliar with any witch of Emerald Woods, but I'd heard of the peddler of rare tonics that supplies Oakbury. Whoever you need, we'll find them."

Lark regarded him with suspicion. "Just like that?"

"Well, I had a feeling this might come up. The Vrykolaka said that she smelled you on me. I can't decide if that's a compliment or an insult. In either case, if they can sense you out, it would probably be within your best interest to sort your shit out." He lowered the pendant back into her hand.

It smelled her on him? Skies above, that was a terrifying thought. "Why didn't you say this sooner?"

Gavriel shrugged. He settled back and laced his hands behind his head, crossing his ankles. Wincing, he readjusted his position.

An impossible thought came to Lark. Why he might not tell the others what she was, or the potential danger she'd brought to the world. "You weren't... protecting me?"

"No." Gavriel sat up. "Absolutely not. I was waiting to use it to my best advantage."

Lark shook her head. "I find that utterly nonsensical. You're the one who wanted nothing more than to escape me. You have the trust of my companions, and you have enough information to discredit me to them. Yet here you are, sitting on your ass. You've tipped your hand; you were looking out for me."

"Let's get this straight." Gavriel leaned in close. She tried not to notice he smelled of warm hearth, leather, and something both sweet and bitter like the Northern wind. "Just because I'm not going to kill you, does not mean that we're friends or that I even like you." He dropped to his sleeping roll, his hands tucked behind his head. "Besides, I can always change my mind."

She bit her lip, desperately trying to keep the grin off her face. "Whatever you say, Gavriel." She glanced over at the pages lying on the floor of his tent.

"Leave those. I'd like a chance to study them more before I ask your healer to spend some time writing copies." Gavriel sighed and closed his eyes. "I'll just tell him Kenna gave them to me yesterday and I was so delirious I completely forgot."

"But I was going to tell them everything Kenna said."

"I know. But you shouldn't, not yet anyway. We have a good thing here. I can finally rest without worrying about getting a knife in the back until I make it to Koval, and you need as much help as you can get. We need to make sure you're worth the trouble before we give them a reason to drop you." He cracked an eye open. "And before you say anything, remember I am looking out for my own best interests. Which don't include you."

Lark nodded, feeling light despite the heaviness of her mortal body.

"Goodnight, Demon. Enjoy your reprieve from my list." He closed his eyes and shifted to get comfortable.

"Goodnight," Lark said as she kicked his foot with no real strength behind it.

She made her way across the camp, back to her tent. As she settled into her bedroll, she found it softer than she remembered. She turned to lie on her side, the promise of sleep lulling her deeper into the restful void of the world.

CHAPTER 24

"*W*ho's coming to town with me?" Alistair bounced on his heels, eager as a pup. He had coin burning holes in his pockets and a devilish glint in his eye that promised poor choices. "I want to get a jumpstart before the market sells out."

Lark caught the meaningful glance he tossed Langford's way.

The brilliant green of spring leaves surrounded their campsite. The trees seemed to have thickened overnight, guarding their space, and the occasional fragrant breeze shook through leafy branches. Their soft rustle, peaceful compared to the call of a bird who'd awakened Lark long before she was ready. It resumed its call. Lark never thought she'd accuse an animal of sounding smug.

She rubbed her tired eyes and leaned closer to the warmth of the fire, equal parts enchanted and annoyed with the noisy creature.

"I'll go with you." Langford sipped his tea from a steel cup, a quiet storm in his grey eyes. "Since you turned down my proposal at our last fireside meeting—"

"You can't keep bees Langford! It's impractical and their incessant buzzing drives me mad, you know that."

"—I find I'm running low on honey." Langford tapped his fingers against the side of his mug. The metallic *ting* punctuated the challenge in his voice.

"Your tea not sweet enough to your liking, Langford?" Alistair angled a dark brow. His eyes were brighter than the verdant leaves they sat beneath. "I'm sorry, but my invitation was more for you to window shop while I make purchases."

"Don't come running to me when you get another scratch that goes *septic*."

Alistair sighed. "It was honey you needed?"

"Among other things. I'll jot down a list and accompany you, just to make sure we get everything we need."

"Sargon's flaming knickers," Alistair muttered.

Langford frowned. "You know I hate it when you blaspheme."

"You shouldn't have taught me the names of your gods, then."

"Aren't we heading north?" Lark asked cautiously. She needed to find Kenna's contact. "I thought we got the horses for that very journey."

"Patience, woman," Alistair said. "We've maintained a close distance to a few towns for quite some time. We need to prepare. We will be journeying to remote locations, and without close access to roads for a time." A lazy smile stretched across his face. "Plus, I need one more frolic for the road."

Langford's jaw clenched, a muscle feathering his cheek. His soft, pale face had gone uncharacteristically hard.

"Ugh. You're so predictable." Daciana's voice was a welcome sound. She'd been scarce since crossing paths with Kenna. She'd plaited her thick, black hair over one shoulder, a leather cord holding it in place. "It's fortunate I'll be going with you to ensure we have some coin left for travel." Her hazel eyes met Lark's.

Lark gave what she hoped was a reassuring smile. There was no need to spew her troubles all over the breakfast they shared.

Daciana gave her a knowing look before tossing a large raspberry into her mouth.

"Spoilsport," Alistair mumbled.

Lark dragged a stick through the dirt, carving nonsense symbols.

She needed to speak with Daciana. With Gavriel it was easy, he already knew what she was and despised her. But Daciana was her first human friend. Lark couldn't bear the thought of Daciana looking at her with disdain as Gavriel had. Although, Lark's kinship with Gavriel seemed to have improved by leaps and bounds since the previous night.

She glanced in his direction. Gavriel crossed his eyes at her, his mouth bulging with the inhuman-sized bite of apple. One of her apples from the canvas satchel at her feet.

"Tea?" Langford held a second cup out across the hearth.

Eagerly, Daciana leaned forward to claim it. "Always."

Hugo still hadn't made an appearance, and likely would not for another hour.

"I want to get going," Alistair whined.

Daciana rolled her eyes. "Ready the mounts while I eat. I want to be back early. We travel at first light tomorrow, and the horses will need plenty of rest."

"Yes, sir." Alistair said, snatching Langford's cup of tea and sauntering off.

Langford merely shook his head and pulled the leather jack from his bag. "I'm off to get water," he said.

Lark nodded and slipped an apple from her stash to follow Alistair, relieved when he veered off to collect the saddlebags. It gave her another chance to see her horse in private.

Lark approached the hitching post Hugo had fashioned the day prior. "There's my good girl," she murmured, holding a palm out to the chestnut mare. Apple blinked her large dark eyes and lowered her head. Lark ran her hand along the white diamond patch on her forehead. Something swelled in her chest as she stared into the creature's gentle gaze. "I brought you something." She lifted the fruit toward Apple's mouth, letting her eat it from her hand. "I would have been here sooner, but Hugo wanted to keep you all to himself." Apple nudged her shoulder, searching for another treat. "I'm sorry, that's all I have. I promise to have Alistair get us some more. A whole bushel." Apple nudged her a little harder.

"Animals are an excellent judge of character."

Lark turned to see Alistair leaning against a nearby tree, a saddle on the ground at his feet. "Either that or they are easily bribed with snacks." He pushed off the tree, walking up to them. "I told you not to get attached."

"Who couldn't get attached to this face?" Lark pressed her forehead to Apple's. "I want to keep her."

He frowned. "Lark, you know you can't. Once we go north, we have to sell them."

"Why?"

Alistair hesitated. "We took a chance letting you in. So far, you've been a good fit. A few surprises thrown in for good measure, but by and large you're a worthy investment." He ran his hand gently down Apple's side. "I will, however, need you to extend the same courtesy of trust we've given you. Rules are rules. If you don't like them, nothing's keeping you."

"Are you threatening to kick me out?"

"No." He shook his head, and a solemn expression stole across his face. "Not at all, but I'm telling you not to push this." He gave Apple a firm pat before turning to strut back to the saddle he'd abandoned on the ground. "We'll take this one with us today, but I'll give you first choice when we ride north. It's the least I can do."

Lark ground her teeth and nodded, walking away without a parting word. The action tightened something in her chest, like the time she'd swallowed a piece of bread without chewing it properly. Alistair wasn't making any sense. For what reason could they need to abandon the horses? Perhaps for coin, maybe that was it. Maybe there were sparse seasons and they couldn't afford any luxury, so the horses would be first to go.

"What's wrong?" Daciana's voice cut through Lark's thoughts. She stood several paces away, her pack slung over her shoulder, and worry creasing her brow.

"Alistair won't let me keep Apple." And without the decency to explain himself.

"Oh, Lark. I'm sorry." Daciana's face fell into a forlorn expression for the briefest of moments.

"What do you have to be sorry for? It's Alistair's fault."

Daciana said nothing. Instead, she turned her gaze to the sky, and exhaled a long breath. "It's always strange not being under the refuge of trees. It makes me feel exposed."

Confused by the sudden turn in the conversation, Lark looked up at the vibrant green leaves. Dappled sunlight fought to find its way to where they stood. "The constant cover makes me feel caged. I look forward to the open sky."

Daciana's smile turned wistful. "Some cages are of our own making. We can never escape them." Her eyes were pinched with something unspoken and full of longing. An ache Lark had seen in her own reflection before she stopped looking. The pain of a life half lived and a wish abandoned.

"Ah, listen to me. So dreary, and on market day!" Daciana's pitch-perfect impression of Alistair pulled a sudden laugh from Lark's chest. Daciana patted her on the shoulder. "Be safe, we won't be long." She hesitated. "Stay close to Hugo. I know you trust Gavriel, but I'd worry less if I knew you were being smart."

"Don't worry about me." All Lark got in response was a skeptical look. "Off you go, bring me back more apples, please."

"Langford will have to make you his famous cider," Daciana said, before heading off to the hitching post where Alistair waited.

Lark made her way back to camp, not at all surprised to see Hugo finally up and seated by the fire, a steaming cup in his large tattooed hand.

"I was told to stay close to you." She settled beside him. "Am I to take that literally?"

"If I had to babysit you to keep you alive, you'da been dead last night, aye?" Hugo leveled her with his rich brown eyes, worn lines around the edges, but sharp enough he missed nothing.

"Aye," Lark mimicked back, swiping his hot mug of tea and taking a long pull. A smoky yet citrus flavor spilled over her tongue and warmed her belly.

"You'll be helping me today."

"How's that?" Lark muttered into the mug, her voice echoing against metal.

He grabbed the wooden short bow he'd crafted last night and placed it on her lap. She lowered the cup to the ground and ran her hands over the smooth surface. The craftsmanship was beautiful, a perfectly sized grasp etched into the handle for her hand to fit. The hemp string held firm when she gently tugged against it.

"It's beautiful."

Hugo snorted. "It's not for looking at. We'll begin training when I'm done eating."

"Pardon?"

He snagged his mug of tea back. "I told you, we need an archer."

"THE MOST IMPORTANT thing with a recurve is consistency." Hugo paced behind her. Hours of lessons had drenched the back of her tunic with sweat. The muscles in her arms shook. "Your stance keeps changing. You'll never hit a target twice without consistency."

Lark groaned, her pull arm trembling, threatening to loose her nocked arrow. It didn't help that Gavriel had taken it upon himself to train nearby. Never once did he acknowledge her, so focused on his task. The speed of his knives distracted Lark from her own training. It certainly wasn't that he'd lost his shirt somewhere along the way—his back, thick and corded with muscles, glinted with sweat. That was definitely not it.

"Hugo." Her voice came out in a whine, but the pain spoke louder. "I can't hold it."

"That's because you need to build your strength. Where are your feet?"

Lark adjusted her stance, positioning her feet shoulders width apart. Bending her knees slightly, she ignored the creaking sensation in her joints. She angled her hips to align parallel with her wobbly arrow.

"Good, how's your posture?"

Forcing her spine to straighten, she elongated her torso, despite her protesting muscles.

"Shoulder?"

Almost imperceptibly she lowered her pull shoulder, offering her neck the slightest hint of relief.

"Anchor point."

Lark tucked the bowstring under her chin, breathing through her mouth. Her focus narrowed to the hastily posted target in the distance, a coiled, circular form of straw Daciana had crudely painted Alistair's face on. She said it was for extra motivation.

"Release."

Lark released. The arrow sailed through the air with a whistle, straight for its mark. It landed, sure and true in the middle of her target—

Before bouncing off and hitting the ground.

Lark spun to gape at Hugo. "What? I don't understand, I hit my mark."

Hugo grabbed a second softened leather quiver full of arrows. When did he have time to fletch all these? "Do it again."

Lark wanted to cry. Her muscles wanted to cry with her—to curl up in a ball and sob until nothing was left but sweat and tears and salt on her battered body. But she was more than this infernal task. She'd led countless souls to their path, felled Undesirables with nary a thought. And now she was real. Flesh and blood and bone.

She wiped the sweat from her upper lip, yanked an arrow from his quiver, and nocked it again.

"Good. Watch your stance."

BY THE DAY'S END, Lark could no longer lift the bow, and her arms throbbed at her sides. She couldn't even push the hair from her face, and salt stung her eyes. The sun sat low in the sky, bathing the forest in warm hues of burnt amber.

Gavriel paused his training to mop the back of his neck, occasionally glancing over to watch them.

Hugo regarded Lark with a twitch of his mustache. "We're done for the day. Get some rest."

"But I haven't sunk an arrow yet," she said, panting. "I'm not leaving 'til I do." She'd shoot until the last rays of the sun disappeared from the forest. Leaving her blind.

"Then you'll never leave."

Lark blinked the sweat from her eyes. "You don't think I can do it."

"I know you can't." Hugo was already collecting her fallen arrows. "Not with that bow." He jerked his chin at her hand by her side.

Lark gripped it tighter. "Why not?"

"The pull strength of that bow isn't heavy enough. You'll need to work your way up for the power behind it to pierce a target at this range." Hugo slipped the arrows into the quiver. "Even more so if you wish to penetrate armor."

"Do you jest?" She tried to throw the bow to the ground, but it slipped uselessly from her shaking hand. "Is it your goal to watch me fail?" Her voice steadily rose while her blood burned in her veins.

"Not at all," Hugo said, voice smooth and calm in the face of her anger.

"Then what was the purpose?"

"You need to train your muscles in the proper form. You're not strong enough yet for a heavier pull." He slipped the strap of the quiver over his shoulder.

Gavriel crept toward them at a glacial pace.

Lark balled her hands, wincing at the newly formed blisters. "You could have told me as much."

"Why?"

Gavriel paused his approach, indecision written on his face. He turned to head back toward camp, likely to avoid their conversation.

"Truly? Perhaps because not telling me is manipulative, condescending, arrogant, unhelpful." Her vision swam with tears. "Need I go on?"

"I don't see it that way." Hugo furrowed his brow, a disapproving frown evident even behind his bushy mustache.

"Look at it however you want." Lark brushed past him. "But I'm done being toyed with."

With each step, her anger dimmed, and the pain set it. She'd over-reacted—she should be grateful he was helping her. But the feeling of being manipulated and treated like a child in need of guidance, no questions asked? It burned.

Lark stumbled into camp, her body heavy and aching. Throwing herself into her tent, she barely had time to register how filthy she was. Her bedroll would need a trip to the stream if she laid in it without washing. Before she could change her mind, her eyes slipped closed, and sleep engulfed her.

Lark awoke in her darkened tent, disoriented and slicked with sweat. An orange glow seeped through the worn stitches. The light flickered, never ceasing its dance. She sat up, head spinning and mouth dry. Her muscles screamed their protest. Lark tried to stretch, but her body was still wound tight. She should have drunk water, washed, and tried to loosen her muscles before she rested. Now she was a coiled ball of pain.

Biting her lip, Lark forced her leg to straighten, crying out at the abrupt twisting in her calf muscle. Breathing through it, she massaged her leg, silently pleading for the pain to subside. She almost didn't notice the small bag at the foot of her bedroll. Inside she found a small piece of cloth wrapped around several pieces of willow bark. A smile tugged at the corners of her mouth. She tucked a piece between her teeth, chewing until relief spread through her sore muscles. She'd have to thank Langford.

Lark tucked her spare clothing under one arm and made her way out of her tent. Everyone sat by the fire having dinner. She limped over, her face burning with every step. Gavriel noticed her arrival first, his eyes assessing her before lowering back to the plate he balanced on his lap.

"You look like shit," Alistair said.

"I feel worse," Lark said.

Langford handed her his canteen of water. She drank it down, swallowing thick, greedy mouthfuls.

"Thanks. For the water and the willow bark. I doubt I would have made it off my bedroll without it."

Langford gave her a puzzled look before twisting his head to look at Gavriel, whose eyes held a vigil watch over the ground.

"You're welcome," Langford said, his voice filled with uncertainty.

Lark turned to Daciana. "Are we still set to leave at first light?"

"Not exactly." Daciana's eyes sparkled in the firelight. "We'll talk after you've had a moment to wash."

Lark grinned and tugged her bundle of clothes closer. "I smell that bad huh?"

Gavriel snorted.

"No." Daciana ignored him. "You just look like you need it."

With a quick nod, Lark slipped away.

FINALLY CLEAN AND feeling human again, Lark eagerly dug into her dinner, ravenous. Someone had cooked venison over the fire. Without care for table manners, she shoved the meat into her mouth with her fingers, filling her cheeks and barely waiting to swallow before piling more in.

"Easy, killer."

Lark looked up, still chewing, to see all five of her companions watching her with varying degrees of amusement.

Alistair grinned at her. "You keep that up and you won't be our little Lark anymore."

Lark ignored him and resumed her task of filling her belly as quickly as possible. She almost didn't notice a large hand reach over toward her plate. Black symbols peeked out the bottom of a sleeve, encircling a thick wrist. Ready to slap it away, Lark darted her attention to the offender.

Hugo paused for a moment, his hand outstretched, and dropped half of his portion onto her plate. With a grunt of thanks, she set back to work on devouring her meal without looking at him again.

"Perhaps now's a good time to discuss our next course of action." Daciana eyed Lark.

"Careful. I think she bites," Alistair said.

Lark bared her teeth at Alistair, earning a playful growl.

"We can't leave until this matter is settled," Daciana said.

The smile vanished from Alistair's face. "It's not our problem."

"Blazing infernals, it isn't."

"It's not. We were hired to fulfill a service. We fulfilled that service. Our job is done." Alistair errantly kicked at a rock near his boot.

Daciana glared at him. "We can't abandon them. Even you can see that."

Alistair rolled his eyes and maintained his rigid posture.

"What's going on?" Lark's attention shifted back and forth between Daciana and Alistair.

"Talbot's men have been harassing the girls at the tavern. We weren't as inconspicuous"—Daciana shot a dark look at Gavriel—"as we'd planned. Think about it, the night of his death, two unfamiliar girls were seen working there, one of whom was presumably the last to see Talbot alive. They're still searching for us and trying to pull information those innocents don't have. We never had a chance to clean up after ourselves or point them in another direction. We've put those girls at risk."

"That's life!" Alistair blurted out. "We saved countless lives from his operation. It'll take weeks for them to reorganize without him. By then hopefully, the populace finds a way to protect themselves." He tossed a handful of dirt into the fire. "We've done our part."

"How did you discover this?" Lark asked, setting her plate down on the log beside her.

"One of my contacts passed along the message. Remember the boy who brought our disguises?"

Lark nodded, remembering the boy who came to the inn.

"When we were in town today, he brought me the missive from

one of the girls." Daciana's eyes met Lark's. "They need us. We can't leave them to face this."

"We won't." Lark shook her head. "Of course, we won't. What do they need?"

"Right now, they need trust. All they're asking for is a meet-up. What we decide to do, is a course we haven't set."

Lark nodded, absorbing the information. "All right, where's the rendezvous?"

Daciana hesitated. "That's the thing, they're wary of messages getting intercepted." She wrinkled her nose. "They'll send for us at a time and place of their choosing. They have eyes everywhere; we just need to be seen within the town."

Lark exhaled a heavy sigh. The precarious nature of this mission was suspect. But she hoped she was in the business of cleaning up after herself. "I don't like it, but I suppose I understand the concern."

"There's more."

Oh, for skies sake. "More?"

"They only want us to go. You and me. If they spot anyone else, they won't make contact."

Heavy silence fell over the group.

"If this reeked any stronger of a trap," Gavriel said. "You'd be able to hear the swinging cage above your heads."

"Thank you!" Alistair shouted loud enough to make Langford jump. "That's what I said."

"Of course, it's a trap," Daciana bit out between gritted teeth. "But the girls are scared, and this is still our obligation."

"You say obligation, I say death warrant."

Arguing erupted between Daciana and Alistair. *Of course it's a trap.* Daciana seemed so cavalier in the face of certain betrayal. She must have a plan. And Lark owed the innocent girls who took the fall for her mistakes. Gavriel wouldn't have given their position away if it weren't for her.

"What's the plan?" No one heard Lark over the squabbling. She cleared her throat to repeat herself.

A sharp, piercing whistle rang out, and Lark covered her ears. The shouting stopped as everyone turned to Hugo.

"Quiet," he growled, before nodding to Lark.

"What's the plan?" Lark repeated.

"Absolutely not!" Alistair cut his hand across the air in front of him. "We need to travel. As scheduled." He shot an incredulous stare Daciana's way. "*You* know I'm right."

Daciana ignored him, meeting Lark's stare. She held her hands over the fire, a coy smile playing on her mouth. "The plan is, we walk into a trap."

Lark sucked in a breath. Ceto once said her desires blinded her. That she failed to see everything at stake around her.

Lark was determined to prove her wrong. "Sounds fun."

AFTER MORE ARGUING and threats of dismemberment, Alistair finally conceded.

They agreed to give Lark a couple of days for her muscles to heal. Then, Lark and Daciana would go into town alone and wait. The idea of walking straight into a trap still set Lark's teeth on edge. But if she could choose anyone to watch her back, it was Daciana.

As Lark ambled toward her tent, heavy footsteps followed behind. She turned to see Hugo a few paces away.

"We need to talk."

She crossed her arms. The action, reminding her how sore she was. "So, talk."

Hugo sighed. "How are the arms?"

"Fine." She bit down on her lip. She wouldn't resort to yelling. Again.

"You're angry."

"Observant."

Hugo ran a large hand over his face. "I'm not very good at this."

"Manners?"

"Smartass," he grumbled. "I'm sorry if you were insulted by my methods. Maybe I was right, maybe I wasn't. But let me ask you this." He leveled her with his piercing stare. "Had I told you the bow couldn't land the mark, would you have pushed past the point of comfort?" He edged a step closer. "You pushed through the pain. That's what I want from you. I don't want your best. I want better than that."

Of course, his choices were born out of strategy. But it still stung.

"I don't want to send you into danger without knowing I've done everything I can to ensure you can handle yourself. Most people train their whole lives to hone their skill with a bow. We don't have that kinda time. I have a way of getting the results I want. At my age, it's unlikely I'll change my practice. So, if you want someone else to train you, I understand." He turned his gaze from her, discomfort written on his features. "But I'd like the chance to arm you with as many skills as I can in the time we have."

A knot formed in Lark's throat, and she swallowed it down. "No. I want to train with you." Before he could protest, she wrapped her arms around his solid form, resting her head on his chest. His scent of smoke and sun-drenched earth enveloped her. His arms hung out awkwardly off to the sides before one hand tentatively patted her back.

After a moment, he pushed her back by the shoulders, holding her at arm's length. "That's enough of that," he mumbled before ambling off.

Lark grinned at his retreating form. "When do I get my next bow?"

"When you put more meat on your bones," Hugo called over his shoulder.

IT TOOK two days for Lark's strength to return. Alistair's ever-growing impatience cast an unusual tension over the camp. With her bag packed, knife firmly planted in her boot, and bow slung over her shoulder, Lark was ready to go.

Alistair made one final plea for Daciana to change her mind.

"How is it I've become the voice of reason?" Alistair gripped the handle of his cutlass. "It's awfully unsettling."

"You worry over nothing." Daciana patted his shoulder.

"It's too risky."

"You don't think I can handle myself?"

Alistair ran his hand into his thick, dark hair. "Damn it! It's not about that and you know it."

Langford sliced an apple, frying it in pieces over the fire as he ignored Daciana and Alistair's arguing. Lark plopped down beside him.

"You know you don't have to cook those." She reached into her bag and pulled out a fresh apple. "They're meant to be eaten off the tree."

"You've never had cooked apples before?" Langford glanced at her over his shoulder. "You poor, ignorant creature."

"Don't be an ass. We're leaving soon."

"Ah, yes. I nearly forgot about that." He shook the cast iron frying pan over the flame to loosen the browning slices. "It's not like those two have been arguing on a constant loop."

"It seems to happen a lot," Lark said with casual disinterest. She hoped he'd elaborate without further prompting.

"They disagree on almost everything. But when it comes down to it, he respects her above anyone else." Langford wore a self-deprecating smile. Bitterness hardening his tone. "Yours truly included."

"So long as they don't burn down the camp."

"No promises."

Langford pulled the pan away from the fire, placing it on a log beside him. Using a fork, he arranged the apples on a plate, dousing them in cinnamon. He grinned, displaying his masterpiece proudly.

"Ladies first."

"I can have one?"

Langford raised his brow at her, gently blowing on the browned fruit. "Of course."

Lark eyed him with suspicion. She grabbed a piece between her thumb and first finger, examining it with care.

"Gods, woman, just eat it!"

Lark popped it into her mouth. The sweet, softened flavor and full-bodied cinnamon burst on her tongue.

She tried to grab more from Langford's plate while he swatted her away, grinning.

"Did you make enough for everyone?" Gavriel's voice startled Lark, temporarily distracting her from stealing more apple slices. She hadn't even heard him approach.

Seizing the opportunity, Langford rose to his feet. With his free hand, he guarded his plate. "I'll finish these in private. Be safe!" he called out, before he disappeared behind the flaps of his tent.

Lark took a bite of her apple. "There goes my breakfast."

Gavriel huffed a soft laugh, watching her. "Nervous?"

"No, not at all." The lie was bitter on her cinnamon-coated tongue.

"You should be." He reached over and snatched an apple from her bag, his eyes locked on her as he sank his teeth through the skin. She forced her gaze up to the trees, hoping the heat on her cheeks wasn't noticeable.

"Daciana knows what she's doing."

"Hm. Maybe so. But it would be unwise to walk into a lion's den without a healthy dose of fear. Fear can make you sharper, hone your focus. It's a myth that fear is a weakness. Fear is a blade, and sometimes the only difference between life and death."

"So, what do you fear?" She leaned in close. His scent was becoming increasingly familiar.

"Many things," Gavriel whispered, also leaning forward until they were face to face. "It keeps me alive."

She could feel his breath on her face, smell the crisp tartness of it. The memory of sealing her lips over his sprang to mind, and a deep ache pulled from within. What would it feel like now, as a human?

Lark would never kiss him again without his permission, and he'd never grant it.

His eyes drifted to her lips as if sensing the same thing. He brought his apple back to his mouth, taking a loud bite right in her face.

"Ass," Lark said, pulling back. She tried not to dwell on the swift thumping of her heart.

Gavriel laughed, and rose to his feet. "Fare thee well on your trip, Demon. Try not to die." He turned and strode away from her.

Lark watched his receding form until she could hold her tongue no longer. "Gavriel," she called. "If fear isn't a weakness, what is?"

He didn't break his stride as he called over his shoulder.

"Love."

CHAPTER 25

*B*rookhill's market square bustled with activity. Last time they'd been here, Lark didn't have the time to explore the town. Now she stopped at every vendor, her curious gaze roving over their wares. Rows of decorated stalls lined the perimeter of the square as customers meandered through. Swaths of fabrics fluttered in the gentle breeze in greys, blues, and browns. In greens the color of a forest on a sunless day, and blacks dark as the night sky void of stars. Lark eyed her cloak, worn with holes and fraying edges, but she pressed on.

Lark crossed the square to a stall littered with bells and baubles, shiny and elaborate as the sun glinted off metal shapes. But that wasn't what captivated her. Various musical instruments sat atop the wooden table. Lazing in a chair within the stall, the seller plucked the strings of an etched lute, playing a gentle melody. The intricate designs along the body of the instrument consisted of vines and leaves, swirling and curving against the smooth wood. The seller's head was downcast, a blue, wide brim hat obscuring his face.

Lark approached, entranced by the soft emotion of his notes, and the seller looked up. Warmth emanated from his dark gaze and his tan skin creased with lines and wrinkles as if he spent all his days smiling in the sun. He offered her a wide grin.

"See anything you like, girlie?"

Lark ran her eyes over the countless flutes, deerskin bound drums, and a few simpler designed lutes. Her gaze landed on a beautifully crafted fiddle. Its rich, stained wood caught the light of the midday sun, and a yew tree with deep, gnarled roots appeared to have been burned into the surface of the instrument. How was such a technique achieved without damaging the fiddle? She reached tentative fingers toward it, pausing to look at him.

He nodded. "Go ahead."

With a delicate hand, Lark lifted it from the cart, running feather light touches along the body. "It's beautiful."

He reached behind him to grab the bow. "Go on, give it a try."

Lark shook her head, cheeks burning. There was no earthly reason for her to be so drawn to this instrument. "I don't know how to play."

"Want me to show you?" He gave her a secret smile.

Nodding, she handed it back to him.

Lifting it expertly to rest on his shoulder, he lowered his chin and dragged the horsehair bow across the strings in a slow sweeping legato. The tone reverberated through Lark. Grinning, he began stroking his bow against the strings in earnest, fiddling swiftly and proficiently.

Lark bounced on her heels in time to his playing, and warmth spread through her. He swayed his body with his playing, drifting over notes faster. The upbeat tempo pulsed through her, as his music washed over her. Every note, every chord tugged at a place in her soul —long buried, long forgotten—and a swell of euphoria filled her chest.

He ended with a flourish, and Lark clapped hard enough her palms stung.

"That was wonderful!"

He gave her a low bow, tipping his hat.

Lark pulled two silvers from her pocket. Alistair would kill her, but it was worth it. "I can't buy anything, but I can thank you for the song." She placed the coins in his hand.

He smiled, his fingers closing around the coins. "The name of the young lady who shows kindness to an old troubadour?"

"My name is Lark, good sir."

"Bartrand Rigglesby, at your service." He dropped in a low bow and pressed a courtly kiss to her knuckles. "I shall compose a song in your name. Dear, sweet, Lark."

Lark grinned back at him. With a quick dip of her chin, she scurried off to find Daciana.

Daciana stood frowning at a Smithy cart, short swords, daggers, and easily concealable blades glinted in the midday sun.

"The seller proclaims these are of Kovalian make," Daciana said without turning to Lark.

"Oh, that's good isn't it? I've heard they're of higher quality."

Daciana huffed a short laugh. "It's a lie. There's no way he can forge Kovalian steel." She pulled an ornate short sword from the pile. Intricate filigree weaved around the hilt in gold. Daciana tested the weight, her frown increasing. "Just as I thought, this is a fake. It would hardly aid me in a fight." She dropped it atop the others with a metallic clang.

A fight. Lark swallowed and hoisted her new bow higher over her shoulder—the bow Hugo had replaced her practice bow with. This ashwood recurve was carved with care. Detailing of roots and branches ran along the grip like etched veins. Lark marveled at its beauty, which earned her a scowl from Hugo as he explained to aim for the throat, eyes, any vulnerable spots.

Lark was both eager and filled with dread at the prospect of needing it.

SEATED across from Lark at The Tawdry Steward tavern, Daciana rolled her shoulders, scanning the room with the fierce stare of a predator.

"You're not being very—"

Daciana shot a dark glare her way.

"—inconspicuous," Lark finished.

Daciana was getting easier and easier to set off. Lark worried that one harsh word would result in a bloodbath of epic proportions. Daciana's rigid posture relaxed by a fraction of an inch.

"Seriously, are you all right?"

Daciana gave her a tight smile that failed to meet her eyes. "Of course, just itching to get this over with."

Lark nodded, unconvinced. "You know, it would be okay if something was wrong. If there's something I should know—"

"It's not that. I just can't believe I'm beginning to think Alistair was right."

Lark lifted a hand to her chest. "Please don't utter such blasphemy!"

Daciana chuckled, taking a sip from her tankard of ale. "I think you've been hanging around him too long."

"We should make more friends."

"No doubt."

Lark surveyed the warmly lit tavern as she gripped the smooth wooden tankard. The room was a sea of unfamiliar faces, some flushed red with drunkenness. The last time she was here, she was on display and tripping over her feet as she searched for Talbot. Gavriel had been lurking in the shadows, nearly hidden from view, but she'd recognized him instantly. Warmth flooded her cheeks at the memory, and she shoved it away to remain focused on the task. From the corner, a minstrel struggled to play his lute over the noise of dozens of conversations and booming laughter. Lark tipped back in her seat to get a good look at him, but it wasn't Bartrand, the musician from the market.

A guard donning the blue and white colors of Ardenas walked by their table. Was he one of Talbot's men? Was the entire city guard under his rule? Lark resisted the urge to shield her face behind her hand and instead stared down at the woodgrains in the table. He wouldn't recognize her. But still, dread knotted her stomach until he swept past, not even offering her a second glance. "You don't think we could have brought back up?"

Daciana pinned her with a knowing look. "Our surest way of tipping them off is by bringing Alistair or Hugo."

Fair point. From what Lark heard, Alistair's reputation preceded him. His antics at every tavern and brothel in Ardenas didn't help. Though, Lark couldn't help but think that was intentional. And Hugo was the opposite of discreet with his hulking build and the tattoos adorning every inch of skin, save for his face.

"What about Gavriel?" The expression Lark received was enough to convey exactly how Daciana felt about bringing Gavriel. The assassin had yet to endear himself to the warrior, a fact not lost on Lark. "Fine, not him. Langford?"

Daciana frowned. "Langford isn't ready. When we find the right fit for him again, perhaps."

"Has he gone on a job before?" Lark tried to imagine mild mannered Langford with a blade in his hand, moving stealthily through the dark, to no avail. "What happened?"

Daciana refused to meet Lark's stare. "It isn't mine to tell."

Before Lark could respond, she caught sight of a fair-haired serving girl who kept darting nervous glances their way. Lark lifted her chin, making an obvious show of seeing her, before lifting her tankard to gesture for more. She'd only had water, not wanting to test her tolerance.

The serving girl hurried over, jug in hand, and stopped at their table to fill their empty mugs.

"Trouble?" Daciana angled her head a fraction of an inch. As if sensing the air.

The girl's brown eyes widened, and she shot a wary glance at the door. She started to pour the ale, only to slip and spill it all down Lark's leggings and onto the floor. The girl dropped to the floor, using her apron to mop up the spill, and Lark slipped out of her chair and lowered into a crouch beside her.

"Two doors down," the girl whispered. "Leave out the back way and go two doors down. To the old warehouse." She stood and scrambled away, leaving a confused and wet Lark still on the floor.

Lark stood, peering over at Daciana.

"Well?"

"I guess we've made contact."

THE DARKENED alley did little to convince Lark this wasn't a trap. She thumbed the knife Hugo gave her, bow and quiver tucked neatly beneath her cloak. Her leggings felt tight with dried ale as she took deliberate steps around the piles of filth and waste on the ground. The flickering light of the lampposts didn't reach her steps, the shadows claimed the street.

The moon was close to full. Such a wondrous thing, the way the night sky could change. Thanar only ever crafted a round moon, never changing, just like her. But the mortal moon had swelled from the last time she looked upon it.

At the large, oak door, Lark's throat tightened, her blood quickening. What had Gavriel said about fear? It made one sharper, focused. Hopefully that was true.

Daciana pushed the door open. Gaping darkness greeted them. Daciana grabbed the lantern that hung from the wall, the squeal of the key rang loud against the silent space. A small flame erupted in its glass encasement, offering a hint of light in the dark.

The large, windowless storage room was empty, except for a few large crates along the walls. Sharp shadows loomed over them, carving the space with black shapes.

Once, Lark was bred for darkness. A being forged from the gloom of a shroud. Like sinking to the bottom of the ocean, utter quiet in perpetual night beneath the surface. But now, her mortal instincts told her not to stray far from the light.

Sharing a quick glance, they searched the warehouse, each taking the opposite wall to check for any hidden visitors. They circled back to the door they'd left propped open.

"Strange trap," Lark said.

Daciana pulled her blades from their sheaths. Lark tossed back her cloak to tug her bow into a lowered position.

A shape appeared in the doorway, and a powerful scent of rose filled the room, both sweet and musky. Lark yanked an arrow from her quiver and nocked it, gritting her teeth against the added strength of the pull.

The strike of a flint, a torch was lit, illuminating the room. Flickers of flame danced along opposite walls, dueling for dominance. But in a room so large, the dark swallowed the light.

A woman stepped through. Her black hair was coiled at the nape of her neck, not a strand out of place, her pale face, severe. A grim line formed her mouth and her eyes were so dark they almost looked black. She paced up to them, casually and assured. Her fine, satin gown of burgundy and lace swished with each step. "You can lower your weapons, I'm not here to hurt you."

"I'll be the judge of that," Lark said, but Daciana placed a hand on her bow to lower it.

"Who are you?"

The woman ran her unyielding gaze over the two of them, thorough in her assessment. And her disappointment. "Neera."

"Are you the one who sent for us?"

"I am." Neera's voice was like the low scrape of a dry throat. "You've caused quite a stir in my place of business."

"Wait, you own The Tawdry Steward?" Lark asked with a laugh. "Did you choose the name?"

Neera turned her sharp stare on her. Her lip curled in disgust. "The name, along with everything else I handpick for my business, is a calculated decision. You foolish girl."

Lark tried not to smile. "Your business needs some new clientele."

"Are you so ignorant? I have built this establishment brick-by-brick. In a perfect world, I'd meet my monthly quota without finding new bruises on my girls. But this is the way of things. I can either rise above, or crumble beneath the weight of it all."

Lark's hands fisted by her sides. She understood all too well the limitations of being born to a world too small. "Well, you've done a fine job. If you don't require our help—"

"Help? Dear girl, do you really think you could ever help me?" Neera's features slanted in disgust.

"You sent for us under the guise of needing help. Forgive us for assuming you'd accept it." Daciana maintained her calm composure.

"Are you not the ones who killed Sir Talbot? Left his men's bodies in the hallway?" Neera blinked at them. The edges of her ghostly pale face tightened. "It would be in your best interest to choose your next words wisely."

"Technically, he killed himself," Lark said. The others were Gavriel's doing.

Daciana silenced her with a harsh look before turning back to Neera. "We apologize if we placed you or your girls in any jeopardy."

"You put my whole enterprise in jeopardy." Neera's eyes held a flash of rage, before they cooled to calculated indifference. "He was one of my most loyal patrons. Beaten to death, skull bashed in when he was most vulnerable. Half-naked, on display for the world to see. How am I to expect anyone to dally among my wares if they fear being murdered with their pants around their ankles?"

Lark snorted. It wasn't funny. Far from it. But the sheer absurdity of it all pulled the involuntary reaction from her chest, and Neera shot her an icy glare.

"You're not being threatened by his men," Daciana said. It wasn't a question, it was an accusation. She gripped the hilt of her dagger.

"Why would they threaten me when I've promised to deliver you to their charge?" Neera's mouth curved into a hint of a smile.

Lark's stomach sank like a stone. They'd known this was a trap. But still she'd held out hope it was under duress to lure them out here like this.

Perhaps hope was a human failing.

Daciana eyed Neera, tracking every movement. "We came to help. Don't turn this into a bloodbath."

"I don't care what you came for. You are no longer my problem. You or your spider."

Lark searched Daciana's face for a hint of understanding, only to be met by granite.

"I assume this belongs to you." Neera half turned to the doorway. The unmistakable sound of armored footsteps rang beyond the threshold, before a squad of guards filed in. Lark raised her bow, her nerves easing the effort it took to nock the arrow. She took aim at the throat of a faceless guard. Faceless, because that's how she needed to see them. A means to an end, nothing more.

Daciana spun her daggers into place, lowering into a crouch.

"I wouldn't do that if I were you," a low voice called from the shadows.

Lark's gaze snagged on something in the corner.

Kneeling between two guards, hands bound behind his back, was Gavriel. His face was a vicious mockery of the Gavriel she knew. An ensnared animal. The gag pressed into the corners of his mouth. A gash through his brow, and blood trailing down his cheek. Swollen bruising encircled his eye and tinged the line of his cheekbone.

Shit.

"Lower your bow, lest you want to see more of his blood spilt." A blade pressed against Gavriel's neck. He bit into his gag, as if trying to use his teeth to free himself.

The bumbling fool.

Lark dropped her bow. It clattered to the ground, echoing off the walls.

"I found him creeping along the walls of my place like a spider. I called the guard and informed them you'd sent along a spy to infiltrate my humble business." Neera raised her chin at them. "Is it not enough to steal from my pocket?" She gave a dismissive wave of her hand and turned to a stern looking man with a crop of dark hair and sharp brown eyes, as if he spent most of his days searching for trouble. "Captain Andros, I'll consider this matter settled and I expect you to keep your promise of loyal patronage."

Andros nodded even as he scowled. "Yes ma'am. We can take it from here."

With one last look of disgust, Neera swept out of the room, her

255

burgundy gown and overpowering perfume trailing behind her. Daciana looked like she was thinking of a dozen different ways to kill that woman.

"You can drop those too," Andros said to Daciana.

Daciana held her blades out to the side and dropped them unceremoniously onto the floor. Two guards immediately swarmed her, pulling her hands behind her head as they searched her. Her expression never wavered from calm indifference as they found dozens of knives, daggers, her axe, a short sword. Lark marveled at how much she was able to stash in her clothes.

Andros rounded on Lark, his nose inches from hers. Wariness and age lined his face and the corners of his dark eyes. He grinned and held out his hand. With shaking fingers, Lark turned over the knife Hugo had given her, wanting nothing more than to slap the smug smile from his face. "You'll regret this," Lark said.

Andros' smile turned feral. "Check this one thoroughly."

He turned on his heel, walking back to where Gavriel struggled against his binds. He leaned in close to whisper something in his ear. Gavriel's expression turned murderous as he fought even harder.

Someone tugged Lark's arms out to the side, yanking her cloak and quiver off her back. Hands roughly patted her down, running over her arms and legs. A kick in the back of her leg dropped her to her knees, her gaze never straying from where Gavriel twisted to get free.

A sharp tug on her hair yanked her head back, and her eyes pricked with tears.

The last thing she saw was a cloth covered hand that smothered her nose and mouth.

And then darkness.

CHAPTER 26

*T*he ground beneath Lark was moving.

A jarring bump knocked the side of her head against the wood floor. Uncurling her legs, Lark tried to sit up. But her arms wouldn't move. Fear tightened in her chest as she glanced around. Her hands were bound behind her back. Thick rope burned her wrists as she twisted. More rope encircled her ankles, keeping her feet pressed together.

Lark wriggled her arms down her back, pressing her heels to the floor as she struggled to fit her hands beneath her backside. She rolled to her side, pulling with all her strength, and gritting her teeth. The rope tugged with an audible groan against the delicate skin of her wrists. Folding her legs, she yanked her hands past her feet until she pulled them through.

Lark rested her head against the splintered planks of the dingy floor. Deep brownish-red stains had seeped into the grains. She rolled to her back, and dark, hazy spots filled her vision. Blinking them away, she gazed up at the aged wood ceiling. The low light of a fading day crept through a small, barred window, too narrow and too high for escape.

Memories of a dank warehouse flooded back to her. Daciana's

hands behind her head, her eyes cold and calculating. Gavriel, bound and bloodied, fighting to free himself. The cold terror that gripped Lark's heart at the sight, squeezing until she could scarcely breathe. And then darkness.

A grunt sounded from the corner.

Lark sat up, her head spinning.

Gavriel. He leaned against the opposite wall, watching her, his wrists shackled in irons behind his back, his mouth gagged. His unyielding stare surveyed her, traveling over every inch in concentrated assessment.

"Daciana?" Lark rasped. She winced at the sensation, like swallowing glass. How long had it been since she last drank?

Gavriel's gaze flickered to the corner. Daciana laid bound—and far too still. Her dark hair hid her face and pooled on the wood floor. Lark scooted toward her, ignoring the aches in her arms. Another bump jolted her. They were in the back of a wagon. A traveling prison.

Gavriel observed her efforts. The bruising around his eye was already yellowing at the edges. How much time had passed?

"Are you all right?"

Gavriel raised his blood-crusted eyebrow and shrugged.

Lark kept wriggling, propelling forward with her bound feet, to where Daciana lay. They had stripped her of her cloak, and blood stained the neck of her threadbare tunic, but Lark couldn't find any wounds. She pressed her ear to Daciana's chest, listening. Her heartbeat was steady and strong. Thank the skies. Shackles and heavy chains gripped Daciana's wrists, connecting her to an iron ring on the floor. Lark was the only one bound by mere rope. She tried not to take offense by that fact—by the assumption she was less of a threat. It would serve her well when they managed to escape.

"Do you know where we're going?"

Gavriel nodded.

Lark dragged herself to his side and pulled the gag from his mouth and brought it beneath his chin.

He winced at the movement, the corners of his mouth were red and raw.

"Are you all right?" His baritone voice rumbled through her.

Lark ignored the concern in his voice and what it did to her stomach. "You said you knew where we're going."

"Isn't it obvious? They're taking us to the coast. Most likely to sail to Koval and sell us to work in the mines." His mouth tightened, and he cast his eyes to the roof of their cage. "If we're very lucky."

Lark nodded. She'd reaped enough souls from the mines of the Bereft Coast to know. The mines were where people were forgotten. Worked to death until they were nothing more than ash and dust and a distant memory. Though, not everyone made it there. Some were carted off and sold in the market, where all manner of horrors awaited them.

"We can't let that happen." Lark grabbed his face in her hands, pulling him to look at her, even as the rope bit her wrists with the action. "I won't let that happen."

His eyes bore into hers, searching. The gold flecks against dark green were like catching rays of sunlight filtered through a forest of pine. He looked away when the wagon slowed. "They'll be checking on us."

Lark shoved the gag into place, apologizing when he grunted in discomfort, and rolled back to her side just in time for the door to swing open.

"Oh, you're awake. Good, I was worried they overdosed you." An unfamiliar man with a thick beard and an ill-fitting guard uniform hauled himself into the wagon. He wore the colors of Ardenas, blue and white, with a plain breastplate poorly fastened in place. He huffed across the cramped space until he stood over Lark.

Gavriel stiffened.

"Don't try anything stupid," their captor warned, kneeling before her.

Lark scurried away from him. He grabbed her by the rope encircling her ankles and yanked her forward.

"Relax lass, you're not my type. Besides, I prefer to be the one tied

259

up." He offered Gavriel a wink, and Gavriel glared back. The guard grabbed Lark by the back of the head and yanked her forward to drink from his canteen.

The water sloshed over her chin, filling her mouth and throat. She coughed at the sudden loss of air.

He dropped her abruptly, and she fell back against the floor. Shaking his head and muttering something about being ungrateful, he slammed the door shut behind him. The sharp click of the lock echoed off the four close walls of the cabin.

Lark leaned up, kicked off the wall, and scooted back to where Gavriel sat. She yanked his gag out again. "What have they done to Daciana?"

"They gave her an extra dose of the same toxin they used on us."

Whatever they'd given them, it was potent. Lark wished she knew what properties it contained. It was worth having in their gamut of tactics. "How long was I out?"

"Two days."

So long? That must be why she felt famished. Her stomach growled in response.

"I'm thinking it's some sort of concentrated form of valerian and Sleep of Death," Gavriel said. "Not to worry, it's more to promote deep sleep than anything else. When we'd take shifts at all hours, the night watchers would use it to get rest during daylight. It's probably harmless." He glanced over at Daciana, curled on her side, and frowned. "They were quite frightened of her after she kicked one of them in the jaw. I'm pretty sure he bit off a piece of his tongue."

"It's no more than they deserve."

"I should think so. I thought Daciana was going to kill them, bound and all. I'm still convinced she might. She didn't take too well to their threats toward you." Something hardened in Gavriel's voice.

Lark cast her eyes elsewhere. A squirming in her chest made her shift uncomfortably. "We can't go to Koval. I need to find the woman who can connect me to the Otherworld. Every second we delay the tears get worse."

"One crisis at a time," Gavriel said, a hint of annoyance in his tone.

A low groan came from the corner. Lark dragged herself over to Daciana. Daciana sat up, a groggy expression on her face. At least she was awake.

"Thank the skies! Are you all right?" A dangerous giddiness spilled through Lark. Perhaps hysteria.

Daciana's eyes widened as she took in her surroundings. "We need to get out of here."

"Yes. I have a plan. Well, not a plan, more of a rough idea. Fine, I don't have any ideas but yes, we'll get out of here." Lark grinned at her.

Daciana shook her head. "You need to get away from me. Now. Over to Gavriel." She kicked, trying to push Lark away.

Confused, Lark reached a hand toward her. "What are you talking about?"

"Go! You can't be near me, please go!"

"Okay..." Lark moved back toward Gavriel, and worry coiled in her belly. "Daciana, tell me what's going on."

"If we don't get out of this cart before sundown..." Daciana exhaled a long breath. "I don't want to hurt you."

Daciana was worried about harming her? Lark shook her head. "Why would you hurt me?"

"I wouldn't, but I can't take any chances."

"You're not making any sense." Lark leaned back, her hair spilling over Gavriel's shoulder. He turned his face as far from her as possible.

"Do you trust me?" Daciana's stare was intense and pleading.

"Of course, I do. Do you trust me?" Lark fired back. If Daciana was worried about harming her, the least she could do was say why.

Daciana sighed. "You know I do."

"Then tell me what happens at sundown." Lark knew she was being unfair, but a small part of her was wounded by the notion Daciana had something she couldn't tell her.

Even though Lark held a secret or two.

Daciana opened her mouth, closing it before any words slipped out.

Lark fought back the ache in her chest, leaning into Gavriel further. In the far recesses of her mortal heart, she mourned this simple truth: Trust only went so far.

"Could you please not do that?" Gavriel's voice came out strained, through gritted teeth.

"What am I doing?" Lark turned to look at him, taking in the line of his jaw.

His eyes slipped closed as he exhaled. "I don't feel like breathing and eating your hair."

Lark pushed away from him, cursing both of her travel companions as they edged closer and closer to a life of slave labor. Her confined ankles bounced with frenetic energy.

Daciana had curled back in on herself, angled as far from them as possible.

This wasn't supposed to happen.

Lark traded everything to be free—weakened compared to her previous form, but free to choose her path, free to live her life, free to *feel*. But ever since she stumbled into this world, it was a constant pendulum swinging between extremes. Joy and despair. Fear and triumph. Were mortals slaves to their own emotions?

Lark glared at the blood-stained floorboards, and hot tears filled her vision, threatening to spill over. Her human emotions still felt too large to contain. Like being cut off from feeling for so long had dimmed her ability to hold the sensations of humanity in one body. Those traitorous tears trailed down her cheeks, leaving burning shame in their wake.

"Are you crying?" Gavriel's voice had gone uncharacteristically soft.

"No," Lark said, her voice thick. "You're crying."

A low scrape that sounded suspiciously close to a laugh rumbled in his chest. "It's not all bad." His eyes searched her face. "There's something to be said about manual labor. I mean, I've heard it can be back-breaking, and many die never seeing the sun again, but you'll have a productive sort of day. Not many can say that."

Fresh tears rolled down Lark's cheeks as her chest tightened. Another life, another cage.

"Oh, that was meant to lighten the mood," Gavriel said, his tone soothing, apologetic. "It's not going to happen. We'll get out of this, and I will personally see to it you fix the mess you caused. I promise." He gave her a crooked grin. "That was another joke, but my promise is true."

Lark wiped her cheeks. Why did he care?

"Didn't you want to escape Ardenas anyway?"

Gavriel frowned. "Yes, but not like this. I'd rather spend my days in hiding as a free man, if possible. And besides," he said, as he nudged her with his shoulder. "I'm not leaving until I help you."

Her voice left her lips in a hushed breath. "Why?"

"I owe you a life debt and I'm not leaving you until it's paid." His voice was hard and fervent. His sharp jaw clenched as his scarred mouth thinned in a firm line. His unyielding gaze scorched her skin in its relentless pursuit.

Lark ignored the heat on her cheeks and the way her heart pounded. "So, how will we get out of this?"

"Oh, that. Well, we have Daciana. We can get out of anything so long as she protects us."

Lark gave a watery laugh.

A soft smile spread across Gavriel's face. He gestured with his shoulder for her to come closer. "Come on, I don't mind eating some hair."

"Don't ruin it." Lark leaned her head against his shoulder. Hesitantly he let his head rest atop hers. His familiar scent of autumn's return enveloped her, and she closed her eyes.

LARK STARTLED. Having settled comfortably in her position at Gavriel's side, she'd almost nodded off. She turned to see Gavriel's eyes closed, his mouth relaxed of its usual grim line. A silvery veil of moonlight spilled through the bars in the small window, casting an ethereal glow about the space.

Lark glanced over at Daciana.

Daciana's usually calm face was twisted in anguish. Teeth bared in excruciating effort.

A slick creeping dread slid through Lark's blood, freezing her veins. "Daciana?" Her voice wavered. "What's wrong?"

Gavriel stirred, cracking an eye to peer down at Lark.

Daciana's breath hissed through her teeth.

Lark scooted toward her, concern winning out over fear.

Daciana's eyes widened in panic. "Don't!"

"What's happening?"

Daciana twisted away. A sheen of sweat shone against her forehead. "Lark, please," she said, biting into her lip hard enough blood stained her teeth. "I have to do this as quietly as possible." She grunted, flipping to her back, arching as far as the chains would allow.

Lark edged closer. Desperately trying to slow the rapid pounding of her human heart. Light-headed and numb, she reached out with shaky, bound hands.

"What's wrong with her?" Gavriel asked, alert concern sharpening his voice.

Daciana opened her mouth in a silent scream, her eyes clamped shut. Her back exaggerated its arch, snapping the chain across her body hard enough to fling it across the cabin. Her arms, still shackled behind her back, yanked out of their sockets with a sickening pop. They hung, dangling at an unnatural angle.

Lark ignored her human instinct of repulsion at the ghastly sight. She swallowed both fear and bile as she crept closer.

Somewhere behind Daciana, the iron shackles dropped heavy against the floor. She rose on her haunches, throwing her head back so her black curtain of hair hung down over her calves.

Lark froze. Paralyzed as she watched her friend twist and bend in silent agony.

Daciana threw herself forward, landing on her chest. Rising to her hands and knees, she dipped her head. Her face fell hidden behind a dark wall of hair. A low growl emanated from her chest as she curled in on herself.

The back of Daciana's tunic ripped open, revealing dark grey fur.

"Get back!" Distantly, Lark heard Gavriel call to her, but it faded to the background of the blood thrumming in her ears.

Daciana's hands shifted, the bones cracking under her dark skin. They reformed into large claws. Dark, grey fur sprouted over them. She shook off the remnants of her human clothes, lifting her large furry head to stare at Lark.

Lark released a tight breath, tension never ceasing its death grip on her throat.

Daciana's hazel eyes stared back at her. They were Daciana's eyes, there was no doubt about that. A low growl rumbled from the wolf.

"Well, shit." Lark's voice came out soft and breathy. Holding her hands out in front of her, she crept closer to the wolf. To Daciana.

The wolf's eyes tracked her, assessing.

With careful movements, Lark lifted her hands in supplication.

Another low growl loosed from the wolf's chest. Deep and cautionary.

Lark froze.

"Slowly make yourself larger." Gavriel's hushed whisper filled the heavy silence.

Lark shook her head. "I'm not dominant over her. We're equals."

"What?" Gavriel hissed. "For fuck's sake, get away from it!"

With eye contact locked in place, never wavering, Lark tried to pour every ounce of trust into her stare. Letting her face reflect the feelings she knew so keenly in her soul. This was her friend. She would not hurt her. Lark blinked slowly, dipping her chin.

"I see you there. I trust you." Despite Lark's certainty, her voice was a feeble, quivering thread.

The wolf's hazel eyes bore into hers, intelligent and assessing. She lowered her snout ever so slightly, letting her haunches sink to the floor, and she sat in a less defensive posture.

A tight laugh left Lark's mouth. "You're a wolf." The words were absurd, but the fact was hard to dismiss. "I have so many questions." She did have so many questions, best reserved for a time when she could get proper answers.

Werewolves weren't unheard of, but they were rare. In the mortal world, the belief in werewolves wasn't so common, about as common as the belief in the old ways. The belief in monsters and Undesirables. But werewolves weren't Undesirables, they were alive. Lark hadn't heard of any wolf reapings in years.

Skies, did Kenna know? Did the boys?

None of it mattered. This was her friend, her ally. There would be time for questions after they escaped.

Lark grinned, her heart hammering in her chest. "Could you help me with these?" She held her hands out, still bound by rope, giving Daciana enough space to close the distance herself.

"What in the infernal nethers is happening?" Gavriel's voice held an edge of panic

Lark shot a glance at him. He appeared ready to throw himself between them.

The wolf raised her head, sensing the air. Tail raised, she took slow assured steps toward Lark, each action measured and testing.

Lark gave a small smile, nodding.

The wolf sniffed at the rope before clamping her razor-sharp teeth over it and roughly gnawing through it. The tattered remains fell from Lark's wrists and fluttered to the floor. A smile pulled at Lark's mouth, and she flung her arms around the wolf's neck. Gavriel sucked in an audible breath.

She pulled back and searched Daciana's lupine face. She was still gorgeous. All raw power.

Lark untied her ankles, kicking her legs free. After they were out of this filthy, reeking wagon, she'd never complain about feeling trapped by the forest again.

Gavriel twisted in his shackles. "I still need to pick these," he said, a sullen tone to his voice.

"Wait, the only way this will work is if he comes in all the way to check." Lark gave an apologetic look to Gavriel, before yanking his gag back in place. "We can't tip them off too early." She settled back in her spot against the opposite wall, pulling the bindings over her legs and tucking them underneath her to appear taut.

Lark caught Gavriel's eye, then Daciana's. She nodded toward the corner and Daciana trotted over to the shadowed junction beside the door, out of sight.

"Okay, are we ready?"

No response greeted her.

"I'll regard that as a yes. Now, Daciana, when he comes in, I need you to incapacitate him." Lark sucked in a deep breath, readying herself. One thing her altercation with Talbot had taught her, the ease with which one overlooks that which they perceive as weaker than they.

A mortal failing.

"Hey! I need assistance!" Lark hollered, hoping only the one lackey would check on her.

For a moment, the steady roll of the wagon wheels didn't waver, and no one answered. Until their speed slowed to a crawl, and finally the traveling prison halted.

Wiping the grin from her mouth, and twisting her face in an expression of pain, Lark waited.

The door slammed open, bashing against the cabin wall. Sharp moonlight shot across the wagon floor, lighting up all the bloodstains both faded and fresh.

"What do you want?" The man barked as he stomped toward her, stopping to loom directly above. He'd ditched his tight-fitting breastplate and was clad in only his Ardenian tunic.

Lark squirmed. "I need to relieve myself."

He raised his eyebrows. "You think I give a shit? Piss in your pants."

Gavriel had scooted far enough to nudge the door shut with the heel of his boot. Darkness bloomed against the tight space.

The man spun on his heel.

"What in the—"

Daciana leapt into action, tackling him. Claws raked through his skin like a knife through butter, leaving his chest in ribbons. Wet blood glinted in the dark and pooled beneath him.

Lark threw herself forward, clamping her hands over his mouth, closing off his scream. She locked eyes with him, absorbing his terror.

The last seconds of his mortal life, a burden they shared. Then, slowly, his gaze lost focus. Pain dimming, life fading. Cold emptiness left in its stead.

Lark hauled herself off him, staggered to the corner, and dropped to her knees. Her stomach heaved, purging the small amount of water she'd been given and scorching bile. She wiped her mouth with the back of her hand, and blinked the tears from her eyes. On deceptively steady legs, Lark approached the lifeless man and shoved her hand in his pocket, searching for keys. She tried not to think about who might come to collect his soul or what they'd see when they looked at her.

Daciana sat down beside her, and Lark ignored her blood-stained jaws, yanking a set of lock picks from the guard's trousers. Finding Gavriel's side, she dropped to one knee and pressed the lock pick into his hand still shackled behind his back. He closed his fingers over hers, holding her in place.

"Wait," he said.

"We need to hurry." Lark pulled her hand free, unable to stomach the contact. The final breath of a dead man still burned against her palm. "They'll notice he's missing."

Hugo once told her, killing never got easier. It was a burden they carried with them for the rest of their walk on this plane of existence. What if he was right?

What if he was wrong?

Gavriel rubbed his wrists, standing close to Lark. "We should search him for weapons."

Lark couldn't stand how soft his voice sounded. She gave a nod and knelt, searching with numb hands.

Gavriel managed to find an unremarkable short sword and a dull bladed dagger. He held both out to Lark. She plucked the dagger from his palm. He brandished the short sword in the air as if it were the finest rapier.

"Stay behind me."

"Stay behind Daciana." Lark made to pass him, but he held up a hand.

Gavriel's eyes narrowed. "Just, don't do anything stupid."

"Like what? Trail you and get captured forcing us to surrender?"

Gavriel exhaled. Mouth tight. "Fair enough."

Lark pushed past him and pressed her ear against the door. With luck, they wouldn't be traveling with a large party. She listened to the various muffled voices on the other side of the door. They didn't have long.

She turned back, looking between Gavriel and Daciana. The wolf sat poised, ready for attack. Gavriel stood, sword at the ready, waiting for her signal.

Lark leaned against the wall, behind the hinges of the door. Now it was only a matter of time until someone came looking for the dead man in the center of the wagon. His sweat and blood were a greasy film on Lark's palms. She wiped her hands on her leggings.

After a heartbeat or two, the door swung open, and moonlight trickled across the floor.

"If you damaged any of the merchandise Lonnie, I swear to the gods..."

Lark grabbed him, yanking him inside and spinning to press him against the wall, her blade pressed to his throat. It wasn't as sharp as she preferred, so it would take more force on her part to cut the skin.

"Don't speak," Lark whispered. "Don't say another word lest you want to end up like him."

His eyes darted behind her, to the mangled mess of human remains on the floor.

"You—"

A flash of a blade, severing his jugular, and blood poured over her hands. Lark gaped at Gavriel, her stomach rolling.

Gavriel shrugged. "You gave him fair warning."

"Next time," Lark said as she stepped back, letting his body drop. "Give me fair warning."

THE NEXT GUARD TO enter was smarter than the last, choosing to remain silent when told.

Lark pressed a blade to his thin neck, taking shallow breaths to avoid inhaling the scent of his fear. His curly red hair clung to his forehead, matted with sweat. "How many of you are there?"

His brown eyes darted around wildly.

"You can speak." Lark shook him.

"There are five armed guards." He swallowed audibly. "Two mounted."

"Seven in all?"

"Yes, ma'am."

"Seven?" Gavriel asked. "That's it? Insulting."

Lark shot him a dark look before turning back to the sweating man. "Why are you doing this?" she demanded. "Where is your conscience that you can drag innocents into a life of shackles?"

He shook his head.

Rage mounted in her chest—rage at the sins of these men, at the sins her hands had committed. At the helplessness of awakening, bound and drugged, at the call for blood that ignited her senses. "Answer me."

"Is there an answer that'll stay your hand?" Gavriel asked. "You know what needs to be done. Don't draw it out."

Lark offered a quick nod. Where was Alistair's sense of right-eousness? His unwavering faith that what they were doing was right? The lesser evil? She searched, plundering the very depths of her soul in search of that comfort.

She never found it.

Turning back to the man, she looked him square in the eye.

"I'm sorry." She meant it. She meant it as she plunged her blade into the side of his throat, yanking it back out with a squelch. She meant it as her stomach dropped with the fresh wave of warm blood painting her hands. Lark took a step back, colliding with Gavriel's firm chest.

His hands found her shoulders, steadying her, and she shrugged out of his hold. Daciana waited patiently, her hazel eyes watching intently.

Gavriel sighed, frowning. "Seven isn't that many, especially if we just took out three of them. But he could have been lying. Make it quick, make it clean if you can. I'm eager for this night to be over."

Lark braced a hand on the splintered wood of the door. "As am I," she said, as she tugged it open.

Two guards a few paces away spun to face her. They paled when they saw Lark's blood red hands. Yanking their swords from their sheaths, they barreled toward her, and as they drew near, Lark stepped aside.

The grey wolf came leaping out and sank her teeth into the throat of the nearest guard. His eyes glazed as the pall of death and blood-loss muted his face. A second guard raised his sword to strike, but the clash of Gavriel's blade halted its path toward Daciana's back.

With a vicious smile that promised death, Gavriel spun the sword away. The sharp metallic clash of steel cut through the air. He advanced with razor-sharp reflexes, parrying each strike and dodging faster than the armored guard's attacks. The smile only grew on Gavriel's face. He was an ever-moving target, like a wisp of smoke.

Two men rushed to flank him. Disarming his first opponent, Gavriel spun his sword behind his back, parrying and counter-striking. He possessed more grace than this bloody skirmish deserved.

Lark spun the dagger in her hand, flipping it into a more natural position, and lunged for one of Gavriel's attackers. She plunged her knife into the gap in the guardsman's armor under his arm. She wrenched the blade free and slammed it into his eye.

Pulling back, she gave a wide berth between herself and yet another human life snuffed out.

Gavriel cut down the other with a swift slice across the throat. The sight was both grotesque and beautiful. Stunning violence—its harmony both whispered and bellowed.

A deep growl was Lark's only warning before the grey wolf pounced.

Lark watched, numb, as the wolf tore out another guard's throat. Blood dripped down her mashing jaws, and the moonlight illuminated a halo of light around her lupine features. The visceral beauty of raw power unleashed, of bloodlust curdling the air.

Someone yelled. Lark blinked, trying to decipher the sound. But all that remained was unintelligible resonance. Like being shoved underwater.

Before sharp pain bloomed in her chest.

Lark gaped at the protruding arrow. Everything narrowed to the bloodied shaft jutting out from her blood-stained tunic. Her shaking fingers ghosted against the spine of the intrusion. Fire lanced through her chest at the contact, and a cry ripped from her lips. Her legs gave out, and the whole world tilted as she hit the ground.

"Lark!"

She heard Gavriel's outcry. Felt his blind terror. Lark's dimming gaze trailed down to the blood-stained sand. Cold crept through her, dancing along her veins, and her eyes fluttered closed as she succumbed to the darkness once more.

CHAPTER 27

*N*ereida had warned Lark she knew nothing of pain. Lifetimes as a Reaper had dulled her senses, including any concept of agony.

The witch was right.

Lark sucked in a breath through her teeth, and the world came catapulting back into focus. The sharp light of the moon on the glistening sand, and the pain. She winced as her sudden consciousness brought the scorching sting of the arrow lodged in her chest.

She tried to sit up, but a strong hand held her firm.

"Be still," Gavriel said, his voice tight.

Lark focused on the crease of his brow and the blood splattered across his face. Reaching a shaking hand toward him, she ran her thumb along the scar on his cheek. He caught her hand and lowered it to her lap. But he didn't let go.

Gavriel's eyes darted between her face and the arrow protruding from her chest. She followed his gaze.

"Can you pull it out?" Lark asked weakly.

"I have nothing to staunch the bleeding or ease the pain."

She nodded, and the motion made her vision spin. "How do we get it out?"

"I need to cut off the arrowhead, so I don't cause more damage removing it than it caused going in."

Lark swallowed down the tang of blood on her tongue and tried to keep her voice steady. "That sounds simple enough."

"I can't remove it if it's close to any major arteries or your heart. I won't be able to stop the bleeding in time." He tightened his grip. His hand was so much larger than hers. The rough calluses on his palm—a sensation she was determined to commit to memory.

"How can you tell?" A fresh wave of pain pulsed in her chest. The shock was wearing off, every nerve waking again.

She thought of all the harrowing wounds she'd inflicted on others without a thought to how they suffered. Her gaze fell to the sand, to the limp, lifeless body nearest her. Who was here collecting these souls?

Gavriel inspected the entry wound closely, squinting to see in the pale moonlight. He exhaled a breath of relief. "It appears to be closer to your shoulder, and it went all the way through. Small mercies."

"Oh, how lucky I am." Lark's words tasted bitter, and coated in blood. The undercurrent of hysteria added a sharp note of fear she was distinctly trying to ignore.

A small smile tugged at his mouth, stretching the scar against his lip. "As I said, I have nothing for the pain, nor to stop the bleeding."

"Use your shirt."

Gavriel's smile turned teasing. "We're filthy, I'm not putting grime and disease in your open wound."

Lark was sure she had a retort ready on her tongue, but her mouth wouldn't cooperate.

"If I had a flame, I could cauterize it." He looked at her, uncertainty etched on his face. "But it would hurt."

"This hurts."

The grey wolf padded over, nudging the side of Lark's head with her snout.

"Skies, this is so strange," Gavriel muttered. "Give me a moment to see if I can't find a torch on any of them." He placed her hand down on her stomach with more gentleness than she thought he possessed, and hurried over to the mass grave the road had become.

Daciana whined, tilting her head.

"I'm fine." Lark chuckled, wincing at the sting it caused. "I just... have you ever had a bad day and thought to yourself 'there's no way this could get any worse' and then you get shot by an archer?"

The wolf somehow managed to throw a sardonic expression her way, earning her another painful laugh.

Gavriel approached, carrying a blazing torch. Warm light spilled across his face, illuminating every bruise and gash. Along with the tight line of his mouth. Kneeling by Lark, he yanked a serrated dagger he'd looted off a slaver corpse from his pocket.

"This would be a lot easier with a second set of hands." He heated the blade over the flame. Propping the torch against a rock, he gently lifted her to sit up. "You're going to want to move. Don't."

Lark rolled her eyes. A regrettable action that sent her vision spinning again. "Were those supposed to be words of comfort?"

Gavriel rose to his feet and yanked his belt off. Folding it in half, he brought it to her lips. "Bite down. This is going to hurt."

Blinking up at him, Lark took a deep, steadying breath. She opened her mouth and sank her teeth into the leather.

With the first swipe of steel against the shaft, she groaned into his belt. Each pass of the blade vibrated through her, and panic mounted in her already crowded chest.

"Don't move." Gavriel ran the blade forward and back with enough efficiency to suggest this wasn't his first time cutting an arrow loose.

The arrowhead dropped to the sand with a whistle, and Lark inhaled slowly. The cool night breeze carried the coppery scent of blood. Gavriel steadied her shoulder and gripped the rest of the arrow invading her body.

Lark met his gaze, silently pleading.

His eyebrows lifted in apology before he yanked.

The tug in her chest ripped the air from her lungs in a muffled scream. Lark sobbed against the leather between her teeth, and she gripped his shoulder, digging as hard as she could to keep from flailing.

Lark's vision darkened, and she fought to maintain consciousness.

"Lark, stay with me. I need to pull harder." Gavriel squeezed her shoulder, shaking her. "I need you to try not to follow the pull of the arrow. Stay firm so it comes free." His voice was hard and desperate.

Nothing else existed outside of his hand, tugging at the very bottom of her well of strength. Lark shifted her unfocused gaze to his face. To the beads of sweat along his forehead. His furrowed brows. His dark green eyes that appeared black in the shadows. Tears rolled down her cheeks as she nodded.

Grimacing, Gavriel yanked, pulling the shaft free from her chest.

Lark fell forward, gasping, and warm blood trickled down the front of her tunic.

With a curse, Gavriel shifted behind her and hauled her against his chest. Lark was vaguely aware of his heart hammering against her back. Black spots danced in her vision. She tilted her head back to look up at him.

Gavriel braced one arm across her chest, holding her against him while the other held his blade over the flame of the torch. The sharp line of his jaw was clenched so hard it looked like his teeth would ache.

He brought the dagger back, heat radiating from the steel. He ripped the neck of her tunic enough to expose the entry wound and angled the blade over it. He paused to offer his only warning.

"Don't watch."

Blazing steel pressed against her chest, and a sharp cry tore from Lark's throat, muffled by the belt between her teeth. The blade scorched and seared the wound closed, and her scream turned guttural, something primal howling in pain.

The acrid smell of burning flesh burned her nose and sent a fresh wave of dizziness through her.

When he finally lifted the dagger, she collapsed against him. Everything had gone hazy, and Lark's eyes fluttered as she clung to consciousness. She let the belt fall from her mouth, unable to keep her jaw tight.

A warm hand rubbed down her arm.

"I have to close up your back."

Lark pressed forward, her forehead resting against packed sand, silvery and sparkling in the moonlight. She twisted her neck to look at Daciana. The wolf sat watching and unable to help. Gavriel yanked Lark's shirt high enough to expose her spine. Likely he didn't want to ruin the garment by ripping the back too. Had he given her a chance to gather her words, she might have told him not to bother.

He didn't wait.

He seared more skin to close the exit wound. This time she couldn't scream. The pain devoured her voice. When the dagger hit the ground with a twang, Lark knew he'd flung it away upon finishing. Likely never to hold an edge again.

All strength in her limbs dissipated, and stars swam in her vision. Gavriel lifted her, and without thinking, she turned her face toward the solid wall of his chest.

"If I can find the concoction they used to make us sleep, do you want me to give it to you?" His warm breath fanned against her face.

Lark forced her hazy eyes to meet his. "Don't think I'll need it." The words dripped from her lips, heavy and liquid as they rolled off her thick tongue.

"It'll help with the pain. Please."

She shook her head. No, she didn't want to be drugged again. If she could avoid that particular experience for the rest of her human life, she'd be grateful. Gavriel sighed heavily with disapproval but said nothing.

There was only one remaining horse—the other must have fled during the fight. Gavriel lifted her into the saddle, and Lark gripped the reins with shaking hands. He swung in behind her, wrapping one arm around her waist, the other wrestling the reins from her uncooperative hands.

The wolf padded up to them, her intelligent eyes watching. Waiting.

"Can you find us a place to stay for the night?" Gavriel asked, tucking Lark against his chest.

The wolf took off running.

Gavriel urged the horse into a steady canter. Even as the tug of sleep beckoned, Lark's fading awareness whispered of how close she'd been. Of being carted off, sold, and disappearing as if her mortal life never existed.

The wind rushed through Lark's ears and tangled her hair. It carried the faintest scent of wood smoke. Grassy hills, bathed in moonlight, stretched endlessly before them. The forest would be a welcome refuge once more.

Lark sat higher in the saddle, groaning at the aching through her chest. She would find a way to reach Ferryn. Find out if the witch had held up her part of the bargain. She'd reach the woman in the woods. As long as she had the necklace from Kenna—

Lark's hand flew to her neck in a panic. The necklace was gone.

"We have to go back."

"That's madness. They'll soon discover their missing party. We need to put as much distance between us as possible," Gavriel said.

"Kenna's necklace is gone. We have to find it."

"I know where it is." Gavriel's breath ghosted against Lark's neck. "Andros confiscated everything when they captured you. He has it."

In a haze of memories, she recalled The Captain's sneer. The cruelty twisted on his unremarkable features.

"We need to get it back." A fraction of her strength had returned to her voice. Though her eyelids were getting heavier by the moment.

"Oh, I intend to."

The image of Gavriel struggling against his binds as they disarmed her was seared into her mind as surely as the scar she now bore on her chest.

Andros would answer for his crimes.

Lark leaned her head against Gavriel's solid chest. Her eyes slipped closed as the sweet relief of unconsciousness descended over her weary body.

GAVRIEL QUESTIONED his sanity in trusting a wolf to find shelter, but she proved her effectiveness. Daciana led them to a shallow cave at the edge of the forest. A relief that they would only have to watch one entrance for an attack.

The smell of wet stone greeted them, but it was a far cry from that filthy slavers' caravan.

Despite feeling restless, Gavriel needed the break to clear his thoughts. He immediately offered to take the first watch. Lark looked like she wanted to argue but lacked the strength.

Good. She needed the rest more than he.

Lark.

She laid on her side, the only comfortable position to sleep with her still-healing wound. Her face, smoothed of pain, and her long, dark eyelashes rested against the top of her cheek.

He turned away, staring into the blue pall of the night. He didn't want to look at her. Or remember she smelled sweet, like autumn and sun-ripened apples. He didn't want to think about her. Or the terror that gripped him over the past few days. Now, her sleeping form was a comfort. She looked serene almost. But hauled off in the back of the slavers' caravan—the stillness of drugged sleep—the memory of her limp body, bound and tossed into the wagon, still filled him with dread.

It could have been a lot worse.

In his youth, he'd begged the Masters of the Guild to consider putting a mark on the prime orchestrators of the slave trade in Koval. But challenging an operation that large required more than piss and vinegar, and it wasn't their jurisdiction. If the king permitted indentures to remain, to challenge that was to invite war.

Ardenas and Koval had long reached rapprochement. More of a 'live and let live' sort of policy. The Guild of Crows held their power in Ardenas, remaining as little more than whispers in Koval, unlike the Den of Lions, brash and arrogant, spilling blood for sport. They were a mockery of what it meant to hide in the shadows. Their flair for theatrics always disgusted Master Hamlin, and he credited their failure to the fact they always got caught up in public political schemes. The Lions had become little more than hired thugs, and turned to hosting the gauntlet at Aelcliff on the farthest edge of the Western Desolates. Death for honor, what a ridiculous idea. The Crows were above that.

Gavriel learned not to question. Not when he owed his very life to the Guild. The stone fortress. The training. The punishments. He was a weapon forged within its walls. His heart, body, and damned soul belonged to his home.

Only it wasn't his home anymore. It was his executioner.

None of that mattered so long as he had a purpose. He'd aid Lark to prevent more death and destruction. He'd get her to the Emerald Woods to meet with the sorceress, or whatever she was, and find a way to repay his debt.

Follow her into the damn void if that's what it took.

But where he once had strength, Gavriel found nothing but weakness. He hadn't anticipated how sloppy he'd become in his time on the run. His mistake in Brookhill was a stark contrast to the skill he relied on. He followed Lark and Daciana, intending to offer help from a distance. When that demon stopped to examine the instruments in the market, he lost himself. So impractical. He had to get closer to see what she was up to, and the moment her eyes lit up as the fiddler played, the sight struck him. He'd drawn closer still, shrouded beneath his cloak, to observe her. The way she moved to the music.

But when she smiled.

He was a weak man. Weaker still, because the memory of her face lighting up still haunted him. Though it was preferable to the moment his stupidity was on full display in that warehouse. When he kneeled in his shame as they caught her, all because of his mistake. And he was powerless to stop them.

She wasn't a demon.

She was Lark.

His head screamed her name over and over.

And when the arrow pierced her chest, and the blood roared in his ears. One thought remained.

Lark.

Lark made a soft sound in her sleep as she shifted.

Gavriel reached over to push a red lock of hair from her face, but he stilled.

What was he doing?

He retreated, stoking the fire with a long stick instead.

Not two months ago, he didn't even know this girl. Now he had a former Reaper hounding his thoughts, assassins of the Guild hunting him, and monsters roaming the earth?

There was also the matter of her werewolf friend. He'd almost forgotten about that. Between trying to escape and dealing with Lark's injury, he hadn't managed to process that information. Should he just learn to accept all matter of monsters as fact, and save himself some time and shock?

Gavriel ran a hand over his face, debating for the millionth time why he hung around.

He had his practical reasons. A life-debt needed to be repaid. There was also the advantage of having extra sets of eyes at his back so long as he was in Ardenas. But with each passing day, they seemed more and more like excuses. Explanations from afterthought rather than his driving force.

Once more, he looked over his shoulder at the sleeping girl with the auburn hair. The realization dawned; he had come to count her as a friend.

He'd had worse ones.

LARK AWOKE SORE AND HUNGRY. She braced her hand against the cold stone and sat up. Gavriel sat beside her, tending the fire. The muffled sound of wind skirting through the trees crept into the cave. A soft, low hum of melancholy. The shadow of the flame danced along his sharp jaw, the orange glow softening his features and deepening the scars adorning his face.

"How do you feel?"

He'd caught her staring.

"Starving." Lark glanced around, taking stock of her surroundings. They hadn't had the time to properly loot the corpses they paved the road with, and the sparse cave was an echoing chasm of all they had lost. "Where's Daciana?" Neither wolf nor warrior was anywhere to be found. Lark couldn't remember the journey here. Or laying down on a makeshift bedroll consisting of hers and Gavriel's cloaks.

Not waiting for an answer, she stood, only for her knees to buckle.

"You know you were shot yesterday, yes? Stop before you keel over. She's fine, and hopefully returning with breakfast soon."

Lark willed her head to still its spinning cacophony. Gavriel was right, but panic crept along the edges of her chest. Was it concern for Daciana, or something else?

Gavriel sighed. "I'm quite comfortable and I'd prefer to stay that way. But if you're determined to follow her, I'll just wait for you to pass out and carry you back." He shrugged, turning his back on her to face the fire again. "Your choice."

Lark was in no position to track her. Fabric wrapped around her chest and shoulder in a tight band. She prodded at the dark covering, a shock of pain lanced through her.

Gavriel made a noise in the back of his throat. "Don't touch it. We need to keep it covered for at least another two days."

They'd escaped, she'd been shot, and Daciana—

Daciana was a wolf. A werewolf. A living, breathing, entity of equal parts humanity and primordial ferocity.

Were there others? Where was her pack? From Lark's understanding, though limited at best, werewolves were fiercely loyal to their pack. Leaving one was agony. Like the severing of a soul.

The few times the soul of a werewolf had been reaped, it was never in isolation. Entire packs tended to band together both in life and in death. But it had been many years since Lark heard of any werewolf reaping.

Lark's hand drifted to her bare throat. She'd lost the talisman. The one Kenna promised would guarantee the hedge witch's help in contacting the Otherworld. Gavriel assured her they would return to pay Andros the visit he deserved, but that did little to assuage the unease in her gut.

Lark resumed her thorough study of Gavriel's face. His dark hair and the scruff on his face had grown. It suited him.

Scuffling footsteps rang from the mouth of the cave. A shadow darkened the entrance to their makeshift camp. Daciana stood, clad in a white, oversized tunic and black breeches she fastened with a rope around her slim waist. Her dark, windblown hair cascaded over her shoulders, along with a burlap sack.

"Thank the skies," Lark gasped. She wanted to leap from her seat and throw herself into Daciana's embrace. "Will you please get over here so I can hug you properly?"

Daciana breathed a tight laugh and glided to Lark's side, was that gracefulness a wolf attribute? She placed a gentle hand on Lark's arm, careful to avoid her injury.

Lark wasn't as careful.

She threw her arms around Daciana's neck, and a cry of pain ripped from her lips.

"What did I say?" Gavriel's voice was laced with annoyance.

"I didn't touch it." Lark refused to look at him. She ran her gaze over Daciana's face. Her hazel eyes, full of kindness, hinted at something heavier.

Lark hesitated, unsure how to begin. If she wasn't careful, a million questions would spill out.

"Did you bring food?" Gavriel asked, momentarily saving her the trouble. "Lark's bound to pass out if she doesn't eat soon."

When had he started using her name? The sound of it on his lips sent a thrill through her.

Daciana arched her brow, probably wondering the same thing. "I did." Reaching behind her, she grabbed the satchel. She pulled out an apple, handing it to Lark with a smile.

Lark grabbed it, cradling it in her hands. "You spoil me."

Daciana shook her head. "Eat. I've no doubt you have a thousand questions burning in your mind."

Daciana knew her so well. Needing no further invitation, Lark sank her teeth through the skin of the fruit. "So," Lark began around a mouthful of apple. She needed to rely on tact to broach the subject of Daciana's unearthed secret. "You're a werewolf."

Lark never had an abundance of tact.

Daciana nodded.

Gavriel stared into the fire, looking at neither of them. He was good at that—appearing disinterested while absorbing every word around him.

"Born or bitten?" Lark avoided using the word cursed. It seemed to convey something about Daciana that she didn't believe.

"Born. I came from a long line of wolves."

Interesting. She must be very powerful. "You are bound to the moon?"

"I am. Though I had the chance to master my, *legacy*." Daciana's mouth curved around the word with great care. "I walked a different path." She clasped her hands in her lap, the picture of poised calm. But her pulse jumped in her neck. It was a precarious thing. Knowing when to push and when to pull back.

"You have control as a wolf. Your mind remains your own." Lark wasn't asking. Never for a moment did she fear the wildness of the animal, for bright inquisitive intelligence shone in those hazel eyes.

"I—yes," Daciana said. "But there's always a moment I'm not sure if I'll remain. If the wolf is more than I am."

Lark took a large bite of apple, struggling to form the words around it. It was a stall tactic. Perhaps by the time she swallowed she'd sort out how to respond. Gavriel finally lifted his head, if only to watch her attempt speech with her cheeks full of fruit.

"Do the boys know?"

"They do. After months of traveling together, I had to tell them. It didn't feel right to let them put their lives in my hands, nor mine theirs, with such a secret stretching between us. And it made it easier to slip away for each turn without arousing questions."

Lark swallowed, hunger giving way to a different pit in her stomach. Now was as good a time as any to tell Daciana the truth. She'd put it off long enough—a temporary omission, a tactic for survival until she could be sure her human life wouldn't end before it began. Without Daciana, Alistair, Hugo, and Langford, Lark wouldn't have made it this long.

"I need to tell you something."

Gavriel's head snapped toward her direction. The weight of his stare was impossible to miss. Lark ignored it, keeping her eyes fixed on Daciana.

"I'm willing to listen." The warmth in Daciana's voice gave her pause, but only for a moment.

"That day you found me, you remember, yes?"

Only Daciana could be so gracious and patient, offering nothing more than a polite nod.

Why were her palms sweating? Lark wiped them on her leggings. "The day you found me was my first day walking as a human in the mortal realm." The hum of the wind cutting through the mouth of the cave was the only sound against the crackling of the fire.

Any reaction Daciana felt remained concealed behind her well-crafted and familiar veneer of calm. Daciana tilted her head almost imperceptibly. "What were you before?"

"A Reaper."

Silence.

Lark wanted to cast her eyes down to the ground, the fire, her boots, anywhere but the maddeningly composed expression in Daciana's eyes.

"Ah. I suppose that explains it then," Daciana said with a shrug.

"Explains what?" The loss of Lark's voice and the pain of walking for three days? Because that still didn't make sense to her. Likely Nereida did that just to toy with her.

"I always sensed something more in you. I thought you had to be something interesting," Daciana said with a wry smile. "That, and you smelled different when I found you." Her tone was nonchalant as if they were talking about the weather. "Not that you smelled bad. Just, other. I had a feeling there was more to you than it seemed. But you looked so lost. And small. And naked."

Gavriel cleared his throat.

Lark shot him a glare, heat burning her cheeks. "It's not like the transformation left me the opportunity to pack an overnight bag!"

"I didn't say anything." He held his hands up.

Lark turned back to Daciana. "You said I *smelled* different?"

"Of course." Daciana grabbed an apple from the satchel. "I was in the Twisted Woods for my transition when I found you. I didn't feel like waking up with animal blood in my teeth, so I went where no living things should be." She gave Lark a knowing look. "Lucky for me you were unconscious; otherwise, I doubt you would have let me help." She bit into her apple, pointing at Gavriel. "And you knew this about her."

Gavriel nodded, mouth set in a firm line.

"I'll be damned," Daciana said. "You know a Reaper isn't the same thing as a demon, right?"

"Yes, yes. I know, we've already had this conversation." Gavriel scowled.

Of course, Daciana knew enough not to be frightened. Kenna was well-versed enough in all matters of creatures. Though it begged the question of how a werewolf and a hunter managed to cross paths without bloodshed. Perhaps Kenna was a progressive sort.

"Do you have any questions for me?"

Daciana chewed thoughtfully. "Were you always a Reaper?"

"No. I was mortal once. When I died, instead of moving on, I was chosen to become something else." Lark fiddled with the end of her tunic. "That's how Reapers are made."

Daciana didn't even blink. "Do you remember your mortal life?"

"No." Lark always mourned the fact she couldn't remember. She'd once asked Ferryn if he remembered. He'd told her he remembered his life in a distant, detached way. Like hearing someone tell the same story so many times you envision it as your own memory.

Lark was always a blank slate. An empty page Thanar seemed far too keen to scribble on.

"There's more. Kenna knows what I am."

Daciana froze. "Kenna."

Lark ran a hand through her hair, knotted from the wind. "Yes, and she thinks when I became mortal there might have been some unintended side effects."

"Meaning?" Daciana raised an eyebrow.

"More Undesirables are coming through." Lark exhaled a tight breath. "The timing is... rather damning."

A heavy silence fell over them.

Lark took it as permission to continue. "So, I need to see the woman Kenna told me of, in the Emerald Woods."

Daciana said nothing. Her unyielding stare spilled ice through Lark's limbs, freezing her veins in terror. What happened between Kenna and Daciana to garner such a reaction from the mere mention of her name?

The crunch of teeth piercing the flesh of an apple from Gavriel's direction broke the spell.

"Kenna gave me her talisman to show the woman to aid me in contacting my friend. So, I can sort out if I caused more Undesirables to cross through." Maybe then Lark could finally live her life in peace.

"Where is that necklace again?" Gavriel asked, a little too innocently.

Lark shot him a dark look.

He offered a boyish grin that dimpled his cheek in response.

"Andros has it."

Daciana's mouth tightened. "Then I guess we know where to head next."

She made no mention of Kenna. Of how the necklace came to be in Lark's possession in the first place. Only resolute determination.

"I'm sorry," Lark said. "I don't know what history you share with Kenna, and maybe I should have respected the fact that you didn't want her help. But I wasn't sure if you'd understand, and I couldn't—" Lark clenched her fists as something swelled in her chest. She cut a glance in Gavriel's direction. "I couldn't bear the thought of you looking at me the way he did."

Gavriel's face flashed with shock.

Daciana fixed Lark with a meaningful stare. "You have nothing to apologize for. I trusted you'd tell me your story when you were ready, and you did." She let a warm smile curve at her mouth. "I can hardly fault you for waiting when I did the same. It changes nothing. You are still you, and I'm still me."

There were still plenty of unasked questions between them. But they could wait for another time.

Gavriel watched Lark, his dark green eyes regarding her intently.

Laughter burst from Daciana. A fit of giggles punctuated by a snort that echoed against the cave walls. She waved her hands, finally getting a handle on her unbidden mirth.

"I just thought of how the boys are going to react."

CHAPTER 28

*N*ight fell before they breached the outskirts of Brookhill. Lark tied the grey mare they'd liberated from the dead slavers to the hitching post on the edge of town. Daciana and Gavriel had insisted she ride to stay off her feet for another day or so. But by now the pain in Lark's chest had subsided to a dull, constant ache.

The market vendors had all but closed down their shops for the night. Bartrand, the traveling musician, was the only one who remained. Perched atop his cart of goods, plucking the strings of his lute under the light of a burning lamp post.

Keeping to the shadows, they crept along the sides of the stone buildings. Following the path to the barracks.

Rowdy patrons of the Tawdry Steward echoed through the square. With luck, most of the guards would be out patrolling or reveling. Lark didn't think she could stomach any more killing. She couldn't bear to think about the men they'd slaughtered in their escape, though they were never far from her thoughts. Freshly spilled blood seared like a brand.

Shoving the thought from her mind, Lark pressed closer to the darkness.

They reached the back entrance of the barracks. Gavriel kneeled and examined the iron lock barring their way. He cocked his head, studying it with a frown.

Lark scraped her fingers through her hair, keeping her voice low. "Can you pick it or not?"

"If I had my set of lock-picks, I could pick any lock in Ardenas," Gavriel whispered back.

They needed to get in. Lark wasn't leaving without the talisman.

"Thankfully, this isn't locked." Gavriel stood and pushed the door open. He sketched a bow before stepping aside.

Gaping darkness greeted them.

"Keep a close watch, and should things go south, remember the meeting spot," Lark said. They'd agreed to flee to the forest, to the clearing they'd found. It appeared to be an abandoned campsite. Hopefully, whoever used it wasn't coming back.

"Try to stay out of trouble," Daciana said, flicking Gavriel's nose as she passed him. Lark didn't bother hiding her grin.

The rickety stairs to the upper barracks promised an ill-timed creak. With great care, they crept to the upper level. Light leaked under the door at the end of the hallway.

Lark and Daciana pulled their borrowed weapons from their sheathes. Daciana remained hidden as Lark strode into his office.

Andros snapped up in his seat, and a few papers fluttered from his desk at the movement. His eyes widened and his sword arm twitched.

Lark aimed her blade at his chest. "If you value your life, you won't move a muscle." She pressed closer. "I have no qualms with searching your corpse." Sweat broke out along her palm. Her words were true. A terrible burdensome truth.

Andros raised his hands in surrender. "Whatever you think you're doing, don't."

Heat flared in Lark's chest, and she ground her teeth. "You're not in any position to be making demands of me."

"It's not a demand, it's a suggestion I'd heed if I were you."

"You're not me. And I'm not you. I'd never sell human lives for coin." Lark's stomach twisted at the memory of the fate they'd narrowly missed. The fate countless lives were still plagued by.

Lark took in the cramped, untidy office he kept with critical eyes. His narrow bookcase, crumbling beneath the weight of too many books, and his worn throw rug. The unraveling stitches appeared faded. Bright Ardenian colors of blue and white had turned grey and beige. If someone lined his pockets for his aid in slave trade, why were his quarters in such a shabby state? It mattered little, nothing, in fact.

"I want my things back." If he'd sold Kenna's talisman, Lark would offer him up to the next Undesirable she found.

Still holding his hand up, the other snaked behind his chest plate to yank the leather cord free. "You mean this?" The glowing blue pendant sprang free, clanging off his armor.

It hummed as it swung back and forth, glinting in the dim candlelight.

Lark pointed with the edge of her short sword. "Put it on the desk."

"Wait." Andros cleared his throat. "I think we can reach an agreement."

"As do I." Lark surged forward. "You can agree to do as I command before my patience wears thin."

"Now, I don't think you're as ruthless as you claim to be. I'd wager you're a smart young lady far in over her head."

Lark rolled her eyes at the insufferable man. "You're very perceptive. Care to tell me what I've been missing all along is love? A big strong man such as yourself can show me the ways of the world if I'd only trust you to care for me?" She shoved her blade a hairsbreadth from his throat. "Don't patronize me again."

His throat bobbed. "I only mean to have a civilized conversation. Is that too much to ask?"

The unmistakable sound of Daciana's footsteps thudded against the dirty floor. "Yes." She sauntered into the room, brandishing her sword. She cut a glance toward Lark. "He talks too much. I grew bored of waiting." They didn't need her on lookout anyway, the barracks was empty. A foolish mistake on Andros' part.

"Can't say I blame you," Lark said.

291

Daciana turned the force of her stare on Andros. Her mouth twitched. "Give her the pendant."

Andros shot a desperate look Lark's way. "What's to stop you from killing me once I give it to you?"

"What's to stop her from killing you now?" Daciana had a point.

With a sigh, Andros yanked the cord, pulling it over his head and tossing it onto the desk.

Lark grabbed the talisman, pocketing it as her heart hammered in the throat. The pendant trembled against her thigh. But now wasn't the time to be distracted by its strange magic. "My knife and bow. Where are they?"

He shook his head, his expression turning incredulous. "You can't be serious?"

Lark pressed the edge of her sword to his throat. His skin began to weep blood at the contact. When she stole the lives of those guards on the road, that was in service of survival. It was them or her. And she'd always choose to live.

If she took Andros' life, she'd have the chance to commit every moment to memory. To make room in the darkest corners of her heart to carry it with her. This wasn't survival. This was a slow trickling pass of judgment.

"Where are they?"

"The closet."

Daciana kept her sword trained on him, while Lark searched his room, sifting through the mountains of objects. Cloaks, a pair of hardened leather boots that appeared two sizes too small for Lark, a bundle of dried lavender that crumbled in her hand and filled the air with a light floral scent. She stilled when she came across a small wooden sword, a child's toy. A wave of nausea rolled through her gut before she continued her search.

"For the record," Andros called from his seat, "I don't make it a habit of selling people. That was Talbot's trade. I merely found myself —" He paused as if searching for the right words. "I found myself otherwise engaged when those deals went down. You were specified by Neera to receive a fitting punishment for your crime."

Daciana advanced on him, causing him to jump in his seat. "That makes you a monster and a coward."

Andros had no response.

Finally, Lark found her bow and quiver and her knife. She held it up for Daciana to see.

"Hugo gave you that," Daciana said.

"He made it for me." Lark curled her fingers around the handle. Testing the weight and the balance.

"No, he didn't. He made it for—" Daciana clamped her mouth shut.

"Let me guess, not your story to tell either?" One of these days, Lark would find a way to convince her to share all these secrets.

Daciana answered with a coy smile. "She catches on."

Lark slid the dagger into her boot and sighed in relief. She slung her bow and quiver over one shoulder. Home again. Stepping out of the way, she allowed Daciana a chance to pilfer when something caught her eye.

Sticking out beneath a pile of cloaks was the fiddle she'd admired from Bartrand, the traveling musician. Golden roots glimmered along its rich body. Such exquisite craftsmanship. Lark snatched it up, feeling around in the pile of stolen treasures until her fingers closed around the horsehair bow. She placed them on the chair nearby.

Lark turned to face Andros. "Where did you get the fiddle?" Bartrand seemed in good spirits when she caught sight of him; likely he didn't even know it was stolen.

Andros' dismissive wave did little to temper her mood. "The one trailing you had it in his possession."

Gavriel? Why would he steal a fiddle?

Daciana emerged from the closet of artifacts Andros had collected. Her posture, straighter under the weight of the many weapons she'd hidden all over her person.

"Are we done here?" Andros spat at them. "I wish to be free of you."

"Not quite," came a voice from the window behind them. Gavriel lounged, one leg on the windowsill, the other draped on the floor. "We have one more matter to settle." Despite his relaxed posture, the venom in his voice was unmistakable. Dark enough to give even Lark an unbidden chill. Gavriel was every bit the assassin Emric claimed. His black hood hid most of his face, save for his dangerous smile. The dagger he'd looted from a slaver corpse glinted in the candlelight as he ran a finger along its edge. Gavriel dropped his hood, leveling the full force of his stare on Andros.

"You," Andros hissed. "You're a dead man."

"Maybe. But then again, so are you."

Andros' face twisted in disgust. "I should have slit your throat myself."

"Yes." Gavriel regarded him with a thoughtful expression. "You should have."

Before Lark could protest, the gleam of Gavriel's blade swept like lightning through the air. Blood sprayed against the reports cluttering the desk.

A harsh breeze from the open window blew out the candle, smothering them all in sudden darkness. The wisp of smoke from the charred wick slithered out into the night air, and the smell of blood and burnt tallow filled the room.

GAVRIEL KNEW he shouldn't have come. Lark and Daciana were more than capable of handling Andros. But that same itch had returned, the one that compelled him to shadow them in the first place. One look at the man poised behind his desk and Gavriel's fury returned, deafening.

If Lark noticed the tremble in his blood-covered hands, she didn't let on. Instead, she gave him a wide berth as he searched for his belongings. He found his daggers and short sword, but swapped them for a set of higher quality, and added to his collection. Ardenian smithies still had a lot to learn about how to hone a blade. Unfortunately, Andros had no Kovalian weapons in his stockpile. But the dirk he found with the stunning blood groove, and the Ardenian skinner with the gut hook were fortunate finds. Practically name day gifts, if he'd ever celebrated his before.

Gavriel rifled through the stack of obscurities, cursing under his breath when he realized what was missing.

"What are you searching for?" Lark stood at the opposite end of the room.

Gavriel rolled his shoulders, shaking off the flare of annoyance. "It doesn't matter."

She crossed the room, snatching up the fiddle and bow and tossing them to him. He caught them with ease, marveling at her boldness, to risk destroying the instrument.

"Is this what you wanted?" She lifted the stubborn set of her jaw.

"No." Gavriel placed them on the floor. "This isn't mine, but I'm sure it'll fetch a hefty sum."

"We know you were listening. You heard Andros tell us it was yours."

"He was mistaken." Gavriel held her stare, daring her to contradict him.

She narrowed her eyes at him. Assessing. There was something heavy and penetrating about her amber gaze, and Gavriel fought the urge to squirm.

"That must be it." Lark relented, sounding anything but convinced. "What are you missing?"

"It's nothing. We should move on."

Lark glanced over at Daciana, who gave her a quick nod. "Fine." Lark stomped over to the window, throwing one leg over the side and disappearing into the night.

Daciana flashed him a grin before strutting past and slipping out the window after Lark.

Gavriel took one last survey of the room, moving a few papers around in search of his prize. He'd recently run out and it had been months since he'd last had a chance to stock up the delicacy he'd found in the market. Seizing his opportunity, he'd purchased a hefty bag of the stuff, keen to ration it accordingly.

Of course, that and all his personal effects had been taken when he was foolishly captured. How he'd managed to misstep so spectacularly was no great mystery.

It was Lark's fault.

After Gavriel witnessed her deep admiration for the fiddle and retreated to his shadows, he'd returned to purchase the damn thing. He thought he might... he didn't know what he thought actually. It was impulsive and reckless. It put a target on his back to drop that much coin in broad daylight. It was no wonder he'd had eyes on him after that foolish transaction.

Gavriel yanked the drawers free of the desk, without a care for how they landed. There'd be no hiding this scene as it was. He debated flipping the desk over.

"Where did you put it, you churlish little shit?"

Andros' vacant eyes told him nothing.

Gavriel stalked over to the window, but something caught his eye on the bookcase. A corner of a green satchel stuck out behind one of its many volumes. He ripped the book from the shelf, revealing his bag of contraband that had been taken.

A grin spread across his face as he opened it, plunging his fingers in. He produced a small piece of dark chocolate, the size of his thumbnail. He popped it in his mouth, savoring the bitterness undercut with a hint of sweetness that melted on his tongue. There was considerably less left, meaning Andros had likely indulged in quite a bit of his supply. The bastard.

Turning to regard the room, he glared at the fiddle. It sat there, mocking him. Gavriel grabbed it and stuffed it in his bag before he could think about it. Pulling himself through the window, he gripped the sides of the building where the stone jutted out. He shimmied down until he was close enough to the ground to land with a soft bend in his knees. Still grinning with his triumphant retrieval, he bounded into the bushes, eager to find Lark and apologize for his actions that seemed to bother her.

Though he didn't know why they should.

She wanted Andros dead too, hadn't she? He never thought she'd be squeamish about death. For all her bluster, was it possible her new human heart was far more fragile than he thought?

Perhaps it had something to do with the fiddle. Though, that didn't sound right either.

Gavriel quickened his pace as he neared the rendezvous they'd agreed upon. Back when the plan was for him to keep watch and meet them after they retrieved their belongings.

It didn't bother him they hadn't waited beneath the window. If she was pissed, it would be good for those two to have a chance to speak without him. Perhaps Daciana would smooth things over. She had a knack for communication, especially when it came to Lark. Gavriel couldn't help but envy how easy it was for her. To say and do the right thing.

It seemed everything he did pissed Lark off.

In the clearing up ahead, the outline of a figure kneeled on the ground.

Daciana. She was alone.

Gavriel's stomach tightened.

Lark was nowhere in sight.

CHAPTER 29

"*W*here is she?" Gavriel tried to keep the strange mixture of panic and rage at bay.

Daciana said nothing. The predatory calm on her face only confirmed his fears.

The round moon bathed the clearing in cold light. Even the shadows were more blue than black.

"Gavriel Pearson, as I live and breathe."

Gavriel turned to see a familiar figure, clad head to toe in sleek black leathers. His blond hair was shorn close to the scalp, and a vicious grin split across his face. His mouth was always too large for his features. "Connor," Gavriel said. If only Daciana would answer the call of a nearly full moon and bite Connor's face off.

"Is that any way to greet an old friend?" Connor asked, placing a hand to his chest and feigning insult. "And here I thought you'd be glad of our reunion. I've even been regaling old stories with your little friend here."

A silvery mane appeared from the tree line across the clearing. Sorscha, another Guild assassin. The pristine buckles of her black leathers gleamed as she dragged Lark in tow. Lark dug her heels into the dirt, clawing and fighting despite the rope encircling her wrists.

Gavriel's lips curled back in a snarl as Sorscha dumped Lark at Connor's feet.

Connor placed a possessive hand on Lark's head. She recoiled from his touch. He grabbed a fistful of her auburn hair and yanked her head back, exposing the long column of her throat. Sorscha rested the curved edge of her saber against Lark's pulse.

Lark ceased struggling, but her eyes still held a murderous glare.

He'd kill them.

He'd kill them all.

If Daciana didn't get to them first.

"So, life on the road appears glamorous." An angry scar cut through Connor's right eye, glinting in the moonlight. Gavriel had been the one to give him that scar. He'd be receiving a few more this night. Connor grinned. "There's something to be said for the rustic life."

Gavriel didn't need to glance down to know his clothes were torn, frayed, and discolored. "And the life of a traitor?"

"That's rich, coming from you." Connor leaned close to whisper in Lark's ear. "What has he told you? If you knew the truth, I doubt you'd find his company charming." His eyes, bright with glee, darted back to Gavriel. "Did you tell her what we used to call you?"

Gavriel had heard this same song and dance a thousand times. It'd been years since Connor's words landed any blows. Bringing up his first assignment used to send him in a violent rage, but that urge had been beaten out of him long ago. So rather than take the bait, Gavriel focused on Lark.

She stared back with keen amber eyes. Liquid honey and fire.

"Leave her out of this."

"You're the one who dragged her into this, brother." Connor chuckled and pressed closer so his lips moved against Lark's hair. "Did he tell you what he is?"

Lark's throat bobbed. "Connor," she said in a calm voice that raised the hairs on the back of Gavriel's neck. "You won't live to see the sun rise. Not unless you let me go, right now."

"Oh, sweetheart. We haven't even started yet." Connor's smile turned savage. He shot another dark look at Gavriel. "We had a name for men like him. Father slayer. Only a real bastard is jealous enough to kill his own father. Didn't want to share your whore of a mother, is that it?"

Gavriel ground his teeth. In all this time, Connor still hadn't managed to form better insults.

"Shut your mouth," Lark growled, and Connor twisted his hand in her hair. Her face tightened.

"Connor." Gavriel dropped his voice dangerously low. He knew Connor well enough to recognize when he was goading him. Feeling around for a nerve to press. "They have nothing to do with this. Let them go and we'll settle this."

"See, that's where you're wrong." Connor yanked Lark to her feet, pulling her close to him. "She deserves to die knowing what kind of company she keeps."

"Gavriel." Lark said his name with the force of a whisper. Like a confession. Or a farewell. Something clenched in his chest at the sound.

Connor was a dead man.

He'd hand deliver him to the Netherworld himself.

Sorscha had backed off, now angling her sword at him. Gavriel trained with her enough to know her weaknesses. For one, she never had a very strong stance. Now that the edge of her blade was no longer at Lark's neck, it would be easier to disarm her and knock her off her feet.

In his periphery, he noted a hooded archer in the tree with his bow trained on Daciana. A bow crafted to resemble the flaming wings of a phoenix. Only one archer from the Guild was stupid enough to value craftsmanship over practicality. Gregoir. His twin, Hazel, must be nearby. They were never far from each other.

There were, no doubt, more assassins waiting in the shadows. Connor was too much of a coward to attack without numbers.

This would be bloody.

"You know the bounty on your head, Pearson? It's enough to pay off a lifetime of debt. I can *buy* my freedom with the coin your pretty corpse will earn me."

"They'll never let you leave, Connor. People like you are a liability. That's why they never gave you marks of higher rank." Gavriel smirked as Connor's face reddened. "They know how little you're worth."

Lark angled her wrists to the side of her hip, fingers creeping up Connor's side. Toward the dagger he wore at his waist.

Connor glanced down at her. "I never did catch your name."

A muscle feathered in her jaw. "Lark."

"Lark. That's right, Hazel mentioned it when we trailed you. Pretty name." He grinned down at her. "Is Gavriel your lover? Hazel was quite certain of it. I heard he put up quite the fight when the Captain of the Guard handed you over to the slavers." He glanced up at Gavriel. "Thank you, by the way, for dealing with him. He proved to be a bit of a thorn in my side. That's what happens when you toss scraps to beasts. They come back for more."

"You always talked too much," Gavriel said, annoyance temporarily winning out over anger.

Connor laughed and returned his attention to Lark. "You didn't answer my question."

A breathy laugh escaped Lark's lips. "You're coming off a bit desperate, Connor."

"Mouthy, huh? What if I cut out your tongue and keep you as a pet. Can you be trained?" He looked up at Gavriel. "You won't mind, will you?"

Lark's fingers closed around the hilt of the dagger. Spinning away, she yanked the blade free. Using the binds on her wrists as a garotte, she encircled Connor's neck, and pressed the edge of his dagger against his throat.

Gavriel's sword was already free from his sheathe and in his hand. He caught the end of Sorscha's saber before she could cut Lark down, and knocked her back, causing her to stumble over her poor stance.

Connor held his arms out the side, laughing. "Whoa, easy there. I'm all about role-reversal, sweetheart."

301

"Shut up," Lark said through clenched teeth.

Daciana leapt to her feet, sprinting toward them. Gavriel yanked a dagger from his belt and tossed it to her.

Gavriel threw a glance in Lark's direction where she still pressed a dagger to Connor's throat. "I'll deal with him."

"I need insurance," Lark said, eying the tree line.

Gregoir would never shoot to kill. Hazel was the one who handled all his dirty work. But Gavriel didn't have the time to explain that. "You're spry, just dodge the arrows."

Lark scowled before she kicked Connor to the side and held her wrists out. Gavriel hacked through the rope without hesitating, and Lark yanked her knife from her boot, taking her place back-to-back with Daciana.

"I need you to deal with the others." Gavriel eyed three advancing assassins whose faces were still shrouded beneath their hoods. Connor was so predictable. "And watch the wound in your chest. You're still healing."

"On it." Lark flashed him a smile, a dimple creasing her cheek.

How Gavriel had never noticed that before, he wasn't sure. He pushed its dizzying effect out of his mind as he stalked over to Connor.

Connor had regained his footing and a few weapons. His murderous grin belied the tension in his jaw. "Come on, you coward."

Violence thrummed in Gavriel's veins. "Try not to beg."

Connor spat at the ground, already circling.

The two assassins regarded each other with predatory stares. A swift thrust parried, and the clash of steel rang like music in Gavriel's ears. He reveled in the familiar cadence of this dance. Brandishing his blade high, he met Connor strike for strike. Like old training exercises.

Oh, how he'd missed this.

LARK COULD ONLY GLANCE in Gavriel's direction, as Sorscha advanced. Swift and lethal.

Lark kicked Sorcha's thigh, having observed her faulty footwork against Gavriel, and dropped into a crouch, sinking her blade through Sorscha's leather boot. Sorscha screamed, pinned in place by the long dagger. Lark yanked a narrow stiletto knife from Sorscha's belt and plunged it beneath her chin. The wound spurted violent red and the gurgling sound of Sorscha choking on her own blood filled the air. Lark swallowed the bile that rose in her throat as warmth gushed from Sorscha's neck, down her arm.

A surge of pain swelled in Lark's healing chest. Sore was better than dead.

The archer had yet to shoot. Lark couldn't count it as mercy. Likely a tactical maneuver. He could have taken them out whenever he pleased.

She needed a bow.

Daciana snatched up Sorscha's sword, still wielding Gavriel's dagger. She crossed both blades with expert finesse as she dueled her opponent. A flash of steel and a sharp ringing of metal sang through the air. The assassin was lightning fast, spinning and leaping like the acrobats in the traveling circus. But when facing someone as lethal as Daciana, style over substance was a terrible idea.

Fed up with his performance, Daciana landed a firm kick to his chest, knocking him back before slicing her sword across his gut. Lark turned in time to shield her eyes from the entrails that dropped. The unmistakable thud in the grass churned her stomach.

The ghost of a moon spilled its silvery light across the blood-soaked grass. How long it would take for the rains to wash it away?

The third assassin she'd forgotten stepped in her way. Lark stopped short of barreling into him. His eyes were dark and expressionless, and a giant axe rested over one shoulder.

Shit.

He swung his battle axe, Lark stumbled and fell hard on her back, just missing the edge of the blade. He lifted it again, intending to cleave her in half, when a dart speared the side of his throat.

Lark scrambled back as he dropped his axe into the dirt, his hand flying to his neck. He plucked the small, feathered needle from his skin, staring at it in disbelief. He lifted his gaze to Lark's as if waiting for an explanation before his knees buckled. He landed face-first in the slick, moonlit grass.

Lark's hands pressed into the earth as she stared at the massive man, at the axe glittering beside him. The back of her leather leggings was damp with dew. Morning wasn't far.

A roar ripped through the air, yanking her from her shock. Lark jumped to her feet, dashing toward the two men battling.

Connor lunged, his face twisted in anger. Gavriel met each thrust with fierce calm. Lethal and measured.

Lark took half a step forward when a firm pair of hands grabbed her arm.

"This isn't your fight."

Lark turned to see a familiar set of ice blue eyes framed by bronze skin, and raven black hair braided down her back.

The woman who hired them to take out Talbot. The one who demanded her name.

Hazel.

"You?" Lark yanked her arm out of her hold. "You set us up?"

The assassin's eyes narrowed. "On the contrary, Lark. I saved your life." Hazel gestured to the man lying a few paces back, dart still clamped between his fingers.

Lark turned back in time to witness Gavriel parry a particularly heavy blow. "Why would you do that?"

"You gave me a good laugh, last we met." Hazel watched Gavriel and Connor duel with a neutral expression. "And I don't see why any more of my brothers should fall in service to Connor's lust for Gavriel's death."

"You also belong to the Guild."

"Yes, my orders were to kill Gavriel and return home."

Anger flared in Lark's chest, and her grip tightened on the hilt of the sword she still carried. "I won't let you."

Hazel arched a dark brow at the movement. "Put that away, before you hurt yourself. I'm not here for him."

Lark didn't trust careful words. "What are you here for?"

"I'm here to make sure my little brother doesn't get himself killed. He has a knack for getting into trouble and following the wrong man."

"Connor's your brother?"

"No." She gave Lark an exasperated look. "The man aiming his bow at your friend is."

GAVRIEL HADN'T SPARRED with Connor for a long time. The last time they'd gone head-to-head he'd handed Connor's ass to him and humiliated him in front of everyone training that day. But it seemed Connor had taken that lesson to heart. Shame can drive a man farther than dedication. But Connor was all brute force, his finesse waning with exhaustion.

Gavriel's strength was also flagging. But his ability to remain focused and quick, master of his emotions, was always his greatest strength.

In his periphery, a flare of dark red hair danced into sight. Gavriel chanced a look. Lark was standing with Hazel. Far too close for his liking.

His distraction cost him a slice deep in his thigh. He snarled through the pain, boring his teeth in Connor's direction.

Connor smiled back, panting with the effort. "Don't worry Gavriel. Hazel knows not to touch her; she's saving her for me."

Red filled Gavriel's vision. So much for being master over his emotions. He lunged forward with renewed vigor. His offensive strikes were hard enough to reverberate down the steel and ache in his hands. He didn't care—he'd wipe the scum that was Connor Briggins from the face of the earth. His pulse pounded in his head, drowning out the metallic clang of the blade's heavy strike.

"I don't get what she sees in you."

Skies even in the face of exhaustion, Connor ran his damn mouth.

"How she doesn't see how bloody your hands are, Pearson." Connor grunted as he met Gavriel's strike just in time. "I'm doing you a favor here. You can die, your honor preserved in her memory." He grimaced, trying to mask it with a smile.

Gavriel glanced back at Lark, unable to help himself. She seemed to take a step toward him—when a flash of burning pain cut across his abdomen. He jumped back and placed a hand just beneath his ribcage. His blood was warm against his palm.

"Avalon's tits! Have you really lost your touch?" Connor laughed even as he staggered forward.

Gavriel's vision spotted. Fatigue and lack of nourishment were beginning to take their toll. Perhaps he had lost his touch.

Gavriel surged and brought his blade down hard enough to knock Connor's sword from his hands. Using the momentum, Gavriel knocked Connor flat on his back and kicked his sword away, advancing on his retreating form.

Even on his ass in the dirt, disarmed, bloody, and beaten, Connor still managed to appear smug. Gavriel leveled his blade against his sweat-slicked throat.

"I won't be the last," Connor promised, blue eyes darkening. "They'll never stop hunting you. You'll never know peace." He glanced in Lark's direction where she stood watching. "She'll never be safe either. Mark my words, one day, they'll find her and gut her before they put you down like the dog you are. And my only regret is that I won't be around to watch."

Gavriel cocked his head. "I thought your only regret would be dying a failure. By the hand of some bastard Father Slayer." He swept the edge of his blade across his throat, quick and clean. The blood that poured from his wound, only half as satisfying as the shocked expression frozen on Connor's face.

Gavriel rolled his shoulders, trying to shake off the residual rage. The slice across his gut burned something fierce. Soon enough, all his muscles would ache. He really should train more. He turned, violence still humming in his veins.

But the sight of Lark running toward him rooted him to the spot.

He could do little more than stand there paralyzed as she leapt toward him, throwing her small body against his.

He staggered back, his knees almost giving out. Her scent of sunlight and sweet apples filled his senses, instantly calming the roaring in his head. Of their own accord, his arms wrapped around her, the bloody sword still hanging limply in one hand.

She was warm and real and right in his arms—a thought that terrified Gavriel more than anything else, but in that moment, he surrendered to it. Breathing her in and thanking the skies she was all right.

LARK DIDN'T KNOW what possessed her to embrace Gavriel. But she breathed in his familiar scent and willed her heart to stop pounding. He was alive. He was safe. He was here.

Lark pulled back to look at his face. His dark green eyes bore into her. She couldn't name the emotion in his expression. With a shaky hand, she brought her fingers to his cheek, wiping away the flecks of blood on his skin.

She wasn't ready to face the fear in her heart. The way it thudded against her ribs even as his arms, solid and firm, sent relief through her. She needed to stay focused on the task at hand. Once they regrouped—

Blind terror seared through her.

They hadn't dispatched the archer yet.

"Daciana," Lark breathed, unable to articulate the sudden dread that coiled in her gut.

Gavriel's expression melted into cool anger. "Hazel," Gavriel said, voice low and dangerous.

"Gavriel," Hazel purred as she approached. The sound of it immediately set Lark's teeth on edge. The intimate familiarity behind it was enough to convince her of certain implications.

"Call off your dog," he seethed.

Hazel gave an amused expression before waving her hand dismissively behind her.

A heartbeat or two later, a hooded man came tumbling out of a large oak tree, landing light on his feet with barely a sound.

Lark ran over to Daciana who crouched over the corpses of their kills. Daciana wiped her bloody blades on their trousers before sheathing them with calm indifference. Lark pulled her into a tight embrace.

"You need to stop acting so relieved whenever we survive." Daciana huffed a laugh against Lark's head. "I'm starting to doubt your faith in me."

Lark laughed and shook her head. "Never."

Daciana and Lark approached the assassins still regarding each other with a careful distance. The distance of knowing someone too much and not at all.

"So, you've taken to keeping interesting company," Gavriel said, his voice tight.

"As have you," Hazel said. "I had the pleasure of meeting Lark after she fulfilled the contract I placed. When I caught wind of your involvement, I had to return to see what kind of trap Connor would set for you." She placed a hand on his arm. "You really should be more careful where you're seen."

Gavriel shook off her touch. "You should be more careful who you align yourself with. Give me one good reason not to bury you and Gregoir right now."

The archer made no move to remove his hood, Though his jaw stiffened.

Hazel tipped her head back and laughed. "Oh Gavriel, how I've missed your dour moods. I have no interest in fighting you. Or your friends. You see, I quite like having you on the run. It's granted me temporary freedom. I've discovered a knack for business ventures, and I don't even have to get my hands dirty. Once you're slain, we all return to the Guild to take up our positions once more." Her expression darkened. "I have no wish to return to that."

Gavriel gave a grim nod, refusing to meet Lark's questioning stare.

"You will have nothing to fear from us. But you have to be more careful. If I hadn't been among Connor's men, I don't know who would be standing here now." All humor had bled from her tone.

"I know. Thank you."

Hazel nodded. "Don't mention it. Just disappear." She glanced over her shoulder at the man she'd shot with a sleeping dart who was starting to rouse. "You should go. Sorrel won't stay under much longer. Your weapons are behind that fallen trunk. Get your things and go."

Lark nodded, turning to leave with Daciana and Gavriel, when Hazel caught her arm.

"Hang on. I need to speak with you. Alone."

Lark debated ripping her arm free of her hold. Instead, she nodded.

Hazel waited until Gavriel was far enough away that despite his suspicious stares over his shoulder, he couldn't catch her words. "Don't let anything happen to him, Lark. I'm serious."

Lark considered her words carefully. "I can't promise that. But I can promise"—she leaned in close to whisper—"should anything befall him, it's because I'm already lost to the abyss."

Much to her surprise, Hazel smiled. "That's fair."

CHAPTER 30

*N*ight covered the forest. The sky, laden with clouds, was an oppressive blanket, tucking the moon away and offering Lark no comfort. The flutter of wings unseen shuddered in the dark.

Daciana led the way, torch in hand. The flames cast a warm glow on her rich skin, illuminating her high cheekbones and narrow chin. The side of Gavriel's face caught the light of Daciana's torch, revealing the sharp line of his nose and strong jaw. In the gloom of a night void of stars, their faces were all Lark could see.

Camp couldn't be far off. So long as the others hadn't moved on in their absence. How many days had passed? At least a week since they set off on a mission that should have taken two days.

"What if they've gone?" Lark asked, breaking the silence.

Daciana slowed her steps to glance over her shoulder.

"We were longer than expected," Lark continued. "Perhaps they've packed up, left to move north as we planned. They have all the horses, only three riders without us."

"They wouldn't do that," Daciana said with a slight shake of her head.

"If they thought we were dead? They wouldn't move on with their lives if they thought we weren't coming back?"

"No, they wouldn't."

"Why not?"

"Because." A deep gravelly voice sounded from behind. Lark spun on her heel, feeling blindly for the arrows in her quiver. A large shape loomed in the shadows. "Daciana's too stubborn to die."

That familiar voice, laced with annoyance, was a beautiful sound.

Lark dropped her arms, relief weakening her limbs. "Hugo. Thank the skies."

Hugo stepped into view, the warm light of Daciana's torch banished the shadows from his lined face and tattooed neck. His mouth twitched behind his dark mustache. "I could say the same about you."

Lark launched herself toward him, whether he liked it or not. To her surprise, Hugo caught her with ease, as if expecting the onslaught of her silly affection, and wrapped his thick arms around her.

"Welcome back, kid."

LARK WRUNG her hands in her lap, dreading the task that lay before her. She'd announced over the fire a truth she needed to share with them all. It was time.

Surrounded by trees, linen tents more inviting than any inn she'd stayed in, and the circle of stones they'd lined the fire with, she should have felt at ease.

"What is it?" Alistair called out, amusement written on his face. "We've put coin on guessing your story, I'd like a payout sooner rather than later."

Lark met his eagerness with bewilderment. "You placed wagers?"

"Of course." Alistair appeared insulted she hadn't assumed as much.

"There may have been a particular scenario I deemed most likely," Langford said with a wave of his hand.

"Hugo?"

He frowned at the ground. "I'm not proud of it."

Lark was sure she would have laughed, had the sound not been trapped in her throat. She darted her eyes around the campfire, searching for the strength to continue. Until her gaze settled on Daciana.

Daciana missed nothing. "She knows what I am." All sounds of laughter and banter ceased, the sudden silence smothered the camp. "How could she not? We were bound in the back of a slaver's caravan when I turned."

Alistair cursed. "Are you serious? You watched her change? I've only been begging her to bring me during a full-moon for ages."

"That's really not what this is about." Daciana exhaled a long-suffering sigh.

"I got to see it too," Gavriel said with a sly grin.

Alistair narrowed his eyes, dark brows drawing together. "Now you're just being mean."

"The point is, she knows." Daciana ignored Alistair and turned to Lark. "No more secrets. Tell them."

This would take tact. Diplomacy. Elegant wording. It was a chance for Lark to make them understand by using carefully cultivated language.

"I was a Reaper."

Lark never was one for careful words.

Everyone stilled.

"I beg your pardon," Langford leaned forward, two fingers tucked behind his ear. "A what?"

"A Reaper, of souls. I guided the deceased to the afterlife." Lark thumbed the seam of her tunic. Her throat tightened around the words. "I've only been human for as long as you've known me."

For a few heartbeats, no one spoke.

Lark cursed herself for being so stupid. Even Gavriel had hated her for what she was. No one welcomed death with open arms. Except for Daciana, apparently.

"Well," Alistair finally said. "I don't think any of us won that pool."

LARK CLOSED her hand around her new bow. Gingerly turning it over between her hands. This Ashwood was carved simpler than her last bow. She tested the pull. The string groaned, bending the limbs in a beautiful arch. The twinge through her chest and shoulders told her two things: this was a stronger bow, and she needed to allow her injury more time to recover. Then she'd shoot several quivers full.

After last night's confession, she'd disappeared to her tent the first chance she got. Things felt different now. Weightier. Though they'd all offered interesting theories regarding what they'd thought her origins were. Alistair had assumed she'd fled an arranged marriage to an elderly lord somewhere in Koval. Ridiculous.

Langford guessed she'd grown up in a family of zealots. Hidden away from society as they prayed to the Warriors and Paragons of Avalon. An interesting thought since he was the only one who seemed worried whenever Alistair blasphemed.

And Hugo. His guess came the closest. He bet she was a spy, imprisoned by duty. A soldier following bad orders until her conscience told her to run.

"Why aren't you training?" A rough voice, edged with disapproval, rumbled down at her.

"I wasn't aware I'd committed to a training session this morning." Lark turned away, avoiding Hugo's calculating expression. She pushed past him, hoping he wouldn't choose this moment to become chatty.

"We thought we lost you."

Lark halted her retreat, turning to look over her shoulder at where Hugo still stood.

"Would that have been the worst thing?"

"Don't be stupid."

Lark spun to glare at him.

Hugo advanced surprisingly fast. "I knew Daciana would be fine. The girl's damn near unkillable. Gavriel, I don't give a shit about, so no loss there. But you?" He narrowed his dark eyes. The crooked slope of his nose wrinkled. "I had no idea if you were a corpse."

Lark clenched her fists against the tightness in her chest. "That would have mattered to you?"

"Yeah, kid. That would have mattered to me. To us all." His expression tightened. Even beneath his thick dark beard, it was evident he was clenching his jaw. "We sent you off with hardly any training. If something happened, that'd be on us."

Hugo said us. But somehow it felt like he carried the burden alone.

"Even still? After last night?"

Hugo shook his head. "Is that what this is about? You think you can scare us off? You wouldn't believe the shit I could tell you, the things I've done. Pull your head out of your ass and listen to me. You're one of ours now. Nothing in this gods-forsaken world is going to change that."

Lark swallowed, her throat dry. This open-arms acceptance would take some getting used to. She wasn't entirely certain she deserved it. "You don't know what I see when I close my eyes. I can't help but think I've done something terribly wrong by coming here the way I did."

When she closed her eyes, she could see Ferryn's face, twisted in anguish—the echo of fear that gripped her whenever her mind was quiet. Or worse, his face smoothed of any emotion, a blank slate that Thanar could rewrite as he pleased. How long before he realized Ferryn was involved in saving Gavriel?

Hugo's expression darkened. He took a step closer and placed a large hand on her shoulder. "If you think you're facing any of this alone, you haven't been paying attention. Your fights are our fights."

DACIANA AND ALISTAIR sparred as Lark approached the designated clearing. Langford sat against a large oak tree with an apple in his mouth, furiously sketching in his worn leather-bound notebook.

Daciana was the picture of control, each lunge a display of finesse and measured power. Knowing the wealth of power beneath her placid composure made her all the more imposing.

Alistair was all style and flair. Grinning and flicking his wrist with each slash of his cutlass. Lark had no doubt Daciana could take him, but she couldn't imagine too many swordsmen skilled enough to overpower his technique. Gavriel, maybe. That would be a match worth watching. Perhaps Langford would bring snacks.

Lark focused on watching the skirmish and almost missed Gavriel's appearance in the clearing. He took his place on the far end and began his warm-ups. Even beneath his tunic and leathers, his finely honed physique was impossible to ignore. The broad muscles in his shoulders rippled as he stretched, limbering up.

Lark's knee bounced as a light-headed sensation came over her.

"He's going to pull his stitches, the fool," Langford muttered as he followed Lark's gaze to the assassin.

Lark had almost forgotten the strike Connor snuck in when Gavriel was distracted. She was so relieved when he still stood and Connor bled out in the grass, and he didn't complain the entire trek back to the others. Perhaps she should check on him later—

"Oh, Lark!"

Alistair's voice pulled her attention from the sight of Gavriel doing pull-ups off a thick branch. "Your turn, love."

"For what?"

He gestured to the array of weapons behind him. "I want to see what you can do, *Reaper*."

"It's Demon," Gavriel called from across the way. "She prefers to be called Demon."

Lark gritted her teeth as heat washed over her cheeks. "I don't *prefer* to be called anything other than my name."

Alistair sketched a bow. "Of course, Lady Lark, please grace us with a demonstration."

"And who shall I face?"

"Me, of course." Alistair placed a hand over his heart. "It would be an honor to cross steel with you."

Lark laughed. "All right, then. I'll warn you, I've learned a thing or two." She yanked Hugo's dagger from her boot and crossed the way toward the sparring circle.

"If you'd be so kind as to peruse my special selection. Reserved for only the finest opponents." Alistair gestured to the canvas tarp beside Langford, folded in on itself.

The man grew stranger by the day. Lark yanked back the covering, to reveal a long scythe.

Langford laughed, emitting a few snorts as he clutched his stomach and kicked his fine boots into the ground. Lark spun to find Alistair watching her with a far too innocent expression.

"What? Not to your liking? I also have this if it's more your style." He held up a sickle he'd kept behind his back, face finally falling into his devilish smirk.

Daciana shook her head. Mirth danced in her eyes.

"I hate you," Lark said, still smiling. Knowing that wasn't the truth. Not even a little bit. This was what family felt like.

This was home.

THE JOURNEY NORTH brought Lark ample time for reflection. The air carried the all the promise of summer and the bite of spring's farewell. When the sun slipped below the horizon, the wind held a northern chill Lark wasn't accustomed to. Days passed, traveling in near silence. Nights ushered in exhaustion. They'd all collapse on their bedrolls after eating dinner.

Lark didn't mourn the temporary loss of their fireside chats. There was a sense of purpose in pushing beyond her physical limits each day. Toward her goal. The proof of her effort was in every ache of her muscles. In how quickly the hypnotic seduction of sleep overcame her.

Too tired to dream.

Even Alistair found his voice lacking in entertainment after the first three days.

One evening, Langford found Lark doubled over behind a tree. Her stomach burned like she'd swallowed a blade, and warmth spilled between her legs. Without so much as a remark, Langford disappeared, only to return with a folded cloth, and flowers with white petals and yellow pistils.

"Now that I'm familiar with your cycle, I'll try to have chamomile tea ready for next time," Langford said, crouching beside her.

"I don't want tea," Lark said through gritted teeth.

"It's for the pain." Langford handed her the dark cloth. "And this is for the blood."

"Thank you," Lark said, feeling foolish for not recognizing her own courses. She'd thought her pain resulted from something she ate.

"It's no hardship. I do the same for Daciana's. Only it's a different sort of cycle..."

Langford must brew something to take for the transition. It looked horribly painful.

He made no mention of helping her, apart from keeping Lark supplied with chamomile tea every time they stopped to make camp. After a few days, the cramping subsided and she no longer had to disappear to change the cloth for her blood.

Traveling with three horses meant doubling up for some and taking breaks from riding when the terrain proved too narrow.

Lark hid her surprise the first time Gavriel asked to ride with her.

After composing herself and giving a quick nod, he'd swung in behind her. His large hands settled at her waist before they trotted on. Lark tried not to think of how warm and firm his thighs felt against her backside. His solid arms wrapped around her and filled her veins with fire. Every contact seared like a brand and Lark was sure she'd lose her mind. It didn't help that they slipped into wordless riding partners whenever it was her turn with Apple, which was most days.

Hugo insisted he hated riding, and Daciana made the horses nervous. Those two seemed more than happy to take the most frequent breaks and walk alongside their companions.

Alistair constantly darted glances between Daciana and the horses. As if watching for any signs they might get spooked. His insistence that Lark avoid attachment with the horses made much more sense now. Each day that brought them closer to the next moon, the tension in his shoulders tightened. How much of everyone's burden did he share?

Shadows lined Alistair's face, darkening with each passing day. When he caught Lark watching, he'd slip into his rakish smirk. But when Lark was free to examine him, she saw how he white-knuckled the reins. His brilliant green eyes filled with concern every time they passed over Daciana. He carried the weight of the world behind his devilish smile and easy swagger.

Lark tightened her grip on the reins. What did people see when they looked at her?

A tugging at Apple's bridle yanked Lark from her thoughts. Gavriel pulled himself into the saddle behind her, situating himself far too close. She squirmed and he tightened his hold in response. The heat of his body shot tingles along her skin. A breeze ruffled the ends of Lark's hair, carrying the scent of wet soil and something else. Something distinctly Gavriel.

"What is that smell?" The minute the words leapt from her mouth, heat rose on Lark's cheeks.

"I'm sorry?" Gavriel's warm breath fluttered against her ear.

"You always smell sweet, but earthy. I've been trying to place the aroma and it's driving me mad." Poor choice of words. "I mean, it's annoying me."

A soft laugh escaped his lips. Reaching into his pocket, he pulled out a small cloth bag and handed it to her. "Is this what you mean?"

She dug her fingers into the leather, dyed-green satchel and pulled out a small dark brown morsel.

"Are these sweets?" Lark turned in the saddle to face him. "Have you been sneaking sweets?"

"Sneaking? No, why would you think I was trying to hide it?"

"You've never pulled this out in front of anyone; you've never eaten it in front of me." Lark turned it over between her fingers, inspecting it. "You've never offered to share."

"Why would I share?"

"I knew it! You are sneaking it. You're a greedy little sweets hoarder."

Gavriel tried to grab the bag from her, but she held it out, extending her arm as far as it went. "Give it back." His voice was more of a growl. So, the assassin had food aggression?

"I think not. I want to see what all the fuss is about." Lark popped the piece she held into her mouth, letting it crumble on her tongue. It had a deep flavor. A little bitter for her taste, but not bad. "This is what you've been hiding? Hmm, maybe I should take your supply off your hands."

Gavriel made a low whining noise in the back of his throat. "Lark, please. That's the last of my stash 'til we make it to the next town."

She clicked her tongue. "Poor little Gavriel. Serves you right for not sharing. Didn't your mother teach you any manners?"

He wrapped his arm around her as he stretched to grab the small satchel. Thick, corded muscle held Lark firm. Pressed against him, she tried to ignore the flare of heat that bloomed at the contact.

"Give it." His words were strained between clenched teeth.

Twisting away, Lark slipped from the saddle.

Gavriel's grip tightened. Lark's head flung back as the sudden force yanked her short of hitting the ground.

She lifted her eyes to Gavriel's face, suddenly inches from hers. His warm breath, as sweet as the chocolate she'd just stolen. His forest green eyes darted to her mouth, once, before finding their way back to meet her gaze.

"I got you, Lark."

The sound of her name rumbling deep in his chest did funny things to her stomach.

Lark righted herself and tugged her tunic smooth. With a deceptively steady hand, she placed the bag in his palm and tried to ignore the searing touch as his fingers grazed hers. She had other things to think of. They were a mere matter of days from reaching the edge of the Emerald Woods. Oakbury was on the outskirts, and the perfect place to resupply.

Lark needed to tell the others of her plan without arousing concern. Without knowing exactly what she was walking into, she couldn't allow them to follow. They had enough to worry about, and she didn't want to add another shadow to Alistair's crowded eyes. If all else failed, she and Gavriel might have to sneak away in the night.

The thought stirred a sudden thrill through her. She smothered it before it could take root.

Gavriel was only bound to her by obligation, nothing more. Her foolish notions were born of loneliness and inexperience. It was in her best interest to remember that.

Even if he was warm and smelled like leather and dark chocolate.

CHAPTER 31

"All right, we'll put it to a vote. Camp here for the night or power through the pain so I can spend the wee hours of the morning between a pair of lovely and expensive breasts. Hands? Anyone? Anyone?" Alistair asked with his hand high above his head.

Lark glanced up from her task of wiping the sticky sap from the endless pine trees against her softened leather leggings. They'd left the road and taken once again to the forest, a supposed shortcut, but days spent breathing the cool scent of pine and damp earth gave Lark doubt.

Alistair searched everyone's expressions for a glimmer of agreement.

He found none.

Alistair had a way of switching his scoundrel mentality on and off like an oil lamp. Raising and lowering the flame at will.

"Fine. Have it your way. Langford's will have to do."

Langford choked on his water, coughing and sputtering rivulets all down his tunic. Lark patted his back.

"You'll keep your hands to yourself, Alistair. Your urges are your burden alone," Daciana said.

Alistair wagged his eyebrows at Langford. "Not if the bottles of wine I stashed in your pack remain intact. Then all bets are off."

Lark pretended not to notice the charming flush that crept up Langford's neck. Or the small smile he twisted his mouth to hide as he rummaged through his pack. He pulled out two bottles. "Alistair, you know I hate this trick."

Alistair shrugged. "How else shall I dazzle you with my cunning? The expensive stuff is in Daciana's care, of course. Lark, if you would be a dear and examine the contents of your pack as well."

Skies above, what a pest.

Lark placed her bag on the ground, weary of all the times she'd been less than gentle with it. "You could have at least told us you were hiding glass in our bags."

"Yours isn't glass," Alistair said, bouncing on his heels. "And that would have ruined the dramatic reveal."

"It also would have made them less likely to shatter."

"Oh, hush."

Lark dug her hand around until she found a clay jug. Alistair's rum. Glaring up at him, she yanked it from her bag. "Where did you get these? And how did you even manage this? I checked my pack this morning." Lark had heard tales of Alistair's light fingers, his ability to pickpocket a man while looking him in the eye. But Alistair was the source of these stories, so she assumed them to be exaggerated.

Alistair leapt forward with eager fingers to snatch it from her. "Ay, that's a good lass. The broken down caravan Hugo and I searched wasn't quite as empty as I led you to believe, and I have my ways. That's all I'm going to say." He gazed fondly at the jug as if staring upon the face of a lover. "I'd have stashed it in Gavriel's but he was already carrying precious cargo."

Lark turned on Gavriel. Desperate curiosity gnawed at her. "What does he carry?"

Gavriel gave Alistair a murderous glare. "Nothing."

"Why would you carry an item like that if you had no intention of sharing it?" Alistair crossed his arms and angled his head.

"You found his chocolate?" So much for raiding his stash later.

"Lark." Gavriel's voice held a warning. He wrenched his pack out of reach and stomped off to tie up the horses.

Lark followed, ignoring whatever Alistair offered in response. Her gaze was fixed on Gavriel's bag he'd placed on the ground as he wrapped the reins around an ash tree. The spring breeze wafted through the forest, carrying the scent of fresh rain. It rattled the buckle on Gavriel's unguarded bag.

What could he possibly carry that he didn't want her to know about?

"Don't even think about it."

Lark found Gavriel watching her with a threat in his eyes. "One can't help but wonder—"

"Leave it alone." Gavriel resumed brushing the horses, ignoring her.

Lark's arm snaked out to grab his pack, but Gavriel was quicker. His hand clasped around her wrist in a bruising grip, yanking her forward, and Lark stumbled, laughing high and bright.

"I'm sorry. But I won't be able to sleep until I know what's in there." She grinned as she lowered her voice to a whisper. "Is it indecent?"

"Skies, woman." Gavriel dropped her wrist in disgust. "It's personal and private. That should be enough."

"It may be personal, but it won't stay private long. Not among us anyway."

Gavriel muttered to himself as he resumed grooming the horses.

"I'll ask Alistair."

"He'll enjoy knowing something you don't. He isn't likely to let that go."

"Then I'll have to get him drunk," Lark said with a smile that promised mischief. "I've found spirits to be just the thing to loosen even the tightest of lips."

THE FIRE BURNED bright that evening, flames dancing amongst the shadows.

The wine bottle was once again pressed into Lark's hand. She thumbed the glass, smudged with everyone's fingerprints, and took a deep drink. Warmth spread in her belly and hummed in her head. She passed the bottle to Hugo, and he passed it off to Daciana again without taking a drink. No surprise there. Lark couldn't remember ever having seen Hugo partake.

Daciana grinned at Lark as she slugged it back, nearly finishing it. She passed the last of it to Gavriel who handed it toward Langford without so much as a sip.

"Of course," Lark muttered.

Gavriel froze. "Why, 'of course'?"

"Because you just don't seem like the type to relinquish control." Lark settled back, crossing her arms. They were heavier than usual.

Gavriel laughed. "Oh? And you are?"

"Deflect all you like. I still find you utterly predictable."

Gavriel's eyes flashed dangerously.

Alistair made a move to take the bottle from Langford, but Gavriel snatched it back, holding it out of reach. Alistair grunted as he lunged for the bottle, but Gavriel was faster in his sober state.

Heat washed over Lark's cheeks under the force of Gavriel's stare. The air between them thickened, and his dark green eyes bore into her, a challenge written in them. He downed the rest of the bottle, ignoring the sound of protest from Alistair.

Lark grinned, tempering the thrill that ran through her. "Are you sure you know what you're doing?"

He gave her a crooked smile that dimpled his cheek and sent something fluttering in her stomach. "Are you, Demon?"

LARK'S MUSCLES were loose and weightless, as though she floated atop a river current. She tipped her head to watch the embers float up in the dark sky. The hum of drink buzzed in her head and loosened the coil of tension she'd grown accustomed to.

Her gaze dropped back to Gavriel across the fire. His expression was difficult to read as he watched her.

The gentle hum of the conversations around her filtered in and out of her awareness. It was the pleasant sound of warm laughter and idle chat. But she wanted to hear music. She remembered that traveling musician with the beautiful fiddle. The one Andros swore was in Gavriel's possession. In her foolish anger, she'd left it behind.

What a waste.

Not that she could play, but she suspected Langford might. He had the sort of elegant hands that seemed destined to create something of beauty.

"It's a shame we haven't any music," Lark said, wiping the back of her hand across her mouth. "I would love to dance."

Gavriel stared at the ground.

Alistair halted his conversation with Daciana, before sliding a gleeful expression Lark's way. "Would you now?"

"Oh, yes." There was no room for hesitance when wine warmed her belly with courage. "I haven't had occasion to dance yet in this form."

"You've never danced," Alistair said, running a hand over his chin as he glanced over at Gavriel. "What a shame. I've found when you lead a life such as this, you can't wait for fate to intervene. You could die tomorrow, never having danced. Such a pity. Isn't that a shame, Gavriel?"

Gavriel refused to acknowledge him.

"Who says we need music to dance?" Daciana jumped to her feet, far more lithe than she had any right to be. She marched over to Lark. Bending in a deep bow, she extended her hand. "May I have this dance?"

Thoughts of maiming and dismemberment dissolved. Lark giggled and clapped her hand in Daciana's. "But of course, my lady, I thought you'd never ask."

Daciana pulled Lark to standing. Clumsily, they waltzed around the fire, tripping over each other and cackling with each misstep. Alistair gruffly hummed a tune for them, though no one could quite keep a tempo.

Lark's foot hit Langford's, knocking them off balance, their movements getting sloppier with each pass around the fire. Lark's sides ached with laughter as Daciana dragged and spun her in circles.

"I want to lead!" Lark angled Daciana back in an exaggerated dip. Too far back. They toppled over in a heap on the ground, legs tangled. Breathless, they lost themselves to another bout of laughter.

Lark hadn't realized mirth made it difficult to breathe.

"You are, without a doubt"—Daciana said, in a voice on the edge of breaking—"the worst dancer I've ever had the misfortune of pairing with."

"Why thank you," Lark said, tipping her chin. "I aim to impress."

Disentangling their limbs, they heaved themselves to their feet, tripping back over to the fire.

Lark plopped herself down next to Gavriel. "I don't suppose you dance."

He was still staring at the ground. "You truly wish to dance?"

"Was that not dancing? I admit that was the extent of my knowledge."

"No, that's not what I—" Gavriel clamped his mouth shut tight as if forcing the words to slow. "Do you desire to hear music?"

Lark turned, ready to tease him, only to find something both soft and intense in his eyes. Her stomach flipped; a different sort of shiver crept along her skin. "Yes."

"I'll only be a moment." Gavriel nodded, leaving her side and taking his warmth with him.

True to his word, Gavriel appeared a moment later, pack in hand. He gave her a sheepish expression before reaching into his bag. "If I catch even a whiff of ridicule, I'm smashing the damn thing. Understand?"

Lark nodded. A tingling of energy buzzed in her veins. She shifted, unable to sit still.

He pulled out an elegant horsehair bow. The polished redwood gleamed in the firelight. Gavriel wore a bracing expression, and out came the beautiful fiddle. The one she'd admired from the musician's stand. The one he swore was not in his possession when he'd been captured, despite Andros' claims.

"You said it wasn't yours."

"I lied."

Lark ran her gaze over dark cherry wood, lacquered to a bright sheen. Intricate carvings of golden leaves, branches, and roots swirled along the body of the instrument, a wild forest captured on its smooth surface.

"You stole this?"

Gavriel frowned. "I'm an assassin, not a thief."

Lark bit her lip, gaze darting between the man and the instrument. "Why would you buy this?"

He balanced the bow across his lap and the base of the fiddle against his knee. "You seemed to like it."

As if that didn't build a million more questions in her throat.

Lark swallowed them down, asking only one. "Can you play?"

"I can." The corner of his mouth lifted.

Something tight and shaky curled in her chest, coiling around her heart. "Play me a song."

Gavriel gave a short nod before lifting the fiddle to rest between his shoulder and chin. If the others made any comment on their exchange, Lark didn't notice. All the world had narrowed down to him and this beautiful instrument. Fiddle and bow were delicately balanced in the same hands she'd witnessed commit enough bloodshed to last a lifetime.

Gavriel's eyes never left hers as he dragged the bow across the strings. Her skin goose-pebbled as a chill crept up her spine, settling at her neck. He glided back and forth across the strings, a haunting melody filling the space between them. Still, his eyes never left her face. The hairs on the back of her neck rose, and her skin hummed as he played. Unnamed emotion thickened her throat, her vision blurring from unshed tears. Her heart pounded against her chest as she watched and listened. Felt his music pour through her. Fill her with everything she'd never known as a Reaper. Everything she dared to want as a mortal: hope and crushing sadness, familiar yet new. It was a memory that didn't belong to her, and yet her heart soared. It plummeted. Rising and falling in time with the sweep of his bow.

Everything else fell away until there was only she and him. His notes and her fractured heart beating away as he played. His song was a lifeline to her very soul, tugging her out of the mists and into somewhere new and inviting. Something once lost, found.

Gavriel flourished his last arpeggio, ending the trance. He cleared his throat, lowering the fiddle to his lap.

Lark blinked away tears, missing one as it rolled down her cheek, and Gavriel wiped it away with his thumb. The warmth of his touch seared her skin with a fire she longed to burn in. He seemed to catch himself and snatched his hand away.

The absence of his touch doused her with cold. Lark wiped her cheeks with both hands. "Forgive me, that was beautiful."

"There's nothing to forgive," Gavriel said, voice thick. "But I didn't give you anything to dance to."

The air between them was too charged. Lark struggled to find words. Any words. They had all flown from her head.

"Remedy that, you fool!" Alistair called from across the fire. "We could all do with a jig, none of that maudlin drivel."

Gavriel gave Lark a wry smile and lifted his instrument again. With precise strokes, he began an upbeat tune, fingers dancing over the strings. Lark's heart quickened as he deftly fiddled his way through the song. She felt a tap on her shoulder.

Langford bowed before her. "My lady, I know I shall pale in comparison to the great lady Daciana, but would you do me the honor of this dance?" He extended his hand.

"The honor would be mine." Lark gave Gavriel one last look as she stood. Langford led them through the dance with far more grace than any of them possessed. Despite her obvious shortcomings, he managed to glide them round and round the fire. Picking up speed with Gavriel's furious playing.

Lark glanced over to see Hugo watching, a small smile on his face.

Daciana and Alistair danced around the fire, their faces bright with laughter. Alistair's hand kept snaking down her backside, which Daciana was quick to slap away.

Langford spun Lark, and as she turned, she caught sight of Gavriel. Though his forehead was pulled in concentration, he wore a grin as he played—a grin she wished she could bottle up and save. She wanted to always remember this moment. Right now. When everyone was smiling, the fire was warm, and nothing could touch them.

Lark tipped her head back and laughed, full and deep, as Langford continued to spin her effortlessly. The dark trees spun against the night sky, waltzing with her as Gavriel played. She clung to the moment as it was happening. The fleeting rightness of a memory as it formed, and she was more alive than she'd ever been her entire existence.

AFTER THE DRINKS had run out, and Alistair was unconscious, the general energy began to die down.

Langford shuffled off to bed as Daciana called out, "Goodnight."

Gavriel finally retired his fiddle for the evening, sweat glistening on his forehead. He was so precise in everything he did. Be it packing, playing the fiddle, killing a man. What weren't those hands capable of?

"You play beautifully."

Gavriel smirked at her. "I know."

"What a relief you aren't plagued by false modesty."

Gavriel's responding laugh curled around her. "Perhaps not. But it doesn't mean much. It isn't a practical skill to have."

"I disagree. The gift of music is an incredibly valuable skill."

Gavriel pulled his pack closed, eying her. "Did you enjoy it?"

Something tugged in her chest. Making it difficult to breathe. Lark nodded. "I did."

"That's all the purpose it needs."

Her stomach fluttered as heat washed over her face. They stood in silence for a moment. The night air, their only witness.

"I was a child the first time I saw a fiddle. Master Hamlin kept one in his office. I guess my eager hands lacked the discipline to keep from touching things I shouldn't." He gave her a crooked grin. "Lucky for me, my superior was an understanding man and seized an opportunity to teach me a lesson. He forced me to learn, to practice for hours as punishment."

Lark laughed. "A fitting punishment, indeed."

"I had training to attend. While the others my age had time to rest between sessions, I had to discipline my mind and hands through the exhaustion. No breaks, no rest."

Lark had no idea what he'd been through. What life had wrought for him thus far. His hands weren't clean, but there was a rare beauty to his spirit she found herself drawn to. Before she could think better of it, she placed her hand over his. Gavriel stilled, staring at where their hands joined.

"I'm glad I met you." She didn't know what possessed her to say it. But there they were, the simple yet traitorous words. Hanging between them.

He slipped his other hand over hers. The blazing heat sent a shudder through her. He pinned her in place with the intensity of his stare. "I'm glad you found me. I'd still be lost were it not for you."

Lark swallowed against the knot in her throat. "You'd be dead. Although depending on where you ended up, I daresay you'd have found some enjoyment in the afterlife."

Gavriel ran his thumb over the back of her hand, the simple act jolting through her and searing fire in its wake. "That's right; I suppose you found me twice in this life."

The sweet scent of wine and chocolate mingled on his warm breath. The scar across his cheek was close enough to touch. The seemingly permanent frown line reserved for her, smoothed for once. His face was open. Hopeful. She'd never seen anything so beautiful.

Without thinking, Lark wet her lips. His eyes darted to her mouth, and his lips parted. If she rose up on her toes and pressed her lips to that scar, what would it feel like?

The memory of the kiss she stole, the binding promise to inherit his death and spare him, came barreling through her. Of everything they'd suffered. Every choice, every sacrifice made, led her here to this moment, this path. She'd already claimed more than the balance owed her. It felt like tempting fate to allow herself this.

Lark pulled back.

Gavriel's face fell. "Lark, if I—"

"You did nothing wrong." She ignored the sharp crack in her heart as she took another step back. Icy cold rushed through her at the loss of his warmth. "It's late."

He nodded, his eyes growing distant.

She bit the inside of her cheek, cursing herself for being so foolish. So selfish. Perhaps in another life... but this life was already tipping the scale.

"Goodnight Gavriel." She turned and fled before she had a chance to change her mind.

CHAPTER 32

*D*espite summer's impending arrival, mornings had a crisp bite. A wet chill that seeped beneath the skin until the midday sun thawed the cold from each evening.

The week spent on the road was tense, each moment laden with unspoken words between Lark and Gavriel. So when the forest thinned and a road lined by a low stone wall came into view, Lark felt a surge of relief.

When they arrived in Oakbury, they found the Walden Inn and Tavern and retired their horses for the night. Upon crossing the threshold of the stone clad building, Alistair was greeted by the innkeeper, a portly woman with a wide smile. She yanked him into her arms with enough force to crush a small bear, hugging him to her chest.

"Don't you dare let this much time pass between visits again!"

Alistair laughed, extricating himself from the embrace. "Why, Mrs. O'Connell, you know I'd never allow it intentionally. I haven't had a decent meal since the last time I was here."

"Oh sit! Sit!" Mrs. O'Connell ushered them in, offering a polite pat to Hugo and Langford and kissing both of Daciana's cheeks. She wore her cornflower hair in a messy coil at the nape of her neck, unruly strands sticking out in all directions. She wiped her flour-covered hands on her homespun dress, adding more white dust to the russet fabric. She turned to Gavriel and Lark. "And who might these folks be?"

"That's Lark and Gavriel." Alistair had his feet crossed atop one of the round wooden tables, fingers laced behind his head. "They're utterly debauched and a terrible influence on me."

Of all the ridiculous things. Lark shot him a glare, and Alistair grinned.

"I don't believe that for a second." Mrs. O'Connell turned back to them, a small smile on her face. "Any friend of Alistair's is a friend of mine."

"You may come to regret that sentiment," Langford called from his seat.

"Hush now, boy." She opened her arms and enveloped Lark in a none too gentle embrace. She smelled of flour, cinnamon, and warmth. Lark found herself hugging her back and reveling in the odd sort of comfort that came with embracing a stranger.

Mrs. O'Connell pulled back and placed her hands on Lark's cheeks. "You look like you could use a good meal." She peered at Gavriel. "And you look like you could use a bath."

Gavriel had the grace to look somewhat embarrassed, hands errantly dusting his clothes.

He appeared so normal—

—for an assassin covered in grime from travel.

"Never mind that." Mrs. O'Connell patted his arm. "Come, sit, I'll fetch you a warm supper."

"And ale!" Alistair hollered.

She smacked his legs, pointing to the floor.

With a sigh, Alistair pulled his boot-clad feet off the table and sat upright in his seat.

It was beautiful. His ability to make a home in so many places, care for people, and find himself in their hearts as well.

"So, where's Mr. O'Connell?" Lark was quite pleased with herself for remembering the mortal customs of marriage and name exchange.

Judging by the knowing grins she received, she'd made a miscalculation.

Mrs. O'Connell laughed, a deep hearty sound. "There never was a Mr. I gave myself the title to keep the pestering men at bay. Never needed a man, not one day in my life, thank you very much."

"Oh, of course," Lark said, feeling foolish for asking.

"But one day, I'll wear you down," Alistair said, arching a brow and offering a rakish grin.

Mrs. O'Connell shook her head at the ceiling and swept away to prepare their dinner.

Alistair leaned across the table. "I'll be hitting town square tomorrow in search of a job. I can offer you each a stipend for the market. You're free to do what you want wherever you want. Just don't spend all my coin."

As much as Lark longed to explore the village, having one carefree day as a human, she couldn't. She had to get to Emerald Woods and find the woman Kenna spoke of.

The fantasy she'd had all those months ago flashed in Lark's mind: carrying a basket of flowers, passing them out to villagers. When she was a Reaper with little more than dreams and longing.

Lark pushed the thought away, and picked up a wooden spoon, eager to taste her next meal.

WHEN THE HOUR WAS LATE, and they'd all retired to their rooms, Lark grew restless. Alistair had procured private quarters for her, Daciana, Gavriel, and of course himself, while Hugo and Langford shared one of the larger rooms the Walden Inn offered. Lark and Daciana had offered to share, but Hugo was quick to grunt his dismissal and claim his side of the shared bed. Lark stifled a smile at the thought of Langford and Hugo fighting over blankets and sleeping space.

This was the first room Lark had all to herself since fleeing the Otherworld. Her narrow bed was tucked in the corner, cotton blankets folded down, waiting for sleep. A lone candle in its brass holder sat atop a tidy end table, flickering beneath the open window. She paced the short length of her room and ran her hand impatiently through her hair. Tomorrow she would search for the witch in the woods, and she still hadn't told the others. A slippery unease wound its way in her gut. Was she actually experiencing guilt for not telling Alistair, Hugo, and Langford her plan? That would be impossible. She had nothing to feel sorry for; it was her business she was under no obligation to disclose.

Then why did it feel strangely close to lying?

Before she could change her mind, she opened her door and padded down the hall to Gavriel's room. With a quiet knock, it swung open as if he'd been expecting her. Her breath caught in her throat under the sheer force of his stare. A map of scars and muscles hewn for destruction greeted her. Unburdened by clothing. Lark's cheeks burned.

"I'm sorry," Gavriel whispered. "I've been listening to you pace around your room for the last half an hour. I'd been wondering when you'd come to me."

Lark scowled on instinct. He certainly thought highly of himself. "Why would you expect me to come to you?"

"Because we need to form a plan to slip away." His eyes narrowed in suspicion. "Did you think I had something else in mind?"

Lark debated walking back to her room and leaving him out of her plans. Fewer headaches that way.

He sighed, opening the door further, his arm still bracing it, so she had to duck under to enter. He shut it behind her, tension in every movement as he approached his washbasin. Without a word, he splashed his face, cupping water to rub over the back of his neck and the top of his head. Flickering candlelight danced across the firm planes of his chest and stomach.

Lark averted her gaze. "If you expected me, you might have put on a shirt."

She kept her eyes on the wall, tracking the wood grains. His answering chuckle slithered through her, filling her with a dizzying warmth.

"There, I'm decent."

Lark turned back to see him sporting a dark loose-fitting tunic, neckline unlaced.

He most certainly was not.

Clearing her throat, and her mind, she regarded him with what she hoped was a neutral expression. "You know what we need to do tomorrow."

"We can take two horses; travel will be faster that way." He leaned against the wall, arms crossed.

"I'll ask Alistair tomorrow; make sure they can part with them."

Gavriel tensed. "You can't be serious."

Confusion cleared away any hint of lingering heat. "Why's that?"

He pushed off the wall, stalking over to her. "You'd jeopardize this, to ask *permission?*"

Now she was annoyed.

Lark rose to her feet, her hands fisting by her sides. "I'm not asking permission to go. I'm being considerate to their needs."

Gavriel scoffed. "And what of more pressing needs? I thought this was imperative to the fate of the world. Or is your need to be liked more important than saving thousands of lives." He glared down his nose at her.

How did he get this close?

She met his disgust with equal disdain.

"How dare you presume to know my motivations? You jump to conclusions and treat them as fact before your head has a chance to catch up."

"All I know is, they're not going to let you leave with their mode of transport."

"You're all-knowing now, Gavriel? My, what a useful skill that must be. Tell me, can you predict where I'm planning on hitting you?"

"You think because they've made peace with what you are that they'll let you go unchecked?" He shook his head at her. "You're not that stupid."

Lark couldn't help it. As a Reaper, her rage had always been a cold measured animal. A creature of ice and stone. She could quietly storm, roiling inside and never so much as crack. Emotion was a fleeting thing. Slippery like an eel, she couldn't hold onto it for long.

As a human, her anger was wild. An unchecked forest fire, waves crashing against the surf. All uncontrolled energy. Gone were the days of her quietly smoldering. Instead, an inferno raged within her. One she couldn't quell no matter how hard she tried, and she hated that her form betrayed her like this in front of him.

She clenched her fists, and hot traitorous tears filled her vision, scorching their way down her cheeks. She willed them to stop, to cease their travel and call a retreat.

But humanity was wild, and answered to no one.

Gavriel's face twisted, regret written across his features. He reached out to her, "Lark," he began. "I didn't mean it to come out that cruel." He edged closer but stopped when she took an equal step back. With a sigh, he sat on his bed and ran a hand over his face. "I don't want to see anyone stand in the way. This task is as much mine as it is yours. And I'll be damned if I sit by and let anyone interfere."

"Why do you care?"

"It's important, isn't it?"

"Right, but why do *you* care?"

Gavriel swallowed, lowering his eyes to the floor. A heartbeat passed before he spoke. "Everything that's happened, all that you've had to do, it's my fault." He lifted his stare to regard her. "If your escape caused any holes in the barrier or whatever keeps monsters from this world, I share the blame for those."

"I don't understand."

"If you hadn't saved me, you wouldn't have been punished and forced to flee your world."

"You think I wouldn't have chosen this path were it not for you?" Lark shook her head. "I already told you, I hated being a Reaper. I've wanted to be human long before you were even born."

"But you could have taken your time, done it right. Saving my life forced your hand." Gavriel's voice had gone quiet.

Lark crossed the room and grabbed him by the chin, forcing him to face her. The look she earned was decidedly cross. "I made my own choices. Now I live with them. And knowing how all this plays out, I'd still do it. I'd save you a thousand times, Gavriel, because it was my choice, and no one will ever take that away from me."

Gavriel gazed up at her, his expression softening. His green eyes searched her face, eager in their pursuit. He stood, the sudden motion jarring her to take a step back.

"I promise to do everything to ensure that choice wasn't in vain." He placed his hands on Lark's arms. Where his hands touched, her skin burned. Even through the cotton tunic she wore. She swallowed, her throat thick.

"Even if it means"—he bore his eyes into hers, unwavering intensity scorched through her—"asking permission to borrow horses."

Lark rolled her eyes and shoved him off.

Gavriel flashed her a boyish smile that made her knees weak. "You're right, you know. My way would only lead to further complications. We do it your way." He crossed over to the door, leaning against the wall and grasping the handle. A silent dismissal. "By your leave, madam."

Quelling her disappointment, Lark gave a short nod and strode past him and into the hallway. Glancing over her shoulder only once, she could have sworn his face was twisted in indecision. Like he was warring with himself over words left unsaid.

But that would be absurd.

She made her way to her room. Closing the door on the night.

"Of course, you can take the horses, love," Alistair said as if the sheer notion of confirming with him was ridiculous.

Even though they all knew he'd pitch a fit if she hadn't.

They all sat at what had become their usual table in the corner by the hearth. The lattice windows nearby let the early morning illuminate the steam coiling out the top of Lark's cup and Alistair's pleased expression.

"Thank you," Lark said, distrusting his agreeable nature. Perhaps he was content to be in a safe place among civilization for once.

"Sure, sure. Do you need any supplies? I'm assuming you and Gavriel will share a tent should your errand run late."

"That won't be necessary, it should only take the day."

"Splendid. Well, safe journeys, we'll see you for dinner tonight, yes?" Alistair clapped her on the back.

Who knew what put Alistair in his good moods? Maybe he found a warm body to lay beside last night.

"Lark, I almost forgot, since you'll be requiring the horses I will ask you to complete a favor for me upon your return." Alistair flashed her a grin. "Thank you so much."

"Hold on. What kind of favor?" A price yet to be determined didn't sit well with her.

"Just a job, nothing you can't handle."

"Might I inquire after what this job entails?"

"You may."

"But you won't answer."

"Nope." Alistair beamed, before patting her on the arm. "Hurry along, we all have places to be. Langford, you're with me today." He beckoned with a wave of his hand.

Langford downed the rest of his tea, wiping the corners of his mouth with a napkin. "As you command."

"Careful, lest I think you enjoy spending the day by my side." Alistair winked in Langford's direction.

Langford snorted. "Perish the thought."

"We should get going." Gavriel stood, shifting his weight from one foot to the other.

"I can accompany you if you wish." Daciana sat, breaking her bread into small pieces between her fingers and popping them into her mouth.

"I won't say no to an extra set of eyes watching my back." Lark slid into the seat beside Daciana, ignoring Gavriel's impatient energy. She traced the grooves in the wood table. "But are you certain you want to come?" This was Kenna's contact, after all.

Daciana took a swig of her tea. "Why wouldn't I?" She cast an amused look at Gavriel, noting his tense posture. Turning back to Lark, a mischievous grin spread across her face. "Unless you'd prefer some alone time with this one."

Lark scoffed but it somehow lacked the intended effect. "Why would I want that?"

Daciana held up a hand. "All right, give me ten minutes; we'll be on our way."

Lark nodded, standing and stretching her arms over her head. "We should ready the horses."

Gavriel gave her a strange look before he strode for the door. Lark followed, but as she passed Hugo, she gave him a reassuring pat on the shoulder.

Hugo caught her hand. "We need to talk."

"I have the stronger bow you made me. And I have Daciana. I'll be fine."

He stood, his chair groaning against the floor. "Right. Let's talk." He gestured toward the back door.

The summer morning was warm and damp with dew, and the dawn chorus of early birds had yet to end. Lark smiled and breathed in a lungful of wet air. Hugo turned to face her. "I don't trust the assassin."

One of Hugo's finer qualities: he spoke straight and to the point.

"Hugo, he's proved time and time again he's with us. You know he's saved my life once or twice." And gotten her captured a time or two, but who was keeping track? Lark regarded Hugo's scowling face and tried not to laugh. This was ridiculous. A mortal man treating her like a child. She'd been a Reaper more years than he'd been alive.

And yet. A small ember of warmth unfurled in her chest at his concern.

"I'm not talking about that." He placed his hands on his hips and regarded her with a hard expression. "Men like that, they don't last long. And I don't like him making a target outta you. You deserve better than that."

"We're all targets, aren't we?"

"Yeah, well." Hugo shook his head. "I'd be wary of a man with that many enemies. There's only so long you can keep your guard up before something slips through."

Some wounds never healed. Never knitted back the flesh once parted. Impervious to time and distance.

Lark grasped his shoulder. His large hand covered hers, patting it once. Perhaps one day he'd tell her of his hurts.

If only she could make him understand his concerns for her were unfounded. Gavriel and she might dance around each other, but their alliance, or whatever it was, was finite. The day was fast approaching where they'd part ways.

"Thank you. It's nice for someone to care enough to worry."

He nodded.

"But you needn't. I'd hate for you to waste any time or energy on it. So, I relieve you of that burden."

Hugo narrowed his dark eyes. "It's my job to worry."

With a slight shake of her head, she pulled him into one of her hugs that always made him cringe. This time he hugged her back, wrapping a thick arm around her and crushing her to his chest. She felt his hand on the back of her head.

"Be safe, kid."

CHAPTER 33

*K*enna's instructions were simple: *"In the heart of the Emerald Woods, head as far west as you can until you hit the lake. You'll see her place."*

They rode hard and fast despite the unfamiliar forest. The thought of hearing Ferryn's voice, of seeing him again, propelled Lark through the dense trees.

The Emerald Woods buzzed with life. Light filtered through branches, sparkling against the dew covered ground. The trees disappeared into the sky, ancient and unyielding to time. Moss had claimed and softened their trunks, and violet mushrooms adorned their roots. It was like something out of a dream. A haven of vibrant greens and deep browns. The damp air carried the scent of overturned earth and recent rain.

When the trees thickened, and the ground darkened without the warmth of the sun, Apple reared up on her haunches, almost unseating Lark. She clung to the leather reins, firmly planting her heels to keep from falling. Beside her, both Gavriel's and Daciana's mounts had been similarly spooked into halting at the same spot.

Lark swung a leg over, dismounting and running soothing hands down Apple's mane. There must have been a very good reason they dared not venture deeper into these woods.

"We must be getting close. Can the horses sense this?"

"Animals instinctively avoid danger. Survival of the species and all that," Gavriel said with a frown. "Seems stupid not to take this as a warning."

Lark bit the side of her cheek. It might not be safe, but it was necessary.

Daciana sighed. "Guess we're traveling the rest of the way on foot." She slid from her mount, leading her horse over to a tree to tie the reins.

The sudden loss of speed sharpened the sounds of the forest. The rustle of small animals rooting around in the underbrush. The hum of the cicadas in the distance.

"I don't like the idea of leaving Apple here," Lark said. She reached into her pocket, fingers closing around Kenna's pendant.

Gavriel crept to Lark's side. "I know, but she'll be safe." He ran a hand down Apple's mane. "Won't you now?"

Apple gave him nothing.

"She doesn't like you," Lark said with a smile.

He frowned. "She just hasn't warmed up to me yet. I'll grow on her though."

Lark rested her forehead against Apple's. "Be safe. Any sign of trouble, you run. Otherwise, wait here for me."

"Wait, you're not going to tie her up?" Gavriel regarded her with an incredulous expression.

"No, I'm not risking her being trapped if something happens."

Gavriel crossed his arms. The strength of his frame was evident as he stared down at her. "You risk her wandering off and getting lost."

Lark ignored him and gave Apple one more pat before continuing west. It couldn't be far now.

343

THE CRYSTAL-CLEAR LAKE came into view. The placid water was like a glass mirror, reflecting the forest's height in its image. Lark took cautious steps forward. There was no cottage. More forest lay beyond the lake—endless trees.

Daciana placed her hands on her hips, thumbing her daggers. "What exactly did she say?"

"Travel as far west as you can until you hit the lake, then you'll see the cottage." Lark hoped she remembered correctly.

Daciana's mouth thinned in a firm line. Gavriel hung back, watching them as he leaned against a tree and drank from his waterskin.

"She must have been mistaken," Lark said, rising onto the balls of her feet and staring intently into the distance.

"Nope, she's just a pain in the ass." With a quiet sigh, Daciana strode into the lake, the water lapping against her ankles. "That's what I thought."

Lark frowned. There was nothing there. Just the calm waters of a lonely lake tucked into the forest.

Daciana grabbed Lark by the wrist, yanking her forward until lake-water spilled into her boots.

"Daciana!" Before the litany of curses on the tip of Lark's tongue could tumble from her mouth, she caught sight of it.

Across the lake sat a small cottage. Smoke billowed in thick tendrils from an aged brick chimney. Overgrown moss and vines capture the façade of the hut, as if at any moment the forest would swallow it whole. The surrounding trees reached out their branches to reclaim it.

Lark dragged her foot free from the sand that tried to swallow her boot.

"Where are you going?" Daciana watched Lark with thinly veiled amusement.

"I'm going around. Now that I know it's there, I'll just walk along the water's edge until I find it."

Daciana's full lips curved in a knowing smile. "It doesn't work that way, Lark."

"I'll see you on the other side." Lark took off, uncaring if Gavriel or Daciana followed. They could swim if they wanted to. But one thing Lark was not going to do was spend the day in wet clothes.

SOAKED TO THE BONE, Lark stood before the sun-faded cottage door, thick droplets rolling off her clothes and landing heavily upon the earth.

Daciana was right. As soon as Lark made it a few paces away, her feet stilled and she couldn't remember where she was going. After a dozen more tries, Lark relented. It was some sort of warding spell to keep the cottage from view. The only way of access was across the lake or in this case, through it.

Lark assumed soaking wet clothes would be uncomfortable against mortal skin. What she didn't account for was the weight. The leather was heavy against her thighs, tight and unforgiving. When Lark returned to the inn, she'd luxuriate in a scalding hot bath. She swept a hand across her forehead, pushing back the water-thickened hair that clung to her face.

"There's a boat for our trip back across the lake," Gavriel said.

A small comfort that failed to lift Lark's mood. Balling up her fist, she knocked against the aged wood door. It swung open, and a young woman appeared. Deep chestnut waves framed her warm umber face, her large dark eyes scanning them warily.

"Are you the hedge witch?" Lark offered no pleasantries. She'd left those at the bottom of that blasted lake.

"I'm the one who decides who enters and who is sent on their way. What do you seek?" Her voice was thick and rough. The girl lifted her sharp chin to look over Lark's shoulder at Gavriel. "Surely not a love potion with a strapping man like that watching your flank."

Gavriel cleared his throat.

"I was sent here." Lark snaked her hand into her pocket, her fist closing around the talisman. "Kenna told me the witch would help me."

The girl's dark eyes roved over Lark in a calculating fashion. "Kenna sent you?"

Lark yanked the pendant from her pocket, holding it out so the glowing blue stone and wood-carved mountain range dangled between them. It hummed on the end of the black leather cord. Vibrating through Lark's palm like it was eager to be seen. "She told me to show her this." Lark didn't know why, but she was anxious to tuck it away.

But the girl wasn't listening to her. Instead, her eyes were transfixed by the swinging necklace, her gaze traveling with it. Her eyebrows furrowed, and she opened the door wide enough for them to enter.

Lark hastily tucked the talisman away and glanced around the small cottage. Living greenery dominated every surface. Leaf-dusted vines snaked up the walls and across the ceiling. A black iron kettle rested over the hearth where a small fire crackled. Tempered glass window panes spilled beams of sunlight across the floor and through countless decorative glasses that donned every surface.

"Nethers, take that reckless fool." The girl slammed the door shut, blowing dark strands of hair from her face. She stomped past them; the floor groaned with every step. Yanking a chair out of the way, she kicked back the rug, revealing a trapdoor with a thick iron ringed handle.

Lark and Daciana shared a look.

"Well, get in."

Lark glanced over at Gavriel, who was running a hand across the overcrowded bookshelf. "Are you the witch?"

The dark-haired beauty heaved a sigh that held the weight of a thousand lifetimes. "I am who you seek."

Lark tried to school her expression into one of neutrality but based on the answering scowl she received; she was unsuccessful. The witch appeared far too youthful to hold all the knowledge Kenna promised. But humans had surprised Lark before, and undoubtedly would again.

The witch shook her head and wrinkled her narrow, elegant nose in disgust. Gathering her skirts, she began descending into the cellar. She paused before her face dipped out of view. "Whoever's last, close the damn door."

The three of them stood in stunned silence.

Kenna had mentioned the witch hated when she sent people her way. Apparently, not an overstatement.

Gavriel gestured with a wave of his hand. "Ladies first."

LARK'S BOOTS squelched as she dropped from the last rung to the dirt floor. She crept down the narrow passageway—the dimly lit room at the end was both a beacon and a warning. A sense of striking familiarity settled on Lark's shoulders. The unnerving parallel to the last time she sought out a witch's help.

Lark entered the cramped room. The girl furiously gathered materials, vials of unfamiliar liquids, and a silver-handled mirror. The shelves teemed with jars of obscurities. Lark leaned in for a closer look, half-expecting to find eyeballs and tongues.

Rueberry Preserves.

That was anticlimactic.

The witch bustled around the space. The wind she created in her wake stirred the candlelight to dance in shadows across the walls.

Lark was unable to smother her curiosity. "What are you doing?"

She didn't even deign to glance Lark's way. "I'm preparing."

"For what, exactly? I haven't even told you my request."

The witch blew a dark strand of thick hair out of her face impatiently. "If Kenna sent you bearing that talisman, it's safe to assume whatever you're asking of me is both important and dangerous enough to put her at risk. That stupid, foolish girl!" She slammed the books down on the table, rattling the glass, and turned on Lark. Lark had to take a step back to keep their noses from touching. "That pendant in your hand is her only warning, her only protection against all of the miserable souls that crawled out of the Netherworld, and those who failed to cross over. If Kenna had half a brain in that head of hers, she'd have written a note like a sane person."

Lark felt the shift in the air when Daciana and Gavriel entered the room. "I know what a hunter's talisman is used for. If Kenna thought she could part with it, she must have had faith in her abilities to sense one coming. And honestly, you wouldn't have found a hand-scrawled note to be unreliable? Possibly forged?"

"That is neither here nor there." The witch waved her hand dismissively. "I am, however, very curious to know what garnered Kenna's interest." She studied Lark intently with eyes of ebony. "Who are you?"

Lark lifted her chin under the scrutiny. "You haven't even told me your name."

"I am Inerys. I'm the one the village girls seek when they're lovesick. The one called upon for women whose labor will kill them. The one they beseech when men sicken and waste away, leaving no one to provide for their families. I am the light and hope for the mortals who are lucky enough to know of me." She narrowed her eyes at Lark. "Now tell me who you are."

"My name is Lark." She exhaled a steadying breath. "And I need to contact the Otherworld."

Inerys' dark brows knitted together. "Tell me everything."

INERYS THREW BACK her third draught with a swift toss of her head. "If I'm going to do this, I'm going to need every advantage." She wiped her mouth with the back of her hand.

"Kenna didn't indicate any danger by asking this of you." Lark watched Inerys scurry around the room.

"Either she's overly confident in my abilities or very stupid." Inerys slammed a heavy tome onto the table. "Either way, I'm both flattered and furious."

Inerys grabbed Gavriel by the arm, yanking him none too gently to sit at the table. "You look sturdy, and your will is strong; you're my tether. If I start to lose my hold on Lark or this plane, you need to pull me back."

Gavriel paled. "Daciana might be better to—"

"Listen here, boy." Inerys placed her hands on Gavriel's shoulders and brought her face close to his. "If anything happens to me, Lark's not coming back."

The scar across Gavriel's cheek tightened, a muscle feathering in his jaw.

"If you want me to ask the wolf to keep her soul here, I will. If you don't have the strength to keep her from crossing to the ether and never coming back, tell me now." Inerys stared him down, unyielding.

Lark shot a glance at Daciana. "Who said she was a—"

"I can smell a wolf in my own home, thank you very much." Inerys turned back to Gavriel, regarding him with an expectant glare. "What say you, boy? Are you strong enough to call us back, or do I need to ask her?"

Gavriel shook his head. "No. I'll keep you both here."

Lark ignored the strange warmth in her belly at the intensity of his voice.

"Good boy," Inerys whispered, patting him on the cheek. She grabbed a small vial of clear liquid from the shelf and handed it to Lark. "Here, drink this."

Lark tipped it between her lips. It tasted of salt, like bracing sea air. "What is it?"

"You have to open yourself up to receive communication," Inerys explained, grinding her mortar and pestle. "It's Waking Nightmare."

Lark gripped the vial in her hand tight enough the glass began to shudder. Waking Nightmare. The very poison that claimed Emric's life and nearly Gavriel's.

Lark's stomach roiled.

Gavriel leapt from his seat. "You've killed her." He yanked the sword from his scabbard.

Inerys smirked, continuing to grind away, amusement written in her motions. "Relax, hero. She'll be fine. Waking Nightmare is harmless if prepared right."

"I know what Waking Nightmare does to a person." His words snaked out between his teeth. The promise of violence slithering through them.

"Oh, so I suppose you're the expert, and I can retire." Inerys set the bowl down on the table. "Waking Nightmare is meant to open your awareness beyond mortal senses. The hallucinations its victims experience are just that last flare of the elixir working before the body shuts down." She shook her head. "They aren't hallucinations at all."

Gavriel didn't look convinced.

It made sense how Emric could see them plain as day. Lark had always assumed it resulted from being in the place between life and death, like the first breath after awakening from a dream.

"Gavriel, she'll be fine I promise." Daciana turned to regard Lark with the full force of her stare. "You have my word."

Lark nodded. She wet her lips, still tasting brine.

"If she dies, witch"—Gavriel pointed with the tip of his blade —"you'll beg me for a quick death."

Inerys gave him a slow, sultry smile. It stretched across her deep bronze face like a sun setting the sky on fire. "Countless men have tried to make me beg and failed. You can put your weapon away, she'll be fine. So long as you uphold your task."

After a moment's hesitation, he sheathed his sword and sat. His gaze flickered to Lark, and she could see fear in his eyes, as if he was waiting for the first sign of symptoms to arise.

With a trembling hand, Lark set down the glass vial. If Daciana was sure she'd be fine, she should focus on that.

Inerys turned to Daciana. "Roll up your sleeves."

Daciana frowned but did as commanded. Inerys grabbed a bowl and began smearing some dark substance up and down Daciana's forearms, across her forehead and down each cheek. It carried the scent of low tide and rotting eggs.

Gagging, Lark lifted an arm to block her nose. "What in the skies is that?"

"Protection," Inerys said. "She needs to be invisible should anyone hitch a ride back with us. And ready to cut them down."

Daciana didn't flinch, nor did she balk at the noxious odor. "I understand."

Inerys returned to Lark. She grabbed the handled mirror and placed it on the table beside them. Yanking her chair forward, she sat opposite Lark, arms out, palms up. "Think of who you want to communicate with, scream the name in your head. And when you're ready, lay your hands upon mine."

Lark nodded, lifting her hands but Inerys pulled away.

"This will take a considerable effort from me, Lark. You must ask your questions and return. Don't tarry. Every moment you spend there, it will be harder for me to hold on to you."

"I understand."

Dark brown eyes met Lark's stare as Inerys once again placed her hands, facing up, on her thighs.

Lark reached over, placing her hands in hers. Eyes fluttering shut, she filled her mind with only one thought.

Ferryn had better be listening.

LARK OPENED HER EYES. A haze of grey mist permeated the air, filling the yawning space with a sense of despair. A vast nothing stretched around her with no end in sight. She had the vague inclination that her heart hammered in her chest, but it felt distant.

Lark stood, detecting no sound of her chair scraping the floor. She edged a step forward. Her body barely registered the sensation. Like wading into a dream, devoid of any sense of touch.

It was as if cleaving her soul from her body had dumped her back into the Otherworld, but an Otherworld yet to be written by Thanar. Without his illusions, is this what her world would have been?

She'd forgotten how numbed off from sensation she'd once been as a Reaper. The reminder filled her with dread she only half-felt, and a lonely desolation crept into her heart.

This was usually when she'd yank herself from her dreams, awaken safe in her mortal body.

But she was far from her body.

And awake.

"Ferryn!"

Beyond the mist was more... nothing.

"Ferryn, where are you?"

The dull hint of panic filled her chest, an echo of consciousness. Like trying to recall a memory already half-forgotten.

She called for Ferryn again. Why wasn't he answering? Could he not hear her, or was he unable to respond? What if Thanar punished him, what if wiped his soul clean?

Lark tamped down that thought, unwilling to chase its end. She couldn't afford to lose hope, not here. If Ferryn couldn't hear her, she needed to call someone else. Someone attuned to perceive her call. Loyal enough she could trust.

Only one came to mind.

If anyone could hear her, it was Leysa. Thanar's seer. All mortal deaths passed through her awareness, divided among her acolytes, and disbursed to Reapers. The gatekeeper to all human souls. She should sense Lark's soul, crying out to her.

But would she answer?

"Leysa!"

There was no answer to her call.

What would Ferryn say if he could see her now?

Little bird, is it your sole intention to brood yourself into oblivion?

She could almost hear his voice, laced with sarcasm and disapproval.

How much time did you spend pining to be among the humans? Now you're what, bored already? So determined to be miserable.

She let her eyes slip closed, desperate to hear his voice in her head, perhaps the last shred of her friend she had left.

Oh, I get it. You missed me.

"Always."

All right you've had your pity party, now get back to the task at hand.

"You don't command me."

Now, now. Let's not pull rank here.

"Why aren't you here?" Lark cracked her eyes open, seeing nothing but grey mist shrouding the horizon.

Call Leysa again.

"Leysa!" If no one answered, was it a failure or something worse? What if they couldn't answer? What if Thanar knew she'd try to reach someone, and sealed off any chance at communication?

What if he sensed her and answered her call?

"Larkin!"

Lark spun toward that soft, lilting voice she'd come to know her many years in the Otherworld.

Leysa's ethereal face slowly came into view. Her pale hair fell in gentle waves down her back and worry lined her wintry blue eyes. "Larkin, you can't be here!" She ran to her, skirts billowing against the movement. "You have to leave."

"What's happening in the Otherworld? Why can't Ferryn hear me?" Lark searched her face.

Leysa shook her head, her thin fingers clutching the periwinkle sash of her gown. A shadow passed over her face. "Everything's changed. There's no time to explain."

"Wait," Lark said. If nothing else, she needed to find a way to repair the veil. If what Kenna said was true, this was her one shot at finding a way to repair what she caused. "I must know. The state of the veil—are more Undesirables slipping through?"

Leysa shook her head. "That's the last of our worries right now. You must know how vulnerable you are here."

Lark knew full well how defenseless she was. That Undesirables were drawn to weakened souls, and souls in transition. Parted from her body, Lark was both.

"Leysa, please."

Leysa bit her lip. "Yes, the veil has weakened, like unraveling threads of spider silk."

Kenna was right. When Lark passed through and made new tears, it weakened the veil. And Nereida failed to keep her word. "It was me, wasn't it?"

"Oh, Lark." Leysa ghosted a hand along Lark's chin. It was strange, the phantom sensation of touch. Lark had almost forgotten how much the mind attempts to supplement. "This has been a long time coming. The board has been set for centuries; they're only now getting around to the game." Leysa tipped Lark's chin with a whisper of delicate fingers. "Don't think on it. You've finally gotten your wish. Enjoy it, Lark. You deserve it."

Enjoy it? But she could not. It was madness, an incessant scratching in Lark's head. No matter how much she gained—no matter how many wishes granted and desires realized—there was always a price. "What about Ferryn?"

Leysa froze, her fingers still in midair.

Lark yanked Leysa's hand away from her face. "Where's Ferryn?"

Leysa settled her fathomless gaze on Lark. Her eyes sharpened to glacial points. "Will knowing truly help?"

Ceto once accused Lark of burying her head in the sand, of choosing ignorance. Knowing might not help, but damned if she was going to turn away from this. "Where is he?"

"Lacuna."

The dream world. A hellscape for Reapers. Forced to walk amongst the mortals, but never seen, never existing. Neither living nor dead. The isolation of being all but erased. No one would hear his voice, see his anguish. He'd never feel the wind on his face. All sense of touch, stripped from his being.

In the Otherworld, their senses were dulled. But Thanar had done his best to create illusions of sensory experience. In Lacuna, they were cut off from any sensation, save for hearing and seeing. They could see life pass without them, and hear their cries fall on deaf ears.

It would drive him to madness.

But at least there was a chance of finding him. Lark held to that pulse-point.

"Why?"

Leysa angled her head, her eyes full of pity. "He was convicted of aiding and abetting a criminal escape."

Lark slipped from her cell into Nereida's domain. Her will brought her to the witch-queen, not Ferryn. How could he be so stupid?

"Oh, Lark. You mustn't blame yourself. Ferryn confessed to his crimes. He owned his actions as you do yours, I'm sure."

Lark flexed her hands. If she could get him out of Lacuna, the first order of business would be a firm slap upside the head for lying. "He didn't help me escape."

Leysa's delicate mouth curved in a sad smile.

Lark knew she didn't believe her.

"I'm getting him out. Whatever it takes."

"Careful." Leysa raised a chiding finger. "Mistakes are born of desperation."

Lark knew full well what desperation could lead to. "I'll keep my wits about me."

Leysa didn't look convinced. "Lark, I must insist you leave."

She was right, Lark had tarried long enough. It was fortunate no Undesirables had sniffed her out already, but to linger was to tempt fate.

"Thank you, Leysa, for everything." Lark squeezed against Leysa's gentle grip and it was like her hand was asleep. The sensation was there, in a detached way.

"Thank me by abandoning your quest to find Ferryn."

"You know I can't do that."

Leysa nodded. Pale tendrils of hair framed her soft face. "I know. Now go. Your connection must be wearing thin, and I'm sure we've attracted a fair amount of unwanted attention by now."

Lark nodded, appraising Leysa one last time. Her cheeks lacked the usual flush of rose she applied daily, and her eyes had dulled to the blue of a sky threatening to cloud over. How much of a toll did the weakened veil take on her friend? It was true, Leysa had been a friend to her, but Lark had always been too morose to appreciate it. There were so many things she'd let slip by when she was under the haze of self-loathing.

"Thank you."

"Go!" Leysa pushed her away.

Lark had the vague sensation of tumbling backward.

Falling

Never landing.

Through a yawning chasm of nothing.

CHAPTER 34

Lark jerked in her seat as her soul plummeted into her body. A flash of ice seared through her veins, like falling to the bottom of a forgotten well.

She lurched forward, retching. Her stomach heaved, but with nothing to spill onto the floor, her muscles contracted sharply around her empty gut. Every muscle twitched at the rejoining of body and soul. Damp clothing against her cool skin slammed back into her awareness. The weight of her mortal body was a beautiful welcome as she gagged and her vision spun. When she lifted her head and wiped the tears from her eyes, she caught sight of Inerys.

Inerys' head was thrown back, eyes rolled to reveal only the whites. Blood seeped from her nose, down her chin, and pooled on her chest.

Inerys rasped a sharp breath, her eyes rolling forward to glare at Lark. "I... said... to... hurry." Dark eyes flashed with rage as she jerked her chin up.

A weak groan sounded from behind. Lark turned, ignoring the wave of dizziness that darkened her vision. Gavriel slumped over in his chair. Blood trailed from his ears and nose.

Lark stumbled over to him, taking his face between her hands. "Are you all right?"

Gavriel offered a crooked grin, blood in his teeth. "I'm great. Don't I look it?"

Unable to stop her smile, Lark shook her head. "You look an awful lot like the first time we met."

He raised an eyebrow, his eyes glassy. "I seem to recall receiving a kiss that day, so I'll consider that a compliment."

Ignoring the responding flutter in her stomach at his jest, she glanced over at Daciana. "Are you all right?"

Daciana sat perfectly poised in her seat, crossed-legged, and sword resting atop her thigh. She shrugged. "I'm fine. My leg is starting to fall asleep, though."

Lark wiped the blood from Gavriel's face. Her finger caught the groove of the scar across his mouth.

He watched her with an unreadable expression as his intent gaze swept over her features.

The panic that filled her chest echoed its painful reminder. Even as she took stock of his well being, finding him whole and unharmed. Even as relief bloomed between her ribs, spreading soft warmth through her icy body.

Gavriel lifted a hand as if to push the hair from her face, and Lark's throat tightened. If she weren't selfish, she'd focus on the fact that she'd failed. That she still didn't know how to find Ferryn. That he was punished for an act all her own. Instead, she zeroed in on the way Gavriel's hand flexed suspended in midair. A fierce want surged through her. A need for him to close the distance and put her out of her selfish misery.

He lowered his hand to his lap.

"Did you find what you were looking for?" Daciana asked.

Lark unwillingly tore her eyes from Gavriel's face. "Not exactly. Ferryn wasn't there. But I was able to make contact. Things are more complicated than I thought." That was putting it mildly.

"Where is he then?" Gavriel asked.

Answering for her crimes. "Somewhere he shouldn't be. I have to get him out."

"Of course," Gavriel said, his voice resolute.

How could Gavriel be so certain when she was not? Sometimes it seemed like her entire human existence was chasing something destined to remain out of grasp.

"It isn't vital to save him," Lark said. "Not in the grand scheme of things."

"It's vital to you, isn't it? That's reason enough."

Ferryn's safety was crucial, at least to her. Though Lark was starting to feel more insignificant with each passing day. Like she was little more than the space between two stars. Inconsequential enough to fail to notice.

Gavriel saw her, though.

"I am never helping anyone ever again." Inerys rasped out behind them before unceremoniously vomiting onto the floor.

A HESITANT SUN hovered low on the horizon, its orange glow peeking through the trees. Lark stepped out into the early evening, taking her first full breath once she'd passed through the threshold of the cottage.

"If I never see you darken my doorstep, it'll be too soon," Inerys said. "Good luck with everything, and next time you need help—ask someone else."

Lark spun around as Gavriel and Daciana followed out of the small cottage after her. She couldn't leave without asking. "What do you know of reaching Lacuna?"

Inerys crossed her arms and leaned against the doorway. Fly-away strands of dark hair caught the burning glow of the setting sun. "Is that where your friend is? You'd be better off having a funeral pyre for his memory." She said it as if it was set in stone.

Lark couldn't bring herself to accept Ferryn's loss. Not when Gavriel stood as proof that even fate holds no certainty.

But destiny was a greedy beast. What did she have left to barter with?

"Oh, don't give me that look. The truth is a rancid swill, but a mercy compared to sweet lies. You'd chase your end, venturing after him."

A sapling of hope dug its roots in Lark's chest. "So, you're saying there's a chance?"

Inerys regarded her with an incredulous expression before a laugh burst from her chest. "With blind optimism like that, I'm beginning to doubt you ever were a Reaper." She shook her head before disappearing into her home, leaving the door wide open.

Lark and Daciana exchanged a glance.

Inerys reemerged with a heavy tome. She tossed it to Gavriel, who caught it unsteadily and cradled it to avoid bending the pages. "There you go; I've done my part a thousand times over. I bid you all farewell."

"Thank you. For everything," Lark said. Inerys was another person who aided her when she didn't have to. For every horror Lark encountered, there seemed a ray of hope in defiance. Humanity was such a funny thing. The hideous beauty of it all.

Inerys smoothed out her skirts and sniffed. "No need to thank me for sending you off to your death."

There was no flicker of fear in Lark's heart. Death was a familiar animal by now. "Until we meet again."

Inerys gave a curt nod before stalking into the house and slamming the door shut. For a moment they all stood there, Gavriel still delicately handling the large ancient book.

"Is it just me?" he asked, breaking the silence. "Or did she seem disinclined to ever help us again?"

"Your instincts are sharp as ever," Daciana said flatly. "Shall we make our way back to the horses then?"

Lark held out her hand for the thick book. Its mottled grey cover might have been black once. Where Gavriel had held it, the heavy coat of dust was disturbed.

"Yes, we should, thank the skies we'll be taking the boat back.

This book appears minutes away from disintegrating." Lark turned it over in her hands. "Looks like I'll have some reading tonight." After a bath of course. The first time she sunk her shivering, aching limbs into the warm depths of the oak barrel tub was near euphoric. She'd heated enough pots over the fire to fill the tub up to her shoulders. After sitting in damp clothes for hours, she deserved another scalding soak.

The old row-boat glided across the smooth surface of the lake, the soft ripples shattered the illusion that the water was made of glass. The gentle hum of cicadas and hypnotic call of crickets filled the air with a summer song.

They reached the shore, and Gavriel leapt out, yanking the dinghy to the bank. The moment Lark set foot off the boat and onto dry land, she glanced back. Inerys' cottage was gone, vanished as if it never was. Lark smiled. Inerys was a clever witch.

"We should have asked her about that spell, the one she uses to hide her home," Lark said. "Imagine if we hid Alistair's spirits, or Langford's books!" Lark turned to gauge her companions' reactions.

The wind tore at Lark's cloak, pricking the hairs on the back of her neck. When had it gotten so cold? She pulled her cloak tighter; a violent shiver wracked her body. Daciana's mouth pulled in a grim line, head canted. Listening.

Even Gavriel stilled.

The forest had fallen quiet, all sounds of life, silenced.

"Lark," Gavriel said. "We should go."

A figure stepped out of the tree line. "Oh, but I've only just arrived." His velvet-smooth voice cut through the clearing. The being's shock of white hair glowed against the darkening forest. Two black horns curled from either side of his head to stand at sharp points. His angular face twisted in a wicked smile that failed to meet his silver eyes. With skin like the moon, it clashed against his fitted black leathers.

Lark's mouth went dry. She knew what matter of beast took this form. The enticing shape of horrible promises. Unearthly handsome.

This was a demon.

Lark darted a glance to Daciana who'd already brandished her sword. Gavriel thumbed his daggers by his side.

The demon sauntered over to them, silver eyes zeroing in on Lark. "Well, well. Is this what all the fuss is about?" His voice was full of indulgent amusement with an undercurrent of violence. "From what I understand you've caused quite a stir."

Gavriel stepped between them.

The demon clicked his tongue. "It's rude to interfere in a private conversation." He waved a hand, as if swatting a fly, and Gavriel's body careened through the air, hitting the earth with a sickening thud.

Lark rushed toward him. But the demon lurched forward, grasping her arms. Paralyzing her in place. She fought against the ice spearing through her veins—

—but she couldn't move.

"Now, where were we?" He leaned in close, running the tip of his sharp nose along her neck.

Lark ran through the litany of holds Alistair practiced with her. Just in case he released her from his compulsion. All she needed was a distraction. As if sensing her trail of thought, the demon's grip tightened. Her eyes darted to where Gavriel laid on the ground. Daciana hovered over him, checking his vitals. She met Lark's gaze and held a finger to her lips.

The demon hadn't noticed Daciana yet.

The noxious substance Inerys had coated her with must have still been in effect. But for how long? Daciana pinned a meaningful glare on the demon. As if to say, *keep him talking.*

"I know what you are," Lark said, keeping her voice steady as her chest clenched and her legs shook against whatever spell held her captive.

"It's rude not to ask for my name, you know." The demon sniffed as if affronted. "But I wouldn't expect a lowly creature like you to care a thing for decorum. I am Balan."

The name didn't land with any familiarity. He was a low-level demon. "How did you escape?" Demons weren't permitted access to the mortal world. They were under strict orders to remain in the deepest pits of the Netherworld. Fed the scraps of the blackest souls.

"Who said I escaped?" Balan's voice caressed her skin, making Lark want to scrub herself bloody to erase the sensation. "I heard you calling; I had no idea how desperate you were to be found." He pulled back and tilted his head. "A curious thing, to be remade. Tell me, did it hurt when she reformed your flesh? Knit you back together and stuffed your soul into this"—he ran a long finger down her neck—"meat sack?"

Lark swallowed the bile that rose in her throat. "You talk too much. Are you bored scrounging from the dregs of the Netherworld—little better than a sewer-rat?"

The demon scraped out a low chuckle, running a rough hand through her hair. "There's a new world order, thanks to you." He tilted Lark's head back, tugging on her hair tight enough her scalp burned. "How foolish are you to flaunt your weak, defenseless form?" He brought his full lips to her jaw, close enough his words landed in a feather-light touch against her skin.

"What makes you think I'm defenseless?" Lark bit out.

"Your pathetic human has nothing on me, little Reaper." Balan's mouth curved against her. His teeth scraped a line of ice against her skin. "Should we bring him with us?"

A shadow of movement slinked out behind the demon. Lark couldn't help but smile.

"I wasn't talking about him."

Daciana sank her blades into his back, and Lark wrenched free of Balan's grasp. Shock splashed across his face before it turned to fury. Inerys' concoction was effective at subterfuge, rendering Daciana invisible from the monsters of the Netherworld. But he could see her now. His silver eyes blazed as he appraised the warrior.

Gavriel stood, blood trailing from his forehead and blades glinting in the fading twilight.

Balan spun around. His face twisted in a feral expression. "I'll gut you for that, you little whore."

Daciana smirked at him, the action lighting up her face. Both dagger and short sword raised in challenge. "You're welcome to try."

Balan hissed, lurching for her. His hands curled into black claws sharp enough to rake ribbons through human flesh.

Daciana spun out of reach.

Gavriel threw himself at the demon's exposed flank, landing quick and expertly aimed stabs into his lower back. Balan threw his head back and roared. The ground trembled beneath their feet.

Lark whipped her bow into position, and nocked an arrow, aiming for his throat. Resting the string against her cheek, she exhaled and released.

It landed with a sickening squelch. Dark blood spurted from Balan's mouth, and he crumpled. As he fell, he slammed both fists against the earth. A wave of energy rushed outward, launching Daciana, Gavriel, and Lark back.

Lark's head smashed into the dirt, rattling her teeth. She groaned. Every muscle in her back seized in protest. Twisting to the side, she tried to right her vision against jarring vertigo.

Heavy footsteps shook the earth. Until Balan hovered over her, glaring down as he yanked the arrow from his throat and tossed it to the ground. The gaping wound began to heal, flesh stitching back together. He crouched down to grip her by the neck, lifting her with ease.

"No more foreplay. We're leaving." Balan snapped his fingers.

Nothing happened. A choking sound ripped from Lark's throat as the demon squeezed.

"Interesting," Balan said with a sharpened edge to his tone. "It seems I can't take you with me." His lip curled, and his silver eyes narrowed.

Blood pounded in Lark's ears, a steady tempo beneath his words.

"When you fall, and believe me little Reaper, you will fall, I've been promised an eternity with you."

Lark gasped for air and scratched the large, clawed hand gripping her throat. The toes of her boots scraped against the ground.

"I can be patient." Balan squeezed even tighter.

Black spots danced across Lark's vision.

With a look of disgust, he dropped her body into the dirt.

Lark gagged, coughing and sputtering for air. Her hand flew to her throat.

The air around the demon began to stir with wicked promise, a dark veil of shadows wrapping lovingly around him. A snarl froze on his face before he vanished.

Lark coughed again, the hoarse rasp in her throat promised bruising, and a sharp burning pain flared up her side. She'd landed on a root—its thick thorns glimmered with fresh blood. She curled, her hand flying to her dripping wound. Balan was strong. A low-level demon was stronger than her now.

How far she'd fallen.

Warm hands were suddenly upon her. Lark lurched, panic mounting in her chest, only to find Gavriel and Daciana.

"Are you hurt?" Blood matted the side of Gavriel's hair and forehead.

"I'm fine." It could have been so much worse. A fact that made something slippery and hot ache in Lark's gut.

"Can you stand?" A thin river of blood trailed from the corner of Daciana's mouth, but she appeared unharmed.

Lark nodded, accepting Daciana's hand as she stood. She stumbled, fire lighting up her side. Lark winced, pulling back the hem of her filthy tunic. Three deep, angry gashes were torn through her skin. As the air hit the wound, it carried a sharp sting.

Gavriel uttered a curse at the sight, immediately falling to one knee and grabbing bandages from his pack. "Daciana, I need you to dip this rag in the lake."

Daciana nodded once before running back to the water.

Lark braced her hands on Gavriel's broad shoulders as he worked. The corded muscles tightened with each pass of his hands. He carried so much tension. It was a wonder he didn't complain of constant aches. A bead of sweat trailed down his neck. Lark tightened her grip experimentally.

Gavriel blinked up at her. His hands stilled their task of lifting away the layers of fabric that were caught in the edges of her wound. "Did I hurt you?"

"No, you didn't hurt me."

He resumed his gentle exploration. He didn't notice the shiver it ghosted through her. A searing pain pulled a gasp from Lark's throat, and Gavriel stroked his thumb against her skin soothingly. "What in the infernal nethers was that thing?"

Lark glanced down to find Gavriel studying her intently. "You know your endearing name for me?"

"What? Demon?"

"Yes." Lark wet her cracked lips. "Now, you've actually met a demon."

BALAN SAID Lark was to belong to him once she passed through.

Nereida had given her word she would bypass Thanar upon her death. But Lark hadn't expected her to sell her soul to a random demon.

"There has to be a way to kill it." Daciana whipped her head to look at her. "I *will* find a way."

Lark laughed, the sound clanging in her chest. "To what end?" She'd signed the binding contract with a glimmering bone-shard and sealed her fate without understanding what it truly meant. Nereida was the holder of that contract, not Balan. "You'd crush an insect only to find the entire colony still awaiting."

"I don't care. You're not going back."

Lark turned away from the resolute expression on Daciana's face. "We all have to die someday. There's no way to stop the inevitable." Fate. Destiny. There could be no escape.

"We will find a way," Gavriel said, voice low and dangerous.

"How?"

"However we have to." His chest rose and fell with the anger that stirred beneath his skin. The exposed feeling of helplessness giving way to rage.

It was a fool's hope. Even Gavriel must have known, there was nothing to be done.

Lark tore her eyes from his simmering glare. The horses were tied just past the thicket of dense brush, although in the dark it was impossible to know for certain.

Lark's foot caught something large and solid. She jolted, nearly landing face-first on the ground. But a strong hand gripped her arm, anchoring her.

She didn't even need to look to know whose hand burned through her.

Instead, she glanced down at what she'd tripped on. Night obscuring her vision, she lowered into a crouch and reached down. Thick blood, cooled and already beginning to coagulate, coated her fingers. Tufts of hair and viscera left behind.

"The horses..." Gavriel trailed off.

Lark pushed down the wave of despair and vile self-revulsion.

Another thing to add to the ever-growing list of horrors she caused.

"Come on." Daciana's soothing voice wrapped around her. Her arm settled around Lark's shoulders, urging her forward through the dark forest. The Emerald Woods were more vast than Lark realized. The trees were too thick for moonlight to find the forest floor. Wind shivered through heavy branches, before the air calmed and dark silence filled Lark's ears.

The horses were dead. Apple...

Lark's eyes stung, and her throat thickened. How many others would suffer on her account before her time was up?

Ferryn. Thanar banished Ferryn to Lacuna as punishment for her crime. She knew Thanar would suspect him. In the earliest days of her human life, the image of Thanar and Ferryn in that throne room, of Ceto cleaving his head from his neck in a sick, twisted form of justice, had plagued Lark's dreams. But Ferryn would never have been implicated, even if Thanar dipped into his mind, it would prove his innocence. So why did Ferryn confess to helping her?

Lark hadn't known of Ferryn's ambition until shortly before she fled. He only wanted the balance to succeed, and it was her foolish fascination that landed her in trouble. Never had she apologized for blaming him, for letting him carry that burden. And now, he seemed determined to carry all the weight of her choices. She'd spend whatever was left of her mortal life trying to free him. But time always seemed to slip from her grasp. Did all mortals feel this way?

Daciana stilled, canting her head to listen.

A rustling sound came from beyond the trees. Lark's knife found its way into her hand, slipped from her boot before her mind could catch up.

The sound of twigs snapping had Daciana brandishing her sword too. Likely, Gavriel had silently slipped his blades into his hands as well.

Lark squinted into the darkness, trying to see farther than her human eyes could in the absence of daylight. Searching the obscured forest for any sign of attack. Heavy thuds against the earth pricked the hairs on the back of Lark's neck. She gripped her dagger, angling the curved blade in a readying hold.

Apple loped out of between the trees, looking decidedly unimpressed.

Relief flooded Lark as she rushed forward, throwing her arms around her horse's neck. "Thank the skies." Hot tears spilled down her cheeks. Searing a trail through blood and grime. Apple gave her shoulder a slight nudge in response. As if telling her to buck up. Or demanding a treat.

In her already crowded chest, Lark found a glimmer of joy.

CHAPTER 35

*I*mages of butchered horses, Balan's sinister face, of her friends' corpses all desecrated in a variety of gruesome ways, hounded Lark's dreams.

The talisman sat heavy in her pocket. Kenna had entrusted her to find answers, but she'd only succeeded in uncovering more questions.

Lark stared down at her breakfast. The events of the night before still churned her stomach. With a sigh, she pushed her bowl away. She didn't even have an appetite for Mrs. O'Connell's sweetened cream and oats.

A large hand thrust the bowl back in front of her.

Startled, she looked up to see Hugo frowning down at her. His eyes were dark with disapproval and even behind his thick mustache, his mouth was tight.

"Eat, we're training in an hour. You'll need your strength." He eyed Lark when she made no move to lift her spoon. Leaning in close, he hissed through gritted teeth. "Eat or I'll damn well force-feed you, then make you run 'til you puke."

ONLY WHEN LARK WAS PANTING, arms and legs quivering with exertion did Hugo relent and allow her to rest. She abandoned the attempt to sit with dignity and dropped to the ground with a grunt. Small blades of grass and dirt clung to her sweat-slicked skin. They'd trained, strength and stamina building from running and muscular resistance, until a high sun claimed the sky and warmed the land. Across the valley, mist curled from the dew sodden ground.

Pinpricks jabbed her lungs as she sucked down each breath. The stitches in her side Langford had expertly sewn during the night, ached in protest. She'd get an earful later, and she'd be sure to blame Hugo.

Hugo lowered himself to sit beside her, gazing out at the low dips of the valley. Propping herself up on her elbows, Lark studied him. Age and weariness had left their marks on his face. He'd torn the sleeves off his tunic, baring his thick, muscled arms. They flexed beneath black swirls and symbols.

"Your tattoos, what do they mean?"

Hugo frowned at his broad shoulder and grunted. "Stupidity."

"You'll have to give me more than that."

The ghost of a smirk played on Hugo's mouth, but he remained silent. His dark eyes surveyed the horizon. Lark had so many gnawing questions for him—she wasn't accustomed to mortals who weren't inclined to share. Death loosened lips almost as surely as wine.

"Loyalty, duty. These are easy for a simple mind to grasp," Hugo said. "There's no thought, no question. It's when you're faced with decisions that things get muddled."

A breeze blew over Lark's skin, cooling her sweat. She shivered. The memory of holding Gavriel's name in her hand—the mark Ferryn gave her. The moment she chose to chase a different path, filled the spaces in her head.

"What sort of decision?"

"When I chose to have something all my own." Hugo ran a large hand over his face. "Maybe if I'd just let her be, things woulda turned out different."

A charged silence fell over them, stretching between them with a sharpened edge.

Whoever she was, it hadn't ended well.

Lark's hand itched by her side. She reached down to yank the curved knife from her boot, turning it over in both hands. Light glinted off the blood groove that ran half the length of the blade and illuminated the carvings in the steel. They matched the symbols covering Hugo's body. Curious things, mortals. Deriving strength and hope from lines and swirls.

His eyes darted over once before settling back on the expanse that lay before them.

"Who was the original owner?" Lark held the knife out, the handle toward him. Perhaps this was an easier answer to give.

"Csilla." The name was a whisper on his lips. He wrapped his fingers around the knife handle. "From the moment I saw her..." He laughed, but it came out tight. Like his chest was unwilling to part with the sound. "I was gone, wrapped around her little finger."

Lark smiled, hugging her knees to her chest and leaning her head to the side. "Tell me more about Csilla."

Hugo ran his finger over the etched symbols. "She was the only pure thing in my life. The one thing I got right." His mustache twitched to the side. "She was stubborn as a mule, digging her heels in the dirt."

"Hmm... that doesn't remind me of anyone."

"She was too good." He handed the knife back. "Life has a way of stamping out anything too clean."

Lark slipped the knife back in its rightful place in her boot. "She was your lover?"

"She was my daughter."

"Absolutely not. This is a terrible idea."

Alistair placed a hand on his chest, doing his best to look insulted. "Have you so little faith in my ability to formulate a plan?"

Daciana crossed her arms. "No, just this one."

The waning light of the day spilled through Daciana's window as Alistair and Daciana melded into one of their usual debates. Lark suspected Alistair came up with these plans with the sole intention of provoking Daciana. He got far too much enjoyment out of their little spats.

Sitting on the well worn quilt atop the bed, Lark adjusted the cards in her hand so the nameless Paragon, the Mother of Arcadia, was in front. Lark studied the face card. It was of a figure shrouded in white, rays of the sun bursting out from behind her form. The mortals couldn't know what the Mother looked like. Neither did Lark. Her name was lost to time as punishment for creating Arcadia, the only circle in the Netherworld that offered comfort after death.

Now she was a faceless card in a mortal game.

"Oh, come on." Alistair threw his hands up as he paced Daciana's room. The floorboards creaked under his feet with every pass. He'd insisted they all meet there to discuss the job he'd picked up at the market. Alistair was being cagey on the details, as usual. "It's the perfect plan. Langford is a Brenner, that name still carries considerable weight."

Daciana nodded, her face stern. "I'm with you on that."

"And we have it on good authority that the Brenner name will be included on the list as a formality. Even though Langford's father hasn't left Blackwall in years." Alistair froze, his impossibly green eyes transfixed on Langford. His throat bobbed. Like he wanted to say something, but the words were stuck.

Langford shifted, coughing into his fist. Blackwall was a wealthy fiefdom in the northern region of the Koval, closely aligned with the crown and well-regarded. So what in the blazes was Langford doing in Ardenas with Alistair's crew?

"That's not the part of the plan I'm objecting to." Daciana crossed her arms.

"And then," Alistair continued, ignoring her. "We send someone capable on his arm to pose as the charming Lady Brenner."

Daciana tapped her foot.

Lark fought a smile. She looked up from her hand to peer across the bed at a red-faced Langford. He frowned at his cards. It was generous foresight that he brought the game to pass the time while they argued. Hugo had claimed the small pinewood chair in the corner, opting to bring his knife and a piece of wood to whittle. It appeared to be another knife handle. Gavriel silently stood, leaning against the wall and surveying them with a calm focus he must have honed from years waiting to take a killing strike.

Lark tried to ignore the way her stomach flipped whenever his gaze snagged on her.

Alistair gestured to her. "Which is where Lark comes in."

"No." Daciana poured every ounce of power and authority into that one word.

Alistair threw his head back with a loud sigh. "Must we have this argument every single time?"

Daciana crossed her legs, leaning back in her seat. "Only so long as you insist on making the same bad call."

"It's not a bad call! Just because you don't like it, doesn't make it wrong." Alistair crossed to sit on the bed, jostling Lark and Langford and spilling the deck of cards. "No offense Dac, but you're not exactly inconspicuous. You draw all the attention in the room."

"He's got a point you know," Lark said, eying her cards. "That night at the tavern with Talbot, not a single man could keep his eyes off you."

"I wasn't watching her."

Lark ignored the flush that crept up her cheeks at Gavriel's response.

"See?" Alistair dropped his hands to clap Lark on the back. "Dac, you're far too noticeable. We need someone unremarkable—to blend in and play the part of Langford's empty-headed wife."

"Thanks, Alistair," Lark muttered.

"Anytime," he said dismissively. He grabbed Daciana's hands, pulling them to his chest. "At some point, you have to let the baby bird fly from the nest."

Daciana yanked her hands from his. "I know, but I don't like sending anyone in without me."

"I know." All signs of humor bled from Alistair's tone. "I don't either. But we have no choice."

"We could wait for a more opportune time to go after Adler."

Alistair shook his head. "He doesn't open his home often; this is the perfect chance to rifle through his things. And the coin is ready now." He leaned his elbows on his thighs, lacing his fingers together in front of him. "This is a non-confrontational job. They go, they dance, they slip away, they come back with a few well-guarded secrets." He grinned. "Hopefully, positively carnal ones."

"Why does our source need secrets?" Langford peered over his cards.

"Secrets are currency. Security," Gavriel said, breaking his silence. "Blood can be spared by the whispered threat of a few well-collected secrets."

Langford sighed, propping his head on his fist. "Why *specifically* does our source need secrets? What's the angle?"

"The angle is, get in. Gather dirt on Adler. Get out," Alistair said with a pinched expression.

Langford narrowed his eyes, holding his stare. If he had more to say, he kept it to himself.

"I just don't see why you accept jobs without specifics, and why it has to be Lark instead of me on the inside," Daciana said abruptly, breaking the spell and redirecting the conversation back to the conflict she and Alistair had been squabbling over for the better part of an hour.

Holding up his fingers, Alistair began counting them off. "One, she owes me for the horses. Two, she's efficient and less noticeable. Three, they look like a believable couple. Watching them dance confirmed it. They could easily pass as a boring, lifeless, no passion left, scheduling sex for special occasions like holidays, and namedays—"

"We get it."

"—couple. Whereas you"—Alistair waved a hand up and down her body—"are far too attractive to be anything less than the hit of the ball. If I send you, there'll likely be a sex riot and poor Langford here will have to go searching room to room on his own." He lowered his voice to a conspiratorial whisper. "And we both know how that would go."

"What exactly does a sex riot entail?" Lark asked.

Alistair flashed her a savage grin.

"Don't answer that," Daciana said, voice strained. "And I am capable of entering a room without starting a *sex riot.*"

"Should things go tits up, I need to know I have you on the outside to sort it out."

And there it was. At the end of the day, Alistair always had a plan. And his care and loyalty to them were never forgotten. Not completely.

Daciana exhaled a tight breath, but the resignation was there. "Fine, but I won't be kept out of planning a single detail."

"Of course." Alistair dipped his head in a slight bow. "Now, first things first." He pointed to Lark. "This one needs a dress, and they both need masks. Maybe I can send Hugo shopping."

Hugo grunted in response.

"Wait, why do we need masks? I thought we were on the guest list." Lark shot Langford a questioning look.

"It's a masquerade ball," Alistair said with a grin. "I'm almost jealous. Next time, we'll find a way for me to join. They almost always end in orgies."

Lark's chest constricted. No one said anything about an orgy. She glanced over at Gavriel. He smirked and shook his head, rolling his eyes at Alistair's remark.

Thank the skies. Lark wasn't ready for that undertaking. At least not in a group.

"Deal again." She tossed her truly awful hand to Langford. "This time give me better cards."

An easy smile lit up his face. "I don't control the cards Lark, fate does."

The corners of her mouth lifted. "Well, maybe it's time fate answered to us."

THE SUN DIDN'T MAKE an appearance the next day, carefully tucked behind a greying sky. But the air held a charge. The promise of a storm.

Lark found herself alone in a nearby field, her arms wrapped around her knees as she stared up at the dark sky.

Everyone else had matters to attend, and she supposed she did too. But this felt vital. If she was going to suffer an eternity of damnation anyway, she'd experience the feeling of raindrops against her skin. Just once.

A thought occurred to her as she waited for the clouds to burst. There were still many things she hadn't had the chance to experience yet. She'd never felt a true rainstorm upon her skin. There were misty days and hints of rain, but never a true tempest she longed to be caught in. She'd never tasted those powdered puffs of sugar spun dough Alistair described once, light as air and sweeter than honey. Never had a kiss graced her human lips.

She'd kissed Gavriel when she was a Reaper, and his life depended on it, but it was more of a ruthless attack against an unwilling participant than a kiss. He brought it up so casually when they were in Inerys' cellar, and she didn't think he'd noticed the impact those words had on her.

Likely because he'd kissed many times. Dozens of women. Ran his hands over them and bedded them. Lost himself in them. Humanity was still new to her, but Lark was no fool. She caught the passing glances he received. The thinly veiled lust reflected in the eyes of passersby. It was a wonder she'd never seen him with anyone, but it was none of her business.

He was not hers.

He could do as he pleased.

As could she, if she chose to.

Lark wasn't ignorant of the mechanics of it. The memory washed over her: of fumbling hands in the Otherworld, of torn seams and clumsy rutting. But all she'd felt was empty, the ghost of sensations. Because she wasn't human—she wasn't alive.

As a mortal, she could imagine it would be a completely different experience.

It was no secret both Alistair and Langford had their share of amusements. Indulgences of whatever desire they held that evening. Alistair more so. Men, women, sometimes in groups. The word to describe Alistair was insatiable. But she'd seen Langford take a gentleman to his quarters once or twice.

Even Hugo had his admirers. But none made it to his bed.

Daciana seemed to have no interest in taking lovers, even for just the night.

Lark didn't doubt if she'd asked Alistair, as a friend, he'd agree to it. So she wouldn't be sent to the Netherworld completely ignorant of human touch. But it felt like a betrayal. A betrayal to whom, she wasn't exactly sure.

If she were being honest with herself, the only person she could imagine drawing back that particular curtain with was Gavriel.

She'd thought of it. More often than she should. The way he always clenched his jaw in annoyance at her. The way his eyes lit up when he teased her. When his expression would soften at the sight of her pain. His broad chest that flexed with every training exercise he insisted on performing half-naked.

Lark lifted her face to the sky. Her eyes slipped closed as she waited for the cool rush of rain.

"Storm's coming, you should get inside."

She cracked an eye, to see Gavriel striding up to her.

"I know it is. That's why I'm out here." Lark resumed her silent beseeching of the rain to fall.

Gavriel settled down next to her, a moderate distance, but she swore she felt the warmth radiating from him. "The washing accommodations not to your liking?"

Lark smiled, a sigh slipping from her lips. "Are you so bored you've come to pester me?"

"Do I need to be bored for that?" He gave her a crooked grin before turning his face up to the sky. "It's kind of nice out here."

"Mhmm." The familiar scent of him washed over her, distracting her even more than his presence already did. Heat spread through her belly when he shifted and his knee brushed the side of her leg.

"Langford is busy studying that book the witch gave you?"

Like a bucket of cold water, the fire was doused. "Yes, he seemed quite eager to begin."

After they'd returned from the Emerald Woods, she'd told the others of what they'd gone for; To seek counsel from the Otherworld, only to find Ferryn was trapped in Lacuna. The moment Langford caught sight of Inerys' dusty old tome, his eyes lit up in excitement. 'Research-boner' is what Alistair had called it. That Lark insisted Inerys referred to this task as a death wish did little to dim Langford's enthusiasm.

Gavriel and Lark sat side by side for a few heartbeats, neither saying a word. The dark sky hovered over them like a warning.

But Lark was never very good at heeding warnings.

"What's it like, sex as a human?"

Gavriel coughed, his cheeks burning bright red—it was an image she'd carry for the rest of her life.

"Why are you asking me that?" His voice was laced with irritation and embarrassment.

Lark shrugged. She hadn't meant the words to spill from her lips, but she didn't regret them. She couldn't even find it in herself to be embarrassed, not when Gavriel held the lion's share of discomfort on his normally stern face. "I thought you might educate me." At the panicked look on his face, she added, "I meant in theory Gavriel, not in practice. You can stop looking like an ensnared rabbit desperate to flee."

"I look nothing of the sort." His words were tight in his mouth as if he were clenching every muscle in his body. "Aren't there books you can read on the matter if you're looking for theory?"

"Probably," Lark said with a nod. "I could always ask Alistair."

The glare she received was worth all the gold that lined their pockets, as far as she was concerned.

"That would be a stupid idea."

The sky seemed to rumble in agreement. A rush surged through Lark. As if the energy of the impending tempest was filling her with electricity.

The first few drops that fell from the sky landed on her arm, a cool reprieve against her skin.

It was starting.

GAVRIEL WATCHED Lark's eyelashes flutter as the first few drops of rain kissed her face. He almost reminded her they'd be soaked through like drowned rats, but the words died in his throat. A carefree smile stretched across her face, dimpling her cheek and crinkling her golden eyes. Her auburn hair fluttered in the breeze.

The words she'd spoken not moments ago still burned in him. He'd need to plunge into an ice-cold stream or river. But he was not some green youth, equipped with little more than blood flow and impulses. He'd spent enough nights beside a warm body to know he always woke up cold.

Lark was different. She was warmth. Every inch of her, from the heart she wore on her sleeves to the fire in her eyes. He couldn't be certain a taste of her would be enough. She was an itch he'd never scratch, even if he did give her a demonstration of everything she asked of. And more.

It was better this way. Hers was a sweet torture. One he'd endure for the rest of his days. Though he knew his were numbered.

The clouds opened up; a crack of thunder bellowed across the sky. Raindrops fell heavy and fast. Pelting them with a violence only a summer storm could rouse. Lark tossed her head back and laughed. The sound was still the most beautiful music he'd ever heard.

Her intoxicating scent mingling with the smell of rain nearly drove him to madness. A sudden urge jolted through him—to grab her and seal his mouth over hers and take and take until there was nothing left standing between them.

Instead, Gavriel watched her laugh, her arms wide, embracing the storm she demanded.

He found himself laughing too, squinting against the rush of moisture dripping into his eyes as it slid off his brow.

She turned to him, joy lighting up her face as she beamed at him.

Skies above, she was beautiful.

CHAPTER 36

*L*ark took an unwilling sip of her cold tea. Morning crept through the tempered glass windows like a hesitant visitor. Pale light spilled across the oak tables, illuminating every groove of the grains. The tavern was nearly empty, only a few scattered patrons were seated as the barmaid milled about. It was too early for those who'd spent the night carousing and indulging.

Sleep hadn't come easily to Lark, plagued as she was with thoughts of Gavriel. She rose before the sun, eager to forget all images of him and how he looked soaked through. There was something about the way the rain carved the outline of his muscles, of his broad shoulders and sharp curves of his arms that made Lark's belly tighten. His hair was longer than when they first met, clinging to his forehead and neck as he laughed up at the sky. She wanted nothing more than to peel the wet layers off him and trace each path the rain sluiced down his skin.

With a groan, Lark ran a hand down her face, ignoring the familiar ache—the ache she still didn't know how to deal with properly.

She had more important things to worry about. Like how in the blazes she was going to repair the veil. What she was going to do about her apparent debt to the Netherworld. And how she was going to free Ferryn.

Langford dropped in a seat opposite her, and Inerys' tome landed on the table with a thud. The dark circles beneath his stormy eyes stood out against his pale skin.

"Did you sleep at all last night?" Lark asked, taking another sip of tea.

Langford huffed a strand of dark hair out of his eyes. "I might have drifted off at some point." He turned his head to summon the server. Backward letters were stamped across his cheek.

With a laugh, Lark reached over and rubbed her thumb over them, smearing more than cleaning.

He wiped his face with his sleeve. "Did you wish to hear the good news or the bad news first?"

"I only want good news," Lark said, cradling her cup in both hands. "I've opted to purge my life of all bad things." Maybe someday that wouldn't be a jest.

"Good luck with that. According to this manifesto, the Forbidden Shrine holds unspeakable power that no mortal has ever possessed. We should have little trouble locating it. Thankfully it wasn't called the Hidden Shrine. Or the Impossible to Find Shrine, right?" Langford laughed, a slight snort wheezing through his nose.

Lark waited for him to continue.

Langford scraped a hand through his untidy hair. "That's the good news, I've managed to decipher the general location indicated in the text." He cast his eyes up to the rafters, muttering to himself as he deliberated in his head.

"Out loud, Langford."

"Yes, sorry. I was thinking it shouldn't be too hard to get to, provided we can gain access to a ship at Emeraude Port and hike into the Forbidden Highlands." He paused. "Oh, I get it. The Forbidden Shrine is in the Forbidden Highlands. That's not exactly clever is it?"

Lark bit the inside of her cheek. Gain passage on a ship and sail for what two weeks? More? The Forbidden Highlands were in the northernmost region of Koval. A steep mountainous region too harsh for any settlements. They'd need enough supplies to last the journey.

"Don't look so dour. Alistair knows a captain that might take us. Provided he's still on good terms with her." Langford rubbed his jaw. "Perhaps that wouldn't work at all..."

"You haven't even told me the bad news yet." Lark grabbed his hand and shook it to get his attention.

"What? Oh yes, I'm sorry. Barely functioning here." He yawned, wide and slow.

Lark slid her tea in front of him and waited for him to continue.

"Thank you." Lanford took a deep swig. "The bad news is we'll have to face trials of sorts. Tests of character, strength, will..." He trailed off, tipping his head back and downing the rest of it. "Anyways, I couldn't get a real sense of the specifics, but I think we could manage. At least I'll have two weeks aboard the ship to get some research done."

Dread coiled in Lark's gut at the thought of putting them in harm's way. She should demand they steer clear of this. To deal with this on her own. Ferryn was her responsibility, not theirs. But even she could recognize a losing battle.

And her pride had to allow the truth. She needed all the help she could get.

"Fine. But if any of you die, I will be angry with you."

Langford grinned. "That sounds reasonable."

HOW ALISTAIR MANAGED to get the largest room, equipped with a table and chairs, was beyond Gavriel's understanding. The man was about as charming as a gnat and somehow his quarters harbored a double window facing the forest, enough walking space Gavriel could complete his training maneuvers, and a bed fit for three people. Gavriel claimed a wooden chair, a far safer surface than the large bed Alistair had undoubtedly taken advantage of, and waited for him to explain why he called a meeting.

"I have a job for you."

Gavriel studied Alistair's eager face. Unless it was to shadow Lark at the ball or to collect another round of drinks, Alistair could shuffle off to the Netherworld.

"Not interested."

Alistair frowned. "You can't say that until you've heard what it is."

"I'm preparing you for my answer. That way your inevitable disappointment is lessened by the knowledge of it coming."

Alistair examined him. "You are rather sassy today. Do you need some spare coin to lessen the ache in your trousers?"

From the other side of the round table, Lark stifled a laugh. Nearly choking on a bite of apple pie.

Gritting his teeth, he leveled Alistair with a glare. "No."

"Are you sure?" Alistair grinned at him. "I've found it works wonders for the soul. Even aids in digestion."

"Oh, now you're making that up," Daciana said.

Alistair arched a dark brow. "You should try it sometime."

Images of Lark grinning at a dark sky weeping rain, her tunic drenched and clinging to every inch of her, flooded Gavriel's mind. She was somehow hard and soft. Sharp lines honed from training and smooth curves he wanted to map with his hands. He cleared his throat, hoping his face wouldn't betray his thoughts.

"What's the job?"

"I need you and Hugo to go collect someone who's been wrongly imprisoned."

Gavriel frowned. "That doesn't sound like our kind of job."

"I decide what sounds like our kind of job," Alistair said. "And the reward says it is."

Gavriel rolled his eyes. Alistair's greed and his libido were his two driving forces. "What's his crime?"

"Doesn't matter. Get him out. Get him to safety." Alistair took a swig of his ale, a mustache of froth clung to his upper lip. "We get paid."

As if anything was that simple.

Gavriel should have known that was the wrong question. He

glanced up at Alistair's arrogant smile, still coated in foam. "Who hired us, and what's he paying?"

Alistair's smile faltered. He ran the back of his hand across his mouth. "My sources pay for discretion with enough gold crowns to book us all passage aboard a ship sailing to Koval." Alistair's eyes darted over to Lark. "To the Highlands."

"Alistair..." Lark said, warning in her voice.

Alistair held his hand up, interrupting her. "It's done. Now I'm indebted to a certain Captain Ingemar, but it's no matter." He gestured to Gavriel. "Because you and Hugo are going to make sure we don't end up indentured to her by completing this task."

Of all the moronic things.

Gavriel wanted to grasp him by the neck and squeeze. He glanced over at Lark, noting the pinched expression on her face. He didn't want to add to her stress. "When?"

"Three days from now, you'll need to leave in two." Alistair plucked an invisible thread from his jacket. "It's a day's ride from here."

Three days. That would be during Lark's mission to Adler's masquerade. While she was at the ball, collecting information, Gavriel had planned to follow them and remain in the wings. Just in case. There was no way he was disappearing *a day's ride away* while they infiltrated the estate.

"Not until after Lark and Langford return," Gavriel said with a shake of his head. He sensed the subtle shift in Lark's posture.

"I'm going to have to agree with Gavriel on this one," Daciana said, forking a buttered carrot from her plate. "Should things go south, it would be helpful to have a second set of eyes."

"You know that isn't possible," Alistair said. He dropped into the chair beside Daciana and propped his boots up on the table, smug superiority radiating off him. Gavriel wished Mrs. O'Connell would sweep in and smack him. "If the prisoner hangs, we aren't getting paid. Hugo's already agreed, being the smart, hardworking go-getter he is."

Gavriel lifted his chin. "And what if I refuse?"

"If you refuse"—Alistair motioned to Lark—"you forfeit our coin. And how then, will we afford passage to the Highlands? Our poor little Lark will have to forget about her friend in need."

Gavriel shot a glance Lark's way and was met with her golden gaze. Her tankard vibrated against the wood table, and he knew that if he looked underneath, he'd find her knee bouncing.

"I should also mention that the same client hired us for both jobs, quite determined to bring down Adler. I think we all share a mutual goal here, no?" Alistair looked far too pleased with himself.

"You mean to say, you took two jobs from the same source, and if one of them goes wrong we'll all be implicated?"

Alistair frowned. "I'm more of a glass-half-full kind of guy."

Gavriel clenched his hands, clamping his mouth shut tight enough his jaw twinged.

"Besides," Alistair continued. "The ball is the perfect distraction to make our job of extracting the man simple. Easy even. Adler's diverted most of his guards to this function—"

"Putting Lark and Langford at risk."

"—making the task of sneaking in and out of Stormfair easier. And Daciana will be on the lookout for any pesky messengers riding to the estate with news of the man's escape. If you're half as good as you say, there should be plenty of time for everyone to complete their missions and make it back here for a drink before Adler even notices."

Too many moving parts indeed. None of this sat right. Plans that relied on numerous things going right usually ended in disaster.

"I'll cover them, Gavriel," Daciana said, her expression fierce.

"Fine." Gavriel rose to his feet and stalked off. He didn't need to look back to know Alistair was grinning.

CHAPTER 37

*T*he earth smelled fresh and warm from the heavy rainfall as Gavriel and Hugo headed south to Stormfair. The trees swayed in a balmy breeze, their dense leaves shaking off the last of the storm.

Gavriel glanced over at Hugo, tightening his mouth to keep from smiling. The large man sat upon his mount, shoulders high, elbows in, discomfort written in every clenched muscle. He considered suggesting he keep his posture loose, or else he'd feel this journey deep in his back for days, but he doubted he'd listen.

Gavriel regretted borrowing Apple for the journey. Now he was duty-bound to protect Lark's horse. Especially after she'd turned those wide amber eyes on him, forcing him to swear an oath that no harm would come to the animal. She missed a great opportunity; under the full force of that stare, he would have sworn to anything.

Images of the day in the rain swam in Gavriel's mind, an unwelcome fire ignited in his belly at the memory of a stolen moment. A risk not taken. That day in the field, rain coated her face, and her bright, open smile was directed at him. Him. As if he could ever be worthy of someone like her. As if he'd ever deserved a second thought.

He wished he could be that kind of man. Someone she could count on when the blight of the world had been eradicated and he was no longer hunted. He'd kiss her senseless at the end of a long day, cook her those damn sweet apples she was obsessed with. The kind of man who'd hold her through the night—without awakening in a pool of sweat, blade at her throat. Forgetting for a moment he was safe and she was supposed to be there.

Memories of pain burrow deep into the mind. He doubted he'd ever dream without images of death and blood filling his vision. Despite all this, he couldn't stand the thought of losing all hope. It was selfish, really. Holding onto this notion of a future that could never be. Clinging to this half-formed wish of a better life.

He knew that wish included her. It was her.

But he was never meant for such things.

Their parting words still ached somewhere deep in his chest.

"Adler has a reputation for cruelty."

"Yes, Gavriel, I know."

"I don't want to see anything go wrong. It would be difficult to extract the two of you should you fail."

Lark crossed her arms, her beautiful face scowling. "You're being super-fluous. This was covered already."

"I would feel better if I were going with you."

"Need I remind you, that last time you decided to drop in on a job, you got caught."

"Technically, we were all caught."

"I don't need advice from you. I just need you to do your part and let me do mine."

He stared at her, willing the words to form.

Be safe. Skies above, promise me you'll be safe. If anything happens, I'll raze the entire town to the ground, but promise me you'll be there waiting for me.

He didn't say any of those things.

"I'll see you in a few days."

The sooner the task was done, the better.

HUGO'S GUARDSMAN uniform of blue and white looked tailor-made for him. Knowing Alistair, it probably was. Stormfair was one of the few towns wealthy enough to afford guards in Ardenas. Hugo wore a mail coif, which was fortunate since the hood covered his tattooed neck, but he'd forgone the breastplate. Another detail Alistair was keen enough to keep in mind. Stormfair was a peaceful town, and The Crooked Bottle Inn was more of a quaint visitor attraction than a raucous tavern. If Hugo showed up donning full plate armor, he'd gain immediate attention.

Hugo wasn't the only one donning a disguise for their task. When the stone-laid wall of the town came into view, Gavriel stashed his usual black attire with the horses, opting for a simple homespun cloth patched together in varying shades of brown and tan. He was a common thief. Not a killer.

Not today, at least.

They'd already incapacitated the on-duty guard at the gate, Lindon was the fellow's name, before they slipped in and kept to the small wooded area within the town's boundaries. There was one last detail to take care of.

Hugo gave Gavriel one last look. Then his large fist collided with Gavriel's face.

They'd agreed a bit of realism would go a long way.

Gavriel's nose gushed blood, dripping in thick streams over his mouth and down his chin. Why the man had to aim for the nose was beyond him.

Hugo examined his knuckles, before yanking thick leather gloves into place. Right over the swirls of ink. He grabbed Gavriel by the arm and dragged him away from the side of the building, through the center of town. Passersby kept their heads down, paying them no mind as Gavriel staggered in worn boots through the square.

In the center of town stood a large stone fountain. Seven large cannons spurted water, creating a steady gurgle in the pool. In the middle towered the stone head of a bear, mouth agape for water to rush out the bronze pipe. The steps leading up to the fountain were worn with age, and moss had sprouted in the cracks. It was a warm day. If there were any children in the town, Gavriel expected to find them splashing in the water, filling the air with laughter and wreaking havoc.

But all was quiet. Only the sound of the trickling water filled the air as Hugo dragged Gavriel past the fountain.

Stormfair was a somber place. Strange, since it was home to one of the best markets in Ardenas.

The two guardsmen on watch eyed them curiously as they approached. Hugo stood at attention, yanking Gavriel roughly with him.

"What's going on here?" The man narrowed his shadowed eyes at them. Both guards were pale, their faces etched with dark circles of sleepless nights. Alistair was right, the security around here was stretched thin.

"I'm detaining this pile of filth." Hugo shook Gavriel with enough force to rattle his teeth.

Hugo was enjoying the charade a little too much.

"Uh-huh. And who are you?"

"Recruit Morin, sir." Hugo lifted his chin. "I transferred so Lindon could care for his wife. I heard their child was due any day now."

"Ugh, that's right," the guard said with a smirk. "She looked right ready to pop. I can't believe he got the time off for it though. He must be greasing the right palms, eh?"

Or he was unconscious and tied to a tree.

Hugo's expression didn't so much as flicker. "Where are the cells?" Before the guards could respond, Hugo kicked the back of Gavriel's leg, sending him onto his knees in the dirt. "I caught him trying to pickpocket someone in the market. I haven't turned him out yet, I figured we'd do that in his holding cell."

The guards looked Gavriel over curiously. "Let's see what he's got."

Hugo pulled a bag of coin from Gavriel's pocket and tossed it into the eager hands of the guard.

"That's mine," Gavriel said. It wasn't much more than a few silvers and copper bits, but still. He was saving up for more chocolate.

"A thief's property is forfeit." Hugo glared down at him.

The guards exchanged a private glance before giving him a nod. "Take him to the furthest building on the right. There should be a cell available. He's arrived just in time." The guard sneered, revealing a large chip in his front tooth. "Tomorrow's hangin' day."

Hugo hoisted Gavriel up and yanked him along. The heavy door slammed shut behind them, as they descended down the stone steps to the dungeon. The air grew thick and damp, and the musty scent of sweat and decay enveloped them.

This wasn't his first dungeon Gavriel was dragged to. Probably not the last either.

It was a small hold—only three cells and a straw-covered floor. But judging by the number of guards still on-duty when most were stationed at the ball, Gavriel suspected this town rarely saw crime.

Hugo dumped him into an empty cell and pulled the door shut with a clang.

Gavriel rolled his tight shoulders. Had he known he'd be tossed around like a rag-doll, he might have stretched.

Hugo turned and marched over to where a young guard lounged against the wall. "You're relieved. It's my shift."

"I thought I was taking the overnight."

"I don't question my orders," Hugo said gruffly.

"I should make sure with the Captain."

"You do that." Hugo edged a step closer. "Go interrupt his dinner with his pretty little wife and ask him. I'm sure he'd welcome the intrusion on his evening for a pissant like you."

The young guard seemed to hesitate as if weighing the outcomes of either decision. He gave a curt nod and scurried away.

Gavriel leaned his elbows on the bars, arms hanging through. "I didn't know the Captain's wife was pretty."

Hugo grunted. "I didn't even know he had a wife."

Gavriel laughed. "You coy bastard." He could have sworn he caught the ghost of a smile on Hugo's lips.

A wavering voice floated over the adjacent cell. "Please, let me go. You've got the wrong man."

Gavriel cocked his head. He approached the adjoining bars and peered through to assess the boy within.

His pale, unkempt hair hung in dirty clumps over his shoulders. Blue eyes darted about. Skinny arms and legs peeked out from the filthy rags hanging off of him. So, this was the prisoner they needed to free. Alistair neglected to tell them he was barely old enough to grow hair on his balls.

"I've never heard that one before. Next, will you say you were set up?" Gavriel said.

Hugo shot him a warning look that he ignored.

"I was set up!" the boy squeaked.

Alistair hadn't given them any specifics on his crimes. Were Gavriel still a member of the Guild, he'd follow his orders without question. But things were different now. Blood was spilled too easily these days, and setting this boy free could cause as much harm as drawing the blade across his throat himself.

"Does it matter? I'm going to die tomorrow."

"It matters to me." Better the boy thought his death was imminent. Gavriel found men were far more willing to spout truth in their final moments.

Gavriel pushed his cell door open, half surprised Hugo hadn't locked it, and stepped over to the boy's cell door. He produced a lock pick from his boot and frowned at the boy cowering in the corner. Inserting the pick, he began deftly maneuvering the lock open. "This might take a moment. But I assure you, once I get this door open, I will have the truth." The tumbler clicked, and with a satisfied sigh, Gavriel swung the door open. "There we are. Now you were saying?"

The boy stood, trembling. "They think I'm possessed. By a demon."

Gavriel frowned, casting a private look Hugo's way. That was a new one.

"Demons don't need to possess you. Not right now anyway. They walk freely in their own form."

"I'm not saying I believe it! I'm telling you my charges. They blame me for... unspeakable horrors. They say I did it, and when I denied it and swore to the gods of Avalon, they claimed I was possessed and didn't remember doing it. The monster is still out there. And before it kills again, it'll be too late for me."

Gavriel stared at the ground, trying to wrap his head around the boy's story. He turned to Hugo, assessing his reaction.

Hugo's face was a mask of neutrality. The man knew how to play his cards close to the vest.

Gavriel was impatient to get this over with and get back to Lark. Maybe he'd even be able to follow them to the ball.

You know you can't do that.

Damn his conscience. The voice of reason.

"We're here because someone thinks you're valuable enough to rescue."

The boy's shoulders sagged in visible relief. "You mean, I'm free?" his filthy face split in an eager grin. "What are we waiting for, let's go!"

"Not so fast, boy. We do this our way. I have pressing matters that need attending, and I can't very well see to them if I'm strung up by my neck." Gavriel wiped a hand down his face. "You do exactly as we say, without question. By the looks of it, you're already more trouble than you're worth."

"Fine. But my name isn't boy. It's Declan."

"I don't care what your name is," Gavriel said. "I only care that we get this done. With as little excitement as possible. Think you can handle that?"

"Yes." Declan nodded, voice tight and face twisted in annoyance.

CHAPTER 38

*L*ark traced her fingers along the edge of her crystal-adorned mask of silver leaves.

She wished she could have seen Gavriel one last time before he rode off. The way they'd left things still sent a gut-churning wave of regret through her. But she pushed the thought from her mind. She had more important things to focus on.

Lark glanced across the carriage Alistair had "borrowed." Langford donned a simple green doublet to match her with silver buttons and trim. He'd tucked his sleek grey dress trousers into pristine black boots. His dark hair, usually untidy, was swept back and sculpted to a slight bouffant, edged to one side, his blue-grey eyes made even more striking behind the simple black mask he wore.

"You look handsome."

His mouth quirked in an answering smile. "You look astonishing."

Lark's cheeks warmed, and she smiled. Alistair had combed, braided, and pinned her hair in place. She'd been shocked at how capable his hands were, so nimble in their styling, which he was quick to explain:

"Have you ever found yourself face to face with a woman's husband, in her bedroom, post-coitus? You learn a thing or two about survival."

Images of Alistair pretending to be anything other than the cad he was brought a grin to her face.

Lark ran her hands down the green gown, cataloging all the weapons she'd stashed beneath her skirts. She couldn't bring her bow, but Daciana had ensured she made up for it in blades. Lark's fitted bodice covered enough for modesty while still plunging a deep neckline trimmed in delicate silver leaves. The deep green—Langford's choice—offset the dark red of her hair, and the cut of the dress emphasized the curve of her waist, flaring out to a wide skirt that hid her dirk and daggers.

Lark was grateful she wasn't wearing Alistair's choice. The black gown, if you could call it a gown, exposed her entire midsection. The skirt billowed to the ground, in sheer panels, and the top, little more than a breastband, had black glittering branches jutting out from the shoulders like spikes for impaling. It was the sort of dress Thanar would have sent to her chambers, demanding she wear it for one of his absurd gatherings.

She'd made the right choice. Green felt like life. And she'd had enough death for many lifetimes.

"Are you nervous?"

Lark turned to find Langford studying her. "Maybe. Are you?"

"Oh yes," he said before peering out the window. "It's been a long time."

With a thousand questions begging to burst from her lips, she clamped her mouth shut. Now wasn't the time to delve into a history Langford would prefer to forget. Though one thought refused to be silenced. "Why are you so sure your father won't attend?"

Langford stiffened, a muscle feathering in his jaw. "My father wouldn't lower himself to cross the sea to Ardenas. It would be a little too much like chasing after me. Even after all these years, his pride wouldn't allow it."

Lark studied him, the stubborn set of his jaw, the ice in his eyes. What pushed him so far from Koval, from a life of luxury and advantage? It seemed they were all running from something. But she needed Langford here with her. Not wherever his mind went when he gazed out the carriage window at the rolling scenery beneath a dark sky. "Want to go over the plan again?"

"We mingle, we dance, we drink, you leave, I face judgment by a court I had no desire to ever deal with again. What more is there to plan?"

"Why did you leave?" So much for keeping focus on the task at hand.

Langford's mouth thinned in a firm line. "I didn't fit the role I was expected to play."

Lark thumbed the seam of her gown. As the son of a lord, Langford must have felt the weight of responsibility. What did Thanar always say, 'the sins of the father are the sins of the son?' Mortals were so quick to shape their children in their image and expect them to carry the torch even after the flame had been extinguished.

"You're much more than whatever they planned."

Langford shrugged, returning his gaze to the window.

"Do you have any advice for me?" Lark would be a fool not to ask.

He regarded her with an incredulous stare. "You're asking me?"

"Yes, you seem familiar with this setting. Is there a fork I should avoid? A particular way to bow so I don't offend and end the night in the stocks?"

"You're mocking me."

"No." Lark grabbed his hand. "If there's one thing that's become clear, it's that I don't know nearly as much as I thought I did."

The corner of Langford's mouth lifted. "I could have told you that."

"See? That wisdom? So valuable."

He patted her hand and straightened in his seat. "Follow my lead. Do not speak unless spoken to. You're the outsider here, you can't seem too eager, too hungry for interaction. You'll appear weak and common. Act bored, and when you do respond, leave it polite and vague." He leveled her with a serious stare. "Every instinct you have is wrong."

Lark sat stunned for a moment before releasing a long breath. "Wow, Langford. I had no idea what a tyrant you are."

"You, Daciana, and Alistair might be masters of your weapons. But that will serve you little here. A well-placed word can yield so much more bloodshed than the tip of your sword."

THE LARGE STEPS LOOMED OVER, leading up to the grand estate. Marble statues depicting sterile recreations of Paragons stood vigil over the gilded arches lining the top of the staircase.

Langford offered her his elbow. "My Lady?"

With a tight exhale, Lark slipped her gloved hand through, settling her other upon his bicep. Her mouth pulled into a smile. "My Lord."

Her slippers made clattering sounds against the pale stone staircase, filling Lark's ears and setting her teeth on edge. Each step was steeper than the last. As if they were walking to the gallows rather than into a party.

"Remember everything I told you and breathe," Langford whispered, his breath fluttering the few strands of hair that had slipped from her style on the journey.

A woman in a jade gown and peacock feather mask gave them a curious glance.

Langford leaned in again. "Pretend I said something scandalous."

Lark attempted a shy smile, looking up at him from under her eyelashes and feeling ridiculous.

Langford made a noncommittal noise. "We'll work on that."

The grand atrium, carpeted in crimson and trimmed with ornate gold, led to large double doors, manned by two stern-looking guards. Distant music and laughter fluttered through the cracks.

A scribe wearing a gold mask and a red tunic bustled over to them and began furiously scribbling his quill against the rolled parchment atop his podium. He dressed as if he was another ornament matching the estate. A crimson ribbon tied back his long blond hair at the nape of his neck. Even beneath his mask, his face was pinched and sullen.

Langford cleared his throat as they approached.

The scribe tossed them a withering glance. "State your name."

"Langford Brenner."

His mask framed eyes widened in shock. "Gods, Lord Brenner's son?"

"Am I not on the list?"

The scribe recovered quickly, his distaste resuming hold of his expression. "Oh no, you're on the list. Your family is always included in my Lord's considerations."

Langford angled his head. "I am most grateful for his kindness."

"May I ask who this lovely young lady is?" The scribe didn't so much as look at Lark, even as he complimented her. So many words. Few truths. "So I can announce you."

Langford placed a hand over hers where it sat at the crook of his elbow. "This is Lady Sereia Brenner. My wife."

"How nice." He still hadn't glanced at Lark as he scribbled with his little blue quill. "This way." The sour-faced scribe swept an arm out in front of him.

The guards pushed open the large doors and the full force of opulent colors—swirling in flourishing gowns—slammed into Lark. The music swelled and crashed through the grand room. Laughter and smiles half-concealed behind masks in an all-consuming ocean of vibrancy. Lark was adrift with only Langford's firm arm as her anchor.

The heavy doors closed behind them. A note of finality in their thud. Lark was distantly aware of their names ringing out.

Large golden eagles adorned the balconies above the dance floor, their wings outspread in mid-flight, and crimson draperies hung in arches on either side of the great room. Countless attendees, ornately dressed and hiding behind their masks, milled about. Most paid them no mind, continuing their private conversations.

Lark and Langford reached the bottom of the staircase. Tables lined the hall, overflowing with all sorts of decadent temptations. Chocolate coated fruits, clusters of violet and green grapes, meats glistening with butter and spices, and bread so thick she'd need the dirk strapped to her thigh to cut through it. Lark's mouth watered.

They crossed the smooth marble floor, approaching the man she assumed to be Adler, where he waited on the dais. He was outfitted in a red military jacket (curious, since those were Kovalian colors), and his polished epaulettes and ash brown hair glinted in the light of the hundreds of candles throughout the hall.

That seemed like a fire hazard.

"Langford Brenner." He extended his hand. "You honor my home with your presence."

"The honor is mine, Adler."

Adler didn't so much as flinch at the informal use of his name. According to Alistair, he'd accumulated his wealth through trade and investment. He was likely used to the discrepancy of respect between old and new money.

Langford gave one firm shake before pulling back. "I've neglected your kindness for far too long."

Adler shook his head, his gloved hand cutting through the air in a dismissive wave. "Nonsense, you're always welcome. No matter how much time has passed since our last meeting." He turned his gaze on Lark, who resisted the urge to stiffen her posture under his thinly veiled scrutiny. He had the face of a man who was handsome once, before years of frowning took their toll. His eyes were a warm brown in color, but that was where the warmth ended. "Speaking of which, much seems to have changed since last we met. Did my ears deceive me? This is your wife?"

"She is indeed."

"It's a pleasure to make your acquaintance," Lark said with a smile she hoped was pleasant rather than frantic.

"The pleasure is mine, my lady." Adler accepted her hand and yanked her toward him. "She is a treasure." His eyes never left hers as he placed a kiss on her knuckles. Her skin burned through her glove, and she had to fight the urge to rip her hand away. Finally, he lifted his eyes to Langford. "But you already knew that. I'll have to borrow her for one dance, with her husband's permission of course."

Lark bit down on her tongue. Langford told her, every instinct she had was wrong.

"Of course. It's the least I could do after shirking your invitations for so long." Langford's mouth curled into a pleasant smile that failed to meet his eyes.

Adler let out a loud laugh. "Quite right. Perhaps I should see how far this favor can take me?" He gave her a wink.

Lark's forced smile began to ache.

Adler dropped her hand. "Enjoy the party. Eat. Drink. Dance. I'll find you later."

A promise or a threat. Lark couldn't tell.

Once they were away and hidden behind a pillar of an outer balcony looking over the garden, Lark placed a hand to her stomach and exhaled a long breath.

Langford came close, resting an elbow on the stone above her head. It would appear to anyone walking by, that they were lovers engaged in a private conversation.

"That was sickening."

Langford cracked a smile. "That was nothing. You'll have to withstand a lot more than that to last the night."

"Can't I just stab him?"

"I warned you. Don't take it to heart. You need to put it away for the evening." His eyes bore into her from behind his mask. "Come, our absence will be noticed if we aren't seen drinking and smiling soon."

Even as a Reaper, the games and schemes of court intrigue disgusted Lark. Social climbers were always desperate to find themselves in Thanar's good graces. Back then, she'd barely had access to any real emotion or reaction. As a mortal, every heightened sense and emotion served as fuel to the flame.

Langford pressed a chalice of wine in her hand, giving her itching fingers something to close around that wasn't someone's throat.

"Bring it to your lips frequently, but don't drink."

She rolled her eyes, lifting it to her mouth.

The ballroom was a throng of glitter, feathers, and wicked smiles peeking beneath their chosen facades. A woman in a midnight gown —sparkles glimmering along her décolletage—swooped past and offered Langford a heavy-lidded glance he ignored. Lark slipped her hand into Langford's, though she doubted it would deter any determined ladies from their interest.

Lark needed to break away, to begin her search. Perhaps she could retire to the privy to "freshen up." Lark couldn't even find it in herself to be proud that she remembered the mortal practice. Maybe that was all wrong? What instincts was she supposed to trust when Langford said they were all wrong?

A headache began to throb in her temples.

Before Lark could ask how she should slip away, a hand reached out and clapped Langford on the back. "Langford, you old cankerblossom. Is that really you?"

Langford's hand tightened in hers, his posture stiffening.

An obscenely handsome man in a panther mask stood behind them. He grinned, his hand still claiming Langford's shoulder. His long black hair trailed over his shoulders, and his deep brown skin took on a golden sheen in the candlelight. He eyed Langford in a way that had even Lark's stomach fluttering.

Langford's tight face smoothed into an easy smile. "Ryker." He turned, keeping Lark's hand in his and pulling her with him. "I see you haven't changed a bit."

Ryker laughed, shaking his head. "Not at all, but look at you. You've filled out nicely haven't you?" He glanced at Lark with his rich brown eyes. "Who's your little friend?"

"Sereia is my wife," Langford said, wrapping an arm around her.

"Sereia," Ryker said. "You're certainly not what I was expecting." He grabbed Lark's hand and pressed a quick kiss to it. "Although Langford never does what's expected of him." His tone had an edge to it—an unspoken shard of tension.

Lark glided her hand up Langford's chest, angling her head up to him. "Darling, while you two catch up, would you miss me terribly if I freshened up?"

Langford tore his gaze from Ryker to stare down at her.

Lark waited. This would be the perfect out, but only if he felt like he could manage without her. Mission or not, she wouldn't abandon him if anything in his eyes asked her to stay.

Running his hand down her arm in what would appear to be a soothing fashion, Langford nodded. "Of course, my heart, don't tarry."

"As my lord commands."

Lark sauntered away, knowing her exaggerated movements were for neither of their benefits. Certainly not Langford. And something about the intensity between him and Ryker confirmed no amount of her charms would work on him either.

She was almost to the doors when she caught sight of a mountain of chocolate-dipped strawberries on the golden table along the wall. Her eyes widened, and her mouth watered. She paced over and plucked a large one from the platter. The fruit was half raised to her mouth when she caught sight of one of the minstrels. He donned a fine turquoise doublet, with silver detailing along the seams. He swayed, his bow caressing the violin. A soft smile stretched across his creased face.

Bartrand, the traveling musician she met at the market. He seemed to have moved up in the world. She stuffed the fruit whole into her mouth and moved through the crowd toward him.

"I should have known it was you," Lark said around a mouthful of sweet yet tart berry and rich chocolate. "I could recognize your talent anywhere."

Bartrand opened his eyes, his expression confused. He wore no mask—a relief to Lark to have one true face to look upon. His weathered features broke into a beaming smile. "Dear, sweet Lark. I didn't expect to see beauty of the likes of yours here."

"Nor I yours," she said with a grin, bouncing on the balls of her feet in time with his playing. The compulsion of his music pounded in her blood, too strong to ignore.

"I wrote that song in your honor, as promised. Would you care to hear it?"

If only. "Not here, not tonight. But someday I demand to dance to that song."

He bowed his head slightly as he continued to play. "As the lady wishes."

She offered him a curtsy before dancing away.

With each step, the buoyant joy in her heart dimmed. She couldn't wait any longer to begin her search.

She passed through the alcove, to the furnished antechamber where more attendees were getting... comfortable. Writhing bodies occupied the long, plush benches of gold and crimson. A fugue of heady lust and incense thickened the air with dark promises. Lark ignored the heat that rose on her cheeks and pushed through until she was in the servant's hall. Fewer guests loitered there, and the servants who bustled past were too busy to notice her.

Lark strode up to a statuette of Adler's likeness, pretending to examine it while she ran through the layout Alistair had drilled into her head for days. Casting a bored look over her shoulder and confirming no one was watching, she continued down the second corridor, past rows of portraits.

Sprawling before her, the silent hall of arched ceilings and closed doors awaited—floor to ceiling of white marble with swirls of grey. Muted. Like all the color had been sucked out and deposited in the ballroom.

Lark tried the doorknob of the last room, only to find it locked. Reaching into her bodice, she produced one of Gavriel's lockpicks and began working on the lock, as he'd taught her when they'd practiced on Alistair's door. It popped with a satisfying click before she swung the door open and slipped through.

The room was elegantly decorated, understated. Ivory and gold cast the empty chamber in soft ethereal light.

Yanking her gloves off and stuffing them into her bodice, Lark crossed the room to the window and pushed it open. Throwing a leg over the sill, she paused, summoning her courage. She hadn't even begun, and already her chest tightened. It struck her as if her body was protesting mortal danger. She pushed her human feelings aside and continued with purpose.

In the light of the moon, a maze of greenery and marble statues peered up at her, and a warm breeze carrying the scent of Adler's prized roses ruffled her skirts. The ground, so far below, sent her head spinning.

The outer gardens weren't open to partygoers. If she plunged to her death, the night air would be her only witness. Who would come to collect her? Nereida swore Lark would come straight to her should she die, but what if Thanar came? Would he drag her soul back to the Otherworld?

Lark couldn't dwell on that thought. Not when she needed to steady her nerves.

Lark tiptoed along the narrow ledge of stone. Arched up on balls of her feet, she locked her elbows tight to keep as close to the wall as possible. Turning her head, her ear skimmed the stone facade.

What was Gavriel doing? She imagined he would be sipping ale by the fire when they returned to the inn. He never did see her in her gown. Would he have failed to hide his reaction? She'd caught the way he looked at her sometimes when he thought she wasn't watching. The way his eyes darkened—

Lark's foot slipped, and her heart plunged to the pit of her stomach. She froze, listening to her quickened pulse. That's what she got for letting her mind wander. Exhaling a shaky breath, Lark regained her footing, her blood thrumming in her ears.

A bead of sweat rolled down her back, taunting her with its descent.

The large balcony finally seemed within reach. A whimper escaped her mouth, as she strained against her flagging strength. Blinking back the moisture in her eyes, Lark crept a few more paces before lunging over the railing. She collapsed in relief, sprawled on the cold stone with her skirts in disarray.

As the tremors subsided, she sat up, smoothed out her gown, and fixed her hair.

Her absence would be noticed soon.

The outer lock to Adler's private chambers was simple enough to pick, a gamble they'd taken, and relief sang through Lark's limbs. Alistair had told her not to bother attempting the inner door, likely fitted with a far more complex series of locks than she had the ability to master in such a short time. This door wasn't so protected because only an idiot would take the time to scale the outer wall to reach his balcony.

An obvious oversight on Adler's part.

With great care, she slipped through, not wanting the night breeze to disturb the room. She crept to the large desk. Starting from the bottom, she tugged each drawer open, sifting through documents and parchments. Letters of business, travel expenses, tax collections. Nothing of any interest. She turned to survey the rest of his chambers. The rails of his large four-poster bed were carved from walnut and adorned with crimson canopies.

Were those manacles on his bedside table?

Lark repressed a shudder at the image. Careful to put everything back in its place, she swept over the room. Checking drawers, the dressing table, the bookshelf. Finding nothing worth keeping.

A large oil painting hung beside his bed. Adler's naked form, proud and unabashed, stared out from the portrait. From where she stood, the angle of the portrait jutting from the wall appeared off. Lark approached the painting, trying not to make eye contact with his crotch. Undoubtedly, the painter had been very generous with his or her brush strokes.

Lark ran a finger down the edge of the ornate frame, snagging it behind the golden rim. It swung open, revealing a hole cut out of the wall behind it. A single envelope, wax seal already broken, begged for closer inspection. Squinting in the moonlight, she peeled back the folded edges.

A flush of warmth flared up her cheeks.

This was a *very* private letter indeed.

From the wife of a close friend, it appeared. Lark tucked the letter into her dress. Alistair wasn't entirely clear on what he wanted, only that she was to gather information damning enough for leverage. A twinge of discomfort coiled in her gut at the thought of getting paid to help blackmail someone she had no prior knowledge of.

A creak ripped Lark from her thoughts. The hairs raised on the back of her neck, and her heart jolted.

The glass door of the balcony had slipped open, pushed by the wind. Shaking her head at her foolishness, Lark crossed the room and shut it, twisting the lock in place. Her eyes drifted to the large wooden desk once more. There had to be something she missed.

She pulled his top drawer open again. This time, she lifted the documents out, placing them atop the desk. She ran her finger along the underside of the drawer until she found the seam. She lifted the false bottom, revealing what Adler had wanted to remain hidden.

Pages upon pages. All unfolded, seals already broken. The image appeared to be a wolf sigil. The Mayor of Stormfair's crest.

That was where Hugo and Gavriel went to extract the prisoner.

These were personal letters between Adler and the Mayor. Lark smoothed out the creased page and squinted in the dark with no light save for the moon.

...another child was discovered. We dug as fast as we could, but he was long dead before we unearthed him. I didn't dare tell his parents the coroner deemed him living when he was buried.

How many more children must we lose before justice is served?

There's talk of people leaving the village. We're cursed with a blight that steals their children from their beds. I don't know how much longer I can keep my citizens from relocating.

I've promised to find their killer before he strikes next. Based on the pattern, I've less than a month.

I'm at the end of my rope. You have to help me.

Or you can consider Stormfair a relic of the past.

-Bronn

With numb fingers, Lark folded up the letters, stuffing them beneath her dress. Her stomach was a pit of ice. She placed his documents back in the drawer in the same order she'd found them in. Children were being murdered. And here they were collecting secrets for coin.

Her head spinning, Lark crossed the room and leaned against the doorframe. She exhaled a steadying breath. Now was not the time to spiral. She had to be smart. Finish the task that lay before her first. One step at a time.

Lark pulled her gloves from her bodice and yanked them on.

Cracking the door open, she slipped out in the hallway, soundlessly closing it behind her. She smoothed her skirts and glided down the vestibule. Her footsteps echoed on the marble floors.

A guard donning oxblood leathers and gold buckles rounded the corner. He jumped when he saw her.

"You're not supposed to be here." He was young. New enough to Adler's employ that he hadn't learned to mask his emotions.

"How embarrassing! I must have gotten turned around searching for the privy." Lark pressed a gloved hand to her forehead. "I fear the wine's gone straight to my head."

The guard pursed his lips as if debating his response. "I can escort you back to the ballroom if you need, my lady."

Lark plastered what she hoped was a beaming smile devoid of any thought on her face. "I have great need of you. Though perhaps you might lead me to the washroom first. I never did find it." No need to be accompanied under guard back to the ballroom.

"Of course, my lady." He offered her his arm.

Lark slipped her hand through, pretending to marvel at his firm bicep. If only Alistair were here to see her. No doubt he'd be brimming with pride.

"Do you make a habit of rescuing damsels in distress?" She bit her lip as she glanced up at him. He wasn't unpleasant looking. He wore his black hair short, dark eyes glittering behind his mask. He gave her a crooked grin, his eager gaze darting to her neckline

What a prince.

"Let's say I have a vast skill set. Ready and willing to assist in any area necessary."

"Of that, I have no doubt." Lark was fortunate his vanity was so easily flattered.

His answering smirk reeked of pride. As if he'd already sated her with his presence alone.

Music and conversation fluttered down the hall in soft waves.

Easing their stride, Lark leaned in close enough her whisper ghosted against his ear. "I have to see to my husband. Meet me in the gardens in an hour."

His answering smile was triumphant. "As my lady commands." With a bow of his head, he meandered away, pausing to throw a meaningful glance over his shoulder.

Lark openly scanned him head to toe, biting the side of her lip for his benefit.

He tossed his head back with an agonized sigh before marching out of sight.

Taking a deep breath, Lark squared her shoulders before she once again descended into the vipers' nest.

CHAPTER 39

"*W*here have you been?"

Lark ignored Langford's glare as she emptied his glass of its contents. Right down the back of her throat. She grabbed at a passing tray, snagging a fresh chalice of wine. Another server bustled by carrying a platter filled with tiny, frilly cakes. She lunged toward him, arousing a few nearby gasps. She'd earned this. If the dried sweat between her breasts was any measure.

The documents concealed beneath her skirts scraped against her bare legs. She pushed thoughts of the letter's contents from her mind; she couldn't afford to yield to anger at the moment.

Lark held the tiny pink cake, adorned with white ripples of icing, between her thumb and forefinger. Such a delicate little thing. She popped the entire cake in her mouth. Rich, chocolate sponge infused with thick raspberry filling exploded on her tongue.

She washed it down with a sip of her wine, letting her mind wander. Would Gavriel enjoy that particular dessert? The unbidden image of his large hand holding such a pretty little cake made her snort, choking on her wine.

"I told you not to drink it." Langford frowned. "What did you find?"

"Not here, dance with me." Lark downed the rest of it, warmth buzzing in her head and deep in her belly. She grabbed Langford's hand and led him onto the crowded dance floor.

"Have you any idea what I've had to contend with?" He possessed a fluid grace even in the face of his frustration.

"I'm sorry if the party was an inconvenience while I shimmied my way above certain death."

He tutted. "Don't be dramatic. Tell me you found what we need."

"I'm not sure." She had the scandalous letters between Adler and someone he called his 'thirst-quencher.' Lark stifled a shudder at the memory. There was also the matter of Stormfair. If Adler was involved in any sort of coverup, that was far more damning than a few dirty letters.

"Damn it all to the fiery pits of the Netherworld."

"Right, I'm the dramatic one. Has it been so terrible? It seemed you and Ryker had a lot to catch up on."

"That"—Langford said through his teeth—"is none of your business. We need to leave."

Lark nodded. It would be a shame to leave before they collected enough information, but without confidence there was more to unearth, every moment they stayed was a mounting risk. If Adler discovered anything missing from his quarters—

"May I cut in?" Adler's voice jolted Lark from her thoughts. He stood off to the side, the bemused expression on his face at war with his dark stare, cold and penetrating.

Langford released her waist. He offered a curt bow to Adler and marched off the dance floor. Lark focused her attention on the man standing before her. With a slight curtsy, she placed her hand in his and let him spin them into the center of the crowd.

"I must confess," Adler whispered far too close for comfort. "I find your connection with Langford most curious."

Lark gave a tight smile, stomach flipping. "What can I say? We fell hard and fast."

He chuckled. "No, I mean I find it fascinating you think anyone would believe he prefers certain feminine charms."

410

Dread coiled in her gut like a threatened snake. "I don't know what you're talking about."

"My lady," he said, his tone admonishing. "Let's not pretend we don't know of his preferences. I've long been aware of his penchant for, shall we say, more virile energy."

Lark clenched her teeth. "My husband's preferences are none of your concern."

"Oh, come now, don't be that way. I have no ill will toward the lad. He can do whatever he pleases. I'm merely curious what Lord Brenner, Langford's father, makes of all this." Adler twirled her, and Lark's vision spun. "Wystan was bereft when Langford took off like that. No one objected to his preferences, flesh is flesh and all that, so long as he fulfilled his duty."

Lark swallowed, trying to deafen the roaring in her ears. In the face of her silence, Adler continued. "All great houses need heirs. Not bastards tied only by blood, but legitimate heirs. It was quite the scandal when Langford disappeared from his lands right before he was due to select a wife. And here he waltzes into my home with you on his arm. Most curious indeed."

Lark tried to reign in the anger that coursed through her. It was pathetic, how much a bottom-feeder savored gossip. But there was safety in the distraction. The real danger began when he examined too closely. "You overreach, sir."

Adler angled his head, an infuriatingly smug smile on his face. "So direct. I admire that in a woman."

He spun her across the room, maneuvering her around the vast array of gowns. Of silk and lace and tulle. A dizzying menagerie of false smiles and wicked eyes. As the song ended, Lark tried to take a step back, but Adler held her firm. She glared up at him. His eyes were sharp with calculation.

"There's a saying in Koval, one I've grown quite fond of." Adler angled his head, his ash-brown hair shimmered. "A sneaky mouse always finds the poison."

Lark pushed him away with enough force he relented. "I don't know what you're talking about."

411

Adler bowed his head, a conspiratorial smile on his face. "Of course, my lady. Enjoy your evening."

Lark stumbled away, her head spinning, and she sucked in a deep breath. They needed to get out of here. Mission or not, they had to go. If Adler was onto them, it was too dangerous to mount another search. What she'd collected would have to be enough.

Hopefully.

A warm hand grasped her wrist and yanked her behind a pillar. The stone dug into Lark's shoulder blades. She glared up the offender, about to shove her way through when she caught the desperation in his crystal blue eyes. The urgency of his expression, even half-hidden behind his fox mask, struck her. His pale cornsilk hair hinted its retreat from his forehead, and grey whiskers dusted his square jaw.

"I was hoping to catch you before you disappeared," he said quietly enough only she would hear. "But it seems you were determined to dig without the proper tools."

Lark stiffened against his hold. Was this Alistair's contact, or one of Adler's men? Determined to back her into a corner? "My own hands are the only instruments I trust."

He sighed. "Please let's speak plainly. I'm not one for the double talk of court, it gives me a headache."

This conversation was giving Lark a headache. "Fine, speak plainly. Tell me your name."

He bent his head closer to hers. "Davin. Davin Callahan. I know you didn't search Adler's private office, because any schematics you had access to would have left that room off the map. Why didn't you wait for me to find you?"

How was she to know he'd find her? She couldn't just stand around waiting all night. "Don't you think, you shouldn't be seen with me right now?"

Davin stared her down, hidden behind the face of a fox. His hand flexed at the small of her back. "Perhaps, but frankly, I don't care."

Lark's jaw clenched. "You may not care, but you're not the one risking your neck."

Davin's blue eyes sharpened, giving way to a steely gaze. "I have far more at stake than you know."

"We all have more to lose than we're willing to admit. Let's get to the point."

He gave a curt nod. "I want a specific document implicating Adler on his dealings in Koval."

"What is he—"

"I wasn't finished," Davin hissed and his eyes flashed dangerously. "I want that document brought back to me, tonight."

"That wasn't the deal. I bring my findings back to my base, and we complete the handoff at the time specified." Lark narrowed her eyes up at him.

Davin's mouth tightened against any retort he may have had. "You'll find what you require in his private office. Out the doors, down the hall, and through the library. Behind the case of poetry, you'll take the stairs. His vault is sealed with a passcode."

"Do you happen to know this passcode?"

"No, of course not. But his most trusted assistant, Cliffton, does. He's monitoring the guest list this evening."

Lark remembered the stuffy scribe at the door. She doubted she could charm him into giving it up. Threats of violence it was then.

"Anything else?"

Davin leveled her with a pleading stare. The years shone on his face. "What I want more than anything in this whole world, is my son to be free and safe."

"Your son?" The mission for Hugo and Gavriel. Their mission, divided into two jobs, one to infiltrate, and one to extract.

"Yes. Adler was tasked with assigning blame to horrendous crimes, and rather than find the actual bastard responsible, he pinned it on my son. Why do the legwork, when you can blame an easy target, and come out looking like a hero? He has my hands tied. His influence far outweighs mine. If we can discredit him—" his voice was a whisper, though it whipped through her "—I might have a chance at keeping my son from the noose."

Lark swallowed. The air in the room, heavy with uncertainty.

Davin's son stood accused of a crime he hadn't committed, thrown in the cell of the Stormfair dungeon. The child-killer the mayor of Stormfair was desperate to bring to justice. Had Adler condemned an innocent man to silence those families? The letter beneath her skirts pressed against her like a blade promising to draw blood.

"I have no doubt your son is already out of harm's way," Lark said. Davin's posture seemed to relax. "And I'll do whatever it takes to ensure Adler has nothing left to his name but shame and disgrace."

Davin's eyes shuddered closed as he exhaled a long breath. "Thank you. Go, now. I've bribed the musicians to play a jig next, it should be very raucous and disorienting." He offered a small smile, before disappearing into the crowd.

Lark found a very flustered-looking Langford, who had amassed a following of eager young ladies. Lark gripped him by the sleeve and yanked him away from his crowd of unwanted admirers, earning a few dark glares in the process.

"Apologies, ladies," Lark said over her shoulder as she dragged him away. "I require my husband's attention." She pulled him out onto the balcony overlooking the gardens. Below, a bold couple enamored enough not to care for privacy ardently expressed their affections among the rose bushes.

Langford turned to follow Lark's line of sight, giving her a crooked grin. "Oh, don't worry, that happens all the time."

A large dark hand gripped a milky white thigh. Even from the balcony, the desperation in his hold was palpable enough to steal the breath from Lark's chest. The shadows offered privacy, but not even the darkest shade could hide the ferocity of their want. A fierce ache Lark couldn't quite name tightened in her chest.

"What did Adler say?"

Langford's voice cut through Lark's thoughts, and she tore her gaze from the couple. "Nothing important. But the contact approached me, he told me to search Adler's study. It wasn't in the castle schematics."

Langford turned to brace his hands on the balcony, oblivious to the rising crescendo of the coupling down below. "A secret room?

That sounds like the right place. But if Adler is onto us, we need to go while our heads are still attached to our necks."

Lark shook her head. "I don't see that we have a choice."

Langford leveled her with a solemn expression. "There's always a choice, Lark. No matter the stakes, you can always choose to walk away."

Was there any truth to that? It was a lovely thought, the freedom to leave any path determined to remain dark. She could leave with what little they had, knowing Gavriel and Hugo had likely already rescued the boy. Though a life on the run wasn't truly freedom, and they'd likely lose some, if not all, of their payment. Or she could stay and see this through, risking her neck. Get paid, and see Adler fall.

An easy choice to make.

Langford studied her. "Where do we need to go?"

"We need to see someone first."

"I don't like the sound of that."

"THAT WAS BRILLIANT," Lark whispered to Langford as they crept through the darkened library. Its cathedral ceilings threatened to echo the barest of sounds, and glimmering motes floated in the streams of moonlight that crept through the tempered glass windows. Adler had an impressive and untouched collection of books if the thick layer of dust was any indicator.

"You said you needed the combination, I got the combination," Langford said through clenched teeth.

"When my threats of dismemberment proved fruitless, I figured you'd step in. I just didn't expect you to be so..."

"So, what?"

"Calculating. I figured you'd seduce him with your charms. The charms I unfortunately lack."

Langford rolled his eyes. "Don't be so crass. Sex and violence, that's the only way you think to gain what you wish?"

"Mostly, yeah. How did you know he was skimming off the top of Adler's account books?"

"They're all skimming off the top, trying to scrape off more than they deserve. This whole court is a scourge in need of eradicating."

Lark stalled in her tracks, eying Langford's shadowed silhouette. "That savors quite strongly of bitterness, dear husband."

Langford nudged her toward the bookcase of poetry. "Yes, well, it's part of my charm."

Among the shelves of books, *Sonnets of Lace and Love* peered out from the stack. The only book not coated in a thick layer of negligent dust. Langford made a noise in the back of his throat. "Of course, he reads that drivel."

Behind the wooden case, carved into the wall was an alcove, stone steps disappearing into the shadows. Moon-soaked windows illuminated the library, but a truer dark crept in as they descended to the lower levels. Lark skimmed her hand along the uneven wall, fingers snagging on a cold torch. She turned to Langford, sticking her hands in his pockets.

"Excuse me," Langford said, tone thick with disapproval. "I'll remind you to keep your hands to yourself, wife. I haven't had nearly enough wine for this."

Even in the dark, Lark grinned. "I need to light the torch."

"Why didn't you say so?" The strike of flint, and a spark flooded the space between them with a tease of light. Another strike and a flame erupted against the brazier. "There we are." Langford's voice echoed against the dank walls of stone. He hoisted the torch from its stand and handed it to her.

A few steps brought them to Adler's oak door. Lark grasped the heavy iron latch—it was rough and cool against her palm. Her wrist twinged as she pushed the door open. It was heavier than she thought, but why wasn't it locked? Maybe a secret room didn't need locks. Another oversight on Adler's part.

Lark swept into the room and lit a standing candelabra in the corner, revealing a simple, sturdy desk and stone slab walls. They were bare, save for a small portrait of a watery landscape.

Remembering the portrait in Adler's study, Lark swung the painting away from the wall. A series of interlocking numbers were etched into a complicated steel device. This form of security was too advanced for Ardenian locks. This was of Kovalian make.

"Langford, the passcode?"

Langford scrolled through the numbers until the latch clicked and the safe door came loose. He pulled it open and fished out a thick pile of documents, handing Lark half to sift through.

She sat at the desk and thumbed through the stack of paper. Document upon document of Adler's unsavory business ventures. His capitalism of the slave trade in Koval. Receipts of taxation in many towns he had a hand in, Stormfair the most lucrative. It made sense he wanted to protect his holding there.

A personal letter caught Lark's attention. She pulled it from the stack and smoothed it in her hands to read. "Langford, he's being threatened by the head of merchants in Koval."

"Let me see."

Lark handed him the letter. His eyes widened, and he glanced away from the page to regard her with an incredulous expression. "They don't like the percentage he's been cutting himself." His eyes returned to the letter. "Interesting."

"Interesting enough to take with us?"

Langford nodded, stuffing it into his pocket. "It seems Adler's appreciation of Koval fails to extend much further than his decor."

"What do you mean?"

Langford laughed. "Didn't you notice his guards? Those were Kovalian colors, not Ardenian."

The entire castle was adorned in gold and crimson. Lark hadn't realized it was a blatant disregard of Ardenas.

"My eyes can barely function right now. I still don't know what I'm searching for." Lark resumed her search, sifting through his trade letters and documentation. A particular name leapt out from one of the pages. *Davin Callahan.* She snatched the paper up.

Shipment 347- eleven men, six women, four children. Inspection—passed.

"Our contact is his business partner." His son wasn't the only one

Davin was protecting. Lark kicked back her chair to stand and handed Langford the page. "Skies, I'm so blind! Look at this."

He crinkled the parchment in his grip. He studied the page, his frown only deepening. "Did Davin really expect us not to read these? Adler behaves like he's begging for King Zaire's favor, but if he were to discover Adler's debt to the Kovalian Merchants Guild... " At Lark's puzzled expression, Langford sighed. "You really should learn more about the world. Slavery is legal in Koval—"

"Yes, I'm well aware of that fact," Lark interjected.

"Ardenas regards it as unlawful, but who controls the law?" Langford waited expectantly.

"Each town seems to have its own guard."

"And who pays the guards?"

Lark frowned. "The ones with the deepest pockets."

"Now you're getting it." Langford handed the document back to her. "It's prohibited so only a few can make the highest profit. Adler and Davin are trying to cheat the system, and all it would take is a letter from the Kovalian Merchants Guild, sent to the right person, for the entire operation to implode. Do you think Ardenians will rejoice when they learn the truth?"

"They'd call for blood."

"Right you are, and enough coin could result in the dispatching of the Crows."

Lark pressed her fingertips against her temple. Every new piece of information only complicated matters. "That's who employs the Crows? Wealthy men bickering amongst themselves for power?"

Langford held his hands up. "I'm merely postulating, but yes. The coin has to come from somewhere, and I wonder at how such a facility has lasted this long. Someone is keeping the Guild of Crows employed, and payment isn't gratitude and smiles."

Lark stuffed the document into her bodice. She wouldn't be giving any of this information to Davin, that much was certain. "We need to leave."

Langford scrambled, trying to collect everything up neat and orderly.

"Just shove it in and let's go. Daciana should be waiting for us on the other side of the walls."

The unmistakable scrape of the wooden door against the stone floor pricked the hairs on the back of Lark's neck.

"I wouldn't be too sure of that." Adler's voice emitted from the shadows. For the love of the skies, this was not happening.

Adler stepped into the room, flanked by two guards. One was a blond, twitchy-looking fellow who kept darting glances about the room. The other, Lark recognized from their encounter earlier. His dark eyes were narrowed, his mouth tight. The image of him waiting in the gardens, for a liaison that was never going to happen brought a smile to her face.

"Adler," Lark said. "My husband and I were merely looking for a private spot to enjoy each other."

Adler nodded, puckering his lips and furrowing his eyebrows. "Oh, yes dear, I'm sure that's what you were doing." He gestured to his guards who started toward her. "Bring them where they can enjoy the utmost privacy."

Lark grasped for an idea—anything to get them out of this. "Don't you want to know who sent us?"

Adler laughed humorlessly. "I already know Davin sent you. He never did master the game of two faces." He edged a step closer. "My dear, you have nothing to offer. Absolutely nothing I want from you. Just do yourself a favor and keep that pretty mouth shut. Lest my guards decide you have something they want."

Lark snarled, her heart quickened. "Threaten me with that again, I'll cut your pathetic sack from your body"—she glared at the guard advancing on her—"and feed it to you."

The blond guard, to his credit, stilled.

Adler smirked, mirth shining in his eyes. "I like you. Pity you fell in with the wrong company. I shall drink a toast to your memory tonight." He turned to Langford. "You, I won't miss so much."

"A mutual sentiment."

Adler sighed, tugging on his glove. "Torren, I trust you can handle this?"

The young-faced guard Lark had assumed to be newly appointed gave her a vicious smirk. His dark eyes flashed. "Oh, yes."

"Good. Make sure they're in the next shipment, and if they give you any trouble, dispose of them. Wystan will never know what became of his son." Adler leveled Langford with a mocking smile. "Then again, you're already dead to him." He turned on his heel and ascended the stairs.

Lark itched for one of the many blades stashed beneath her dress. The blond guard lunged. She dropped and yanked Hugo's dagger from its sheath along her thigh. Kicking his leg out from under him, she sank her blade into his shoulder.

His groan of pain was musical fire to her senses. An unbidden thrill sang through her veins.

Lark yanked her knife free and dug her fingers into the bloody hole. He doubled over as she angled the edge of her blade to his throat, and lifted her head to give a triumphant smile to Langford—

Langford was on his knees. Hands behind his head and mask ripped off. His eyes held a desperate terror as Torren held the edge of his sword against his throat.

Shit.

Lark tugged on the guard's blond roots. "Unhand him before I release—" She paused and leaned down to whisper in his ear. "What's your name?"

"Rylen," he squeaked.

"Before I release Rylen from the earthly confines of his mortal body."

"You think I give a shit what happens to him? Go ahead, spill his blood. This one will die before you have a chance to come after me." Torren tightened his grip on his sword. "What's his life worth to you, huh?"

Langford's eyes widened.

Lark pulled her dagger away and shoved Rylen to the side. He scrambled away, keeping a wide berth.

"Don't just stand there." Torren nodded his head in Lark's direction, urging his companion on. "Unless you want me to search her,"

Torren said. "She didn't meet me in the gardens, I'm curious what she's hiding under there."

Rylen wrinkled his nose and sheepishly took Hugo's dagger from her grip. "That won't be necessary." He patted her down with a tentative touch, blushing when he pulled the hidden documents from her bodice. He kneeled, lifting her skirts enough to see every blade Daciana had hidden along her thighs.

"You packed heavy tonight," Torren said, grinning. "It's a good thing I didn't stick my hand up your skirt. I'd have lost a finger."

Lark glared at him. "You still might."

The stack of knives and daggers on the floor at Lark's feet grew by the second. When Rylen finally freed the final blade and the last of her hope, he placed it atop the mound and stood to clap her wrists in irons.

Langford's shoulders hung low in defeat. She tried to offer the most reassuring smile she could.

Earlier he said there was always a choice. Well, this was her choice. Whatever it took, she was getting them out.

421

CHAPTER 40

*G*avriel flung open the door of Walden Inn and tavern. Most of its tables were empty, and a dying fire stirred in the hearth. The scent of burning embers mingled with musty ale.

He wanted nothing more than to throw back a stiff drink and receive a biting word from the fire-haired girl he swore he hadn't raced back to see.

"Where is everyone? I want to give Lark a chance to insult me before I wash the stench of the road off." Gavriel could already imagine the look on her face, nose wrinkled in disgust.

Alistair sat in the corner, feet up on a nearby stool, crossed at the ankles. He stared into the fire with the bleak look of a man searching the flames for answers. "They haven't returned."

She should have returned last night—this morning at the latest. "What do you mean, they haven't returned?"

"I mean, they aren't back yet." Alistair lifted his head to regard him with glazed eyes ringed in dark circles. The glow of the hearth carved dark paths along his golden-brown skin, deepening his face.

Hugo placed two large tankards on the table, sliding one over to

Gavriel and keeping one to himself. He removed his scabbard and lowered in his seat with a contented grunt.

"They aren't back yet," Gavriel said, still staring at Alistair.

With a weighted sigh, Hugo rose to his feet. Wordlessly buckling his weapon back into place and leaving his stout untouched.

Gavriel swallowed against the vise in his throat. "Aren't you coming?"

Alistair glanced up at him. The haunted look on his face made him searing to look at. "Someone needs to be here if they come back."

The air threatened to choke him. Gavriel recognized signs of panic within his body. He had to separate them from his mind, to overcome the senseless pounding in his chest and the way his skin burned. This was a minor setback. They could have been detained for any number of reasons. And yet. "You sent them in there. You sent Lark with *Langford* as her backup."

"Daciana's with them too."

"A lot of good she can do where you stationed her."

"I did the best I could."

Gavriel tightened his grip on the edge of the table. "Don't pretend their lives hold equal value to you. We all know who's expendable in your eyes."

Alistair slammed his hand on the table hard enough to rattle the full tankards, foam sloshing over the sides. "None of my people are expendable." He retreated, turning his desolate stare back to the fire. "But I have to trust they know what they're doing. Daciana will find a way. She always does."

Gavriel's jaw clenched. He wanted to shove Alistair face-first into the hearth.

A steadying hand on his back brought him back to his senses. "Come on, if we ride hard, we can make it there by daybreak." Hugo pushed him toward the door, and out into the night.

Gavriel would neither rest nor relent until Lark was safely berating him for his impulsive actions.

With the ghost of a moon at his shoulder, he plunged deeper into the darkness.

LARK RUBBED HER TEMPLES, staring at the dingy floor. The stone bench was hard against her thighs, and her fine gown did nothing to stop the cold from seeping into her bones.

Langford paced the tiny cell, unable to keep still long enough for Lark to think straight.

"This is not good. This is bad. We are well and truly screwed."

Lark's hands fell to her lap as she glanced up at him. "If there were ever a time to use the word, it's now."

He glared at her, feet never ceasing their travel back and forth. "Fine, we're fucked."

"There you go."

Lark surveyed their surroundings. Stone walls, no windows, bars running along the side of the passageway. Where was Daciana? Wasn't she stationed on the outer perimeter for such an occasion as this?

"Gods, this is bad," Langford said with a groan.

"I wouldn't try to get their attention if I were you."

"Ugh Lark. Now's not the time to blaspheme."

She bit down on her retort, glaring at the solid stone wall instead. Langford was a man of logic and reason, yet he slipped into faithful paranoia as easily as an overworn coat.

"I knew we should have left after Adler danced with you. It was our last warning, and we ignored it." Langford's hands were on his hips and his brow furrowed in anger desperate to keep terror at bay.

"A miscalculation," Lark said, resuming her assessment of their surroundings. The door appeared sturdy, but perhaps she could pry the hinges loose enough to use the weight of it against the door jamb. Pry it free with what? She had nothing on her besides her gown and ridiculous mask.

Lark yanked it off her face and threw it to the corner. Its sharp metallic clank against the stone did little to ease the hardening of her stomach. It had been foolish to continue their search. Adler never would have detained them publicly; his vanity wouldn't allow it. He'd waited until the party could continue uninterrupted. And Lark walked right into his trap.

Langford watched her with an unreadable expression. "I'm sorry."

"Why are you sorry, I got us into this mess."

"No. It's my fault." He sat beside her and stared down at his hands, twisting the silver ring he'd worn to keep up the ruse of marriage. "I don't know what happened. I just"—he swallowed, eyes refusing to meet hers—"froze."

Lark angled her body as best she could on the narrow seat to face him. "That's nothing to be sorry for. That could happen to any of us."

Langford snorted. "I highly doubt that. I can't imagine Daciana paralyzed in fear. Alistair forgetting he's even carrying a weapon and pinned to the spot like a coward." He ran a hand into his dark hair. "Hugo would have snapped the man's neck before you'd even completed your heroics."

"Sometimes the only difference between death and survival is a healthy dose of fear." Gavriel's words, once spoken over the fire, came to mind. *Fear can make you sharper, hone your focus. It's a myth that fear is a weakness. Fear is a blade.* The image of Gavriel's face was a welcome intrusion on her thoughts but Lark pushed it away. She bumped Langford with her shoulder, earning a small smile. "Perhaps your heart was trying to tell you something."

"My bladder didn't have to chime in."

Lark's bright laugh echoed off the dank walls. "You didn't really piss yourself, did you?"

"Ugh, Lark. Don't be crass." Langford slung an arm around her, placing a quick kiss on the top of her head.

She leaned her head onto his shoulder. His touch was a warm comfort, like basking in the sun. Lark was learning how different each type of touch could feel. "A question for a question?"

Langford angled his head to smirk at her. "What are we, twelve?"

"It keeps the panic from setting in."

Silence fell over them, weighty and deafening.

"What was it like being a Reaper?" Langford asked, voice soft.

Lark's gaze found a crack in the wall. A black vein spidering in two directions in the grey slab. "Numb. Lonely. It was too quiet." Like all the light of the world had been dimmed. A soft glimmer of what could be. A hint, a taste but never satisfying. A thirst never quenched and hunger never sated. She'd been slowly starving while everyone around her failed to notice or care.

Langford's arm tightened around her.

"Why don't you go on jobs anymore?" Lark glanced up at him to find his answering expression one of discomfort.

"Is this not answer enough?" He gestured around them.

"You know what I'm asking."

He sighed. "I used to go on missions all the time. Usually, as a decoy, while Alistair and Daciana handled the real danger. The last job was supposed to be a quick haul. We had the schedule and guard rotation and everything. I was to meet with the dealer at the nearby tavern and discuss my desire to invest in a great business venture. Meanwhile, Alistair and Daciana made off with the goods. In and out, no trouble."

"I take it things didn't go as planned." The easier the plan, the bigger the oversight.

"The man we were stealing from had hands in every pocket, including the inn where we stayed. He didn't take too kindly to a respectable investor such as me being seen with the likes of Alistair. Said it seemed, 'fishy'—his words, not mine."

"Clearly."

"Next thing I know, I'm knocked over the head and waking up tied to a chair in his sitting room."

"Langford—"

"Wait, I'm getting to the good part." He wet his lips. "We sat there. Him sipping tea without offering me a cup. Me counting my heartbeats, sure they were going to cease from terror alone. All the while waiting for Alistair to show his face after he uncovered the ransom note." Langford shook his head. His smile didn't reach his eyes. "Want to know the worst part?"

Lark nodded, unsure of what to say.

"It was the moment I knew Alistair wasn't coming for me. As the hour grew late, seconds ticking by, I felt it in my gut. He wasn't coming. He had the haul, he had Daciana. What was I worth to him?"

Lark touched her fingertips to his cheek. "But he did come back."

"Yes, he did. He came back for me and handed the goods back to that bastard, receiving a brutal beating for his trouble too. But right before he made the trade, I could see it. It had been a tough call for him. He'd almost left me to die. I was barely worth it." Langford bit down on his lip, his grey eyes downcast. "After that, I couldn't bring myself to go on another job. I know my worth. I can do more if I'm not underfoot." He gestured around them again. "Case in point."

"Langford, you know he doesn't think that." Lark placed a hand on his shoulder, forcing him to look at her. "And you must know how valuable you are. To all of us. You're not underfoot. You're vital."

Langford took her hand and threaded his fingers through hers. "It's my turn, Lark. What exactly is the story with you and Gavriel?"

Warmth flooded her cheeks. "What do you mean?"

Langford raised an eyebrow. "You bring an assassin back to our camp, ignoring the fact that he wants to *kill you,* and somehow you lure him into following your every move like a little lost puppy."

"I'm just more charming than the average person?"

"No. That's not it. The truth please."

Lark sighed. Did she even know the truth anymore? "Things with us have always been... complicated."

Langford remained unmoving in his expectancy.

"I received the mark to reap his soul."

"Reap, as in he was dying?"

"Yes. And rather than lead his soul to the afterlife, I saved him." Images of dark green eyes, glassy and fading swept through her mind. Blood dripping out the side of Gavriel's mouth as he gazed up at her. Her heart gave a painful lurch.

Langford frowned. "What was killing him?"

"Waking Nightmare."

He scoffed. "Some poisons expert he is. Waking Nightmare is one of the first you should learn to identify by taste and smell. Utterly fatal, but equally conspicuous."

Lark couldn't halt the smile that stretched across her mouth. Ever the scholar, Langford. "Perhaps you should tease him for it next time you see him."

"Oh, you bet I will. If we survive."

"Don't say that. We were doing so well with our distraction." Lark rubbed her goose-pebbled arms, cursing the wretched dress for not bearing sleeves.

"You're freezing." Langford began unbuttoning his green doublet.

"Langford, I don't think you need to strip just yet."

He rolled his eyes. "I'm wearing another shirt under this, get your mind out of the gutter, woman." He unbuttoned it far enough to yank over his head, revealing a white linen shirt beneath. "Here," he said, handing it to her. "You can't freeze to death if you're to get us out of this."

Lark pulled it over her head and shivered against the warmth it still held from his body. "I'm working on it."

"Work harder," he muttered before sinking to the floor, back against the wall.

Footfalls echoed in the distance. Lark scrambled to grasp the bars, pressing her face in the narrow space for a better look.

Rylen approached, holding a tray with bread and water. His eyes darted around nervously as he stopped a good distance from their cell. He wore a new uniform, one without the hole she'd stabbed into his shoulder. "I need you to clear back from the bars." He held up the tray higher with one hand, the other remaining locked against his side. That shoulder must have really been bothering him. "Do you want to go hungry?"

"Isn't that a waste of resources if they're just going to kill us in the morning?"

Rylen wore a tight expression on his boyish face, but gave no answer.

Lark drew back from the bars, allowing him ample space to open the slat at the bottom and slide it through. The tray scraped against the hard floor, and the slat squealed with rust as it fell closed. When Rylen turned to leave, she lunged for him. "Wait!"

His shoulders tightened, eyes darting to the door to the dungeons. The only escape.

"I have one last request. Please." If this didn't work, Lark would have to employ a different tactic.

She hoped for his sake it worked.

Rylen exhaled a sharp breath, turning back to face her while remaining out of her reach. His oxblood uniform accentuated his muscled form, though he bore the posture of scared youth. "What is it?"

"The knife you took from me—"

"I can't give you a weapon!"

"I know," Lark said. "But my father carved the handle. I don't need the blade, I just..." She let her eyes blur with unshed tears. He answered with an uncomfortable expression. "I don't want to die without a piece of him with me." If she could get Hugo's knife, she might be able to work the lock... or reach her hands through the bars and threaten Rylen into giving up the keys.

Rylen hesitated, glancing around as if someone might be listening.

"Please."

Rylen met her gaze with eyes of spring after a fresh rainfall. Finally, he reached into his pocket and produced the knife in question. Hugo's knife. He held it by the blade's edge, turning it over and inspecting the handle's carvings. "I know what you're capable of with this."

"I know. I'm sorry for that. In my defense, you were trying to imprison me."

Rylen regarded her with a calculating expression. Holding the blade close as if debating handing it over to her. "This would give you comfort?"

Lark nodded and reached through the bars, waiting.

Rylen's mouth pulled into a sneer. "What makes you think I give a shit about your comfort?"

Lark didn't need to school her expression into one of shock.

He edged a step closer. "What's this handle worth to you, anyway? A finger? A hand?"

So, Rylen's claws only came out when there were bars safely in place between them. *Coward.*

He tapped the edge of her dagger against the steel bars. He didn't notice Langford's hand snake out through the tray slot along the bottom. He grabbed Rylen's ankle and yanked. Rylen went careening back and hit the stone floor with a thud.

Lark sank in a crouch and grabbed Hugo's knife. Reaching over, she helped Langford drag him closer to the side of their cell.

Rylen scrambled, trying to kick them. Lark sank her blade through the bars and into the meat of his calf. His howls of pain swallowed each sickening squelch. Lark squeezed her eyes shut, slowly exhaling through her mouth and pushing down the sick churning in her stomach.

It was brutality or death.

Yet another easy choice.

Langford fumbled with Rylen's pockets for a set of keys. Lark wasted no time yanking her blade out and plunging it in again and again. Until his ruined calf lay in tatters of flesh, muscle, and blood.

Rylen's screams turned guttural.

"It'll do no good if he alerts every guard in the damn estate," Langford said through clenched teeth.

"Well can you blame him? Look at his leg. I doubt it'll heal right." Lark gestured to the bloody mess of gore.

"You bitch," Rylen spat.

"Name-calling? You take things to a personal level I'm uncomfortable with, Rylen."

"I got it!" Langford set to work on the lock, trying each key to find the correct match.

Rylen dragged his body away, leaving a messy trail of blood in his wake.

"Hurry, hurry, hurry," Lark murmured under her breath.

Langford didn't look up from his task. "Would you like to do this?"

"No, no. You've got it well in hand." She stood up on her tiptoes to peer over his shoulder. "He's almost to the door, he's pulling himself up, he's lost a lot of blood. Credit where it's due, the boy knows how to take the pain."

"Yes, we'll be sure to send a recommendation for promotion to his superior."

The beautiful sound of the key turning and unlatching the lock echoed in their cell. Swinging the door open with a roguish wink, Langford stepped back. Lark swept past and advanced on Rylen, faster than he could open the heavy door to the stairwell. She stepped on his mangled calf.

Rylan cried out in agony and grabbed her ankle.

Lark toppled, landing on harsh stone and yanking him into a headlock. Rylen thrashed, and Lark's head hit the floor, black spots dancing across her vision. She grit her teeth and squeezed until she felt his muscles go lax and he collapsed on the floor at their feet.

Her practice with Alistair finally proved useful. Perhaps she'd tell him so.

HUDDLED behind a pillar in the abandoned hall, Lark focused on the weight of the blades she'd strapped back into place, even as she mourned the absence of her bow. Langford had retrieved most of their belongings, save for the evidence they were sent in the first place to collect.

After they were safe, Lark planned to ruminate over that failing.

"It seems most of the guests have retired for the evening."

Langford scowled. "That's a polite way of saying they're debauching their way through the corridors and guest wings."

"I'm saying I think the ballroom's deserted. We might be able to sneak past and out through the hedge maze." Might, being the operative word. "I hope Daciana hasn't ventured in here looking for us."

"Let's worry about getting out of here alive, then we'll worry about her."

Yanking him with more force than necessary, Lark pulled them out from behind the marble pillar. Distant voices echoed from down the hall. Lark shoved Langford into a nearby room, tripping over his feet in the process.

"Lark—"

She clamped her hand over his mouth. Her pulse pounded in her neck and palm as she listened.

Langford breathed through his nose, all the while glaring at her.

Turning her head, Lark strained to hear. When the sound of their footfalls passed by the door, Lark pulled her hand away and wiped it on her dress. "You made my palm all sweaty."

"I didn't exactly enjoy tasting Rylen's blood on your hand."

She pushed past him, into the room. It appeared to be little more than another parlor for entertaining guests. Stepping on top of an ivory chaise lounge, she pushed open the large picture window and peered out. Thankfully, it led straight to the outer gardens. They were one floor below where she'd already skirted the wall to Adler's quarters. The hedges could provide a decent cushion.

Lark turned back to regard Langford with a look of triumph.

His eyes widened and he shook his head. "No, no. Absolutely not. No."

"You can keep saying no until they discover we're missing and come looking for us."

"We'll fall."

"Speak for yourself."

Langford crossed his arms, dark brows knitting together. "Fine, I'll fall and die. And won't you feel sorry?"

"Only if I don't fall."

He contorted his face in disapproval. "I find you somewhat less charming than you think."

"Come now, husband, you don't mean that." At his unwavering expression, she sighed. "We've got to try. We'll go slow, and if you fall... I'll fall too."

Langford narrowed his eyes at her. "Don't be stupid." He ran a hand through his dark hair. "Just don't get us killed."

"As you command."

Exhaling in a short huff, he strode over to where she waited. "Let's get this over with. With any luck, we'll be dining in the heavens of Avalon, or the Walden Inn, by sunup."

She placed a hand over her heart. "From your words to the gods' ears."

He wrinkled his nose. "It's even worse when you agree with me. Go on then."

Lark tore her shoes off, not caring where they landed and climbed out the window. The cool, night breeze kissed her cheeks and tangled her hair, and the thick scent of roses carried on the wind. She crept across the narrow ledge. It was easier without those ridiculous slippers.

Langford appeared on the ledge behind her, his dark hair dancing in the wind. His gaze found Lark's, and if she wasn't mistaken, she detected a glimmer of excitement there.

They inched along until they got to a particularly tall hedge. This was their chance. At worst, they might break a bone. So long as it wasn't their necks, they'd be fine.

Langford followed Lark's gaze. "You can't be serious."

"They look soft enough."

"Lark."

"What? We can't stay on this wall forever. Every moment we're stuck here we risk exposure. We need to drop."

He shook his head. Jaw set.

"Langford. Please, trust me."

"I don't want to." He glanced down again, his brow furrowed. A look of stern calculation crossed his face. Without warning, he let go. Falling backward through the night air.

Lark's scream caught in her throat.

Langford landed in a heap within the thick dark hedges, plunging straight through and out of sight.

Lark's blood pounded in her ears as she waited.

One breath.

Two breaths.

"Ouch." Langford's voice was the single most beautiful sound she'd heard that night. Perhaps her entire life.

A laugh of relief burst from Lark's chest, tinged with panic and hysteria. He staggered out, emerging with small twigs and leaves sticking out of his hair. Spreading his arms wide, he gave a short bow before spitting out a small leaf.

It was her turn. Shifting to face out, Lark pushed her back as far against the wall as she could. Her throat constricted. The shadows of velvet indigo beckoned, and the bright sliver of the moon illuminated her path. Lark took a deep breath, and the wall fell away.

Her stomach dropped, burrowing its way to the deepest part of her.

She swallowed the wind and her eyes watered. The ground rushed up to meet her.

Fast.

Too fast.

CHAPTER 41

*L*ark's landing wasn't graceful.

With a groan, she rolled out of the hedge. Leaves and twigs clung to her hair and dress. Her face and neck stung, covered in scratches from the unforgiving shrub. She should have fallen backward like Langford, but she wanted to see, to feel, to taste every moment of this mortal life. Including possibly the worst idea she'd ever had.

"Are you all right?" Langford asked, pulling greenery from her hair.

"I'm fine. But we need to go."

With a quick nod, they set off running, skimming along the estate walls and ducking behind ornate hedge sculptures. Langford threw himself behind a shrub shaped like a giant eagle taking flight. If they weren't fleeing for their lives, Lark might consider this fun.

Stifling a laugh, she fell in place behind the likeness of a generic Paragon of virtue, straight out of the tales of Avalon. She glanced up at the large, unfurled wings shaped from tight leaves. The arms of the warrior were outstretched as if welcoming an embrace. Mortals knew little of Avalon. Of how much the Warriors and Paragons didn't deserve their loyalty.

Voices rang out from around the corner of the outer wall. Lark and Langford took off in the opposite direction. If she could just find a break in the outer perimeter, they could duck out. The wall was too high to climb, even standing on Langford's shoulders.

Where in the blazes was Daciana?

A hiss came from behind a rounded shrub. Lark's ears pricked as she squinted into the shadows, searching for the source. She shook Langford's shoulder to get his attention. He furrowed his brows in confusion until the hiss came again.

An oversized cap topped with a wide feather poked out from behind one of the leafy, green globes. A skinny boy came into view, beckoning them with a short wave of his hand. The bells on his minstrel doublet tinkled with the motion, and he flinched.

Lark and Langford exchanged a silent questioning look. If they ignored him, would he alert the guards? Better to be safe until they weren't out in the open. Lark gave Langford a nod, and they crept after him, weaving through the dark garden toward the estate.

The boy led them to the cellar's entrance. He yanked the wooden doors open without making a sound and waved them in. Swallowing her objections, Lark descended the stairs, Langford at her back.

"Quickly now, we haven't much time," a voice rang out. The cellar doors closed behind them with a heavy thud, and ice speared through her.

"Show yourselves." Lark was grateful for the steadiness of her voice, even as her heart hammered in her throat. They'd made it too far to walk into a trap now. They'd leave this burning wreckage of a mission empty-handed, but they would leave.

The turn of a lantern key squealed and illuminated the small space. A flame danced behind its glass encasement.

Five unfamiliar faces, all wearing varying degrees of disapproval, looked down on Lark. She eyed each of them warily, assessing what exactly she'd gotten them into.

"Finally." The beautiful sound of a familiar voice rang out. Daciana elbowed her way through and flung her arms around Lark.

Lark hugged back, sagging with relief. Daciana was here. They were safe.

"How?" Lark asked, releasing her.

Daciana grinned. "You didn't really think I'd let you into the estate without any of my contacts."

Lark glanced at the boy who'd found them in the gardens. Each time he fidgeted, the little bells on his costume tinkled. "And if we hadn't broken out of the dungeon?"

Daciana scoffed. "Am I meant to do everything myself?"

Langford let out a groan. "How about we escape?" He glanced at Lark. "Unanimous agreement? Good, let's go."

"Wait. You'll be needing these."

Lark squinted in the low light to see the lined face of the minstrel, his arms full of various fabrics that tinkled from little bells sewn in them. His rich brown eyes twinkled in the half light.

"It's you," Lark said, mouth tugging. Something about the troubadour never failed to put her at ease.

"Hello again, sweet Lark." Bartrand handed her a bundle of clothes, tossing the rest to Langford. "Put those on, we haven't much time."

Lark held the garments out for inspection. Brightly colored stockings, one leg red the other violet, striped short pants with little tinkling bells, a violet tunic, and a red vest.

"Oh, these too." He handed her a pair of red slippers, toes coming to an impish point. He reached behind him and grabbed a red slouching hat with a peacock feather and emerald brooch. Lark watched helplessly as he placed it atop her head.

A laugh burst from Langford's mouth, which he smothered with a cough.

Lark pulled the weapons from their sheaths beneath her skirts and handed them to Daciana, who tucked them all away in her pack. Lark yanked her stockings and short pants into place. They were surprisingly comfortable. She frowned at the tunic, glancing up at Bartrand.

His expression melted into panicked understanding, "Oh of course!" He turned his back to her, circling a finger for the rest of his merry band to grant her privacy.

Lark pulled what was left of the torn and bloodied gown from her raw skin. Once everything was in place, she tapped him on the shoulder. Hesitantly he turned, his face widening in a warm smile. "You look a vision. It's a shame you aren't a bard. We'd love to have you on our crew.

A few of his musicians exchanged nervous glances.

"You're too kind." Lark glanced over at Langford, whose outfit was of the same style as hers, if less loud in color. The muted browns and greens looked surprisingly cunning on him.

"Are we ready?" Daciana asked, rolling her shoulders.

"I'm ready," Langford said with a stretch of his long arms overhead. "I'm ready for a bath, and a glass of red wine—"

"That's a bit premature. I need to know you're ready for what comes next."

Panic flared in his eyes as his dark brows knitted together. "What comes next?"

THEY PLODDED THROUGH THE GARDENS, mixed in with Bartrand's band of musicians. Even Daciana sported a fetching little outfit, one Lark hadn't noticed until they left the safety of the crawl space. It was a simple garb of green and black, without the little bells Lark was beginning to loathe as they tinkled with each step.

They just needed to make it to Bartrand's wagon.

There was always tomorrow to worry about how they'd get their coin for passage across the sea—for how she'd contact Ferryn. The painful twist in her stomach at the thought of him, alone in Lacuna, was a constant reminder of how badly she'd failed him. Never mind the tear in the veil, releasing more Undesirables upon the world.

What had she touched, that she hadn't spoiled?

Gavriel.

A small warmth tinged with guilt burned in her chest. No matter what happened, how many lives were lost, how the world burned, she couldn't bring herself to regret saving him.

A curious thing. To be so sure of one single act and utterly lost in all else.

Voices carried over the tall hedges. It was foolish to count on missing the patrol. Two guards strolled into view. Thankfully, they weren't the ones who'd detained them. Torren would have recognized Lark. Wounded pride held grudges not even the shadows could hide. And Rylen... had anyone found him yet?

Bartrand wore a tight, anxious smile. He ran his palms together. "Good evening gentlemen. I trust your night was pleasant." He offered a short bow of respect they didn't deserve.

"Where you off to?" The guard speaking wore no mask, his beady eyes and wide nose crinkled in disgust.

A third guard stepped into view, maintaining a cautious distance. He gripped the pommel of his sword.

Daciana stiffened.

"We have concluded our set for the night, we're off to our lodgings to enjoy the fruits of our performance." Bartrand was perfectly mannered, but even that didn't halt the sneer that spread across the guard's face.

"Oh? Is that right?" The guard's beady eyes lingered on Lark. She fought the urge to glare at him. "Why do you need so many?" He glanced at Langford. Lark prayed he wasn't searching for two escaped prisoners—that he was just a run-of-the-mill creep.

"You can't fathom the depths of our work, our craft," Bartrand said, but the guard raised a hand, silencing him.

"You." Beady eyes pointed at Langford. "What do you do?"

Without missing a beat, Langford grabbed the lute off the back of the nearest musician, its cherry wood body glinted in the moonlight. He began plucking the strings in a simple but elegant melody.

Langford grinned, self-satisfaction radiating off him. He was far more skilled and valuable than he gave himself credit for.

Beady eyes closed his hand over the neck of the lute, silencing the music. "Enough," he said roughly before turning on Lark. "What do you do?"

Lark's mouth went dry. She couldn't play an instrument. Blasted damnation, they were going to be exposed, and all because of her. She was the one who'd been noticed when she went rummaging through Adler's room, the one who insisted they go down into his office even though he knew what they were up to, and now her musical ignorance would be the cause of spilled blood.

Palms slick with sweat and heart leaping in her throat, Lark wet her lips. "I sing."

His mocking smile appeared unconvinced. "Sing for me, little bird."

Lark ground her teeth and pushed down the flutter in her stomach, tucking away the urge to yank her blade free. With a deep breath, she searched for words to a song, any song, that she could muddle through and be done with this night forever.

A vague memory tugged at the back of her mind, and she closed her eyes. An inkling of a thought, a dream, one she couldn't be sure was even hers, undulated invitingly at the edge of her awareness. Slowly, the words began to form. And a song she'd never heard, not in this lifetime, took shape.

"Gentle winds, blow you still to my arms
Through the night, it's hard to see
May the stars light your path without fail
Bringing you home to me
Though your steps may be slow and weary
And your heart, heavy
You'll be safe in my warm embrace
Even if only in your dreams
Sleep now without fear of waking
Let your soul come to me
Darkness calls, and sleep it beckons
I'll hold you there in your dreams."

Lark cleared her throat, now thick with the unfamiliar sensation of singing as heat bloomed across her cheeks.

Bartrand beamed. "See? I run a tight crew, all talented in their own right. But we really should be going." He made to put an arm around Lark and walk away when the grate of steel unsheathing rang out.

"The girl stays." Beady eyes pointed his sword at Bartrand. His mouth pulled into a dark grin. "We'll let her go in the morning. I give you my word."

Bastard. They were never going to let them go. They'd only grown tired of the game. Lark yanked Hugo's dagger from her short pants.

Beady eyes lunged. Rather than spin out of the way and risk anyone nearby, Lark caught the edge of his blade with her dagger, parrying it away. But she couldn't very well fight a broadsword with a knife, not if she wanted to get away clean. "Daciana, a little help."

Daciana had already pulled an ax from her pack. She swung, catching steel, and pivoted to slam her boot into his groin. Lark slashed her dagger across his throat. Another life lost, another soul gone. As he bled out on the impeccably manicured lawn, one guard fled to call for reinforcements. Another headed straight for them, his mouth was a line of grim determination.

Daciana tossed Lark a blade from her pack and took off running. That guard wouldn't get far.

Lark spun the unfamiliar dagger in her hand, testing the balance. It was one of Daciana's double-edged knives, her haladie. The twin edges curved so elegantly, blood grooves begging to be filled.

The guard lunged toward Langford first.

That was a mistake.

Any ounce of mercy vanished as Lark launched herself between them. Halting his blade, she advanced, forcing his retreat. Blocking and slashing until she pinned him against the dense hedge. Blood pounded in her ears; her vision darkened around the edges. Leaving only this moment. This man. This life she was determined to end.

"Lark!" Langford called.

Lark turned just in time to block a sword from running her through. Where did this guard come from? A flick of the wrist, and his throat wept blood. She couldn't bring herself to mourn another kill. Anyone coward enough to aim for her back deserved as much.

Langford appeared between her and the forgotten guard against the hedge. He raised the lute over his shoulder and swung. It crashed against the guard's face, wood splinters flying. The guard dropped, unconscious and bleeding. The lute hung limply by Langford's side, its strings coiled away from the wood of the rich body.

Someone gasped at the ghastly sight of the ruined lute.

Bartrand's mouth hung open. Eyes wild, he stared as if seeing Lark for the first time.

A smile spread across Daciana's blood-splattered face. "Everyone good?"

Lark nodded, faintly aware that she couldn't feel her legs. She handed the trembling knife to Daciana, turning her attention to Bartrand's incredulous expression.

"Are you all right?"

"I—I," Bartrand stammered, glancing around at the bloody scene before him. Three corpses, their throats lay open and bleeding. An unconscious guard with his face bloodied from the ruined lute that silently mocked them.

Bartrand lifted his gaze to Lark's before saying with a shake of his head, "I think I need to do some rewrites to your ballad."

CHAPTER 42

Gavriel spurred his horse faster, muttering a curse under his breath. He'd left Apple at the inn and chosen a nearby palfrey its owner would sorely miss. He rode hard through the unforgiving night. If any harm had come to Lark—

No. He couldn't chase that thought. She could handle her own.

Distantly, his name carried on the wind.

If they were lucky, her delay was nothing more than her penchant for distraction. She was probably holed up in a little tavern, feasting on apples and ale.

The thought offered little comfort. Gavriel recognized a pretty lie even of his own making.

"Gavriel!"

The voice came louder this time. Gavriel tossed a glance over his shoulder to where Hugo rode, barely keeping pace.

"Stop, damn it!"

Gavriel pulled on the reins, easing back to a canter. Every muscle in his body tightened with the action. He needed the speed. "We're wasting time."

Hugo's dark eyes flared as he shook his head. "You'll kill your horse."

"I will do no such thing." Gavriel twisted his grip on the reins, the audible creak of leather filled the silence.

"You will, and then you'll never make it in time." Hugo fished out a waterskin from his pack, tossing back a long draught before offering it to him.

Gavriel ignored it. "In time for what exactly?" His jaw clenched hard enough he wouldn't be surprised if he cracked a tooth. Lark might get all starry-eyed from Hugo's grunts of "wisdom," but Gavriel had little patience for men of no action.

Hugo blinked, expression unreadable. "Do you think this ever stops?"

Confusion and anger warred in Gavriel's head. "What in the skies are you talking about?" While Hugo prattled on in vague riddles, Lark could very well be facing her death.

"You're always going to be racing to her. Trying to shield her from something you can't control. Every day, these are the stakes, boy. If you can't find a way to keep your head, you'll never make it." Hugo's gravelly voice grated against the quiet night.

"I think I preferred your silence."

Hugo scraped out a low chuckle. "You're going to let your horse trot a bit before it keels over, and you're going to listen. I won't tell you this story twice."

Gavriel bit down on his retort. Coiling energy pulsed in his veins, begging him to ride off and leave Hugo in this dust. But the bastard wasn't wrong. If he killed his horse, he'd leave Lark in the hands of fate.

"I was a blade for hire for a while. I broke away from an old life and needed the coin. Had a particular skill set."

Credit where it was due: Hugo wasn't one to weigh down a story with unnecessary words.

Gavriel nodded, staring off at the dark road of patted dirt. Pebbles crunched beneath his horse's hooves.

"Enough time went by, and I got too comfortable. Got it in my head I could make a life, a simple one, but one that was mine. I was dumb enough to find myself a wife."

Gavriel snorted. Dumb, indeed. In the dark, he could feel Hugo's glower. "I'm sorry, I can't imagine anyone tolerating you."

"If you think I'm a hard ass, you shoulda met Lena." Hugo's voice tightened over the name.

Cicadas hummed in the distance. Without the wind to fill the space in his head, Gavriel wished Hugo would speak.

"So, what happened?"

"Make enough enemies, safety no longer exists. Home is nothing more than a fixed target." Hugo sighed and straightened in his saddle. "At least you know Lark can take care of herself."

Shame flooded Gavriel's chest. He'd suspected Hugo had suffered some sort of loss. Skies help him if he had children.

Once Lark was safe, and the world was as right as it could be, the honorable thing to do would be to leave her. Let her have a chance at a human life, free from the shadows that hounded him. Yes, it would be the honorable thing to do.

But Gavriel was not an honorable man.

Gavriel turned his attention back to the road. To the river of moonlight leading the way.

Hugo was right about one thing; he would always be racing to her. Clawing his way across the earth under an apathetic sky to find her. He urged his horse back into a gallop, nearly missing the curse Hugo grunted in his direction.

Gavriel would ride his horse into the ground if it meant a fighting chance to save her. He wasn't sure what kind of person that made him, and he didn't much care. He wasn't here to deserve her.

"Is it too soon to celebrate?" Langford's boyish grin dimpled his cheek.

After bidding farewell to Bartrand and his crew, they took to the woods to avoid detection. After the mess they'd left in the gardens, it wouldn't take long for the guards to storm the roads searching.

"Celebrate what, exactly?" Lark aimed for a teasing tone, though she couldn't mask the bitterness. "Completely botching the mission? Or are we celebrating the fact that we won't be able to pay for passage across the sea?"

Langford blinked at her owlishly. "Celebrate the fact that we're alive?"

"I suppose there is that." Such a human thing, wasn't it? When all else failed, the simple act of surviving was enough.

"I hate to disagree with you," Daciana said, flashing a grin. "But we didn't leave empty-handed." She pulled out a dagger from her pack, the jewel-encrusted handle shimmering even in the dimness before dawn's breaking. The pommel, a large, glittering ruby, cast shards of red light against Daciana's hand. Even the blade was forged in gold rather than steel, garish in its design, and completely impractical.

"Where did you get this?" Lark ran her finger along the grooves. The jewels on this dagger could set them up for a comfortable month while they found more work.

"A lady has her secrets." Daciana slipped it back into her pack. "And that's all I'm going to say on the matter."

Secrets indeed. Daciana had probably made her way into and out of the estate while Lark was still clunking around searching for damning evidence. That sneaky wolf.

"Do you think we've made it far enough to travel the road?" Langford called over his shoulder. "These shoes weren't exactly made for roughing it."

Lark glanced down at her pointed slippers, caked in mud and torn in places. "We could take the road for a bit. But if we hear anyone coming—"

"Yes, yes. We take to the trees like woodland creatures."

Their return was long overdue. But Alistair hadn't seemed worried last time, Lark couldn't imagine he was too fraught with concern. He trusted Daciana's skills too much for that. Though, Lark did too.

Did Gavriel worry? Of course he did. He barely agreed to his own mission since it meant being away when they infiltrated Adler's estate. At least he hadn't followed them this time. He was probably sulking by the fire. When they returned, he'd jolt upright in his seat, and recover by remarking on her clothing. But he'd wear his relief far too openly for an assassin who should have mastered his facial expressions better by now.

Lark straightened her ridiculous hat, standing a little taller.

By the time they found the dirt-packed road, the first hint of the sun's ascent peeked from the horizon. The darkened sky bled into a reddish hue low on the landscape. Rosy sweeps of color across the union of sky and earth bathed the brow of the hill in faint light.

Feet aching, covered in blood and grime, and dizzy from exhaustion, Lark smiled. For each human pain, came the reminder of how false Thanar's imitations were. He never mastered the still beauty of a quiet morning, or how the sunrise could set the sky on fire. His renditions lacked the depth only life could offer.

In the distance, the clop of hooves on dirt came as a warning. Lark spun to face Daciana, finding an expression of annoyance.

So much for taking the road.

Lark leapt to one side, Daciana tackled Langford to the other, rolling down the gorge and into the thicket.

Dust clouds rose from the wrong direction of the road, but Lark had no way of knowing if Adler's guards had already traveled by and doubled back. Two sets of horseshoes galloped straight for them, with a speed reserved for pursuit.

Lark rolled onto her back and stared up at the lightening sky, her heart hammering in her throat. She'd torn her stockings. Her knees stung, and fresh blood bloomed across her exposed skin.

Two horses and their riders raced past where Lark held her breath. Lark propped herself up on her elbows and poked her head up out of the gorge to see who had passed.

Two men rode as if trying to outrun the dawn.

She squinted, trying to make out the shapes of their ever-diminishing silhouettes against the bloody sky. A thick, burly man rode beside a lean, defined man. His broad shoulders, framed in black leather—

Lark leapt out from her hiding spot, sprinting down the road. Her hat flew from her head, landing somewhere behind her.

"Wait!" she called, ignoring the burning in her legs. Her voice was swallowed by the blanket of early morning silence, and her eyes blurred from the wind whipping her face. "Gavriel!"

In the distance, his horse reared, and he halted in the middle of the road. Gavriel turned to look in her direction. He swung his leg over, dropping to his feet, and sprinting to meet her.

Lark's heart squeezed in her chest as she propelled herself forward. He was a lifeline. A beacon. Not even feeling the aches in her feet anymore, weightless in her body, she raced toward him with abandon.

He was here. He'd come looking for her. Skies, what an imbecile.

Lark slammed into the hard planes of Gavriel's body, her arms wrapping around his torso, as she pressed her cheek into his chest. Inhaling his familiar scent, mixed with sweat. Gavriel's hands grabbed at her, as if he was unsure where to touch first. Running over her arms, gripping the back of her head, before settling on wrapping his arms around her and burying his face in her hair.

"Skies above." Gavriel's voice was ragged. "I thought..."

Lark pulled back to look at him. Terror was still written on his face, tightening his green eyes and etching dark shadows beneath them. His lips parted as he scanned her face again and again. He cupped her cheek and ran his thumb along her skin. His whisper of a touch, achingly gentle.

Her nerves flared. "I'm here. I'm all right."

Gavriel's brows knitted together, and he rested his forehead against hers. Lark brought a shaky hand to his face.

His mouth was so close, and yet the memory of the first kiss she stole, to save his life, left an uneasy feeling in her gut. She lifted onto her toes, bringing her lips close enough to his, the warmth of them burned against her skin.

"Can I kiss you?" She couldn't wait for permission that first time, and even as she drowned in need, she would wait this time.

"Please." His guttural voice lanced through her.

Softly, she pressed her lips against his. Warmth flared in her belly, heat rushing to her cheeks. She pulled back to see his face twisted in what looked like pain.

"Wha—"

Gavriel's mouth sealed over hers, swallowing the unasked question and deepening the kiss. He tasted rich and sweet like that chocolate he was so fond of.

Lark gripped the front of his black tunic, her hands slipping beneath his jerkin, and pulled him to her. She was afraid to break contact, as if he'd vanish and this moment would evaporate.

Every inch of her was ablaze in the fire his skillful mouth stoked. She whimpered. He answered with a growl and a tighter grip on her body. Pressing her against him. The contact scorched through her in liquid heat.

Lark grazed her teeth against his lower lip. Angling her head back, Gavriel placed searing kisses down her neck before sinking his teeth into her throat and soothing the hurt with a sweep of his tongue. The desperate mewl that escaped her lips seemed to startle him to his senses.

Gavriel pulled back long enough to catch his breath, a smile playing on his lips. "I'm sorry," he said, panting.

Lark gave a shaky laugh. Her pulse pounded in her ears. Why was everything throbbing? "Don't apologize. Just do it again."

Gavriel's mouth curved in a crooked grin, stretching the scar she'd just been kissing. "As you command." He pressed his lips to hers, gentle this time. Taking his time to explore her mouth in soft, sweeping touches.

When the unmistakable sound of a throat clearing froze them in place.

"Please don't." Hugo's gruff voice yanked them back to the present.

They were standing in the middle of the road.

With three very uncomfortable companions. Well, two uncomfortable companions; Daciana seemed pleased.

"Yes, please refrain from another ghastly display," Langford said, covering his mouth with one hand while the other remained perched on his hip. His eyes sparkled with amusement.

Daciana grinned, one finger pressed to her lips, her eyes wide with glee. "It's about time."

Lark stepped away from the warmth of his solid build, smoothing her hair and adjusting her troubadour vest.

Gavriel seemed no better off, hands shaking as he smoothed the tunic beneath his leathers she'd rumpled.

"It's good to see you, kid," Hugo said with a certain fondness he reserved for her.

They needed to get back to Alistair and figure out the next part of the plan. A plan that had gone so awry, she wasn't sure how far the reach of these consequences extended. Would there be retaliation? Langford had used his family name to gain access to the ball. That was sure to cost him.

Lark stole another glance at Gavriel.

His heated gaze lit flames in her belly all over again. An unwilling smile tugged at the corner of her mouth.

Despite all the uncertainty that lay before them, it was hard not to cling to this small glimmer of hope.

He was the tether. One she'd gladly be bound to, if it meant keeping that flicker alive.

⚘

It had taken most of the day to make it back, and warm light spilled against the weathered door to the familiar inn. Sun-faded wood swung open at Lark's touch.

The tavern was starting to fill with the early supper crowd. Lark stood on tiptoes to see over the Walden Inn and Tavern's patrons.

In the far corner, Alistair stood by the hearth, gripping the mantle.

Langford froze as they passed through the threshold.

Alistair lifted his head. An expression of shock and relief transformed his features before he charged over, shoving a man out of the way and spilling his ale. Alistair didn't even spare him a glance, as he threw his arms around Lark and Langford. "I would have never forgiven you had you not returned."

Langford cleared his throat. "That's actually the very reason we escaped, isn't that right, Lark?"

"Oh, yes. Fear of Alistair's ire."

Alistair wore his crooked grin, though it didn't meet his bloodshot eyes. "At least you know what's good for you." His hand fell away from Lark's shoulder, but his grip on Langford held tight for a heartbeat before he relented. "And of course, my goddess divine who never disappoints." He swept past and yanked Daciana into a full-body hug she barely tolerated before stepping out of it.

"I need a long hot bath to wash the memory of the night off me."

"Is that an invitation?" Alistair asked.

Daciana rolled her eyes before patting Lark on the shoulder and pushing past.

"A bath sounds perfect. I couldn't stop fantasizing about it when we were stuck in that filthy dungeon," Lark said.

Alistair shot a dark look her way. "I'm going to need a full report on what in Sargon's flaming knickers went down—"

"Yes, yes. Tomorrow, first thing." To the abyss with his needs. "Good night! I'm sure if you have any burning questions, Langford would be more than happy to fill you in." As Lark climbed the stairs to her private rooms, she smiled at the sound of familiar steps trailing behind her. She pretended not to hear him and continued on her path, slowing her pace. When she reached her door, she leaned against the threshold.

"Did you also interpret my comment about bathing as an invitation?" She peered up at Gavriel. "Or were you hoping to sneak up on me and persuade me?"

The storm brewing on his face doused her smile.

"Had I wanted my presence to remain unknown, it would have been."

Lark ignored the sinking feeling that something was terribly wrong. "You look like you're about to be ill."

"I don't want you to get the wrong idea. About earlier."

Something cold coiled in Lark's gut. She searched for the right words, the ones that didn't stick in her throat. "Could you be more specific?" Her voice wavered between her lips. "I have lots of ideas every day."

Gavriel sighed "Lark, let's not... complicate things. I swear to aid you in any way you require. Isn't that enough?"

Lark could only stare as her dizzying thoughts competed for dominance. Was he really so fickle? Tears pricked behind her eyes as something tightened in her throat. She wanted to demand answers, to grab him and shake him until he made sense. She fisted her hands by her side instead, clamped her mouth shut, and nodded.

Gavriel reached out a shaky hand, tucking her hair behind her ear. The touch of his skin burned. Pain and need in equal measure coursed through her.

"Forgive me," he whispered, before dropping his hand and disappearing down the hallway.

Leaving Lark alone with her chest cracked open.

CHAPTER 43

"*H*ow are you supposed to take out your enemy if you can't hit a log?"

Lark gritted her teeth as she nocked another arrow, resisting the urge to aim at Hugo. The rope creaked with each swing. "It's too fast."

"You expect your enemy to stand by and wait for you to line up your shot?" Hugo paced behind her. "Maybe you're hoping they'll turn around and bend over to give you a nice round target."

Lark loosed the arrow, missing the log and hitting the tree behind it. They had taken to the forest across the valley to practice aiming at moving targets. So far, Lark had only succeeded in missing. She ripped another arrow from her quiver.

"Easy, don't take it out on the equipment." Hugo's deep voice rumbled behind her. "Breathe, focus. Lead the target. Anticipate to land your shot. Rely on your anchor point, keep your stance consistent. You're aiming with your whole body, not just the arrow."

Gavriel's face swam in Lark's mind. His look of despair as he crushed her hope to a fine powder. He hadn't made an appearance at breakfast that morning.

Lark released, skimming off the log.

"You're distracted," Hugo said with a sigh. He plopped himself down on a nearby boulder. He crossed his thick arms, wearing his signature frown. "Out with it."

"I'm just tired," Lark said, swinging her bow beside her. Sleep had eluded her the night before. Memories of a heated kiss and a cold rejection made it impossible to relax. "It's been a long couple of days."

He angled his head, waiting.

Lark kicked a small rock with the toe of her boot. "Gavriel is hard to read."

Hugo offered no reaction. A silent, frowning statue.

"He does one thing and says another." Lark was no fool. Gavriel wanted her just as badly as she wanted him. She felt it in every lingering stare, every charged moment of silence. He spoke of complications, but it felt like a cheap excuse.

Hugo cleared his throat, shifting on the rock. "Sometimes, what the heart wants isn't good for it. He knows what he wants and what he's willing to lose. If he's willing to lose you, then he's a bigger ass than I thought."

Lark's mouth tugged in a small smile. It didn't change anything. But it loosened the tight knot in her belly. "Thanks, Hugo."

"Yeah, yeah. Now hit the stump, we don't have all day to sit around and moan about boys."

"Yes, sir!" She snatched her bow off the ground.

His frown deepened. "Lark, you need to learn this. The day will come when the difference between surviving and dying comes down to one arrow."

Lark glanced down at her bow hanging loosely in her hands.

"You need to make every shot count. Under every circumstance, I want to see you hit your mark. Even on the hards days. Failure is a luxury people like us can't afford."

"What kind of people are we?"

His mustache twitched, the ghost of a wry smile behind it. "The kind short on luck."

"Really? It would seem to me we're running entirely on luck at this point."

He jerked his chin toward the log that had stilled. Urging her to get on with it. "Who can tell the difference?"

Lark smiled, pulling and nocking an arrow. Finding her anchor point right where it always rested, against her cheek. "The difference lies in how we regard it."

"Less talking, more shooting."

LARK RUBBED her aching shoulder as she stared into the fire.

She mourned the fact that Apple stayed behind with Mrs. O'Connell, but they couldn't bring the horse across the sea. She'd be safe, and happy, and well fed judging by barrels of oats and sacks of apples Mrs. O'Connell lugged into the stable.

After bidding farewell, they'd packed up to move east. Cutting through the forest was the fastest way to the coast where they'd board Captain Ingemar's ship and sail to Koval. The ship docked at Emeraude Bay, at the port. Under different circumstances, Lark would be eager to explore the town overrun by "merchants." But each moment she delayed, Ferryn suffered alone in Lacuna. If Lark was lucky, it would take less than a fortnight on the ship. But before they could take to the sea, they needed the cover of the forest. At least until after the full moon.

Daciana cradled the cup of valerian tea Langford had brewed her. Her eyes darted to the darkening sky. The moon was not yet full, but by tomorrow's eve, it would be round and bright.

The memory of Daciana, bones cracking and limbs twisting at odd angles as she transformed, still pricked the hairs on the back of Lark's neck. Daciana experienced such potent agony each month, with nothing but a mild tea for comfort. Lark would have to find a way to help her. Someone had to know of one. If not to halt the transformation, at least to lessen the torture.

Another important task to add to the list.

Daciana caught Lark's eye and leveled her with a disapproving look. As if she could tell what she was thinking.

Lark schooled her expression into one of innocence and aimed for a safe topic of conversation. "What can I use on my shoulder? Hugo's training exercise might leave me at a disadvantage should we encounter anyone in need of dealing with."

Hugo maintained a neutral expression, staring into the fire. He took another bite of his supper.

Rolling her arms, Lark kneaded her shoulder, trying to work out the knots. "Langford, do you have any more of that willow bark you gave me? Last time Hugo ran me this ragged it was a real lifesaver." She'd found it on her sleeping roll when she awoke. It gave her aching muscles a chance to recover.

"Oh, right!" Langford speared a potato off Daciana's plate as she held it out for him. He waved it in front of him. "That wasn't me. Afraid I was all out then, and I'm all out now because the whore-monger insists on prioritizing his libido over our medicinal needs." He glared at Alistair.

Alistair took a long swill of his wine before clearing his throat. "I will forever approve of that order."

Lark's gaze shot to Gavriel who was chewing and staring at her. Why the man insisted on watching her when she was nothing more than a "complication" was a mystery. She exhaled a long breath, too sore and irritated to listen to Alistair and Langford squabble. It was worse than when Daciana and Alistair went at it. At least with Alistair and Daciana it seemed they were equals, and emotions save for annoyance were never involved.

When Langford and Alistair fought, there was an air of desperation to it. An edge she couldn't quite name.

It felt too intimate to witness.

Lark stood with an embarrassing groan. Gavriel's eyes followed her movement. Annoying bastard. "I need to clear my head."

Daciana nodded. "Not too far, yeah?"

"Yes, mother."

The sky had dimmed. The waxing moon, near to full, illuminated the grass and leaves in silver. Trees swayed in the gentle wind that blew through the forest.

Lark followed the ribbon of moonlight and took careful steps over fallen trunks and roots clawing their way to the surface, making sure not to trample any flowers in her path. Especially the ones tucked away for the night.

When the buzzing in her head was finally silenced, and the sounds of the night took its stead, she leaned back against a large oak, tipping her head up and listening. The chorus frogs sang in the dark. Branches creaked and leaves rustled above, shivering in the wind.

Lark's eyes slipped closed as the swath of warm night air enveloped her.

"You shouldn't be out here alone."

Gavriel's voice sliced through the calm night.

Lark whipped her head, scraping the back of her neck to regard him. He leaned against a nearby tree.

"What is the matter with you?" Lark placed a hand on her chest, trying to slow the rapid pace of her heart.

"I told you if I wanted to avoid detection I could." He pushed off the tree and approached. "I didn't even have to try very hard; you must be distracted."

"You're an ass." Lark ran a hand through her hair, trying not to bristle at how easily he snuck up on her.

"You're mad."

"I'm annoyed."

Gavriel's expression remained hidden by shadows, but the light caught the scar across his cheek.

"We shouldn't be out here," he said, glancing back in the direction of camp.

"*You* shouldn't be out here." Lark crossed her arms, aware of how petulant she sounded, though failing to care.

"Do you at least have a weapon?"

She glared at him. Though in the dark it likely lacked the full effect. "Yes, Gavriel. Contrary to what you seem to think, I do have functioning logic and reason. I didn't traipse out into the woods alone, unarmed, hoping you'd follow me."

He stared at her. His face, unreadable. With a slight shake of his head, he stepped away, toward camp.

Lark's chest hollowed. The burn of his kiss three days prior still lingered on her lips.

"Why?" She couldn't halt the word from leaving her mouth.

Gavriel stilled. "Lark..."

"Tell me. I deserve to know." She charged up to him, blocking his path lest he got any ideas of fleeing.

"I can't have this conversation." He tried to push past her.

Her hands shot up to shove him in the chest. "Why not?" She wasn't going to let him walk away. Not without a real explanation.

"Because I can't stand being near you!"

She recoiled, his words stinging like a slap. And in that moment she was a Reaper again, saving his life and earning his contempt in return. When would she learn he'd never been hers to begin with?

Gavriel ran a hand down his face, exhaling abruptly. "That came out wrong. I meant... Ah! Words are impossible around you."

Lark blinked back the haze in her eyes, willing her mortal body not to betray her this night. She would not cry in front of him.

"I meant"—he edged a step closer—"I lose all sense in your company."

"I rob you of both your ability to speak and to think?" Lark's voice maintained a deceptively even tone. "That must be awful."

Gavriel was close enough Lark could almost feel the tension radiating off him. "It is. The worst form of torture. It's enough to drive a man mad."

"And do I? Drive you mad?"

"Yes. No. I mean"—he furrowed his brows, lifting a hand to pinch the bridge of his nose—"It's maddening to be so close and not touch you."

"So, why don't you?" She reached out, but he backed several paces away. Lark remained rooted to the spot. The abrupt distance was harsh and cold.

Gavriel shook his head. "It's a terrible idea."

"I've heard worse ones."

"No. This. Us. Everything is complicated enough. What happens when we fix the barrier between worlds? When you're free to live your life? Could I expect you to tether yourself to me?" His chest rose and fell with each breath.

"What I want is for me to decide." Lark would never let someone else determine her fate. Not even Gavriel or his fear.

"I'll never be a free man." He shook his head. "The Guild will always hunt me. Do you want to live that way?"

It was a fair question. One Lark never thought of. All she'd wanted was to live. To feel. The circumstances of what life she'd lead were inconsequential. It was too large a question to answer this night. The truth was still unknown and too great to unearth. There was only one certainty. "What I want is you."

"It feels like asking for more than I deserve." He ran a hand over his mouth, watching her with an unreadable expression. Something flashed in his eyes, a resoluteness to his gaze.

Gavriel advanced with the speed of an assassin. Lark instinctively retreated until she felt a tree at her back. He searched her face, scanning every feature. As if searching for the answer to a question he couldn't bring himself to ask.

She held her breath, staring up at his face in the moonlight. The slash of his scar was more exaggerated in the pale glow of the night filled with stars.

"Command me to go," he said, his voice ragged and pleading. His eyes begged her. For what, she wasn't certain. "Tell me to leave, and I shall."

Lark wet her lips, and his gaze tracked the movement.

"Stay," she whispered.

He crashed his lips to hers, his mouth feverish and sweet. His hands found her hips and squeezed. Lark wound her fingers around the back of his neck and held him tight against her as if he might change his mind and pull away. When he deepened the kiss, a gasp escaped from her lips. He swallowed the sound, a low groan emanating from his throat.

His hand fisted in her hair and he yanked her head back, exposing her throat to him. His scorching mouth trailed down her neck and back up to her ear. "Lark," he whispered against her jaw before he claimed her mouth again.

She pressed every line of her body to his so there was no space between them. The heat of him sent warm flutters spiraling through her body.

"Tell me what you want."

"Everything," Lark gasped.

He pressed her against the tree, his lips on hers, squeezing her hip tightly enough to bruise. His thigh slid between hers. The sudden jolt of heat between her legs made her lightheaded.

He pulled back, watching her with ravenous eyes. He cupped her face, running his thumb along her jaw. "Skies, you're beautiful."

Lark felt his other hand slowly trailing toward the top of her leggings, his fingers dancing over the lacings. His eyes never left hers. She hid nothing from him—let her every desire be written across her face. But still, his fingers froze, waiting.

"Please," her voice was a soft whimper.

His hand slid beneath the waist of her pants, trailing beneath the band of her smallclothes. At the first slide of his thumb between her legs, she let out a startled gasp. He watched her intently, his gaze devouring her every expression as he worked her closer and closer to release.

"Gavriel." His name was a reverent prayer on her lips.

Sparks lit in her vision, and the tightness in her stomach grew with each pass of his thumb. Suddenly his fingers filled her, and she couldn't remember what existed outside of his touch. This feverish hot climb to something she couldn't understand. Her body tightened and stretched like she was about to snap. Tears pricked at the corners of her eyes, and she clawed at his shoulder, needing to anchor herself to something.

Needing more and less. Unsure of how to voice what she wanted.

Lark's eyes found his. Gavriel pressed his forehead to hers. "Let go," he whispered against her lips.

She crashed over the edge, clenching around him. The violence of her release dragged the air from her lungs.

He kissed her viciously, devouring every sound she made as he slowed his ministrations and let her gradually come down. Languidly, he withdrew his hand from her, kissing away the little noise of protest she made.

Lark sagged in Gavriel's arms, weightless and boneless in the aftermath of overwhelming sensation. Even her vision had gone hazy. She blinked away the fog and studied his face. His lips were swollen, his hair disheveled. Color bloomed on his cheeks and his eyes blazed. She'd never seen him so undone. He was impossibly beautiful this way.

Lark cupped Gavriel's jaw, pressing her lips to his. He trembled at her touch. As the feeling returned to her legs and her vision cleared, Lark eased them away from the tree. She pushed Gavriel down into the grass and straddled his waist.

His eyes burned with lust as he stared up at her, though his mouth spread into a grin that made him look years younger. She kissed that silly grin. Again and again. Wishing she could always make his face light up like that.

The first roll of her hips pulled a groan from his chest, and he closed his eyes.

Stars danced in her vision as she tested another roll of her hips.

He grabbed her by the neck, pulling her down in a fierce kiss. When he released her, they stared at each other for a moment, as if they were unsure of how they got there. The delicious fire still curled low in her belly, urging her to take all she could.

With steady hands she began undoing his laces, reveling in the way he gazed up at her. In hazy, yearning awe.

The sound of twigs snapping echoed through the trees, and Lark jolted. She stilled, holding her breath.

Gavriel sat up, one hand flat against her back, the other unsheathing a short sword at his waist.

Her knife had already found its way into her hand. She tilted her head, listening, her heart hammering in her chest. Gavriel stared into the darkness, rubbing soothing circles on her back.

"It's nothing." The sound of his whisper was a knife cutting through the laden silence of the night.

"It's too quiet," she murmured, still searching with mortal eyes and seeing nothing.

He pressed a quick kiss to her mouth. Then another. Frowning at her stiff posture. He placed his blade in the grass beside him, hand cupping her chin. "You're making me self-conscious. This is some of my best work."

Lark glanced down to find him smirking. "We should head back."

"If that's what you want," he kissed her again.

She melted against him, his kiss dulling her reason. "I'm serious," she mumbled against his lips, before breaking away. "This is me leaving."

Gavriel captured her mouth again. "I can see that. You must be awfully concerned." He rolled on top of her, pressing himself closer. Evidence of his arousal scattered her thoughts. She was feverish with need.

Lark's hands found his lacings once more, giving a hard tug.

He laughed, low and deep, and the sound rumbled through her. She'd go up in flames if she didn't get these damn trousers off him immediately.

His hands found hers, gently pulling them away.

"You're right. Not here. Not like this." He pushed himself up, reaching for her hand. "You deserve more than a quick rut in the woods." Lark ignored the offer of his hand, straightening her clothes and standing on her own. It was petty to be disappointed, especially after he'd already tended to her needs. But it had done nothing to smother the fire that burned in her veins. A fire he so easily doused in himself.

"I want to take my time with you." Gavriel grabbed her hand, yanking her to his chest. "I don't want you to stifle the noises I draw from you." He tipped her chin, kissing her frown. "And I intend to draw a scream or two."

Lark wrinkled her nose, her shame giving way to mild amusement. "I doubt you could do that."

He grinned, kissing the tip of her nose. "Is that a challenge, Demon?"

Lark's mouth tugged into an unwilling smile. "If you're thinking about sneaking into my tent, think again." The image of the assassin creeping into her bedroll while the others slept, having time and privacy to explore each other, sent a thrill through her.

"Actually, I was thinking I might need to touch you one more time before we head back to camp." He brought his lips to her ear, sliding his hand into her smallclothes. "If it pleases the lady."

"If you insist." Lark hated how weak her voice sounded.

Gavriel chuckled darkly in her ear; his breath ghosted a shiver over her skin. "Oh, I do."

Lark thought she'd be ready for it this time, but at the first brush of his thumb, her legs gave out. He held her firm, showering her with kisses and murmurs of praise. Lost in the moment, she almost missed the sound of footsteps approaching in the dark.

Lark fisted her hands in his tunic, panic mounting in her chest. "Gavriel, stop."

Immediately he yanked his fingers from her, worry creasing his brow. "What's wrong?"

She bent down to yank the knife from her boot, scanning the darkness.

The forest had stilled. Noises of nocturnal creatures, and even the hum of the wind, fell silent. The only sound was the unwavering footfalls of someone in the dark. Someone who wasn't trying to quiet their approach.

Someone heading straight for them.

"Shit." Gavriel searched for his weapon in the grass.

Three women appeared in the clearing. A thick tension in the air followed their steps. Like darkness at their beck and call. Their dizzying beauty and nakedness were the least remarkable things about them. A grand pair of membranous wings flared from each set of shoulders, veins spidering along the edges, talons gleaming in the moonlight.

These weren't women.

A bolt of fear lanced through Lark's chest.

Undesirables.

CHAPTER 44

"*W*ell, don't stop on our account." The dark-haired woman placed a hand on her generous hip, regarding them both with ravenous black eyes. No, she was no woman, Gavriel was certain of that much. Behind her, two more beasts stood waiting. Their hair, the color of snow and ash. The pleasant warmth in his body from finally, finally having Lark in his grasp was doused with a cold bucket of reality.

Armed with little more than his fear, Gavriel stepped in front of Lark, and, *of course,* she pushed her way to his side. Just once, would it kill her to allow him to stand between her and danger?

"Whatever you think you've found," Lark said, her voice low and dangerous, "you are mistaken. I'd leave before you make a mistake that can't be undone."

Gavriel recognized false bravado when he heard it. Still, it would be in both their best interests for Lark to shut her damn mouth.

"Oh, I think you're exactly what we've been looking for, Larkin." The monster grinned, revealing long sharp teeth. "The mortal you've brought along is a bonus."

Lark stiffened. "Crawl back to the deepest pits of the Netherworld, before I remind you just how insignificant you are."

Maddening woman. Gavriel needed his weapon before she goaded the beast into attacking. The dirk tucked in his arm sheath, the stiletto beneath his jerkin, and the Ardenian skinner in his boot meant he wasn't completely helpless. But the distance of a sword would be a greater comfort, especially if these monsters had claws.

He wracked his memory, sifting through pages from Kenna's bestiary. There'd been plenty that took the shape of naked women, but he couldn't remember one with wings. The closest was the Manananggal, but they were grotesque creatures, split in half to leave their legs behind. They were also a bitch to kill.

Skies, he hoped these weren't Manananggals.

He glanced at the spot in the grass where he'd lain beneath Lark, in hopes of seeing the glint of steel.

"You've forgotten how insignificant you've become, little Reaper." The creature sneered. "You don't have power anymore, quit pretending you're not the prey here. You and this delicious morsel you brought."

Gavriel clenched his teeth, swallowing the acid that spread on his tongue. They'd have to rip through him first.

"Leave the mortal out of this."

"Lark." Gavriel couldn't halt the edge to his voice "Stop talking."

Lark glared at him. That was fine. She could be angry. So long as she kept breathing, she could curse his name for all he cared.

"You're in no position to be making any demands. So long as we bring you back in one piece, we're free to do as we please." The creature leveled her black eyes on Gavriel, dragging them up and down his body in blatant hunger. "And it would please me to devour his insides while they're still warm."

Gavriel suppressed a shudder. Fear was his weapon. He accomplished many kills alongside his fear. This would be no different.

He just wished he had his skies-forsaken sword.

He yanked his stiletto knife from the sheath beneath his jerkin.

Lark spun her dagger in her hand. "Have it your way."

When the beast advanced, Lark sank into a crouch, spinning low to slash its belly.

It shrieked, spreading its wings. The stench of death and decay blew against Gavriel's face.

The two flanking beasts roared as they twisted their hips, angling side to side. Snaking their bodies in a violent sway.

Damn it all to the blazing nethers. Gavriel knew what was coming.

Their torsos split like stretched seams along their midsections. Useless legs and bottom halves hit the dirt with a bloody squish. Gore and viscera trailed behind the three creatures as they leapt into the sky—wings wide and spines protruding like tails.

Rutting Manananggal.

"Shit," Lark said, flipping her dagger so it glinted in the moonlight.

As the Manananggals launched higher in the sky, they screeched. The sound, like claws raking against Gavriel's eardrums. This was part of their little dance. Manananggals were known for playing with their food. Flying in and out of range, sometimes picking up their prey to drop through the air, only to catch them again. A game of terror and release. Whatever it took to prolong the pain.

It wouldn't be long before they descended again.

Gavriel dropped to the ground, feeling around for his sword. He needed a weapon that would keep him out of range of those claws.

Lark sank to her knees to help.

Gavriel ground his teeth. Another mistake on his part, and Lark was in danger. Again. If his urges hadn't gotten the best of him, they wouldn't be searching the ground for his weapon. But at least he'd followed her out here. Skies only knew what would have happened had she been alone when they came.

Gavriel was well aware of his chances for survival. But damned if he was going to let her go down with him. If he died before tomorrow came, at least he knew what her kisses tasted like.

That was something he could carry to the afterlife.

"Lark," Gavriel said, unsure what he was going to say.

"I know," Lark said quickly, continuing her search.

She was right. Better to save his declarations of affection for when they were safe.

467

His fingers curled around the tip of the blade, and thick relief washed through him.

"I got it!" Lark said, tugging his sword before he could warn her. The blade sliced against his palm in bright, searing pain.

Gavriel cursed, curling his hand onto itself, dark blood leaked between tightened fingers. Wonderful.

Lark yanked part of her sleeve off, wrapping it around his hand and tying it tight enough, he winced. "Hasn't anyone ever told you not to grip it by the sharp end?"

Smartass.

"I think I heard that somewhere before," Gavriel said, grimacing. "We need a silver blade or salt. Or sunlight."

Lark's face fell. "So, a miracle then?"

Gavriel stood, bouncing on his feet to limber up for a fight they wouldn't win. "No, you need to go back to camp and get me Langford's sea salt." He'd stay and fight those things. Whatever it took to give her a chance at escape.

The weighted thrum of wings shuddered through the air. They were coming back.

Even when Lark scowled she was beautiful. "I'm not leaving."

Three sets of moth-colored wings flapped into view. Their monstrous half-bodies trailed what should have been vital organs behind. Gavriel angled his weapon, falling into a stance as natural as breathing.

"We need to salt their lower halves so they can't reform before sunrise." If she'd only listen to reason, perhaps Gavriel had a shot at getting her out unharmed.

"I'm aware of the properties of Manananggals," Lark said through gritted teeth. "So, we fight 'til sunrise?"

Stubborn demon.

ALL THE CARNAGE seemed to amount to nothing. No matter how much those creatures bled, no matter how much gore hung off their torn frames, it made no difference. It staunched no rage in their attacks.

Gavriel's strength waned. His sword arm trembled under the weight of his attacks. Were his foe human, he could exploit their weaknesses. As it was, the only advantage he had was too far to use. And his weakness was Lark.

Her scream skittered down his spine, and he searched for her in the dark. Three gashes ran the length of her back, glimmering with wetness in the moonlight. He couldn't get to her, not without turning his back on the creatures. Another rake of claws against his cheek stung, and blood dripped down his face. He roared in helpless fury. He'd gut the filthy creatures for every mark they laid upon her. And only when their rotten blood painted the ground, would he be satisfied.

Claws gripped Gavriel's shoulders, burrowing into his skin. His body slammed to the ground, and he swung blindly, hacking off the limb within reach. The decayed arm dropped to the ground as the creature howled, throwing its head back and cascading long white hair down its back.

But it wasn't enough. It was never enough. Gavriel fought and dragged his way through this blighted world, only to fall.

In the end, everyone falls.

Lark cried out. Gavriel turned to find her suspended above the ground, held in the air by the dark-haired beast. Blood dripped down her face. Before he could react, the other two creatures pinned him down.

"Do you know what we do to mortals?" The acrid stench of death blew against his face as he kicked and fought. "We feast on their innards while the heart still beats. While the blood is still warm."

Gavriel growled. They pressed him down into the dirt, one behind his head, and one over his chest, their wings flapping rancid air around him.

"He looks strong. I bet it'll feel like hours before he dies."

If there was one merciful god in the entire rutting sky, they wouldn't let him die like this. Not in front of her.

Gavriel's eyes found Lark's, and the whole world narrowed to her face—to the fierce desperation in her gaze. Every unspoken promise. Every moment stolen. Each aching regret. Raw and consuming.

The sound of flesh ripping filled his ears.

But there was no pain.

The beast's arm hit the ground with a heavy thud. Daciana stood, poised over Gavriel like a damn Warrior of Avalon. Her blade high above her head, her face splattered with blood.

The creature shrieked, and Daciana slashed her blade across its neck. Its head toppled to the ground, its mouth still wide in a silent scream.

The Manananggal whose claws dug into his shoulders released him, beating its wings erratically as it tried to back away. Gavriel turned and grasped it by the end of its spine and yanked it back like the tail of an animal. Daciana swept her sword again, and another head fell to the ground with a satisfying thud.

Gavriel scrambled to his feet, his knees shaking. As soon as he found his voice, he should thank her.

Daciana caught him. "I have salt and silver. Tell me you have some fight left in you."

A wail of outrage rang out. The third creature dragged Lark higher into the sky.

Gavriel ran, a slight limp in his step toward the spot where its legs waited to be rejoined.

"Gavriel!" Daciana tossed a small canister to him.

He caught it before it was swallowed by the dark and dropped to his knees beside the bisected torso. With shaking hands, he ripped the lid off the canister and dumped white sea salt over it.

The beast screeched, climbing higher into the sky while dragging Lark along with it. Lark kicked and flailed.

Gavriel's heart leapt into his throat. If it took her much higher, the fall would kill her.

Lark's boot snagged on a branch, she twisted her leg around it, grappling to stay close to the ground.

Daciana sprinted over; her blade gleamed in the moonlight. "Lark, catch!" She tossed it up. Lark reached for it, only for it to miss her fingertips and plummet to the ground.

Gavriel leapt forward and clambered up the tree. She would not fall. He would not let her fall.

The beast tugged harder, and a cry ripped from Lark's chest.

Daciana tossed her blade up once more, and Gavriel caught it. But Lark was still too far for him to reach her. The wet hilt was warm and glistened with blood in the palm of his hand. He found Lark's eyes, the desperation in them surely mirrored his own. If it took her away, he'd follow them to the pits of the Netherworld to get her back.

He threw it up to her, handle first.

When her fingers closed around it, he breathed a sigh of relief.

Wasting no time on parting words, Lark thrust the sharp blade under the beast's chin. Dark blood showered the side of Lark's neck and shoulder. Lark stabbed and stabbed and ripped the blade through flesh until the top half of its head fell away with a sickening squelch. Its arms went slack, and both Lark and the winged torso fell through the darkened sky.

Gavriel threw himself forward, wrenching a muscle in his shoulder, as he grabbed Lark's forearm, stopping her short. She dangled from where he gripped her with every last shred of his hope and strength. With a grunt, he pulled her to him. Lark let the sword fall from her grasp, her feet finding purchase on the tree branch. Gavriel crushed her to his chest, shaky breaths escaping his lungs as he held her against him. She was here. She was alive. She was all right. He pulled back, needing to see her. Her amber eyes were still wide with terror and glassy with unshed tears. Blood painted her cheek and coated her freckles. He couldn't decide between yanking her into his arms or just staring, committing every feature to memory.

He nearly crumpled when she lifted a delicate, shaking hand to trace his face. The ache of her gentle touch was enough to bring a man to his knees.

"I thought I lost you," Gavriel said.

For once there was no retort. No glib remark to lessen the tension. Lark pressed her forehead against his. When the first wave of tears rolled down her filthy cheeks, he gripped her chin and tilted her head up to look at him.

Only a quiet broken noise left his lips before he pressed them to hers, desperate and greedy. She wove her fingers into his hair. He needed this anchor. This moment. This truth.

Finally, they broke apart, their breathing ragged. He pressed soft kisses to her blood, dirt, and tear-stained cheeks, her forehead, her nose, her hair, until she began to shake in his arms.

"You're going into shock," Gavriel said softly, bundling her closer to him. "Can you climb down on your own, or do you need me to carry you?"

Lark nodded. She climbed down the tree and landed on her feet upon the soft grass. She swayed.

Before Gavriel could leap down, Daciana was upon her, checking her for injury.

"We need to get you cleaned up. Both of you." Daciana frowned as Gavriel climbed down the tree. "There's a creek not far from here. Head east and I'll meet you with some clean clothes." She eyed Lark one more time, as if unsure if she should let her out of her sight.

"Just give her a moment." Gavriel recognized the same look of shock Emric wore after his first kill. The way he crept into Gavriel's room and shook in the corner, offering no words to explain. He didn't need to.

The quiet sounds of the night had returned, the chorus of frogs resuming their calls. Cicadas hummed in the distance, and a gentle wind shook the leaves. But loudest of all was Lark's silence.

ark had never sailed. If she had in her previous mortal life, she couldn't remember, but as a Reaper, there never had been any need. Souls lost at sea tend to stay lost. A fact that she'd never considered before. But as a mortal, she trembled at the thought of spending eternity at the bottom of the black, unforgiving depths. The thought soaked through her skin and settled into her bones.

Lark gazed down at the water sloshing against the dock, imagining the trip that stretched before them. Koval was vast with many places Lark once dreamt of experiencing without the tether of a human soul to reap. The Royal City, home of King Zaire, was the largest center of trade in all the world. But they wouldn't be venturing south, they'd veer north to the Forbidden Highlands. For Ferryn. He mattered more than Lark's desire to lose herself in unfamiliar places.

Heavy footfalls boomed across the wooden dock. A woman stalked toward them with a murderous gait, her cutlass gleaming in the midday's sun. Her black hair swept across her deep complexion in the ocean breeze, and her narrow, brown eyes glared at them from beneath her cunning, off-kilter hat.

Captain Ingemar. Alistair had been cagey on the details of the mysterious Captain, who would be aiding their trip to Koval, and now Lark had a sense of why that might be.

"Alistair, you slimy son of a bitch." Captain Ingemar gripped the hilt of her sword, her elegant nose crinkling in disgust. "I thought I told you never to set foot in my port again."

"I thought you said she expected us," Daciana said with a sharp glare.

Alistair frowned. "Did I...?"

Ingemar lifted her slender chin. "Give me one good reason not to slit you, nose to navel, Alistair."

Alistair pulled a coin purse from his satchel. "I believe this is the sum for lodging and passage as previously agreed upon."

She narrowed her dark eyes at him. "I should have known it was you. The whole exchange reeked of your schemes."

"If the coin is no good—" Alistair stashed the small satchel into his breast pocket—"I suppose we'll go elsewhere." He turned on his heel.

"Wait."

He stilled, spinning with a puzzled expression on his face. "Yes, Ingemar?"

"Captain Ingemar," she bit out. "And you might be a filthy bilge rat, but coin is coin. I honor my deals." She held out her hand.

Alistair grinned. "A fact I know all too well. There is honor to be found, even among thieves—"

"You know nothing of honor," Ingemar said. "But payment speaks for itself. Now get on my ship and out of my sight before I change my mind." She stormed back to her Galleon, each step like thunder across the dock.

The ship waited in the harbor, dozens of sailors readying her to take to the sea as the sails billowed in the breeze. Whatever slight Alistair had committed must have been grave indeed for such a frosty reception. It was a wonder she was letting them board her ship at all.

The Savage Jewel, painted in large, white letters, gleamed along the portside of the large ship. The figurehead of an intricately carved lion curved from the bow. Poised to attack, claws at the ready. Great gaping jaws spread wide to reveal large, sharp teeth.

Lark hoisted her pack higher over her shoulder and followed Captain Ingemar.

LARK PUSHED OPEN THE SMALL, round window in her private cabin. A gust of salty air swept through the room, instantly calming the tightness in her chest.

Lark turned to survey her quarters for the next two weeks. The smell of wet sawdust still hung in the air. A narrow bed, chained to the wall, jutted out to suspend above the floor, and a small unlit lantern swung from its hook. She dropped her pack on the meager bedside table. It was nailed to the floor with a single drawer that wouldn't open.

She'd slept in worse.

Not that she'd get much sleep.

Every time she closed her eyes, she saw that moment.

Gavriel trapped beneath the Manananggals, their claws raised and ready to slice open his belly so they could feast on his flesh and viscera. The instant his eyes sought her face, and it was written plain as day.

He was going to die.

In her dreams, Daciana didn't make it in time. Nearly a week had passed and Lark still couldn't shake the memory from her mind each time she closed her eyes. In her nightmares, she was paralyzed as they devoured his insides. She heard his screams—smelled the tang of his blood as they ripped him apart, and was powerless to stop it.

Sleep was a terrifying thing these days.

Lark plopped down on the bed, and a thick cloud of dust tickled her nose. She sneezed into her sleeve.

She should go up on the main deck, stay out in the open air until dinner. But she still couldn't face Gavriel. She'd done her best to avoid him since that night. Once or twice, she felt the burn of his hand against hers, a silent question. And she'd pulled away.

Lark curled in on her side on the narrow bed. Staring at nothing but the floating dust motes in the beam of sunlight that stretched across the small room.

WHEN HER DOOR BURST OPEN, Lark sat up, knife in hand, and heart in her throat.

The doorway framed Daciana's silhouette.

Lark rubbed her face, wiping the last vestiges of her nightmare from her mind. Though she'd done her best to stay awake, the lull of the sea and exhaustion got the best of her. She'd slept long enough the room was dark. She rolled over to light her lantern, illuminating the tight room and Daciana's expectant expression—and the bottle she swung in her hand.

"What's that for?"

Daciana eyed the brown glass bottle. "I believe it's for consumption." She raised an eyebrow. "Although, since it came from Ingemar's stash it's wise to be wary."

"*Captain* Ingemar."

Daciana settled down on the narrow bed beside Lark. "Yes, of course. Captain." She shook her head, casting her eyes to the ceiling. "Alistair really knows how to pick them."

"They were lovers?" Lark brought her knees to her chest. Perhaps that was the wrong word. Alistair was open with his sexual conquests. A little too open. He once drew her a diagram detailing an orgy he attended. But 'lover' was a word she'd never heard him describe his bedfellow as.

"Allies," Daciana said, uncorking the bottle with a pop. "Which is a far worse betrayal, if you ask me."

Lark considered her words carefully. In her time as Reaper, she'd heard all sorts of tales of love from mortals. It seemed heartache was near destined to follow any romantic attachment. Expected, even. Perhaps that was why the betrayal of an alliance was a far greater offense, at least in Daciana's eyes. A slight compounded by the sheer shock of it.

Either that or she was speaking of her own experience.

Daciana took a long swig, furrowing her brow at the taste. She handed the bottle to Lark.

Lark dangled it by its long slender neck. "I'm not in the mood."

"You might not be, but I am. Are you going to make me drink alone?"

Lark huffed a laugh as she brought the bottle to her lips, tipping it back to let the liquid slide over her tongue. She grimaced at the vaporous, bitter flavor. But the pleasant warmth that tingled in her belly was a welcome relief to the near-constant knot that made its home there.

Daciana swung her leg back and forth from the edge of the bed. "We haven't spoken about that night."

Lark froze, dread seizing in her veins. There was no doubt to what night she referred. "I haven't wanted to."

Daciana angled her head, quiet calculation written on her face. "Not even with Gavriel?"

Lark's eyes slipped closed as she fought against the headache already mounting at this conversation. "No."

Daciana held her hand out for the bottle. After taking a quick sip, she lowered it to her lap, rotating it in her hands. "It's been a long time since I've been grateful for my... inheritance."

Lark wanted to respond, but the words wouldn't come.

"If I hadn't been so close to my transition," Daciana continued. "I wouldn't have heard you."

Lark could almost feel the claws of the Manananggal, gripping her tight enough to tear skin. Could almost hear the steady beat of its wings flapping as the ground fell away and Gavriel remained. Pinned beneath those monsters.

Daciana grabbed Lark's hand, ripping her out of her thoughts. "I also found myself grateful for everything Kenna has taught me. It seems our time together wasn't in vain."

This was the first time Daciana brought Kenna up.

"What happened with Kenna?" Lark couldn't halt the question.

A shadow passed over Daciana's face. "She's a hunter, so she knows these things. I always carry a silver blade. Too many beasts require it."

Lark should have stopped pressing, but she didn't. "What happened between you two?"

Daciana withdrew her hand. Her gaze fell to the floor as she began twisting the silver ring on her middle finger. "Sometimes, finding the person you'd burn the world for is the worst sort of curse. I know how you felt that night, Lark. I know how it stays with you."

Daciana carried the weight of so much and maintained an honor Lark couldn't claim for herself.

Swallowing against a thick throat, Lark leaned over to grab her pack. Shoving a hand in, she yanked Kenna's talisman free. Mountains and sky dangled from her fist.

"You should have this," she said, passing it to Daciana. "In case anything happens, I want to make sure it gets back to Kenna."

Daciana's brows knitted together as she frowned at the pendant before pocketing it. Lark wasn't sure if she'd just added to Daciana's burdens, but it felt right that she carry Kenna's talisman. Lark hadn't even noticed if it warned of the Manananggals' approach.

"I'm sorry I couldn't protect us."

Daciana shook her head. "We protect each other, and without apology, Lark."

Did they though? How many times had Daciana saved her? And Gavriel...

Lark swallowed. "I almost... he almost..."

Daciana waited patiently.

"I almost lost him."

Daciana nodded. "But you didn't."

"But I was powerless to stop it. I couldn't..." she trailed off, words failing her again. She bit the inside of her cheek.

Daciana wrapped an arm around Lark's shoulders. "We all feel powerless. Don't you get it, Lark? Every day is a gamble. You can't rig the game."

"So, I'm to accept that I have no control over any of it?" Bright, burning anger was bottled within Lark. She'd crawled her way out of the Otherworld for this control that always seemed to elude her.

"You have some, but some things are left up to chance."

Isn't that what she wanted? To be free of fate?

"I can't be certain fate's hand isn't in everything." The more Lark fought to escape, the more her actions seemed preordained. That no matter how hard she tried, she was at the mercy of a power far from her grasp. She couldn't shake the feeling that Gavriel was always meant to die, and fate would have balance. One way or another.

"A life led by chance is accepting the fact that shit is going to happen. Whether we like it or not." Daciana took another swig. "But you can't sit here and dwell on what could have been. That isn't living."

Lark glanced down at the floor, her eyes tracing the grains of wood in each plank. "I feel so lost."

"That's how we all feel."

Lark fidgeted, needing the weight of this conversation to lessen. "Even Alistair?"

"Especially him. I could tell you so many stories, though I'll need more of this." Daciana offered the bottle to Lark in a silent invitation.

A slow smile tugged at Lark's mouth. She grabbed it and took another deep swill. It tasted less bitter this time. "Tonight, every story is yours to tell."

Daciana grinned. "Deal."

LARK GRIPPED HER STOMACH, laughter rippling through her in waves that clenched her muscles and filled her eyes with tears. Every time she thought she had it under control, she and Daciana would look at each other and fall into another fit.

"I can't believe—" Lark wiped her eyes—"Langford didn't think to find the nearest bush for privacy. Did he really think shitting his pants was the less embarrassing option?"

Daciana hit her teeth off the lip of the bottle as she attempted to drink. "I think he thought he could keep his ass clenched through sheer will, despite his sick belly."

"Ah, poor Langford."

"Yes, those first few weeks with us were difficult for him." Daciana nodded, an abrupt somber tone dissolving her mirth. "He was so lost and scared. The first time we saw him traveling the road, alone, and in far too fine clothing in tatters, Alistair took one look at him and tucked him under his wing for safekeeping."

Lark frowned, her face sore from smiling. Her stomach was beginning to sour. "Langford told me about his last mission, the one where he got caught. Alistair took his sweet time collecting him."

Daciana leveled her with an intense stare. "You have no idea what that day did to Alistair. I've never seen him like that."

Something gnawed at Lark's gut. Either the rum or the conversation. "He let Langford go with me to the ball."

"That was different, he had me on the outside to make sure Langford would have someone watching his back."

So that was why Alistair wouldn't let Daciana go in her stead. Lark suspected Langford held a torch for the man, and if Alistair cared for him too...

"Should we help them along?"

"Hmm? What's that now?" The glass bottle distorted Daciana's voice as she spoke against it.

Lark leaned back against the wall, sinking into her dingy mattress. "We could play at matchmaking." It would solve a few of their problems. Like rationing coin and herbs.

"If you think matters of the heart are so easily settled, then you haven't been paying attention."

Truer words had never been spoken.

Lark slipped Hugo's knife from her boot, running her thumb down the hilt in a soothing motion she'd been doing more often. The shapes in swirls carved into the wood were so similar to the ink Hugo bore on his skin.

Daciana glanced at it. "He told you who that belonged to then?"

The blade and blood groove caught the lantern light. The steel glinted like a moonlit sea. "His daughter. But he said nothing more."

"Those markings are Vallemerian," Daciana said. "They're the symbols of someone who fought for their place in the mountain pass arena. Each kill is a fresh tattoo, inked immediately after the fight while the wounds still bleed. But there's honor to each death. Every man and woman who enters accepts that death is watching and ready to claim them."

Lark had never reaped a Vallemerian warrior, though she'd heard of the mountain pass arena. If each mark represented a kill, how many had fallen beneath Hugo's blade? Had she ever seen him with his tunic off? "Hugo's entire body…"

Daciana laughed. "Yes, I know. It's insane. Makes you wonder what happened after that."

"What do you mean?"

"In Vallemer, he'd be a hero. Practically a paragon. He's alive, so he either won the title of Bjornskinn, or he deserted." Daciana frowned. "And I can't see him deserting."

Lark ran her thumb along the hilt again. Hugo carried many secrets, including the origin of his ink. The last time she asked, he called it "stupidity." What changed from the first time he entered that arena to the last time he left it? And which marks were worth carving into his knife? The ones he celebrated, or regretted?

"He didn't even know me when he gave me this," Lark said.

Daciana nodded, taking another drink of rum. "He loves you, you know. They all do."

Love. It was strange to think how she always assumed Reapers couldn't love, and to an extent, she couldn't. But the fierce loyalty and she felt toward Ferryn, and now toward Daciana and the others… that was love, wasn't it?

"You don't seem to understand how important you are to all of us. Why?"

It was a fair question. One Lark had pondered herself more times than she could count.

"I don't know. Maybe something in me is broken. I can't believe I would be worthy of anyone's loyalty and devotion."

"Do you question mine?"

"Of course not. But that says more about you than it does me."

Daciana hummed. She pressed a finger to her lips. "What about Gavriel?"

Lark's shoulders tensed. "What about him?"

"I told you my hearing was heightened that night."

"So?"

Daciana's mouth split in a knowing grin. "Lark... c'mon."

Something hot and slippery sank in Lark's gut as heat flared in her cheeks. "Daciana... did you hear us?"

Daciana threw her head back and cackled. "I did! You seemed determined to get him out of those leathers. Were they too tight to maneuver? It can't be very comfortable."

"Daciana, stop." Lark hid her face in her hands. "Forever stop this conversation."

To her credit, Daciana smothered her smile with her hand even as laughter still danced in her eyes. "I'm sorry, I don't wish to embarrass you. I aim to point out that you seemed somewhat trusting of the assassin who harbored a wish to kill you not two months ago."

Lark yanked the nearly empty bottle from Daciana's grasp, taking a swig. The burst of warm spices and a hint of vanilla swept through her mouth. Warmth bloomed in her body, casting a haze over the sharp edge of humiliation. "Perhaps I'm drawn to death out of habit."

Daciana snorted, yanking the bottle back with no real force behind it. "Aren't we all?"

LARK TRIPPED DOWN THE CORRIDOR, trying to count the doors.

Which room was Gavriel's?

The fog of rum clouded her ability to see straight.

Or walk straight.

Despite the lift in Lark's mood from her conversation with Daciana, there was still someone she needed to speak with.

Lark's boot caught on a raised plank of wood and crashed her to the floor. She rolled onto her back, groaning at the spinning hall, and flung an arm over her eyes, so her knuckles rested against the dingy floor. Once the floor stopped moving, she'd crawl her way back to her room.

Easier said than done on a ship at sea.

She heard the unmistakable sound of door hinges creaking. Perhaps if she was very lucky, whoever it was would ignore her and allow her a moment's misery in peace.

"Lark?" Gavriel's voice was amused. "Why are you lying down in the hallway?"

Damn it all to the blazing pits of the Netherworld.

She lowered her arm to see him standing above her. His black tunic parted to show the firm muscles of his chest, and a soft smile tugged at the corner of his mouth.

Skies, he was handsome.

Lark tried to sit up.

Gavriel dropped into a crouch, one hand against her back, the other held out in silent offering. Placing her hand in his, Lark tried not to remember what those hands had done to her a few nights past. Flames lit up her cheeks and his smile broadened, as if he could sense what she'd been thinking.

Finally upright, Lark yanked herself free of his grip to dust herself off. If only she could get through this with a modicum of pride. "I had actually come to speak with you." Though her head was abuzz from drink and nervous energy, her voice came out clear.

Gavriel raised a brow. "And you thought to find me on the floor in the hall?"

"Well, no." She leaned forward, almost losing her balance. "I was taking a break." It was a perfectly rational explanation. "Before I continued my journey to your room."

Gavriel pursed his lips, fighting a smile. "I see. It's a good thing I found you when I did. Now you needn't complete such a perilous journey."

Lark sucked in a deep breath, calling on her strength to steady her nerves. She hoped she hadn't waited too long to seek him out. How fickle exactly was the nature of mortals? "Can we please speak in your quarters?"

Surprise shot across his features. Had she not just told him she intended to find him there?

"Of course."

Gavriel remained a pace behind her the rest of the way to his door.

Lark managed to walk in her best approximation of a straight line, though the floorboards were trying to leap up at her. When she entered his room she immediately sank to the floor, bending her legs to hug her knees.

Gavriel leaned against the desk, bracing his hands on either side of him. He looked up at her expectantly.

"I think I understand why you didn't want the complication. Between us, I mean."

A muscle feathered in his jaw. "Enlighten me."

Lark tried to recall Daciana's words. "Finding the person you'd sacrifice the world for, it's a curse. Especially because humans are so fragile."

Gavriel's expression hardened. "Is that how you feel?" He was angry? But that didn't make sense.

"Not exactly."

Damn his penchant for silence in the face of uncomfortable conversations.

"When you almost... when I almost..." Lark didn't notice a tear was trailing down her flaming cheek until it dripped down in the space of her neck. Irritated, she wiped it away. "I can't handle the idea that I'm not strong enough to protect you. To save you. What did you say about me once, death follows me and dwells in my shadow?"

His face fell at her words. "Lark—"

"No, but you were right. How could I live with myself if I brought death to your doorstep? Don't you get it? That's all I've been trying to stop." She bit her lip, fighting the tremble in her chin. "And I don't know if I can."

Gavriel pushed off the desk, and lowered to his knees beside her. "Lark, you can't protect everyone from everything."

She nodded, still refusing to look at him. "I just thought being human would be easier. I didn't account for these feelings of help-lessness."

He huffed a quiet laugh. "Someone oversold what you were bargaining for."

No, they hadn't. Every moment of every day was a gift. One she'd trade her soul a thousand times for.

Lark bit the inside of her cheek. Unsure if she should say the words dancing on her tongue. "I was supposed to kill you after I saved you. Thanar commanded me to restore the balance." Her stomach roiled at the memory. "But I couldn't. I knew I'd never let any harm come to you. Whatever the cost."

Two fingers lifted her chin to face him.

He wiped away her tears with the pad of his thumb. "Lark, you must know. I would die a thousand times if it meant knowing you."

Lark took his hand, edging closer. His familiar scent consumed her, and she wanted nothing more than to lose herself in him. She traced the scars on his cheek and mouth.

His lips parted, and his breath warmed her fingertips. When she ghosted her touch along the scabbed claw marks against his cheek, he stilled.

"You're back," he said. "Does it hurt?"

Memories of the Manananggals, of a night fraught with terror and pain. Of sharp claws raking down her back and whispered threats in her ear of what they would do to Gavriel while he still lived.

"No," Lark said. "Not anymore."

The intensity of his stare was her undoing. Unable to halt the impulse, she pressed her lips against his.

He grabbed and deposited her into his lap. She wrapped her legs around him as she deepened the kiss, threading her fingers through his hair. A soft groan rumbled in his chest as he ran his hands up and down her back, before running a hand up into her loose hair. Gripping possessively.

Gavriel parted her lips, sweeping his tongue into her mouth. He pulled back enough for Lark to regard him in a daze. His green eyes that were nearly black as they devoured her with unbridled want.

"Gavriel," was all she managed to gasp before his mouth was upon hers, swallowing the sound of his name on her lips. She pressed closer, sending a jolt of heat through her as she created friction between them.

His hand flew to her thighs, whether to stop her or pull her tighter she wasn't sure. She rolled her hips again, feeling the bite of his fingers against her thighs. "Demon," he hissed.

A breathy chuckle left her lips ghosting against his, and he began to trail scorching kisses down her neck to the base of her throat. She pressed down harder against his lap, earning a growl that reverberated through her. He flipped her flat on her back and knelt above her. Caging her body.

Gavriel exhaled a tight breath as he stared down at her, eyes burning through her. "You have no idea the things I want to do to you." His baritone voice had darkened with promise.

Lark couldn't breathe. "Show me."

"Not tonight."

She glared at him, deciding to test the strength of his resolve. She pressed open kisses to his mouth, lowering them back down to the floor.

Gavriel broke away, grasping her wrists together. "Not tonight, Lark."

"Why?" She couldn't bring herself to feel ashamed of the desperation in her voice.

"These days have been hard on me too." The fire in his eyes subsided to something less starved. To something fond and gentle. "Allow me a night with you near, so I can be sure you won't vanish on me again."

Lark nodded, and her throat thickened. Gavriel released her wrists and tucked his arms under her knees, lifting her against his chest.

She grumbled her protest, earning a quick kiss before he tossed her onto the bed. She reached for him, but he batted her hands away and crossed the room. He shook his head with a dazed smile as he filled a cup with water from the pitcher in the corner. He handed it to her.

Lark drank it down. She hadn't realized how thirsty she was.

When she felt him pull on her boot, she yelped. "I can undress myself, thank you."

He rolled his eyes as he tugged her boot harder, yanking her down the bed and nearly spilling her water. His eyes darkened in a way she was beginning to recognize and busied himself with her other boot. "Allow me this."

Lark sighed as a smile twisted its way across her mouth.

Gavriel climbed onto the tiny bed, having no choice but to press himself against her. "Don't get fresh with me, Demon. We're just sleeping tonight."

"Is this my penance for avoiding you?"

He tucked a strand of hair behind her ear. "If you like. I prefer to think of it as my reward for surviving you."

Lark huffed a laugh as he pressed gentle kisses to her hair. "You know you could claim the full reward..."

"Well, perhaps you haven't earned my reward yet." He smirked. "You ever think of that?"

She pressed an eager kiss to his lips, lingering long enough for him to break the contact first.

"Behave," he growled in her ear.

A shiver ran through her. Lark made no such promises. But the warmth of his solid body against hers as he held her tight against his chest was too strong a pull to resist. Soon her heavy eyelids fluttered shut, and sleep claimed her against the gentle rocking of the ocean.

CHAPTER 46

*L*ark awoke with a thick tongue and dry mouth. Her head pounded its reminder never to raid Ingemar's stash again. Lark groaned as her stomach rolled. Curse Daciana and the bottomless rum.

Bright light assaulted her eyes. Lark groped for something to cover her face, her fingers running down a solid form.

The whole night came flooding back. Whispered confessions and hungry, scorching kisses, threatening to consume her whole.

"Good morning." Gavriel's voice was still thick from sleep. The deep rumble coiled something low in her belly she was ill-equipped to feel at the moment.

Lark grumbled her response even as her stomach fluttered.

"Not so good morning, I guess."

She pressed her hand over his mouth, and he began placing light kisses on her fingers. Lark opened her eyes to find him gazing down at her.

"Hello," she whispered.

Gavriel's mouth curved into her favorite smile. "Hello, yourself. Had I known what a blanket thief you'd turn out to be, I never would have insisted you stay the night."

Lark glanced down to find his coverings wrapped around her legs several times. As if she tossed and turned until cocooned. She sat up too fast, regretting the movement. "My head..."

A strong hand squeezed the back of her neck.

"In my experience, it's wise to eat and hydrate after a night of carousing."

"I wasn't *carousing*, you ass."

"Be nice, or I won't fetch you breakfast." Gavriel lowered his hand to rub soothing circles against her upper back. "Rest, I'll be back shortly."

Without needing any further invitation, Lark slumped over, nestling under the covers. His lips brushed her forehead, and then silence. Lark wasn't surprised Gavriel could leave the room without making a sound.

Everything hurt. Her eyes. Her head. Her body. Her hair.

Yet in the far recesses of her mind, something glimmered. A spark of excitement her rum-addled brain still recognized. She snuggled deeper into the blankets that smelled distinctly of Gavriel.

On the upper deck, Lark found Langford. He stood hunched forward, elbows resting on the railing as he looked out over the sparkling water. The wind whipped through his dark hair.

The sea beckoned; white caps gleamed in the midday sun. The surface of the water was rough and wild, raging against the impossible blue of the horizon.

Lark couldn't help but imagine falling overboard, how the ocean might swallow her up. Her heart quickened its pace as a thrill ran through her. Such a wondrous thing, the call of the void. A strange and fleeting urge she quickly tucked away.

Lark leaned on the rail beside Langford. She licked her lips, tasting salt. "Fancy seeing you here."

"I hope you're faring better than Hugo. He's been holed up in his room. Never acquired his sea legs, it would seem."

Poor Hugo. If he felt anything close to how nauseated she'd been last night, and for the whole trip, she couldn't blame him for hiding. Though it would do little in the way of aiding his seasickness. Alistair had mentioned something about fixing your eye on the horizon and staring straight ahead if the motion was too much to handle. "Has he not tried breathing some fresh air? Staying above deck?"

"Of course not, the stubborn oaf." Langford yanked a small vial of clear liquid from his pocket. "If you'd give him this tonic the first chance you get, he might actually take it from you. I brewed it for him, and naturally, he insisted he was fine." He shook his head, dark hair hanging in his eyes. Thick with salt and sea mist.

Lark took the delicate bottle and tucked it in her pocket. "I'll see he takes it."

He nodded, staring out at the ocean.

Langford was always easy to be around. His presence had a way of soothing any worried edges. He deserved to be happy. If Alistair was who he wanted, skies help him, there had to be a way. She could lock them both below deck until they emerged victorious in their hearts' desires.

Though that seemed problematic.

"You're all right then?" Langford's voice cut through her thoughts. His blue-grey gaze, thorough in his assessment.

Gavriel and Daciana hadn't been the only ones to notice her inner turmoil. "I am."

"So, Gavriel's trouser snake does have magic healing properties?"

"Langford!" Lark smacked his chest. "You're lucky I don't pitch you over the side for such a remark."

He grinned. "I'm merely pleased there's a man eager to sate you, *wife*."

Lark's cheeks burned even as she laughed. "If you must know, *husband*, nothing happened last night. So, I'd appreciate a moratorium on this conversation."

"Fine then, keep your secrets. But when things do progress, you'll tell me?"

Lark cringed. "Lecher?"

Langford snorted a laugh. "Hardly, but unless you want a mini Gavriel running around, you'll need one of my brews."

Lark shuddered. The thought of being responsible for a child sent a whole different sort of panic climbing up her throat. "I don't want that."

"As I thought. I'll mix something up for you. It will taste unpleasant, but at least you can rest assured your activities won't yield new members to our little crew."

Lark was beginning to rethink jumping overboard. "Please talk about the Shrine."

Langford's face transformed into eagerness. Ever the scholar, ready to share his findings. "What do you wish to know?"

Lark gripped the rail. "Everything."

LARK CATALOGED everything Langford told her over and over as she made her trek back to her room.

Despite the danger, she had to do this.

There was a chance Ferryn might have information Leysa had been unable or unwilling to share. But selfishly, Lark needed to see him. To know he was all right. Or as much as one can be, living in Lacuna.

Not living.

Existing.

But there was still so much they didn't know about the Shrine. After delivering the tonic to Hugo—who was rather green in the face and grunted a quick thanks before slamming the door—Lark meandered back to her quarters. What would Ferryn say when she finally found him again? Would he be angry with her? Would he even be Ferryn anymore?

He'd sworn the oath to Thanar before his banishment. How much of him was even left? Thanar could have wiped his soul blank before sending him off to his purgatory.

Even as she thought it, something about it didn't feel right. How much of a punishment would Lacuna be if Ferryn was no more? Thanar would want him to suffer if he thought he had anything to do with her escape. As much as that hurt, there was comfort to be found in that truth.

A STEADY POUNDING at her door jolted Lark from the book she'd been reading. With flaming cheeks, she tucked it away. There was nothing shameful about raiding Captain Ingemar's library. But this particular volume was one of more *carnal* energy. She'd have to wait until later to discover what happened next.

Well, she knew what would happen next—

"Open the door before this madman kills me!"

"Alistair?" Lark stood and crossed the room, unlocking and yanking open the door. "What are you talking about?"

The sound of stomping down the corridor had Alistair leaping past her. He grabbed her by the shoulders and swung her around to use as a shield.

Gavriel filled the doorway with his impressive form. Lark smothered the way her blood hummed in his presence. The book she'd been reading didn't help.

"You can't hide behind her. Get out here now."

"What did you do, Alistair?" Lark asked, shrugging out of his hold.

Alistair took a step back, fumbling with the lapels of his jacket. "I may have asked our favorite assassin to seduce the fair Captain."

"You said distract," Gavriel hissed.

"Right, right." Alistair waved him off. "I might have let it slip he was interested in her treasure trove."

"Ugh." That made the list of terms Lark never wanted to hear again in reference to private bits. Part of her wished she could have seen the exchange if only to witness how Gavriel managed to sidestep Ingemar's advances without insulting the woman.

He did sidestep them, didn't he?

"But it was for good reason that I needed the Captain indisposed," Alistair said.

"What was the distraction for?" Did it really matter? No, but Lark failed to quell her curiosity.

Alistair had the good sense to appear sheepish. "Yes, well, let us regard that as private personal business..."

"Alistair..." He'd caused enough trouble as it was. He hardly deserved the courtesy of privacy.

"We played cards last night, and I lost something of value and wanted it back."

Lark should have expected something like that. But what would warrant a secret retrieval mission? Alistair wasn't sentimental about items.

"You sent me to distract her while you stole something you rightfully lost?" Gavriel's voice had gone dangerously low. "That is not what we discussed."

"Semantics," Alistair said with a wave of his hand. "I'll take care of it," he added when he caught sight of Gavriel's murderous expression.

"That will be difficult to manage if you're a dead man."

Despite how alluring it was to watch them go hand to hand, Lark had no intention of letting this issue progress. "Get out, Alistair."

Alistair raised an eyebrow. "Are you going to spank him?"

"Out!" Gavriel grabbed him by the collar and shoved him toward the door. Alistair laughed as he was tossed into the hallway. Gavriel slammed the door and turned to face her. "You have to believe me. I had no idea she would proposition me so *forcefully*."

"I wouldn't underestimate the captain. If Alistair put you up to it, I'd wager she could smell his plan a mile away." Lark crossed her arms, needing to do something with her body. "So, how did it go down?" She attempted to sound casual, but by the look on his face, she'd failed.

"Are you asking me if I let it go too far?"

Damn her mortal heart and the way it thumped in her chest. "What's 'too far' to you?"

Something softened in his expression. "The minute her intentions were clear, I put a stop to it."

Lark hated her foolish human reactions. How much her chest swelled and lifted at his response. "You failed Alistair's little mission then?"

"I don't give a fuck." The low timbre of his voice sent a thrill through her nerves.

Lark exhaled a shaky breath. "Depending on how *forceful* she was, I'm sure she knew what you were up to. Likely, she wanted to put you on the spot to see if you'd crack."

A small smile played on his mouth, though the tension remained. "It couldn't possibly be my charm?"

"Of course, not."

Gavriel canted his head to the side. "You don't find me charming?"

A rush of nervous energy coiled in her chest. "No, as a matter of fact, I don't."

His soft smile shifted into something else altogether. "Oh?" His eyes burned into her as he approached. "I find that hard to believe."

Lark stood her ground but shifted her weight from one foot to the other under his stare. He tracked the movement.

"That's because you're an ass." She cursed how breathless she sounded.

He invaded her space, running his thumb along her jaw. His distinct scent enveloped her and made her head spin. "That may be so"—his breath ghosted against her lips—"but you didn't seem to mind last night."

Lark scoffed. "You're the one who stopped it."

A ferocious hunger burned in his eyes; his fingers curled against her jaw, holding her in place. "Tell me what you want."

She was liquid fire. Entranced by the way he held her at the precipice. She wet her lips, letting the fire smolder in her veins. "Would you have me beg?"

The sinful way his mouth curved made standing difficult. "For starters," he said, and the words sank beneath her skin. "Lark, what do you need?"

She searched his face. Raw need, vicious hunger, and a tinge of fear. A naked vulnerability. She ran her thumb over his scarred mouth. "You... everything."

He kissed her, fisting his hand in her hair. His mouth turned brutal against hers in its pursuit to taste and devour. Backing her against the wall, he pressed his hips into her. The contact seared like a brand.

Lark yanked at his black tunic, and his answering chuckle slithered through her. He helped her lift it over his head, tossing it to the floor. She ran her hands down his firm chest, wanting to touch, to explore, to savor.

Bending his head, Gavriel tried to claim her mouth once more, but she held out a hand. "Allow me this," she said, echoing his words from the night before. She resumed tracing his chest, his shoulders, his stomach. Her fingers running over corded muscle and scar tissue.

"You test my patience," Gavriel said in a tight voice.

Lark hummed, placing a soft kiss on an old wound on his shoulder, and he inhaled a sharp breath. She moved to his collarbone where another faded scar received a feather-light kiss. She pressed her lips to each old hurt.

He'd seen a lifetime of bloodshed. She marveled at what he'd survived—this bright and beautiful soul she craved. This burning beacon of light she'd managed to find in the darkness. That always called to her. Even back when the only marks she bore were on her soul.

She needed to acknowledge every hurt that failed to keep them apart.

Lark kissed her way down, lowering into a crouch and pressing her mouth against a jagged scar along his hip bone.

Gavriel grabbed her wrists and yanked her up to him. Tucking a strand of hair behind her ear, he pressed his lips to hers, gentle at first. But it gave way to something heated and primal. Slotting his thigh between hers, he pressed against her, eliciting a soft cry. He lifted her, and she wrapped her legs around his waist.

Gavriel yanked all the covers off her narrow bed and onto the floor. "I don't trust the bed to withstand this," he said with a sheepish grin.

Heat flooded Lark's body at his words.

Gavriel laid her onto the cushion of blankets. His movements were slow and gentle as he tugged each of her boots off, his eyes never leaving hers. He took care with each motion as if trying to give her every chance to stop him.

But Lark had little patience left.

She yanked her tunic over her head, leaving her clad in only her breastband.

Gavriel stared at her, one of her boots still clasped in his hands. He surged forward, hands running over her stomach, over her sides, and up her back to where her breastband knotted. He tugged it away, leaving her chest exposed in the cool air.

"You're so beautiful," he murmured as he ran his hands over her. Her skin goose pebbled under his attention.

Lark squeezed her thighs together, seeking the friction he'd given her before. Gavriel glanced down at the movement, and with nimble fingers, untied her laces and yanked her leggings and smalls down her legs, tossing them over his shoulder.

She lay bare before him. Lark had never given thought to whether her form was pleasing or not.

Gavriel ran his gaze over her, unabashedly drinking in every inch. The predatory edge to his stare burned through her.

He must have found her pleasing.

"Skies," he whispered. "Where did you come from?"

Before Lark could remind him exactly what she was, he pressed hot, feverish kisses to her mouth.

He frowned at the scar on her chest. The arrow bolt from the slaver. Lark placed her hand over the scar, he didn't need to think about that right now.

Gavriel grasped her hands. "Don't," he said, staring down at her. He lowered his mouth to the spot and pressed an achingly gentle kiss to it. He found each of her scars and pressed his lips to them.

Lark squirmed, half delirious from the fire raging in her veins at every maddening touch. "Gavriel," she whimpered.

"I told you, I'd need to hear you beg."

Lark could hear the self-satisfaction in his voice, but he began kissing her neck and throat, working his way down. He lingered on her breasts. When she threaded her fingers into his hair and tugged impatiently, he huffed a laugh against her skin and resumed his exploration down.

When Gavriel settled between her thighs, he cast one more adoring look up at her. Waiting to catch her eye.

She looked down, heat washing over her face at the image.

His mouth descended on her, hot and greedy in his exploration. Lark gasped, as a sharp surge of pleasure speared through her. Overwhelming and humbling. Her hands fisted in his hair, and Gavriel grunted in approval as he resumed his unforgiving pace. She arched her back, unable to handle the way her muscles twitched, and her chest expanded. When he added his fingers she keened, crashing violently over the edge.

Gavriel worked her through it until she trembled and tugged at him to stop. He rose over her, caging her body as he smoothed the hair from her face.

Still dazed, Lark glanced up at him to find him gazing back. Her heart clenched in her chest, and she brought his mouth to hers, tasting herself in their kiss. She dipped her fingers beneath the waist of his pants and closed her hand around him.

Gavriel hissed a sharp breath, his eyes flashing dangerously. "Demon."

Lark ran her fingers along him steadily until he pulled her hand away and sat up. She tugged at his laces.

He batted her hands away and unlaced them with expert dexterity. He kicked off his boots and yanked his pants off, tossing them into the corner. She followed the trajectory, realizing each article of clothing landed in opposite corners of the room. If they needed to dress quickly, it would be a scavenger hunt.

He knelt between her thighs and studied her with such intensity.

If only she possessed the words to tell him how she felt. How her heart could feel both full and fractured by this moment. This was what she always wanted. She was here, this was real. He was real. The way her mortal body stretched to contain her anticipation and joy damn near hurt. Her emotions were too big. Too bright. Like trying to stare into the sun.

Lark pressed her lips to his and poured everything into that kiss.

Gavriel slowly filled her, watching for the first sign of discomfort. He must have remembered her question, that day in the rain, and what it meant. Lark's heart leapt into her throat. The last time she tried this, she was a Reaper. But she was human now as every nerve flared to life under Gavriel's touch. He sank deeper, his brow furrowed as if in pain.

Lark clung to him as he stretched her. The slight burn mingled with desperate pleasure the deeper he went.

This was real. This was life.

Gavriel plunged into her completely, and she tossed her head back against the floor. The dizzying effect filled every corner of her soul. It was overwhelming, beautifully vicious in the rightness of their joining.

Lark cried out, bringing a hand to cover her mouth.

Gavriel snatched it away. "No." His voice, hoarse and pleading. "Let me hear you."

Lark's skin felt too tight to contain her as if she'd somehow outgrown her shape. She gripped Gavriel's hips, anchoring herself.

Each movement deep within dragged a cry from her lips. It tugged at something she couldn't name. She gripped him tighter, unable to voice what she needed.

"Gavriel," she sobbed.

His fingers found the bundle of nerves that sent stars exploding in her vision. She keened, and her release crashed over her. He set a punishing pace as she crested and he chased his end.

Lark slid her hands down Gavriel's back, along his spine and sweat slicked skin. Gripping him tightly as he filled and stretched with each thrust. When she started to shake, Gavriel lifted her hips and stilled, an aching rush as he found his release. His eyes claimed hers, and in the final seconds, Lark swore she saw fear. The all-consuming fear of wanting. But in an instant it vanished, and his face softened with affection.

He collapsed beside her, sweaty and panting through his boyish grin. Lark curled toward him, and he tugged her closer—she fit against his side as if she was always meant to.

"How did I find you?" He asked, voice soft with wonder.

She stared into those dark green eyes that glimmered with gold in the right light. The ones she'd imagined each day and night since the first time she saw him, pacing the room where Emric was fading. "I found you," she huffed with a small smile.

He kissed the top of her head.

Her heavy limbs draped around him as the pull of sleep beckoned. It tumbled her under its hypnotic embrace. Only this time, Gavriel tumbled with her.

CHAPTER 47

*L*ark's eyes fluttered open. She stretched, smiling. The slight burn between her thighs was a welcome reminder of the music their bodies had made.

Gavriel.

Memories of heated kisses, of plummeting over the edge, lit a fire deep in her belly. She made a quiet noise of contentment, rolling toward him. Gavriel's eyes were still held shut by the throes of sleep. He'd rolled away from her in the night. Flat on his back, he tensed and twitched. He shook his head back and forth, teeth clenched as he grunted in his sleep.

"Gavriel," Lark whispered, afraid to startle him but unable to leave him at the mercy of his dream. "Gavriel, wake up." She touched her hand to his forehead, and his skin was clammy beneath her palm.

He shot awake and grasped her wrist tight enough to bruise, wrenching a cry from her lips. Gavriel rolled on top of her, trapping her beneath him. He glared down at her, gripping her wrist in one of his hands, the other squeezing her throat.

She gasped for air, and her heartbeat thrashed in her ears. Clawing at the hand on her throat, she dug her nails into his skin.

Gavriel's eyes cleared and his glare morphed into panic. He

released her throat and tossed her wrist as if it burned. Wonderful air filled her lungs.

"Skies, Lark!" Gavriel leapt off her. "I'm so sorry."

Lark's chest heaved, and her mind quieted its dizzying assault. She rolled toward him, keeping her hands safely in view. "It's all right."

He edged further away; his brows furrowed over widened eyes. His body was rigid. Tensed as if ready to flee at any moment.

"Gavriel, please." Slowly, Lark inched closer. Careful not to alarm him with quick movements.

His eyes widened anyway. "Did I hurt you?"

"No," she swore, shaking her head. "You didn't hurt me." She reached a tentative hand to cup his jaw.

Gavriel froze, his mouth fell open as if he would speak. But instead, he melded into the touch and swept her into his arms. His warm, distinct scent enveloped her and restored the tranquility of her mood.

They all had suffered. Had awoken from terrors with no sense of what was real. She would not shy away from Gavriel.

Lark kissed him, soft and questioning. An invitation. He stilled, letting her gentle exploration of his mouth go uninterrupted. When she ran her tongue over the scar bisecting his lip, he groaned and engulfed her mouth in a deeper kiss. He rolled on top of her. But that wasn't what she wanted this time. She gave a firm push against his chest. Gavriel stared down at her, questioningly. His eyes held an echo of fear. If he didn't trust himself with her, Lark would show him how much she trusted him.

She hitched a leg around his calf and spun him to land on his back with a soft huff of breath. Straddling his hips, she rose over him.

"Do you intend to have your way with me?" Gavriel's mouth curved. He seemed to relax as he tucked his arm behind his head. "Do your worst."

"Don't challenge me, mortal."

His grin only widened.

Lark scooted down and without warning took him into her mouth.

501

He hissed, hands fisting the sheets. His head fell back, and he bit down on his lip.

Lark was familiar with the mechanics of using her mouth on a man, but theory and practice were two very different animals. It was a bit awkward at first but judging by the deep sounds she pulled from his chest, he took pleasure from her attention. Her jaw began to tire, but her body hummed with warmth. It was intoxicating, this level of trust. She cast a glance up to see his cheeks flushed and his expression tight, like he was trying to hold onto that last shred of control. But she wanted him undone and holding nothing back.

The passion humans were capable of was both thrilling and humbling.

When Gavriel caught her stare, his eyes flashed dangerously. He grabbed her wrists and yanked her up to him. She went willingly, her mouth crashing against his. Before he could get any ideas about flipping their positions, she rose over him, shoving his shoulder hard enough to flop him back into the blankets.

Lining him up with her entrance, she gave him one last glance. One last instant for their eyes to meet and for her to pour every word she couldn't breathe into the air between them. Before she sank onto him.

Gavriel's grip on her hips was desperate. Lark moved slowly, unsure of the rhythm and following instinct alone. She reveled in every noise she drew from him as she set a languid pace. Like they had all the time in the world to explore the depths of their needs.

In his arms, there was no death, no darkness, no destruction waiting for her. Only this moment. This bright, burning light he filled her with. And for the longest and shortest of moments in a mortal's life, they were lost in each other.

ALISTAIR TOSSED his head back and groaned, almost falling off his log. "Are we almost there? I don't know how much more I can take."

The rest of the group ignored him, tucking into their meager dinners as dusk embraced the camp.

Ever since they'd docked at the port south of the Bereft coast, things had been tense. The trek to the Forbidden Highlands was taking longer than anticipated. They'd managed to stock up on supplies in a small coastal village outside Koval's capital. But there was only so much coin left after paying for return passage aboard Ingemar's ship. Captain Ingemar had several more trips to make and ports to stop in which gave them over a month before they needed to meet at the docks.

The wind whistled through the camp, rattling the tents. The fire rebelled against the onslaught, and embers shot in every direction. Lark shivered, and licked her plate clean. They'd been running low on rations and had to cut down servings. It didn't help that the deeper they trekked into the Highlands, the scarcer the wildlife. Perhaps it was the extreme temperatures. Days brought sweltering heat where Lark was certain her blood was roiling beneath her skin, and nightfall swept fierce winds through the trees.

But the silence of a forest without birds felt like a warning.

Lark lowered her plate, staring down at it in dismay. A large potato-wielding hand crept into her periphery, depositing it onto her plate. Lark caught Hugo retreating to his side of the fire. She opened her mouth to protest when he gave her a resolute shake of his head with a stalwart frown. There was no point in arguing, especially when her stomach gurgled in response.

"I have informed you of this already, likely ten times each day." Langford's smooth voice cut in. "When we see the stones marked with this symbol—" He held up his notebook for the thousandth time to pan over the group. Langford's elegant sketch of a crescent moon on its side, woven with an intricate knot, glared at them. "I'll be able to decipher the remaining distance." He slammed his notebook down with a resolute thud.

Alistair narrowed his eyes. His expression lacked his usual ease of nature. "You're grouchy."

"I'm not grouchy." Langford didn't bother meeting his gaze. Instead, he peered absently at his notebooks.

"You are, and it's bringing down group morale. Right?" Alistair glanced around.

Lark had crammed her mouth with the potato Hugo gave her and managed an unintelligible sound in response. She chewed rapidly, eager to come to Langford's defense.

"You're the only one complaining," Gavriel said before glancing over at Lark and smiling.

Things seemed unnaturally tense between Alistair and Langford. Different from before. The good-natured ribbing always held an undercurrent of something more. But lately, Langford met Alistair's quips with open hostility. Had something happened on Ingemar's ship? Lark had been preoccupied for the duration of the journey and hadn't the faintest idea what the rest of her companions had been up to.

Gavriel rested a warm hand against her lower back. Flushing, she glanced over at him. He wore a predatory grin, as if he too was thinking of how preoccupied they'd been on the ship.

"Don't start with that," Alistair called from across the fire, pointing at Lark and Gavriel. "It was jolly good fun to listen at your door—"

"Excuse me?" Lark could kill him. It would save rations.

"—but I am not going to lose sleep tonight because Gavriel shrieks like a girl when he climaxes."

Gavriel raised a brow before he glanced down at Lark. "Perhaps he requires a demonstration?"

Hugo cleared his throat, visibly uncomfortable with the conversation.

Lark took pity on him, changing the subject. "Alistair, did you ever manage to retrieve what you lost?" He hadn't told her what it was, or if he'd been successful in his mission while Gavriel distracted Ingemar.

"I did." Alistair's gaze darted to where Langford stared dutifully down at his notes.

Lark caught the action and the tension that rippled between them. "What was it exactly?"

Alistair frowned; his hands twitched by his sides. "It was nothing."

Langford stiffened.

Daciana caught Lark's eye. She frowned and gave a short shrug.

One thing was for certain, the sooner they got to the Forbidden Shrine, the better.

"THERE'S ANOTHER ONE HERE, we must be getting close." Langford ran a tentative hand over the smooth stone, avoiding the knotted crescent moon etched into the surface. The narrow path was packed with dirt and pebbles. It carved its way over large grey slabs of glistening rock and weedy slopes. They'd been traveling for miles since the first symbol had appeared and each time they found another one, with their destination nowhere in sight, it felt like a sick joke. Taunting and mocking.

Lark's belly growled with hunger. They were all hungry.

Her boot snagged on a root, and she hurtled forward. Hugo caught her before she could hit the ground.

Lark smoothed out her clothes and glanced up at Hugo. "Thanks. What would I do without you?"

"Watch your feet when you walk," he grumbled. "Especially on uneven terrain."

If Hugo didn't insist on piling her plates with his meager rations, maybe he wouldn't be so agitated.

"You know, I cherish these heartwarming chats," Lark said.

"You spend too much time with Alistair."

The sky was a feud between cloud and sun. Fleeting light pushed through the gloom and sent minerals in the crags sparkling before cover won out and shrouded them in grey once more. Lark eased over the slick rock face. The landscape was littered with giant stones. Slabs of minerals jutted from the ground at awkward angles as if trying to halt their approach.

Lark wiped the sweat from her brow and pushed down the feeling of unease. They should heed the land's warning.

Daciana passed her a waterskin. Lark tipped it in her mouth just enough to wet her tongue before handing it right back to her. She wasn't sure when they'd find freshwater again, they couldn't afford to run out.

"It's here!" Langford cried, peering at his notebook as he pointed.

An array of boulders blocked the path. Lark stood on tiptoes to see around the obstruction. Glittering limestone led the way to the mouth of a cave. But it wasn't like any cave Lark had ever seen. An etched archway bearing the crescent moon on its side framed the opening, and a jagged staircase led the way up.

"Basalt columns," Langford said in awe. "But what are these doing here?"

A sense of wrongness flooded Lark, urging her to turn back. There was a reason this place wasn't drawn on the maps of mortals. Why it took Langford translating Inerys' ancient text to find it. Lark rubbed her arm to ward off the chill that gripped her.

Daciana fixed her with a knowing stare. "You feel it too?"

Lark nodded. Her blood pounded in her veins. They should turn back. They should leave. Her soul beseeched her body to listen.

But there was no way in the abyss she was leaving without seeing Ferryn.

Gavriel edged toward her, placing a hand on her arm. "What's wrong?"

"You can't feel it?"

He frowned. "No."

Lark turned to Hugo. He gave a short shake of his head.

"If anyone says the words, 'I got a bad feeling about this,' I'm betting everything in my pocket we're immediately ambushed," Alistair said.

"I wouldn't worry," Langford called to her, ignoring Alistair. Though his expression remained dubious. "It's probably ancient wards to fend off travelers. Likely the magic has weakened over time, so you and Daciana are the only ones sensitive to it." Though his voice remained confident, his face was shadowed in doubt.

They continued up to the strange archway. There was no door, just gaping blackness that seemed to devour the light.

Before Lark could change her mind, she stepped into the darkness.

PINS AND NEEDLES pricked her skin—skin that felt too tight. Stretched, and ripping at the seams. Gradually, the tingling dissipated, and a cool air enveloped her. Ancient warding magic. Lark had no desire to ever step through a warded door again.

She sucked in a deep breath as the smothering feeling lifted away. Glancing back, she searched for the others—

—there was only stone. As if the entrance she'd just come from had been swallowed by the cave. She pressed her hands against the cool, rough surface. It didn't budge. Had it closed behind her? Why hadn't she heard it?

Lark willed the panic to remain at bay. She couldn't dwell here. There was nowhere to go but deeper into the earth, and there was still the matter of finding the power hidden in the Shrine to reach Ferryn.

The only path was a simple tunnel. It glittered with hundreds of glowing minerals. Like the cave had swallowed the night sky.

Again, she listened for the others.

But the stone remained silent.

Lark pulled her bow from her back and nocked an arrow; for what, she wasn't sure. But she gripped her bow, running her thumb over smooth ash wood.

In the distance, a light flickered across the cavernous wall. Lark dropped into a crouch and tried to move with the same silence Gavriel commanded. The way he could sneak up on her, even in the forest.

A single bead of sweat trickled down the side of her face.

All at once, the air flattened, and the light evaporated. Lark froze.

Slowly, she pulled the arrow. The groan of the string was harsh against the thick silence.

She swallowed down the terror that climbed up her throat and crept forward. Her arm trembled against the weight of the pull.

She could loosen her hold, but fear is a funny thing, and holding her bow taut felt necessary.

A flash of light flooded the cave, blinding her.

Lark tripped over the uneven floor and landed hard on her side, rattling a few teeth. The clatter of her arrow against the stone reverberated off the walls. With a groan, she sat up and braced her hand on the floor of the cave—which was smooth to the touch.

It wasn't rough stone, but polished marble.

Lark blinked, and as her eyes adjusted, dread settled in the pit of her stomach.

This wasn't the cave.

Golden archways lined the side chambers in designated vestibules, and cathedral ceilings loomed above. Lark squinted against the harsh glow she now knew could never rival true sunlight.

It wasn't possible.

She was in a very familiar throne room, a place she hoped she'd never see again. A place she traded everything to escape.

Lounging on the throne upon the dais, black hair hanging in his dark eyes, was Thanar.

His angular face twisted in wicked amusement, lips parting to reveal white teeth.

"Larkin. At last, you've returned."

CHAPTER 48

*I*t couldn't be real.

Panic flooded Lark's body, and she shook her head in disbelief. She couldn't be in the Otherworld. Scraping her nails against the smooth marble of Thanar's throne room, she tried to blink away the image. It had to be an illusion. It had to. But no matter how hard she tried to expel the vision of ivory and gold, she remained on the floor of her former prison.

"You seem confused," Thanar said. The sharp edges of his face had smoothed in amusement. "You shouldn't be. You knew you'd always end up here."

"Where is here exactly?" Lark clenched her fists as rage and terror battled for dominance.

Thanar chuckled and rose to his feet, his black robes billowing behind him. "You had to have known, I'd never let you leave that easily."

"You didn't *let* me do anything. I escaped." The pounding in Lark's head intensified.

"Did you?" Thanar cocked his head at an angle, a predatory movement. "That doesn't sound quite right, does it, Larkin?"

The fire in her blood cooled, ice taking root in her veins. Panic fluttered in her chest, and she tried to shut out his lies. She had escaped. She had lived as a mortal. Everything was real.

"I've lived, Thanar." Lark spit his name like a curse. Never before had she addressed him by name. A brief, dizzying excitement shot through her. "My life is no longer yours to influence. You can't keep me here."

"Your life?" Thanar towered over her. He peered down over the sharp slope of his nose. "Why Larkin, did it ever occur to you that your life was a trick of fate? That every decision you've made, every experience you've gathered, was someone else's influence? Even that mortal you're so fond of, nothing more than a memory of a pretty face I plucked from your mind?" He smiled fondly and tucked a strand of hair behind her ear. "You don't remember swearing me the oath?"

Stricken, Lark stepped back. Away from his touch. "That never happened." Her voice was a breathless whisper.

"When I seeped into your mind and tore away that precious wall of yours, did you ever truly expel me?" His mouth curved, deepening the shadows on his face. "Or did I plant that little thought?"

The memory of that day flooded Lark's mind. Of bracing against the pain as he invaded her soul and forced his influence in. Of crying out on her hands and knees as he shredded through her awareness. How hard she tried to force him out, days spent by her window fighting the impulse to allow his power to weave through her soul.

Had he truly won?

No.

It couldn't be. She'd fought hard to get to the mortal world. Dragged herself free of that giant yew tree. She'd lived; felt cold, and fear, and pain; she'd felt warmth and tasted food and drink and Gavriel's mouth and—

"That's impossible."

"Oh Larkin, you of all people should know impossible is a word the mortals use to feel like they have control." He leveled her with a dark stare. "When you know they don't."

Lark's stomach roiled, and her knees shook. She'd faced too much.

Felt too much for this to be her reality. She'd seen skies Thanar could never recreate. She had people she loved, people who counted on her.

"I don't believe you."

Thanar raised a dark brow as he smirked. "You're lying. I can taste your fear. Your doubt." He circled her with his hands tucked behind his back. "Let's test your theory. It's your word against mine." He regarded her with that predatory stare. "Sit down."

Lark's body slammed to the floor before her mind could catch up. This couldn't be real. This couldn't be happening.

"Lie back."

Her head crashed against marble; her hair fanned around her face. "No," she gritted out between clenched teeth.

Thanar stretched his long body beside her, resting his elbow on his knee. "Kiss me," he whispered. His voice was soft. Tender even.

Lark shook her head, fighting every instinct in her body to submit. To obey without question. She didn't swear the oath. She didn't. There was no reason for his will to dominate her so. Sweat beaded along her forehead and trickled into her hairline. Her muscles trembled.

"Kiss me," he repeated with a sharp edge to his voice.

The pressure mounted in Lark's head, threatening to explode. Her teeth sank into her lip, fighting against the impulse to submit. Her blood burned through her, screaming at her to comply. She squeezed her eyes shut; a tear pushed its way down her temple.

She had torn her human skin on that yew tree, felt the warmth of her blood stuck to her skin. Daciana had clothed her, saved her, befriended her. Hugo had pushed her, challenged her, and trained her. And Gavriel.

Gavriel had mapped every line of her body. Her mortal form responded to his in a way Thanar could never craft.

She was real.

And she would not submit.

An inhuman noise ripped from Lark's lips as something snapped. A cleaving of her soul from something that tried to claw its way in.

The pressure dissipated, and Thanar vanished as if he never was.

A laden silence filled Lark's ears and wrapped around her as once again, darkness returned.

CHAPTER 49

*C*hest heaving, Lark scanned the darkness, afraid Thanar would reappear at any moment.

She cursed her mortal eyes for taking so long to adjust. Gradually, the faint glow of bright minerals that painted the cave came into view.

Lark ran trembling fingers through her hair, pushing it from her sweaty forehead. The lingering echo of terror pounding in her chest lessened with each pulse, quietly pushing its way out of her system.

Langford had mentioned something about a trial, a test of will. Was that hers?

She scrambled to her feet and snatched her bow off the ground. She readied her stance, bracing herself against whatever should happen next.

At the farthest side of the rounded cavern, another tunnel opened up, leading deeper into the stone. Shouldering her bow, she yanked her knife from her boot. Easier for cramped quarters. Though she doubted any enemy attack would be hand-to-hand combat. No, this was an attack on her mind.

The last residual tremor left her body. She pushed away thoughts of Thanar and focused on the task at hand: find her way to the heart of the Forbidden Shrine, contact Ferryn, and figure out how to escape.

She only hoped the others were all right.

Lark crept up to the path, running her hand along the rough surface of the stone. The solid touch anchored her. The vision of Thanar in the Grand Hall had been just that; a vision. With renewed determination, she pushed her way forward. Deeper into the fissure.

The tunnel narrowed, pressing in on her, and panic clawed at her throat. Each breath shortened as the walls scraped against her shoulders. She turned to the side and edged her way along. One foot in front of the other. Slowly, the cramped space began to widen. When the walls no longer grazed her shoulders, Lark exhaled a sigh of relief.

She couldn't imagine Alistair or Gavriel fitting through that tight space. Definitely not Hugo. The thought of them trapped in this skies-forsaken cave... Lark shuddered.

At the end of the tunnel, Lark came upon a door, fashioned deep into the stone, with a simple iron ring handle. Bright light seeped through the cracks from beyond.

Lark grasped the cool iron ring, swung the door open, and shielded her eyes against the brightness. After becoming accustomed to the dark, the light was a sharp assault on her senses.

Lark blinked as her eyes adjusted to the sun-soaked room. Underground, deep in a tunnel burrowed into a mountainside—the sun couldn't reach her. And yet, daylight reflected off walls of glittering crystal, dancing in a glimmering spectrum of color—a spectrum Lark had only seen when rain and sun held union in the sky.

In the center of the room stood a figure donning a shroud of the purest white. Their face was obscured by a silver trimmed hood. Delicate hands reached up to lower the cloak, revealing a woman so beautiful, she was searing to look at. Her skin was of a rich tone, deep brown and full of light, a single sunburst tattoo glowed in the middle of her forehead. Her black hair sparkled with a thousand stars and her large green eyes held the depths of a thousand lifetimes. And the regret.

"Who are you?" Lark couldn't be certain this wasn't another vision.

"I have been called many names. None that would hold any meaning for you, child." Her voice was soft chimes, soprano melodies whispering in the wind.

"What shall I call you then?" Lark thumbed the knife in her hand, unsure if she'd need it.

"Solana will do just fine," she said with a smile that could thaw a glacier.

Lark glanced around the room, seeking every exit and every item that might come in handy as a weapon. But there was nothing. In the large gold and crystal room, there were no doors save for the one she entered. No windows. No furniture. Nothing.

But this being.

Solana must be the source of light. Somehow.

"Forgive me, Solana"—Lark gestured with her knife, waving it around as she spoke—"but I don't suppose you'd tell me if you were going to attack me, or if I'll be needing this."

Solana chuckled, regarding her with a warm expression. "No, child. No harm shall come to you. Not here anyway."

Careful wording always put Lark on edge, but she stashed her knife in her boot. "So, you're the heart of the Forbidden Shrine? I don't think that was mentioned in the book." Langford would have told her as much. He'd never miss a detail like this.

"You can't believe everything you read," Solana said softly. "Or in some cases see, hear, feel... think."

"What is this place?"

Solana's elegant brows furrowed as if she was displeased by the question. "This is the home of both nightmares and deepest desires. The place where fears are made flesh and wishes are chains. Only the strongest of will have made it this far." She raised her chin as fire danced in her eyes. "And those who are lost... their energy feeds this place."

Lark's mouth went dry. "What do you mean?"

"The dreamers—those souls held enthralled in their minds—their lives are the price for the ancient magic of this place."

Those who couldn't break free of their visions would die to fuel the horrors of the Shrine. Though Solana said something about deepest desires...

"You have made it farther than any have in so long," Solana said. "You will be granted one wish. No more, no less."

Lark blinked. That was not what Langford had told her. He said she could harness a power beyond mortal reach. Was Solana that power?

Blasted damnation.

If the others were trapped in nightmares, how long did they have to escape before the Shrine claimed them? Lark ran a hand through her hair, cursing the cave for walling her in without Langford.

Solana watched her with all the patience of an ancient being.

"Why are you here?" Lark asked, not sure why it mattered.

"It is my punishment."

Lark didn't like the sound of that. She needed to ask questions that would yield specific answers. "Who punished you?"

Solana angled her head. "My former master. Sargon."

Lark's jaw dropped so fast she was sure she pulled a muscle. "The bastard who runs Avalon?"

Solana's expression remained unchanged. "I do not adhere to the principles of Avalon. I mourned the souls who never made it to paradise and made it my mission to find some way to create a small oasis in the Netherworld."

"You created the circle of the Netherworld for souls unjustly punished." Solana had betrayed the highest god of Avalon, the master of them all. She forged a path in selfless pursuit. Leysa had told Lark of the being who defied the laws of the heavens. The one whose name Sargon erased as punishment for creating another path to peace. Arcadia. The bright light of the Netherworld, and the only hope for mortals who fail to make it to Avalon. "You're the mother of Arcadia."

Solana frowned. "I only meant to bring light to the darkness. Suffering in life shouldn't be rewarded with more suffering in death." She glanced away, her expression unreadable. "When my actions were called into question before Sargon, I was given a choice. Destroy Arcadia or remain here until I change my mind."

"And you chose to remain here, granting wishes rather than destroy Arcadia?"

"What would you have done?"

Lark bit the inside of her cheek. A few months ago, perhaps she would have done the same. But now? She would have fought. Brought down all of Avalon if she had to.

"You look lost," Solana said, watching her. "What did you come here hoping to find?"

Redemption. Hope. Ferryn. It mattered little. Fate was determined to block Lark's path at every turn. Lark knew what she had to do, even as her stomach turned to lead. She lifted her chin. "I know what my wish is."

Solana raised her eyebrows, nodding once for Lark to continue.

"I wish for your freedom."

Solana stilled, the action so like Thanar it ghosted a chill up Lark's spine.

"My freedom?"

Lark nodded. She would find another way to save Ferryn. "I wish for you to be free. Free from this place, free from Avalon. Free to do whatever you desire." It was the least she could do for the Mother of Arcadia. "Could you make it impossible to enter this cave once my friends and I depart?"

Solana shook her head, face still frozen in shock. "The magic of this place is very old. I lack the power to dismantle it."

Disappointment curled in Lark's chest. It was worth a shot. "Fine, then just your freedom."

Solana swept up to her, her skirts billowing in her wake. "Is that truly your wish, mortal?" Her voice held an edge of desperation. Of hope. "Because you have to be sure."

Lark nodded. She was sure. Even as her hope of seeing Ferryn again grew heavy, she was sure. "Yes. That's my wish."

The stone around them groaned, the sound a lament of mourning. Lark braced herself, unsure what to prepare herself for. Another vision? The cave collapsing?

A low rumble shook the floor, reverberating through her body. It didn't feel violent, it felt disappointed.

When the room stilled, and only glorious silence remained, Solana's face broke into a radiant smile. Like the sun rising over the horizon and bathing the valley in gold. "What is your name?"

"Lark." Perhaps freeing Solana would earn her some goodwill with Nereida. The witch seemed sympathetic to the plight of mortals, more than Thanar ever was.

Solana clasped Lark's hands. "Thank you, Lark." She regarded her with a thoughtful expression. "What would your wish have been?"

There was no harm in telling her now. "I wanted to free my friend. Or at least find him so I could figure out a way to free him."

"Where is he?"

"Lacuna." Where he couldn't feel, or taste, or smell. Where he was nothing more than a ghost watching the world pass without him. Where no one would ever know the sound of his laugh. Solana spoke of the worst sort of punishment—Lacuna was it.

"I can't help with that." Solana wrung her hands.

Lark's heart sank. It shouldn't have come as a surprise. But they'd come all this way for nothing. Solana's powers must only work through wishes, and Lark used hers.

"I thought I could speak to him."

"You could contact him, but even I don't have the power to release souls from Lacuna."

Lark nodded. It was what she came for, if nothing else, then to see him once more. "I need to see him."

"Follow me." Solana led Lark to the side of the room.

With a flick of her wrist, a small door materialized. Solana tugged the door open and reached in. Gently, she pulled out a small, golden lantern. Simple in design but exquisite in quality. Like the very sun had been woven into the gold filigree. She held it out to Lark.

"This lantern will light the way to any world. You will be free to enter and leave. However many travel by lantern may leave by lantern. I'm sorry to say, you can't bring your friend back. At least not without condemning someone else to his fate."

Lark grasped the lantern. As soon as she touched the warm metal, magic sang in her veins. A sweet lilting song that ran like a current through her whole body. "How does it work?"

"Turn the key, and the flame will ignite. No pesky mortal laws of reality. It will illuminate the dark, show you what those mortal eyes can't see. Then visualize where you wish to go. The lantern will guide."

This was the artifact in Inerys' book. This was her way to Ferryn. "Thank you."

"Thank you," Solana whispered back, and her green eyes sparkled. "If you ever need a favor, or a friend"—she nodded down at the lantern—"use it."

The Mother of Arcadia was every bit as gracious as Leysa had said. "I will."

With one last radiant smile and a quick ruffle of Lark's hair, Solana stepped back. She turned to the wall and spread her arms wide. The stone tumbled away, revealing a bright path of gold. "I can't halt the magic that creates the nightmares, but I can give you an easy way out."

Before Lark could respond, light burst from Solana's skin. Lark shielded her eyes, and when the last rays of light dimmed from behind her hand, Lark lowered it to find she was alone again.

Without a moment to spare, Lark set the lantern on the floor and turned the key. A blue flame blazed in its chamber, flickering behind the glass. She closed her eyes, imagining Lacuna. The torture of losing the sense of touch, of taste, smell. To silently scream as life passed by and one was nothing but a figment of memory. Her heart clenched as she envisioned Ferryn. His long blond hair and piercing eyes. His impish expressions that softened his angular features. The warmth she could almost feel, even as a Reaper, whenever he embraced her.

Lark pushed deeper, searching for him. Calling to his soul like he was her tether. Beseeching his answer, so she might finally find him.

She lifted her head, sweat stinging her eyes.

She hadn't left.

Lark remained in this ridiculous room, gathering dust, while the others were likely still trying to find a way in, or worse—trapped in their visions. She should have waited to test it out with Langford. Disappointment ached in her chest at her failure.

"Damn it all to the fiery pits of the Netherworld." Lark reached over to turn the key and lower the flame.

"Could you wait to do that?"

The hum of a familiar voice broke something in her chest.

She whipped her head to see him, exactly as she remembered. His long blond hair hung loosely over his shoulders. His blue-green eyes sparkled with amusement as he lounged against the wall. Immaculate as always.

Ferryn.

He was here. He was here. By the skies, he was here.

CHAPTER 50

$\mathcal{L}$ark leapt into Ferryn's arms, a strangled cry ripping from her throat.

He squeezed her tight and pressed his cheek to the top of her head. "I expected your anger."

"I don't care. I am angry. Furious, actually. But I can't believe you're here." Lark pulled back to look at him. Ferryn was just as he was the last time she saw him across the crowded room as Thanar delivered her sentence. Time was a mortal construct Ferryn wasn't bound by. His sharp cheekbones still appeared crafted by the gods themselves. He even wore the same black hardened leathers and boots. Lark tried not to glance down at her road-worn clothing. "You haven't changed a bit."

He caught a strand of her hair and held it between his fingers. "It's darker. I like it." He studied her face. "You look…"

"I know, I know. Nereida warned me of the species discrepancy. I'm not nearly as beautiful as you are."

He shook his head. "No, I was going to say you look happy."

"Of course, I'm happy. You're here, you're—" Her unbridled joy dimmed as reality sank in. It was a miracle he hadn't been driven mad by now, trapped in Lacuna. How could he take the fall for her actions?

Lark punched him in the arm, expecting to see his usual flair for dramatics whenever she hit him.

Ferryn didn't flinch. He made no move to indicate he felt it at all.

"Why did you confess to aiding me? You had nothing to do with my escape."

Ferryn's face was uncharacteristically somber. "Is that really why you went through all this trouble to find me?"

Lark bit the inside of her cheek. It was more than that, more than guilt. There was much at stake and she needed information about the Otherworld and the state of it all…

It was guilt. It was soul-crushing guilt. The selfishness of knowing she couldn't be happy until this burden was lifted.

Mortals really were despicable creatures, greedy in their feelings.

Ferryn's face softened. "It wasn't your fault. If you've come looking to right any of your wrongs, this isn't one of them." He braced a hand on her shoulder. "You can let it go."

"That's not the only reason."

He exhaled a long-suffering sigh and folded his arms across his chest. "Pray tell, what is so urgent you had to seek aid from a witch, travel across the sea, hike the Forbidden Highlands, traverse the Forbidden Shrine and surpass your inner demons just to find me?"

"How do you know all that?"

"Did you think I wouldn't keep a close eye on you?" A grin lit up Ferryn's face, almost reaching his eyes. "I'm dying to hear all about Gavriel."

Lark groaned. Somehow hearing Gavriel's name only sharpened her guilt. "Not now."

"If not now, then when?"

Lark ignored his question. "I had to make sure you were all right. When I left, I didn't think of how much my actions would affect you. And when I learned what had befallen you…" Thanar had to have selected Ferryn's punishment with her in mind.

Ferryn bent his head to meet her stare and ran his hands down her arms. "It's not so bad. I can keep tabs on you, which is something I wouldn't have been able to do in the Otherworld. I get to witness everyone's private business, and no one will ever catch me."

A tight laugh pulled from Lark's chest. "You always were a busybody."

Ferryn placed a hand over his heart. "You dare insult me? After everything we've been through? I have half a mind not to even tell you the good news I've been sitting on this whole time."

"And what's that?"

"Ah, ah, ah." He wagged a finger in front of her face. "I demand you answer a few of my questions first. You can't get something for nothing. That's absurd!"

Her dear Ferryn. Unchanged by months in Lacuna. He was stronger than Lark realized.

"Fine, you get three questions, then you're telling me whatever it is you're hiding."

"How gracious of you." He sat on the floor, patting the space beside him.

"One: how was sex with the assassin? You certainly did go at it a lot. Was it more of a learning curve? You know, practice makes perfect?" Ferryn's words flowed from him without pause for breath before he rested his chin in his hand, waiting expectantly.

"You know I'm not answering that. I should whip you for looking in on a private moment."

His face scrunched up in disgust. "I did nothing of the sort. I conveniently found myself elsewhere whenever you two were indisposed."

"You can go wherever you wish? At any time?" That didn't sound as awful as Lark thought.

"Yes. Think of Lacuna as existing in this world. I can imagine myself anywhere. See anything. But that's the only indulgence I'm offered. Here, give me your knife."

Lark yanked it from her boot to place in his palm.

He closed his fist over the blade and yanked. The sharp ring of steel echoed in the empty chamber. Ferryn shook his head as Lark reached for him. "I can't feel it at all."

"It's like what we were, only worse." Lark ran a hand over her face. "And no one can hear you."

"Okay, first of all, I've told you this, being a Reaper was not that bad for most of us. I enjoyed the food, the wine, the sex. Everything you denied yourself." He pinched her cheek. "My grumpy, little biscuit."

Lark swatted his hand away.

"Second of all"—he stretched out on his side, resting his head on his hand—"I never said I was alone."

Skies, had Thanar condemned another Reaper for her actions? "Who's with you?"

Ferryn glared at her. "You still haven't answered my question."

Lark clenched her teeth. "It was good."

"Good?! Do I need to have a talk with the boy? He knows where to put it, right?"

"Ask your second question, Ferryn."

"Aw, that's adorable. Second question: Did you sell your soul to Nereida?"

Ferryn was going to be so furious with her. "I did. But only by accident."

He blinked owlishly. "Well, if it's only an accident." He stood, hands finding his hips as he glowered down at her. "How could you be so foolish?"

"Me?" Lark rose and shoved him. He didn't even budge. "You're the one who got himself banished to Lacuna for no good reason."

"I have my reasons. But you could have had everything. Damn it, Lark!"

Lark turned to glare at the floor. He had his reasons. So did she. "It was the only way I could be sure Thanar couldn't get me." Out of desperation mistakes are borne. How many times had she been warned?

Ferryn exhaled a sharp breath. "We'll figure out a way to get you out of it. You didn't fight for your freedom to end up a dog on her leash."

There was no way out, but she wasn't going to argue with him. "What's your third question?"

Ferryn studied her. It was still a shock to see his face drawn up in intense expressions. "Would you do it differently, if given the chance?"

Despite his protests, it was her fault he'd been trapped in Lacuna. Her actions led him to his fate, all while she was too busy altering her own. But it was more than that, wasn't it? She should have died when she first crawled out from under that dead tree in the forest of decay and pestilence. Were it not for Daciana she wouldn't be here. She wouldn't have made it off that forest floor.

Was it fate that crossed their paths? The very thing she was desperately trying to escape?

Hugo, Alistair, and Langford. They'd all prepared her for fights she wouldn't have walked away from. Given her counsel, she hadn't known she needed.

And Gavriel. Skies, she couldn't imagine a world without him in it. The thought of letting his mortal soul slip away filled her chest with a violent ache.

"No. I would not alter my path." Lark bore the weight of the truth in those words. Of whatever it said about the kind of person she was.

"Then I'm satisfied," Ferryn said with a smile. He wrapped his arm around her shoulders.

Lark leaned into him, quietly mourning the fact that he couldn't feel it. Such a lonely existence it must be.

She'd been honest when she said she wouldn't change the past if she could, but that didn't mean she had to accept the direction she was going in now.

"We have to get you out of here."

Ferryn glanced down at her. "Didn't I tell you the good news? I have a plan."

But why did that strike fear in her heart? "All right then, let's hear it."

"That tone will get you nowhere, young lady. Haven't you ever heard the expression..." He trailed off, tapping his sharp jaw. "Something about honey..."

There was no time for his games. Too much was at stake—too much hanging in the balance. She didn't even know where the others were. Or how they were faring. What matter of nightmares might lurk in their minds?

"Oh, Lark. You'll never enjoy anything if you always take every little thing so seriously." At her murderous expression, he rolled his eyes. "Fine. What do we do? *We*"—he gestured between them—"do nothing. I have a plan. One that doesn't involve you."

"Are you serious?"

"As the plague. I haven't just been sitting on my shapely ass."

"No, you've been spying on me." How dare he suggest she do nothing to help him escape? If he thought she'd sit this one out, he was sorely mistaken. "After everything I've caused, I can't leave you to face this alone."

Ferryn shook his head. "Things were already changing in the Otherworld. Long before you broke the rules."

"That's what Leysa said. Why was I blind to that fact?"

"Lark, what do you want me to say?" For the first time in all her years with Ferryn, his age shone in his eyes. "You didn't want to see anything. You were consumed by your lust for mortality and by fear of Thanar's obsession." He placed a hand over hers. "Rightfully so, I might add, that you closed yourself off."

Lark looked upon the face of her oldest and dearest friend. The one who'd seen the worst in her. There had been times she'd been woefully unfair to him. They'd both made mistakes, it would seem Reapers were no better than mortals on that front, but the sheer magnitude of how much they cared for each other, how much they were willing to sacrifice for each other, never wavered.

"What do you need me to do?"

The surprise on Ferryn's face quickly melted into a warm smile. "Why Lark, are you considering following my lead on this? Doing exactly as I say without question? Relinquishing your steadfast grip on control and letting me take charge for a change?"

"I'm already regretting this."

"Too late! I need you to stay as far away from contacting me as humanly possible."

"But—"

"No." He pressed a hand over Lark's mouth.

Impatiently, she pushed it away.

"I'm quite serious. I have a plan. We'll get ourselves out. But the only way this plays out is if you stay as far away as possible. I promise I'll find you. You need only control your urge to run around the earth searching for me. As difficult as that may be."

Lark recognized a losing battle. "Fine. But you still haven't told me why you confessed to aiding my escape."

A shadow passed over Ferryn's face. "Someone else was accused of that particular crime. I didn't think it was right for that person to bear the brunt of the punishment."

"Who?" There wasn't another Reaper who'd have helped her.

"You wouldn't believe me."

Could it be Leysa? She was a kind friend. She'd hinted at certain musings of loyalty back when she'd first reaped Aislinn's soul and condemned Corwyn's. Was she accused of aiding her?

"I see that look. Busy puzzling away. I'd hate for you to strain a muscle thinking so hard." Ferryn gave her a crooked grin.

"Who was accused?"

Ferryn lifted his eyes to the ceiling. "Who was assigned to guard you, hm?"

Guard her? Why that would be—

"Ceto? Thanar thought Ceto would help me escape?" Lark scoffed. "Idiot. But why would you protect her?" Ceto certainly didn't deserve it.

Ferryn hesitated, finding the floor infinitely more interesting than he had a moment ago. A heavy silence stretched between them.

"Um, Ferryn?" Lark asked. "Don't you and Ceto hate each other?"

"Hate," he whispered. "Yes, I suppose it feels that way sometimes."

Lark's head spun. They hated each other. Antagonized each other. Ceto's very presence made Ferryn clench his fists in anger. She'd verbally eviscerated him for sport on more than one occasion. He'd delighted in goading her for entertainment.

They hated each other.

Memories of lingering looks, uncertainty etched on their faces. Ferryn's eyes, how they followed Ceto's steps for a heartbeat too long.

"Oh skies," Lark groaned. "You love her, don't you?"

"I never said love." His quick defensiveness only confirmed her suspicions.

"What were you thinking?" Lark pinched the bridge of her nose, reminding herself of how little control she had over her pull to Gavriel.

Gavriel.

"Shit. I have to go." She stared up at him. The last time they parted, she'd never gotten to say goodbye. This time, the act of saying goodbye snatched the air from her lungs.

No way of parting would ever feel right.

Ferryn yanked her again into a rib-crushing hug. She tucked her head against his chest, folding herself into his arms as tightly as she could. It occurred to her: he didn't have a scent to wash over her. Nothing to anchor this moment in her mind to more than a memory.

"Next time I see you, I'll be able to feel this." Ferryn sniffed. "And probably smell you. You look like you've taken to dirt bathing."

It felt wrong to let go, but she had to trust he'd find a way to escape.

Stepping out of his embrace, Lark retrieved the lantern. Fingers hesitating on the key.

"Thank you for finding me." He gave her a pained smile. "Next time, I promise I'll find you."

Was that enough to believe in?

"Goodbye, Ferryn." Lark started to turn the key; the blue flame shuddered.

And when the flame vanished, so did he.

CHAPTER 51

*L*ark followed the path laid in gold, gripping the lantern between sweaty palms. Seeing Ferryn had momentarily lifted a weight from her chest, but now she was consumed by thoughts of what the others were facing. What sort of horrors ensnared them? Had they escaped, or was the Shrine holding them captive?

A strangled cry rang from behind the stone wall. Lark startled, nearly dropping the precious artifact. The wall was solid stone, containing no cracks or fissures where sound could escape. She leaned closer, expecting to feel the cool press of stone—

—but she met no resistance. Instead of a solid surface pressing against her ear, she felt nothing but dank air. Solana's words hovered at the forefront of her thoughts. *It will illuminate the dark, show you what those mortal eyes can't see.* Lifting the lantern, Lark turned the key, and blue flame flickered to life. The wall dissolved away to reveal another narrow passage swathed in darkness. A clear warning to turn back and follow the light to freedom.

The lantern vibrated in Lark's hand. She trusted it to guide her.

Ahead, a low growl reverberated off the stones. The path opened up into another cavernous alcove. At the center of the room, trembling on her knees, was Daciana.

Lark swept to her side, setting the lantern down and grabbing her hands. "Thank the skies. How did you get in here?"

Daciana's eyes remained unfocused, sweat beading her brow as tremors wracked her body.

"Daciana?"

Her eyes snapped to Lark's face—her pupils were blown wide enough her eyes appeared black. Lark refused to shy away despite the uncertainty creeping up her spine.

"Lark." Daciana's breath stuttered through her teeth. "This place isn't meant for us."

"What did you see?"

Daciana's face relaxed fractionally, and her eyes cleared. "We need to find the others." She rose on legs far steadier than they ought to be. Lark followed after her. Daciana swept her long black hair into both hands and secured it with a leather cord at the nape of her neck. "You vanished from sight the minute you entered the shrine. When I followed..." She trailed off, her brows knitting together.

That must have been when she entered her vision. Lark couldn't imagine what would leave Daciana shaken.

Daciana busied herself with checking her weapons. A quick touch of the hand to each blade she armored herself with. She lingered on the haladie at her waist, gripping the hilt. The tension in her shoulders lessened and her spine straightened.

***

LARK AND DACIANA navigated the endless pathways and openings, with nothing but a slight pull from the lantern to guide them. Lark cast a sideways glance at Daciana, whose expression remained resolute and devoid of any tells.

"Stop staring at me." Daciana's mouth quirked in a small smile. "You're searching for something you won't find."

"And what is that exactly?"

Daciana sighed, thumbing her daggers impatiently. "You're looking for cracks—a way in so you can assess, and fix." She added with a wry smile. "But it's unnecessary. I am not fractured."

"I never thought you were. But you always let me lean on you. When are you going to let me bear some of your burdens?"

Daciana's face softened, and she placed a hand on Lark's shoulder. "Such a gentle-hearted Reaper."

Lark snorted. "You're just as contrary. The wolf who's really a mother hen."

"And don't you forget it. Lark, I promise we'll talk. Just not now."

The lantern tugged in Lark's hand. At the end of the path was another rounded room carved from stone. It was dark. Lark turned the key, amplifying the blue flame and casting the entire room in its glow. Langford stood alone, his back to them.

"Langford!" Daciana called.

They raced over to where Langford stood.

"Thank the skies you're—" Lark's words died in her throat.

Langford's expression wasn't one of fear or anguish. It was serene, one of soft contentment.

"Langford?" Lark's voice trembled as he looked right through her. "Langford!" She grabbed his arm to give him a shake. The instant she made contact her ears buzzed, and her stomach dropped. The stone room melted away, bleeding into something else.

Transporting her to a place she'd never seen before.

Sunlight filtered into the room, and beyond the windows, fields of blue cornflowers swayed in the breeze. A glass vase of freshly picked wildflowers perfumed the air with the promise of a long spring, and the modest cottage was sparsely furnished, though piles of books dominated every surface.

"Lark?" Langford sat in a leather armchair, a book open on his lap. His pleasant but befuddled voice penetrated the hazy cloud of her mind.

She wasn't in the Shrine anymore. Just as she'd materialized in

Thanar's throne room, she now stood in an unfamiliar cottage. Had she really fallen into Langford's vision? And how could she break them out?

Langford regarded her with vague confusion. "What are you doing here? It's good to see you, of course, but I didn't know we were expecting company."

"Langford, where are we?" Lark still clutched his arm. He frowned at her hand.

"It hasn't been that long since you've visited, has it?"

"I've never been here." Lark's head spun, and panic crept up her throat. If this was his vision, was it a memory? What was she about to witness?

"Oh, I get it," Langford said, nodding. His eyes crinkled with amusement. "Alistair put you up to this didn't he? I only wanted a fresh coat of paint; he's the one who insisted a new color meant we had to rework the entire layout."

Alistair? When did he and Alistair ever live in a cottage? And where in the abyss was Daciana?

A slow creeping realization dawned on Lark. This wasn't his fear. This wasn't a memory—a past trauma serving as his cage. No, this would be far harder to rip him from.

This was a wish.

A fantasy.

Sorrow filled her chest as she looked at him—the youthful expression of joy that illuminated his face, his relaxed posture.

"Langford," Lark said, keeping a firm grip on his arm. "This isn't real. We're in the Forbidden Shrine. Trapped in your vision. You have to let this go."

His face scrunched up in confusion. "You aren't making any sense." He tried to pry her off him. "Do you need help? Alistair will be home any minute we'll give you anything you require."

Home. This was home. A life. A fantasy crafted with Langford in mind. A quiet, peaceful existence with Alistair.

"Langford," she said, this time with more force. "This isn't your home. This isn't real. The real Alistair is likely trapped in a vision too."

Langford gave her a pitying glance. "I don't know what sort of trouble you're in. But I assure you, Alistair is fine." He stood and attempted again to pry her hands off him. "Is it Gavriel? Did something happen to him?"

Madness. This was utter madness. Like talking to a wall.

"Yes. Something has happened to Gavriel. And Hugo. And Alistair." Lark tugged on him. "I need you to come with me."

The front door creaked.

Alistair appeared, clad in his usual black leathers and fine crimson tunic. He kicked his boots off. When he looked up, dark hair fell in his eyes as he grinned. "What's going on here?"

"Lark was just telling me you're in trouble and need my help." Langford stared at her with that same damned pitying expression on his face, like she was the one trapped in a false perception.

"Well, she was right. You wouldn't believe the crooks trying to pass themselves off as merchants." Alistair undid his belt and rested his cutlass in the corner.

"You're one to talk," Langford said.

Alistair arched a dark brow, and mischief glinted in his eyes.

Lark was losing control of the situation. She had to figure out a way to snap him out of it. Langford valued logic and reasoning. She'd have to force doubt to penetrate this haze of contentment.

Langford pulled out of her grasp. Lark lunged forward, afraid if they broke contact, she'd lose the connection and perhaps even lose the chance to enter his vision again.

She stumbled forward, her fingers grazing the sleeve of Langford's tunic. She closed her eyes. Surely she was falling back to the Shrine. But when she opened them, she was still in the cottage, breathing in the scent of spring sunlight and wildflowers. Alistair held her in his arms. He must have caught her when she fell, and his face was exactly as she remembered. His shocking green eyes framed in thick dark lashes, down to the dark scruff along his golden-brown jaw. The Shrine painted quite the portrait for Langford.

A sobering realization crashed over Lark. She was trapped with Langford. Until he let go of this wish, she'd be imprisoned alongside him.

Lark pulled herself out of Alistair's hold.

He regarded her with an air of curious amusement. "You're acting stranger than usual."

Lark looked past him to Langford. "Langford, please, you have to remember."

Langford braced his hands on the slab of oak that formed the kitchen table, eying her with less pity and more impatience. "I don't know what you're talking about. Stop speaking in riddles."

"I'm not speaking in riddles!" Lark shot toward him, only for Alistair to find his way into her path. Blocking her. Protecting him.

"Nothing you've said makes any sense to me," Langford said calmly, pressing a hand to Alistair's chest to ease him out of the way.

Alistair's face was a storm of uncertainty but he placed a soft kiss on Langford's temple and begrudgingly stepped out of the way.

"Please, speak so I can understand." His eyes searched her face. The scholar's never-ending hunt for the truth.

Part of Lark didn't want to tell him. Didn't want to crumble this safe wall of comfort around his mind. Around his heart. But she had no choice.

"When did you and Alistair buy this home?"

"I suppose it's been, what, a year now?" He glanced at Alistair, his brow furrowed in confusion.

"Yeah, about a year," Alistair called back.

"What event preceded the purchase of this house?" Lark's hands fisted, squeezing the blood from her knuckles.

Langford's expression grew suspicious. There it was, that hint of doubt.

"When was the last time we were all together? Hugo, Daciana, Gavriel, all of us, before you bought this house?"

Langford cast his eyes to the ceiling, searching for the answer. "We were... hiking to... a cave of some sorts."

Relief bloomed in Lark's chest. "Yes. Why were we going there?"

His eyes bore into hers, scanning her face for duplicity. Realization dawned on his features. "The Forbidden Shrine."

Alistair leaned against the table. "Something wrong?" he asked, pushing hair out of Langford's eyes.

The anguish that broke across Langford's face was enough to rip the air from Lark's lungs. "We never made it out." His voice broke over the words.

"Hmm?" Alistair ran his thumb along Langford's jaw.

Lark hated what she had to do next.

"Think, Langford. Does this feel real to you?"

Langford ran his eyes over Alistair's face. Again and again. "No," he finally said.

For a moment, a stillness overcame the illusion, casting each detail as a rendered portrait. Void of life. Flat. Motionless.

Except for Alistair, whose eyes still held an intense flame. A fierce longing.

The cottage around them melted away to reveal the dark round room made of stone. The dank air of the Shrine blasted Lark in the face.

She'd done it, she'd broken them out of his illusion. But why did that make her feel worse?

Daciana grabbed Lark's arm. "Where were you?"

Lark's gaze remained transfixed on Langford. His tight shoulders and crestfallen expression.

Without answering Daciana's question, Lark started down the path to the next dreamer.

"WHAT HAPPENED TO US?" Daciana asked. "Did your book explain this?"

Langford sighed and lifted his gaze to the low ceiling. "Not in so many words. I suppose it makes sense in hindsight, but the simple answer to your question is, no."

Lark clenched her jaw, holding back a litany of apologies.

"All right, what's the complicated answer?"

"Well," he said, clearing his throat in the way he always did before launching into a carefully crafted explanation. "As long as we're postulating among friends, I'll recount a passage hinting at the *Trials of Will*. I think each trial was cultivated to target our specific weaknesses." His voice broke on the last word. "Meaning, whatever you saw was designed specifically for you."

"The Shrine means to trap us, and consume us. That's what fuels the magic here, life forces," Lark said softly.

They fell silent.

She should tell them about Solana. About Ferryn. But there would be time for that later.

The path opened up into another alcove—a yawning chasm of darkness. The lantern glowed softly in the shadows, blue light and pitch-black devouring one another in an endless battle for dominance.

Lark twisted the key, and the blue glow flared.

A large body was slumped in the corner. On his knees facing the wall.

Lark's heart climbed up her throat.

Hugo.

She passed the lantern to Daciana. "What happened when I grabbed Langford? I mean, on your end." Important questions she hadn't wanted to ask after Langford freed them from his dream.

"You froze," Daciana said, eying the lantern with suspicion. "But your eyes... there was nothing. They were empty."

Lark nodded. "Right, that's because I wasn't here. I mean, I was here, but I was also there."

Daciana narrowed her eyes. "You went into his vision."

"Yes!" Lark cried with more vigor than necessary. Likely, on the verge of hysteria.

"You want to go in again?" Daciana cocked her head in Hugo's direction.

"Once I'm in, I can't get out. Not without Hugo leaving the dream."

What would she witness in his mind? They'd all speculated about his colorful background. She knew it was bloody. A tangled mess of death and destruction, paid for by coin until the final debt proved too steep.

"Can I get you out?" Daciana's expression was calculating. Always searching for every exit, every advantage, every weakness.

"I'm not sure. If I take too long, I need you to go on and find Alistair and Gavriel." Lark's throat constricted around his name.

"No," Daciana growled. "I'm not leaving you."

"I didn't say leave me. Get them out and come back but don't wait too long." Lark's stomach flipped at the recollection of Solana's words. The magic fed on the lives it stole as they were held enthralled. "This place, it thrives on these dreams. The cave devours the energy of its dreamers. Don't wait long for me."

Hesitantly, Daciana nodded. "I'll come back, if it comes to that."

Before Lark could respond, Daciana yanked her into a tight embrace. Lark squeezed her eyes closed as she hugged her back.

"Be safe," Daciana whispered.

"Be smart," Lark said, releasing Daciana from her embrace.

"When has that ever been a concern when it comes to me?"

"Never. But there's a first time for everything."

Langford stepped forward, placing a steadying hand on Daciana's arm. "She'll be fine. If she could pull me out of it, she'll have no problem with Hugo." He offered her a half-smile. "He actually listens to you."

Turning to Hugo, Lark strode up to him without hesitation, and placed her hand on his shoulder.

HUGO SAT at a large wooden table. Blue linen drapes framed every window. A saucepan simmered on the stove, and a fire crackled in the blackened hearth.

Lark was in the seat at his side, clutching his tattooed arm.

He startled, spilling the cup of tea he was holding.

"Hugo," Lark hissed. "We have to go. This isn't real." Skies help her, he'd better listen.

Hugo raised a thick brow. Before he could respond, a pretty, fair-haired woman bustled into the room, carrying a tray laden with bread, meats, and cheeses. The thick smell of glazed ham wafted, and Lark's stomach rumbled.

"Well don't just sit on your arse, get up and help me, you oaf!" The woman blew a lock of pale hair from her face.

Hugo leapt up and grabbed the tray, placing it on the table. "Yes, boss," he grunted.

Wiping her hands on her apron, she appraised Lark with an unreadable stare. "Who are you?"

Lark's mouth went dry, her heart plunging into her stomach. She stared at the woman who was still waiting for her response, hands perched on her hips.

"I'm—" Lark wasn't sure how to explain to the figment of his vision who she was. "A friend of Hugo's."

She smiled, raising a pale brow. "Is that so?"

"Lena, give it a rest." Hugo's voice was a plea, as though he was at the mercy of this little woman.

"What? You bring one of your *colleagues* home with you and I can't ask a few questions." Lena waved her hand. "Be quiet, Hugo, we aren't speaking to you." She faced Lark, angling her head to the side. "You have a name, yes? Let's hear it."

"Lark." She couldn't play along much longer.

"Hmm, Lark. My husband has never mentioned you before. You a recent recruit?" Lena's brown eyes held a razor-sharp focus. Lark had the distinct impression she'd never be able to hide anything from this woman.

Better to sidestep any real explanation.

"Yeah, something like that." Lark hadn't been with Alistair's group for long. It wasn't a lie.

Horror struck her with a pang in her throat. Was she falling enthralled by his vision too?

Lena's eyes softened. "So young?" She drummed her fingers

against the table. "Well, I hope you're hungry. Hugo's promised to make dinner tonight." She reached into a cupboard and pulled out two leather tankards. "Because you and me, we're drinking."

"Lena. Now's not a good time." Hugo's eyes darted back and forth between his wife and Lark.

Lena threw him an impassive stare.

He sighed and rose to his feet, fetching a bottle out of the tall cabinet—Lark doubted Lena could have reached it on her own. He placed the bottle in her hands without letting go. Before Lena could protest, he pressed a kiss to her lips.

"That's not how a man kisses his wife." Lena grabbed him by the pauldron and yanked him toward her, claiming his mouth for a kiss Lark was more than a little uncomfortable to witness. She'd try to remember that next time she and Gavriel got carried away, though the image of that tiny woman overpowering Hugo was sweet enough to bring a grin to Lark's mouth, even as she turned away.

Lena pulled from the kiss first, pushing him toward the kitchen. "Away with you." She rounded on Lark and plopped in the seat opposite her, dark bottle between them. "Here. You're a guest in my home, and I'll have you treated as such."

"We should be going," Lark said, tossing a meaningful glance Hugo's way.

But he wasn't watching her.

"Da, I can't find my field journals." A soft voice thickened by the same brogue Hugo spoke with carried from the other room. "I'm meeting Shaye down by the river soon and I need our findings." A girl, a few years younger than Lark's mortal form, rounded the corner into the kitchen. Her long black hair hung down her back in a straight, sleek curtain, and her dark eyes matched Hugo's. Lark gripped her drink tight enough the leather groaned.

"I don't know where it is, heart. Where did you last have it?" The look on Hugo's face as he gazed at his daughter—as he watched his Csilla—was enough to punch a hole in Lark's chest.

"I'm not sure." Csilla glanced around the room, dark hair fluttering wildly. When her eyes landed on Lark, she smiled. "Hello."

"Hello," Lark croaked, casting a pleading glance at Hugo.

Hugo's face tightened, his mouth hardened in a firm line behind his beard. "Lark, let's step outside for a moment." He yanked her from her seat, and dragged her toward the door. Lena and Csilla watched with matching expressions of confusion.

When he shut the door behind him, Lark staggered toward the tree in the front yard. "Hugo, I'm so sorry but this isn't real, none of this is real."

He regarded her with a grim expression.

"You don't believe me." Lark ran a hand into her hair. This would be harder to break him out of. She'd have to smash his heart to bits. Remind him exactly why this couldn't be real.

"No. I know," Hugo said. "Of course I know."

He knew? "Then why are we still here?"

He ran a large hand over his jaw and turned back to look at the house. His house.

"Listen, kid," his deep voice rumbled. "I know what I've done. And the things I've lost. There's no getting around that. I know it isn't real. But I couldn't pass up this chance."

"To see them again?"

"To say goodbye."

A weight settled over Lark's shoulders. She wished she could bring his family back to him. To erase whatever decisions led to the moment of their demise. But whether it was fate or chance, it was out of her hands.

All she could do was lead him back.

"Give me a minute," Hugo said as he headed back toward the house.

Through the window, Lark watched as Hugo claimed Lena's mouth in a fierce kiss. She seemed to laugh at him, taking his affection in stride. He wrapped Csilla in a tight embrace, his hand finding the back of her head. He pulled back and cupped her face. Lark couldn't make out what he was saying, but Csilla nodded in response.

When he walked out the door, a weary pace slowed his steps. A flash of pain stole across his face before it smoothed into grim determination.

He gave her a quick jerk of his chin. It was time to go.

Lark grabbed hold of his hand, threading her fingers through his. His palm was warm against hers.

Then the world spun.

CHAPTER 52

*A*fter what felt like miles of tunnels and cramped passages, they reached another alcove.

Lark sensed him before she saw him. She raced through the opening to find Gavriel down on one knee in the center of the space, trembling. She lowered to her knees in front of him. The lantern clanked against the stone floor.

His face twisted in pain, beads of sweat glistening across his brow. His pupils were blown wide enough his eyes appeared black.

"Gavriel." She reached for him.

He made no move to respond or acknowledge her presence.

Lark cast Daciana a pleading glance. "Same thing goes. If I take too long, you need to move on and get Alistair."

Daciana nodded.

"I'll stay." Hugo's gruff voice scraped through the blanket of silence. "I'm not leaving you, kid."

Lark swallowed against a dry throat and turned back to Gavriel.

"Gavriel," she whispered. She placed her palms against his clammy cheeks, and the shadows along his unshaven jaw dug into her skin.

The world melted away.

LARK STILL HELD either side of his face when she materialized.

They stood in a large hall. It lacked the extravagance of Thanar's throne room, but it still set Lark ill at ease. Grey, stone walls and floors with simple braziers burning at each corner, all iron and sandstone. She'd never been here before.

Gavriel stood, blades drawn at his sides, staring at her incredulously. "How can you be here?"

Lark pressed her forehead to his. "Did you have any doubt I'd find you?"

Gavriel flinched away. His green eyes were glassy with unshed tears, his short hair matted with sweat and blood.

A sharp metallic scent filled Lark's senses.

The floor was painted red, crimson coated, in a thick viscous river.

"Gavriel?" Her eyes leapt back up to his face, searching as terror burrowed deep in her belly. "What happened here?"

The heavy clang of his daggers hitting the floor reverberated through her. Gavriel's face fell, tears finally spilling down his cheeks. "I couldn't stop."

Lark wrapped her arms around him without thought. Holding him close and surveying all that spread out around them. Bodies stacked upon bodies. She couldn't decipher any of their faces through the gore. The aftermath of a violent storm.

That's what he was. In the darkest corners of his mind. Lark had nearly forgotten all that he was capable of. What lay dormant.

She tightened her hold on him, heart fracturing at the way he leaned into her touch with desperation. She'd never shy away from him. From all that he was. How could she? When every part of her, even the blackest spaces of a heart not meant for this world, called for him.

"Gavriel, none of this is real." She ran a hand in soothing circles across his back. "We can't leave until you acknowledge this isn't real."

543

Gavriel lifted his head to look at her with red rimmed eyes. He kissed her, all fire, need, and despair, demanding and consuming until her head spun. When he pulled back, they were both breathless.

"How can this be a dream when you feel so real?" His brows knitted.

Lark cupped his jaw, wiping away a spot of blood with her thumb. "Do you trust me?"

Gavriel's expression melted into one of confusion. Before he could answer, the large double doors swung open. A man strode in, his grey hair pulled back at the nape of his neck and a grim expression on his stern face.

"Master Hamlin," Gavriel said. He snatched his dagger from the floor and yanked Lark behind him.

Master Hamlin scanned the landscape of corpses with detached disinterest. "I see you made quick work of your assignment."

"I did as you commanded."

"And you did so with aplomb." Master Hamlin frowned. "With a finesse born of pleasure."

Gavriel stiffened, and Lark tightened her grip on his arm. This wasn't real, but Gavriel's terror felt as real as the linen of his tunic she twisted between her fingers.

"Come now, Gavriel," Hamlin chided. "There's no shame in taking pride in your work."

"There's no pride in slaughtering," Gavriel said.

"I taught you better than that, Gavriel. You know not to chase honor." Hamlin spoke in a cool, even tone. "Remember what happened last time you lost your way."

Gavriel began to tremble. The blade shook in his hand, casting a quivering light on the blood-soaked floor. The action was so contrary to what she'd come to expect from him. Lark stared up at him, dread coiling in her chest as he refused to meet her gaze, and the hairs on the back of her neck stood on end. She tugged on Gavriel, but he didn't move.

"And what's this?" Hamlin peered at Lark. "You missed one." His eyes found Gavriel's face as his mouth firmed. "Dispose of it."

Gavriel froze, the trembling in his muscles ceasing to an implacable stillness. "Leave her out of this."

"You've brought this upon yourself. Have you learned nothing from earning the title of father-slayer?"

Gavriel winced.

Lark gripped his arm tighter. She'd have to remember to kill the real Hamlin after they escaped.

"Finish it," Hamlin demanded.

Gavriel turned to face her, agony contorting his face.

A chill ghosted down Lark's spine. Why was he looking at her like that?

He cupped her cheek with heartbreaking gentleness. His touch, both a balm and searing heat. "I could never hurt you," Gavriel said before he released her face. He raised his blade between them.

Lark thought she knew fear. She'd felt the crippling weight, the thorn wedged beneath skin.

But Lark had never known fear like this.

"Gavriel, please."

He brought his glinting dagger—still coated in blood—to his own throat.

Lark grabbed the blade. It sliced into her fingers, fire and blood filled her cupped palm.

"Lark!" Gavriel gaped at her. "I'm not going to let you die."

"Neither am I, you ass!" Lark grabbed his face, wincing at the stinging across her fingers, not caring that she smeared her blood all over his cheek. "This isn't real. I need you to trust me, damn it."

Gavriel searched her face. "I do trust you."

"We're trapped in the Forbidden Shrine, and if you don't come with me now, we will die." Lark shook him, realizing what she needed to say. "*I* will die."

His eyes widened, and he grabbed her hand. "I believe you," he whispered fervently. "I believe you."

The room tilted. Features melted away, betraying the vision. Like candle wax rolling away from a flame.

545

Gavriel pulled back, still clasping her hand, to peer around the room. "This really is a dream..."

Hamlin pulled his sword—

And the room shattered into a thousand pieces.

GAVRIEL WAS INSTANTLY UPON LARK, yanking her into a breathless embrace.

"I'm sorry," he murmured into her hair, hands running down her back.

Lark burrowed her face into his chest. Breathing in Gavriel's familiar scent, she let the solid planes of his body anchor her. He was alive. His mind was free. She pulled back and placed a hand against his chest. His gaze softened as his hand found hers, threading their fingers and squeezing. Pain sliced through her palm. Her startled cry pulled everyone's attention to them. Daciana found her first, grabbing her arm and yanking it to inspect her hand. "How did this happen?"

"I grabbed the wrong end of a dagger." Lark smiled, remembering Gavriel doing the same thing when they faced the Manananggal.

Daciana shot her an unimpressed look, releasing a sharp breath. "You sustained a real injury inside a vision. Why are we not more concerned?"

"It's unfortunate, though not surprising," Langford said. His cool hands found Lark's wrist, and he held her palm out. The wide gash across three of her fingers was puffed out and raw. Bits of fat and tissue poked out.

Langford uttered a curse. He released her wrist and felt around for his pack.

Hugo crouched next to it, yanking open the flap to produce wrappings.

"I need the honey too," Langford said. "The light's too poor. I can't sew it up in here. Once we get out of this gods-forsaken cave, I'll take care of it." He shook his head, smearing honey into Lark's open wound and mumbling to himself.

Lark grimaced, tearing her eyes from Langford's busy hands to study Gavriel.

He watched her with a thinly veiled expression of guilt. "Did you find Ferryn?"

She winced as Langford ran his thumb along her wound. "Yes, but I can't get him out."

Gavriel's fingers curled under her chin, tipping her head up to face him. "Once we get out of here, we'll find another way." His face still bore the echoes of pain he'd worn so freely in his nightmare.

Langford tied the wrapping tight against her fingers, and Lark hissed. "You're all set for now. But unless you want to suffer permanent nerve damage and never hold a bow again, I suggest you keep that hand out of trouble." He stood and wiped her blood off his hands with a dirty rag. "It shouldn't go septic, provided we find Alistair and get out of here before any rot can set in."

Lark scanned his tense posture, the worry tightening his shoulders. "Your bedside manner is atrocious."

Langford's mouth quirked. "And you are most qualified to make such an assessment. I don't think I've ever had a more frequent patient. And considering how often Alistair is after me to stitch him up after a night out, that's saying something." He folded his bag shut and slung it over his shoulder.

Lark bit her tongue, hoping whatever state Alistair was in wouldn't require medical attention.

LARK'S HAND ached with each pulse of blood through her fingers. Holding the lantern high with her good hand, she pushed onward.

She could sense Langford's desperation, and it settled over her like a dense fog. After what felt like lifetimes, they finally reached another alcove that opened up into a large space.

Lark hurried in, her footfalls echoing against stone. The blue lantern illuminated the wet cracks in the cave walls. She swung around, searching until she found Alistair lying on his side in the far corner. She rushed over and sank to her knees beside his unconscious body. He'd been under longer than any of them. There was no telling what this was doing to him. What it had already done.

Lark reached for Alistair, hovering mere inches from touching him.

"Wait." Langford's voice stilled her movement. "Are we certain, she's the one who should go in?"

"Are you volunteering?" Daciana angled her head, honestly assessing.

"No, of course not. But she's hurt and we don't know what she'll face... what Alistair has been exposed to... and I just thought..." he trailed off, his hands shaking.

"Perhaps he's right." Gavriel took a cautious step toward her.

"I got you out, didn't I?" Lark said as gently as she could. Langford still flinched. "And you."

Gavriel sighed and nodded.

"There's only one person Alistair will listen to," Langford said with a tight expression. "Daciana."

Daciana stiffened and gave a solemn nod. "I will go."

"No. The task is mine."

Lark would not let Daciana traverse the depths of Alistair's mind.

Lark was a souls' guide for longer than her friends had been alive. She'd been forged for this purpose alone. They were all here because of her, and she'd be damned if she was going to allow the Shrine to keep any of them.

No. She would not let Daciana do this.

Langford's eyes blazed with the same fear that must have shone in hers when it was Gavriel's life on the line. She'd bring Alistair back to him. She might not be able to lend words to this promise, but still, her heart swore it.

Lark placed her hand on Alistair's arm.

FEATHERS AND PIECES of broken furniture cluttered the cramped room. Wood splinters littered the floor. The acrid stench of vomit, whiskey, and blood permeated the air as the fire crackled in the hearth, casting tall shadows to flicker against the wall.

Lark still clasped Alistair's forearm. An empty glass hung loosely in his fingertips. He stared at the wall, his dark hair hanging in his eyes.

"Alistair?" Lark released his arm.

He didn't even acknowledge her presence.

Bruises covered his puffy knuckles—bloody and swollen.

"Alistair," she said louder, pulling him from his trance.

Alistair turned to give her a puzzled look. Blood dripped down the side of his head, trickling from his nose, and his lip was split open. He glared at her with red glassy eyes, the striking green of his irises a startling contrast. "What do you want?"

Lark hesitated.

The bed lay on its side; the pillows ripped to shreds. Down the middle, a deep gash ran the length of the mattress like someone had taken a dagger and torn through the canvas and straw. An end table sat in a heap of splintered ruins, and along the floor, shards of glass glistened in the warm light of the fire.

Alistair wore no shoes, the bottoms of his feet were raw and bloodied.

"We need to go." Lark gripped him by the arm. He yanked out of her hold.

"I'm not in the mood to play," he grumbled. "Find another room to earn your coin."

She'd seen him worse for wear after a particularly rowdy evening, but never like this. This couldn't be a fantasy. But it was hard to believe this was his greatest fear—getting drunk and destroying a room at an inn.

"Look, love." Alistair's mouth lazily formed the words. "I'm sure you're very… skilled, but if you don't get the fuck out of my room, I'll toss you out on your ass."

Was he too drunk to recognize her? Lark's anger flared, dream or not. "Alistair, get your ass up." She grabbed him and yanked him to his feet. To the abyss with finesse. "This isn't real. We're trapped in your mind, you and me both."

He shook his head, shoving her away. "I don't know what game you're playing at, but whoever you are"—he yanked his cutlass from his belt, swaying on his feet "I want you out." He pointed his sword at the door.

"Langford will have my hide if I don't get you out of this." Although then she'd have bigger things to worry about. Like being trapped forever.

Alistair startled, his eyes widening and almost lucid. "How dare you speak his name? Who do you work for?"

"You don't know who I am?" That was going to make it infinitely harder.

He glared at her, ignoring the question. "How do you know his name?" His back straightened, the promise of violence sobering him enough the blade didn't tremble.

Lark raised her hands. "Langford is my friend. Just as you are my friend, Alistair."

His face crumpled. He glanced at the floor as he fought for composure. He raised his cutlass again, even as the tears rolled down his cheeks, trailing through blood and soot. "I'm in no mood for riddles. I asked you a question. How do you know his name?"

"And I already answered," Lark said, her hand itching for the dagger in her boot. "Langford is my friend."

"Why do you speak of him in the present?" Alistair took a step toward her. "If you're his friend, then I'm sorry to be the one to tell you." The anguish on his face twisted his features beyond recognition. "Langford is dead."

Lark's eyes darted around the room. The destroyed furniture, the shattered glass on the floor, the bloody fingerprints painting the walls. "You think Langford is dead?" She tried to maintain a neutral tone. If she was going to talk him out of this, she couldn't set him off.

"I know he is." A sob broke loose from his chest. "I saw his body."

Lark wracked her brain for any thread she could tug on. The story Langford shared with her in Adler's prison cell floated to the surface. The job they'd gone on. He was to pose as an investor and was captured. That was the night he was sure Alistair would leave him to die. In Alistair's worst fears, did he let him die?

"Alistair, who do you think killed him?" At his frustrated growl, Lark amended. "Who killed him?"

He ran his sleeve under his nose. "I didn't get there in time."

His worst fear was that he didn't make it to Langford before he was killed. He'd been transported to that rewritten memory. That was why he didn't recognize her. His stubborn mind had crafted his fear so expertly; it was as if they hadn't met yet. How in the blazes was she supposed to convince him to trust her if he didn't know her?

"Alistair, Langford didn't die." Lark took a step toward him. "You saved him. This isn't real. You have to believe me."

He eyed her with uncertainty before his face fell again. "I held his lifeless body. He was gone. Lost to the abyss. And there's nothing you can say to convince me otherwise."

Well, shit.

Lark backed away from him. The madness in his eyes was enough to send an icy chill down her spine. She'd seen Alistair spar, and even drunk, he could disarm her before she pulled the knife from her boot. Still, she reached for it. Alistair lunged, slicing her arm. Lark bit her lip as a thin line of red erupted along her skin.

This was not her charming, playful friend Alistair. This was the darkest part of him. The part that lay sleeping behind easy smiles and friendly banter. The part that never saw the light of day.

When her back hit the wall, Lark knew her luck had run out. Wetting her cracked lips she tried to smile. "How about a drink? You seem like you could use one."

Alistair's eyes were fire and madness. He angled his sword against her throat. "Who sent you? Was it that bastard Vincent?"

"I have never heard that name in my life." Lark couldn't breathe as her chest tightened.

"Don't lie to me!" Alistair bellowed in her face. "He killed him. And then he sent you to torture me, is that it?" He braced a hand on the wall beside her. "Should I send him your head?"

This wasn't happening. This wasn't happening.

"Alistair, you're my friend. You don't want to hurt me." Lark's voice shook.

"You do seem familiar. But I've crossed paths with countless traitors and backstabbers in my line of work."

The light in his eyes had gone out. There was nothing but darkness. She'd drown in it here, in his dream. In the pits of the Shrine. Would she awaken to see Gavriel's face once more?

Before his blade could tear through her throat, a hand grabbed his arm, yanking the sword away. Lark scrambled to the far side of the wall.

Langford gripped Alistair's arm tightly, unspoken emotion bleeding across his face.

Alistair's eyes widened, shock claiming his features. "How?"

"This isn't real. Whatever you've imagined, it hasn't happened," Langford said, his voice tight. "We all have to leave, now."

Alistair reached a shaky hand up to Langford's face, and Langford stilled.

"You were dead. I saw you," Alistair whispered. "I held you. You were gone."

Langford peered into his gaze with fierce honesty. "I'm here now."

With a sob, Alistair threw his arms around him, burying his face in the crook of his neck. Langford squeezed his eyes shut, arms coming around him.

Lark stepped closer, wary of how much time they'd spent here. "Langford, we need to go."

He nodded and pulled back to look into Alistair's eyes. "We aren't here Alistair. You need to let this go so we can return."

Alistair stared at him as if he was seeing the sun for the first time. Grief and adoration spilled across his face. "Lead on, I'll follow you."

Lark reached a hand to Langford, who grasped it firmly in his. Cautiously he held his hand out palm up to Alistair, a silent question. Alistair threaded his fingers in his.

The room fell away in ripples. Pieces snatched away by an invisible current. Until the glow of the fire too, was torn away.

And the darkness greeted them once more.

CHAPTER 53

*L*ark's eyes fluttered open to find Gavriel peering intently at her face. A broad smile of relief transformed his features.

"Hello," she whispered.

"Hello yourself, Demon." His grin only widened.

Lark dropped Langford's hand and winced. The blood from the slice across her fingers had slowed but the ache of it squeezed like a heartbeat.

Langford and Alistair realized they still clasped hands. Langford pulled away and paced over to his pack with red cheeks.

Alistair seemed dazed as he watched him go. He looked as though he might follow after him, but when his eyes landed on Lark, a new sort of anguish crossed his features.

"Lark, I'll never forgive myself for what I almost did." His expression was worn and weary, just as it had been in his nightmare, and the sight of it clawed at Lark's chest. She never wanted to see him look like that again.

"What did he almost do?" Gavriel asked dangerously.

Lark ignored him. "There's nothing to forgive. Besides, I was expecting worse."

"What did you expect?"

"Far more nudity." Obviously.

He grinned, and relief washed over her. There was the Alistair she knew.

"That would have been preferable." Alistair's gaze snagged on Langford who was busy rummaging through his pack. Alistair schooled his expression into a rakish grin and strode over to Daciana. "There you are, you gorgeous creature. I hope you had a better time than I did."

Daciana gave him a gentle shove, a relieved smile brightening her face. "You know better than to ask."

"I never learn, do I?" Alistair's gaze kept finding the back of Langford's neck.

"I think it's time we moved on," Hugo called out, sheathing his knife and standing. His dark eyes found Lark. The shadows they bore were more telling than he'd ever been.

"Tell me that lantern of yours will show us the way out," Daciana said.

If Lark hadn't gotten all turned around, she might have remembered where Solana opened that passage. The easy way out.

Gavriel snatched it up and handed it to her. The gentle hum of the lantern called to her, wrapping around her hand and tugging at her ribs.

Lark staggered as they made their way through the tunnels. Spending so much time in the visions of the others had left her drained. How were they faring? Alistair had spent the most time trapped out of all of them. Lark cast a glance his way. Shadows hid his face. She'd bet all the coin she didn't have that he needed rest.

Once they were free.

The lantern tugged her forward, a tether between the object in her hand and a place deep within her. Like the souls she reaped. It felt like lifetimes ago, finding the pull between her soul and another.

A distant, glimmering light beckoned, and the lantern buzzed in Lark's hand.

"We're almost there!" she called over her shoulder, her eyes seeking Gavriel's.

They exchanged a glance, the intensity in his gaze enough to send a thrill through her. They were so close. And then she could collapse in his arms and sleep. And eat. And sleep. And familiarize herself with every inch of him. And then sleep again.

They crossed the threshold to the room where she'd found Solana and spoken to Ferryn. The room felt larger without him as if he'd filled and stretched the space, and now it sagged under the loss. Lark took solace in the fact that he was likely watching her now, shaking his head at how ridiculous she was.

"Just this way," Lark said, lowering the lantern. The beaming, golden hallway Solana had opened up for her remained. Lark was all too happy to put this awful place behind her. Daciana seemed of the same mind, casting her with a genuine smile as they picked up speed.

"I never thought I'd be looking forward to Hugo's cooking," Alistair said to no one in particular.

"I'm ready to see the sky again." Hugo's rough voice echoed against the walls.

Before Lark could respond, a wave of dread crept over her. A distant putrid fog encroaching on the edges of her mind. Maybe it was this place, or the lantern, or that echo of otherness she and Daciana seemed to share. But she felt it.

A low rumbling sounded in the distance. Lark froze, peering over at Daciana, who angled her head. Listening. Another low echo, deep in the bowels of the Shrine.

Something was coming.

"Run!" Daciana commanded.

Lark sprinted toward the passage, the door at the end feeling farther and farther with every step. She gripped the lantern by the handle tight enough to feel it bite into her skin.

The fear in her mortal heart left a bitter taste in her mouth. Her boots slammed against the stone floor, jolting through her muscles.

A shrill screech sliced through the air.

Manananggals.

The winged beasts flapped their mottled wings and filled the air with the smell of death and decay. Segmented harpies shrieked and slashed.

Half-dead creatures with antlers jutting from almost human, hateful faces. Flesh hung from their bones as they growled and spilled rancid saliva on the floor.

Wentikos.

Lark swallowed the bile that rose in her throat. It should be impossible for these many Undesirables to swarm in one place.

The limestone hall was large, even larger with dozens of monsters blocking the exit. Gavriel and Hugo slashed at a few nearby creatures. Lark slipped the dagger from her boot. Her awkwardly bandaged hand throbbed. Mocking her.

"Lark," Daciana gripped her shoulder. "Run for the door."

At the farthest end, Lark could see the outline of a door carved into stone. Would it even open?

Lark ran. Dodging and ducking. Black spots filled and threatened to darken her vision. She was so close to the etched door she could almost taste freedom.

Alistair got there first, slamming shoulder-first into the stone. Sunlight peeked through the crack, and Lark almost sobbed in relief. They'd make it. The bright sky called to them, beseeching. They were so close. The others weren't far behind—

A sharp cry rang through the hall.

Lark turned, and her heart jolted in her chest at the sight.

Langford hung in the air, gripped by the bloody talons of a harpy. The creature raked its claws down his back, and he screamed. Suspended above the ground, his blood dripped onto the stone.

Alistair yelled something Lark couldn't understand before he shoved past her, running toward Langford. Daciana caught Alistair by the arm and hurled him toward the door.

"Get this open," she demanded, pulling a sword from the harness on her back. She swung it in a circle to loosen her wrist and darted toward the beast.

Gavriel leapt into the air, catching the harpy by the ankle. It sank lower to the ground under his weight, before releasing a mighty roar and dropping Langford.

Langford hit the ground with a heavy thud.

Hugo hauled Langford's arm over his shoulder, dragging him toward the door. Daciana stood poised, ready to cut down any attacks at Hugo's flank. She yanked her haladie from her belt and slashed it across the belly of a Wentiko, spilling fetid innards on the stone floor.

Alistair sagged in relief when Langford was within reach. Pulling him into his arms, he pushed the door open and tugged him out into the sunlight.

Where was Gavriel?

Lark's chest tightened as her pulse thrashed in her ears.

The harpy lifted Gavriel higher into the air. He sliced his blade against the back of its calf. The creature howled in agony as it flailed, loosening Gavriel's grip. He slipped, plummeting to the ground. The sickening crunch of bone as his ankle twisted at an unnatural angle rang through the air. A scream got caught in Lark's throat, and she ran for him.

She wouldn't let him fall. She couldn't watch him die.

Hugo caught Lark around the waist and threw her toward Daciana, who was already yanking her through the door.

"Go, I've got him." Hugo's voice betrayed his terror.

"No!" Lark fought to escape Daciana's impossible grip, but her strength had fled, and fatigue weighed down her limbs. She'd spent too much energy in the dreams of the others.

She couldn't leave him. She couldn't leave him.

"Kid, I promise, he'll be fine," Hugo said, face set in grim determination.

Daciana scooped up the lantern. Her arm, unyielding in its hold around Lark's waist. Lark gripped Daciana's shoulder with trembling hands, needing to hold on to something.

"We have to go," Daciana said. "I promise I'll go back in and get them."

Hugo swung his blade as he came to Gavriel's side and hoisted him up. Gavriel's eyes found Lark's. Pain mingled with relief in his expression. Undesirables surrounded them, beginning to close in.

Daciana dragged Lark through the door and into the blinding midday sun.

As soon as they crossed the threshold, the lantern's flame snuffed out and the door slid shut behind them.

Lark whipped her head to stare at the stone.

There was no trace. The rock face was smooth.

As if it had never been a door.

"No..." Lark yanked herself out of Daciana's loosened hold to feel around for the opening.

All she felt was solid unwavering stone.

"No!" She beat her fist against it. Ignoring the pain that flared up her hand. "Daciana!"

Daciana's eyes widened.

Hugo and Gavriel were sealed in the cave.

The Shrine was to be their tomb.

CHAPTER 54

$\mathcal{G}$avriel watched the door close behind her, sealing shut, and relief washed over him. Lark was out. She was safe. Without thinking, he leaned onto his ankle, and a jolt of pain shot up his leg. He blinked the sweat from his eyes, ignoring the way they burned.

"You with me?" Hugo's gravelly voice called to him over the shrieks and screeches of the monsters closing in.

"I'm here. You got a plan?" Gavriel tucked his dirk back into his arm sheathe, and yanked the dagger from his hip. He recognized the different monsters from Kenna's bestiary. Manananggal needed silver; he flipped the silver blade into ready position. Wentikos must be pierced through the heart. And Harpies? Well, they were a pain in the ass, all claws and screeches, but easy to kill.

"Yeah," Hugo said. "Don't die."

"Works for me."

Unable to lunge and slash, Gavriel made do with keeping his weight off his ruined ankle and swiping at any who came too close. At his back, Hugo sliced with surprising agility for so large a man, cutting and slashing with all the dexterity of a skilled duelist.

"Where did you train?" Gavriel called over his shoulder. Gavriel had recognized the lion tattoo Hugo always tried to hide, that could have been forged by a skilled ink threader, but a fighting stance was drilled into one's head until it was as natural as breathing.

"What?" Hugo growled, hacking off the arms of a screeching harpy. The horde was thinning, though not fast enough. Dozens of beasts against two men—one of them injured. Gavriel didn't like those odds.

"I doubt we'll get another chance to speak." Gavriel blocked a swipe from a clawed hand, severing its wrist with his blade. Black blood poured over his boot.

Hugo remained silent, and the clash of bones and steel filled the air.

Gavriel continued. "Your style gives you away. Your stance and perry especially. Were you a Lion?" The Den of Lions. The rival assassin's guild, almost equal to the Crows. But they'd get caught up in political affairs, so their successes ebbed and flowed like the tide. Whether or not they were in favor always came down to a matter of dates and titles.

"What if I was?" Hugo kicked the antlered head of a Wentiko with impressive force.

"Nothing. My curiosity would be sated." Though, it was a wonder how a Vallemerian warrior become a Lion. Gavriel gave up on getting answers and gritted his teeth through the pain. His swollen ankle throbbed, and his arms grew heavy. "Hugo, I'm not going to last like this. Take the silver blade, and I'll buy you time."

His words were true yet bitter. He'd never see Lark again. Never tuck a strand of her dark red hair behind her ear. Never see those amber eyes glare at him. Never taste her mouth again.

"Don't be stupid," Hugo said with a groan as a set of talons ripped up his arm. "I promised her I'd get you out."

"Don't you know not to make promises you can't keep?" Gavriel panted through the effort of staying upright and keeping the creatures at bay.

"That's it, get low."

Gavriel sank to the ground, using his short-sword to slash the legs out from under another beast. It landed with a thud amongst the mass of bodies that littered the floor.

Hugo lunged and wielded his sword with as much finesse as Gavriel had ever seen in a trained killer.

"Don't let them aim for my legs," Hugo said.

Gavriel positioned his weight onto one knee, cutting and blocking.

Hugo struck again and again. Showering Gavriel with blood and gore as he severed heads and limbs from bodies. The putrid smell of death and rot was overpowering. Worse than the time Connor knocked him into the shitter hole.

Hugo forged a path of destruction, leaving mangled limbs and segmented carcasses in his wake.

Gavriel grunted as his steel collided with beast after beast. His swings were losing momentum. "Hugo, I can't hold them off."

"Stay with me, boy." Hugo threw his weight forward as he deflected and slashed. Again, and again. He swung wide, cutting down another. And another.

The last beast let out its death cry as Hugo slammed the blade of his dagger through its throat, spilling black blood over his hand. Its corpse fell to the floor. The thud echoed through the now silent hall.

Hugo held out a hand, yanking Gavriel to his feet and holding him steady.

Mounds of carcasses and limbs decorated the stone floor. More than he cared to count.

"Remind me again why you hardly go on missions?" Gavriel asked, hobbling along as Hugo led him to the wall.

"Don't like to."

Fair enough.

They reached the wall where the others had escaped—where the door should have been. Gavriel hadn't planned on surviving that horde. Now the threat of entrapment beneath rock was his next battle.

"Any ideas on breaking out of here?"

Hugo lowered him to the floor. "We should do something about that ankle, then we'll figure a way out."

"I love it when you take charge."

Hugo leveled him with a frown. "We already have one Alistair. We don't need another."

Gavriel laughed, tipping his head back and running his hands down his face. Deliria from exhaustion and pain sent his thoughts racing to the corners of his mind. The time he found a stray cat and snuck it into the Guild to feed. The other boys found it while he was running drills and strung the animal up over his bed. He cried until Master Hamlin came to his quarters and ushered him into the courtyard. He received five lashes for his infraction but was gifted with the task of lashing each boy who participated in the creature's demise. The crack of the whip never sounded more righteous.

He glanced down at Hugo as he eased his boot off. His ankle had swelled to thrice its normal size. That was going to make travel difficult. Gavriel braced himself for the pain. Before Hugo could set his ankle, the unmistakable sound of footsteps echoed down the hall.

A tall figure stepped from the shadows, shrouded in black. A flash of white hair and black horns gleamed in the light. Piercing, silver eyes regarded them with amusement.

The demon. The one who dared try to claim Lark as property. A broad smile spread across his sharp face as he stepped over the bodies littering the floor. Raising his pale hands, he delivered a slow clap.

As if this day couldn't get any rutting worse.

"I must say," the demon said smoothly. "This is impressive."

"What do you want?" Gavriel tried and failed to stand.

The demon grimaced as he sidestepped more corpses. "What is with you mortals and your lack of propriety? You must have meant to ask for my name, but your injuries impeded your sense of decorum. I am Balan."

"I don't give a fuck about your name, what do you want?"

Balan frowned. "You know what I want. Or, I suppose it's who I want."

Gavriel could scarcely feel his ankle anymore as rage shot through him. "She isn't here."

Balan's smile only grew, revealing impossibly white, sharp teeth.

His black leathers gleamed, not a buckle out of place. "You're her little pet, aren't you? She'd notice if you went missing."

Gavriel's blood burned with the need for violence. "She already thinks I'm dead. It won't matter."

"But you're not dead," Balan said with a sweep of his hand. "And I have no intention of killing you. I merely want what's owed to me."

"You can't have her." Gavriel would rip this creature apart with his bare hands before he let that happen.

Balan gave him an indulgent smile. "That's not exactly up to you, is it?"

A low rumbling from the alcove filled the hall—growls and screeches echoing in the distance.

Hugo unsheathed his weapons.

"Did I forget to mention I didn't come alone?"

For fuck's sake, not more of those monsters. Gavriel's knees threatened to buckle.

"We don't have much time." Balan swept forward. He grabbed Gavriel's ankle, and Gavriel hissed. It burned, searing fire through his nerves before it dulled to a warm pulse. The foot righted itself, muscles, tendons, and bones reforming as if it never happened. "There that's better. Can't have you hobbling around the Netherworld, can I?"

Hugo lunged, bringing the blade across Balan's throat, and blood spilled down the front of his pristine leathers. Balan gripped his throat, glaring. With a wave of his blood-drenched hand, he sent Hugo careening against the wall. The impact of his body hitting solid stone echoed in the cavernous hall.

Balan stomped over to where Hugo pushed himself back up to stand. "That wasn't very sporting." His voice gurgled through his bleeding throat.

Gavriel tested the weight of his ankle—and lunged.

The demon whipped his head in his direction, his flesh, already knitting itself back together. He held out his hand and squeezed it into a fist.

Gavriel's throat compressed. His pulse pounded in his head as his airway locked tight.

Balan's face twisted in rage as he held his fist tight for another heartbeat, before opening his hand.

Gavriel sank to the floor, air filling his lungs as he coughed and sputtered.

Blood coated the side of Hugo's head as he held dual blades out at the ready. "You're not taking him."

Balan chuckled, pulling a white handkerchief from his pocket and wiping the blood off his hand before dabbing at his neck. "Oh, yes I am. You're a darling to worry, though." He dropped the sodden cloth to the floor, taking a step toward him. "Besides, you're about to be very busy. Why don't you let me worry about him."

Hugo lunged toward the demon, slicing his blade through his chest.

Balan shrieked an inhuman sound. "You filthy maggot! Do you know how difficult it is to sew leather without puckering?"

A laugh ripped from Gavriel's chest.

Balan glared at him. With a wave of his hand, the blade slackened in Gavriel's hand and hit the floor with a twang. Gavriel's feet shuffled forward of their own volition, like they were attached to puppet strings. He threw a panicked look at Hugo, whose own face wore an expression of shock.

"That's better." Balan patted him on the head and turned to Hugo. "Well, whatever your name is, I can't say it was a pleasure meeting you." He grimaced down at the slice in his leather chest piece.

The growls and screeches grew louder with every second.

Hugo's expression morphed into a calm acceptance. He dipped his head in a quick nod.

"Hugo..." It was the only thing Gavriel could think to say.

Hugo gave a soft smile."Lark can take care of herself," he said before his face hardened. "But be sure you deserve her." He turned toward the creatures flooding in from the narrow corridor. He limped toward it. Even using the space as a bottleneck wouldn't be enough. Hugo was weakened by the first wave. The floor was heavy with corpses. If only they'd had more time to rest and recover. If only Hugo had seen to his wounds before the demon appeared. If only—

Hugo readied his blades and lowered into his stance.

Gavriel's hands shook. He stood, frozen in place. He had to find a way to break free. To fight by Hugo's side. With his healed ankle, the two of them could handle this horde.

Gavriel fought with every ounce of strength he had left to break free from the compulsion, gritting his teeth as he pushed and wrestled against his locked muscles. A bead of sweat worked its way down his forehead as he trembled against invisible binds.

Gavriel heard it before he saw it. The howl of pain. Distinctly human.

Hugo was completely overrun. The arm of a Harpy thrust deep into Hugo's gut, reaching in past its elbow. A hateful sneer froze on its face as Hugo lopped off its arm—before slumping to the ground. Gavriel watched in horror at the trail of viscera that pooled beside him. Hugo's eyes met his, for a heartbeat or two, before they lost focus. Leaving them wide and empty.

The thrumming in Gavriel's ears deafened him.

He was gone.

Hugo was gone.

CHAPTER 55

"We can't leave them there." Lark paced the same patch of earth, tangling the fingers of her good hand in her grimy hair.

"We won't." Daciana's hands ghosted along the rock face, her brow furrowed.

Hugo and Gavriel were up against those beasts, armed with nothing but their blades and wits. And Gavriel's ankle...

Helplessness crushed Lark's chest, making it difficult to breathe. They couldn't survive on their own. She needed to find a way in.

Langford sat on a nearby rock, easing his shirt over his back. The claw marks marring his unblemished skin were deep and angry, and the stench of rot permeated his torn flesh.

Lark tugged Langford's shirt the rest of the way, dropping it to the ground. "What else do you know about the Shrine? Why is the door gone?"

Langford stared back at her with eyes red-rimmed and glassy. "I don't know."

"What do you mean, you don't know? You're the one who studied the tome!" Something sharp and cold burrowed in her gut. She was the one who led them here. She'd lost Hugo and Gavriel to the darkness. This was her fault.

"Lark." Alistair's voice cut in, dangerously low. "Langford's wounds need tending. Give him a chance to breathe."

Lark refused to sit idle and accept this fate. "I need a way in. The longer we wait, the more we risk." A small voice in the back of her head whispered, *they could be dead already.*

Alistair grabbed her by the wrist, dragging her away.

"Don't you think I know that?" he hissed, tugging her closer. "I want more than anything, to go charging back in there. But first, we need to assess the damage. You're no good in a fight with that hand, and Langford needs medical attention. When he's all fixed up and not about to pass out, you can barrage him with all your questions."

"That could be too late. We need to move fast—"

"Damn it, Lark!" His verdant eyes blazed. "We need to take care of what's in front of us first. Before we lose everything."

Lark glanced over to find Daciana thumbing her daggers and studying the stone wall. Each moment they spent arguing could be Gavriel and Hugo's last. She yanked her wrist from his grasp, glaring at him. "What if it was Langford in there?"

Alistair looked like she'd just slapped him.

Without waiting for his response, she turned to where Langford struggled to reach his back with the pot of honey in his hand. Lark should have learned how to make a poultice like the one he placed on her back after the Manananggal attack. His wounds did appear to be festering. Skies knew what sort of infection he might face. Lark took the clay jar from his shaking hand and dabbed the honey tincture against his wounds. She never intended for any of this to happen.

"Does it look bad?"

"No," Lark said quickly. "Once it heals, you'll bear rather fetching scars."

He snorted. "At least we're still focused on what's important."

Langford grew quiet while she continued working on his back. They were all so calm about the fact that Hugo and Gavriel were trapped. Lark's stomach burned with each moment that passed.

"This is all my fault," she said, soft enough for his ears only. "I'm the reason we were even in the Shrine. I still don't know why I thought this was the answer." Foolishness. Naïve hope.

Langford hummed. "Have you considered the artifact you possess?"

"The lantern is only meant to show the way, not create a way..." Lark stilled, realization dawning. In her panic, she'd forgotten: Solana had told her to call on her should she need anything.

"Alistair!" Lark tossed the clay pot into his unsuspecting hands. "Finish him up."

Daciana had already grabbed the lantern and held it out to Lark. "You have an idea?"

"Maybe." Lark twisted the key and ignited the small blue flame. "I don't know if it will work, but we have to try."

She squeezed her eyes shut, imagining the beautiful being. Solana's smooth dark skin that seemed to glow, her long black hair that shimmered like a thousand stars. The iridescent sunburst tattoo in the middle of her forehead.

Solana. Solana. Solana.

Lark poured every ounce of her remaining strength into screaming that name in her mind over and over. Forcing every corner of her fragile heart to seek her out.

A violent gust of wind blew through the air, and Lark's damp hair danced in the breeze. And when it ceased, a quiet calm settled over her. Silence—suspended in midair.

Lark opened her eyes.

Solana wasn't there.

Lark glanced down at the lantern in her hands. Blue flame rippled behind the glass. "I don't understand, why didn't it work?"

"What's not to understand?" A smooth voice crooned.

Unease pooled in Lark's gut. She remembered that voice. She turned. A long body clad in dark leathers leaned against the stone wall. His blinding white hair gleamed in the midday sun, black horns curling from either side of his head.

Balan.

"You took the word of a paragon at face value?" He arched a dark brow—a severe contrast to his white hair—smirk tugging at his mouth. "Come now, you know better than that. Has being remade dulled your mind too?" Balan pushed off the stone and sauntered over. His black leathers creaked with the movement.

Daciana unsheathed her blade faster than Lark could blink. In the corner of her eye, Alistair brandished his sword, angling himself in front of Langford.

Balan tsked. "Now, now, there's no need for violence. I'm merely delivering a message." He held his hands out to the sides in a display of innocence.

Lark yanked the knife from her boot, wishing her hand could bear the strength of her bow.

"It would seem we got off on the wrong foot last time we met." He placed a hand over his chest. His black horns glinted in the sunlight. "I apologize for my part. You see, you caught me by surprise, and I was under the impression I could force you to take a little trip south with me."

Lark swallowed the fear that climbed up her throat. "What's changed?"

"It would seem there are a few parameters in place preventing me from claiming what's owed. But being the forward thinker I am, I found a remedy to that particular nuisance."

"You certainly enjoy the sound of your own voice." Lark tired of his games. Her gaze snagged on his chest. A rip cut through his black leather, pale skin peeking out.

Balan laughed, rich and deep. "And why shouldn't I? I'm the most interesting company I've had in a long time." A wicked grin stretched across his mouth. "That is until your little pet came into my possession."

Lark's breath caught. Her knife hung limply in her unfeeling fingers. "You're lying."

"Am I? Must be a different Gavriel in the Netherworld."

Rage flooded Lark's body, launching her forward before her mind had time to catch up—only for her blade to meet air. Balan had vanished as if he never was. She spun around in time to see him materialize behind her.

"Lark, let's be rational here. I didn't have to tell you right away, but I did. Let's call that a show of good faith."

Lark's heart thundered in her chest. "Or, I could gut you and spill your entrails on the ground."

Balan grinned. "You're a feral little thing, aren't you? That'll be fun." He smoothed his leather gambeson, running his hands errantly down his chest. "But I'm here to deliver a message. Nothing more. What you do with it is your choice."

Lark's first choice was to rip an arrow from her quiver and aim for his throat. She settled on gripping Hugo's dagger, now slick from her blood.

Balan held up his hand, ticking off his fingers as he spoke. "One, Gavriel is in the Netherworld providing some much-needed entertainment. Two, if you wish to free him, you must willingly come down and bargain for his life. Three—" He paused, his face going blank. "What was three? Oh, yes! Your burly fellow, Hector? Hubert?"

"Hugo?" Lark's voice came out strangled—terror constricting her throat.

"That's it! Hugo! That was going to bug me all day. Yes, Hugo is dead."

Lark's heart plummeted to the pit of her stomach, hollowing her in its descent. Blood roared in her ears.

"That's not possible," Daciana said, her voice shook.

"Afraid it is," Balan said, with a false expression of pity. "Being ripped apart by twisted souls will do that to you."

It couldn't be true. It couldn't be true. Lark's stomach churned as she turned the news over and inside out. She crouched, unable to stand, and gripped the sparse grass and dry dirt, ignoring the twinge in her hand.

The demon watched her curiously, his head cocked to the side. "You seem distracted, should I run down the list again?"

Daciana's cry of rage ripped through the air as she threw herself at him. Her blade sank into his chest.

He snarled and waved his hand, blowing her back to land against the ground beside Lark with a heavy thud. He ripped the dagger out, examining it with an expression of distaste before flinging it to the ground.

"You'll have to be cleverer than that to kill me, wolf."

Daciana bared her teeth in a snarl. "I swear on the blood of my people, I will rip you apart."

For an instant, Lark swore she saw fear on Balan's face, but it melted into amusement.

"Perhaps." Balan returned his gaze to Lark. "Until we meet again. Sooner rather than later, I hope." His silver eyes flashed. "I'd hate to get bored with your pet." He raised his hand and snapped his fingers, vanishing.

Lark's head spun. She turned to Daciana, searching for any sign of doubt on her face.

All she found was despondency.

"He didn't mean it." Alistair swayed on his feet. "He was lying, wasn't he?"

Gavriel had been taken to the Netherworld.

And Hugo.

He couldn't be gone.

A cry ripped from Lark's lips. Her stomach heaved, but it was already empty.

CHAPTER 56

$\mathcal{L}$ ark nocked another arrow, aiming for the log she'd suspended from a tree with a rope. Blinking back the haze of tears, dirt, and sweat, she pulled the string taut. Tension stretched through her bow, through her arms, until they shook with the effort.

She released—the arrow sailed through the air and missed her swinging target.

Lark prepared to nock another arrow. She ignored the flare of pain in her fingers when she pulled the string. The fresh stitches were wet with blood as she ripped them open again.

She felt feverish with every gust of wind that blew over her sweat-soaked skin. She exhaled a ragged breath, finding her anchor point. Muscle memory.

Mortals are funny things. She felt her grief in her bones at the news of Hugo's death, but now it was tucked away like her mind held private chambers for such an occasion.

She released the arrow, not bothering to watch its trajectory. Her hand burned, and the loose wrapping darkened with blood.

"You opened up your stitches, didn't you?"

Lark turned to find Langford watching her. He held his shoulders low as he avoided tugging on his back. The bandaging that wrapped around his entire torso peeked out the top of his white tunic.

Lark held her palm out. He grabbed it with both hands and a feather-light touch, unwrapping it with deft efficiency.

Her mangled fingers greeted them; stitches ripped open in places where tissue poked through.

"It needs a complete redo." Langford met her gaze with sunken eyes. His dark hair stuck out in every direction, like he'd been yanking on it. He looked like he might say something. A word of comfort, or even acknowledgment of the shit the world had suddenly become.

That it was a little darker without Hugo.

Langford sighed. "It looks like you hit your target."

Lark glanced over her shoulder to see the log had slowed its swinging to a gentle lull.

Her arrow, stuck square in the middle.

As LANGFORD STITCHED up her fingers again, Lark watched Alistair. He leaned against the same tree he'd taken ownership of since they made camp the night before.

They hadn't ventured far from the Shrine—it seemed wrong to leave Hugo behind. They settled for edging back into the forest of the Forbidden Highland path.

Daciana paced back and forth—her familiar caged animal energy. Each pass held more agitation than the last.

Langford's mouth had thinned in a firm line as he expertly sewed Lark's fingers shut once more. His brow creased in concentration, and his boyish features drawn tight. "Try"—he said, voice strained—"not to rip them out again."

"I won't. Where I'm going, my bow would make little difference anyway."

Langford's posture stiffened, and he lifted his head to regard her with a calculating expression. He looked like Langford again.

"You're going after him."

"Did you ever doubt I would?" Lark's voice was even and steady. There was much to fear; the weight of doubt was crushing.

But Gavriel was a beaming light of certainty.

"No," Langford said, taking his time to wrap her hand, slowing his movements to a glacial pace, as if this was the only time they had.

Lark didn't know what she'd face—what she'd find in the Netherworld.

The memory of the mortal girl, Aislinn, crept into her mind. The courage she mustered before sprinting toward her unknown.

Lark would have to access that same mortal courage.

When Langford finished, Lark cupped his face with her good hand. He threaded their fingers. There was so much to say. So many things she wanted him to hear before she left.

"Thank you," she whispered.

A muscle feathered in his jaw.

Daciana was still wearing a path into the same patch of grass. She lifted her head to regard Lark, feet never ceasing their trek. "What do we do now?"

Lark exhaled a long breath, mustering her dwindling strength. "You know what I must do."

Daciana stilled. "You can't be serious."

"I'm not leaving him there."

"I'm not saying that you should, but we need a plan, we need—"

"No, Daciana," Lark said, gently. "This is the only way."

She couldn't let Gavriel stay in the Netherworld. Suffering in her stead. If she had a chance to save him, damn the consequences, she had to take it.

"I can't let you do this." Daciana's voice broke. Her lovely face crumpled, anguish twisting her normally calm composure.

A hole punched through Lark's chest. Angry and raw. "Daciana, do you trust me?"

"That isn't fair."

"And still, I'm asking. Do you trust me?"

Daciana hesitated, her eyes finding the ground. "Yes."

"What's this now?" Alistair staggered over to them, nearly losing

575

his footing on a loose rock. He looked tired, drained. Wrung out like a wet cloth.

Daciana cleared her throat. "Lark's going after Gavriel."

"No, she isn't," he said, without missing a beat. "Not without a plan."

"I have a plan."

"No, you don't. Plans take days, weeks even. Not a few hours off by yourself shooting target practice."

"That's not—"

"Furthermore," Alistair continued, blowing over her response. "Do you think this is what Hugo would have wanted? For you to go running down there, sacrificing yourself for the sake of impatience."

Lark's hands clenched into fists, a spark of pain lighting in her hand at the action.

"You're a bastard," Langford said. He leveled Alistair with the force of his steely gaze. "How dare you wield Hugo like that? He isn't another one of your schemes to hide behind."

Alistair regarded him with a searing expression. "Do you think Lark's death honors Hugo in any way?"

"No one said she was going to die."

No one said it. But they all knew.

"You can't expect her to leave him there, Alistair," Langford said, a challenge in his voice.

They stared at each other, the air heavy and tumultuous between them. Finally, Alistair's eyes softened, and he gave an almost imperceptible nod. "Right. Dazzle me with this plan of yours."

"I'll use the lantern to enter the Netherworld. Find Gavriel. Get out." Lark refused to look any of them in the eye. She couldn't handle their scrutinizing gazes.

"Simple. Elegant," Alistair deadpanned. "Daciana will go with you."

There was no way Lark could let her set foot in the Netherworld. "None of you can come with me. Not this time."

"Lark, be reasonable. We can't just let you—"

"You're not letting me do anything. Let me be clear, I'm about to venture into a world you all know nothing of. A place only I am familiar with. I appreciate how much you want to protect me, really I do." Lark eyed the three of them. "But where I'm going, you can't follow. I can't worry about you down there."

Silence descended. Smothering the air around them until there was hardly room to breathe.

Lark yanked her bow and quiver off her shoulder and handed them to Langford. She knelt to pull the Hugo's dagger from her boot. Feeling both lighter and heavier without the familiar weight of it. She handed it to Daciana.

"Keep these safe for me." Her stare darted between Langford and Daciana. "I'm going to want them back."

Langford tightened his lips as he cautiously held the bow and quiver to the side. Daciana frowned at the knife in her hand before stepping forward and yanking Lark into a tight embrace.

"Promise me, damn it," she hissed. "Promise me this isn't the last time I'll see you."

"I promise," Lark whispered as she hugged her back. The lie left a bitter taste on her tongue.

ALONE AND ARMED with naught but the mysterious lantern, Lark made her way down the steep hill. She'd left the others at camp in search of a secluded spot to try to slip through the veil to the Netherworld. Dense woods and large minerals gradually gave way to sky.

Lark came upon an ancient yew tree, its branches heavy with vibrant green, each leaf turned upward, awaiting the kiss of rain. Gnarled, twisted limbs reached out to warn her.

A storm brewed in the air.

Lark twisted the lantern key, and the blue flame erupted. Holding it out, she let her eyes slip closed. A gentle rush of breath escaped her lips.

She called to Gavriel. Beseeching and beckoning.

Memories of his scarred mouth flashed through her mind. Of heated kisses and shaky embraces. The scent of his blood and the feel of his soul tugging her so long ago, when she was but a conduit to guide him to the afterlife. Her thoughts swirled, never landing for longer than a moment, endlessly scattering in a breeze that never touched her skin.

Her head spun in a dizzying cycle of thoughts and images. Memories both remembered and forgotten. The drag of his bow against the strings of his fiddle. The flash of his eyes when he kneeled bound and gagged in that warehouse. His softening gaze as he stared up at her with blood trailing from his mouth.

Lark couldn't clasp onto anything. Ceaselessly flying and falling with no tether to follow.

The lantern slipped from her hand and dropped to the earth—the sharp clang of metal echoed in her ears.

The lantern was meant to guide her. It worked in the Shrine. What if that was the only place the magic was strong enough? Solana hadn't answered her call for aid—perhaps the magic simply wasn't strong enough to summon the goddess. But how else was she expected to travel to the Netherworld? Was Balan hoping she'd call to him?

A horrible revelation struck Lark. She was supposed to die. That's how she'd enter the Netherworld. To end her life, hoping Balan would honor his word and free Gavriel.

That wasn't going to happen.

Lark snatched up the lantern. The blue flame still blazed in its chamber. Lifting it high, she let her mind reach for the Netherworld. For darkness. Despair and longing. For a life cut short, and a life lingering far past youth. A dwindling candle, burnt down to the last of the wick. She searched for the call of peace and rest. The last page of a book. The bitter edge to a soul of unrest. A mournful wail of a sinner's lament. The torment of regret. All the wicked songs she knew by heart.

She felt a tug through her hand. Through her soul. Along the dusty, clouded edges of her awareness. All but forgotten in her mortal form. Some small part of her, the human sense of survival, trembled against the enchanting hum of the lantern.

Swallowing her fear, Lark took a step forward, refusing to shrink away when the buzz of magic seared her hand. As if the lantern itself was eager to make this journey. Another step forward and the right-ness of it sang in her veins.

The air before her glimmered. Like a veil made corporeal. Lark lifted her wrapped hand toward the reflections of light refracting. When her fingertips reached the edge of the veil, warmth flooded her being. Like a sudden gust of summer air.

Without hesitating, she stepped through. Leaving the mortal plane behind.

DARKNESS SURROUNDED HER, and the acrid taste of smoke lingered on her tongue. Only the small blue flame illuminated the space of nothing before her.

Lark's skin buzzed with magic. Like a thousand needles piercing her nerves. It was worse than entering the Shrine. Every instinct in her human body screamed the wrongness of this place. Of entering the Netherworld as a living mortal.

In the distance, a shape began to take form.

A red door, holding vigil in the dark, silent hallway.

Whatever Lark faced, whatever lay before her, she accepted it. Welcomed it. Soon enough it would all be over and Gavriel would be back where he belonged, where he always belonged.

An ache hollowed out her chest. She had hoped that place was by her side.

But fate had other plans.

The door swung wide, revealing a familiar room. Unchanged since the last time she'd been here, begging for aid.

Lark stepped in and scanned Nereida's quarters with mortal eyes, curious if it would appear different. Her staggering number of books covered every surface—some flipped open, some worn—with leather binding holding on for dear life. More books stacked in piles on the floor, and across the desk that seemed to wilt under the weight. The same bookcases traveled floor to ceiling with countless tomes wedged in to fit. The black leather chair sat by the fire that crackled in the hearth.

"Well, well. I sensed an intruder, but I didn't dare hope it would be you."

Lark spun to find herself face to face with Nereida, witch-queen of the Netherworld. Her pure white hair was braided in a crown around her head, not a strand out of place. A black, leather corset cinched her flowing white tunic, and her black leather breeches were tucked into thigh-high boots. Her violet eyes glimmered with amusement as she canted her head to the side, and delight curled her plum-painted lips.

"You can't be surprised to see me, Nereida." Lark clenched her fists, wincing at the searing pain as she tested the limits of her twice stitched fingers.

Nereida clicked her tongue, grabbing Lark's hand for closer inspection.

"You poor, sweet thing. You haven't been staying out of trouble, have you?" She regarded Lark with a knowing smile that dimpled her full cheeks. She seemed to take Lark's silence as answer enough. "Good. It's much too fun to avoid." Nereida ran her thumb over the bandage.

Lark stiffened as the sensation of skin stretching and reforming burned in her hand. It was irritating like a swarm of insects crawling along her nerves. When the feeling passed, Nereida deftly unwrapped Lark's hand to reveal her healed fingers.

"That's better, isn't it?" Nereida ruffled Lark's hair before turning on her heel and striding over to her leather seat. She collapsed with a satisfied groan. "Tell me, to what do I owe the pleasure of your visit, little Reaper?"

She knew damn well why Lark was here. As if Nereida couldn't sense one of her demons dragging a mortal to the Netherworld. If she'd lost sight of what her minions were doing, Thanar must be proving a great challenge indeed.

"Gavriel was brought here, despite being very much alive." Lark's blood burned in her veins, scorching along in a current of rage. "Give him back."

Nereida regarded her with a thoughtful expression. "We need tea. I'll have Khronos fetch us some." She raised the delicate bell poised on the end table beside her chair.

"I did not come here to play games with you. Your demon stole a human from the mortal realm to force my hand and call in our bargain early. I was meant to have a human lifespan. *My* death, its conclusion. Have you no honor left?"

"Child, you mistake me for one of your *human* peers." Nereida smiled, the expression anything but friendly. She laced her fingers over her crossed knee. "Remember your place."

Lark wished she'd brought her weapons. If only to have the rush of satisfaction of lodging an arrow through her skull.

"But," Nereida continued, "your plight does require closer inspection."

The air shifted. The edges tinged with darkness before a burst of shadows erupted. Messy white hair and black horns appeared above narrowed silver eyes. The demon who had stolen Gavriel away.

Balan.

"You bastard," Lark cried, leaping to grab him by his throat. It mattered little that she couldn't hurt him here, not in physical form, but it didn't stop the thrum of violence in her blood.

Balan's eyes widened in surprise, his angular face twisted into a smirk. "I guess true love really does conquer all." He grasped her wrist and ripped her hand from him. She bit down on her cry of pain as he twisted her arm.

"Balan," Nereida said from her seat in a chiding tone. "Mind your manners."

With a growl, he released her.

Lark reached for the desk laden with books and parchments and swiped the only weapon she could find: a letter opener. It wouldn't make any difference, which was why she left all her weapons behind. But she found a surge of comfort in its weight.

Balan laughed, the low timbre making her skin crawl. "Is that the best you can do? I must say, I'm disappointed."

"I can carve your eye out, you miserable shit," Lark hissed through clenched teeth. It didn't matter what happened to her. Or how foolish she appeared, waving around a dull little blade. "Where is Gavriel?"

"Balan," Nereida repeated, a warning in her voice. She bounced her crossed leg. Her leather breeches outlined the contours of her thick and shapely thighs. "Where is the mortal?"

He gave her an insincere version of a smile. It stretched unnaturally around his sharp teeth. "He's safe, for now." Balan turned back to regard Lark with a dark expression. "Provided *she* can behave."

"I held up my end. Release him." Lark tested the weight of the letter opener in her hand. The image of sending it soaring through the air and into his eye was a lovely thought.

"You are here." Nereida seemed to consider, and a small smile played on her lips. She stood with a languid, feline grace. A grin stretched across her full, dark lips as she placed a hand on her generous hip. "Bring him to the Great Hall. This is cause for celebration."

"No," Lark bit out through clenched teeth.

Nereida spun to face Lark. A scornful look crossed her features. "You don't seem to understand the position you're in."

"I want to see him. No pomp and frills. Just take me to him so I might assess if *he* kept his word." Lark didn't even glance in Balan's direction. "Then, Gavriel is free to leave. That was our bargain."

"You doubt me, after everything we've been through?" Balan said in a wounded tone.

Lark was well versed in how demons made deals and trifled with technicalities. No, she didn't trust him. She didn't trust any of them.

She wouldn't make that mistake again.

"I'm a woman of my word," Nereida said. "You might doubt him, but you have no reason to doubt me."

"Don't I? Did you not promise to mend the tears with the power you took from me?"

"I only took what you gave freely. And technically, I said I would fix the tear you created. I never said how."

"You misled me." Even though Lark wasn't shocked, all signs

pointed to duplicity, some small, naïve part of her hoped Nereida would deny it. "We struck an accord."

"Words are dangerous weapons, darling. Don't fret, all will be revealed in the Great Hall." Her violet gaze fell on the lantern in Lark's hand. "What manner of trinket is this?"

Lark hid it behind her back. "A parting gift from the Forbidden Shrine. It guided me here." If Nereida took the lantern, Lark couldn't guarantee Gavriel's safe return.

"Oh, you sweet thing. I'm not about to take your little night light." Nereida wrinkled her nose in an affectionate expression. "I have no use for such silly things. And soon, neither will you." She turned to regard Balan. "Bring her to retrieve the mortal. But Larkin—" Her eyes narrowed, all amusement fleeing her expression. Casting her in the role of the terrifying witch-queen. "Don't try anything stupid. I will kill your human, and his suffering will last all of eternity."

A shiver licked up Lark's spine. "I understand."

The storm on Nereida's face melted into carefree amusement once more. "Splendid! Now run along, fetch that man of yours, and I expect to see all three of you in the Great Hall. I promise you he will leave freely. Just not yet."

Lark exhaled a breath rife with tension. What choice did she have? Even if this was a trick, Gavriel would get out; the lantern would guide him. She shoved it into her bag. "Fine."

Balan grinned. "Who knew she could be so agreeable? Tell me, mortal, just how compliant will you be when your rib cage is spread open for me?"

"Your love of hearing yourself speak only confirms my suspicions that no one else can stand your voice." Lark was too impatient to fear his words. Words he loved to whisper in hopes of getting a rise out of her. He could stew in his disappointment.

"And you get the pleasure of listening to me speak every minute of every day for all of eternity." He slung an arm around her shoulders, and Lark shook him off. He laughed as he gripped her arm tight enough to bruise. "And if you think for a moment your time with me will be enjoyable"—he leaned close enough, his breath tickled her ear —"think again."

Before a scathing retort could leap from Lark's tongue, a rush of vertigo washed over her. An abrupt snap—a disconnect within her soul as she plummeted.

Her mind leapt from her body, falling through the ground, and landing miles below. The sensation of falling twice, once in her soul and once in her body, threatened to paint the stone floors with the meager contents of her stomach, and she collapsed.

CHAPTER 57

*W*hen Lark opened her eyes, Balan stood over her, eying her with thinly veiled amusement. "Your pet didn't like my preferred mode of transport either."

Lark sat up, assessing her surroundings that spun from the lag of her mortal body. The damp scent of decay and rot assaulted her senses. The air was wet and cold. Dungeon cells lined the room, iron bars keeping the prisoners of the Netherworld from escaping. Lark tasted magic, a sickly-sweet cloying flavor, and her stomach heaved. It made sense it would take more than iron for certain prisoners.

Lark stood and cursed the way she swayed on her feet. "Where is he?"

Balan wore an infuriating smirk that widened to show teeth too sharp. "Ask me nicely."

"Lark?"

The unmistakable voice called out to her. Hope filled Lark's chest near to bursting as she spun around seeking the sound. "Gavriel?"

"What are you doing here?" Anger sharpened his tone, and it was the most beautiful sound she'd ever heard. Lark ran down the hall to the furthest cell. Gavriel's hands gripped the bars, hands she'd memorized from countless nights of watching him when he wasn't looking.

Gavriel wedged himself between iron bars as far as he could, trying to reach her, filthy and beautiful, as his green eyes sought hers. Blood and bruises adorned his face.

Lark tangled her fingers in his, pressing against the door of his cell.

"You came for me," he whispered, disbelief and wonder in his voice. "Have you gone completely mad?"

Lark laughed, the sound ripping from her chest in a sob. She cataloged every scar on his face and the dark shadows along his sharp jaw.

Gavriel ran a trembling finger down her cheek. "I didn't think I'd see you again. I hoped I wouldn't. How could you do this?" His anger had returned.

"I told you. I'll never let anything happen to you." Lark yanked the lantern free of her satchel. "Use this and return to the mortal world."

She clung to it, her fragile hope, that she could get him out alive. That he could live as a free man. She clung to it with the last shred of sanity in her grieving, exhausted mind.

If he could survive, one good thing could come of this.

His expression turned murderous, sharpening the edges of his face. "I'm not leaving you here."

Lark closed her eyes, tears already filling her vision. "Gavriel, you have to. Only the same number of souls who traveled by lantern can travel back. It's the only way."

"Lark," he growled, his eyes flashing. "I'm not going anywhere without you."

"But—"

"Shut up and kiss me." Gavriel claimed her mouth in a bruising kiss. The tears finally trailed down her cheeks. Her chest ached with the mournful truth she'd already known. Of course, he'd never leave her, no more than she could leave him.

"All right, that's quite enough." Balan ripped Lark away from the cell. "We have places to be." With a wave of his hand, the cell door swung open.

Gavriel stepped out, searching for any hidden traps before he gathered Lark into his arms, pressing her close to his chest.

Lark leaned into his touch, one last time. Closing her eyes and pretending for a moment they were curled up in her tent.

"I'm bored of this." Balan grasped her by the collar and heaved her forward. "Ladies first."

Lark tripped over her feet, nearly landing on the filthy dungeon floor.

"Watch it, Balan," she said, turning to glare at him. She ignored the curve of his mouth at the mention of his name.

"I'd prefer we have special little nicknames for each other once this business is all sorted. I choose 'Master and Commander.' It has a nice ring to it, don't you think? And for you, how about meat sack? It is, after all, what you were always dying to become."

Lark ignored him, eyeing Gavriel. He studied her with a worrying expression. Like he was formulating a plan. Lark shook her head. If there was any chance of him making it out of here alive, they would need to cooperate. She glared at him, willing him to understand, but he only glared back.

Better angry than dead.

A hand squeezed her shoulder.

That was the only warning before her mind vaulted ahead of her body, slipping through space and time, and landing square in the middle of the Great Hall. Her consciousness lurched back into her physical form in a dizzying collision.

Lark doubled over, gripped her stomach.

A warm hand rubbed soothing circles against her back. She lifted her heavy head to find Gavriel watching her with ill-concealed worry. Even though he, too, must be battling the wave of nausea from bleeding through rifts in existence.

Lark stood and blinked, halting the spinning of the massive room. This hall rivaled Thanar's in size. But while the Otherworld strived for recreation of mortal whims and fancies, the Netherworld reveled in its darkness.

Beneath Lark's feet were onyx floors, smooth enough she could see her reflection like a black mirror. The few rounded arch windows within the hall let in the soft white light of the moon. Leaving the rest of the hall shrouded in darkness. Braziers remained unlit. There were no vestibules or private corners. No matter where one stood, even cloaked in darkness, one was exposed.

"Step forward, meat sack." Balan gripped her by the elbow. Gavriel knocked his hand away.

Balan smiled. "Do not forget every allowance you're given is a kindness, mortal." He grabbed Lark again, this time with more force. "If you'd rather sit this out in the dungeon, I'll happily oblige." He dragged her toward the empty dais.

Lark yanked her arm free from his grasp. "The bargain hasn't been fulfilled. You don't own me."

"Yet." Balan's eyes darkened. "Go then, meat sack. Enjoy your momentary freedom. Use it to walk to your fate."

The throne seated atop the dais was far less ornate than the one Thanar had created for himself, but it looked crafted by the very night air—glittering obsidian that claimed the shadows and held them captive. The back of the throne cut in jagged shards that fanned out behind its owner. Sharp enough to slice through mortal flesh.

As Lark studied the seat, the air around it began to shift. A wicked promise. A gossamer curtain parting.

Nereida appeared, sitting sideways on the massive throne. Her thick legs dangled over the side. She waved a hand and flames erupted atop every brazier. Casting the hall in a glow that felt anything but warm.

Nereida regarded Lark with an affectionate smile before her eyes landed on Gavriel. "So, this is the mortal who started it all." She shot Lark a conspiratorial look. "He *is* handsome. Hopefully, he's worth all this fuss." She spun in her seat and crossed her legs, peering down at them. Light from the flames danced across her braided crown of silvery hair. Sitting in the throne of death and darkness, Nereida was every bit the powerful queen. Lark tried to reconcile the image of the distracted witch devouring filthy literature with the calculating enemy before her.

"Before our bargain comes to a close, I offer you something I know your curious little heart will jump at the chance to receive."

"Is it a pardon from my debt?"

Nereida laughed, a bright tinkling sound. "No, silly. I don't trade in pardons. What I offer is information."

Lark pushed down the unease of accepting anything from Nereida. "What sort of information?"

"How aware are you of the state of things since you went on your little mortal holiday?"

"I've heard whispers. The evidence of Undesirables running free, unchecked in mortal lands is rather damning."

Nereida's smile grew. "Yes, sweet thing. I did not mend the tears in the veil. Nor did I cause them." She leaned forward. "There's a new dawn rising. One you had a hand in creating. The world can be remade anew. A world where fate answers to us rather than commanding our submission."

Terror flooded Lark's human heart; a slippery cold feeling took root in her veins. "What have you done?"

"Me? I did nothing but wait." Nereida clasped her hands around her bent knee, kicking her boot in a rhythmic pulse. "Your former master, however, he's the real architect of it all."

"Thanar?" There was no way he'd stand for this. He valued order above all else.

Nereida uncrossed her legs, leaning back. "Didn't you spit on destiny? Wish for a world where one's actions dictate their path?"

Lark didn't respond. Dread burrowed its way deep into her gut.

"This is the only way. We must tear down the barriers between our worlds. Don't you see?" Nereida's eyes lit up with reverential glee. "This is how we master fate. The entire system was corrupted by the gods of the sky. It's only in chaos we can ever be free."

Lark glanced back at Gavriel. His face contorted in revulsion.

Balan frowned.

"This is madness!" Lark turned back to stare down Nereida. "Countless innocents will die if you let all the twisted souls of the Netherworld free to rampage the world."

Nereida angled her head, her expression tightened in frustration.

Like she'd expected Lark to rejoice in this plan. "Perhaps. But it's the only way to break the chains of fate and balance."

"That can't be true." Lark stepped forward, desperation souring her tongue. "There must be another way."

"How many children have you reaped, Larkin? How many good men met their end at the hands of injustice? How many women were beaten and raped, left dying while you waited in the shadows to bring their souls to me?" Her beautiful face hardened. "How many evil souls go on living, while you collect those who might flourish if given the chance? If that is the way of the world, I will not mourn its loss."

Lark bit the inside of her cheek. Warring with the internal rightness of her words. Had she not complained of the very thing Nereida spoke against?

This couldn't be the way.

"There are still innocents out there. You would force death to their door by doing this."

"Death is everywhere. In everything. Each time you kiss your man back there, that sweetness you taste is a promise of death delayed. And besides"—her face smoothed into its mask of indulgent amusement—"the credit isn't mine. I did nothing. I merely neglected to stop it."

Panic clutched Lark's chest and crawled up her throat. If what Nereida said was true, before long the whole world would be overrun. "Why now?" Lark studied the witch-queen. "What's changed?"

Nereida's mouth split in a wide grin. "That is an excellent question, little Reaper. I don't have the power to rip down the veil between our worlds. Not yet, anyway."

Realization dawned on Lark. The sickening revulsion of it was overpowering. "When you took my power. All the strength I'd accrued from guiding souls—"

"A good guess, but not exactly," Nereida interrupted. "You see, it was never your power I needed."

Skies above.

The doors slammed open.

Lark jumped and spun around.

Storming through the Great Hall, cloaked in black, dark eyes murderous, his rage and power palpable in the air, was Thanar.

He had come to collect what was his.

CHAPTER 58

*T*hanar was a tempest of wrath. His raven hair hung in his dark eyes as he thundered through the Great Hall. His black robes hung open, billowing in his wake as Ceto and Nyx trailed behind him. The force of his inner circle.

Though, Leysa was nowhere to be seen.

Thanar barreled straight toward Lark, stopping just short of colliding into her. "You stupid girl! Have you any idea what you've done?" His voice rumbled through the hall.

Lark clenched her fists, tipping her head to glare at him. "You forced my hand. I couldn't suffocate under your rule any longer."

Towering over her, his sharp face darkened, nostrils flaring. His impossibly black eyes narrowed. "This is larger than you, Larkin. You've jeopardized everything. Every soul in existence is hanging in the balance because of your petty selfishness."

Gavriel found his way to Lark's side. Thanar didn't so much as acknowledge him.

"Was it worth it?"

Ferryn had asked her the same question. And unequivocally she'd known—yes it was worth it, and she'd do it again. But now, she hesitated.

So much was lost.

The balance of life and death.

Hugo.

"Come now, Thanar, you can't blame her, can you?" Nereida interrupted before Lark could formulate a response. "In fact, I think today is a good day to air our grievances. Get everything out on the table," she smirked at him, resting her head on her fist. "I hear it can be quite cathartic."

Ceto stiffened. Memories of what Ferryn told Lark in the Shrine spilled into her thoughts. Maybe Ceto was dying to know how he was. If she loved him, she must be agonizing over it.

Nyx's mouth curved in the barest of smiles.

Something big was coming.

"I won't entertain this madness." Thanar seized Lark's arm in a bruising grip. "We're leaving."

Lark ripped free of his grasp. And reached for Hugo's knife—

The one she'd left topside with Daciana.

Gavriel grabbed the ancient being by his black robes. "Over my dead body."

Thanar's mouth curved in a cruel smile. "Interesting choice of words. So be it."

Lark shoved her way between them. "You won't harm him." She glared up at the face of her tormentor. Lifetimes of cruelty she'd witnessed him wield. Countless moments of terror she'd faced.

She wouldn't fear him now.

Thanar's eyes widened in surprise for but a moment, before they narrowed. "You will do as commanded." He grasped Lark's shoulders. "I will be sure of it."

"No!" Gavriel cried out, as Lark braced herself to be swept away to the Otherworld.

Nothing happened.

Nyx let out a bark of laughter while Ceto remained silent.

Thanar's expression melted into confusion, before shifting to outrage. He whipped his head to glare at Nereida still lounging on the throne watching curiously. "What's the meaning of this?"

She shrugged, her mouth quirking to the side. "It's not my doing, old friend." She pointed the toe of her boot at Lark. "Ask her."

Thanar stared at Lark in horror. "What have you done?"

Warm triumph spread through Lark's body as she shoved him back. "I made sure you'd never own me." The satisfaction that curled in her chest at finally being able to utter those words to him was nothing short of euphoric.

Thanar shook his head, his eyes widening. "How could you do this?" He turned to Nereida, stalking toward the dais. "Release her at once."

"I don't take orders from you. Besides, I already told you, no more secrets. Today is a good day to set yourself free!" She lifted her hands to the vaulted ceilings and dark chandeliers that glistened in the firelight. "Tell her the truth, or I will."

A muscle feathered in his jaw; his dark brows knitted together as he glared Nereida down.

"Tell me what?" Lark asked. Whatever it was, she needed to know.

"Thanar's dirty little secret," Nereida said, her eyes never leaving Thanar. "Isn't that right, Commander Ceto?"

Ceto stepped forward, never once glancing at Thanar. "Yes, your majesty. That is correct."

Thanar's expression turned murderous, his face twisting and hardening into the expression Lark knew so well. "You dare to turn on me? After everything I've—"

"What have you done for me? You mean denying my ascension, in favor of *her*?"

Lark fought the urge to shrink back at the hostility in Ceto's voice. She wasn't wrong. Lark never wanted his favor, and yet he kept her close.

"Or what about that punishment you leveled, so many years ago?" Ceto continued, beautiful fury splashing across her face. "You thought I'd forgotten, but I never did. I honored your balance, I turned him in, and I gave up everything for you. But when it was your precious Lark—"

"Priamos was—"

"Don't speak his name!" Ceto's voice echoed in the dark hall, reverberating off the unforgiving onyx. Her mouth curved in a cruel sneer. "You reap what you sow, Thanar. And you sowed your downfall the first moment you saw Lark." She took her place at Nereida's side, Nyx trailing behind her.

The fearsome Commander and Spymaster, answering to the Queen of the Netherworld.

The ground beneath Lark's feet tilted. She fought to stay upright, though her body sagged under the weight of the truth. Ceto and Nyx were Thanar's enforcers, the ones all Reapers feared would collect them to face his punishments. They were unswervingly loyal, always watching and reporting. And here they were, abandoning him.

That conversation in the Otherworld dungeon felt like lifetimes ago, Lark's last day as a Reaper. Ceto's words came to mind.

"You want to change fate? Tell me, what would you sacrifice to meet that end? What would you give?"

How many sacrifices had Ceto made?

Thanar's face warred between rage and grief.

Nereida sighed. "Isn't it so much better to rip the bandage off? Rather than letting the wound fester?" She grinned. "Your turn Thanar."

"Nereida, please." His voice was a guttural plea.

Lark crept closer to the two gods staring each other down.

Nereida turned to Lark, her smile softening. "You were human once, yes?"

What was she getting at? "That's my understanding."

"But you don't recall your human life, do you?" Nereida's violet eyes were alight with excitement.

"No." Lark didn't, but Ferryn remembered. She envied him his human memories.

"Is that typical of Reapers?"

"I suppose it happens when you exist long enough to forget." That's what she'd always told herself. And being a Reaper was a ceaseless existence. Living in such certainty of time was still a new concept.

Nereida nodded, not in agreement but acknowledgment. Like

Lark had provided the correct response. "Once upon a time, long ago, there was a young girl named Larkin Byrne."

Thanar stiffened. "Nereida, I beg of you—"

"As much fun as it is to watch you beg," she said with a coy smile, "interrupt me again, and you'll find out exactly how much influence I've been granted."

Much to Lark's shock, Thanar shut his mouth and quietly glowered at her.

Somehow that was more unsettling than anything she'd ever witnessed from him.

"Now, where was I?" Nereida hummed in thought. "Oh, yes. There was a girl named Larkin Byrne. She was a kind and beautiful soul. So caring." She rolled her eyes. "So soft.

"One day, her father sold her to pay off his old gambling debts. In all the world—not just Koval—it was quite common for men to sell the women they owned into indentured servitude until their debts were forgiven, or dowries replaced, or any sort of lovely reason you can think of for a father to cart his daughter off like chattel.

"What he didn't know was, he'd failed to negotiate the terms and sold her into a lifetime of servitude." Nereida lifted her finger into the air with a dramatic flourish. "But all was not lost. For, in the depths of her despair, in the darkest horrors of her cage, hope blossomed. Within the walls of her prison, she met a man whose name has been lost to time. But this man cultivated joy in her little heart."

Nereida lifted her head to regard Gavriel. "You there, step forward, handsome mortal. You need to hear this too."

Gavriel stepped forward, standing close enough to Lark, she could breathe him in.

"This man had the gift of song. And when their master's punishments grew too loud, this man would play her music. Such wonderful music to drown out the sound of lashings and screams. Care to guess what instrument he played?"

"The fiddle," Lark breathed, sure her heart was about to hammer through her chest.

"Yes!" Nereida clapped with delight. "He played the fiddle. There was more than one occasion when he'd play a lullaby, and she'd sing to the frightened children at night to help them sleep. So romantic."

Lark exhaled a stuttering breath. Her entire body was numb, save for the warmth in her hand where Gavriel slipped his fingers through hers. His hand tightened.

"While they were falling in love, there was another who watched from afar. The first echoes of love in his black heart awakened him from his centuries-long slumber." Nereida grinned at Thanar whose face had fallen in anguish. "He had seen many souls lost from that castle. Too burdened by what they'd faced in their mortal lives to move on. When he went to investigate why so many souls had been lost on their journey, he found the girl.

"She was a bright, beaming light amongst a sea of darkness. This ancient being fell for the mortal." Nereida sighed, casting her eyes to the ceiling. "I love a good tragedy."

Lark's stomach rolled. She felt a tug as Gavriel pulled her closer to him. He wore a kindred expression of fear in his eyes. Tearing her gaze away, she nodded to Nereida to continue. "What happened next?"

"What always happens in a romantic tragedy? The girl and her mortal held a private ritual at nightfall by the ancient yew tree. Binding their souls, for what else did they have to offer each other? They didn't realize that they'd stirred ancient magic in their coupling, nor did they understand the lasting effects of their bond."

Lark's eyes widened in horror. "Do you mean we, I mean they—"

"Don't skip ahead," Nereida chastised. "Let a storyteller weave the tale. They made plans to run away but only after Larkin could be sure her disappearance would land no one in trouble." She laughed, the sounds echoing through the cavernous room. "Such a sweet thing. Unfortunately, it mattered little. Someone had spotted them returning that night and reported it to their master."

Lark gripped Gavriel's hand. A lifeline when everything else felt like it was crumbling.

"Her death was known by the fates. Written in blood and foretold by the great seer, Leysa. When she received the mark, something urged her to report this particular mortal to Thanar." She glanced over at him. "Would you like to take it from here?"

Thanar silently glared, his face a dark storm.

Of course Leysa had a hand in her fate. But where was she now?

Ceto's eyes met Lark's as if sensing her thoughts.

Nereida continued. "He was beside himself with grief. This bright and beautiful soul that danced before his very eyes would be snuffed in the cruelest of ways. Details of her impending death circulated his mind, driving him near to madness. Unable to handle her fate, he nearly tore down Avalon to reach the weavers of destiny.

"It was lucky for him he had such a caring friend who only needed to nudge him in the right direction." Nereida winked, and a dimple creased her round cheek. "He'd never win a war with Avalon, and the mortal girl was going to die anyway. Why not lead her from the path ever so slightly so she might move on in peace rather than risk the eternal torment of her soul failing to move on? Twisting and reforming into something else."

"An Undesirable." Lark felt like she was floating, tethered to her body but not really there. As if her mortal mind was trying to protect itself.

Mortals were funny things.

Nereida nodded. "Not the kind you're used to though. More of a lament of regret that echoes in the same place for all eternity."

"The girl waited by the yew where they'd sworn the bond—where they'd delved into ancient magic they couldn't possibly understand and left their mark upon the earth. But her love wasn't the one waiting for her. A group of guards was stationed nearby, ready and waiting to catch the poor girl." She sucked on her teeth, agitation evident on her beautiful face. "What do you think they planned for her?"

Lark knew. Her very soul was unraveling as the witch spun her tale. A story long-forgotten that echoed within her very bones.

"Thanar arrived before they could force her legs apart and taint the earth with her blood."

"Skies above," Gavriel murmured.

Lark glanced over at Thanar whose downcast eyes would not meet hers.

He was a monster. He'd tortured her and threatened her with the worst possible punishment. He couldn't be anything else in her eyes. And yet—

"What next?" Lark demanded, strength returning to her voice. She dropped Gavriel's hand, taking a step toward the dais. "After the mortal girl was no longer in danger, what did he do?"

"He told her of her destiny. Her death in all its inevitability. How he wished he could spare her, for if there was a soul worth altering the balance for, it was hers. But he could not. Not without ripping a tear in the veil that keeps everything in place. His precious balance."

Thanar snapped his head up, a murderous glint in his dark eyes. "Without the balance there is chaos. Unnecessary death. It is my responsibility to uphold the safety of the mortal world."

"And how did that work out for you, Thanar, dear?" Ignoring him, Nereida continued. "With a single touch, he ended her life. A kindness in his eyes, for she died without pain, without fear. What he didn't account for, was her anger.

"She refused to move on until her man was safe from his fate. Thanar couldn't allow this. Her soul needed to depart or else be lost to the abyss for all time." Nereida arched an elegant eyebrow. "So, he *dragged* her to the other side. Her fingers clawed at the earth as she was ripped away from the mortal world and her love."

Lark felt the sensation of dirt and blood and leaves caked beneath her fingernails. The ache in her chest at leaving the mortal man behind to face his death alone.

"And she became a Reaper," Lark said. Everything made sense now. How she was the only one who couldn't enjoy their existence. How it never felt right. Why she was the only one who dreamed. She'd been displaced the entire time.

Nereida studied her. "Indeed, she did. But when she was pulled unwillingly through the veil, a tear was formed. The first of many. The forest died that day, never to be home to a living creature again."

The Twisted Woods. Where Daciana found her. Where Lark crawled out of the ancient yew tree and took her first breath.

Nereida stood and strolled down the dais to circle Thanar with predatory grace.

Ceto and Nyx stiffened but remained in place.

"No matter how much he tried, he never could bring that soul back. She'd been wiped clean as soon as she crossed over. Forever existing as a painful reminder, a torment of his own making. He'd destroyed that which he loved most." Nereida canted her head to the side. "A fitting punishment for everything he's caused. But that's a story for another day."

Ceto exhaled a tight breath. Lark met her gaze only to find anguish and regret.

Nereida paused for dramatic effect. "The soul he cherished was lost to the abyss. Or so he thought. I prefer to think of her as dormant; she came back in the end."

Lark stared at Thanar, trying desperately to see past all the cruelty. It was like trying to force the last piece of a puzzle that didn't line up.

Realization dawned on her. "You said it was never my power you were after."

Nereida smiled affectionately. "You're so sweet to bring us full circle. That's correct, I don't want whatever power you manifested in your time as a Reaper. Did you really think I'd need it?"

Of course, Lark was nothing compared to the goddess of eternal suffering. "You said as much, I suppose it was foolish of me to expect the truth."

"I told you your power had to go somewhere. Might as well allocate it to me," Nereida said with a shrug. "But more importantly, there was a little kernel of power that didn't belong to you." She cut an eager glance Thanar's way. "You took a bit of his soul when you crossed over. It was a matter of acquiring it so I might gain a foothold in the Otherworld."

Thanar looked so small. Unremarkable. Like the curtain had been lifted and he'd been exposed as a fraud.

Nereida clapped her hands together. "Don't we all feel better getting that out in the open? I know I do."

Everyone stood in silence. In the aftermath of so many unearthed truths, the air was heavy with tension.

"I feel great," Balan said from somewhere behind.

"What happened to the mortal? The man she loved." Lark already knew the answer, but some part of her needed to hear it.

Nereida grinned. "Why, he's standing right next to you. Handsome as ever."

Lark's heart plummeted to her stomach. So Gavriel had been bound to her. By some unknown magic. How much of their connection was compulsion? "How?" The word constricted in her throat.

"My dear, fate is a powerful thing. He'd never move on until you found each other. How many lives has he lived and forgotten waiting for you, I wonder?" Nereida tapped her chin in thought. "It would be a curious thing to restore all his memories from every life. Do you think his mortal mind could handle it?"

Gavriel was bound to her.

Why did that settle like a stone in Lark's gut?

"He lives now because your soul *demanded* it." Nereida shook her head. "You have far more power than anyone gives you credit. You would be more than an asset to my cause."

"I don't give a shit about your cause. I came to uphold my end of the deal. Nothing more. Gavriel is free to go, and I remain." Lark was too exhausted to face this any longer. She just needed to get him out.

"I won't leave you." Gavriel tugged on her hand.

Vision blurring, Lark whirled on him. "Damn it, Gavriel. All I'm trying to do is save you. Why do you make it so hard?"

He glared at her. "You're asking me to abandon you, and it's not going to happen."

"I want you to live, you insufferable ass!"

Gavriel grabbed her by the arms and yanked her toward him. "I won't let you sacrifice yourself."

Lark glared up at him. Exhaustion and tears hazing her vision. It was all too much for her body to contain. She needed to sink to the floor and curl in on herself and scream.

Nereida held her hands up. "All in good time. There was a reason Thanar was summoned, and not just for my amusement."

Thanar watched Lark and Gavriel with an expression of anguish. "I know why you summoned me, witch. I know what you want from me."

Lark extricated herself from Gavriel's grip. Thanar's expression was intense and full of longing. With a tight exhale he strode up to Lark and grabbed her by the shoulders. His face close enough his breath tickled her mouth as he spoke the binding words: "I swear to inherit the debt she bears."

He sealed his mouth over hers in a rough kiss.

CHAPTER 59

*N*umb.

Lark's entire body had gone numb.

Finally, Thanar released her from his kiss. His dark eyes searched her face for something. A glimmer of hope smoothed his sharp edges for an instant before his face tightened in cold indifference. "There, a new bargain's been struck."

Lark swayed on her feet; darkness blotted her vision. She glanced over at Gavriel, needing to see his face.

Gavriel wore an expression of hurt. Not betrayal exactly, more as if the sight of them pained him. But he held her gaze, unwavering.

"So, it would seem," Nereida said. A satisfied smile warmed her features.

Nereida had outplayed them all.

Lark spun to glare at Thanar. "Do you realize what you've done?"

Thanar lifted his head, dark hair falling in his eyes. His silence, deafening.

"You just handed her everything she needs to destroy the world. To obliterate the balance." Lark advanced on Thanar, itching to strangle him. Instead, she twisted her hands into the fabric of his black robes, shaking him hard enough to rattle her teeth. "Have you nothing to say for yourself?"

Thanar shifted his dark gaze between her eyes and her mouth before responding. "I'm sorry."

Lark didn't know if he was apologizing for now, or long ago. When he dragged her through the earth to an afterlife she wasn't ready to meet. She loosened her grip, stepping away.

Nereida situated herself back on her throne with an eager grin on her face. She snapped her fingers and pointed next to her.

Lark watched in horror as Thanar, the ancient and powerful being, the one who'd struck fear in her heart long before it resumed beating, approached the dais and sat down beside the throne.

How far he'd fallen.

All because of her.

Ceto's face darkened, while Nyx still wore that maddening smile.

"Now," Nereida said. "You two are free to go. The terms of our bargain have been met and you no longer need to worry what happens to you in death." Her dark lips quirked to the side. "Unless you're terribly naughty, then I'll see you again soon."

"What?" A deep, indignant voice rumbled behind her. Balan pushed past Lark and Gavriel. His silver eyes, murderous. "You promised her to me."

Nereida shrugged. "Terms have changed, darling. Learn to adapt."

His hands clenched into fists. "You lied to me."

The witch-queen laughed. The sound, though bright, still raised the hairs on the back of Lark's neck. "Of course I lied, sweet thing. Did you think I'd ever hand anything of value over to you?" She regarded him with pitying amusement.

Balan growled in response. He lifted his chin, firelight danced along his black horns. "Careful, witch. Or you may find yourself without the support you desperately need to wage your little war."

Nereida ran a hand through Thanar's black hair. He didn't so much as flinch, his eyes never leaving Lark. "I have everything I need right here."

With a snarl, Balan turned to leave.

"Balan," she called out, stilling his movements. "It isn't wise to bite the hand that feeds you. You might find yourself starved."

Without so much as a backward glance, Balan stalked out of the throne room. Each departing step echoed through the hall before he slammed the doors shut behind him.

"Is there anywhere you'd prefer I send you?" Nereida asked in a congenial voice. "It can be anywhere at all, there are countless tears, and I'd be willing to make a few more."

Lark would prefer to travel by lantern. To avoid receiving any boon from Nereida in case it came with a price. But she'd traveled alone, and however many travel by lantern are how many can return.

Her heart heavy in her chest, and avoiding Thanar's gaze, Lark gave her a short nod. "I'd like to go back the way I entered." To the yew tree not far from camp. Where the others were either waiting or had given up on her return and bid farewell.

Nereida smiled as if satisfied with that answer. "Of course, sweet Larkin. Close your eyes tight, and envision the place from which you came."

Lark grabbed Gavriel's hand, the warmth in his touch almost searing. She clenched her eyes shut. Seeing the yew tree, green sun-kissed leaves swaying in the summer breeze. The damp scent of earth wafting in the air.

Lark cracked an eyelid to see Thanar one last time before she was swept back to the mortal world.

Thanar stared at her, his eyes black and depthless. Something akin to longing flared on his face. The pain etched there was too much for her to look at, so she closed her eyes on him and the Netherworld.

The last words she heard were from Nereida murmuring to him, "We have so much to catch up on, old friend."

Then the world fell away.

THE WARM, damp earth embraced Lark's body, her head cradled on moist grass. The air held the heavy scent of rain—a reminder of what had been, a promise of what was to come. The warm unmistakable grip of Gavriel's hand in hers sent flutters through her chest.

They'd made it out. They'd survived. Both of them.

Why did she feel so hollow?

Opening her eyes, Lark gazed up at the dense leaves overhead. Verdant and upturned, awaiting another kiss of rain.

The corners of her eyes were wet. As if she'd squeezed them shut tight enough to force unbidden tears out. She turned to find Gavriel watching her quietly. His expression unreadable.

She wanted to open her mouth to speak—to tell him how grateful she was they both lived. That nothing revealed in the Netherworld would ever come between them. That she could push aside the raw terror she felt at the notion that their love was predetermined and not her choice. She sacrificed so much for the sake of choice. And here she'd been playing into fate's hand the whole time.

Lark wanted to tell him they'd figure out a way to stop Nereida and prevent the world from falling.

That nothing had changed between them.

She wanted to say all these things, but the words died in her throat.

Instead, she pulled herself closer, claiming his mouth in a burning kiss that promised everything and nothing.

Gavriel pulled her atop him, yanking her down close enough to press every inch of her against him. To remind them of every inch won, every breath earned, every kiss shared, that they were alive. That this was real.

They ignored the tears that rolled down her cheeks. Pouring everything they had left into each other. Starved for a touch that was real and tangible.

Was love meant to be a choice?

Was it always supposed to be out of her hands? A freefall from a height far beyond what mortal eyes could see.

Under that ancient yew, branches heavy with life, they found answers and questions beneath one another's skin. Searching and burning until all that was left was the hazy sun peeking between the leaves.

CHAPTER 60

*A*s Lark and Gavriel crested the top of the hill, the camp came into view. She surveyed each companion she'd left behind in her quest to rescue him. It had only been a matter of hours, or had it been longer? Time was a tricky thing in the Netherworld. Either way, if Lark didn't know any better, she'd have assumed she'd been gone for a matter of moments given the fact that camp remained unchanged.

Alistair still watched Langford with a forlorn expression drawn on his normally roguish face. Langford ignored him as he gingerly tugged his tunic over his head to change his bandages. He'd never allow a wound to fester.

Daciana had ceased her agitated pacing. She sat on a nearby boulder in utter stillness—a posture Lark had only seen achieved by otherworldly beings—with a bleak, calm acceptance on her face.

As if sensing a change in the air, Daciana whipped her head up and stared at Lark. A misty, radiant smile spread across her face. She leapt to her feet and sprinted toward them.

Lark ran and threw herself into Daciana's open arms. Laughter broke through their sobs of relief.

"I should be furious with you," Daciana said, squeezing her tighter.

"Aren't you?" So many buried emotions catapulted to the surface, edged with hysteria.

"Yes, but I'm too happy to care."

"You all waited for me. You must have known there was a chance I'd return." Lark glanced behind Daciana to see Alistair and Langford approaching.

Langford pulled Lark into a soft embrace, pressing a whisper of a kiss to her hair. Alistair watched with an unreadable expression. When his gaze met hers, his mouth curved into a ghost of his smirk.

"It seemed the least we could do." Daciana clapped Lark on the back. "It wouldn't be the first time you managed impossible odds."

"Nor the last," Gavriel said somewhere behind them.

Daciana stared at him a moment, before grinning. "Oh, come here, we're happy to see you too." She pulled him into an embrace.

And for a moment they were nothing more than old friends, reunited once more.

"I take it that's bad," Alistair said, with a dubious expression on his face.

Lark had just finished recounting the events that took place in the Netherworld. "Yes, Alistair. That's bad. We don't want all the souls of the Netherworld roaming around up here unchecked."

Langford frowned. "How much of a difference will it make? They already seem to find no resistance in entering our world."

"That was a trickle. If things seemed bad before, imagine a flood."

He ran a hand across his mouth, deep in thought.

Lark wasn't ready to face the implications of all that would be. With Thanar's power now at Nereida's disposal, the fall of the mortal world seemed inevitable. But Lark had overcome that power once. She could do it again. "We need a plan. Some way to stop her from dropping the veil. If we can slow her progress—"

"How do you propose we do that?" Alistair interrupted, breaking a stick into little pieces to toss one by one into the fire. "The only answer I'm accepting is, find the nearest tavern and drink ourselves into a stupor while we await the end of the world." He finished with a grin that failed to reach his eyes. "Preferably between two sets of inexpensive breasts."

"Not now, Alistair," Langford said harshly.

Alistair firmed his mouth and glared at the fire.

"We're in Koval, are we not?" Langford continued. "We could gain access to the Great Library. I could peruse their ancient archives." He shrugged as if he wasn't dying to get his hands on those books. "It might provide a lead."

Lark nodded, biting the inside of her cheek. It wasn't a bad plan. Although it did leave her somewhat sitting on her hands, *hoping* for a useful outcome. That wasn't going to happen. "You, Daciana, and Alistair go." She gestured to herself and Gavriel. "We'll find our own way back to Ardenas. I want to call on Inerys again. See if she might know something."

Langford sat up, his eyes widening. "You want to split up?"

"I don't *want* to. But you three should stick to the plan and lodge on Ingemar's ship back. We've already paid and struck the bargain. You just have to be at the docks in a month. We'll meet you at Emeraude Port." Technically the coin paid for all their passage, but Lark was willing to forgo money spent to save time. Every day—every hour —counted against them. "And I don't want to waste your brilliant mind, Langford. You should look into all the research you can find and see if there are any tales of halting a god's whims." That's what Nereida was, though Lark doubted many mortals still revered her or Thanar.

Langford narrowed his eyes. "You flatter my pride, wife," he said, falling on his endearment for her.

"I could flatter other parts of you, husband." Lark was relieved she could still find humor, even after everything.

He laughed, shaking his head and ignoring the raised eyebrows of their companions. "Very, well I second your plan."

"Good. Everyone else?"

"It seems like a good place to start," Gavriel said, eying her with a calculative expression.

"Aye. It'll do," Alistair said with a nod.

Langford rolled his eyes. "Are you certain you wouldn't rather find yourself cheap company while the rest of us save the world?"

Alistair didn't toss back his usual brand of wit. He only stared, firelight deepening the shadows on his face. "If you think for one minute I'm ever letting you out of my sight again, you're stark raving mad."

Langford's mouth parted in surprise, but he schooled his features into indifference, staring down at the ground.

"I'm sorry, Lark, but I have something to take care of first," Daciana said.

Panic flared in Lark's chest. "What's happened?"

"Nothing, yet. But I have matters to attend, and then I'll find you all again. I swear it."

Lark exhaled a tight breath. She'd never force Daciana to follow her, and she'd known there was always a chance they'd part ways. But still, that sense of abandonment crept into her heart.

"Is this something I can help you with?"

Daciana's mouth curved in a sad smile, shaking her head. "Some cages are of our own making."

The familiarity of those words clanged in Lark's head, ringing in echoes across her mind. Whatever Daciana needed to do, it was important. She'd never decide to leave them lightly. Lark trusted her.

"I'll leave you messages everywhere we stay," Lark said. "That way you can track us down."

Daciana grinned. "Like little breadcrumbs."

BEFORE THEY PARTED WAYS, they knew there was one last goodbye they needed to say. The ache of it left a gaping hole in Lark's chest. The shrine wasn't far from where they'd made camp. Lark hadn't been able to put much distance between them without feeling like they were abandoning Hugo.

They couldn't recover Hugo's body. This, she mourned nearly as much as the loss itself. Death wasn't the end but the beginning of a journey. One he'd have to embark on without her. She hoped whatever was happening in the Netherworld didn't keep his soul from moving on, and whoever had come to collect him had done him justice. He deserved peace, more than anyone.

The five of them stood in a semicircle around the pile of small stones they'd made beside the mound of rock that once was their door to freedom. A door he never reached.

Alistair cleared his throat. His eyes, bloodshot. "Hugo was the strongest man I knew. The day I met him, he was stubbornly lifting a carriage out of a pothole in the road. Aiding some stranger to fix his broken wheel. Little did he know, he interrupted my plan to acquire a few extra coins from unsuspecting travelers. He helped them on their merry way, botching my scheme. But he was worth far more than a full coin purse." He stepped forward and placed his stone on the pile before taking his place back by Daciana's side, carelessly wiping his nose across his sleeve.

Gavriel stepped forward, placing his stone atop the mound. "Hugo hated me. That's how I knew he was a good judge of character. His sacrifice won't be in vain." He addressed the stone wall that hid Hugo's remains from the world. "I promise to spend every day fulfilling your command."

"He was a man of few words but keen insight. Wisdom not seen in this world." Langford stepped up, hesitating with his stone before placing it with the others. "I'll honor his memory by remaining brief. He wouldn't have wanted me to drone on about his heroic deeds." He choked out a laugh. "Goodbye dear friend, may the gods reunite you with your family." His voice broke on the last word, and he stepped back.

Daciana squeezed Langford's shoulder before she approached the stone pile. "He was a testament of loyalty. His courage unmatched. He's forever with us because he would never abandon any one of us.

No matter the stakes." She placed her stone but grabbed a small grey pebble from the pile. "I leave my stone to mark his place, but I choose to carry a piece of him with me always. Loyal to the end, my dear comrade." She slipped the small pebble into her pocket, giving Lark a nod of encouragement as she resumed her place.

Lark ran her thumbs over the smooth surface of the rounded stone she held. Her throat tightened, and her legs shook as she stepped up to the neatly piled stones. Panic overwhelmed her as she remembered his body was still entombed in the cave. She let her eyes fall closed, exhaling a stuttering breath.

"Hugo"—she began, her voice hoarse from unshed tears—"didn't care what I was. He didn't care what any of us were, or where we came from." She glanced down at the stone in her hands, worried it was the most pathetic little rock she could have found. She should have spent more time looking.

"Lark?"

She heard Gavriel's voice, gentle concern in his tone.

She waved him off, clearing her throat.

"Hugo was a loving husband and father. He never stopped being those things. Even after he lost his family." With a trembling hand, she placed her stone on top, fingers holding it in place. "And he'll always be family to me," she whispered, before releasing her stone.

LARK AND DACIANA sat side by side as the last few rays of sun bled from the horizon. Daciana was set to leave at first light, but Lark knew as soon as they'd all drifted off to sleep, she'd be off. The night wasn't a foreign or scary thing for her. She'd travel by moonlight with greater ease than Lark tracking the sun.

"I thought I should return these," Daciana said, placing the bow Hugo had carved by Lark's side, and the quiver full of arrows he fletched.

Lark ran her fingers down the etchings of the bow. The subtle designs he always crafted for her. Though he'd frown whenever she remarked on them.

"And this." Daciana pressed the knife into Lark's hand.

Lark closed her fingers around it, hugging it to her chest. "Thank you."

Daciana smirked. "I couldn't let you travel completely unarmed."

"I'm not unarmed. I have a pack full of blades to prove it. I'm beginning to think you're lightening your load for ease of travel."

Daciana laughed. "Perhaps. But now you're armed with far more than a blade." She stared out at the horizon, scanning the expanse before them. "Never forget what a wondrous thing memory can be. It has the power to fuel or destroy you."

Daciana's hand flexed over the hilt of a dagger at her hip. She had taken to saying cryptic things such as this and had a way of telling them things without saying what she meant.

"Is that what you're chasing? A memory?"

Lark let the question hang there, unlikely to receive an answer. She busied herself with slinging her bow across her back and slipping her knife into her boot. The overwhelming rightness of the balance was both swift and staggering.

There was plenty of work to do. Chasing an unknown. It seemed like her path had been predestined for so long. One foot in front of the other. The sudden openness was vast enough to get lost.

Lark glanced at Daciana. "Will we see each other again?"

Daciana smiled. "Of course, we will. And when we do, Nereida will have a lot to answer for."

A vow, and a threat of destruction to come.

There was much to do. And somewhere in Lark's tent, there was an assassin waiting for answers she wasn't ready to give.

Daciana had a mission she wasn't ready to share.

Nereida had a destiny she wasn't yet aware of. An end by Lark's hand she wasn't sure was her will or the will of the fates.

It mattered not.

For one fleeting moment, everything else fell away. Save for the wicked song she knew by heart.

EPILOGUE

Ferryn felt a shift in the air. *Felt.* As if he had access to any sensation.

He leapt to his feet, excitement flooding him. Could it be? Had Ceto really done it?

It was too much to hope for, after everything. But still, he hoped. He yearned and pined and hoped. That his sacrifice, his choice to keep her safe, was enough to earn her trust. Ceto was always just a hair out of reach.

He lifted a hand, pressing against the veil that, like Ceto, should always remain out of reach for him here in Lacuna. Trapped in a world squeezed against the mortal realm. A living ghost destined to descend into madness.

He should never be able to reach the veil. It would always elude him in this prison.

His fingers slipped through. Icy pinpricks against his skin as he pushed his hand through the glimmering veil.

"What is it?" His companion asked. She tucked a strand of golden hair behind her ear. "What are you doing?"

Her curious expression and large green eyes were always questioning. In the early days, she reminded him a lot of Lark in that way.

Only she had a softness Lark hadn't possessed in ages. A naïve hope still burning in her every expression. Her life had been cut short too soon for her to grasp the ugliness of the world, despite what she had faced in death. She never told him what happened to her, but a young, pretty girl like that, her life ending with no cause of illness? He could guess.

"I don't know," Ferryn marveled. "I think"—he pressed his hand through, all the way up his forearm, to his elbow—"the veil feels thinner, accessible."

She gasped. "Do you mean...?"

He nodded, pushing up to his shoulder. "I think..." He didn't dare say it. Didn't dare lend words to his hope. That Ceto had indeed found a way to barter with the witch queen to grant his pardon. A chance to leave. To escape.

He grabbed his companion by the wrist, yanking her hand up to the juncture where his shoulder was pressed in.

She pressed her hand through.

They passed through the invisible wall, coming to stand in the same room they'd been sitting in. They'd grown tired of watching mortals ignore them and had found an abandoned hut to wallow in.

The smell of the hut hit Ferryn first. The dank odor of stale hay and wet earth. He breathed it in as if it were the finest aroma in all the world. He turned to her, knowing he must be wearing the same expression of wonder and euphoria reflected on her face.

He held out a hand to her. "How would you like to feel the sun on your face again?"

Her expression broke into a dazzling smile as she placed her hand in his. The sensation of skin on skin was something he'd missed more than he realized. "I'd say that would be the greatest pleasure since before my end."

Ferryn closed his hand around hers almost shivering. "Oh, you haven't met your end, Aislinn. This is just the beginning."

ACKNOWLEDGMENTS

Foremost, I want to thank my amazing husband, Lance. He listened to me read aloud my earliest and roughest draft, spent years discussing characters and plot beats with me, and never once doubted my dream. Thank you for being the most supportive person I could ever ask for, and for being the love of my life.

My beautiful wildling. This book wouldn't exist without you. You brought magic back to my life. I love you more than I thought capable of.

Friel Black. My writing soulmate, my best friend, and the first beta/alpha reader I ever had. This book wouldn't be what it is without you. I'm so grateful to have found you. You are an inspiration and a bright light in my life. You're my editor, my confidant, my dearest friend, and my sister. I love you.

Elle Caldwell. My writing sister of blood and gore. I'm so lucky to have found my witchy sisters in you and Friel. You are such a remarkable friend and if I ever needed backup in a knife fight, I'd choose you. In the solitary world of writing, I found my coven.

My sisters, Jess and Sam, for believing in me when I wasn't ready to admit to myself how important this was. I love you both.

My parents for supplying me with endless stacks of books growing up, taking me to see every LOTR movie, and being as, if not more, excited than I was when I finished the discovery draft of SOW.

Kate Khavari. My CP, my cheerleader, my sounding board. Your friendship, your belief in me, and the way you challenge me while encouraging me is such a blessing. I cherish you and your giant heart.

My beta readers, Emmalee, Robert, Eleanor, Amber, Clara, and Liz. You folks... you've done so much for me! You read my book when it was still a hot mess and helped me strengthen it. I'm so fortunate I found such an amazing group of people to help me. You guys hold a special place in my heart, always.

Devon, my fated friend who I didn't meet until after you left the state, I'm so glad I found you. Your insight, and our long conversations about theology, religion, mythology, and The Room mean the world to me.

Brandi Gann and Stella B. James. You girls make every day fun, even on days when it's hard to smile. Thank you for being such bright spots in my life.

Freya Inkwell. You might just be one of the kindest, sweetest, most supportive people I've ever met. I'm so glad I know you.

Fran and her AMAZING work on my cover design. Right from the very first message, you saw my vision. Your patience and understanding have been such a joy.

All the incredible writers I've met through Instagram. This is one of the kindest, most passionate communities I've ever belonged to.

JAIME! You didn't think I'd forget you, did you? Never. Thank you for playing Zorro and the princess with me, (and sorry for stabbing your eye.) We spent our childhood playing make believe and embarking on epic quests. I wouldn't be who I am today without your friendship.

And last but not least, you, reader. Thank you so much for giving my book a chance. For taking time out of your busy life and precious time to step into my world. You are the one making my dreams come true.

ABOUT THE AUTHOR

 C.A. Farran is an emerging author of dark fantasy. She's addicted to video games, Kit Kats, and energy drinks.

Farran grew up by the sea on a steady intake of fairytales, renaissance fairs, and mythology. She's always felt a profound connection to horror and dark fantasy, spending her childhood searching the woods for monsters and magic.

Now, she spends her days photographing nature in Maine with her two cats; Commander and Demon, her husband, and their wildling.

This is C.A.'s first novel, but her short story "Safe Travels" can be found in the anthology "Frontiers: Past, Present, and Future" by Owl Hollow Press.

To stay updated on her shenanigans, check out cafarran.com